Walter Dobius was a powerful man

Being cooperative with Walter Dobius was simply a matter of survival. He was the most powerful political columnist in the nation and with the right turn of a phrase he could either make or break a senator, a governor, perhaps even . . .

But no, that was impossible. This was America, a democracy; that sort of thing just couldn't happen here. Or could it?

Walter Dobius was a powerful man. He believed all things were possible—and this time he was determined to prove it. . . .

CAPABLE OF HONOR

BY ALLEN DRURY

A DELL BOOK

*Dedicated to all the many sincere and
objective newspapermen and -women, in Washington
and elsewhere, who are not a part of Walter's world*

Published by
DELL PUBLISHING CO., INC.
750 Third Avenue
New York, N.Y. 10017

Note to the Reader

MOST OF THE CHARACTERS in this novel, and the background of most of the events in it, have appeared in its predecessors, *Advise and Consent* and *A Shade of Difference*.

In *Advise and Consent* (1959) will be found the story of the nomination of Robert A. Leffingwell to be Secretary of State; the accession of Vice President Harley M. Hudson to the Presidency upon the sudden death of his predecessor; the successful Soviet manned landing on the moon; the death of Senator Brigham Anderson of Utah; the appointment of Senator Orrin Knox of Illinois to be Secretary of State following the defeat of Bob Leffingwell by the Senate. There, also, will be found the marriage of Orrin's son Hal to Crystal Danta, the marriage of Senate Majority Leader Robert Munson of Michigan to Washington hostess Dolly Harrison, and many other episodes leading into later books.

In *A Shade of Difference* (1962) will be found the visit to South Carolina and New York of His Royal Highness Terence Wolowo Ajkaje, ruler of Gorotoland, with all its explosive effects upon the racial problem in the United States and the United Nations; the beginnings of the rebellion in Gorotoland which produces major events in *Capable of Honor;* the early stages of Ambassador Felix Labaiya's activities in Panama, also inspiring major events in this novel; the opening moves of California's Negro Congressman, Cullee Hamilton, in his race for the Senate; the opening moves of California's Governor Edward M. Jason in his campaign for the Presidential nomination; the death of Senator Harold Fry of West Virginia and his decision to entrust his son Jimmy to Senator Lafe Smith of Iowa; and many other episodes leading into later books.

Running through both previous novels, through this and through *Preserve and Protect* yet to come—as it runs through our times—is the continuing argument between those who favor the responsible use of strength to oppose the Communist drive for world dominion, and those who hope to find in diplomatic negotiation and the refusal to employ force the surest path to a secure and stable world society.

Contents

PART ONE
The World of Walter Wonderful   11

PART TWO
The President's Book   289

PART THREE
Ted Jason's Book   361

PART FOUR
Capable of Honor   517

Major Characters in the Novel

Harley M. Hudson, President of the United States
Lucille, his wife
Orrin Knox, Secretary of State
Beth, his wife
Governor *Edward M. Jason* of California
Ceil, his wife
Patsy Jason Labaiya, his sister
Selena Jason Castleberry, their aunt
Valuela Jason Randall, their aunt
Herbert Jason, their uncle
Senator *Robert Durham Munson* of Michigan, Majority Leader of the United States Senate
Dolly, his wife
Senator *Stanley Danta* of Connecticut, Majority Whip of the Senate
The Speaker of the House
Representative *Cullee Hamilton* of California
Senator *Lafe Smith* of Iowa
Representative *J. B. "Jawbone" Swarthman* of South Carolina, chairman of the House Foreign Affairs Committee
Senator *Tom August* of Minnesota, chairman of the Senate Foreign Relations Committee
Robert A. Leffingwell, Director of the President's Commission on Administrative Reform
Walter Dobius, a columnist
Helen-Anne Carrew, another columnist
The executive chairman of The Greatest Publication That Absolutely Ever Was
Members of Walter's world
The working press

AT THE UN

His Royal Highness *Terence Wolowo Ajkaje*, 137th M'Bulu of Mbuele; "Terrible Terry"

His Royal Highness *Obifumatta Ajkaje,* his cousin; "Prince Obi"
Vasily Tashikov, Ambassador of the U.S.S.R.
Krishna Khaleel, Ambassador of India
Lord *Claude Maudulayne,* Ambassador of the United Kingdom
Kitty, his wife
Raoul Barre, Ambassador of France
Celestine, his wife
The Secretary-General
Members of Walter's world
The working press

AT THE CONVENTION

Hal Knox, son of the Secretary of State
Crystal Danta Knox, his wife
Mrs. *Mabel Anderson,* widow of the late Senator Brigham Anderson of Utah
Roger P. Croy, National Committeeman from Oregon
Mrs. *Esmé Harbellow Stryke,* National Committeewoman from California
Mrs. *Mary Buttner Baffleburg,* National Committeewoman from Pennsylvania
Miss *Lizzie Hanson McWharter,* National Committeewoman from Kansas
Mrs. *Anna Hooper Bigelow,* National Committeewoman from New Hampshire
Joe Smitters, Bill Smatters, Bob Smutters, John Smotters, Buddy Smetters: county chairmen
Senator *Fred Van Ackerman* of Wyoming, spokesman for the Committee on Making Further Offers for a Russian Truce (COMFORT)
LeGage Shelby, national chairman of Defenders of Equality for You (DEFY)
Rufus Kleinfert, Knight Kommander of the Konference on Efforts to Encourage Patriotism (KEEP)
Booker T. Saunders, a hero
William Everett Hollister II, another hero
Frankly Unctuous, an Anchor Man
Members of Walter's world
The working press

PART ONE

THE WORLD OF WALTER WONDERFUL

1

"THE LATEST wacky rumor in this wacky city [reported one of the Washington *Evening Star*'s many lady columnists in Monday's paper] is that Patsy Jason Labaiya, sister of Presidential Likely Gov. Ted Jason of California and wife of Panamanian Ambassador Felix Labaiya, will run for the U. S. Senate. Of course at the moment Patsy's a legal resident of the Canal Zone, but her friends ['There's a euphemism,' the columnist thought with a grim little smile, x-ed out 'her friends' and wrote in 'those close to the Jason camp'] advise her that this doesn't make any difference.

"They say she should follow the Golden Rule of other F.F.P.'s (First Families of Politics) in their search for power in this power-hungry town:

"Go where it is and grab it.

"Patsy may yet wind up running from New York, which would give her and Big Brother Ted the sort of continent-spanning alliance so ravenously sought by others in an earlier era."

Well, is that a fact now, Patsy thought spitefully when she read the paper in the privacy of her Dumbarton Oaks study, where the teletypes rattled on with their afternoon budget of news about humanity's most recent day on the road to wherever humanity was going. *Is* that a fact.

Recalling how the columnist had cooed at her only yesterday at the opening of the International Students Fund drive at the Shoreham, Patsy was tempted to call her right then and there and tell her what a two-faced tramp she was. This impulse, so often characteristic of the mood with which Washington's higher-placed denizens regard one another in the uneasy relationships imposed upon them by the haphazard imperatives of politics, gave way, also characteristically, to less violent thoughts. The matter of who uses whom for what is always of paramount importance in the lovely capital, and personal antagonisms are quick to yield to more pragmatic considerations.

Patsy calmed down.

For Patsy had plans—in the cause of her brother, Patsy always had plans—and in them the lady columnist of the *Star,* along with many another powerful personage in the beautiful city now muffled in the last heavy snowfall of winter, was destined to play a prominent part.

In fact, she might as well start playing it right now.

"Darling," Patsy said into the telephone a moment later, "I'm so glad I could reach you. You are always so BUSY. Such an example to us idle ones!"

"Yes, Patsy dear," the columnist said. "Did you see my item today? Is there anything in it?"

"But, darling," Patsy protested. "You mean you printed it without KNOWING? I didn't know you girls worked like that!"

"Us girls," the columnist told her with a sardonic chuckle, "move in mysterious ways our wonders to perform. It is true, isn't it?"

"I don't know who told you—" Patsy began with a well-managed show of indignation, and then dropped it for a more confiding tone. "Oh, well, dear, you always know EVERYTHING. I do marvel at how you do it."

"It is true, then," the columnist persisted. Patsy laughed.

"*I* didn't say so," she pointed out. "You write what you please, but just remember *I* didn't say so. Darling," she went on, becoming more intimate, "I wanted you to be the first to know—and this IS true—about the exciting thing I'm going to do."

"What's that, have a baby? Better late than never, I always—"

"Now, stop," Patsy said, not so cordially. "Really," she added gaily, taking the opportunity thus afforded, "You can be so bitchy, darling. So REALLY bitchy. No, it's what I'm going to do for Walter Dobius."

" 'Walter Wonderful'?" the columnist asked, a note of genuine interest mingled with the sarcasm with which political Washington always used this famous nickname. "What are you going to do for that little—for that statesman-philosopher of the press before whom we all fall down and worship?"

"I know you don't, darling," Patsy said smoothly, "but he really is a statesman. He really is. Everybody reads Walter. His column is in hundreds of papers—436, to be exact, he's just picked up the Walla Walla *Union Bulletin—*"

"You *have* been checking on him, haven't you? O.K., I'll grant it, everybody reads Walter. And you want him to come out for Ted, because this will influence nine-tenths of this sheeplike profession who always follow baa-ing at his heels. And so you're going to do something for him." She snorted. "Something quiet and modest that nobody will know about, I'll bet, typical of the way the Jasons operate. The thing I love about your family, Patsy, is that you're so unobtrusive. It's so hard for the country to find out what you're doing."

"There you GO again," Patsy said with a merry peal of laughter. "Naturally I don't want to keep it quiet, darling, or I wouldn't be talking to you, would I? I can't think of any other earthly reason for talking to you. Can you?"

"Mmmm," the columnist said thoughtfully. "Maybe I just shouldn't mention the Jasons at all for a while. How would that be?"

"Don't be silly, darling, we can't be ignored, we're too big, you know that perfectly well. Anyway, this is an exclusive you're getting, you know."

"Well, what is it?" the columnist demanded. "I have to be at 'Vagaries' for Dolly Munson's party at three, and it's going to take an hour to get there in this snow. I can't sit here yakking forever."

"Oh?" Patsy said sharply. "What's Dolly up to? She didn't invite me."

"I should hope not," the columnist agreed with a happy laugh. "Not to a tea for Beth Knox."

"What we do for Walter Dobius will be ten times more important than that," Patsy promised with a certain grimness in her tone. "Particularly with the award, and all."

"What award?" the columnist asked, and then added thoughtfully, "That's right, Friday is his twenty-fifth anniversary as a national columnist, isn't it? That would make a good occasion."

"And with the people I'm going to invite," Patsy said with a calculated increase in excitement, "and the speeches that will be made—"

"And the publicity of it all, the sweet publicity," the columnist said. "To say nothing of the assist for Ted. O.K., sweetie, how would this be—" and Patsy could hear her typewriter tapping as she mused along—

" 'What promises to be the biggest event of this or any
other social season is shaping up for this coming weekend
when the Jasons (Gov. Ted and Ambassadress Patsy, that
is, America's coming political team) throw an all-out wing-
ding to honor the writing anniversary of America's most
distinguished political commentator, Walter Dobius.

" 'Walter Wonderful,' as he was originally dubbed by
Lyndon Johnson—it's the nickname by which he is still
fondly and respectfully known to political Washington—
completes his 25th year of syndicated columning this Friday. That's the night the Jasons have chosen to confer on
him the Jason Foundation's coveted biennial Good and
Faithful Servant Award. 'GAFSA' was won two years ago
by Robert A. Leffingwell, now director of the President's
commission on government streamlining.

" 'Washington is scrambling for invitations to this affair,
which promises to bring together everyone from the President'—shall I say the President, Patsy?"

"You can say the President," Patsy promised, adding to
herself, *He'd better come, the old fathead.*

" '—from the President to the copy boy who picks up
Mr. Dobius' column at his charming Leesburg estate and
rushes it to the syndicate office in Washington to be sent
out to his 436 newspapers across the country.' " The columnist paused. "How's that copy boy touch, Patsy? Don't
say I never did anything for the Jasons. If you're lucky he
may even be colored. That would wrap it up."

"That will do very well, thank you, darling," Patsy said
with dignity. "As a matter of fact, I had thought of the
copy boy myself. And he is colored. So there."

"That does it. Can I spread the word at Dolly's?"

"I'd rather you didn't."

"Can't I tell them they're all invited?" the columnist persisted with her wicked little laugh.

"I'll let them know," Patsy said coolly.

"Beth and Orrin Knox too?"

"I'm not ready to say anything yet about the guest list.
And I don't want a lot of speculation, either. I'll give you
plenty to write about in the next couple of days if you'll
just be patient. After all, it's exclusive."

"Unnhunnh," the columnist said. "Exclusive until the
next phone call you make. All right, we'll do it your way as
long as it *is* exclusive. The minute I see something in the
Post that I haven't got first, we'll start doing it my way. I

still think a hint of friction with Beth and Orrin would in-
trigue—"

"Darling, when did anyone have to HINT at friction between us and the Knoxes? It's built in, as long as he per-
sists in thinking he has a right to be President."

"Yes, I know; only Ted Jason has a right to think that.
Incidentally, how come you don't run for the Senate in
California instead of New York? You aren't afraid of
Cullee Hamilton, are you?"

"Because New York is—" Patsy stopped abruptly and
chuckled. "Oh, no, you don't. None of this entrapment,
now. Who said I was running from anywhere? Anyway,"
she added, more tartly, "who says I'm afraid of Cullee
Hamilton? He isn't such a shoo-in, even if he runs. And
who says he is? He hasn't announced yet, has he?"

"Nope," the columnist agreed comfortably. "But he
will."

"Well," Patsy said, still tartly, "I repeat: who said *I* was
running from anywhere?"

"I agree I think it's a fool idea," the columnist told her
with a deliberately infuriating indifference. "But I suppose
you think if Jason money could buy California for Ted it
can buy New York for you. Who knows?" She yawned
elaborately into the telephone. "You may be right. Lordy,
I've got to run to get to 'Vagaries' by three. Call again soon
when you've got another hot one, O.K.?"

"I certainly will," Patsy said, deciding not to rise to the
bait and argue. "Give my love to Dolly. Tell her I hope she
isn't planning a party for Orrin Knox the same night. That
would be a coincidence."

"That would be a disaster," the columnist said. "I think I
can assure you right now that nobody will give a party that
same night. I'm sure the Knoxes, the Munsons, the President, the copy boy, and the whole wide wonderful world
will be there to honor wise little wonderful Walter." She
gave a sardonic snort. "After all, why shouldn't we? Hasn't
he saved the nation for twenty-five long years? It's the least
we can do to show our gratitude."

Of all the unpleasant people, Patsy thought as she hung
up on the ribald, knowing voice, that one took the cake.
Honestly, that woman. First, floating that ridiculous rumor
about the Senate when she, Patsy, hadn't really even made
up her mind, and then implying that she was afraid to run

in her native California just because Cullee Hamilton, its most famous Negro Congressman, might try for the Senate this year. Jasons didn't scare that easily. Jasons, in fact, didn't scare at all. A couple of hundred millions and four generations of command running back to the Spanish occupation of California saw to that. Jasons went after what they wanted without any qualms. And got it.

And they will this year, too, she promised the columnist. You wait and see!

As for what the columnist—whose name was Helen-Anne Carrew, and who had herself seen them come and go in Washington's restless tides almost as long as Walter Wonderful—thought about that distinguished gentleman, Patsy had to confess that, while disliking the tone, she could not entirely disagree with the diagnosis. There was something quite precious about Walter Dobius, as though he were handing down tablets from a golden sarcophagus in the Smithsonian. But there was also something quite powerful, about him. More powerful, in fact, than about any other single commentator on the American scene.

Regularly his solemnly portentous, more than a little pompous countenance stared out upon his countrymen from the head of his column, as if to say, "Who are you, and what makes you think you know what's going on? Much better you should listen to me, peasants. I *really* know What It's All About."

And such is the obliging nature of peasants that they had long ago accepted this implied self-anointment—which was much more than implied in the title of his column ("The Way It Is") and the general tone of his writings—and concluded agreeably that indeed he did know, and that of all those writing out of Washington, the Bakers, the Drummonds, the Krocks, the Lippmanns, the Pearsons, the Restons, and the rest, Walter Wonderful was indeed the greatest of them all.

"Did you read Walter Dobius today?" someone would chortle in Canarsie, someone would rage in Dubuque. "I do think Walter Dobius is so *astute*," they would tell one another in Kennebunkport, nodding sagely in L.A.

As broad as the oceans, as high as the sky, ran the writ of Walter Dobius to tell humanity what it should do. With a heavy and often slashing turn of phrase (broken at conscientious intervals by determinedly jocular attempts at humor) and a diligent attention to his news sources, that is exactly what he did.

Even more fundamental than his hold upon his countrymen, of course—and the thing that really made him so interesting to Jasons and Kennedys, Knoxes and Rockefellers, and everyone else who had aspirations to power in the powerful city—was his influence with the government and his hold upon the press. The press did not quite, in Helen-Anne's acrid phrase, go "baa-ing at his heels"—it wasn't as obvious as that—nor did certain influential people in the State Department and elsewhere—at least openly—ask him what they should do.

Yet there had been more than one secret meeting at "Salubria" in Leesburg in time of crisis, more than one Chief Executive and Secretary of State who had arrived by furtive helicopter in the lush Virginia countryside to stay a while, receive the Word, and then be whisked away again to the city of their torment and their power. And in news offices throughout the land his columns, a little turgid but filled with the calm certainty that he was absolutely right— for did not things very often move as he said they would, and was not his advice very often followed in the councils of the mighty?—laid down a line that was frequently echoed by editors not quite sure of themselves, local columnists casting about for a subject to fill up today's six hundred words, national commentators needing inspiration with which to face the evening cameras, book and drama critics anxious to maintain their standing at Manhattan cocktail parties, reporters who found themselves awed and impressed by his fabulous reputation and so inclined, often quite unconsciously, to see the news and transmit it with a selection and emphasis that subtly but powerfully reflected his ideas.

Thus Walter Wonderful was a prize indeed, and Patsy intended to see to it that the prize went to her brother in his growing campaign against Secretary of State Orrin Knox for the Presidential nomination that would presumably be left open when President Harley Hudson made good on his promise to step down at the end of the present term.

As Walter jumped, so would many of the news media, much of the academic world, most of that complex of power and superior certainty that had its habitat in plush offices in New York and Washington and other major centers throughout the land. All of these people swore by Walter Dobius, all of them obediently thought as his columns told them they should. There was a network of attitude, non-conspiratorial but quite binding, which controlled the thinking and the reactions of this particular powerful group of interests in America. Walter Dobius nine times out of ten was the man who, in the last analysis, created that attitude if it did not exist, or strengthened it if it existed but showed signs of wavering.

This Patsy knew, and Ted, and Orrin Knox and Harley Hudson and a number of other astute and powerful people, some not so basically friendly to the country as these. Sophisticates in politics, instinctive or self-made students of their well-meaning but sometimes rather erratic countrymen, they were all aware that if you praised the right people, backed the right causes, parroted the right phrases, indulged in the right type of automatic thinking, you could be absolutely sure of flattering news stories, favorable editorials, cordial television broadcasts, helpful reviews, friendly and encouraging references in any one of the thousand and one channels through which a public issue or personality is presented to the American people, and through them to the world.

Thus if Walter Dobius endorsed the shrewd gray-haired gentleman known as Governor Edward Jason of California, his friends, colleagues, and true believers by the millions would also endorse Ted. And if by some remoter chance he decided to endorse the shrewd gray-haired gentleman known as Secretary of State Orrin Knox, the friends, colleagues, and true believers, though gulping and groaning and protesting a bit, would finally, obediently, fall into line behind Orrin.

So it was that Patsy, having launched her well-laid plans in what only appeared to be an impulsive moment, again picked up the receiver, drew toward her over her enormous redwood desk a carefully prepared list of names, and began telephoning around the country. At almost the same moment, three miles across town in Southeast Washington, Helen-Anne Carrew yanked the item about the award banquet out of her typewriter and sent it along to be set in type for tomorrow's paper, knowing as she did so that she was helping to start in motion what was, for all practical purposes, the opening gambit in Ted Jason's formal campaign for the Presidency.

The ways of the Jasons, the columnist told herself as she gave her mouth a hasty smear of lipstick, grabbed her purse and mink coat and hurried out of the *Star*'s busy newsroom, were among the damnedest curiosities in American politics. But, knowing full well the weight of Walter Wonderful, she was ready to bet a sizable amount that they would, in this instance, be more than a little effective.

And now, the Secretary of State thought with an annoyed grimace an hour later, he supposed he would have to go ahead and announce right away instead of waiting, as he had planned, for some definite sign from the President.

"Damn that woman, anyway," he remarked rather absently into the telephone. At the other end of the line, in Dolly Munson's green and gold dressing room at snow-hugged "Vagaries" standing white and secret and warm amid the softly falling drifts in Rock Creek Park, his wife chuckled.

"Watch your language. This line may be tapped."

"It probably is," Orrin Knox said. "By Patsy. What do you think I should do?" he asked with mock solemnity. "Give Helen-Anne a statement withdrawing from the race?"

"Helen-Anne has enough to write about for one afternoon," Beth Knox said. "I think you'd better talk to him."

Her husband made a skeptical sound.

"Ted? You don't think I can get him to withdraw, do you?"

"Not Ted."

"Walter?" The Secretary snorted. "I lost Walter the night I refused to take his advice on Terrible Terry. I was the first Secretary of State in fifteen years who had the guts to say No to Walter Dobius. You've observed the tone of his columns toward me ever since."

"Very pontifical, I've thought. Suitably dignified and profound, as always."

"And full of little knives," the Secretary said. An acid note came into his voice as he quoted:

" 'I think we can begin to see the basic fallacies underlying the policies of Secretary of State Orrin Knox as he attempts to apply to foreign affairs the same techniques he used in the Senate as senior Senator from Illinois. It is apparent now, it seems to me, that methods effective in that distinguished body do not always have the application elsewhere that former Senators sometimes assume. It is time, in my judgment, for the Secretary to reconsider his course. Too much is at stake for him to do otherwise, I believe.' "

Beth laughed.

"You have the tone, all right, but aren't you a little harsh with the personal pronouns? I don't think he uses 'I' and 'my' more than once in each paragraph, does he?"

"I once counted five in two hundred words. Anyway, what difference does it make how many he uses? They all add up to nix on Knox."

"I repeat, watch your language," Beth said with an alarm that wasn't entirely in jest. "You'll let fly with some bright line like that someday and the Jasons will pick it up and run with it. Don't give them any more ammunition than they've got already."

"Oh, is it called ammunition?" her husband inquired. "I thought it was called money. What does Dolly think of this?"

"Dolly is being the perfect hostess and wife of the Senate Majority Leader. She is being as bland as I am under the vigilant eye of Miss Helen-Anne. And that, my boy, is mighty bland, I can tell you. I have conveyed nothing but polite interest in Patsy's plans."

"Which of course doesn't fool Helen-Anne for a second."

"Not one second. I don't really think Dolly likes what Patsy's up to. I don't think Bob will, either. It's so obvious."

"Crude, I'd say," the Secretary agreed. "Unless," he gave a sudden chuckle, "we'd thought of it first, in which case it would have been shrewd and quite all right. So you think I should talk to Walter, do you? What makes you think any talk from me can change that closed mind?"

"I'm sure he thinks exactly the same of you. It could be you're both suffering from misconceptions a good talk could remove."

"You don't believe that," Orrin said. His tone became amused. "Walter's misconcepts about me I'll grant you, but surely not mine about him! But, you're no doubt right, as always. I should talk to him. I should go on bended knee as so many of my predecessors have before me, and say to him, Walter, I should say, tell poor old stupid ignorant Orrin how to run the world, Walter. Walter, tell poor old Orrin how to do it, Walter—"

"Not in that mood, you shouldn't. If you can't do better than that, you might as well write him off and forget it."

"He's gone anyway," the Secretary said, "and with him most of the press. Why shouldn't I write them off?"

"Now," his wife said. "Relax, Mr. Secretary. Relax, Senator. This time, I think maybe we can agree, the stakes are rather high, right? Don't you think you can afford a little patience, even if they haven't been very nice to you? You really are the logical candidate this time, in spite of Ted's ambitions—"

"And fortune."

"Fortunes have been beaten before."

"Not lately."

"Well, it can be done. And if I were you—of course I'm not, and as usual, you'll do exactly as you please—"

"Yeah," her husband agreed in an amused tone. "Oh, yeah. Hank," he said, using the nickname he resorted to in moments of deepest candor, "when haven't I followed your advice?"

She laughed. "I haven't got time to give you a list—the girls downstairs will get suspicious if I powder my nose much longer. Just take my word for it, I think you'd be well-advised to talk to Walter Dobius. After all, you know, he may quite conceivably have to accept you as President if the country does. It will be hard on Walter if the country goes against his advice, but who knows? He's not dumb, and if he decides you're going to be elected in spite of him, he may decide to get on the bandwagon. Or rather, as I expect he would rationalize it in his own mind, come to your assistance and help persuade you to do the right thing."

"Save me from myself," Orrin suggested.

"And save us from you, too. Walter has a terrific messianic complex at heart, you know. He just wants the salvation to be on his terms."

"Who doesn't?" the Secretary said. "As a matter of fact, I don't think Walter's going to have to worry. Harley Hudson will save all of us from me."

At this reference to the kindly, somewhat bumbling but unexpectedly forceful and highly popular occupant of the White House, Beth Knox made a small, impatient sound. Not too impatient, for like most people she too was fond of the President, but enough to express the characteristic annoyance of would-be candidates faced with an equivocal incumbent.

"Yes. I could rather wish he would make up his mind."

"I'm sure he's made up his mind," Orrin said. "He just isn't telling anybody."

"But here it is almost April," his wife protested. "He's paralyzed all of you, so far this year. He's kept a lid on you and Ted both. Nobody's been able to do any real campaigning or run in any primaries—"

"Frankly," Orrin Knox said, "I am deeply grateful to the President of the United States for keeping me out of the ruts and drifts of New Hampshire. If he wanted to let his name go in there, and Wisconsin too, well and good."

"He didn't say he wanted to," Beth pointed out. "The state chairman did it without his approval. Or so it was alleged, in well-informed circles."

"Yes," the Secretary said wryly. "I've thought before this that Harley has turned into a damned sight cleverer politician than any of us ever gave him credit for when he was Vice President. Actually, he's made it quite painless for everybody, up to now. I'm happy to avoid as many primaries as possible, and campaigning too, as long as he makes his intentions clear before the convention. . . . Except that Walter is going to kick off Ted's campaign Friday night and then I'll have to follow suit whether I want to or not, or whether Harley wants me to or not. Damn that woman, as I said before."

"Maybe it's best for everyone that Jasons rush in where more decorous souls fear to tread," Beth remarked. "Maybe we should be grateful to Patsy. This idea of hers may be just the catalyst everybody needs. It might even smoke out Harley. Why don't you talk to him too?"

"I've talked to Harley so many times I'm blue in the face. He's become a master of the sidestep, combined with the fatherly sooth-down. I'd swear at times he's my grandfather."

"Maybe Patsy will do it," Beth said. "Lucille Hudson's here and of course she'll go right back and tell Harley. Why don't you give her an hour or two and then drop in? I don't believe there's anything official going on over there tonight."

"I'm very skeptical it'll do any good," Orrin said, "but it might. Give my love to all the girls—I suppose they're all there?"

"Oh, yes, Kitty Maudulayne and Celestine Barre and many others from the diplomatic crowd; a lot of Hill wives and a good many from downtown. Dolly's done it up right for me. This means Patsy will have the whole town buzzing by tonight, which of course is just what she wanted to do when she talked to Helen-Anne."

"Patsy'll have the whole world buzzing by tonight," the Secretary said ruefully, "which is what she wanted to do when she talked to Helen-Anne."

"Walter, dear," Patsy said with a careful urgency, for she knew as well as anyone how delicate you had to be with Walter, his ego was so monumental and his dignity so insecure, and altogether he was such a pompous little a— but, no, she mustn't let herself entertain irreverent thoughts like that. Most people thought he was God.

"Walter, dear," she said, deciding to try a rush of girlish enthusiasm, "most people think you're GOD. That's why you've simply got to do it."

Forty miles away in Leesburg, in the study she had seen on a couple of occasions, book-lined, leather-filled, glowing snug and cozy in the dark snowy afternoon, she could hear the self-satisfied amusement: a little surprised, as people often were at Patsy, but not arguing with her thesis.

"And some think I'm the devil," Walter Dobius said in his deliberate voice. "You have an intriguing beginning, though. What comes next? What is it that I have to do?"

"You have to let us—you have to be willing to allow us —you have to be prepared to break some of your strongest rules to permit us—"

"Patsy," Walter Dobius said, "you're too much. Stop this phony suspense and tell me what I've got to do. You know very well there's nothing you can't command from me. Now, out with it."

"Well, of course we know you have all the honors in the world and couldn't possibly want another, but—"

"If you're going to give me GAFSA," Walter said, "I accept. I couldn't be more honored. When will it be?"

"Walter, you naughty boy! I'll bet Helen-Anne has been talking to you."

"Not lately," Walter said, a trifle grimly. "No, I just guessed. I think you've made a good choice," he added, quite without egotism, a statement of simple fact. "After Bob Leffingwell's fiasco, the award needs to be made respectable again."

"I think we'll have Bob say a few words before you speak," Patsy said coolly. "I'm not ashamed of Bob

Leffingwell. Nor are you, to judge from some of your columns."

"Oh, no," Walter Dobius said calmly. "I still consider him our best public servant. Considerably better," he remarked acidly, "than the gentleman who became Secretary of State in his place."

"That's exactly why we felt the Foundation should give you the award," Patsy said eagerly. "To show the world that we still believe in the Right Position on things. Which you, dearest Walter, always state so effectively. Goodness!" she said with another burst of enthusiasm. "I really don't know where the country would be without you, Walter!"

"You don't mean that," Walter said complacently, "but I won't argue."

And you do mean that, Patsy thought, so I won't argue either. Twerp.

"Walter," she said earnestly, "this is going to be Friday night—"

"My anniversary."

"Yes. And Ted and I hope that you will deliver a major address. A Major Address," she repeated, giving it the capitals. "It is a sounding board, you know, even though you do have your own in the column all the time."

"Sometimes a different forum lends one's thoughts an extra weight," Walter agreed gravely. "I appreciate the opportunity. Why do you think I'm going to cancel out on the Ambassador of Thailand's dinner Friday night? It takes a lot to make one pass up the Ambassador of Thailand!"

"Walter, you're wicked," Patsy told him with an admiring laugh. "Poor little Boomabakrit and Madame will have to write REAMS to Bankok explaining why you didn't show up. But I do think you should make a major address. Everybody will be expecting it."

"All my addresses are major," Walter Dobius said, again without the slightest trace of either egotism or humor. "This one, though . . ." His voice trailed away and it was all Patsy could do to keep from saying, "Yes?" But he came back strong and she couldn't have been more pleased. "This one," he said with a sudden firmness, "should put things in perspective about the election this year, once and for all."

"No one can do it better than you can, Walter," she said fervently. "In fact, everyone has been waiting for you to speak. People think they know where you're going to stand, Walter, but they don't really know. Millions and *millions* of people really and truly are waiting for you, Walter. Millions and millions can't make up their minds until you explain it to them. You know you must, Walter, and this is the perfect occasion. It needs more than a column. It needs a *speech*."

"I agree, it should be a speech. Supplemented by columns later, of course, all through the campaign."

"Oh, of course. I always say you're one of the most active campaigners in the country every four years, even though you can't enter in directly and always have to be objective and fair."

"I try to be," Walter said placidly. "It isn't always so easy, but I try to be."

"You are," she assured him. "You *are*." A little silence fell, for this was the most difficult part of her call and she knew it must be approached carefully. Among the many other things upon which Walter prided himself was a spirit of fierce independence, going back, he always said, to his "ancestors on the bogs and moors." They had given him, he always said, a desire to "go my own way, all men's servant and no man's slave." He had actually said this, in a speech to the graduates of the Columbia School of Journalism. It had received a tremendous hand, so it must be true. Obviously it was what his worshipers wanted to hear, at any rate. Patsy began cautiously.

"Of course, Walter, dear," she said with an offhand amusement, "some people might think it a foregone conclusion who you'll back this year. Wouldn't they be surprised if they were mistaken!"

"Wouldn't they be," Walter said. Again a silence fell. Patsy decided abruptly to plunge right ahead.

"Walter, we would really look awfully silly if you spoke at our dinner and endorsed Orrin, now, wouldn't we?"

"You would, indeed," he agreed blandly. "D'you think it's a possibility?"

"Walter, you're TEASING!" she exclaimed, aware that he never did, save in a heavy-handed, awkward, not-quite-funny and indeed rather pathetic way. Though she was sure that if anyone ever told Walter Dobius he was pathetic he would have been utterly enraged—and quite shattered, though the world would never know it. He chuckled and went on.

"Just having my little joke. You know perfectly well

who I'm going to endorse, don't you? I should think it would have been obvious long ago."

"If you do, it will be such an ENORMOUS help to Ted. We will always be so GRATEFUL."

"Did I say Ted?" he inquired, so calmly that a real spasm of dismay gripped Patsy's heart for a second.

"There you go," she said, "there you go. Oh, Walter, you must stop, now. You'll give me a nervous breakdown if you act coy about it. I couldn't STAND it!"

"You must remember, my dear," he said, and she could tell he was quite serious now, for the clipped, pompous heaviness his friends and colleagues knew so well was in his voice, "that I do have some obligation to be objective and fair. These aren't just words that one takes lightly or evades, you know. In an honorable profession, these are the stoutest guideposts. For twenty-five years I have tried to abide by them and I shall do so now." He paused, and repeated firmly, "I shall do so now."

"But, then—" she protested.

"I must weigh the facts and reach my judgment quite independently, Patsy. Quite independently. It's the only way I can justify the faith the country has in me. It's the only way I can continue to hold it. Surely you know that."

"You don't have to justify it," Patsy said flatly, "and you don't need to worry about holding it. *You* know that. You only have to worry about doing what is best for this nation in this election. On that basis, I do believe there can be only one answer, Walter. Isn't that right?"

"Why doesn't Ted come to see me?" he asked idly. "I'd like to talk to him."

"Certainly, if that will help you decide on the obvious."

"It isn't that I don't like Ted. I do like him. It may be that I like him very much. But there are factors more important than personal liking to be weighed here. I have a responsibility to judge carefully and choose carefully because, as you say, millions of people are depending upon me to help them make up their minds. I can't take that lightly, Patsy. Some might, but I can't."

"I know you don't, and that's why it seems to me there's only one answer."

"Have him come talk to me," Walter Dobius said again, and Patsy was tempted to snap, "Of course he'll be glad to wait on you, he's only the Governor of California." But she didn't say it, because she knew that Ted would wait on

him, though he would record the humbling little require-
ment somewhere in his mind and eventually get around to
evening things, as he always did.

"The dinner will be at the Statler at eight," she said.
"White tie this time, I think."

"You are doing it up grandly. And Ted?"

"He'll be coming into town around 3 P.M.," she said,
suppressing her annoyance. "Suppose we drive out and see
you then. If the snows are gone."

"Can't he see me sooner? I have to go up to the UN on
Tuesday to cover the Security Council debate on our
threatened intervention in Terrible Terry's Gorotoland.
Things are getting very sticky over there, as you know.
And then I have to speak to the American Medical Association in Cleveland on Wednesday. Which doesn't leave me
much time to get ready for your do on Friday."

"What time will you be back on Thursday?"

"Ten A.M., weather permitting."

"Very well," she said in a level tone. "I think we can be
there at noon."

"Do have lunch with me," he suggested dryly. Patsy
laughed.

"Make it a good one, Walter dearest!"

"I'll tell Arbella to give it the works. By the way," he
said in a needling tone, "have you any message you want
me to give your distinguished husband when I get to the
UN? Or aren't you exchanging messages these days?"

"Felix has had to go back to Panama," Patsy said, and
could have bitten her tongue for letting herself be tricked
into revealing something her husband had told her must be
kept secret for the time being. Of course Walter pounced
on it at once.

"Oh?" he said, a lively interest in his voice. "What's
going on down there?"

"Now, Walter," she said hastily, "don't start jumping to
conclusions."

"What's he going to do, overthrow the government? I've
been hearing some very interesting rumors from down
there lately. How about it, now, Patsy?"

"No, really, Walter," she said earnestly, "there's nothing.
Really. Just something in connection with 'Suerte' I think
—the Labaiya family estate, you know. Just a business
matter."

"Patsy," Walter Dobius said, "I don't think you're lev-

eling with me. But maybe you will on Thursday. If I accept
your award on Friday. Don't you think?"

"Possibly," Patsy said coolly. "We'll talk it over, Walter,
and see."

"And meantime," he said, relenting, "I'll be giving very
careful thought to what I'm going to say on Friday, because this one really will be a major address, Patsy. The
award deserves it, the occasion deserves it, and my hosts
deserve it."

"And the country. Don't forget the country, Walter."

"The country is my constant care, Patsy. I carry the
country with me night and day."

"Oh, Walter," Patsy said, thinking, Oh, *God*. "You ARE
wonderful."

"One has a certain position," Walter Dobius said. "One
has an obligation to keep it up."

2

Now THE WHIRLING globe has whirled six months
and on the face of the land and the surface of the seas the
races of man are engaged in their customary kindly attempts to cripple, hurt, and thwart each other in the name
of world peace and the cold reality of a ruthless self-interest. In the United Nations, in great cities and distinguished
capitals as well as in some not so great and not so distinguished, the game of advantage goes on, and with it a
steady advance in all the subtle and not-so-subtle decays
and attritions of a sad and luckless century. In some
places, most notably in the great white city sprawled along
the Potomac, some idealism still struggles against the deep
disillusion of the times, men still talk earnestly of planning
for a better tomorrow, working for a lasting world peace,
improving the lot of the restless human tide that laps ever
higher against the citadels of law and orderly change that
furnish the only hope of saving a civilization apparently
bent upon its own destruction. Likewise in Moscow and

London, Rome and Paris, Peking and Bonn and many another, men still pay the lip-tribute of a self-defined nobility
to what they are about. But it is apparent now, as it has
been for several decades, indeed ever since the Second
World War ripped apart the fragile fabric so flimsily
tacked together after the First, that many powerful forces
are engaged in policies diametrically opposed to those
which men of good will and good heart might reasonably
be expected to follow if they genuinely wished to save their
planet from its ultimate disaster.

Nonetheless the tasks of government and diplomacy go
on, as do the tasks of daily survival for the individual. People, in the simplest but most powerful cliché men know,
have to go on living. There is a power in this, a forward
surge, a life-force if you like, which ignores the dreams or
failures of presidents and prime ministers, kings and com-
missars. The butcher, the baker, the candlestick-maker
have to go on eating, sleeping, sheltering and begetting.
And on they go, regardless of what is created or ruined for
them at the top.

At the top, men try to make some sense of what they do,
but too often the secret eludes them. Yet they too go on,
for there is nothing else for them to do. They ride the juggernaut, but despite their efforts they do not control it. The
juggernaut also goes on, suffering for a little the attempts
of some to guide it, and then shaking them off as it roars
inexorably on toward whatever fate an obscure and mysterious Providence has in store for it.

In some places the decision as to who will have the
chance to try to guide the juggernaut is made in more orderly fashion than in others. In some places it is done by
election, in others by committee, in still others, less tidy, by
ravening revolution and bitter death. Nowhere is it done
with more exhaustive—and exhausting—care than in the
United States of America, and upon no choice, in these
dying years of the century, does the world concentrate with
a more worried and fearsome attention than it does upon
the choice of the man who will sit in the White House in
Washington.

His country may be confused in its aims, uncertain of its
future, baffled and distressed by humanity's exasperating refusal to see things the way it does, but there is no denying
the awesome power to build or destroy that lies at the hand
of this single individual chosen by all the complex and sub-

tle pressures of a complex and subtle land. It is a land the world simplifies, because in many respects the world cannot understand it, but it is by no means as simple as the world makes out. And particularly it is not simple when it comes to electing a President, for there the range of contributing factors is as wide as the gulf that separates Walter Dobius from the butcher and baker who read him in Canarsie, the people involved as diverse as the whole broad land from which they spring.

In this year in which Orrin Knox will attempt for the third and last time to win the White House, in which the Governor of California will meet him head-on in the same attempt, in which the world will again watch, always fascinated, frequently fearful, and sometimes appalled, while the great Republic teeters and trembles on the edge of what may appear to be disaster but always turns out to be just one more smooth and well-ordered transition of power, the people and factors are various indeed.

Some will be found in Africa, where the chaotic Gorotoland of His Royal Highness Terence Wolowo Ajkaje— "Terrible Terry," the 137th M'Bulu of Mbuele—is at last beginning to explode from the internal pressures of his relatives and the external pressure of the Communists. Some will be found in Panama, where Patsy's husband, Felix Labaiya-Sofra, is flying home for purposes that are perhaps less his own than he thinks. Some will be found at the United Nations and in the Congress of the United States, some at the national conventions of America's political parties. Many will be found in the shrewd, didactic world of Walter Wonderful.

A mother and her little girl, sitting even now by a coldly rushing stream in Utah's Uinta Mountains; a determined if increasingly wry Lothario who represents the dignified state of Iowa in the United States Senate; several distinguished ambassadors; a Negro Congressman from California; Edward Jason and Orrin Knox and their respective families; a Justice of the Supreme Court; Senator Fred Van Ackerman of Wyoming, national spokesman for the Committee on Making Further Offers for a Russian Truce (COMFORT); LeGage Shelby, chairman of Defenders of Equality for You (DEFY); Rufus Kleinfert, Knight Kommander of the Konference on Efforts to Encourage Patriotism (KEEP); the Speaker of the House; certain influential members of the National Committee—all these will be involved in the political battle that will swirl around the White House this year. To it each will contribute, and each extract, what the Lord sees fit to allow; not as much, in some cases, as he or she might desire; more, in some cases, than he or she intends, in these opening stages of a campaign implicit with the ultimate destinies of many things.

To some participants the final rewards will be bitter. But to others—just enough to provide some testimony to their countrymen that the system really does work despite its handicaps, that the good in it really does in the long run triumph over the bad, there will come the knowledge and the satisfaction expressed a year ago by Crystal Danta in a conversation with her father, Senator Stanley Danta of Connecticut, the Senate's Majority Whip.

She had been about to leave for Washington's National Cathedral to marry Orrin and Beth Knox's son Hal, and inevitably in a political family, politics had come up even at that most fundamental of moments. Stanley had raised the thought that Hal might someday wish to follow in Orrin's footsteps and seek public office in Illinois.

"It's a rough life," Stanley commented.

"But capable of honor," Crystal replied.

"Yes," he agreed softly. "Capable of honor."

If it were not capable of honor for some, it would indeed be worthless for all. That it is capable of honor for some saves it for all.

But to get from Here—with Patsy Labaiya just setting in motion another of her clever schemes—to There—with someone (her brother? Orrin? the President? Senator Warren Strickland, Senate Minority Leader and the minority party's likeliest candidate?) safely and honorably established in the White House, is not so open and shut as all that.

Safety is relative and honor takes some nurturing even under the best of circumstances, which a presidential campaign quite often is not. Honor is a difficult thing and apt to get skittish if it is either ignored too much or courted too avidly.

To be capable of honor is not always to achieve it. The thing takes doing.

Particularly will it take doing in this year which the small but powerful group composed of Walter Dobius and his friends has already built up to a peak of importance greater than anything in this century—unless it might perhaps be the last presidential election or, possibly, the one before. Already it is being called the most important— the most crucial—the most vital to the future of the nation —the most somberly fateful for our own democracy and the world at large—the most this—the most that—the most the other. Already it has been hailed with suitable trumpets: FATEFUL YEAR, says *Life;* YEAR OF GREAT DECISION, says *Look;* GOLLY-GEE-WHIZ-GOOD-GOSH-ALMIGHTY YEAR OF YEARS, say all the rest. Upon it they are already concentrating their perceptive typewriters, their knowledgeable microphones and cameras, their profound and endless speculations which, designed in some cases to enlighten and in some to confuse, succeed not too well in either but only add up to a kind of pounding roar which swiftly deadens the minds and dulls the sense of the electorate, until its members become really not very sure of what they think about anything.

This year the cacophony is even greater than usual because of several facts endlessly discussed by Walter and his world. One is the growing national uneasiness concerning the United Nations and the entire American position in world affairs, an uneasiness always chronic but now even greater in the wake of Terrible Terry's visit to the country six months ago and its grave consequences for the United States in the UN. Another is the increasing pressure of Communism which, never relenting underneath no matter what bland soporifics are displayed upon its surface to lull the Great Gullibles of the West, is now being pushed to ever greater pitch. And the third is the fact that someone is running for the nomination of whom Walter Wonderful and his world do not approve.

This last makes it a somber and fateful year indeed, and a note close to hysteria has entered some of the attacks being leveled against the Secretary of State as the time nears for him to make formal announcement of the candidacy which twice before has failed to take him to the White House.

This time, Walter Dobius confided recently to one of his closest cronies, the director of the *Post,* he is "going to get Orrin Knox if it's the last thing I do."

"I'm with you," the director assured him solemnly, and already his paper's editorials and cartoons have faithfully, and on most occasions savagely, reflected his cooperation.

The attack upon Orrin Knox, almost always under way in some sector of Walter Wonderful's world ever since Orrin first set foot in Washington, has never been quite as virulent as it is now. It springs from many things, but two are most immediately the concern of Walter Dobius and all who follow him. The first is the Secretary's conduct of foreign policy during the unfortunate episode created by the visit of Terrible Terry. The second and by all odds the more important is what Orrin, then senior Senator from Illinois, did a year ago to block the nomination of Robert A. Leffingwell to be Secretary of State.

The episode of Terrible Terry, which brought in its train a new inflaming of America's unhappy racial problems and the failure by only one vote of a move to expel the United States from the United Nations, did indeed mark, as Orrin has just remarked dryly to Beth, the first time in fifteen years that a Secretary of State said No to Walter Dobius.

It had not been publicized, it had been done so discreetly that it had escaped the notice of the press, but Walter had stopped by Foggy Bottom one afternoon—he had not quite had the nerve at that time to suggest that Orrin come out to Leesburg—and had proposed a course of action so out of keeping with the situation as it then was and as it later developed that Orrin had laughed in his face. Walter's astonishment was comical.

"I guess you aren't used to having Secretaries of State be so impolite to you, are you, Walter?" Orrin remarked cheerfully. His guest had flushed with anger and there had been little left of the smooth, urbane, all-knowing statesman in his reply.

"You do as you please, Orrin," he said heavily. "You always have and you always will. But don't think it will be forgotten. Don't make that mistake."

"Walter," Orrin said, "the only mistake I make is in letting your reputation fool me sometimes. Sometimes I find myself almost believing you're as profound and disinterested a sage as the public thinks you are. Then something like this comes along and I realize that no, it's just Walter, as prejudiced a Washington operator as the best of them."

"It won't be forgotten," Walter repeated with the same characteristically ponderous emphasis. *"I* won't forget."

"No," Orrin agreed, "I expect not."

And true to his promise a new sharpness had come into Walter's commentaries upon the conduct of the office of

Secretary of State: couched in the far-seeing, decades-long, history-embracing perspective he loves to use, but, in its own more graceful and more competent way, as crudely obvious as any attack by the *Post* or *Newsweek* or anyone else on that particular level of fairness and objectivity.

This, however, is merely the frosting on the cake of what Walter and his world have done, are doing, and always will do to Orrin Knox for his part in defeating Bob Leffingwell.

The Leffingwell nomination, Orrin knows now, was one of those Washington events which, like the exposure of a Harry Dexter White or the unmasking of a Hiss, bring down upon those responsible for it a grim vindictiveness, unyielding and never-resting, on the part of the guilty one's supporters—a vindictiveness which can last for many years beyond the event—last, indeed, until it sometimes achieves its objective of driving from public life altogether the persons responsible. The kind of total commitment to a cause which certain influential circles in the country have given to Robert A. Leffingwell brings in its wake total vendetta when its desires are thwarted.

Vendetta follows Orrin now, everywhere he goes.

Yet of course he could have pursued no other course, once Bob Leffingwell's lying under oath to the Senate about his early Communist associations had brought in its wake the events leading to the tragic death of Senator Brigham Anderson of Utah. Nor, probably, could anyone else involved in the Leffingwell nomination have followed a course any different than he had. It was only in their attitudes afterward that men had a choice and their true natures stood revealed.

Some, like Orrin and Senator Robert Munson of Michigan, the Senate Majority Leader, let the episode go when it was ended, accepted President Harley Hudson's appointment of Bob Leffingwell to a different job in the government, assumed that bygones could be bygones and that other, newer tasks were more important than the constant rehashing of old spites.

Not so the world of Walter Wonderful. Its members, relatively few among the Washington press corps but influential out of all proportion to their numbers, have neither forgotten nor forgiven Orrin's decisive intervention to defeat Bob Leffingwell. In a thousand ways, some direct and obvious, some so remote that many readers and viewers are fooled and only political Washington realizes where the hostility comes from, they attack the Secretary of State. And the Secretary of State, being as human as they are, and less afraid to admit it, fights back as vigorously as he knows how.

He always has. He has always been skeptical of Walter and his friends, he has always given them short shrift and small respect. They have always retaliated by describing him to the country as "impatient . . . tactless . . . too arrogant . . . too ambitious . . . wants too much to be President . . ." Filtering out through columns, editorials, and broadcasts, and from there into the common tongue, have gone certain carefully honed phrases that tag at his heels incessantly.

"I like him," Walter and his world say thoughtfully. "But I just don't think he can be elected."

Or, "He's a nice guy—in some ways he's a hell of a competent guy—but don't you think he's inclined to be somewhat erratic and unpredictable?"

Or, most damaging and always said with an air of disturbed puzzlement, "I don't know *what* it is about him, but I . . . just . . . don't . . . trust him."

Having created in the country a frame of mind in which such smoothly destructive comments spring automatically to the tongue, Walter and his world have then been able to pick them up out of general conversation and relay them back through their columns, editorials, and broadcasts in such a way as to create an unending chain of damning uncertainties about the Secretary of State.

"When you hear it said everywhere about a man that 'you just can't trust him,'" Walter had begun a recent column, "one must necessarily wonder whether you can. Such—for some reason unknown to this observer—seems to be the popular impression of an otherwise well-regarded man, the Secretary of State . . ."

Twice before, this type of coverage has had much to do with costing Orrin his chance at the White House. Now, heightened in virulence by his participation in the defeat of Bob Leffingwell, it has as its basic aim the translation of a carefully nurtured doubt into the Great Misgiving that will decide the votes of millions of Americans and, hopefully, retire him forever from the government.

Thus in this presidential year the issue is joined in its most savage and fundamental form.

Walter Dobius knows the world is waiting for his advice in the matter and he intends to give it.

There is no doubt whatsoever in his mind, as he pulls his electric typewriter toward him and starts its motor humming with a flick of his pudgy finger, that he will carry with him a majority of the national columnists, at least two radio-television networks, several major magazines, a large number of politicians, academicians, and reviewers, and a half to two-thirds of the daily newspapers in the country.

Once, when he had provoked an angry and incautious fury in another candidate to whose destruction he had devoted himself, the hard-pressed Senator had charged that "Walter Dobius is lining up the press against me!" The response had been immediate, scornful, and overwhelming.

"Is the American public being asked to assume," *Newsweek* had demanded in a near-hysteric editorial that teetered between adolescence and apoplexy, "that the influence of one man is so great—or his views so expressive of those of all the most powerful sections of press, television, and radio—that simply by stating a position he can synthesize it and advance its objectives across this whole broad land? Surely the country is not being asked to give credence to such a farcical idea!"

Nonetheless, that was exactly what the harried candidate was asking the country to give credence to. And although they very swiftly succeeded in laughing it down, that was exactly what Walter and his world also gave credence to, for it was entirely true and they knew it. That was exactly the kind of influence he did have, and it was exactly the kind that had been held by several of his predecessors in the long parade of Washington correspondents—most notably, in the middle years of the century, by the commentator to whom Bob Taft, in a scathing comparison Walter Dobius never forgave him, had once referred as "Big Walter."

"I always read Big Walter," the Senator had said, "and after that I don't need to read Little Walter. He always says the same thing."

It has been many a long year since anyone has referred to Walter Dobius as "Little Walter." No one ever will again. No one would dare.

For, as Walter Dobius is calmly aware, while his fingers hit the nervous keys with a tread as determined as his pompous voice, and the first words of his speech begin to take form on the waiting paper, *he* is Big Walter now, and what he and his world think and do about this coming election is almost more important to its outcome than any other single factor. He and his world like to tell their countrymen that they, the countrymen, decide what America will do. Walter and his world know better. They know that they do, and they know exactly how the consensus is reached: in Walter's columns and those of his major colleagues, in certain radio and television programs, at cocktail parties and candlelit dinners in Georgetown, at the National Press Club bar, in casual gossip in the press galleries of the Congress and the State Department, in certain foundation-supported study groups, seminars, and round tables, on certain major campuses, from certain well-publicized pulpits, in certain frightfully daring production offices in Hollywood, in certain solemnly self-important editorial offices in the periodicals, publishing houses, and networks of New York City.

These are the places where America's mind is really made up for it, and Walter and his world know it very well, for they are the ones who do it.

Furthermore, these are the places, and this is the method, out of which comes the picture the entire world is given of America. Certain foreign publications and correspondents are fully as susceptible to the pronouncements of Walter and his world as the most timorous would-be-sophisticate editor in Smalltown, U.S.A. As faithfully as any of his native worshipers, certain distinguished if somewhat sheeplike foreign observers in Washington and New York send home the word.

Around the globe the word spreads out. Not only in Canarsie is a reputation created or an idea destroyed, but in London and Paris, Rome and Tokyo, Bonn and New Delhi as well. One intimate little dinner given by Walter for his world at "Salubria" in Leesburg can do more to set the national and international tone toward a given personality or problem than any number of facts shouted vainly into the wind of their bland and implacable intolerance.

It is not entirely surprising that the members of Walter's world should have a rather high opinion of themselves, therefore, and that quite often in private they should recall with some satisfaction the way in which, over the years, they have steered their well-meaning but really rather stupid country past so many pitfalls—saved her from so many serious errors of policy and belief—and prevented her from turning in her folly and bemusement to so many wrong-thinking and unworthy men.

Not, of course, that Walter and his world ever admit publicly to this protective guidance they believe themselves to exercise over their fey and wayward land. It is one of their strongest tenets that no one must ever be allowed to think that they have any conscious knowledge of what they are doing, or that there is, in fact, a pattern of thinking and attitude and reportage which is followed faithfully by all of them as each new public figure or policy appears upon the horizon. Their countrymen must always be given to understand that no one is more independent than Walter and his friends, none more sternly objective, none less moved by the passions and prejudices that afflict ordinary men. About themselves they drape the mantle of a terrible and terrifying righteousness, even as they engage in the most savage personal attacks upon those who disagree with them, even as they deftly slant and suavely tear down everything and all who attempt to stand in their way.

And yet—while there are those who believe it and say so darkly—it would really be quite naïve to think that this is a deliberate plot on the part of Walter and his world. There is here no Great Conspiracy such as their more conservative countrymen profess to see.

There is, rather, the much simpler, quite naïve, and really quite pathetic conspiracy of just wanting to be popular with the right people in the right places; to take, as Patsy puts it, "the Right Position on things"; to live snug and secure in a nest of parroted certainties about all the frightful problems to which you do not, really, know the answers; and to have the comfortable assurance that nobody is going to be sarcastic about *your* ideas, nobody is going to tear down *your* reputation, nobody is going to treat *you* with ridicule.

Ridicule in particular is a key to why Walter's world became the way it is. Its members simply cannot stand to be laughed at. They know what a weapon ridicule can be, for it is one of the most effective in their own arsenal, a scourge to those they don't like, and a powerful means of bringing into line colleagues who threaten to express an independent viewpoint. Ridicule terrifies them. They do all they can to keep it away from their world and to make sure that it is never, never turned against them.

Once upon a time the members of Walter's world were

young, coming to Washington from all parts of the country fired with an idealistic vision, supported and held high by the determination to tell America the truth honestly and fearlessly regardless of whom it might help or hinder. Then came the swift attrition of the years, the frightening collaboration of time and ambition, the desperate running after the popularity of the inward group. Almost without their knowing it they soon began to write, not for the country, but for each other. They began to report and interpret events, not according to the rigid standards of honesty upon which the great majority of them had been reared in their pre-Washington days, but according to what might or might not be acceptable in the acidly easygoing wisecracks of the Press Club bar and the parties at which they entertained one another. In time it became more important for them to receive the congratulations of their fellows—and at all costs to avoid their sarcastic laughter—than it did to receive the congratulations of a clear conscience.

For just as surely as Washington's seductive glamor corrupts some politicians, so too does it corrupt the world of Walter Wonderful. The process is hardly conscious, seldom sinister. It is just that it is so much more pleasant to be popular with your friends than it is to write the harsh, objective truth. It is so much easier and more comfortable to adopt the automatic, well-polished attitudes of the group than it is to take the hard and lonely road of thinking for yourself. It is so much nicer—and so much more profitable —to be In than Out.

Not, of course—as Walter sometimes realizes, a little uneasily—that this applies to all who are in, or about, or involved with, his world. There are many who came to Washington determined to tell the straight, unslanted truth and have remained true to that high ideal during many long and faithful years of service in the press. There are columnists and reporters who were capable of honor when they came to the capital, and live by honor still. Helen-Anne Carrew, in her raucous, self-opinionated way, is one. There are a good many others, liberal or conservative as it suits them, but alike in their devotion to the truth and their determination to tell it regardless of whether it helps or hurts their favorites, frustrates or assists their enemies.

But their ranks are dwindling and their influence declines alongside the national and international power of Walter's world.

The advantages held by those who believe in the Right Position are too great for the skeptically honest to overcome. Being popular with each other has become the surest road to fame and fortune, and year after year shrewd young applicants, trained in a new school, thinking Right Thoughts, come to Washington, seek their places with an eager ambition, and are fitted smoothly into the mold.

Once—just once—a certain satiric self-knowledge about all this was allowed to creep into a Gridiron Club show. Some irreverent soul managed to have accepted for performance (nobody knew how, when an indignant postmortem was held) a jovially acrid skit in which a row of members dressed as defeated presidential candidates tripped to the footlights. Wistfully they sang:

> "Oh—
> you—
> can—

> "Slant the news,
> Twist our views,
> Warp the facts,
> Give us the ax—

> "*But*—
> *if*—
> *you*—

> "Stand tall in Georgetown,
> Stand tall in Georgetown,
> *Stand tall in Georgetown,*

> "You're—
> all—
> RIGHT!"

This had produced such a raucous cheer from the Gridiron's roster of distinguished political and diplomatic guests that its like had never been permitted again. But from that time forward, "Stand tall in Georgetown!" became, as it remains, a favorite joke in the world of Walter Wonderful.

"Got to stand tall in Georgetown!" somebody will grin, skillfully boosting Bobby, vilifying Dick, sanctifying Adlai, blackguarding Barry. "Better watch out or you won't stand tall in Georgetown!" someone else will chuckle to a friend who has inadvertently been fair to the other side.

Stand tall in Georgetown!

It is the surest way to fame and preferment in Walter's world, and the goal inspires them all.

Or almost all, he thinks with an impatient annoyance as the phone rings loudly in the quiet room and he pauses, methodically turns off the electric typewriter, and lifts the receiver to hear an all-too-familiar voice. There are people in Washington who never will think Right Thoughts, adhere to the Right Position, give him the respect which is his due. Fortunately they aren't very numerous. Most people, he thinks with a tiny smile of satisfaction about his lips as he recalls Patsy Labaiya's greeting, think he's God.

Not so, he remembers as the smile fades and a grim little line furrows his forehead, his ex-wife.

"I suppose I'm interrupting genius again, but, God, Walter, life is so exciting when you're involved that I just couldn't hold back."

"Yes, I know," he said dryly. "What's on your mind?"

"I want to know if you're going to fall for Patsy's line and get suckered in on Ted Jason's campaign. It seems a legitimate inquiry, between us two old friends."

"Are you going to warn me against it?" he inquired politely. "How very thoughtful of you, dear."

"I think it would be stupid. And I don't conceive of you as stupid, Walter. Misled by ego sometimes, but not stupid."

"Oh, I am, am I?" he demanded, his voice losing its customary careful gravity and flaring into the sudden anger only she knew how to provoke. Damnable woman, anyway. It was the reason their marriage had been impossible from the start: she was so disrespectful and she—she made him mad. A snort was her only response to his tone now: it was absolutely typical. "I am not!" he said angrily. "Ego doesn't have anything to do with it!"

"Oh, of course it does," she said impatiently. "You'd just love to be the gray eminence of the White House, dear heart. You didn't make it with Lyndon but maybe you might with Ted. Plus the fact that you still get a thrill out of dragging the press and TV after you. You just love being Walter Wonderful, the swayer of mankind. Come on, now. 'Fess up."

"I have always thought," he said, breathing hard, "that you were particularly obnoxious when you tried to be kittenish. ' 'Fess up!' It's like an elephant with a teacup."

"Come, come," she said briskly, "stop trying to be nasty, Walter. You don't really know how to do it in personal relationships. Dr. Dobius only insults through his column. Personally, I've never thought you really had the heart—not the willingness, but the honest-to-God heart inside you—to be honestly blind-mad at somebody. There always has to be a cold-blooded motivation you can express in some devious, involuted way. Anyway, we're getting afield—the same old field. I repeat, I hope you're not going to be a sucker for the Jasons. Ted isn't worth it."

"Governor Jason," he said coldly, "is a most attractive candidate and one worthy of any trust the country may desire to place upon him."

"Are you quoting? Is that the speech? Oh, it will be one of your smasheroos, Walter, I can see that. But I think you'd be a fool to do it."

"Now, see here," he said, striving hard to put the conversation back on the rational plane from which she always tried to shift it, "surely you aren't suggesting that I should support Orrin Knox? After all he's done?"

"What has he done?" she inquired with a deliberate blankness. "Except be an honest man acting on his honest convictions? I know that's considered rather square in your crowd, Walter, but I've got news for you. A lot of your countrymen still go for it in spite of all the educational efforts you and your pals have expended on them in the past few decades."

"Have you talked to Bob Leffingwell about it?" he demanded abruptly.

"I don't see what bearing that has, but I have. At the Nigerian Embassy last night. At some length. Have you?"

"Not for about a month," he said, relieved that she seemed to be diverted from her personal attacks.

"You should. You might be surprised. He isn't so hot for Ted as all that."

"I don't believe you," he said flatly.

This time she got mad.

"Walter Dobius, one thing I don't do is lie, and you know it. Now, stop that. Get out of your dream world and get with it, for a change. You've lived in that ivory tower too long."

"Nobody else on earth," he said in a grating voice, "has

the colossal nerve to talk to me like that. Now, you stop it."

"Now, you stop it," she mimicked. "You stop shaking poor old Walter's faith in himself. He hasn't got too much, you know."

"Helen-Anne," he said in the same harsh tone, "I'm going to hang up on you."

"No, you're not," she said calmly, "because I'm a smart woman and you know it and you're always ready to pick my brains and so you won't do any hanging up until I've had my say. Now, I've been around this town just about as long as you have, dearie, and I've been talking to some people myself. I think you'll be making the mistake of a lifetime if you line up with Ted."

"What do you care?" he asked bitterly. "All you've ever wanted was to see me brought down. You've always been jealous because I was more famous than you, you've always resented it that my column has 436 papers and yours only has 321—"

"Walter," she said, "stop talking like a petulant child, and listen to me. There's something phony about that candidacy and there always has been. I haven't found out what it is, yet, but I will. Or maybe we all will, all at once. At which time Walter Wonderful, if he's out in front leading the parade, may suddenly find himself in a rather awkward position. Awkward positions, Walter, are something we must avoid, you know, at all costs. Isn't that Rule One?"

"Are you through insulting me?" he asked in a weary tone. She snorted.

"Oh, my, the Dying Swan. I'm not insulting you, love. I'm just trying to get you to be very cautious on this one."

"Anyway," he said, changing to a patient tone such as one would use with a child, which was really all she was under the hardboiled-newspaperwoman exterior, "what is so phony about the Governor of California aspiring to the Presidency of the United States? Harley's predecessor was Governor of California. It's a big state. It's been done before."

"Sure, and people buying their way into the White House has been done before, too. But that isn't the answer to everything. No, I think you'd better think it over. Something tells me this may get quite sticky before we're through."

"You always have been a conservative," he said in a tone popular in his world, the tone that indicates that being conservative is the worst possible sin a body could commit. "You always have liked Orrin Knox."

"I like his guts," she said. "And stop using your cant words on me, Walter. They're ridiculous and they don't scare *me*. You can terrify a lot of our friends in press and television by calling them conservative, but not me. I don't give a damn. I'm interested in what a man is, not in the label you and your pals manage to hang on him. Now: I'm just telling you, and"—her tone became noticeably dry— "in my own small way, Walter, boy, I'm just as infallible as you are—that you'll be making a mistake if you go too far out on a limb for Edward Jason. It's a screwball family, in more ways than one, and having several hundred millions just means that its several hundred million times more screwball. I'd go slow, if I were you. That's all."

"I am so touched by your concern," he said with an equal dryness.

"You should be. I don't show it to everyone."

"Yes, you do," he said honestly. "To a lot of people. You do have a kind heart underneath it all. But why to me?"

"You'll never know, Walter, darling. Maybe because I still love you passionately, in the secret silence of my lonely room."

It was his turn to sound skeptical.

"No doubt."

"Believe it. It's good for the ego."

"Of which you tell me I already have too much. Thank you for calling," he said formally, his voice regaining its customary solemn authority, preparing to bid her farewell. "I appreciate your interest."

"O.K. Back to the drawing board, now! Give 'em hell in that speech. We'll all be there to listen. Just remember what I said."

"I couldn't care less what you say," he told her with a last flare of annoyance. But she only gave her ribald laugh.

"Oh, yes, Walter, dear. Oh, yes. That's the trouble. That was always the trouble."

"Aaaaarrrkh!" he exclaimed, a sound inconsistent with his dignity but expressive of his feelings, and replaced the receiver with rather more vehemence than his vast public

would have associated with the figure of gravely impersonal philosopher-statesman Walter Dobius.

After that for a while, of course, his concentration was
shot and there was little point in trying to go on with his
speech. Helen-Anne always had this effect upon him; it was
one of the main reasons their marriage had broken up. He
just couldn't concentrate with her around the house being
disrespectful and unimpressed and building up her syndication on the basis of her hunches about things which nine
times out of ten, infuriatingly, turned out to be right. And
now she had done it again, with her mysterious nagging
about Ted Jason. Who on earth did she want in the White
House anyway, Orrin Knox? He was beginning to think so,
and if anything was calculated to drive him farther toward
Ted, it was the thought that his ex-wife might be for Orrin.

Except, of course, that as Helen-Anne said, he wasn't
stupid, and he did value her judgment in spite of everything. What on earth had her worried about the Jasons?
They had their foibles, but what Presidential or potentially
Presidential family didn't? In Washington the warts of the
great were considerably more visible than they were out in
the country, but everyone had them and there didn't seem
to him anything noticeably unusual about the Jasons'. Particularly when Governor Jason represented a political philosophy—"moderate" was the label Walter and his world
had begun to apply to him with increasing frequency in
these past several weeks—that offered a position infinitely
more desirable than that of the Secretary of State, with his
annoying tendency to act on the basis of principle instead
of on the automatic catch-phrases that Walter and his
friends had evolved to rationalize the catastrophic changes
of a churning world.

Still, Helen-Anne had been quite positive. He made
again his half-coherent sound of protest and got up impatiently from his desk. The darkness outside was complete,
now, and over the sleepy snapping of the fire only an occasional slap of snow, carried on the vicious wind against the
old home's leaded windows, brought reminder of the bitter
weather raging. Downstairs Arbella would be readying dinner: and by the downstairs fireplace Roosevelt would soon
be mixing the customary Manhattan and placing it on the
antique table by the big leather armchair. One cocktail and

one glass of wine with dinner: the rule was virtually inviolate. But tonight, he thought with sudden viciousness as savage as the wind, he might just have two cocktails and three or four glasses of wine, since Helen-Anne wanted his concentration ruined. He'd really ruin it!

But this, of course, was just a passing thought for Walter Dobius, who had never done anything impulsive or uncareful in his life. In an instant it was gone. Methodically he placed his papers in a neat pile, checked the fire screen to make sure it was snug against the hearth, pressed his forehead for a moment against the icy pane and attempted without success to see out into the dark woods, and then turned and started to snap off the desk light, so that no electricity would be wasted between now and the time after dinner when he would return to resume working on his speech.

As he did so, the phone rang again. He hesitated for a second, then took up the receiver with an impatient hand. The little tinkling tremolos of long distance came to his ear. His expression changed to one of interest and then, as his caller introduced himself, to one of pleased attention. Slowly he sat back down again.

"Walter," the confident voice of Governor Jason said across three thousand miles, "Patsy tells me you're having a hell of a snowstorm back there. I've been on the beach all day at La Jolla. Pity me!"

Walter Dobius chuckled.

"You pioneers really have to rough it, out there in the Far West. Am I seeing you for lunch on Thursday?"

"You are. I couldn't be happier about it. I hope I can resolve then any doubts that you may have."

"I haven't many," Walter said complacently (for at least the Governor of California knew who he was talking to, and showed the proper respect). "I'm sure what there are won't be insurmountable."

"I hope not," Ted said frankly. "Your influence is so great that it would be an enormous help to me if I had your approval—and an enormous detriment if I didn't." He gave a flattering little laugh and added with a flattering candor, "Nothing is more important to me than satisfying Walter Dobius, I can tell you that."

"Yes," Walter said gravely. "I think I probably am in a position to have a decisive effect on your candidacy at this particular moment."

"None more so," Governor Jason said with an equal gravity. "I join Patsy in her delight that you have accepted our invitation to be the recipient of the Good and Faithful Servant Award this year. We look forward with lively anticipation to your speech." He gave an engaging chuckle. "For obvious reasons. What are you seeing of my distinguished opponent these days?"

"Orrin?" The Governor could not see Walter's sour little smile, but he could sense it in his tone, amply enough. "Orrin and I haven't had occasion to chat much, lately. Although," he added thoughtfully, "I intend to talk to him prior to Friday night. I think in fairness I should."

"Is it an elimination contest?" Governor Jason asked with a certain asperity he did not attempt to soften. "I didn't understand your principles were up for bids, Walter."

There was a stunned silence. Finally Walter said coldly:

"Only a man possessed of supreme confidence in himself would venture such a remark to me."

Ted laughed.

"Possessed of supreme confidence in you, Walter. If I had the slightest doubt about your principles, I can assure you you would not be selected for GAFSA if it cost me the White House to refuse you. The Jasons have some pride too, you know.

"Too much, I sometimes think," Walter could not resist. "As for Orrin, I think both you and Patsy take too much for granted about my feelings toward him. He is not an incompetent man, you know, or a poor public servant. In a great many ways there is much to admire in Orrin Knox."

"Very true. He has just one handicap."

"What's that?"

"You don't like him."

"I hope my opposition is not based on so frivolous a foundation," Walter said stiffly. "Really, Ted, I have noted this flippant streak in you before. As I told Patsy, I have a great responsibility to the country. I cannot base my decisions on personal prejudice or passion. The country expects too much of me. It places too great a reliance on what I say. I am too important to it. I can't afford to treat things so lightly."

"That is true," Ted Jason said in an abruptly serious, soothing tone. "I know I shouldn't joke about it, but sometimes the pressures of holding office and seeking office are such that I have to relax a little by joshing old friends. Of course I know how important you are. And of course I respect it. Aren't I calling you now? Aren't I coming to Washington a day early just so I can have lunch with you on Thursday? Who else does the Governor of California put himself out for in that fashion, except possibly the President of the United States?"

"Will you be seeing him when you're here?"

Ted responded with a rueful laugh.

"I would think so. I would think so. Enigmatic Harley the Sphinx of the Potomac has to be prayed to, you know, by all us dutiful supplicants. I imagine Orrin drops in every hour on the hour. The least I can do is swing by on my way through town. Have you talked to him yourself in the past few days?"

"He invited me over last Thursday night," Walter said. "We talked for almost an hour and a half, entirely alone. He said he had been missing me and felt the need for my counsel." He gave a dry little laugh. "That's what they all say. He did most of the talking and I didn't learn a damned thing. So much for my intimate chats with the President."

"Yes," Ted said thoughtfully. "He certainly is playing it coy this time. I wouldn't really be surprised if he decided to run after all, when all's said and done, and just leave me and Orrin out there on a limb of our own devising."

"I have some hopes that after my speech Friday night he will find this difficult to do."

"You're probably right," Governor Jason said. An admiring note came into his voice. "I know of no one else in the nation in a similar position, able, as you are, to force the hand of the President of the United States in such a vital matter."

"I can't force his hand, but I can make it difficult for him to move in certain directions. I do have that much influence with my colleagues and the country, I think."

"It's the colleagues who count, Walter," Governor Jason said, and it was impossible to tell whether he was being respectful or wry, "not the country. Persuade your colleagues, and they'll take care of the country."

"They don't need too much persuading when confronted by a choice between a supremely equipped man and one only half-equipped. My work is mostly done for me. All I have to do is synthesize the mood and start it into action, and the rest will take care of itself. I think I can say without excessive egotism that I can do so."

"Good," Ted said in a relieved voice. "Good. Then I shall not attempt to press you any further as to what your decision will be. As long as I know you are judging matters with the fairness and objectivity so long associated with the name of Walter Dobius, I shall rest content with the decision. I know I need have no fear about it. No one of integrity need fear Walter Dobius."

"I hope not. It has always been my aim to foster integrity in this government and sanity in its policies. I hope that will stand as one of my major achievements when the final record is read."

"It will," Ted assured him solemnly. "It will, by anyone's standards. Very well, then, I shall see you on Thurs—"

"By the way," Walter said abruptly, "why did your brother-in-law fly home to Panama so suddenly?"

"I didn't know he had," Governor Jason said blankly. "Patsy didn't mention it. Has he gone?"

"Yes, quite suddenly. And just on the eve of the Security Council debate on Gorotoland, too. It seems odd."

"It does seem odd. I can call our company people in Panama City, if you like, and let you know what they say."

"If you could, I'd appreciate it. I'm going up to the UN tomorrow to see Terrible Terry and cover the Gorotoland debate. I think it's about time for a column, or maybe several, on the UN. Panama could certainly become the basis for one of them, if Felix is up to anything."

"Felix usually is," Ted Jason said, not bothering to conceal his distaste. "I'll get back to you later tonight."

"Please do. And I shall see you Thursday."

"Looking forward with pleasure," Governor Jason said.

And so much, Miss Helen-Anne, for you, Walter thought with a savage satisfaction as Ted's voice faded. He told himself at once, of course, that the satisfaction was unworthy of him, but still he couldn't help feeling a little of it. She was so damned disrespectful and knowing and unimpressed. He *was* Walter Dobius, Governors of California *did* telephone him cross-country just to stay on his good side, President of the United States *did* call him in privately to get his counsel and advice, his colleagues in the world of Walter Wonderful really *did* follow his lead on policies and personalities. He was indeed as powerful and major a figure as the world believed. What right, then, did a —a *gossip columnist*—have, to attempt to destroy his confidence in himself and try to persuade him that he could be in error on anything? It was laughable, simply laughable.

"Ha, ha!" he said aloud into the snug little study, warm and safe from the snows outside, and instantly felt better for it. "Ha, ha!"

"Mist' Waaaallll—*ta?*" Arbella called from below in her characteristic long-drawn yelp. "Me and Roosevelt's 'bout ready!"

"All right," he called back. "I'll be right down."

This time he actually got out the door before the phone rang, and for a second he contemplated letting it go. But he had always prided himself on keeping a listed number, unlike many of his colleagues, and upon answering it himself whenever possible, so after a moment he returned to his desk and picked it up again. Again it was long distance and he felt even more like saying, "Ha, ha!" to Helen-Anne. The Soviet Ambassador was on the line.

"Good evening, Mr. Dobius," Vasily Tashikov said in the perfectly good English he always pretended he couldn't use when his diplomatic colleagues were harrying him about something. "I was wondering if you were planning to come to the UN tomorrow, and if so, if you might have lunch with me?"

"I am planning to if the storm stops and the planes are flying. I should, I think, be quite delighted. But you must let me be host, inasmuch as I shall undoubtedly be picking your brains, as we say, for my column."

"I know the phrase," the Soviet Ambassador said. "It is I who may be doing the picking, I think. Therefore I shall be host. I wish your advice on how to proceed against the imperialist attempt to thwart the desires of the citizens of the People's Free Republic of Gorotoland."

"I see," Walter Dobius said, a little less cordially. "You realize of course that my country is one of those you are attacking. I may not be able to help you very much."

"I think you can," Tashikov said. "You are a very famous man, Mr. Dobius. Very famous. You are a bridge between East and West, for your fame is universal. Possibly on that bridge we can cross to understanding. That is why I wish to have lunch."

"I am always willing to help if I can," Walter said, flattered in spite of reminding himself that you always had to be on guard, you couldn't trust their apparent cordiality for a second, it always concealed some devious and dangerous purpose. "I should like to think I could contribute to understanding between the two worlds."

(*The Two Worlds* by Walter Dobius, Harper & Row, 341 pp., $5.95, had been one of his most popular books, thirteen weeks as No. 1 on the New York *Times* best-seller list. From it the phrase "positive acceptance" had entered the language: *"We must achieve, if you please, a positive acceptance, not a sourly negative attitude, toward those necessary expressions of Communist self-interest which, while they may embarrass us as a nation and alarm some of our more tradition-bound citizens, are nonetheless the logical expression of the Communist desire to share equally with us the burdens of organizing and running the world."* "Positive acceptance" had instantly leaped into a hundred State Department position papers, a thousand columns, editorials, and broadcasts, speech after speech by the country's more enlightened thinkers. Orrin Knox had referred to it as "the art of positive sinking," which was another reason Walter considered him unfit to be President.)

"You do contribute to understanding," Tashikov assured him. "You always have, more so, my dear Mr. Dobius, than anyone else in your country. Your columns, books, and speeches have built a foundation of good will between us that nothing can change. From 'Mr. K'—that warm, fatherly cognomen which did so much to change your countrymen's attitude toward us!—right on down to 'positive acceptance,' you have always been in the vanguard of those who seek to persuade the United States to abandon her foolish opposition to the inevitable and to be more compliant with our just desires. No one deserves our gratitude more. That is why," he ended in a businesslike tone, "I wish to have lunch."

"You give me too much credit," Walter Dobius remarked, "inasmuch as I assure you my purpose has not been to persuade my country to abandon her opposition to things she honestly feels to be wrong, but only to those things in which certain reactionary native prejudices have blinded our people to your justified self-interest and the necessary adjustments we must make in the cause of genuine world peace."

"We know you are absolutely sincere, Mr. Dobius, that is why we honor you. Shall we say 1 P.M. tomorrow in the Delegates' Dining Room?"

"That would be agreeable to me. I am wondering—"

"Yes?"

"I am very anxious to have a talk with Prince Terry— His Highness the M'Bulu—"

"That lackey of the imperialist warmongers?" Vasily Tashikov cried. "That betrayer of the freedoms of Gorotoland? He will not attend my luncheon, Mr. Dobius, I can assure you of that! Never!"

"But I thought the Soviet Union was a great friend of his," Walter said blandly. "I remember only six months ago in the General Assembly—"

"He is a betrayer!" Tashikov said angrily. "He runs the imperialist errands of Washington and London! He is an enemy of his own people and of all freedom-loving peoples everywhere!"

"I shall be happy to have lunch," Walter said cordially. "I want you to tell me all about it. Then perhaps I can help America understand your shift in position."

"Hurry," Vasily Tashikov advised grimly. "Your M'Bulu will not be there long."

"But I will be, Mr. Ambassador," Walter assured him. "Don't forget my bridge between East and West. It will be there, I think, whatever happens to Gorotoland. Or, for that matter," he added calmly, "the Soviet Union. You can also tell me, incidentally, why Felix Labaiya had to fly home, and what you're planning in Panama."

"One P.M. tomorrow," the Ambassador said in an expressionless voice.

"Surely," said Walter Dobius.

This, he tells himself as he closes the door of the study at last and starts down the stairs to his waiting dinner, is really quite a typical period in the life of Walter Wonderful. The Governor of California, the Russian Ambassador, a few nights ago the President of the United States—these things happen to Walter Dobius all the time. How can Helen-Anne be so imperceptive as to fail to see it, so unthinking as to laugh?

Actually, of course, she isn't. She knows exactly the kind of life he leads, for she shared it for seven years, and on a smaller scale she leads much the same kind of life herself. There is nothing so extraordinary about being called by the Governor of California, invited by the Soviet Ambassador, consulted by the President of the United States—these things do happen, at a certain level of press and politics in Washington. It is just that in Walter's case there is a unique emphasis about it, a special aura, a feeling on both sides that he who calls will receive assistance, he who consults will be given a sage and dispassionate wisdom suitable to the unraveling of great problems, the surmounting of great events. If a few observers sometimes feel that Walter with his enormous influence is more often the used than the user, then that simply shows a lack of perception monumental in its misunderstanding of his position in the story of his times. Walter knows what he is doing, and very few indeed are those who fail to take him at his own estimation.

This has not been happenstance, he can congratulate himself as he slowly sips his Manhattan and stares thoughtfully into the roaring downstairs fire while Roosevelt hovers about and Arbella clatters in the kitchen, nor has it been any fluke such as sometimes occurs when Washington's erratic tides toss surprising jetsam to the top. Walter has worked hard for what he has, and Walter deserves it. He may seem a little precious now, there may be an air of dignity slightly greater (if that be possible) than the responsibility and he has not achieved it lightly.

Patsy may regard him with the spiteful attitude with which she regards most people, Helen-Anne from the vantage point of a special knowledge may feel and express a disenchantment more blunt and open than many dare, the Knoxes may be skeptical, Ted Jason, the President, and many another ambitious politician domestic and foreign may think that they play upon his ego to use him for their purposes, but no one can ever truthfully say that Walter Dobius is not exactly where he should be. He has earned his position honestly and he fills it with style.

What citizen of a land that has for so long been dependent upon his wisdom could, in all fairness, ask for more?

Certainly the list of honors and accomplishments indicates that few do. Pulitzer Prize three times, twice for national reporting, once for international; Sigma Delta Chi Award for Washington Correspondence twice; the Heywood Broun Award; the Raymond Clapper Memorial Award; the University of Missouri Award for distinguished service in journalism; the Overseas Press Club Award, the John Peter Zenger Award, the George Polk Award, and now the Jason Foundation's Good and Faithful Servant Award; writer of the nation's most influential column for twenty-five years; steady contributor to national magazines; special lecturer at ten universities here and abroad in the past twelve years, favorite speaker at the annual conventions of everything from the American Society of Newspaper Editors to Rotary International; repeatedly rumored (though never quite selected) choice for the Nobel Peace Prize; adviser to the powerful in his own land, intimate and familiar of the powerful in many a foreign land as well; statesman, philosopher, counselor, and guide to his own worshipful profession; one of the four or five major figures in the political thought of the twentieth century—

If he has critics, they are minor. If he has enemies, they are mute.

When Walter speaks, the world literally listens.

But it was not always so.

Indeed, when he pauses sometimes to reflect upon his early years—and he does so, quite conscientiously, two or three times a week, because, as he once told Helen-Anne (not entirely, as she knew, in jest) "it keeps me humble"—he is struck with a certain wonderment that he should have reached the pinnacle he has. Not too much wonderment, for that would imply a lack of self-confidence of which no one has ever accused him, but enough to prove that he too, as he is fond of saying, is just as human as anyone else who has climbed the heights in Washington.

From what he is fond of referring to as "the bogs and moors of my childhood" to "Salubria" in Leesburg and all it connotes has been a journey whose ultimate triumph few save himself could have foreseen. When his father brought the family from Saxony's Luneburger Heath to America, Walter was two (his memory of the bogs and moors not quite so vivid, perhaps, as in later years he has become fond of recounting from the public platform). The job his father found, that of a meat cutter in Philadelphia, did not give his family much promise of an affluent future. For most of Walter's childhood and adolescence this remained true. The memory of always living in near-poverty, or on the edge of it, has proved a great goad to the family's second son. From the time he was able, he did menial labor and odd jobs of all kinds to help out, and he did them well and without complaining. It made him a lonely, hardworking, and self-sufficient child who had few friends but much respect. He always preferred it so, and eventually he came to realize the value of it to the particular kind of career he finally found. He emerged from a grueling childhood with a grim inner determination that he was someday going to get out of all this and never turn back. Suddenly in high school he found the means. He discovered that he had been blessed with a certain ability to use words, and with it an air of authority that persuaded his teachers and contemporaries that he wrote with a perception and force unusually impressive in an adolescent. He was on his way.

With this gift—"The Lord was good to me, in my talent," he had remarked in the same Columbia School of Journalism speech that had provoked such hosannas from his hearers and the press—"and I have tried to be faithful to Him, in my use of it"—went a native doggedness and diligence that made of young Walter Dobius one of the hardest-working and most ambitious students ever to edit the school paper and graduate with top honors while doing so. Hard work marked him then and hard work marks him now, filled with honors and power as he is. To this day, Walter Dobius does not relax. He performed then, and he still does, the hard, patient, relentless digging that is the mark of the top reporter.

Whenever a big story broke on campus, in high school or later at Yale, where he edited the *Daily,* Walter was there, his sturdy figure trudging into the thick of it, pencil raised, voice insistent, asking his blunt, demanding questions until he got the answers. Whenever a big story breaks in Washington now, Walter is there, his sturdy figure trudging down the corridors of State Department or Senate, emerging from inside closed committee hearings and secret international conferences ("Now, how the hell did Walter get in there?" his exasperated colleagues demand of one another, but only a secret little smile around his lips betrays his knowledge at their consternation and his satisfaction at having caused it), getting exclusive interviews with visiting heads of state, standing at the President's elbow as he delivers his latest pronouncement on the crises of a disintegrating world. Walter is there because he is Walter Dobius, friend of the mighty, just as he was there in school days because he was Walter Dobius, friend of the mighty. But he is also there, and always has been, because he is Walter Dobius, magnificent and indefatigable reporter.

It is the foundation of his fame and the true basis of his power; and it is the element which perhaps more than any other gives his words the weight they have.

"Walter is a pompous, patronizing, insufferable sh . . . owoff," one of his most famous colleagues remarked thoughtfully one night in the Press Club bar, "but he does go to the source."

And the sources go to Walter and together—or so he tells himself with a secret pleasure he would be inhuman not to feel—they run the world.

(Nowadays the claim is not far from the truth. Two or three times a year in London, for instance, the phone will ring at No. 10 Downing Street and the familiarly casual, heavy voice will say, "Reggie?" (or "Harold?") "I'm just in town for a day or two. I wonder if we could have lunch?" And Harold—or Reggie—will obediently drop everything and oblige, aware that behind the voice lie 436 newspapers, an international reputation, and—perhaps—the key to swaying the opinions of a baffling and erratic ally. Similarly from Moscow or Peking, Paris or New Delhi, there will come from time to time the impossible-to-get interview, the exclusive revelation, handed down by men who find in Walter the surest road to the world's front pages, the most effective channel through which to disclose their purposes and threaten, or cajole, the hearts and minds of men.)

Out of the high school editorship, however, out of Yale after editing the *Daily*, something suddenly seemed to go wrong. There followed a dark period of several years during which the future sage somehow failed to find his place. It was the only time in his life when he came close to doubting himself.

He began with a good job on the Hartford *Courant*. At once he ran into trouble. Possibly, as he long ago became convinced, it was the difficult personalities of his fellow workers that started their immediate mistrust and misunderstanding. Possibly, as one of them indicated years later in a witty and quickly discredited article in *National Review* entitled, "I Remember Walter," it was his own personality which was at fault.

In any event a clash was immediate. Somehow his colleagues got the unjust and unwarranted idea that Walter was after their jobs—not anyone's in particular, just that of whoever happened to be in his way. Actually, it was just that Walter, in his usual hard-working fashion, seemed to get there first on every good assignment. This went on for some eight months, until the day when the paper's top political reporter, arriving ten minutes late for an interview with the governor, found Walter already deep in earnest conversation with him behind closed doors and got the unfortunate impression that Walter was after his job. An ultimatum to the editor followed, and with a mixture of reluctance because he recognized Walter's abilities, and compliance, because he recognized his all-consuming drive for power, the editor suggested that Walter might prefer a larger arena for his talents. The editor murmured vaguely of New York and Washington, confident that in those competitive jungles Walter would either go under or hit the top. Nowadays, long since retired in Darien, he is fond of recounting how certain he was that Walter would do the latter.

But Walter didn't get that impression then, and it was only years later, when he was in the process of mellowing his image all along the line, that he had invited the editor to introduce him when he spoke to the annual convention of the American Society of Newspaper Editors in Washington. On a wave of sentimental applause from the audience, all of whom fondly fancied themselves to be in the same position of constantly helping to boost brilliant young talent up the ladder to success, the hostile aspects of Walter's parting from his old boss had been blurred out and the event had been riveted finally into legend in the form in which both he and Walter now preferred it.

At the time, however, the event had been quite shattering, though then, as now, he did not show his feelings to the world. For several days he went through a considerable hell, wondering quite seriously whether there was any place in his chosen profession for conscientious talent and genuine ability. It had honestly never occurred to him—and it has not occurred to him since, that he might be treading on other people's feelings. He quite genuinely did not realize that it is possible to be ruthless with a certain grace that can save it from being cruel. "The thing I love about Walter," Helen-Anne remarked years later, "is his tact." But even as she said it a curious pain came into her eyes that startled her listeners. "Poor devil," she added, and abruptly changed the subject with some profane comment on the First Lady that diverted them into forgetting laughter.

To this day Walter honestly does not know that he has hurt people along the way, or that he is still hurting them, in his column and in his speeches and, sometimes, in his personal relationships (though these in recent years have been cut to a minimum to permit him more freedom to concentrate upon his work) He just knows that he has certain things to say and certain things to do, and if others get in the way he considers it unfortunate but their own fault for not understanding that their wishes must be subordinate to his. Toward Orrin Knox, for instance, he is sure he has only the kindliest personal feelings but he also knows that Orrin should not be President. In the defeat of that misguided and dangerous ambition any misrepresentation in the column is justified, any smear is reasonable, any cruelty excusable. For they do not seem so to Walter, any more than they do to others in his world. Walter, as he is fond of saying on the rare occasions when someone ventures to criticize him for a particularly savage column, wouldn't hurt a fly. More than that, he is conscientiously generous to those about him. With a sort of horrible, heavy-handed graciousness he goes about his world encouraging other correspondents, figuratively patting younger colleagues on the head (providing they agree with him), giving fatherly advice to those whose own talents are sufficiently great that they can hardly bear to accept it with civility, and generally playing the part of the kindly senior squire. Helen-Anne calls him tactless, his older colleagues call him patronizing, but Walter is absolutely sincere about it. For all his brilliance, he has a childlike inability to sense or understand the personal feelings of others. It is perhaps no wonder Helen-Anne can still feel pain for Walter, who is so self-armored that he cannot feel it for himself.

But in Hartford at the age of twenty-two, this was probably a blessing, for it permitted him to gather himself together without too much difficulty and start off to the Washington upon which his heart had always been set. He had not planned to attack it quite so soon, but later this turned out to be the best thing that could have happened.

Again, however, nothing came right at first, and again he went through several periods of doubt and despair. Working in turn for the Washington *Times-Herald*, and the *Evening Star*, he found himself frequently involved over four or five years in the same kind of difficulty he encountered in Hartford. Everyone respected his talent and disliked his personality. Frictions—always due to the failure of others to understand him—were constant. Attempts to undercut others—always innocent, just because he was so hard-working—were frequent. The *Times-Herald* suffered it for a while and then fired him just before he finally decided that the paper's conservative atmosphere was stifling him and he must get out. *Time* seriously considered making him one of its stars and then decided it had enough trouble with talented egos without giving permanent home to another. (The decision suited them both. Briefly he had thought that a newsmagazine's murderous anonymity might be a convenient shield behind which to attack the growing number of people and causes he considered dangerous to the country. But before they reached their decision not to hire him he had reached his not to accept. He decided that he was proud of his views and would stand by them. He was not afraid, ashamed, or jealous, so he did not need the nameless knifer's cloak.) The *Evening Star*, in its easygoing, tolerant way, endured him for a couple of years until it, too, without ever quite saying so, indicated that he would probably be happier elsewhere. Frustrated and depressed, he came at last to the town's most intolerant, most slanted, most ruthless and most powerful publication, and found that they were made for each other.

Swiftly he learned the knack of the prejudicial word, the smoothly hostile phrase, the sarcastic jape that substitutes for decency, the bland omission of friendly facts, the deliberate suppression of honors and achievements, the heavy dependence upon unidentified "informed sources" who believed, or stated, or predicted, or thought, unfavorable and unkind things about the chosen targets of editorial disapproval.

(His writing, as it became more savage under this tutelage, also for a while showed a tendency to become more precious: he was among the first to litter his copy with such self-conscious Anglicisms as "straight away," "in the crunch," and "early on." And, although research never entirely confirmed it, he was generally believed to have been the originator of the term "hawks" for those who favored a responsible firmness toward the Communists, "doves" for those who fled, wide-eyed and tippy-toe, from the slightest show of force about anything.)

Within a year he was an editors' pet, given carte blanche to roam where he would and trample whom he needed. At the end of two more years, after a series of scoops on the State Department's wavering position papers on Southeast Asia that made his by-line world-famous, after an exposé of an after-hours sex-ring on Capitol Hill that won him both the Raymond Clapper Memorial Award and his first Pulitzer, after a long series of analytical pieces on the two major political parties which gave his publication's readers the point of view they felt they must have, he found himself at thirty with his own column and a contract for syndication that promised great things to come.

And great things came, though for a while they were not as great as he wanted them to be, and certainly not as great as they were now. Dutifully, and often with considerable stylistic force, he upheld the Right Position. With intelligence and skill he urged America to follow a course that to many of his countrymen seemed to place her in ever-increasing jeopardy. Smoothly he advised her to give up her idealistic dreams of a lasting peace and accept instead a condition of permanent negotiation and endless war. Logically and persuasively he encouraged her to retreat from responsibility, abandon courage, acknowledge the inevitable nature of accommodations with the Communists that would steadily weaken her power.

All this he did in the name of a genuine personal conviction and a great determination to be In, not Out. Bitterly he attacked those who disagreed with him or deviated in the slightest from the rigid pattern of thinking beloved of his employers, his major colleagues, and himself. He spoke perfectly, in short, for that world in which he was coming to assume an increasingly prominent and commanding position. With an instinctive flair for the right words and phrases to synthesize its attitudes, he speedily became one of its best-known prophets in those days when it was just hitting its full stride in the campaign, always sincere and usually quite innocent, to cripple America and tie her hands in the face of an implacable enemy who used all means, including the eager if unconscious help of Walter and his world, to try to bring about her death.

And still he was not where he wanted to be. There were, after all, a good many others parroting the same line: Walter Dobius was not unique. For all that his column began to pick up clients with a fair rapidity, it did not, as yet, have anything particularly special to offer. He began to think that it would not have as long as Big Walter lived and he must work in his shadow, for as Bob Taft had so unnervingly noted, Little Walter more and more found himself thinking and writing along much the same lines and in much the same style. There was the same air of superior knowledge and infallible wisdom; the same appeal to a higher reality above the law—and above the ideas of those who dared challenge the Right Position; the same ridiculing of America's naïve belief that firmness and decency together might save the world; even, on occasion, the same angry attacks upon candidates and leaders who dared to disagree with the policies that Big Walter—and Little—believed best for the country.

It was not, in fact, until Big Walter joined the Great Press Conference in the Sky that Little Walter finally came into his own; and then it was only because he had been shrewd enough to gather about him an aura of dispassionate disinterest that concealed his lively partisan emotions as successfully as his idol's had. There had been a brief period when he had thought that excessive partisanship for a given candidate was the right road to fame and power, and for a year or two his columns were filled with undiluted praise for the Texan in the White House. But it turned out that Lyndon had other ideas, and aside from a good many intimate chats in which he was told how much he was loved and how much his advice was valued, he discovered that his vision of himself as another Colonel House, a second Harry Hopkins, a Brother Milton or Brother Bobby redivivus was not to be. He did not need the lesson twice. Although he continued to aid his favorites, he did so with an air of being far above the battle which only served to make his concealed partisanship more effective. And little by little he began to acquire the position of unassailable authority and automatic influence left vacant when his great idol succumbed. "Doesn't he have an ideal life?" he had once asked a friend with naïve wistfulness when Big Walter was at his peak of fame and power, worshiped by all the Right Thinkers and Forward Lookers, hailed universally as a latter-day Socrates, a modern Plato, Paragon of the Nations and Monument of the Age. "He just sits there in that study and writes his thoughts on things and the whole country listens. Isn't that the life to lead?" And now, at last, Walter Dobius could lead it. The years of glory began.

If in the process of reaching them Walter seems to have had little personal life, this is because, essentially, he hasn't. Walter has been an ambitious machine for most of his days, and personal considerations have been peripheral. His parents are dead, he has two brothers and a sister whom he almost never sees; there are three or four old friends from high school and college who have been retained because they are suitably awed (he has no genuinely close friends in Washington, for all the thousands of famous and talented people he knows); and he did marry Helen-Anne Carrew, when he was young in Washington, because he was temporarily bemused by her brains and by the idea that a proper columnist ought also to be a well-wed one, since so much of the capital's news-gathering occurs on the social circuit and contacts one acquires there. Her motivations had been much the same, with the addition of some genuine affection and the feeling that anyone so arrogant as Walter must be vulnerable and in need of protection. But it didn't work, for the reasons implicit in their conversation just now: brains equal to his in some respects, an intuition greater; an equal ambition; a refusal to grant the automatic acknowledgment of superiority which is necessary to Walter if he is to feel really secure and write at his best.

They had stuck it out for seven years, getting increasingly on each other's nerves; had never had children to hold them together because Walter feared it would distract him from his work; had finally parted in a half-hateful, half-friendly way that still prompts Helen-Anne to call him sometimes, as she has tonight, to warn him against some misstep she fears he may take, or to urge modification of some pet thesis he is promoting in his column. Of course he is never able to concede the possibility of a misstep, for his record of success indicates that he makes none; and since he early discovered her conservative bent, her ideas on his public philosophy can be dismissed as typically reactionary, obstructive, and worthless.

This relieves Walter of feeling any ties to Helen-Anne—except, of course, the tie she still exerts by being unimpressed. And that, of course, ties him to her forever.

"Walter Wonderful," Lyndon called him, in lieu of more concrete favors. The nickname, often used with a jealous mockery among his older colleagues in Washington but always echoed with a dutifully respectful friendliness in less knowledgeable circles across the country, has stuck to him ever since. For fifteen years, now, he has occupied his unique position, challenged by three or four, ousted by none, never seriously threatened in his role as (to quote from the preface of *The Necessary Dobius*, a compilation of his columns and speeches published five years ago) "America's philosopher-statesman par excellence and nonpareil," and (to quote from the welcoming address of the Yale trustees when he was elected to join their number) "this beacon-light of the intellect whose rays illumine the murkiest corners of American policy and bear testimony to the nations that all is not wasteland in the Great Republic of the West."

One of his non-worshiping colleagues, scornfully snapping off a CBS special, "Tribute to a Mind," on the occasion of his third Pulitzer and fiftieth birthday, had remarked, "It's a pity Walter died so young." It is true that many of the references to him do have an elegiac, he-has-moved-above-and-beyond-us ring. But it is also true that the overwhelming majority of the tributes he receives are so perfervidly genuine and sincere that only the most grossly irreverent and daring would ever dream of pointing out that Emperor Walter, like so many other Washington emperors, really does not, at times, have on too many clothes.

Thus he goes his way, his influence so pervasive and his ideas so dominant that it can almost be said that he is the principal architect of American thought on most of the major issues of the age. This could be a farcical idea—as *Newsweek* in its hysteria may have noted with the right emphasis but for the wrong reasons—but it is a factual one. He reflects with satisfaction now, as he finishes his Manhattan, gets up from the big armchair, and goes into the candlelit dining room where Arbella has braced his solitary meal with the Georgian silver service and the antique lace tablecloth that are always laid out, be the number of diners one or twenty, that he and the powerful columnists, commentators, broadcasters, writers and reviewers who accord with his views do, in fact, come as close to controlling the country as anyone can.

He knows—and it is both pleasing and flattering—that since the Sixties they have made it virtually impossible for anyone who disagrees with them to receive an impartial hearing in America. They have successfully scoffed and attacked and withered almost every attempt to state the opposing view. They have established such a monopoly on the means of communication that those who venture to assert an independence from them are subjected instantly and automatically to a savage campaign to smear, suppress, or ridicule down. It is no mean accomplishment, and Walter and his world are justified when they reflect, with the smugness born of a secure intellectual hegemony, that their views, and their prejudices, are quite, quite safe.

If their countrymen sometimes show a certain restiveness at this, if on occasion there is some harsh indication—such as, say, a roar of cheers at a public meeting when someone attacks the press—Walter and his world are highly indignant and dismayed. Their consternation is, in fact, quite comical. It is not enough for them to exercise the virtual censorship of American thought that they do, in fact, exercise: it is necessary to their self-esteem that they be allowed to believe that they are getting away with it. One of the few humorous—if not actually pathetic—aspects of Walter and his world is their naïve belief that nobody sees through them. It is shattering to them to realize that while the peasants may be easygoing and too lazy to object very much, they are not fooled. This is upsetting.

But not, of course, upsetting enough for them to deviate in the slightest from the exercise of the dictatorship that they have managed to establish over the American mind. Right Thoughts flood the columns, dominate the airwaves, fill the editorials, news reports, movies, plays and reviews. Right Thoughts are everywhere. Right Thoughts are gospel, and Walter, as Patsy truly says, is their God.

And the gospel he presides over and offers to his countrymen? It comes down essentially to the same basic arguments that first caught the approving eyes of his employers, the same arguments that he and his major colleagues have offered ever since the end of the Second World War, endlessly repeated through every means of communication:

America is declining in influence and therefore unable to meet her problems with firmness and integrity—

Communism is gaining in strength and therefore had best be accommodated, because its advances aren't really very important anyway, and anyway, it might be dangerous to try to stop them—

And a blind fear of atomic war, offered as the final obliterating answer to all who dare suggest that if America will only stand unafraid for the great revolutionary principles upon which she was founded, she can come safely through her perils and achieve in reasonable time the establishment of an honorable and lasting peace.

In the minds of Walter and his world, this last is a naïve and childish idea, a hopeless obsession on the part of far too many of their foolish countrymen. Toward it their scorn is implacable and unyielding. He is readying some of it right now, as he carefully wipes his lips on his damask napkin, pushes back his richly carved chair from the massive old refectory table, and starts slowly and thoughtfully up the stairs to his study to resume work upon his speech.

For that idea and for all who hold it, up to and including Orrin Knox and the President himself, Walter Wonderful and his world have only savage answers. The thought of them brings once more the tight little smile of satisfied contempt to his lips as he snaps on the desk lamp, takes off his coat, sits in his writing chair, and again flicks on his electric typewriter with a pudgy determined finger.

Others may doubt, on this cold, blustery night suspended between winter and spring, the course they will follow in the presidential campaign now getting under way. Others may be uncertain where the best solutions lie for the enormous problems domestic and foreign that swirl about their uneasy, beleaguered land. Others may be humble and afraid, seeing not only the night of snow but the night of ages threatening to close in on America.

Not so Walter Dobius. Walter and his world, now as always, have no doubts.

He flicks a key or two in a tentative, pondering way, and then, without humility or hesitation, begins to write steadily and forcefully into the night.

3

THERE WERE, of course, other perspectives on the night.

Not as simple as Walter's, a portly man at a big desk overlooking the floodlit Washington Monument told himself ruefully as he put down his knife and fork and stared at the fluffy pink-and-white matron eating opposite from a TV tray, was the White House perspective.

For Harley M. Hudson, who actually had the responsibilities Walter and his world thought they did, life was never a simple matter of fears, slogans, and the arbitrary consignment of people and issues to categories labeled with automatic little words. For him life was real and not a shadow play of ego and ambition that led to standing tall in Georgetown. The President of the United States had to stand tall before his country, mankind, history, and his own conscience. He did not find the last particularly difficult, but the other three were sometimes not so easy.

He sighed, a little heavily, and Lucille Hudson gave him an appraising glance.

"Now what are you worrying about? Surely not about being President, again."

"Am I worrying?" her husband said mildly. "I didn't realize it."

"Oh, of course you are. I can always tell. And really there's no cause for it. If Walter Dobius makes a speech and nominates Ted Jason, what of it? Walter isn't the convention."

"Walter is part of it," the President said. "A substantial part."

"He can't stop you," Lucille said calmly. "You know that."

"I know that," the President agreed. "He can't stop me because I'm not going to be in a position to be stopped, since I won't be running—"

"Oh, stuff," his wife interrupted. "Of course you're going to be running."

"I gave my solemn pledge to the Senate and the country when I moved in here that I was retiring at the end of the term. And I am."

Lucille Hudson sniffed.

"Solemn words are all right for solemn occasions. But later one has to get down to what's really practical."

"Oh, one does, does one?" her husband inquired with a sudden humor. "You're certainly getting to be a cold-blooded politician, I must say. Where did you learn all that?"

"Right here in this house," she said. "It does that to one."

"Yes," he agreed, abruptly sobered. "It does. Nonetheless, I have given my word—"

"Harley Hudson," she said, and her face dissolved into the twinkling little smile which, combined with her rosy cheeks, sparkling eyes, roly-poly figure, and infallibly sweet disposition, had long ago prompted Helen-Anne to bring forth her famous private description of the First Lady as "a meringue enigma wrapped in whipped cream inside a marshmallow sundae"—"Harley Hudson, I don't care how many people you've given your word to, the facts are the facts and they're going to produce exactly the situation I've always known they would. They're going to force you to be a candidate for re-election."

"I really don't want the job, you know," he said mildly. She chuckled.

"Look me straight in the eye and say that," she commanded. He obliged. She chuckled again.

"I could almost believe you if I weren't your wife. Ted and Orrin are going to eliminate each other and then there's going to be you. There's got to be. So I don't really see why you don't step in right at the beginning, right now, and say that events have forced you to reconsider and you're going to run. It would save everybody so much wear and tear."

"Can't you hear Walter Dobius and his friends if I did?" the President inquired with a sudden grin. "Poor Walter would have a stroke, he's so dead set on getting Ted in here. About as dead set," he added, the grin deepening, "as you are to get me in here."

"But you are here," the First Lady said comfortably. "That's the difference."

"I really think," he said with a smile, "that you think it's just a picnic. Any normal wife would be worried about the wear and tear on me. She would want me to retire and take it easy. She wouldn't want me to continue to knock myself out in the world's most thankless job—"

"I know it isn't a picnic," she said. "I'm not a fool. It's just that I believe in you and in what you are doing for the country. Furthermore, Harley Hudson," she added indignantly, "ever since you went to Geneva and defied the Russians the country's worshiped you and you know it. So don't give me Poor Old Harley. You love it."

His smile broadened.

"Some segments worship me, but I haven't noticed too many hosannas from Walter and his friends. They've had to go along with the general mood, but you've noticed all the careful qualifications in the columns, broadcasts, and editorials. They don't like anybody to get really tough with the Communists. It upsets them."

"They're worried about the bomb," the First Lady said. He made a skeptical sound.

"And I'm not? My God, I eat, sleep, think, and dream the bomb twenty-four hours a day."

"I know you do. You needn't swear about it. That's the only thing I regret about this office. You use more profanity than you used to."

The President gave a delighted laugh.

"Lucy, you take the cake. I wish I could reduce everything to the fundamental level you do."

"How could you?" she inquired with her sudden little twinkle. "You're a man. Now: why don't you announce at your press conference this week?"

"I don't think I'll have one. I think I'll lie low this week and let Walter and Ted and Orrin produce the fireworks. Anyway, as I say, I have nothing—absolutely nothing—to announce."

"You can't sit still," his wife said. "History won't let you." The buzzer on his phone sounded sharply in the big, cluttered room. "There's history, now."

"No it isn't," he said, reaching for the phone. "It's Orrin. But I guess he's history, too. Hello?"—he nodded across the desk with a confirming smile—"yes, put him on

. . . Hi . . . Why, sure. I thought we had pretty well decided on policy in that area but if you'd like to come by and talk about it again, there's nothing doing here tonight, as you know. We're just having a quiet snack in the upstairs study. I don't mind talking about problems some more, it's all I—Oh, it's you you want to talk about?" He chuckled. "My friend, I could never have guessed. O.K., come along. I'll be here. Right. In fifteen minutes. . . . There, you see?" he said, turning back to his wife. "I don't need to move. I can sit still. History comes to me in this house. I don't have to go after it."

"Harley Hudson," she said, rising and preparing to depart for the family quarters, "if I hadn't already bet with you, I'd bet with you again: come next January you will be right here, right where you are this minute, after being reelected by a landslide. It's inevitable."

"Inevitable's a big word."

"If anything is," she said, concluding a conversation she would recall many times later, "you are."

"Well, don't tell Walter," he said with a grin. "He couldn't stand it."

She came around the desk and kissed him good night.

"I'll let you tell Walter. He only listens to people on his own level. Don't be too late, now."

He nodded.

"I'll try not to. But it depends on the Secretary of State."

Alone in the room that held so much history, in the house where history lived, he sat for a moment after she had gone, staring out at the Monument where it rose imperious and shining into the snow-swept night. The storm was beginning to slacken a little, the savage gusts blowing out of Virginia and the west were dying, soon it would be over and the soft muffling silence of a cold white world would settle over Washington. It was a little late in the year for it, hopefully spring would come tomorrow, but tonight and probably for the rest of the week the capital was still in the grip of the weather, and the mood, of winter.

And not a very happy mood it was or had been, he thought with an uneasy grimness, still reflecting as it did the savage stresses and strains created by his successful confrontation with the Communists at Geneva a year ago and the many problems flowing from the crisis that had arisen six months after in both the United Nations and the United States over the visit of H.R.H. Terence Wolowo Ajkaje the M'Bulu of Mbuele.

When he had walked out on the Soviets at Geneva, in the most decisive action any American President of recent decades had taken with the Communists, the world had not known for some hours whether it would die or live. It had lived, but on different terms and on a different basis from those existing before the Chief Executive had reasserted his country's integrity in the face of an outright ultimatum from its most implacable opponent.

When the M'Bulu, the Communists, and the more child-like and irresponsible of the Afro-Asian nations had almost succeeded in censuring and expelling the United States from the UN because of its racial problem which the M'-Bulu had deliberately inflamed, the reaction within America had been violent and grave indeed. Walter Dobius and his world might argue with a suave desperation that the United States was undoubtedly to blame and therefore should stay in the UN in order to keep the Afro-Asians happy and well-financed while they went about their care-free business of destroying the fragile bonds of world order, but all their millions of words had not been sufficient to stem the tide of feeling in the country. The UN, as always, had been the UN's worst enemy; and not all the bugaboos of possible disaster should the UN collapse, raised by Walter and his world, could conceal the organization's built-in death-drive from a proud and impatient people increasingly convinced that the United States was always destined to get the short end of the stick and increasingly unable to accept the argument that the United States must always be cheerfully willing to.

Upon the President, however, there rested a higher obligation than the powerful carping of Walter's world on the one side, a stronger imperative than the rising impatience of so many of his countrymen on the other. It was true that the UN was in sad disarray, that not all the Right Thinkers in the world could conceal the fatal irresponsibility of its new and inexperienced members, that its sickness infected all of international relations with a cancer second only to that of Communism itself. The argument could not stop there. Weak and wavering as the United States itself had been toward the organization over the years, sadly as its leaders had allowed themselves to be persuaded on a thousand occasions that they must not act with firmness because it might offend some little power that might not like them, still there was something to be gained by keeping the UN alive, and staying in it. Or at least there was something to be gained by an orderly termination, if history, brushing aside the dreams, pretensions, and fears of men, should find termination inescapable.

He was not ready to write the UN off yet, however, ragtag and bobtail hodgepodge of nations and non-nations though it had become. There was still some glimmering, feeble hope of reformation, some last faint possibility that its raucously brawling members would realize at the last moment that every time they weakened it or twisted its rules to satisfy their anti-colonialist hysteria they were only weakening themselves and making more certain the road to their own extermination. Without the UN, most of Africa and Asia would die under the new Communist imperialism, yet every day most of Africa and Asia did everything they could to make the UN die. They were fools, the President thought impatiently, history's greatest fools, and saying that they were still just children was no excuse.

It was time, and past time, that they grew up.

This was perhaps the major headache that would face the next man to sit at this desk, that and of course the never-ending struggle with Communism itself. He had read in many a column by Walter Dobius, he had sat right here last Thursday night and heard him say it in person, that the old fears of Communism were now out of date, that a new era had dawned, that it was no longer wise or even, he gathered, fashionable, to be suspicious of the Russians, the Chinese, and all their vicious little hangers-on around the globe.

He could not in all honesty see how Walter got that way. He could remember these wildly welcomed "new looks" before, these oft-recurring and quick-dying "new eras," the trade, the visits, the desperate attempts—by the West, not by the Communists—to pretend that the basic drive had changed; the determined and unending campaign by Walter and his world to make their countrymen believe that it was somehow stupid and unfair to continue to be suspicious of a system that was absolutely and irrevocably dedicated to the death of their country as a free nation and themselves as a free people.

He could remember all this, and he was not impressed.

These eagerly and repeatedly hailed softenings of Communism that were no softenings at all were the Potemkin villages of the Western mind, or at least that portion of it influenced by "Salubria" in Leesburg. Not one single item of hard fact in more than half a century gave corroboration, yet day in and day out, week after week, year after year, Walter and his friends reiterated their contention that Communism was changing, that it was becoming "mature and civilized," that its practitioners were really human beings as kindly as could be and not human machines dedicated to the destruction of every decency in the world.

Well, he had not fallen for that standard weakness of Presidents which had led most of his predecessors to fancy that their own personal charm, devastating and infinite as it always was, would be sufficient to divert Communism from its irrevocable purpose. The naïve belief that a personal chat could solve everything had not been his. His own confrontation had come in the first week of his Presidency. The stars had been knocked out of his eyes at once and permanently. Thank God for that. It enabled him to read with the skepticism they deserved the suave exhortations to weakness put forth by Walter's world.

Since he could not, aside from some few examples which were known or whispered about in Washington, believe that a majority of those who peddled this line were actually traitors to their country, the President could only conclude that their arguments sprang from a terrible and pitiable fear. They were actually, apparently, so afraid of the consequences of having their country stand up for what she believed in that they would go to any lengths to persuade her to abandon it and crawl away—crawl away, though they professed indignantly not to see it, straight into the darkness the Communists were readying for them.

Again, it seemed to him that a sizable portion of the society he had to deal with should grow up. He could not afford to be patient much longer with children who played so irresponsibly with the heritage of freedom they had been given.

Well: soon, at any rate, he might be able to lay down this burden and let someone else worry about it. If, that is, he could be sure that the hands into which it passed were suitably strong and suitably equipped, by experience and belief, to carry it.

And right here, he realized with a wry little smile as he

looked about the private office where he had already faced so many crises and which had already become so familiar to him in the short space of a year, he was entering the realm of the Rationale of Presidents.

"Let's face it," he said aloud with a humorous air to the silent room, "nobody can handle this job better than I. I don't *want* anybody to handle this job better than I. I don't want anybody to handle this job *but* me. Period. Exclamation point. And twenty-five little stars and asterisks."

That was the truth of it when you came right down to it, just as the First Lady knew, with her feminine logic that was so disinterested in the rationalizings of mere men. If he permitted himself to entertain the thought just a little longer, just a very little longer, he would run again because he had convinced himself that no one else was capable and he simply had to run again. It was as simple as that.

But I can't do it, part of his mind objected, because I gave my word. But, another part objected, your word to preserve and protect the country that you swore when you took office is more important than any word you gave any-one else. And anyway, it added, how could Orrin or Ted or anybody do the job as well as you can with all your experience?

One year's experience, the first part said scornfully.

But more than any other living soul has, the other part rejoined.

Very well, then, the first part said, what do we have to face now? We have Felix Labaiya hurrying home to Pana-ma, which he thinks we don't know—but the White House has unexpected ways of knowing things, and we do. And what does it mean? Certainly nothing pleasant for the Unit-ed States, if Felix's past performances are any indica-tion. . . .

And we have Gorotoland, where Terrible Terry's cousin is raising hell aided by the Russian and Chinese Commu-nists, and where American missionaries at the All-Faiths Hospital near the capital of Molobangwe, and the new Standard Oil installation up-country, may both be seriously threatened at any moment.

And we have our formal warning, issued by me a week ago to Terry's cousin, His Royal Highness Obifumatta Ajkaje ("Prince Obi" in Walter's fatherly columns and the world's headlines), telling him that his trumped-up "Peo-ple's Free Republic of Gorotoland" had better stay clear of

American nationals and American property—and we have, as a result of that, fifty wild speeches in the General Assembly, a thousand condemnatory blasts from Walter and his world, and tomorrow's Security Council meeting to consider "American imperialist aggression. . . ."

And we have the problem of maintaining the American installation on the moon which was established a year ago in the midst of the turmoil over Bob Leffingwell's nomination to be Secretary of State. And the question of whether Clete O'Donnell and his "One Big Union," which controls much of the work at the Cape, are going to permit a needed refueling and crew-replacement ship to go, or whether they are going to strike and hold up the government for some political purpose, which is how Clete likes to use his power. . . .

And the latest screaming by Indonesia at Australia in their running feud, a feud increasingly serious now that Djakarta has renewed its alliance with Peking. . . .

And the strong likelihood of a British election soon, which could mean new problems there. . . .

And such intriguing domestic mysteries as who will line up with whom, what coalitions will be formed, what concentrations of power be created or disbanded, in the shifting, whirling, clashing fandango of the coming campaign. . . .

And so, forever and always, inevitably and inescapably until it is settled, back to the question of who will sit in this house.

For a patient man, he told himself with a wry little smile, he certainly seemed to be impatient about a lot of things. But then, there were a lot of things to be impatient about. The ubiquitous buzzer sounded again. Lifting the phone, he was informed that one of the principal ones was on the way up in the elevator. He frowned for a moment, but when the Secretary of State entered he found the President propped back in his chair with his hands folded comfortably upon his ample stomach, regarding him with a kindly, welcoming smile.

The Secretary's reaction, as Seab Cooley had once described it in the midst of one of their many legislative battles in the Senate, was Orrinesque.

"I must say that's a happy picture," he remarked with a certain amicable asperity. "How do you manage it?"

"By having a clear conscience and always doing right,"

the President responded. "Don't you think I always do right? Some people don't think so, but I do."

"Mmmhmm," Orrin Konx said, dropping with accustomed ease into one of the big leather armchairs, draping a leg over one arm, facing his superior with a quizzical air, "I don't think Walter Dobius thinks so."

"Oh, good heavens," the President said. "Haven't we got better things to worry about tonight than Walter?" He sighed in mock concern. "But no, obviously you haven't. But don't let him get you down, Orrin. He's just a columnist."

"Yes," the Secretary of State said dryly. "He's going to try to take your convention right away from you in that speech Friday night unless you stop him."

The President shook his head.

"Oh, come. You build him up too much. That's how he's achieved the position he has—just by claiming it and persuading otherwise level-headed people to go along with it."

"There's more to him than that," Orrin Knox said. "And they are persuaded. That's the problem."

The President turned away for a moment to stare again, as Presidents are wont to do, at the Washington Monument —tribute to unassailable, unknowable, indispensable George, long since passed into legend, having served his time with honor and gone to glory undiminished, freed from all those torments his successors have to face.

"Yes," he agreed thoughtfully, turning back, "that is a problem. What do you want me to do about it?"

"Make your own position clear," the Secretary said bluntly. "Either come in or get out."

For just a second the President started to look offended and then, remembering who he was talking to, looked amused instead.

"If I want straight talk and firm advice I don't have to read Walter, do I? I just have to have a chat with my Secretary of State. . . . What would be the advantage in that?"

Orrin gave him a shrewd look and let him have it.

"You could resolve the whole thing once and for all. If you're going to run, I'll stop fretting and settle for a plaque on the cornerstone of that latest annex-to-the-annex-to-the-annex-to-the-Annex that my busy planners at the State Department want us to build. If you aren't, then I'll get moving instead of sitting around half-paralyzed waiting for you. As it is, I'm respectful enough to sit still but my opponent isn't. As witness this business with Walter."

"You're respectful, all right," the President said with a chuckle, "but only because you're not sure of what I would do if you barged ahead without my permission. Right?"

The Secretary of State gave him a cheerful grin.

"Oh, that's part of it. But not all—not all. Really, Harl —Mr. President—why do you do this to us? Do you like to see us squirm?"

The President's expression sobered.

"No, I don't like to see you squirm. At this moment, I honestly do not know what to do."

"Well, if you don't know," Orrin said, "then that means you're going to run. You didn't have any doubts a year ago. Now you have doubts. Having doubts, you will resolve them in your favor. Presidents usually do, when the Constitution gives them a chance. Good Lord, you've only served a year in this office. You're permitted to stay another eight. Who would want to give it up?"

The President smiled.

"There speaks a man who has never had it. The imagination runs rampant when it comes to this job. The power— the glory"—he began in a grandiloquent tone which changed to one of wry irony as he went along—"the problems—the headaches—"

"The chance to do what *you* want to do for the country, in *your* way, with the outcome depending on how skillful *you* are at getting your countrymen to go along with it and with *you* having the satisfaction when it works out," the secretary finished for him. "Yes, it's a burden, all right. And you all get to love it in spite of its problems. Let's face it," he suggested with a grin. "Power corrupts—and absolute power is absolutely delightful."

The President laughed in spite of himself.

"Not so absolute. Our friends on the Hill don't allow it to be absolute. The Supreme Court doesn't allow it to be absolute. The country doesn't allow it to be absolute. Walter," he said with a wry expression, "doesn't allow it to be absolute. A thousand and one things don't allow it to be absolute."

"Absolute enough to satisfy any sane ego for as long as life remains."

"All right," the President said, leaning forward and leaning his elbows on the desk, clasping his hands and resting his chin upon them, staring straight at the volatile, impatient, powerful old friend who sat across from him. "Let me tell you how absolute it is. You know how absolute you are in your own department, where any little clerk with the wrong slant on things can throw you off with a carefully phrased position paper. Let me tell you how it is here.

"You see this fancy phone and these fancy gadgets—that all add up to that 'button' everybody's worried about for so many years? What do I have to go on, if I should decide to press it? Well, I have an estimate by you and the Secretary of Defense, let's say, on what a given situation actually is. And on what do you base your assessment of its political realities, and he his assessment of its military aspects? In each case, on somebody lower down, who gives you what he receives—from somebody lower down. And underneath that, there's—somebody lower down. And underneath that —and finally, there we are, back at your little clerk, who may or may not be loyal and reliable."

He frowned.

"Who can possibly have all the facts in a world as complex as this? Our society believes that the President has, because for the sake of its own sanity it has to believe it. But I don't know—no mortal man can know, of his own knowledge—all the facts on which a President acts. The thing is too big. I can't tell you—*of my own knowledge*— that if I push that button, so many ICBM's will blast off for Russia or China or Indonesia. All I know is that somebody below has told me so—and somebody in turn has told him—and he in turn has gotten it from somebody else. I haven't gone to see for myself, I couldn't possibly. I act in the faith that I have been given a true account. The country follows me because it believes I know. But I don't know. What single individual could?"

For a long moment there was a silence in the historic room in the quiet old house that served as the focus for so many hopes and fears in so many strange and varied lands. The Secretary of State spoke very softly when he finally spoke.

"It's terrifying, isn't it?"

"Yes," the President said grimly, "it is terrifying. Are you big enough to face it? That's what I have to know, before I can do anything about this election."

The Secretary of State made an impatient gesture.

"Is he?"

"Don't talk about him," the President said sternly. "I'll get to him. Are you?"

Again there was a silence. The President was aware as he searched the strong and determined face before him that the last sounds of wind had gone, the storm was over. He and his Secretary of State seemed adrift in time without reference to anyone or anything, though of course in their companionate responsibilities they were in reference to everyone and everything that lived and existed on the globe. The President could see that the face before him was thoughtful, but he was not surprised that it was not afraid.

"I think I am big enough," Orrin said slowly. He too stared with a distant contemplation at the Monument. "Of course—who can say for sure, until he's tested? Could you have said so a year ago when you came down here from the Senate that afternoon to take the oath? Certainly"—and he smiled a little at the thought of that now far-off, frightening moment for them all—"certainly not too many of us on the Hill thought you could. Could you have said when you went to Geneva? Again, few of us were sure. But you did, didn't you, Harley? You could. The time came, the demand was rendered—and you could. So, I think, could I." He turned from the Monument and looked directly into the honest eyes across from him, eyes that held now a much greater wisdom, certitude, courage, and sadness than they had a year ago. "Do you doubt it?"

Again there was a silence as the President returned his look with a thoughtful stillness that came from many things he had learned and experienced about men and their characters and dreams in the past twelve months.

"I don't doubt your courage, Orrin," he said finally. "The public record is full of that for the past twenty years. It goes deeper than courage. It goes to—acceptance, I think you might call it—of what this job is, and what it does to you, and what it can do to the country and to all of humankind. You can talk about it. But can you do it?"

"How can anyone do it except you," the Secretary demanded with a sudden exasperation, "if you won't get out of the way and give anyone a chance? Ted and I can't kick you out, you know. You're here 'til you want to leave, that's for sure."

The President started to laugh and then stopped abruptly, with a curious note of unhappiness and questioning and, in some strange way, almost of self-distaste, in his voice.

"I don't know whether I want to stay or leave, Orrin," he said quietly, "and that's the God's truth."

The Secretary shrugged, though it cost him much to do it.

"You want to stay," he said in a voice he succeeded in making indifferent. "So stay."

Again the President uttered a curious half-humorous, half-skeptical, regretful sound.

"It isn't that easy, and you know it."

"I can't help you," Orrin said. "But," he added quietly, "you can help me. If you so decide."

The President sighed.

"Yes, I know that. . . . I want a little more time, Orrin. I haven't quite got the feel of this yet, I need some sign. I don't know what's going to happen in Africa, or in Panama, or Southeast Asia. I don't know what's going to happen—"

"You're looking for justifications," the Secretary interrupted, aware that he might be running the risk of antagonizing Harley, but feeling also that the conversation had reached an impasse, there was no hope of resolving anything tonight even if time was rushing forward and Walter Dobius and his world were about to send the Jason bandwagon racing down the road. "Something is always happening somewhere that we can't see the end of. Time has no stops these days. There are no clarifications in the world, only new confusions to displace the old and so give us some illusion that we are moving ahead instead of churning around, as we very probably are, in an ever-narrowing circle. You can wait forever, if you wait for that kind of answer. . . . Go ahead and run, Mr. President. I'll support you in every way I can and serve you in any capacity you want afterward. Surely you have no doubts on that score."

The President shook his head.

"Oh no, of course not. And of course I'd want you to stay right where you are. If, that is—" His voice trailed away and he looked down at the many papers on his desk in an odd way as though he had never seen them before.

"Well," Orrin said with a sudden decision, starting to rise. "I'm sorry I took your time. I guess we'll just have to ride out whatever Walter says Friday night and play the whole thing by ear."

"I'd talk to him, if I were you," the President suggested. The Secretary paused.

"That's what Beth says," he admitted.

"I don't think it would hurt you. And it might slow him down a little."

"Not if I haven't got your support," Orrin said, trying not to make his emphasis too annoyed.

"Don't forget that I can help—or hinder—Ted, too. If he's wise, he won't encourage Walter to go too far."

"If I know Ted," Orrin said tartly, "he's playing on Walter's ego and hoping he'll go as far as possible. There's one risk you run, you know, Mr. President. You may be underestimating Ted. He may not be as inhibited about waiting for you as I am."

"Well," the President said with an equal bluntness, "I'd like to see him try to run if the President decides to! It would be the end of him politically."

"That didn't stop him in New Hampshire," Orrin couldn't resist pointing out.

The President, for him, looked quite pugnacious.

"And he got soundly licked, and you too, didn't you?"

Orrin grinned and nodded.

"I still wouldn't put it past him to try. . . . Tell me," he said, changing the subject as he saw the thought beginning to sink into the President's mind, easygoing and good-natured on most things but, like all Presidents' minds, touchy and self-defensive when it came to the protection of his own position, "are there any last-minute instructions you want me to give Cullee and Lafe at the UN before tomorrow's Security Council session? I'm planning to call them around nine tonight at the Waldorf. They're attending a party Selena Jason Castleberry's giving for Prince Obifumatta and the People's Free Republic of Gorotoland."

"Oh, dear," the President said with a relieved, humorous expression, diverted from perhaps being forced into a political decision that might cause hurt to someone if it arrived too soon, "oh, my! So Selena's stepping in, is she? If it isn't the Jasons we have to worry about, it's their cousins and their uncles and their aunts."

"Selena's doing her bit," Orrin said. "I understand half the UN and half of New York are there."

"Except His Royal Highness Prince Terry the M'Bulu of Mbuele," the President said with a grim little smile.

"Terry is finding out what it means to be the darling of a

certain segment of America," the Secretary said. "It means you're a darling today and damned tomorrow."

"It couldn't happen to a more deserving fellow," the President said, remembering the high and mighty way Terry had acted on his visit six months ago which had stirred up so much trouble, and recalling also the talk he and Orrin had held with him in this very room, in the midst of it. "But," he added as other implications came to mind, "still not a pleasant matter for us."

"No, indeed," the Secretary said. "He is the legitimate government and we can't let the Communists get in there. So there we are."

"Give Cullee and Lafe my best," the President said. "They know what I have in mind, if necessary."

"They know," Orrin said thoughtfully. "It would be a sensation, right enough. And not on a very major issue. But—" he shrugged. "It's all major. There aren't any minor issues these days. The world turns on every one, for all we know, so we have to proceed on that basis, since the Communists force us to." He sighed. "I'll call you if the boys have anything startlingly new to report."

"I doubt if they will. Personally, I'm going to bed early. I'd suggest you do the same."

"I'll try," Orrin said. He was unable to resist a parting shot. "I hope you have a good talk with Ted, whenever it happens, and manage to impress him with the gravities as well as the honors of the office."

"I look forward to it," the President said with what, for him, was a surprisingly mischievous little smile. "I may not make you squirm, Orrin, but I think it would be rather fun with Ted."

"Yes," the Secretary said dryly. "If what you've just done was *not* make me squirm, then I really feel sorry for Ted. And causing me to feel that, I might add, is quite an achievement."

The President laughed.

"My love to Beth."

"Always," the Secretary said.

It was with an odd mixture of amusement, anger, frustration, and hopelessness that Orrin sat back against the cushions as the driver of his official department limousine guided it slowly over the hushed and slippery streets toward Spring Valley. Very few cars were out, there was only the occasional sound of chains slapping against fenders or the soft susurrus of snow tires creeping cautiously by in the ghostly avenues to break the white silence that held the city. It was one of those curiously deserted and exposed moments in Washington when the past for some reason seems very close, when the figures of complicated Tom Jefferson in his study, or Andy Jackson on a horse, or Abe Lincoln stalking thoughtfully along with his cape pulled tight against the cold, come easily to mind; in which it seems that anything—or everything—might happen.

Or nothing, the Secretary of State told himself wryly. Apparently, as far as the President was concerned, nothing. It had been a good many months since he had seen Harley Hudson so irresolute. This was almost the old Harley, the one who had been a timorous and worried Vice President until the sudden death of his vigorous predecessor had plunged him abruptly into the center of the world's events. After that, Harley had not been irresolute—until now. The irresolution was understandable enough to other men of power. The President had power and he didn't want to give it up: felt, morally, that he should; felt, intellectually, that he could not; knew, actually, that it was entirely up to him and that no one could force him one way or the other; and so was caught on the points of conscience and duty and dilemma in a way that probably made it quite literally impossible for him at this moment to do anything. He had said he wanted a sign, Orrin remembered wryly, while the car skidded slightly at 23rd and Massachusetts Avenue as it swung around Sheridan Circle, and then steadied itself and crept carefully up Embassy Row. Well, Orrin had tried to give him one—it couldn't have been any clearer if he had walked up and down Pennsylvania Avenue outside the White House gates carrying a sign that said FOR GOD'S SAKE GIVE SOMEBODY ELSE A CHANCE. But the President, he knew, had to move in his own good time, though every day, seemingly, made it more difficult for him to move in the direction Orrin and Ted Jason wanted him to.

Actually there was every evidence that he wanted to run again. He had permitted his name to go into the New Hampshire primary and had soundly trounced both Orrin and Ted, each of whom had maintained that their backers had acted without their permission. Of course the President had maintained the same thing, and undoubtedly each of the three had been convinced that his own desire to remain aloof had been quite genuine. Nonetheless, there they all were in the contest, and the President had won by a landslide. Then he had again permitted his name to go into the Wisconsin primary—this time, by dint of vehement insistence and threats of all sorts of dire reprisals against their overeager lieutenants, both Orrin and Ted had managed to stay out and give him a clear field—and again he had won by a landslide.

Meanwhile at his press conferences he had played a game of half-answer and jocular sidestep worthy of his predecessor at his peak. Nobody had pinned him down yet, though many skilled people had tried. And always, for the record, he had firmly and without equivocation reiterated the statement he had made to the Senate the day after his succession a year ago: he would not be a candidate for reelection.

With this combination of noble purpose on the one hand and political flirtation on the other, he had successfully kept the matter in his own hands, and had, as Orrin told him, paralyzed the two potential contenders who were so anxious to succeed him. The Secretary of State who was certainly not one to be let alone by Walter Dobius and his world in such a personally embarrassing situation, found himself subjected to a constant barrage of questioning whenever he exposed himself to the press, be it at formal press conference or in one of those hurried running interrogatories that always accompany the arrival and departure of a Secretary of State before the committees of the Congress.

This was an old game, and both he and his questioners played it with a certain humor; but the constant necessity to deny his own ambitions and maintain with a straight face that he saw no evidence of the President's would sometimes bring him home to the rambling house in Spring Valley in little mood for jovial chitchat. This put an extra burden on Beth, but fortunately her long experience as an old campaigner's wife usually came to the rescue in time.

The more he thought about it now, as the limousine crossed Wisconsin Avenue, passed Ward Circle, and made the final run into Spring Valley, the less patient and less tolerant he felt about the President. Harley was obviously about to be confronted by a major *démarche* on the part of the Jasons in this speech by Walter Dobius, a dramatic rallying behind Ted of all the psychological and actual forces Walter could command. The President could still act, but apparently he was unable to see that his area of action would inevitably be restricted to some degree as soon as all of Walter's friends and supporters came out on Saturday with their columns and editorials, their news reports and their special television and radio playbacks that would, the Secretary knew, flood the country over the weekend. A massive barrage of public opinion, a heavy psychological climate, would immediately be formed in the wake of Walter's speech. The longer the President waited the more difficult it would be for him to escape its oppressive and hampering confines.

As for his own position, the Secretary decided as the car drew up at his door and he bade the driver good night with wishes for a safe journey back downtown, it inevitably would have to be just what he had told Beth earlier in the day. He would have to announce his own candidacy, whether the President liked it or not, and he would have to plunge immediately into his campaign. He had a reasonably good organization in most of the states, party leaders who had supported him twice before in his unsuccessful tries for the nomination and had given active indication they would again. He had a modest amount of money and a few substantially moneyed backers. He had his name and his record. He had Beth. He had himself. He was not afraid of the future, but as he stamped the snow from his boots and removed them, then hung his coat in the hall closet and went along to the comfortable living room where he knew she would be reading in front of the fire, he could have wished that it were arriving a little more on his terms.

"Well," she said, closing the book (*New Myths and Old Realities*, by one of Walter's more outspoken competitors in the great seesaw of American opinion) and looking up with a smile, "how did it go?"

"He wants to run, but he wants someone to tell him to."

"And did you?"

The Secretary made a quizzical sound.

"I certainly did."

"And is he?"

He shook his head in an impatient way.

"Oh, of course not. It will have to be done over and over, and all the while he'll be inching closer and closer.

Suddenly one day he'll find himself in it." He frowned. "Meanwhile, Walter will have made his speech and Ted will be running and I will be running. It will all end up in a very embarrassing tangle. But that's what happens when you have conscience in the White House. The White House always wins, but conscience has to have its day."

"I'm sure he has other motives than just ego," Beth said, and the Secretary nodded quickly.

"Oh, certainly. I'm not denying Harley's integrity or good heart. But—it puts me on the spot, right enough."

"All right, then," she said briskly, "when do we hit the road?"

He gave her a humorously grateful smile and immediately looked more relaxed.

"Hank," he said, "I think you're more bloodthirsty about this than I am. When do you want to hit the road?"

"It would be a little premature before Walter's speech, wouldn't it? He called, by the way. He wants you to call him."

"Oh?" Orrin Knox said. A definite interest came into his tone. "Where is he, Leesburg?"

"Out there in the snow," Beth said with a smile, "spinning his little webs. Probably just putting the finishing touches on his speech for Ted. Why don't you interrupt him?"

"Oh, I will," her husband said. "I will. I just wonder what prompts this sudden contact, that's all."

"Go find out," she suggested. "He won't bite."

He chuckled.

"Maybe I'll bite him."

She smiled.

"I'm sure. But try to find out what's on his mind, at least."

For the first few moments of their conversation, however, this remained a mystery to the Secretary. For his part, Walter Dobius was not in any hurry to enlighten. An intriguing thought had hit him in the midst of his writing, he had taken up the telephone and acted upon it at once. Beth Knox had been surprised and puzzled and had not made any attempt to sound particularly pleased though he knew she must be at this show of interest from one whom the Knoxes, he was sure, regarded as an enemy. It pleased him to play the part of unsuspected friend now, particularly in the cause of so shrewd a jest. He had not believed Beth when she said the Secretary was out. He could imagine their fear of him, their puzzled concern, their worried discussion, their pleased conclusion that he must be leaning toward Orrin and so, finally, the Secretary's decision to call back. It all lent an extra edge of confidence to his voice, the unctuously kindly and patronizing note that was, though he did not know it, among his most infuriating characteristics to those who were not quite as overawed by Walter Wonderful as Walter Wonderful sometimes supposed.

At first, however, the Secretary managed to conceal this. His own tone was politely interested and quite correct.

"It's always good to hear from you, Walter. How's the snow out your way? Pretty heavy?"

"About six or seven inches, I'd say. I'll have a devil of a time getting in to catch my plane to New York tomorrow."

"Oh, are you going?"

"Yes. I was planning to go up to the UN to see Prince Terry and his cousin—"

"Not together, I hope," Orrin interrupted. Walter uttered a cordial, knowing little laugh.

"Hardly. Also, Vasily Tashikov called and invited me to lunch, and so all in all—I really hope I can get up there. It should be very interesting."

"Yes, I suppose," the Secretary said, thinking, I'll be damned if I'll invite you to fly up with me, no matter how you hint. "Are you going to cover the debate in the Security Council, too?"

"What's going to happen in that debate, Orrin? Is there anything I should be looking for?"

Aware that his slightest change of tone was being listened to by an expert, the Secretary deliberately made his voice as noncommittal as possible.

"The usual thing, I suppose. A lot of words—some more mud-slinging at us—a postponement without a vote—a gradual frittering away later in the General Assembly."

"Is that what you expect?" Walter asked in some surprise. "I've been hearing over in your department that there may be something much more dramatic than that in the wind."

"Drama's relative," Orrin said, sounding as bored as possible. "But I imagine your talks with Terry and his cousin, and your lunch with Tashikov, will more than compensate for any official dullness. You seem to be rather partial to Terry's cousin these days, I notice."

"I regard Prince Obi as a remarkable young man," Walter Dobius said.

"So are they both."

"Yes, but Prince Obi, I think, rather more than Prince Terry. Particularly now that he seems to have a really genuine popular uprising behind him."

"Oh, Walter, stop being ridiculous," the Secretary said, provoked to annoyance despite his plans by this dutiful parroting of the line Walter himself had done so much to create in his columns and speeches. "You know that little freebooter has nothing behind him but Soviet and Chinese Communist money. He's depending on mercenaries, Walter. I thought you established the principle in the Congo that nobody should like mercenaries."

"I fail to see that the situations have anything in common," Walter said stiffly. Orrin snorted.

"You don't? Well, look hard. The resemblances are there."

"Are they?" Walter demanded. "A vigorous and democratic young leader—an oppressed people—a spontaneous rebellion breaking out against centuries of oligarchical rule—"

"You said exactly the same thing six months ago about Terry. Now, didn't you?"

"I thought at that time he deserved them," Walter Dobius said sharply. "Now I do not believe he does."

The Secretary grunted.

"Walter, have you ever been to Africa?"

"I was invited to speak a year ago to the Conference of Unaligned Nations in Accra, as you know perfectly well."

"Yes, I remember," the Secretary said. "You gave the United States quite a kicking around, as I recall. They were very pleased. Tell me, do you ever have a good word to say for your own country?"

"Now, that isn't fair," Walter said, a real anger in his voice. "That simply isn't fair. You know perfectly well that I—"

The Secretary gave an impatient sigh.

"I know, I know. It wasn't fair, and I apologize. We seem to be arguing again. What did you want to talk to me about?"

"I wanted to ask you and Beth to come to lunch on Thursday. But I suppose we would only argue more."

"Undoubtedly," Orrin said, allowing a little more humor to come into his tone, "but I imagine Beth and I can make it. I've been wanting to have a real talk with you for some time. When do you want us?"

"Noon, I think," Walter said, quite calm and correct again, the anger beginning to subside as he reflected who he was talking to, after all: just Orrin Knox. "If that suits your schedule."

"I'll make it fit," the Secretary said.

"Very well, then. In the meantime, I assume I'll see you at the UN tomorrow?"

"I think I'm probably going up," Orrin said, "but it's not entirely definite yet. I'm going to put in a call to Lafe and Cullee in a few minutes and see what they advise." He remembered Walter's luncheon date with Tashikov and decided abruptly that Walter might be a bridge between the two worlds, at that, if the situation in the Security Council got bad enough. "Where will you be staying?"

"I'll be at the Waldorf-Astoria, but only overnight. I have to go on to Cleveland to make a speech on Wednesday."

"We may have a lot to talk about at lunch Thursday. Beth will be pleased."

"I, too," Walter said, the pomposity returning, the conversation back on his own ground again, Orrin, difficult as he was, once more in the implicit role of supplicant, as they both understood. "I have some important decisions to make soon. I want to discuss things with you before I make them."

"I appreciate your courtesy," the Secretary said. His voice became wry. "I can't say my views have changed much since the last time you disapproved of them, but it may be helpful for you to get a refresher."

"The decisions to be made are important," Walter repeated without humor, "and I feel I must weigh everything very carefully if I am to do the job the country expects of me."

"So must we all," Orrin agreed, trying not to sound ironic. "Until tomorrow, then, and Thursday."

"I shall be looking forward to it," Walter Dobius said, thinking as the Secretary hung up, Little do you know how much I will be looking forward to it.

"There's a puzzler," Orrin said as he returned to the living room and started to poke the fire. "He wants us to come to lunch on Thursday."

"Alone?" Beth inquired. He paused, the poker dangling from his hand, and gave her a surprised and thoughtful stare.

"He didn't say. I assumed so, but—he didn't say. Anyway, it's what you and Harley have both told me to do today—go talk to Walter. So I am going to go and talk to Walter. Coming?"

"I wouldn't miss it," she said with a smile. "Somebody has to keep you from chopping his head off in the first five minutes."

"I'm afraid I already have," he confessed with a rueful little chuckle. "He began giving me this Noble Young Leader routine on Obifumatta Ajkaje, and I'm afraid I got a little short with him. That's one of the things I can't stand about Walter and his crowd, their damned hypocrisy. They can moon all over a bright young good-for-nothing like Terry as long as he's doing what they want him to—namely, kicking the United States in the teeth—and then the minute he stops that, they drop him and find somebody else to give the big buildup to. They tell the public such damned lies about these people. That's what I can't stand."

"Well," Beth said firmly, "I'd suggest you keep things like that to yourself, Mr. Secretary. You aren't going to change them, and pointing out their hypocrisy is the surest way to make them hate you forever. And that we don't want when you're on the verge of running for President again. Right?"

"I suppose so," he agreed with a grin, "but I must confess I like to twist Walter's tail once in a while. Somebody ought to, or he'll get even more insufferable than he is already."

"I wouldn't be so sure that Walter isn't about to twist your tail," she remarked thoughtfully. "In which case, lunch on Thursday should be great fun."

"Well," he said, "Thursday will have to be Thursday's problem. Right now I've got to call Cullee and Lafe, who no doubt are having great fun themselves at Selena Jason Castleberry's party for Free Gorotoland. They're having fun, and Selena's having fun, and Prince Obi's having fun, and all of Obi's friends and admirers in New York are having fun. What more felicity do you want in the world?"

She chuckled.

"The felicity of a cautious tongue, if you must know."

He tossed her a cheerful grin as he started out of the room to make his call to New York.

"It wouldn't be me. And think how dull that would be!"

"How will we ever know?" she called after. "It's never going to be tried."

But he didn't answer, and after a moment she returned with a quizzical expression to her book, though not before deciding to put in a call a little later to someone who might know Walter's plans, or at least would know enough of how his mind worked to come up with an educated guess about them.

"Darling," cried the gaunt, diamond-drenched woman with the hacked-off gray hair and the gasping eyes—Mrs. Jason Castleberry that was, Mrs. Roger Castleberry that had been, Selena Jason that was, had been, and always would be—"I do want you to come over here and meet Prince Obifumatta Ajkaje. He's a mad, *mad* character and so utterly delightful in his understanding of this whole mad situation in Africa." She glanced quickly around the hectic, shouting, bulging living room of her modest little twenty-room hideaway on Sutton Place and lowered her voice to a hurried whisper. "Not at all like *our* Negroes, you know. In spite of the great danger he's in personally because of this wonderful enterprise he's leading, bringing freedom to his poor downtrodden people in Gorotoland, *he* has a sense of humor about it all, you know. It makes *him* so much easier to talk to. Now, *then*," she cried triumphantly as she shoved forward her companion, the earnest little man from the *Nation*, "*here* he *is!* His Royal Highness Prince Obi—Prince Obifumatta, that is. Darling, where *ever* did you get such a delightful name?"

The tall young Negro who loomed above her in his gorgeous red and green robes smiled down with a beneficent gaze reminiscent of his cousin, Prince Terry, except that underlying Prince Obi's smile there was, at present, a terrible tension that grinned like the smile of death through his outward cordiality. Neither his hostess nor her guests, most of them filled to slopover with liquor, love, and liberalism, seemed to notice this, though it did not escape the two Americans, one white and one black, who stood together at the side of the rocking room. Cullee Hamilton, Representative in Congress from the State of California, and Lafe Smith, junior Senator from the State of Iowa, members of the U.S. delegation to the UN, were under no more delusions about Prince Obi than they had been six months ago about his cousin. Only the emphasis had changed, as though a kaleidoscope had been given half a turn and everything had come up at right angles to where it used to be. It still meant trouble for them and their country.

"My name?" Prince Obifumatta repeated in the clipped, guttural Afro-British accent of his education and upbringing. "I made it up. I knew that someday I would be a famous man and I wanted a name that people could neither pronounce nor forget. So I chose Obifumatta. Actually," he said, giving again the nervous thrust of his savage smile, "it's been in my family for seven hundred years, give or take a few."

"That's what I mean, darling," Selena Castleberry said, giving the arm of the *Nation*'s earnest little man an excited squeeze. "Such a sense of humor. Such a *doll*."

"What is your reaction to this American attempt to suppress your battle to bring freedom and democracy to Gorotoland, Your Highness?" the *Nation*'s little man inquired earnestly. Prince Obifumatta thumped him so fiercely on the back that he staggered.

"Call me Obi!" he directed. "Everybody does. I really have no comment at all, you know I am happy with everyone. I am not annoyed with anyone. Life is wonderful, do you not agree?"

"I do," the *Nation*'s little man assured him hastily, "but I was just wondering if you cared to express a comment—"

"Now, express a comment, Obi, dear," Selena admonished him with a shriek of laughter. "That's exactly why I'm giving this Aid-to-the-People's-Republic-of-Free Gorotoland party you know, so that all these darling people of the press, television, and radio, all these *molders* of American *opinion*, can see you and find out what you think." She gave a coy hoot. "It might make headlines, you know! It just might, now!"

"Headlines are nothing to me," Prince Obifumatta said with a sober air. "Absolutely nothing."

"Oh, *doll!*" Selena cried. "Isn't he just a doll, now?" she demanded of the horned-rimmed glasses, the ivory cigarette-holders, the portentous martini glasses, and the thoughtful, important pipes that swam before her in the dancing room. "He is a doll, a doll, a *doll!* And of course," she added with an abrupt transition to complete solemnity, "one of the Truly Great Men Of Our Time."

"*We* think so," said the man from the *New Yorker*, somewhere behind her.

"*We* think so," said the man from the *Reporter*, somewhere behind him.

"*We* think so," said the man from the *New Republic*, somewhere behind him.

"*We* think so," said the man from the *In-Group Quarterly*, trying to see around them.

"*We* think so," said *Newsweek*, right out in front and smiling up at Prince Obi with a fearfully concentrated gaze, horribly nearsighted but damn it, darling, I hate contact lenses and I will *not* wear glasses to a party.

"I'm damned if *I* think so," Senator Smith murmured to his companion. Congressman Hamilton returned a grim little smile and nodded.

"Tell us what you think of the President's defense of Standard Oil's exploitation of your country," the *New Yorker* demanded with a nervous little giggle, coming closer.

"Tell us what you think of this attempt by Washington to launch a new colonialism in Africa," the *Reporter* suggested, lighting his pipe.

"Tell us what respect you think the United States can possibly hope to retain when it takes so backward and vicious an attitude toward its *own* great Negro people," the *New Republic* proposed, elbowing one of their representatives absently aside as he grabbed another martini from a passing tray.

"Tell us *anything*," breathed *Newsweek*, stabbing Prince Obi unexpectedly in the region of the belly-button with an eight-inch ivory cigarette holder picked up on a twenty-four hour survey of Southeast Asia's trouble spots last spring.

"Yes," shrieked their hostess, "*do* tell us, doll!"

"It would hardly behoove me, as a visitor to your great country, to say anything critical about it at such a pleasant social occasion—" Prince Obifumatta began slowly.

"Yes, yes!" said the *New Yorker* eagerly.

"Yes, yes!" said the *New Republic*.

"Yes, yes!" said the *Reporter* and the man from the *In-Group Quarterly*.

"God, don't keep us in suspense!" cried *Newsweek*. "Out with it, Obi, out with it!"

"But," said Obifumatta, "it does seem to me that in these times of great challenge—"

"In which the United States is playing, at best, a shabby and equivocal part," the *New Yorker* offered quickly.

"—when the eyes of the world are upon this country—"

"Whose people and leaders seem absolutely stupefied by their own lack of intelligence and imagination," contributed the *Reporter*.

"—and when both abroad and at home her attitude toward the colored races of this earth is under such heavy fire—"

"Which of course is God damned well deserved!" cried the *New Republic*, gulping his martini with a feverish concentration.

"—then it does seem to me—"

"Oh, *tell* us!" cried the *In-Group Quarterly*.

"—that there is reasonable ground for criticism in recent events."

"How well you put it!" exclaimed *Newsweek*, extricating the cigarette-holder from Prince Obi's midriff and swinging it about into the eye of the earnest little man from the *Nation*. "Doesn't he put it well, everybody? Doesn't he?"

"He's a doll!" Selena Castleberry assured them, her hacked-off hair a-frizzle, her staring eyes wide with excitement. "I told you all he was a doll. Now you know!"

("We've just signed him to do his autobiography for us," murmured the vice president of The Most Right-Thinking Book Publishers, Inc. "We're going to call it *New Star Over Africa: My Struggle for Justice*, by Prince Obi.")

("We'll make a bid of five hundred thousand dollars plus 30 percent of the gross," offered the representative of The Most Daring Young Right-Thinking Hollywood Producer. "We'll budget it for thirty million, shoot it in Spain, and hire the entire nation of Dahomey to be extras. It'll be the greatest!")

"Oh, *God!*" Selena cried with a sudden yelp of pleased surprise. "There come Poopy Rhinefetter and the Princess Saboko! *Now* the party's complete. Poopy! Poopy, darling! Do bring your lovely bride and come meet the greatest leader of Africa. This *man*," she explained to Prince Obifumatta in a confidential voice that carried clearly over the clutter, the clamor, the raucous, smoke-laden roar of the aching, shaking, quaking room, "is almost as famous as you are, darling. He's worth absolutely untold millions and he's always to be found supporting the most *liberal* causes, and just three weeks ago he married that *lovely* girl, there. The Princess Saboko—your fellow royalty, doll. It was all so romantic. He found her last month, singing native songs at some place down in the Village, and before you could say clip-my-coupons he had eloped with her to Connecticut. The family's absolutely *furious*. Their picture was all set to be on the cover of *Life* this week until you came along, you naughty boy, and they decided to run yours instead. Poopy and the Princess! Poopy and the Princess! Come over here this minute, you delicious dolls, and meet this wonderful man!"

"Where did you say the Princess was from?" Obifumatta inquired.

"Some place in Ghana, I believe," Selena Castleberry said. "Or is it Mali? Or maybe Nigeria? Oh, darling, who cares? She's a princess, she's lovely, she's Mrs. Poopy Rhinefetter. That's all *anybody* needs to know. Poopy, this is His Royal Highness Prince Obifumatta, from Gorotoland. Your Royal Highness, this is Poopy Rhinefetter and Mrs. Poopy Rhinefetter, *Her* Royal Highness. From Ghana. I think. Those marks on her forehead are the marks of her royal birth, aren't they, Saboko, darling?"

"Place dere bime roahll fadder," the Princess Saboko said carefully, while her adoring husband swung at anchor off her left elbow.

"I am honored," Prince Obi said gravely, sounding his most British. "Those are noteworthy marks, indeed. Are you from Ghana?"

"Dat my place," said the Princess, and Poopy, apparently relaxed from some previous engagement, echoed happily, "Dat her place, everybody. Yassuh, boss, dat her place."

"I see," Obifumatta said in the same polite tone. "Whore of the earth," he added pleasantly in Twe, "you are doing well in the white man's world."

"Anus of the universe," the Princess responded cordially in the same language, "swallow your own excrement."

"They *like* each other!" Selena cried ecstatically to the billowing room. "They speak the same language! These two great leaders of Africa are *here* with *us*. Oh, *God,* to think we are making such *progress* in world relations, right here in my humble flat! Oh, it's wonderful!"

"It's the greatest thrill of my life," the *New Yorker* said soberly.

"The moment is really historic," said the *Reporter,* relighting his pipe.

"I'm going to recommend a very strong editorial next week," the *New Republic* announced.

"We shall run one next month," sniffed the *In-Group Quarterly.*

"This sort of thing makes up for everything," *Newsweek* said fervently. "Really for *everything!*"

"And now," Prince Obifumatta said gracefully, "I really must be buzzing off. Tomorrow is a fateful day for Free Gorotoland in the Security Council, you know, and I must rest and prepare." He enfolded his hostess' hands in his enormous paws. "It has been delightful, dear lady. I commend you to the Princess Saboko, who will tell you much of our difficult life in Africa now that she is Mrs. Poopy Rhinefetter. My thanks and blessings to you all."

He waved to the turbulent throng, bowed low, and departed on a burst of approving shouts and applause.

"He's a dreamboat," murmured the *New Yorker* fervently.

"One of the authentic greats of our time," agreed the *Reporter,* sucking deep upon his pipe.

"How wonderful the spirit of unity that binds the great black continent together," the *New Republic* said gravely.

"With people like that in the world," asked the *In-Group Quarterly,* "how can humanity lose?"

"They are both so *real,*" agreed the *Nation.* "What an experience!"

"And the wonderful thing about it, darling," murmured *Newsweek,* "is that these people aren't *dull.* They aren't *ordinary* Negroes, like ours."

"Is this actually fresh air we're breathing out here?" the junior Senator from Iowa asked the Congressman from California as they stood on the stoop in Sutton Place half an hour later waiting for an official U.S. delegation car to work its way through the crush in the narrow street and take them back to the Waldorf-Astoria.

"I've about forgotten," Cullee Hamilton said. He sniffed. "Guess it is—or about as close as New York gets when it isn't breathing the kind they were breathing in there. What a crew!"

"Marvelously enlightened," Lafe Smith agreed, nodding to the Ambassador of Chad and his ample lady, who had emerged beside them into the snowy night. "Prodigiously progressive. Lavishly liberal. A three-thousand-dollar party for a ten-cent cause. Now they can all go home feeling so much better. It's comforting."

"What phonies there are in this city," Cullee said in a curious tone that combined wonder, irritation, and a sort of despairing hopelessness at the prospect of ever breaking through to reality in such an atmosphere. "Six months ago they were giving poor old Terry the buildup and now he's out in the snow on his ass. Not that I mind," he added with a grim little smile, "what they do to poor old Terry. But it's the principle of the thing."

"The principle is consistent enough," Lafe said thoughtfully as their car arrived and they got in. "Tear down your own country and its aims, ideals, and purposes as often and loudly as you can. Support any international brigand who attacks it and attempts to defeat it in world affairs. Tell yourself you do these things out of an enlightened liberalism and a genuine patriotism. Have another drink, and congratulate yourselves on your contribution to the forward progress of humanity. Be gay. Be happy. Be smug. Be secure. *In your heart you know you're right!* Have another drink."

"You sound bitter," Congressman Hamilton said with a chuckle, giving him a friendly slap on the knee as they settled back and the car began its slow crawl through the swirling whiteness that still held the city. The storm that had already died in Washington would linger a while in New York before it moved on out to dissipate somewhere over the lost and lonely reaches of the black Atlantic.

"I am bitter," Senator Smith said. "All that fuss we went through six months ago over Terry, and now we have to go through all this with his cousin. I must confess the UN gives me a terrible sense of being caught forever in a revolving door."

"We'll be off the delegation soon, and after that it will be somebody else's headache. Personally, I won't be sorry. I've got people to see and things to do."

"You're going to run for Senator from California, aren't you?" Lafe said, more a statement than a question. The handsome black face beside him looked genuinely troubled for a moment, the big ex-track star's frame moved uneasily.

"I am damned," Cullee Hamilton said heavily, "if I know, at this point. You see, of all the things that are going to get caught in the squeeze between Orrin Knox and Ted Jason, little Congressman Hamilton from California is one of the most obvious."

"Surely you aren't going to side with Ted," Lafe said as their car crept carefully west on 66th Street in the blinding white. "Somehow I can't see you in with that crowd."

"Except that he's the governor, of course, and it is rather nice to have the governor on your side when you run for the Senate. Not imperative, but nice."

"Buddy, I think you've reached a point where it doesn't matter whether he's on your side or not. Ted needs you, you don't need Ted."

"Which means he's in the mood to bargain," Cullee said. "Which is another factor."

"Which is another factor. And Orrin isn't in a mood to bargain?"

Cullee shrugged.

"You know Orrin. He bargains when it suits his integrity, but he won't otherwise. Which," he said with a sudden sidelong glance and smile, "suits me just fine, because that's when I bargain too."

"You're a pair," Senator Smith conceded with an answering smile, "which is why your problem is relatively simple, it seems to me. You know who you'll back for President when the time comes—if," he interjected dryly, "Harley ever lets it come—and that automatically solves the Senate problem. I don't think you'll have any trouble bucking the Jasons. The rest of the family's like Selena, in varying degrees: they all telegraph their punches."

"Sometimes yes and sometimes no," Cullee said thoughtfully. "Don't make the mistake of underestimating them, particularly Ted. He's the trickiest of the lot. For the moment, I'd prefer to let things ride without forcing the issue, if I can."

"I gather from what Orrin said on the phone just now that Patsy and Walter Dobius are going to force it for all of us. So now what?"

Cullee chuckled.

"He did sound a little annoyed about it, didn't he? It

seemed to be more on his mind than the Security Council debate on Gorotoland tomorrow."

"He just wanted to alert you to what was being planned so you could be thinking—his way. And you are, so he achieved his purpose, right?"

"I guess time will tell," Cullee said lightly. Their car crept into Lexington Avenue and turned south. "How are you making out these days with all your romantic projects?"

"Don't change the subject," Lafe said, "even to that one. I haven't got time for projects these days. I've got responsibilities now, you know." His normally open and sunny face darkened for a moment. "Hal Fry left me some."

"Yes, I know," Cullee Hamilton said softly, his own expression saddened by the reference to the late Senator from West Virginia, former chief American delegate to the UN, whose death from leukemia six months ago had been one of the major tragedies of the last session. "How is his son these days?"

"Healthy," Senator Smith said, with a certain bitterness in his voice in spite of himself as he thought of the smiling, handsome youth sitting serenely in his closed-off world. "Always healthy. But no improvement at all"—he tapped his forehead—"up here. However," he added firmly, "I am determined to bring that boy back if it is humanly possible to do so, and I will. He's in a sanitarium up the Hudson, you know. I go up twice a week now and work with him. The people there say he's beginning to expect me, but I can't tell. He never got to expecting Hal, though he went there often enough, poor guy. But I'm working. It doesn't leave much time for extracurricular activities. And you know?" he added with a curiously naïve air that touched his companion, "I find I don't really mind it much, now that I have something important to think about instead of just me."

"Maybe Hal accomplished something with his dying," Cullee suggested gently. Lafe nodded.

"Hal accomplished a lot of things with his dying. Whether they know it in the UN or not."

"Oh, they know it," Cullee Hamilton said bitterly. "They remember his last speech, though they'd rather not. They're dying themselves, and they know that, too, but they try to keep on pretending it isn't so. . . . I won't mind getting off the delegation. I've had about enough of watching them destroy the hopes of the world with their petty bickering and their insane drive to destroy every rule of civilized behavior that makes any attempt at strengthening world order."

"You couldn't tell Selena and her guests that the UN is dying. They'd scream bloody murder and call you a damned reactionary."

Congressman Hamilton made a scornful sound.

"That crew," he said. And again: "*That crew.*" They rode in silence for a little until Lafe broke it, more lightly.

"And what about your extracurricular activities? Seems to me I see you and Sarah Johnson at an awful lot of UN parties together lately. Is this true love or just relaxation?"

"I don't know. I don't think either of us has thought it through, yet."

"She has, you can bet," Senator Smith assured him. "They always do. . . . Where's Sue-Dan these days? Are you getting a divorce?"

"Seems to me you're getting awfully personal all of a sudden," his companion said with a frown and a note of genuine annoyance in his voice. But on the strength of a good and genuine friendship, Lafe refused to be impressed.

"You know me," he said with his engaging, boyish grin. "What fun is a world without gossip? *I'm* getting a divorce, for what it's worth as an example to you."

"Yes, but you don't love her," Cullee said, his voice so low Lafe could hardly hear it. "God help me, I still do."

"You'd be better off," Lafe said, though he knew he was risking a real explosion if he kept it up. "You know it."

"I know it," Cullee said, "but my heart and my guts and my—the rest of me, don't know it." He brought a powerful fist down upon his knee with a sudden heavy sigh. "Ah, damn it!"

"Where is she?" Lafe asked in a matter-of-fact tone. "Did she decide to go to work for LeGage Shelby in DEFY?"

"Yes, she's jazzing around with that no-good, loudmouth sonny-boy I used to call a friend." Congressman Hamilton said, a frown deepening on his handsome face at the thought of his clever, ambition-whipped ex-roommate and the Defenders of Equality for You that he had put together from the more irresponsible elements of the younger Negro community. "Both of them laughing and sneering at me all day long, I expect. Well," he said darkly, "time takes care of the likes of that. You go down that road, you end up in a smash. Or so my Maudie tells me."

"Who's Maudie?" Lafe asked with a smile. "Another girl friend?"

"She's my sixtyish girl friend. She keeps my house for me in Washington. She's about the only company I've got down there, now Sue-Dan's—gone away. . . . Anyway," he added with a bitter little laugh, "I've got a good excuse not to get a divorce right now. You didn't ever hear of a Senatorial candidate getting a divorce before election day. The voters don't like that."

"If she's running with DEFY, you'd be better off getting one."

"Maybe in Iowa," Congressman Hamilton said, "but out in California DEFY and all the rest of the alphabet go over big, you know. It doesn't hurt me to have a wife and an ex-campaign manager with DEFY. Politically, that is. Other ways, voters wouldn't care about anyway."

"Walter Dobius says DEFY is a sterling symbol of the noblest aspirations of the younger elements of the Negro race, constructive in purpose, democratic in procedure, forward-looking in thought, and profoundly a part of the American dream," Senator Smith informed him solemnly. "Don't you agree?"

Congressman Hamilton snorted.

"What Walter Dobius doesn't know about the Negro race and its aspirations would fill even more books than he's written. And be about equally intelligent, in my opinion."

"That's heresy. In the first degree. Walter thinks he's going to make the whole world hop Friday night when he makes that speech for Ted."

"Won't make me hop," Cullee said bluntly. "He never has and never will. I got Walter's number about ten days after I arrived on the Hill. He came around to give me a few pointers on how to lead the Negro revolution from a back row seat in the House. It was kind of him, but it didn't have much bearing on the realities in that great body."

"Walter pretty well tells everybody how to do everything," Lafe said thoughtfully. "Of all the sad cases of *ego gigantea Washingtonia* I know, I think he's about the worst. The annoying thing about it is that he can write—and he's a terrific reporter—and he really does do a conscientious job, according to his lights. It isn't easy to dismiss him out of hand. He's too damned good."

"He and his pals can swing maybe five hundred thousand votes in California," Congressman Hamilton said matter-of-factly. "That's enough to be decisive."

"But you aren't going to let that influence you," Lafe suggested with a humorous certainty.

"I'm not going to let that influence me. . . . What do you think of this business tomorrow in the Security Council?"

The Senator from Iowa looked grave.

"I think Walter and his friends are going to scream to high heaven if it happens. I think it may very well be a decisive factor in the presidential election. I think it may beat Orrin, if he runs, and it may even beat the President, if he runs. Certainly it will if Walter and his world have anything to say about it. And we know they will."

"You really think it's as bad as that," Cullee said thoughtfully. "Maybe you're right."

Lafe stared grimly out at the driving snow as though all the world's devils were in it, while the car crept slowly down toward the Waldorf.

"Just look at the consequences that can flow from it," he said finally. "War could come from this, buddy. Don't make any mistake about it."

Cullee gave him a a quizzical look.

"It wouldn't if Harley would back down."

"I have the feeling Harley thinks we've backed down long enough. What do you think?"

"Oh, I agree. I've always agreed. But if you think it will beat Orrin and Harley, then it will probably beat me. Because I certainly shan't sidestep the issue, regardless of Jasons or anything else. Nor will you—you run, too, this year, don't you?"

"Oh, yes. And Iowa, I'm very much afraid, is going to be inclined to agree with Walter Dobius—for different reasons, but with the same result for me. But"—he gave his charming grin—"I have a trick or two up my sleeve. Uncle Lafe isn't beaten yet, by a long shot. I've talked Iowa around before, when the right's been on my side. And I will this time, although"—his expression became somber—"it won't be so easy."

"Well," Cullee said as the car came to a crunching halt in the drift in front of the Waldorf, "it may not be necessary. This may go entirely differently tomorrow."

"Maybe. But don't bet on it. . . . Want a nightcap before we turn in?"

Cullee nodded.

"Sure. . . . Oh, oh!" he added with a sudden humorous note as the warmth of the lobby enveloped them and he saw seated across the room a giant ebony figure, looking, though it was obviously trying not to, dejected and forlorn for all its gorgeous robes and haughty air. "Do you see who I see?"

Lafe chuckled.

"I do. Shall we spread a little cheer by inviting him to join us?"

"He sure needs it," Cullee Hamilton said, not without a certain relish. "Boy, does he ever. However, if you don't mind—"

"O.K.," Lafe agreed. "We've had our fill of him, after all. . . . Tell me," he said as they walked on by, not looking at Terry, carefully ignoring his sudden recognition, his eager starting to rise, his forlorn sinking down again as he realized they did not want to see him, "did you ever meet Mabel Anderson—Brigham Anderson's wife?"

"No, I haven't," Cullee said as they entered the bar. Something in his companion's expression caused him to smile. "Oh, that's it, is it?"

"No," Lafe said thoughtfully. "Not necessarily. I got a letter from her today, though. First I've heard from her since she left Washington after his death. . . . She's a nice girl," he added, as if to himself. Then he grinned. "I know what you're thinking—too nice for Lover Lafe. But maybe Lover Lafe is ready to settle down. Who knows?"

"Write her back, by all means," Cullee suggested with a smile. "At once."

"I already have," Senator Smith admitted, with an obvious satisfaction that made his friend laugh.

"We'd better drink to that," Cullee said. "What'll you have?"

"Something for that," Lafe said, "and also something to wish luck to our friend in the lobby. He needs it."

And, indeed, it was clear to any perceptive observer that His Royal Highness Terence Wolowo Ajkaje, 137th

M'Bulu of Mbuele, ruler—as long as he could hang on—of turbulent Gorotoland, outstanding young leader—at least he *had* been, until just recently—of emerging Africa, did, indubitably, need all the cheer he could get.

Life was doing puzzling and unhappy things to the 137th M'Bulu, and he still was in something of a daze about it. His was a sad case. "Yesterday's hero"—as the London *Daily Mail* had put it to the *Daily Telegraph* only this morning in the Delegates' Lounge—"today's bum." It was a strange and unsettling experience for one possessed, but a few short weeks ago, of the unrestrained plaudits and unstinting assistance of all those elements, both in the United States and abroad, who now turned upon him stony and unfriendly faces as they went happily about the business of helping his cousinly rival hurl him from his throne. And all for no logical reason that he could see—except that his cousin, the hated Obifumatta, had managed to capture both the support of the Communists and the attention of all those legend-makers and seekers after truth—the right kind of truth, of course, and the proper kind of legend—who had so recently favored Terry himself with their fond and encouraging regard.

It was very peculiar. Six months ago Terence Ajkaje —"Terrible Terry" to the jet-set and the world's headlines —had descended upon the United States and the United Nations like an avenging black angel riding down a path of light to blast away the enemies of progress. (That was the way he had actually been portrayed, in fact, in a cartoon in the Washington *Post*. Alas, the contrast today! Now he appeared in the *Post's* cartoons skulking out from under a manhole cover in the street across from the UN building, emitting from his mouth such fictitious and unfair comments as, "That ship can't desert us sinking rats!" *Sic transit gloria mundi*, at least on some people's editorial pages, and all in the sad short space of six little months.)

Half a year only separated him from his days of triumph. Those were the glorious days in which he had literally captured the attention of the world when he escorted a little colored girl to school in South Carolina and was stoned and egged for his deed. Those were the great days when, aided by the Communist bloc, most of his fellow Africans and Asians, and such enemies of the United States as Panama's Ambassador Felix Labaiya-Sofra, he had roused the brawling United Nations to frenzy and

come within a single vote of winning censure of the United
States for its racial policies. Those were the times of
Life, Look, Newsweek, the *Saturday Evening Post,* and
Screen Gems; when the New York *Times* vied with the
New York *Post,* the New York *World Journal Tribune,*
and even the *Christian Science Monitor* in heaping praises
on his head; when the English language—except for a few
sourly skeptical editorials in the place where the English
language began—hardly held enough glowing words to do
him tribute. And then—suddenly—disaster. Collapse.
Bursting bubbles. Popped balloons. A pained reaction every time he heard, "The Party's Over" on the radio. Cal-
umny. Criticism. Slander. Libel. Denunciation. The End.

Or almost The End. The End if it hadn't been for the
powers he had done so much to harass six months ago; The
End without the United States and Great Britain.

And why? What had he done, except be the dutiful agent
of all the enemies, both foreign and domestic, of those two
peculiar countries? Hadn't he appeared on all the right television programs, addressed all the right forums, attended
all the right functions (including, he recalled with a special bitterness tonight, a party given by Selena Jason Castleberry "In Aid of Independent Gorotoland"), produced
all the right answers to all the right questions put to him by
all the right interviewers? He had denounced "imperialist
aggression" as self-righteously as anyone, his caustic
strictures on "neo-colonialist adventurism" had rung out
with the best, no one had done more than he to thwart,
besmirch, and demean the United States and the United
Kingdom. Walter Dobius had written a total of ten columns supporting him, Walter's friends and colleagues in
both countries had given him the full treatment to speed
success for his cause and disaster for their own governments. And now it was all gone. Where, and how, and why?

The process had begun, he could see now, with the weird
little riot that had occurred in his capital city of Molobangwe just on the eve of his most triumphant moments at
the UN. When Terry had left dusty Molobangwe to come
to New York seeking immediate independence from Britain and the confusion of the United States on racial matters, he had appointed his mother, aging but still shrewd
and ruthless, to serve as co-regent with his cousin Obifumatta. Prince Obi, scion of one of the royal family's many
cadet branches, had sworn blood oaths and fealty ten times

over, and although Terry realized that he possessed an intelligence and ambition almost as great as his own, he had decided to take the chance of leaving him in command. He had been confident at the time that the Council of Elders who advised the throne would take stern and immediate action if Obifumatta attempted anything disloyal. He was also certain that if the Council failed in such a crisis, his mother would poison Obi at once. He therefore left home feeling quite serene. He had made just one little mistake: although he had secretly accepted Soviet and Chinese Communist aid, like many another ambitious African adventurer he had been sufficiently egotistical to think that he could somehow escape being presented with the bill for it.

The riot in Molobangwe had been the first indication that this was not so. It had been an odd little affair which had swept through the mud-and-wattle town like a vagrant wind one stifling afternoon. It was over in half a day, but not before Terry had turned in desperation to the British, who as always were ironically ready to help those who were in process of booting them out; and not before Obifumatta had seized the opportunity to harangue the crowd, swing it to his side, and emerge as the popular hero. The Council of Elders had not dared act against him then, nor had Terry's mother, even though it was apparent that much more than an afternoon's rioting and fun had been involved. The episode had been a warning to Terry, and when he arrived home from the UN—after a pleasant plane ride that he had shared with Senator Bob Munson of Michigan, the Senate Majority Leader, and his wife Dolly, on their way to a month in Britain and the Continent—the warning was spelled out in language so blunt as to temporarily shock and paralyze him.

It appeared that the Communists, who literally twenty-four hours before had been working with him in absolute singleness of purpose at the UN, were working for different purposes six thousand miles away in Africa. He was not the first African to make this sad discovery, but it struck him with the same dismay, both laughable and pathetic, with which it strikes others in the naïve continent as they harshly, inexorably, inevitably find it out.

The Soviet and Chinese attachés, his smiling friends when he left Molobangwe for New York, greeted him with different faces when he got back. There was a short, ugly conference in the ramshackle old palace that once had housed some of the Christian missionaries who had attempted, without much success, to bring their own brand of progress to Gorotoland. The present-day missionaries were tougher and more to the point. Terry was told that he must form at once a "coalition government" in which Obifumatta would have equal rank and in which Communist-trained officials ("progressive elements," they were called by the world of Walter Dobius) would control the police, defense, and foreign policy ministries of Gorotoland's embryonic government.

At first Terry refused point-blank to accede to these demands. He was reminded sarcastically that the United States and Britain were far away and not really, despite Britain's dutiful gesture, very interested, whereas Communist forces were right here and very actively interested. In the final compromise—which all parties, though they hailed it dutifully, knew would be final no longer than it would take one side or the other to break it—Terry had yielded a co-equal command of the defense ministry and a small share of foreign policy to his cousin. Police control he kept for himself, and equal rank he would not concede, pointing out that it was a matter of blood and nothing he could do anything about. The headlines in the West were very encouraging: COALITION GOVERNMENT SOOTHES TROUBLED GOROTOLAND; and, COALITION LAUNCHES NEW PEACEFUL ERA FOR AFRICAN NATION; and, STRIFE-TORN GOROTOLAND EASED BY POPULAR-BASED GOVERNMENT. Walter Dobius and his world wrote and broadcast millions of encouraging words about it, and all those in the West who feared they might have to take a stand if things got sticky relaxed and took a drink instead.

The "coalition" lasted for just over four uneasy months, after which the Communists made their first attempt to overturn it and murder Terry. He escaped, brought the drifting, mindless street mobs to his side by the sheer impact of his powerful personality, and drove Obifumatta, the coalition "ministers," and their Communist supporters back into the bush. Obifumatta at once appealed to Peking and Moscow for help, received loud pledges from each, and filed an appeal with the United Nations. To Terry's shocked dismay, all those elements in the Western world whose views were symbolized and sometimes synthesized by Walter and his friends at once began to attack him and build up his cousin.

"A genuine popular uprising somewhere on the globe is sometimes one of the healthiest things that can happen to this confused old town," Walter wrote. "Washington this week is faced with its newest problem, but, in a relieved sense, also with its newest hero. Tired to death of 'Tiresome Terry,' the brash and erratic young ruler of Gorotoland, influential leaders here are welcoming with some relief the attempt by his cousin, Prince Obifumatta, to establish a truly democratic regime in the difficult African country."

Who these friendly American "leaders" were, neither Terry nor any disinterested observer could see, since President Hudson's administration, far from embracing Obifumatta, had immediately pledged its support to Terry. But if Walter Dobius said so, a great many of his colleagues and countrymen were ready to believe that it must be true. Favorable reports on Obi at once began to flood the press and airwaves.

"BATTLE FOR FREEDOM," CBS offered: "A NEW LEADER RISES IN AFRICA." "SPECIAL REPORT," NBC countered: "WILL DEMOCRACY WIN IN GOROTOLAND?" Pictures of Obifumatta speedily blossomed in all the places where Terry's picture, so short a time before, had grinned upon the populace. The New York *Times,* moving swiftly to cover the emergency, transferred to Amsterdam the level-headed veteran who had been covering Central Africa and rushed to the scene its youthful expert-on-overthrowing-governments. A flood of dispatches favorable to Obifumatta and derogatory to Terry immediately began to appear.

When Obi's mercenaries, either inadvertently or by design, broke into the All-Faiths Missionary Hospital at Molobangwe and carried off two white nurses into the bush, and when, two days later, one of the oil tanks at the new Standard Oil development in the highlands area of the country was mysteriously set afire in the night, the tempo increased. In Washington the President remarked, at first mildly in a press conference but then more firmly in a formal statement issued three hours later after consultation with the Secretary of State, that the United States would "not remain silent or idle" while American lives and property were under attack. Obifumatta immediately filed a new protest with the UN and the outcry doubled. Walter and his world now had exactly the sort of issue they loved —the brutal, overbearing United States threatening a helpless little noble, honest, Communist-riddled backward nation—and if what they said about it happened to coincide with the Communist line, well, that was just too bad. They were morally in the right, whatever the facts of it, and high and mighty was their indignation.

"Rarely," Walter wrote sternly, "has the United States been in a less graceful or more suspect posture than it is today in Gorotoland. True, two American missionary nurses have been abducted and are, presumably, dead. True, a Standard Oil installation has been attacked. But what were they doing there in the first place? The world has seen too much of exploitation moving behind the cloak of mercy. The nurses may have thought they were there to help the natives of Gorotoland. Actually, they may well have been there as an innocent smoke screen for further adventures by the oil interests of the United States."

"OIL: HOW MUCH DOES IT STILL DICTATE POLICY?" CBS obligingly offered two nights later, devoting roughly forty-five minutes of the hour to Obifumatta and his noble cause, fifteen to Terry and his probable shady tieup with Standard. "OIL: NEW SWORD OF EMPIRES?" NBC riposted twenty-four hours later. "BEHIND GOROTOLAND'S CRISIS, THE SPECTER OF OIL," the New York *Times* Sunday Magazine reported at week's end in two thousand hastily written, characteristically objective words from its youthful expert-on-overthrowing-governments. "OIL," said *Life* simply, with a thousand words of text, seven pictures, and three bright maps.

Caught in this kind of cross fire between the world of Walter Wonderful and the Government of the United States, the 137th M'Bulu of Mbuele, though it took him a little while to realize it, didn't have a chance. Almost overnight, it seemed to him, all his support vanished. The friends who had hailed him so eagerly yesterday hailed him no more. In the sort of strange, fantastic, overnight about-face contortion that Walter and his world are all too frequently capable of, he who had been hero was instantly and forever villain. And the thing that staggered and appalled him more than anything else was that Walter and his world got away with it. Apparently their readers and viewers were not aware of the switch, or if aware, were too bored—or too exhausted by innumerable past duplications of the performance—to protest or be skeptical about it. Within a month any mention of Terry, almost anywhere in the American press, carried with it the automatic addition "youthful adventurer who acquired the throne by strangely suspect methods . . ." or, "suspected friend and agent of the oil interests . . ." or, "leader of the anti-democratic forces striving to keep down the people of Gorotoland . . ." or some other pack-cry honed and polished to do the most damage.

In all this sad disarray of his hopes and fortunes, Terrence Ajkaje had only two things going for him; but they were, while they lasted, substantial. The British Government had immediately announced its support, and the Hudson administration in Washington, unlike some previous administrations, showed no inclination at all to be swayed by the propaganda barrage laid down by Walter and his friends. In fact, a week ago the President had reaffirmed his warning to the rebel forces, and to Obifumatta personally, that the United States would "take immediate and substantial action" if so much as one more American citizen or one more piece of American property were hurt. This was so unlike the decades-old pattern of the United States that for almost a day there was a stunned silence around the globe. Then Walter and his world, the Africans and Asians, the Communists, and indeed all Right Thinkers everywhere, let go with an outraged clamor that made their previous attacks sound like friendly greetings.

It was then that the President had called Walter in to ask his advice firsthand and incidentally let him know that it was not going to be taken no matter how furiously he wrote. It was then that the Security Council decided in a heated emergency session—in which the United States, Britain, and Nationalist China found themselves standing alone against France, Uganda, Ceylon, Chad, India, Dahomey, Yugoslavia, Chile, Cuba, the Soviet Union, Venezuela, and Panama, to take up Obifumatta's appeals "at the earliest possible moment." Only by dint of much behind-the-scenes maneuvering at the UN and in the capitals of the Council members had the United States and Britain been able to secure agreement that if Obi were invited to attend and testify, Terry should be too.

And now here they were, though dismal and different indeed were their respective positions and prospects on this snowy night in Manhattan. Prince Obifumatta, just returned to his suite at the Carlyle (paid for by voluntary contributions from Selena Castleberry, Poopy Rhinefetter, and a host of others anxious to Do The Right Thing), was giving one more gracious interview to one more group of friendly and obsequious questioners from the metropolitan press. Prince Terry was huddled uncomfortably (if six-feet-seven could be said to huddle) in the lobby of the Waldorf, looking fiercely proud and abysmally lonely. Far away in Gorotoland Obi's forces, coached by their Russian and Chinese advisers, were skirmishing halfheartedly in the highlands with Terry's forces, coached by their American and British advisers. A temporary lull lay on the scene of battle as both sides awaited events in the UN; but it was, as the Indian Ambassador had remarked today to the French Ambassador when they met at the luncheon given by the delegation of Cameroon, "an interesting and fateful scene."

"I think we have here the setting for quite a drama," Krishna Khaleel had remarked with a hiss of concern, "though not, I think, a pleasant one, do you agree?"

Raoul Barre had responded with his sidelong, clever glance and skeptical smile.

"The principal players are ready, as always," he remarked. "Someday they will be ready and will actually perform. This may be the time."

"Oh, I hope not," K.K. had responded with a horrified expression. "Think of the consequences."

"The world has worried about consequences for decades," Raoul replied. "It may be tired of worrying about consequences. If it is, consequences will come."

Before the stormy night ended, consequences would indeed come, greatly increasing the tensions against which the Security Council would vote tomorrow, against which Walter Dobius would make his visit to the UN and, on Friday, his speech at the Jason Foundation dinner, greatly inflaming the angers and passions against which the presidential campaign would have to be played out. But for the moment, all that the participants, past and future, could see was what faced them right now.

Most immediately, in the lobby of the Waldorf, all that Terry could see, dolefully, was that he had received a royal snub from two people whose friendship he had every right to expect. It was true that he had been a little hard on their government six months ago, but after all, their government was backing him now, so why couldn't they be more cordial? It was one of those things that left him baffled, depressed, and confused as he decided disconsolately that he might as well go up to his room and watch television.

Except that he knew what he would see if he did: hated Obifumatta, grinning forth from all those flattering programs and interviews, just as Terry himself had done six months ago when he, too, had been America's enemy and the darling of America's most powerful opinion-makers.

"I'm sorry to bother you," Beth said, "but just what is your ex up to with this luncheon invitation on Thursday?"

"I'm damned if I know," Helen-Anne Carrew confessed. "He invited me, too, you know, which really indicates he wants to show off about something. I haven't been to Leesburg in four years. Something great must be under way."

"I'm glad you're going to be there, if you don't mind my saying so."

"Oh, so am I. I wouldn't miss it for the world. It may well be the biggest story of the year."

"I hope not," Beth said in alarm. "Surely it's going to be off the record."

Helen-Anne snorted.

"Nothing is off the record in this town, as you very well know. It's just a matter of timing as to when things go on the record. Some sooner, some later, but they always get there, in the end. Personally, I hope they have a terrible fight. Orrin might as well, he has nothing to lose in that quarter."

"You really think so? I've been telling him he ought to let up on Walter for a while and maybe he'll come around to supporting him, in time."

Helen-Anne snorted again.

"My dear! That hard-nosed little—no, he'll never give Orrin a kind word again, no matter what. Not even if Orrin gets the nomination. It's impossible."

"Why?" Beth asked thoughtfully. "Disagreement over past policies? Personality clash? Ambitions the Jasons can satisfy and we can't? I've always wondered, really, why Walter had such a dislike for my husband. I know he isn't perfect, but still—you'd think a little tolerance, now and then."

"Knowing the two of them," Helen-Anne said, "I'm quite sure that at some point very early in Orrin's career here, he was advised by Mr. Wonderful on some subject or other, and being Orrin, he said, Go shove it—or"—she chuckled—"Orrin's equivalent, because Orrin doesn't say naughty things like that, only hard-bitten old newspaper bags like me do. In fact, I sometimes think that if Orrin would say things like that he'd generate less dislike than he does with that way he has of acting as though he doesn't think you have two brains to rub together if you disagree with him."

Beth laughed.

"At least he's honest about it."

"In a superior way which I suppose he doesn't know and can't help, which is what gripes. Anyway, despite what the other member of a once great journalistic marriage may do, I want you to know that I hope sincerely Orrin makes it. If there's anything I can do for him, I will."

"Why, thank you," Beth said, trying not to sound too startled. "I'm touched. Really. And surprised, I may add."

"I've been giving it some thought," Helen-Anne Carrew said slowly. "The longer I stay in this town the more I become convinced that honesty of purpose is the basic necessity in a good President. It isn't enough to qualify a man who hasn't the other qualifications, but if he has them, as Orrin has, and then honesty is added to it, that's the right combination, for my book. This isn't the smart point of view according to Walter and his friends," she added dryly, "but I like it."

"I wonder," Beth said cautiously, "how actively you would want to be associated with Orrin this year."

There was a thoughtful silence and she thought she had probably gone too far too fast. But presently Helen-Anne answered with a characteristically direct candor.

"There are limits, of course. I can't use my column the way Walter uses his. Although," she conceded with a chuckle, "I do manage to get my licks in, now and then."

"Yes, I know. I've felt a few of them."

"Ouch. All right, dear, if you want me to be honest—do you really think I could do more good in a partisan position—if either the dear old *Star*, tolerant as it is, or the syndicate, would give me leave to do it, which I doubt—than I could do indirectly through the column? I wonder."

"Frankly," Beth said, more moved than she wanted to admit, "I'm quite overwhelmed that you think enough of him to consider the alternatives seriously. That's a tribute we'll remember, whatever happens—a hard-boiled old newspaper bag like you!"

Helen-Anne laughed.

"I have my moments. . . . What did you have in mind?"

"Why, I would think . . ." Beth said with a deliberate air of consideration, "press secretary during the campaign . . . to begin with."

Helen-Anne gave her ribald hoot.

"You're all alike holding out one carrot and then topping it with another, for us poor old spavined hacks in the press. Well, I'll tell you one thing, lovey: if I were to do that job, you can bet your bottom dollar it would *be* done, and done right. That's for sure."

"We know that. Why do you suppose it's being offered?"

"Is it being offered, or is this just pleasant persiflage on a snowy night in the nation's capital?"

Beth laughed.

"Let's put it this way: it isn't being offered after three martinis at Dolly's, is it? We aren't shouting at each other across a crowded room at Perle's, are we? I mean, this is cold-sober stuff, isn't it, girl? What more do you want?"

"Forgive me for being suspicious, but I've played around and stayed around this old town too long. I'm afraid it won't be official until I hear from the man himself. Where is he, by the way?"

"Taking a shower. He was down talking to the President earlier, and—"

"Oh?" Helen-Anne said, instantly alert as Beth had intended her to be. "Any signs of a break in the logjam?"

"I'm sure I don't know what you mean," Beth said lightly, "but, no, there aren't."

"I can't stand Harley's wife for some reason," Helen-Anne said, "but I love him. I'd like to set off an H-bomb under his chair and blast him out of there so our man can get moving."

" 'Our man'? That's a good sign. I think you're softening."

"Helen-Anne *Carrew?*" that lady said in a disbelieving tone. "*Softening?* You're mad!"

"Think it over. It's a firm offer and Orrin will confirm it Thursday if not before."

"I'll be waiting. Sorry I haven't got the angle just yet on what the Leesburg Lion is up to, but maybe I'll snatch it from some passing breeze in the next couple of days. I'll let you know if I do."

"Thanks, dear. You're a real friend. As well as a press secretary."

"We'll have to see about that," Helen-Anne said. "There are a lot of things to be considered before I—Hello!" she said in a startled voice. "What's that? Is somebody trying to cut in?"

"That's funny," Beth said in a puzzled tone. "I wonder what—"

There was a definite clicking on the wire, a sudden urgent voice.

"I'm sorry, Mrs. Knox," the White House operator said, "but we can't seem to reach the Secretary on the direct line."

"I know," Beth said, too taken aback to be entirely coherent. "He's running the—the faucet thing in the shower. What is—can I—"

"Please tell him at once that the President is calling the National Security Council, the rest of the Cabinet and the Congressional leaders to the White House in half an hour and he wants the Secretary there."

"Certainly," Beth said. "Certainly."

"Thank you," the operator said, and went off the line.

"My God," Helen-Anne said, "what's that?"

"I don't know," Beth said hurriedly, "but I've got to get Orrin."

"Call me back and tell me all you can!" Helen-Anne shouted, and Beth shouted back, "I will!" before she slammed down the receiver and hurried up the stairs to recall her soapily oblivious husband to the cold realities of a cold world.

So began, for all practical purposes—and several days before Walter Dobius had thought he would begin it with his speech—the presidential campaign, with all its fateful consequences for so many millions of people. As the news spread out through the night—first a FLASH on the newswires to the effect that PRESIDENT CALLS SECURITY COUNCIL CABINET TOP CONGRESS IMMEDIATE WHITE HOUSE SESSION, and then bulletin after bulletin of speculation, rumor, gossip, and non-news generated by the crew of several hundred nervously talking newspapermen and women who began to converge on the White House press room from their homes and beds all over town

—as it spread on to New York, where it found Terry surprised and delighted as he thought he could predict the consequences, Obifumatta excited and gratified as he thought he could do the same—as it reached all the twittering, clamoring, argumentative members of the UN in the great cold city and found them shocked, appalled, dismayed, and/or delighted according to whose side they were on—as the news swept forward over London and Paris and Moscow (where the corps of student rioters was told to prepare itself for another spontaneous attack on the American Embassy) and Rome and Tokyo and all the rest—as it came over the short-wave on the chartered jet carrying Felix Labaiya home to Panama, and instantly changed and accelerated certain plans of his—and finally as it reached Leesburg and took Walter hastily to the telephone for a futile and angry call—even as it did all these things, its import and impact began to change and shift the emphasis of events even though the event itself, as the nations knew, was only half-completed.

It would not be completed until a decision came out of that hastily called meeting at the White House. It would not be completed until action, or non-action, flowed out of that decision. It would not, in fact, be completed at all, but would simply take its place in the mysterious and fearful story that the years still had to tell, flowing into the ever-broadening stream of events carrying a world too reckless to a fate too harsh.

4

AND THAT, Walter Dobius told himself as he arose nervously at six the next morning, having stayed awake most of the night in gloom, foreboding, and disturbance, was a sample of what happened when you had an inexperienced dunderhead in the White House and a trigger-happy, irresponsible firebrand like Orrin Knox advising him. How on earth his poor country had got into such a tangle, Walter would never know. Certainly, reviewing the many warning columns he had written about Orrin, recalling the innumerable occasions on which he had given the President sound and irrefutable directions on how to proceed, he knew it was not his fault.

Now all he could do, along with men of good will everywhere, was make some attempt, however futile, to help pick up the pieces. The difficulties of this depressed him as he slowly dressed, ate breakfast and got ready to have Roosevelt drive him into town so that he might fly up to a United Nations racked and shaken by the latest fearsome turn of events. This time might be too much. This time, his awkward, ill-led country might have stumbled into the final morass from which neither it, nor the world it could pull down with it, would emerge.

When he had heard the news last night of the rebel capture of Molobangwe, of the slaughter of thirty-five or possibly forty American medical missionaries there and the destruction by dynamiting, with further undetermined loss of life, of the Standard Oil installation up-country, his first assumption had been that of course the United States would proceed like a civilized nation. It would take the matter to the UN and there tempers might be soothed, the crisis might be eased, the dead might be decently buried, and the damage decently forgotten in one more endless, if heated, debate which would prove anew that fine old UN truism: "At least when they're talking they aren't shooting."

This would, as Walter saw it, have been the right and proper thing to do. It is true that it would not have brought earnest good-hearted innocents back to life or really have justified their deaths, nor would it have restored ruined property or re-established broken law, but it would have been civilized, as the later twentieth century understood civilization. It would even, he thought with a bitter protest against all the hotheads and the extremists, have been Christian. It would have turned the other cheek. Above all, it would have kept the United States from placing itself in the position of aggressor.

The rebels who had committed the deeds which had brought from the United States so violent a retaliation were not, in Walter's mind and in the minds, he knew, of most of the UN's clamorous newly arrived nations, aggressors themselves. They were simply freedom-loving children of nature seeking their God-given rights. The aggressors were those who reacted to them and called them lawless and insisted that they be punished. The aggressors were those who refused to concede that freedom-loving children of nature had a right to hurt them and walk all over them. The aggressors were those who said murder and destruction were wrong and should be stopped.

Those were the ones, in Walter's mind and in the minds of all those many millions on all continents who agreed with him, who were in the wrong and deserved the condemnation of civilization in this enlightened, if perhaps somewhat topsy-turvy, century.

Instead, what had happened? Out of the fateful meeting at the White House—which he had tried to prevent by a furiously alarmed call direct to the President, which the President had refused to accept—had come a harsh and shattering decision, as uncontrollable and threatening to the settled fabric of life as the first thunderclap on the open plains: United States transport planes, carrying three thousand Marines, would be sent—indeed were already on their way—to invest Molobangwe. Units of the United States Indian Ocean Fleet would be sent—indeed had apparently been on their way for more than a week, even at the time the President, disgracefully, was telling Walter he didn't know what he would do next—to stand off Tanzania and furnish logistic support. Three squadrons of United States Air Force fighter-bombers, equipped with small atomic weapons, would be sent—indeed were already on their way —for stationing in the nearby Congo, no friend to Terry but less to Obifumatta.

The United States, in other words, stupidly, fantastically, inexplicably, inexcusably, was for all practical purposes going to war. And over what? Perhaps fifty murdered people and an oil monopoly's property! It was utterly insane, as Walter saw it, and not all the President's mealy-mouthed hypocrisies could change the fact.

The President had gone on television and radio after midnight. The broadcast was being repeated every hour on the hour. Walter had just seen it again for the fourth time, and still he could find in it nothing but faulty logic and hysterical emotionalism totally unsuited to the conduct of a great power—the world's greatest power, he thought bitterly, until it got into the hands of two madmen like the President and Orrin. And now God help it! He recalled with a scathing sarcasm the President's words, a sarcasm whose angry vigor had already found expression in the column he had written at top speed at 2 A.M. when he had heard the broadcast in its original delivery.

"My countrymen," the President had said gravely, flanked by Orrin and the Secretary of Defense, with the rest of the Cabinet, top Congressional leaders, and members of the National Security Council ranged behind them, "six hours ago in the African nation of Gorotoland thirty-five or forty of your fellow citizens, medical missionaries and nurses, were deliberately and mercilessly murdered and mutilated by rebel forces running amok in the capital of the country. At the same time, less than two hundred miles away, installations of the Standard Oil Company, protected by treaty and agreement with the legitimate government of Gorotoland, were deliberately and wantonly destroyed by other members of these same rebel forces. An as yet undetermined additional number of Americans were killed there.

"These acts occurred despite the clearest and most specific warning from the Government of the United States, delivered to the rebel forces, as you know, a week ago.

"In that warning, which many of you heard on your television or radio, or read in your newspapers, I said:

" 'The Government of the United States further warns the rebel forces in Gorotoland, led by Prince Obifumatta, that if so much as one more American citizen or one more piece of American property is hurt, the Government of the United States will take immediate and substantial action.'

"Apparently it was decided by those backing Prince Obifumatta that the United States did not mean this, and that it would be safe to try the United States' patience once again because nothing would come of it but an empty protest.

"But now your fellow countrymen lie dead, mercilessly slaughtered in the most cold-blooded and deliberate way. Now American property lies in ruins, mercilessly destroyed in the most cold-blooded and deliberate way.

"What option confronted me and your Government when the news reached me here in the White House two hours ago?"

Here the President paused and then ad-libbed what was, in Walter's estimation, a most inflammatory and propaganda-filled statement.

"It could be you I am called upon to protect.

"It could be your property destroyed.

"It could be you lying dead.

"What would you have had me do?"

It had been quite clear to Walter that this bit of demagoguery had greatly pleased the Secretary of State—he was practically smirking with joy, Walter thought—though most of the other faces ranked behind the President were grave and upset. But not Orrin the warmonger! He looked happy.

"Consistent with the position taken by your Government a week ago," the President said, "and consistent with what I believe to be my obligation to every American citizen— here or anywhere on earth—and to every legitimate American property-holder—here or anywhere on earth—I decided to act.

"I called together my advisers in the Cabinet, the Congress, and the National Security Council.

"We discussed whether to take this matter on appeal to the United Nations, as no doubt some of you would have wished. [My God, Walter thought, *would have wished!* Then he's already done something else.]

"This course," the President said slowly, "I rejected. [*I rejected,* Walter echoed, phrases for his column already racing through his mind: then the President must have overruled a substantial group right in his own house.]

"I rejected it because the challenge was immediate and I felt the response should be immediate. I did not want to wait weeks to have others decide whether Americans had been hurt. I knew they had been hurt. ['Oh, you demagogue,' Walter told the portly figure before him on the screen, *'you demagogue!'*]

"I also knew," the President said dryly, "that others would get the matter to the United Nations fast enough. That was not my worry. My worry was what to do about the facts that existed. My worry was how to act."

He paused and took a drink of water, wiped his lips carefully on a handkerchief, and went on.

"I did act. I have acted. Supported by my advisers whom you see here before you, I gave orders, which are already being carried out, to dispatch appropriate air, Marine, and naval forces of the United States to the nation of Gorotoland. These forces have orders to protect American lives and property and also to restore order to Gorotoland so that civilized law may prevail and all individuals, native as well as foreign, may be protected and safe.

[My *God,* Walter thought savagely, you're going to establish a protectorate. You're going to administer a free and independent nation. My God, how can you ignore what I and all other sane and civilized men have been advising the country all these years?]

"These forces of the United States are on their way at this moment. The first contingents will arrive in Gorotoland at 6 A.M. Washington time this morning.

"They will proceed to carry out their orders.

"If anyone attempts to interfere with them," the President said calmly, "he will be dealt with." He paused and looked straight into the cameras.

"I want you, and I want the world, to know exactly why I have done this. I have done it because it seemed to me that it was time to take a stand. It was time to put a stop to the wanton destruction of American lives and property. It was time to defend the law of civilized nations. It was time to stop the steady slide that we have seen in recent decades toward the complete breakdown of responsible dealings between nations.

[You call *this* responsible? Walter cried in his own mind. You fool, is *this* responsible?]

"It was time to re-establish the fact that when America says something, she means it. Specifically, it was time to re-establish the right of American citizens, as long as they behave themselves, to go anywhere in safety on the face of this globe."

The President's final words were soft but unyielding.

"I have had enough of the other. There will be no more of it.

"I hope you will understand my reasons. I hope you will support them. I have committed you to what I believe to be the honorable course. I hope for all our sakes that you agree."

And then, as always (Walter described it to himself bitterly) there had come that damnable national anthem that fogs over any President's words with a haze of stupid patriotic emotionalism, and the thing was over.

But it was not over, anywhere on earth. The special edition of the *Post* that was delivered to him by special messenger every morning was waiting beside his breakfast coffee, placed there by a purse-lipped, worried Arbella. It was index enough to what would follow.

U.S. MOVES ON (not "in") GOROTOLAND, the headline said. MOSCOW, PEKING ISSUE ANGRY WARNINGS, DEMAND WITHDRAWAL, IMMEDIATE UN SESSION.

"What do you think of this, Arbella?" he had demanded sharply. "Don't you think the President is insane?"

"No, sir, Mr. Walter," she had replied firmly. "They only one way to deal with bandits, I say. I like it."

"Well," he snapped. "There will be plenty who won't."

"That's right, Mr. Walter," she agreed with what could only be the insolence of long association. "I expect you'll tell 'em not to."

And so, by God, he would, he thought as he reviewed once more the column he had written in the night. His mood had been savage and the column was savage. He had changed it hardly at all before he had called the syndicate at 3 A.M. and dictated it so that it could be rushed out at once to replace the rather dull one on gold outflow that he had filed earlier.

"So the triumph of idiocy over reason has come at last," it began. "So we are going to war on a distant continent, for unworthy and indefensible objectives, in a contest in which nine-tenths of the world is automatically against us. So American imperialism is reborn, helped to new life by the monstrous midwifery of Harley M. Hudson and Orrin Knox. So stands the United States, convicted of aggression by its own foolish act. What will history make of so insane, futile, and foredoomed a decision?

"How arrogant they are, these little men who have placed the United States in a position that is an affront to civilized mankind everywhere! How serenely they talk, as though they had all the answers! How savagely has mediocrity achieved its revenge upon all those superior minds who have for decades sought with patient care to weave the difficult fabric of peace. How quickly is all their painstaking effort vanished now!

"The President tells us that he had to decide what to do. Apparently it did not occur to him that civilization has a mechanism, the United Nations, for settling such petty disputes between nations. Apparently he did not recall that the use of force has long ago been condemned by the decent men of all nations everywhere. Using the flimsy pretext that freedom-loving elements in Gorotoland, seeking the just achievement of their just desires, may have inadvertently attacked and possibly killed a handful of Americans and may also have damaged an oil monopoly's plants, Harley M. Hudson has committed his country to what amounts to a state of war in the middle of Africa.

"The President says, 'I rejected' suggestions by some of his advisers that he make the appeal to the United Nations that would have been the only honorable, civilized course. Obviously, then, it was his decision alone, overriding the grave doubts and objections held by many who participated in last night's fateful conference at the White House.

"For this grave crime against humanity Harley M. Hudson will have to answer to history, as will the man who clearly urged him on, Secretary of State Orrin Knox.

"The President talks of his 'warning' to the People's Free Republic of Gorotoland. Did he really believe that any self-respecting government, seeking the full dignity and freedom of its long-suffering, colonially suppressed people, would do anything but reject such a humiliating ultimatum? How could it, and still hold up its head among the nations?

"It was, in effect, an invitation to do exactly what has been done—to punish the United States and so give proof, to those foolish, irresponsible, and shortsighted men who still need proof, that in this forward-marching century the world cannot be run by ultimata from Washington. The response was exactly what could have been expected. And history, it seems likely, will say it was exactly what was deserved.

"What, now, of Peking and Moscow? Are we to assume that they will sit idly by and let the United States work its will in Central Africa? Rightly they fear renewed imperialism, justly they think they see a new attempt to re-establish colonial control. Are they, whose entire modern histories have been devoted, at least in principle, to the battle to spread freedom and peace throughout the world, to do nothing while the world's latest torch of freedom is wantonly and ruthlessly put out by superior force?

"The President and his war-happy principal adviser are sending American boys to die many thousands of miles from home, in an inconvenient and inaccessible terrain that cannot be either easily captured or adequately defended if it is captured. He is throwing away your sons and your money in pursuit of a purpose no decent man can defend, engaging American fortunes and forces in a hopeless war far away at a time when the nation's domestic needs are crying for solution. All this he is doing in the name of the honor of the United States.

"Never has it been so sadly misjudged or so dreadfully defended.

"War is what the President and the Secretary of State are committing in Gorotoland. World war is what trembles on the edge of what they do, waiting only the slightest misstep to unleash its awful nuclear horrors upon a helpless world.

"My fellow Americans, pray for your country. It needs your prayers as never before."

And never before, Walter told himself with an iron satisfaction, had he written truer words than those. And never had he been more confident of their soundness or more certain that he should send them forth to the world. It was insanity that the President and Orrin were engaged upon, the dreadful insanity that can end nations and end worlds.

It was up to him, he realized as he trudged out through the heavy drifts to the car where Roosevelt waited to drive him to the airport, to him and to all other decent men and women in America, to stop it if they could. Helen-Anne thought he never got really angry, did she? Well, this time she'd find out—they'd all find out—that he could.

A thin, bitter line settled around his lips and stayed there. Roosevelt, normally sunny and chatty, made no attempt to talk as they passed slowly over the slippery, drifted roads to the capital in the sparkling morning that had succeeded the world's dark night.

Far below on the East River the barges, tugboats, and freighters maintained their ceaseless commerce; across on Long Island the world was a smudgy gray, clean snow contending with drab buildings, drab buildings winning out. But when he had entered the shimmering glass monolith of the UN Secretariat Building to take the elevator to his office on the thirty-eighth floor, the air had been crisp and clear, the sun had been steadily warming. Winter's last storm would not lie too long on the land. Spring, at any moment, would be here.

And what a spring it promised to be, the Secretary-General thought sadly as he let his black, knobbled old hands rest idly on his desk and stared out the window, not really seeing the lovely day that was developing. What a spring, and how would men survive it to see summer, or the autumn that would follow, or another winter after that? Somewhere along the way in the next few months or weeks or days or hours someone would do something to make it impossible, the flywheel would spin out of the creaking machinery, the whole great game would end, the centuries' old pretense that man could determine his own destiny would collapse in one final, obliterating NO brought on by man himself. Man could determine his own destiny—if that destiny were destruction. That was clear enough. It was beginning to seem increasingly unlikely to him that man could exercise the slightest control if the destiny were to be anything else. That apparently lay entirely with the God or gods to whom man prayed, when he remembered to pray.

Thinking of all the raucous, brawling, undisciplined nations and non-nations that snapped and snarled in the Security Council, the General Assembly, the committees, and the conference rooms that lay below his fragile and impotent aerie, the S.-G. gave a heavy sigh, the sigh of an old man who has seen too much and accomplished too little, in his own estimation, to have made it all worth the struggle. He had come to his office with such high hopes, had learned so soon that the Communists had no intention of permitting him to exercise any real influence upon events, had found himself attacked by his fellow Africans and Asians for his decision to be fair to the white nations, had found all hopes dissipated in the conflicting hatreds and suspicions that swirled constantly like a sickening and fatal gas through all the handsome chambers below. The UN was dying, it had been dying for years, and why had it been given to him, he wondered bitterly, to preside over what might well be its final agonies?

There lay before him on his desk the latest earnest pamphlets of all those well-meaning and good-hearted American organizations which still insisted, in the face of all the evidence, that the raddled organization was a strong and effective force for world peace. He had also seen on their television screens and heard over their radios in defensive, anguished pleas to believe in a dream whose guardians had wrecked it long since. THINK WHAT YOU WOULD DO WITHOUT IT! they urged; DON'T LET THE SKEPTICS TELL YOU IT ISN'T WORKING! Well: he was its Secretary-General, and he knew. Every honest observer in the world knew. Yet here were the Americans, pretending with a desperate anguish to the end, that somehow by sheer incantation and appeal they could put life back into something that was already, insofar as its original purpose of being an effective peace-keeper was concerned, a corpse putrescent and overdue for burial. This was the fact, and not all the desperate pamphlets and all the defensive statements and all the indignant outpourings of scorn upon those who acknowledged the fact could change it in the slightest. Long, too long, after the UN had been weakened and dragged down by its own members into a howling shell of what it could have been, powerful groups in America were still pretending that it was the vigorous and hopeful organization of their long-ago dreams.

The Secretary-General could not understand this on the basis of reason, though he could understand it on the basis of fear. They were so dreadfully afraid of what the world would be like without the shaky symbol, however empty, of their hope of peace. They were so frantically unsure of themselves when confronted by the possibility of a world in which they might have to stand on their own feet, take the consequences of their own acts, be unable to avail themselves of this comforting fiction to which to pass the buck for their own errors. They wanted the UN propped up and kept there so that they could run to it like children and hide their faces in its skirts. But the skirts were empty, the sought-for womblike comfort long gone, if it had ever really existed after the first ten minutes of the organization's life. They knew, as he did, but they would not give up the pretense. They were too afraid.

Not so, ironically, the Africans and Asians who had done so much, with their exaggerated fears of the colonial past, to bring the UN down. It was the greatest thing in the world for them to be able to come to New York, all expenses paid, usually by American money, and live in luxury while they went to the Assembly or the Security Council every day and denounced America to the accompaniment of fine, approving notices in the American press. To use one of those skeptical, ironic, knowing American phrases that so often went to the heart of things, they never had it so good back in the bush. But they did have, back in the bush, the comforting assurance that no matter how irresponsible they were, no matter what they said or did, the UN would continue to exist as long as the Americans could possibly preserve it—a free and protective shield from behind which they could spit out their hatreds of America and make a bitter mockery of its earnest, awkward, well meaning hopes that somehow, sometime, somewhere the world might discover dignity and peace.

And now America had finally given them real cause for hatred, and most of them, he knew, would be in a manic frenzy when the Security Council met at three this afternoon. The President had called him last night near midnight, waking him from a deep yet troubled sleep in which he had been chasing, with dragging feet and arms so dreadfully heavy that he could not raise his spear, some impossibly bright and golden lion in his native Nigeria. He had known at once that something of dreadful import must have occurred. He had also realized that the call was a great courtesy, for he need not have been informed; few others bothered to inform him. His gratitude increased when he realized that the President was actually asking his advice, as much as Presidents ever could.

The President had told him what had happened and had asked that he should do. Did the Secretary-General think that any purpose other than a futile and foredoomed attempt to appease the vague phantasm "world opinion" would be served by refraining from stern and direct action? Did he see any hope of affirmative support in the Security Council or the General Assembly if the United States should go through the procedure of submitting the issue?

"You answer a first question with a second, Mr. President," the S.-G. had said. "We both, I think, know the answer to the second. Therefore the first need hardly have been asked, do you think?"

"Probably not," the President said. "But I felt it should be, out of respect to you."

"Thank you," the S.-G. said, feeling flattered. "I think, in any event, that you need have no doubt that the issue will be submitted to the Council, as it is already seized of Prince Obifumatta's complaint against your ultimatum."

"Call it what you will," the President said, "I felt it had to be done."

"I am afraid Obifumatta, too clever, like his cousin, did not foresee that you were laying the foundation for future action."

"I am afraid Obifumatta has not foreseen many things. Very well. I am sorry to have disturbed you, but I wished you to know what to expect and I also wanted you to have the opportunity to go on record, if you so desired, as being opposed to what I am about to do should I decide to do it."

The Secretary-General had permitted himself a wry chuckle.

"Opposed to what you *will* do *should* you do it," he repeated. "Mr. President, even if I were warning you against it—"

"Are you?" the President asked quickly.

"Each of us must act as his fate decrees."

"I thought as much. Understand me on one thing: I do not minimize the consequences at all. They may be ultimate. But I feel we have no choice."

"The world is becoming full of no choices," the Secretary-General said sadly. "Daily the choices diminish. It is a world of no choices."

"And Obifumatta and his friends have just reduced them further," the President said grimly.

"As they no doubt thought you did with your ultimatum," the Secretary-General ventured. The President sighed.

"There is one-millionth of a chance that they sincerely believe they are in the right. But I do not believe it. I think their actions always spring from the most abysmal cynicism and the most utter contempt for human decency as we understand it. I think this is the essential fact underlying all the others. . . Thank you again. My advisers are waiting for me to tell them what they may advise me to do. May all go well until we meet again."

"Which will be?"

"Who can say? I may address the Assembly myself before this is over. Though not for a while, yet. Events must develop for a time, first. Nothing would be gained now."

"If that is your opinion," the Secretary-General said. "When you are ready—"

"I shall let you know."

"May all go well with you, too, Mr. President," the Secretary-General said, moved by a strange combination of sympathy, understanding, pity, and fear.

"My thanks. Good night."

"Good night."

The S.-G. had rolled back into his pillows, though not to sleep for several hours. Always there was the fear that the United States might be provoked too far; always there was

the possibility that her patience, which usually was
sufficient to withstand any amount of attack, opposition,
disparagement, and contempt, might abruptly snap; always
there was the awesome possibility that she might explode
into some violent and drastic action whose consequences
could not be foreseen, much less controlled. It had happened in Asia, it could happen in Africa. Apparently this
was to be one of the times.

Nothing but disaster lay ahead for anyone, as the Secretary-General saw it. He knew that in the morning he would
have to receive a constant stream of visitors from the
rooms below, all furious, all shouting, all demanding that
he do something. Do something! He had done all he could,
though he would not admit it to them. He had in effect told
the President to go ahead, for he agreed with the President;
though he knew the ultimates of the decision might be
dreadful beyond imagining.

Now the first howling visitor was about to arrive. The
graceful Swedish girl who was serving as his principal secretary this year entered the room.

"The Soviet Ambassador wishes to see you," she said.

The Secretary-General sighed and nodded. Now the bad
day would begin, and in the worst possible fashion. He sat
very still, bracing himself for the screaming denunciation
he knew was about to come.

"Good morning," the familiar voice from the Senate said
with a certain dry amusement. "I hope you're well rested
after our busy night."

"I'm not exactly chipper," the Secretary of State admitted. "You, I suppose, are fresh as a daisy and have nothing
to worry about, up there on the Hill. Don't relax. I'm going
to give you something."

Robert Durham Munson, who was senior United States
Senator from Michigan and Majority Leader of the United
States Senate, uttered his comfortable chuckle.

"I don't doubt it for a minute. What do you want us to
do?"

"The obvious. A concurrent resolution supporting the
President and affirming the determination of Congress to
stand by him until Gorotoland is pacified."

"And the world is made safe for Standard Oil?" Bob
Munson inquired in a mocking tone that parodied all those
who believed as much.

"And missionaries and Americans abroad and honorable dealings between nations and so on," Orrin Knox said impatiently. "We were all agreed on this last night. I just want it put in a form the world will recognize. What's the matter with that?"

"Have you seen Walter Dobius' column?"

"I have."

"It's having some effect, I find."

"So? And are we supposed to run from Walter?"

"No, I'm not saying anything about running from Walter. I'm just saying it's having some effect. I've already heard from quite a few people this morning. Some are quite disturbed."

"Aren't we?" Orrin asked in a scornful tone. "Do the dolts think we went into this lightly last night?"

"No, but people like Fred Van Ackerman and Arly Richardson, for instance, are convinced from Walter's column that there was a terrific split at the White House and that Harley overrode us all and dragged us kicking and screaming off to war."

The Secretary snorted as he thought of Fred Van Ackerman, junior Senator from Wyoming and perennial troublemaker, and Arly Richardson, junior Senator from Arkansas and not much better.

"Seven negative votes out of thirty-one?" he demanded. "That's a terrific split? They're just making trouble, as usual."

"I'm not arguing what the facts are," Bob Munson said patiently. "I'm arguing what Walter Dobius says they are. The two needn't be the same in order to satisfy Walter's followers. His word is sufficient." He made an amused sound. "I see he says you're a monstrous midwife. There's a new description of Orrin Knox."

"Walter's hysterical. I've known him to write some strange things, but this one takes the cake. I think he's gone mad."

"Obviously he thinks the same about you. And, as I say, there are some who are going to agree with him. A great many, I suspect, before it's over. Over there."

"How could we have done anything else?" the Secretary demanded. "How could we—"

"I'm not arguing," Senator Munson said, "I'm not arguing. I was there last night. I voted for it. I'm just philosophizing on the great gap that exists between what a situation actually is and the picture of it that people like Walter can create in the public mind if they have sufficient distribution. I sometimes think there ought to be a law."

"There is. The First Amendment. They all go screaming behind it when you try to challenge their version of things."

"Walter's a special case, though. He doesn't only fight through his column now. He's becoming too big a wheel in the Washington world for small potatoes like that. He's called me this morning. Guess what he wants."

"A resolution opposing it," the Secretary said.

"Exactly."

"He is mad."

"I reminded him that in twenty-five years of columning here he had never yet seen a Congress fail to support a President in an international crisis. He said this might be different. He sounded as though he really thought so, too. Very grim is Walter Wonderful on this bright sunny day. What's this Dolly tells me about him going to receive the Jason's Good and Faithful Servant Award Friday night?"

"So I hear from Helen-Anne. Don't worry, you'll be invited. Quite inadvertently events seem to have played right into his hands as far as timing's concerned. By Friday he should be really wound up and ready to let go with both barrels."

"I suppose Patsy set the whole thing up so he could come out for Ted," Senator Munson said.

"Apparently. Now he'll be in even better shape to do so. Unless Ted supports the President."

"How could he? Wouldn't that be supporting you too?"

"Oh, some people might be broad-minded enough. Or patriotic enough. Or honorable enough. Or some other old-fashioned concept like that. I doubt if Ted will curb his ambitions at this moment, though. If Walter really does represent a major segment of the population, it seems like a bandwagon tailor-made for Ted."

"The neo-*neo* isolationists?" Bob Munson suggested. "How many contortions poor Walter and his friends have had to make in recent years!"

"I feel deeply for them," Orrin Knox remarked. "It's touching to watch Walter, in foreign affairs, stand on his head, rub his stomach, wiggle his ears, peddle a bicycle, and do push-ups, all at one and the same time."

"Nominating Ted is going to hurt you, though. You know that."

"Certainly. I don't minimize it. However, that's still assuming that Harley won't run again. I don't see how he can avoid it, now. Ted isn't the only one who has things tailor-made."

"Oh, I expect this will die down in a week or two, don't you?" Bob Munson asked. "I doubt if it will take any longer than that to get things settled. You'll still be in the running."

"I'm not so sure," Orrin said gloomily. "Who can say how long a crisis is going to last nowadays? We may be in there for years if things don't fall just right. I don't think Peking and Moscow are going to let stability be restored without a contest, do you? As usual, they've got too much stake in chaos."

"It's a devilish place for them to supply," Senator Munson remarked.

"Us, too. But that isn't going to stop anything. Nor do I see why it should. 'Sending American boys to die many thousands of miles from home,' Walter says. Well, isn't that too bad. He sang a different tune with Hitler."

"He always sings a different tune with people he doesn't like."

"Except when he's afraid of them. Unless you assume that Walter Dobius and his crowd are Communists, which strikes me as ridiculous in spite of what some wild-eyed people say, then the only logical explanation of their erratic positions over the years is that they're so afraid of war that they are willing to bow down to anyone who appears to threaten it."

Bob Munson chuckled.

"I believe they would prefer the word 'negotiate' to the words 'bow down.' It amounts to the same thing, but 'negotiate' smells better. Maybe you're right. It's always baffled me, I must say. Well, you want a resolution, then. Have you talked to Bill?"

"The Speaker of the House isn't in yet, so his office just informed me. Rather primly."

"Must be a new girl. I'm ready to go, over here. I'll have Tom August introduce the resolution as chairman of the Foreign Relations Committee, right after the opening this noon."

"I'm sure the Speaker will go along too," Orrin said. "Thanks, old pal. When are we going to get together for something social?"

"The Jason Foundation dinner Friday night appears to be the first opportunity," Senator Munson said solemnly. "I'm sure we're all going to be there, aren't you?"

"I don't know," Orrin said thoughtfully.

"Have you talked to Harley," Senator Munson asked, "and has he seen Walter's column?"

"Yes and yes. Our mild-mannered old friend is not so mild-mannered this morning."

"I'd advise you both to keep calm and prepare for a savage lashing from the press. This is one of those many times in recent years when all of America's finest minds are going to be telling the world that the worst thing in it is America. And those who got her into this."

"It seemed the only thing consistent with honor."

"Not honor as they see it."

"Thank God I don't wear their glasses," the Secretary of State remarked. "Keep me advised on the resolution."

"Sure thing. Keep me advised on the candidacy."

"I want to talk to you about that one of these days soon."

"No point until Harley decides, is there?"

"He's got to say something soon. The time for drift is ending, particularly with Gorotoland on the griddle. I imagine it won't be long, particularly after Friday night."

"You don't think Walter will show his usual restrained and dignified statesmanship, then," Bob Munson suggested.

"Usual restrained and dignified fiddlesticks. He'll be raving."

"The whole thing is such fun," Senator Munson said gently. "Give my love to Beth."

"Likewise Dolly. Keep in touch."

The Speaker, when the Secretary reached him ten minutes later, was equally cooperative on the resolution, equally intrigued by the public hullaballoo.

"Should have thought of the resolution when we were all together at the White House last night. Don't know why we didn't, Orrin. Must have been too many other things on our minds. When you going to announce for President?"

"You think I should, when I'm a monstrous midwife to a third world war?"

The Speaker chuckled.

"Yes, I see where friend Walter got a little heated this morning. I expect he'll carry a good many with him, too. Scare you?"

"No, it doesn't scare me. The only thing I worry about is that it may scare some of the people who want to be for me."

"You can't include me there," the Speaker said with the comfortable assurance that was his from years of unassailable power and control over his unruly branch of the Congress. "Told you a year ago at the time young Brigham Anderson died that I'd be for you, and I am. Folks like Walter been trying to scare me for forty years. They never have."

"Thank you, Bill," the Secretary said with a genuine gratitude. "You're one big plus I have on my side, anyway. You don't know how much it means."

"First, though," the Speaker said, "we've got to blast Harley loose. He may not want to blast, Orrin."

"I'm quite happy either way. Honestly I am, Bill. I think you know me well enough to know that."

"I know, I know, but still. He ought to let us know."

"How much damage is Walter going to do in this Gorotoland business?"

"Quite a lot, I think," the Speaker said gravely. "He called me this morning early, you know. Wants the House to pass a resolution opposing it."

"He's an ego maniac."

"He isn't modest, that's true enough. However, we'll pass your resolution, all right, and plenty to spare. But it won't stop some of 'em making a hellish row."

"Will Jawbone Swarthman introduce it for us?"

"Now, there's an example," the Speaker said regretfully. "Much as I love Jawbone—and I do, you know, I've known him since he was a little tad coming up here when his grandfather was in the House from South Carolina—he can be as slippery and stubborn as one of those Carolina mules sometimes. I'm afraid this may be one of 'em."

"It's going to look a little odd if the chairman of the House Foreign Affairs Committee won't back the Administration in a crisis like this."

"Oh, I'm working on him," the Speaker said. "Don't worry about that. But he's pretty riled up. Tends to agree with Walter Dobius, I'm afraid, that we shouldn't send American boys thousands of miles from home. At least,"—

the Speaker chuckled—"not to meddle in any colored folks' family quarrel, as Jawbone puts it."

"Jawbone isn't a fool," the Secretary said sharply. "He knows perfectly well this is another pitched battle with the Communists. Why didn't he speak up last night at the White House if he had all these qualms? He voted for it then."

"That's what I mean when I say slippery," the Speaker said. "Jawbone's doing a lot of thinking about the folks back home these days. Now that Seab Cooley's dead, God rest his soul, that South Carolina Senate seat's up for grabs, and Jawbone has ambitions, you know. Plenty of 'em."

Orrin made an impatient sound.

"What on earth does he want to go to the Senate for? He's got fifty times more influence as chairman of House Foreign Affairs than he'll ever have as a member of the Senate. What does he want it for?"

"He's never really been comfortable with foreign affairs," the Speaker said. "Jawbone would much rather have been chairman of Agriculture, worrying about all the cotton and taters on the old plantation back home. Plus the fact, Orrin"—the Speaker gave a wry little chortle—"plus the fact, much as I hate to admit it and you must never quote me, that for a lot of people, an awful lot of people, the title of United States Senator somehow means more than the title of United States Representative. They just like to have it."

"And for that Jawbone is going to give up Foreign Affairs and betray his own Administration when it needs him? I'll talk to Jawbone!"

"Now, Orrin, now; Orrin. Easy does it. You can talk to Jawbone, but you let me do some talking first. I think we can ease him around, but it may take a little time."

"This resolution ought to go through at once if it's going to do any good."

"It may just not," the Speaker said. "Better brace yourself, if you and the President are counting on it. It may just not. The folks who agree with Walter can't stop it, but they can slow it down some. Particularly when it's all involved with the presidential election. That makes everything extra touchy."

"Are you going to the dinner for Walter Friday night?"

"Patsy called and invited me last night just as I was leaving for the White House. I told her I didn't know whether I'd be in town, but if so, I might. Be interesting to hear what he has to say. Also be interesting," he added dryly, "to hear what Ted's going to say about this Gorotoland business. I expect he's being asked."

"I'm awaiting a blast any minute. Or he may just be clever enough to keep still. We'll see."

"I'll bet he's under plenty of pressure to speak out," the Speaker said with a chuckle.

"I feel for him," Orrin said, realizing that he had said the same thing to Bob Munson about Walter, and realizing that it came from the same commingling of impatience and contempt for those who could not see their country's best course as clearly as he could. Or, as he reminded himself with the saving grace that kept Orrin Knox from being insufferable, as clearly as he thought he could.

"Darling," Patsy Labaiya was saying at that very moment from the house in Dumbarton Oaks, "you know we're counting on you to introduce Walter Friday night. Why don't you call Ted right now—collect, of course— and consult with him about it? Then you can also tell him that Walter and all his friends back here do hope that he's going to issue a strong statement condemning this latest insanity by the President and Orrin Knox in Gorotoland. Could you do that, darling?"

Downtown in the marvelous gingerbread structure known as the Executive Offices Building, or, more historically and affectionately, as "Old State," the director of the President's Commission on Administrative Reform swung around in his chair and stared across West Executive Avenue at the White House. It was gleaming so brightly in the sun that Robert A. Leffingwell felt he could touch it if he reached out a hand. The snow was melting fast on the roof; as he looked, a large section slid off and doused a couple of photographers emerging from the press room. He could almost hear their shouted profanities as they jumped back. It lent an amusement to his voice that Patsy was quick to notice.

"Well, I'll tell you," he said. "I might or I might not, at this point. I don't just know yet."

"Don't *know?*" Patsy demanded in some dismay. "Well, it isn't any laughing matter, I can tell you that."

"I'm not laughing at you," Bob Leffingwell said. "I just saw a couple of friends of mine get socked by the snow over at the White House. It melted and fell down on them. Anyway, why ask me to talk to Ted? He's your brother. You two are still speaking, aren't you?"

"He knows what I think, we don't have to communicate on a thing like this. It's important that other people talk to him, though."

"It might be important for him to stay out of it for a day or two," Bob Leffingwell suggested. "He can't be hurt by keeping his mouth shut, but he might be if he kept it open."

"I don't agree. I think it's imperative that he say something right now while things are at their peak."

"Do you think that this is their peak? I have a feeling we ain't seen nothin' yet."

"Even more reason why he should speak out," Patsy said firmly. "And you, too, I might add, especially if you're going to be associated with him in the campaign. Have you read Walter's column?"

"Yes, I read it."

"Well, then," she said triumphantly. "You agree with it, don't you?"

There was a thoughtful pause and she repeated in some alarm, "You *do* agree, don't you?"

"I told you, I just don't know," Bob Leffingwell said slowly. "I thought Walter was a little extreme. In fact, I thought he sounded hysterical. It didn't really sound like Walter at all. He's usually so calm and judicious."

"This time he obviously feels very, very deeply. He obviously feels this is THE END."

"Even so," Bob Leffingwell said in an unimpressed voice, "I thought he went overboard. Quite amazingly so, for Walter. I wonder if he's losing his touch?"

"He is *not* losing his touch," Patsy said sharply. "He is just simply frightfully concerned about this insane act by the President and Orrin, that's all. Aren't you?" she demanded in a challenging tone. "Don't tell me YOU'VE gone over to the enemy. That would be the day!"

"Of course I'm frightfully concerned," Bob Leffingwell said with a show of annoyance rare for one normally so suave and self-possessed. "Don't be a fool. Everyone's frightfully concerned, and I'll thank you not to impugn my intelligence or integrity."

"I'm sorry, darling," Patsy said hastily. "I just got carried away. But, REALLY, now, you aren't going to side with Orrin and the President on this, are you? It would be so DREADFUL to have you on the other side. I did so want you," she added forlornly, "to introduce Walter Friday night. It would have made it so perfect for Ted."

"I didn't say I wouldn't introduce Walter. I just said it's a situation that requires some thought and restraint. I don't know if I want to associate myself with everything he says if he's going to be as rabid as he was in that column this morning."

"I still don't think it was rabid," Patsy said stubbornly, "but if you do, I suppose I can't change you. But honestly, you don't want to be with Orrin and the President, do you? It's one of those issues that narrows down to just where *does* a man stand. You've got to make a choice, you know. You can't just sit out the campaign."

"Is Ted going to fight the campaign on this issue? That would be interesting."

"He may be forced to. It may be one of those things a candidate can't avoid, you know. Expecially with the enemy taking the other position."

"Who is this enemy you keep talking about?" Bob Leffingwell asked with some amusement. "If you mean nice old Harley and volatile old Orrin, that seems a slightly fierce way to talk about them."

"I think that's the kindest tone I've heard you use about Orrin since he—since a year ago," Patsy said. "You really AREN'T going over to him, are you, darling?"

"I doubt it very much," Bob Leffingwell said in a voice that was suddenly quite crisp as they both remembered the way in which Orrin, then senior Senator from Illinois, had blocked his nomination to be Secretary of State. "Even so," he said, less arbitrarily, "I think it is easy—dangerously easy—to oversimplify a situation like the present one. I think it is a time to be reasonable and mature in our judgments of it."

"Darling," Patsy said in a wistful tone, "you don't sound liberal at all, any more. You sound just like a REACTIONARY. Don't you think Orrin and the President have oversimplified? Don't you think they should have been reasonable and mature? Don't you think what they've done is dangerous?"

"Of course I do," he said with a renewed impatience. "But I'm not saying I might not have done the same had I been—had I been in a position where my advice was sought. It wasn't. If it had been, I couldn't honestly tell you at this moment what I would have counseled."

"Well," Patsy said, really dreadfully shocked at this apparent betrayal of what everyone on the Right Side had always thought Bob Leffingwell stood for, "I guess if you don't want to introduce Walter, then, we'll just have to get somebody else. But I had so hoped—"

"I repeat," Bob Leffingwell said, "I'm not saying I won't introduce Walter. In fact, I will. But I'm going to reserve the right to qualify my own position as I see fit."

"You want it both ways," Patsy said, though she told herself she mustn't be spiteful, it would only antagonize. "You want to be in both camps at once. I never thought I'd live to see the day when Bob Leffingwell abandoned his principles."

"Perhaps Bob Leffingwell is learning a few," he said crisply. "Give my best to Ted when you talk to him, because I'm not going to, at this point."

"He would value your advice," Patsy said soberly. "That's the only reason I asked."

"My advise is to keep quiet," Bob Leffingwell said in the same crisp tone. "But I don't suppose he'll take it."

Sitting in his office in Sacramento, however, staring thoughtfully down at the crowds of state employees hurrying to work along the walkways of the Capitol, the Governor of California was not being as hasty as his friend feared and his sister desired. It was still early in the West but already the full flood of Eastern opinion was shrieking from the headlines, blaring from the radio, snarling with a suave indignation from the television screens. The little turns of phrase that do so much to tear down something Walter and his world wish to tear down were everywhere apparent to the perceptive citizen:

"The *sudden* and *abrupt* American move *against* Gorotoland. . . . An action *which many Americans themselves* regard as *indefensible.* . . . A situation in which the rebels, *apparently seeking only to establish an independent government free from colonial control,* are suddenly confronted with the *ghastly ghost of colonialism,* strangely revived by the West's leading democracy. . . . A *minor skirmish* and *a few* American lives, transformed instantaneously into *the sort of issue that could destroy the world.* . . .

The President's *inexplicable*, and *many people feel, inexcusable* decision. . . ."

Walter and his world had wasted no time, and dutifully the chant was being picked up in the West as well.

Ted Jason sighed as he looked at the state's morning papers spread across his desk. The homogeneity of Walter's world impressed him anew. It had been increasing ever since World War II until now it was virtually a solid mass of automatic opinion, swinging on cue against this issue, for that personality, as though someone punched a button. From Manhattan to the Golden Gate the cry was predictable, consistent, and virtually impenetrable by any dissenting opinion. When the big boys in the big city spoke, those who considered them the epitome of sophistication wanted desperately to speak like them. In pursuit of that goal, a blanket of conformity stultifying to thought and murderous to genuine discussion lay upon the nation. Orrin and the President, Ted told himself grimly, would have a tough time making their way against it. It wouldn't matter much if the entire populace started out solidly behind them, Walter and his world would do their damnedest to swing the balance the other way. And if, as was certainly the case now, many Americans were divided, uncertain, and confused, the current might be too strong for even the President to overcome.

Should Ted, then, swim with it and seize what advantage he could? The way was open and it could be easy. Perhaps the President, all unknowing, had handed him the key to the White House after all. Quite possibly he had if Orrin ran, and—heady thought—perhaps he had even if he himself should run. Governor Jason was absolutely certain that if he issued a strong statement denouncing the President's decision, the entire apparatus would be his to ride as far and as high as he could. And that, he realized with a cold-blooded calculation as he studied the harshly self-righteous journals before him and remembered the indignant and condemnatory broadcasts he had heard and seen with breakfast, might be far and high indeed.

Still, there were other things. He had to admire the President's guts, taking such an action on the very eve of a campaign: such things were usually deferred until after, when politically it was quite, quite safe. Many a stanch defender of the nation was braver after November than he

ever was before. Harley Hudson had preferred to meet the
issue head-on and do it now. So, too, had Orrin Knox, who
had gone into it with his eyes open, knowing it was to be a
decision that he too must carry should the President retire
and he become an active candidate for the nomination.
Ted Jason, not for the first time, was forced to admire the
courage and integrity of his principal opponent.

And his own courage and integrity? Recalling how Ceil,
very glamorous and Givenchy as always, had paused in the
doorway to look back at him this morning, he had wondered if these qualities were showing signs of the strain
they were under.

"Sweetie, I must dash," she said with her cool little humorous air. "That thing the P.T.A. convention is putting
on, you know, that breakfast for distinguished ladies. Of
whom," she commented with an amused expression, "they
seem to think I am one. I shall try not to make a speech. If
I do, I shall try not to mention Gorotoland. But, my dear"
—giving him that long, slanting glance that he sometimes
felt might penetrate his defenses, though it never had and
they both knew it; but Ceil kept trying in a humorously
halfhearted way—"my dear, what about you? Can you get
by without, today?"

"I don't know," he had confessed. "Do you think I
should?"

"Whatever you decide I shall be for," she said with the
look repeated, the humor exaggerated. "I'm a politician's
wife. I go along."

"That's not responsive to my question," he told her with
his calm, self-possessed smile.

"I repeat," she said with her cool, cordial little laugh,
"I'm a politician's wife. You name it, I'm for it."

"Then you think I shouldn't say anything. Sit down a
minute," he had added impatiently, but with the basic good
nature that underlay all their discussions, "and stop being
the social butterfly long enough to apply that magnificent
brain of yours to it."

"Sweetie!" she cried. "You say the nicest things!" But
she complied and, disposing herself gracefully across from
him at the huge old table gave him a long, analytic stare
which he returned unflinching. "You *aren't* sure, are you?"
she observed finally. "I thought Ted Jason was always cold,
calculating, self-assured, and ruthless. As the papers say.
Not so much this morning, eh?"

"The stakes are very high," he remarked, gesturing at the papers spread about. "Look at this reaction."

"Very high in every way," she agreed, slipping off one of her gloves and studying her long, handsome fingers critically in the sunlight that fell across the comfortable room. "Politically and personally both. I imagine if you hop on the bandwagon it might carry you right on up. I also imagine your voice would be more powerful than any other single voice in slowing the bandwagon down, if you so decided. It poses a problem." She slipped the glove back on, clasped her hands on her purse, and looked at him with her shrewd, level gaze. "I'm glad it isn't mine."

"Tell me what to do," he suggested. She smiled and shook her head.

"I know what honor would suggest, but perhaps conviction is too strong for it. And ambition. It isn't everybody who's lucky enough to have those two coincide. Perhaps you should make the most of it."

"But you don't think I should."

"If it's genuine conviction, why not?" she said, but, as always, he couldn't find the real Ceil in it. The real Ceil was somewhere back inside where he would always pursue in vain. Which, he thought with an ironic little amusement that reached his eyes and was answered in hers, was why he would always keep on pursuing.

"It seems to be genuine conviction with a good many of those," he said, gesturing again at the papers. She nodded.

"And also Walter Dobius and the other big boys say so, so it's stylish. But, I repeat: you can stop it if you will. And very probably, as I say, no one else is in exactly the same position you are of being able to stop it. . . . Excuse me, sweetie," she said with a sudden briskness, "but the distinguished ladies of the P.T.A. are awaiting the arrival of one more distinguished lady in their midst. I must run."

"First Lady of California," Ted Jason remarked with an ironic but friendly smile as she came around the table, leaned down, and kissed him lightly on the cheek. "First Lady of—"

"Don't bedazzle a poor girl's head with dreams. I repeat, I'm that necessary adjunct of politics, a wife. Lead on, Mac-Duff, and whither thou et cetera. I'll try not to mention Gorotoland."

"Good," he said with a smile. "Ceil," he added as she reached the door. She turned back, tall and stunning and willowy but, as he knew better than anyone, shrewd as nails and tough as steel underneath.

"Yes?"

"I think you're somewhat more than an adjunct."

She gave him a dazzling smile and blew him a kiss.

"I hoped as much, but I wasn't sure."

"Oh, get out," he said with a grin, turning back to the papers. "Go on, get out."

She gave him another smile, this time filled with a genuine friendliness and amusement, and did so.

But that, of course, was little help in solving his problem. It was all right for Ceil to advise, as she surely had, that he say nothing to oppose the President and, if possible, support him; but much as he admired his wife's brains and intuitive grasp of politics, the matter was not so simple.

If he spoke out now in support he probably could give the President the extra edge he needed to carry the country wholeheartedly with him; he probably could effectively slow down the world of Walter Wonderful. But what would that do to his own chances for the nomination and election—and what, also, would it do to his own convictions in the matter? He might not be as rabid as Walter—like many on this day who admired and followed Walter, he was a little taken aback at the extreme virulence of his column attacking the President—but he did have very grave personal doubts about the wisdom of what had been decided last night at the White House.

If he spoke in opposition, it would be considerably more than ambition that prompted it. And if he spoke in support, it would in fact require of him more of a conscious effort, more a deliberate forcing of himself into a not entirely comfortable position. Yet speaking in support of course had its imperatives and its appeal, depending upon how seriously one conceived the United States to be threatened by Communism and how actively one thought it should defend its rights and protect its citizens.

He was held by this dilemma for a while, wandering in the gray no-man's-land between conviction and desire, ambition and duty. Which was which, and what was the true nature of any of them? Who ever knew, when the crises came and history said: decide—and you were one of those history had chosen to do the deciding?

He had been sitting thus, staring unseeing at the screaming headlines, the insistent columns, the harshly demanding editorials, for perhaps five minutes when his secretary buzzed and a light flashed on his telephone. Across three thousand miles of a troubled country he heard with a startled surprise and an immediate tension the quiet greeting of its Chief Executive, apparently not at all upset by the gale in which he found himself.

"Hello, Ted," the President said. "I'm pleased to find you in. My luck."

"My pleasure, Mr. President," the Governor said, recovering rapidly and preparing to listen with extreme care to every nuance in the comfortable voice. But the President's next remark made it clear he was not indulging in subtleties today.

"I wonder where you stand, Ted. Perhaps you can tell me."

"Why—" the Governor began. Then he laughed. "You're so direct you leave me momentarily speechless."

"Only momentarily, I hope," the President said in a friendly tone, but not allowing him time to really gather his thoughts. "Well?"

"As a matter of fact, I've been sitting here reading the newspapers and realizing that I really don't know where I stand."

The President chuckled.

"Oh, well, if you've been reading the newspapers you know where you stand. There's only one position with them—or most of them, anyway, the most powerful. The position is that I'm history's greatest scoundrel and World War III is here. Do you agree?"

"I find it difficult to agree with extremists of any kind," Governor Jason said carefully; so carefully that the President chuckled again.

"I could take that personally, you know—at least if I adopted the line about me that Walter Dobius and his friends have adopted this morning. Well, then, if you aren't ready to tell me at the moment, let me put it to you this way: what would you have done?"

"How can I say?" the Governor inquired smoothly, "since I couldn't possibly place myself in your position with all the facts you had at hand when you made the decision?"

"They weren't so very different from what has already been made public," the President said dryly. "I'm not one of the fact-hiding Presidents, you know."

"I do know," Ted Jason agreed, "and I admire you for it. I didn't mean to sound disrespectful, but, really—I don't have the facts, at least as they came to you fresh from Africa last night, so how could I know what I would have done had I been where you are?"

"You might have to face that one of these days."

The Governor laughed.

"That I doubt. Harley M. Hudson is going to be President of these United States for quite some time, I imagine."

"Maybe you can beat Harley M. Hudson on this issue," the President suggested calmly, "if you decide to make it an issue. Or Orrin Knox," he added, so smoothly that it was a second before Governor Jason realized the slip he had made, "or whoever."

"I doubt that," the Governor said, giving no indication he had caught it. "I imagine anyone who wants to run a winning campaign will pretty well have to endorse Harley M. Hudson's position, won't he?"

"Perhaps," the President said. "And perhaps not. That's one reason I'm calling. Do you?"

"I haven't made any statement yet," Ted Jason said, "though of course I've had plenty of opportunity. I'm sticking to 'no comment' for the time being."

"Probably sensible," the President said. "I want you to know, however, that it would be a great help to me if you would endorse my action. Just as it will make us mortal political enemies," he added calmly, "if you don't."

The Governor made an acknowledging sound.

"Suppose I don't do either one, for the moment? What would your reaction be then?"

"I should be disappointed," the President said, "but not actively annoyed. Assuming that in due course you saw your way clear to supporting your President and the leader of your party."

"It's complicated for me a little," Governor Jason said thoughtfully, "because I am not sure what I would have done. I am not sure that this is the wisest course. I am not sure that we should be doing what you have committed us to. Why, for instance, make the issue here and now? Why not some other time, some other place?"

"All places and all times are the same in this onslaught against us," the President said somberly. "It had a beginning, once, many years ago, but once it began it has never stopped, it has never even paused. It is a continuous thing, and it is up to us to decide where and at what time we shall try to stop it. One time is just as good as another, one place as good as another, one issue just as valid as another, for they are all on the same footing in the eyes of the Communists, they are all attacks upon us, and so we might as well look at them the same way. The attack is total. It may be a military skirmish, a cement wall, a diplomatic negotiating table, a cocktail party, a riot, a visit—anything and everything. I simply chose this time and place because I personally—and, I will say, most of my advisers agreed with me—felt that it was time for certain things to stop."

"So you started others," Governor Jason suggested. "Understand me," he added quickly, "I am not being flippant. You will realize that I am trying to be as honest with you are you are being with me."

"I do realize. I appreciate it. I don't want to force you into something you honestly can't accept. I'm not that kind of President, either. But of course if you oppose me I can't ignore it. It's going to have consequences. Inevitably."

"Suppose I were to endorse what you've done," Ted Jason said slowly, "so that Orrin and I were on exactly the same footing as far as support of you is concerned. What would your attitude be in the convention? Would you be neutral as between us? Or would you endorse Orrin? Or would you endorse me? Or," he said, taking a gamble on the President's good nature, "is it all academic because you plan to run yourself, anyway?"

"Will my answer help you make up your mind on a matter which you tell me is one of such fundamental conviction with you?" the President inquired dryly. "Are you for sale?"

"I am not," Ted Jason said coldly, and prepared himself for the explosion his next remark would bring: "Though you seem to be bidding."

But Harley Hudson was a surprising man in a lot of ways to his political contemporaries, and instead of flaring back in anger he simply responded with his comfortable, unperturbed laugh.

"I suppose I deserved that. And I suppose I am, yes. And you still haven't told me. So what shall I do about you, Governor?"

"I don't see that you have to do anything," Ted Jason said, more calmly, feeling suddenly that he was emerging from this conversation the winner. "When I have made up my mind I shall speak out. It will be a matter of conviction, too. Believe me."

"I am sure," the President said, again so dryly that the Governor abruptly wasn't sure that he had won, after all. "I shall look forward with interest. I assume your decision will come fairly soon."

"The way events are moving, I would think so. Will we have the pleasure of your company Friday night at the banquet for Walter Dobius?"

The President laughed.

"Walter does me such honor that I should of course be eager to honor him. But I shall have to think about it. There are many implications in that affair, aren't there, Ted?"

"Only the recognition of a great career of service to the country, as far as I know," the Governor said blandly. The President laughed again.

"Well, we shall have to see. I assume you can fit me in somewhere, even if it is a late acceptance."

"I think we can. In any event, I hope to see you when I am in Washington."

"I, too," the President said. "We must talk about this some more."

"Gladly," Ted Jason said. "Good luck, Mr. President."

"And good luck to you. We shall all need it."

But despite the friendly cordiality with which he offered this final thought before ending the connection with Sacramento, it was with a somber expression and a worried mood that the President turned back to a desk which, like Ted Jason's, was covered with newspapers. He had managed to preserve a fair equanimity and simulate a comfortable unconcern, but he was as aware as he knew Ted was of how important the Governor's position could be at this particular moment.

All the hysterical anger of Walter and his world, all the frantic dismay of the allied worlds of education and culture that were so influenced by it, were already in process of finding their focus in the carefully calculating mind that sat in Sacramento. Not yet had anyone spelled it out, though the President would be very much surprised if Walter did not do it Friday night, but there was just one logical man to lead the opposition to what was being done in Gorotoland. It was so logical, in fact, that the President did not see how the Governor of California could possibly avoid it; unless, of course, he possessed a patriotic devotion to the country's welfare that the President was not ready to accord him.

Yet possibly this skepticism was too harsh and too dictated by his own convictions in the matter, his own need for support. It could be that Ted was honestly opposed. Certainly the President was willing to concede that even Walter and his world, harsh as they were, were moved by a genuine conviction. He was not sure they were willing to concede him an equal honesty of purpose, but fortunately he had a nature charitable and mature enough to be able to concede it to them.

He was struck, as he had often been before, by the strange nature of this America which is capable of arousing such absolutely divergent opinions, most of them quite sincere, as to what is best for her.

Certainly they were divergent today. The President was ready to admit that he had never seen such a universal and vitriolic tidal wave of condemnation as that which was descending upon him. The violent diatribes that had greeted the Johnson administration's firm stand in Vietnam and Santo Domingo, the furious uproar that had greeted his own action in walking out on the Russians at Geneva a year ago—these were the two most violent outbreaks of press hysteria he could remember in recent decades, and neither was the match of this.

"We cannot remember a President more headstrong and impetuous in his abrupt decision to plunge the nation into a course that could mean open war among the great powers," the New York *Times* said gravely.

He could not remember a press campaign more determined to thwart, hamper, and cripple a President in the performance of his duty as he saw it.

And of course those segments of the American commonalty that always know better than everyone else what ought to be done were also reporting in. Students were rioting against him at the University of California campus in Berkeley. The General Board of the National Council of Churches had just issued a statement strongly attacking his action. The head of the AFL-CIO, in his shrewd, sharp-eyed way, was about to do the same. The National Association of Manufacturers and the U. S. Chamber of Commerce, afraid that profits from trade with Communist countries would suffer, were going to follow suit. Two lost souls in nearby Maryland had already purchased kerosene. Herbert Jason, uncle of Patsy and the Governor, brother of Selena Castleberry, Nobel Prize-winning nuclear scientist, was drafting a public letter, aided by the arrogant little professor who had once served as court historian to the most self-conscious Administration in American history and had never recovered from it.

"Mr. President," they wrote: "We feel that we must express the abhorrence that the overwhelming majority of your countrymen feel concerning your invasion of innocent, helpless Gorotoland. As holders of the Presidential Medal of Freedom, we feel we have a right to admonish since we feel we express the overwhelming opinion of America on what your course should be." In Congress, Senator Fred Van Ackerman of COMFORT and Arly Richardson were only the start of a noisy parade. In New York, a distinguished group of actors, artists, authors, scientists, publishers, teachers, doctors, lawyers, were busy with telephone and telegram urging as many of their fellows as they could reach around the country to sign their names to a full-page ad headlined MR. PRESIDENT! STOP THIS INSANITY IN GOROTOLAND! which would appear in sixty-seven leading newspapers tomorrow morning. LeGage Shelby of DEFY, first major Negro leader to speak out, had issued a statement terming the President's action "wanton imperialistic aggression of the worst neo-colonialist type." And in Dallas, Rufus Kleinfert, Knight Kommander of the Konference on Efforts to Encourage Patriotism (KEEP) was calling the Gorotoland decision "an obvious concealed Communist-inspired move to bring the United States into universal disrepute."

And of course the world was reporting in. Moscow and Peking had issued angry statements. London was nervous, Bonn alarmed, Rome quizzical, Paris wry. Eleven U.S. embassies had already been attacked by well-organized spontaneous student rioters, seven tinpot dictators in Africa and Asia had already seized the opportunity to burn down U.S. Information libraries and thus get rid of outside ideas once and for all. The President of Egypt was threatening to close the Suez Canal to American shipping, Morocco had already closed its airfields to American craft en route to Africa. The International Film Festival at Scquircz, Yugoslavia, had turned into a mass protest rally of all the right-thinking movie folk from Bandung to Beverly Hills, and in London an International Committee to Oppose U. S. Imperialism in Gorotoland was being formed by Britain's oldest, most doddering, most pathetic peer.

All in all, Harley Hudson reflected with a wry smile and some return of his normal easygoing humor, it was quite a morning to be President of the United States.

He still had no doubts that he had done the right thing: as he had told Ted Jason, the issue had to be made sometime, and in the last analysis it really made no difference where it was made or over what. The battle was continuous and the decision to bring it to a showdown could be taken whenever it seemed advisable or necessary. Gorotoland might not be the most convenient ground, but then, what would be? No place would be convenient for the United States unless the United States struck first. Until the United States did, the ground would always be of the enemy's choosing.

There was a curiously childlike strain in these protests from some of his more vocal countrymen about "inconvenient and inaccessible terrain." Did they really think the Communists were going to choose terrain convenient and accessible to the United States to conduct their maraudings? He wondered where the perfect ground would be, in the minds of Walter and his world, and what the perfect issue. Nowhere and nothing, he was forced to conclude from their febrile yappings now.

Somehow they wanted the deadly issue between the free world and the slave to be settled without war, without conflict, without controversy, and without any advantage for their own country—not even the advantage of a guaranteed stability, apparently, for that would require force, and force, apparently, was the only thing they really were able to abhor. All else they could swallow, but threaten them with the possibility of force and they would climb the wall, just as they were doing now. It baffled him how such people could sincerely consider themselves to be loyal Americans loyally dedicated to America's preservation, yet he knew the great majority did. It increased the burden of opposing them, for no such tolerance informed their attitude toward him. He was a monstrous midwife who would have to answer to history. He gave a grim little chuckle as he recalled the tart comment of his fellow midwife, when Orrin had first read Walter's column.

"I'm a monstrous midwife helping Walter have a miscarriage of mice," he had remarked. But the mice were not so funny, gnawing as they did at the vitals of the Administration as it sought to meet a deliberate challenge its leader felt had to be met, and in just the way in which he had chosen to meet it.

He pushed the shouting papers aside with a motion that was, for Harley Hudson, surprisingly impatient, and pressing the buzzer on the intercom, asked his secretary to get the chief American delegate to the UN on the line. The screams of Walter's world were so much chaff on the winds of history: he was dealing in fundamentals much more serious than their quivering vituperations.

When Cullee Hamilton answered from U.S. delegation headquarters across the street from the UN the President gave him precise and specific instructions as to what he was to do in Security Council later in the day.

"If you agree with me, that is," the President said. "I don't want to jeopardize your political future. If you'd rather not be the one to do it, you can turn it over to Lafe."

"I don't duck out," Cullee said calmly. "And I do agree with you, 100 percent. In fact, I'd be terribly disappointed if you wanted me to do anything else."

"Good," the President said. "Then we're ready for them."

"Let 'em come," Cullee said.

And come they did, the first wave greeting him as he arrived at the United States delegation building across First Avenue from the UN an hour later. He had asked the driver to take him up to the new apartment house on East 63rd Street to pick up Sarah Johnson, and they had shared a comfortable, if worried, ride back downtown. She was working now in delegation headquarters in an office two floors below his: he found that quite often he was dropping in there. They had also dated a good deal at the endless round of UN dinners and cocktail parties, he had taken her out occasionally for dinner and the theater. A couple of times he had stayed overnight. But, as he had told Lafe, he couldn't have said at the moment exactly what it meant, if it meant anything. Except that she was comfortable—that perhaps was the best word. Comfortable and reassuring, after all the hell he had gone through with overclever, over-ambitious, waspish little Sue-Dan.

Now as the limousine moved slowly through the mid-morning traffic down FDR Drive, they were uneasy about the news from Gorotoland but curiously exhilarated too.

"I only hope we can carry it off," she said thoughtfully.

He frowned.

"We've got to."

"I suppose the roof will blow off the UN today," she said with her slow, amused smile. "I can hear them now."

"Another Hate America day. Sarah, you and I are a couple of no-good nothings, to be running the errands of such an imperialistic, colonialistic, grasping, arrogant, evil nation. How can we live with ourselves?"

"I don't find it hard," she said. "Particularly when I see some of the alternatives."

"They aren't too attractive, are they?" A scornful expression came into his eyes. "Even if they think they are, just because they're black."

"They have egos," she agreed. She gave his arm a sudden squeeze and uttered a gentle little laugh. "So do some others I could mention."

"Do you think I do?" he asked with some dismay, abruptly serious, finding curiously painful the thought that she might be criticizing, however gently.

"In a nice way," she said, squeezing his arm again. "A necessary way, to be in politics, I suppose."

"I don't think I'm too bad," he said, still, ridiculously, hurt. "You have to have a certain self-assurance to stay in the game, but I don't think—"

"Now, I'm sorry I said anything," she said, though still with a gently humorous air. "I didn't mean to upset you. I think you have a very nice ego." She smiled again. "Just the right size to be United States Senator."

"I don't know about that," he said, flattered. "There's a lot of things involved in that."

"Nobody's better equipped," she said seriously. "I'd come out and work for you myself."

"You would? Do you mean that?"

"Why not?" Her tone lightened. "There are worse causes to work for."

"I'll remember that," he said with a smile. "That may just do it. That may just make me decide. I've been hesitating, but with an offer like that I may just have to do it."

"I think you'd better," she said, as the car swung off the Drive at 42nd Street and prepared to double back past the UN to U.S. headquarters. "We need people like you."

"Do you really mean that?" he asked, quite touched by her suddenly earnest tone. She gave him a quick look.

"Of course I do. This girl doesn't say things she doesn't mean."

"That," he said soberly, taking her hand in his, "is why I like this girl."

"Now," she said, flushing and pleased. "I don't know whether you mean that."

"Same as you," he said simply. "I don't say it unless I mean it."

For a moment they looked at one another with a candid, trusting gaze that withheld nothing. He was about to speak, impelled by some instinctive knowledge that this was the time to do it, to accept what was offered, to give up Sue-Dan once and for all, evil and unhappy as she was and evil and unhappy as her influence over him had been, to commit himself to the future and be thankful he had found it. The words were almost out when the chauffeur suddenly rapped on the glass, rolled it down, and asked, politely but with a noticeable tremor in his voice, "Do you want me to try to go right through, Mr. Hamilton? It looks as though it might be—kind of hard."

And now they could see ahead that First Avenue was filled with a swarming mob that washed from the UN esplanade to the steps of U.S. headquarters. Traffic was rapidly backing up on either side of it; four or five mounted policemen were trying vainly to push back the marchers who surged against the door of the U.S. building; sirens were beginning to sound in the city as police cars screamed toward the area. Banners and placards bobbed through the crowd:

DOWN WITH HUDSON THE WAR-LOVER! . . . HANDS OFF GOROTOLAND! . . . OBI, GREAT! HARLEY, NUTS! . . . DEFY DEFIES YOU, MR. PRES-IDENT! . . . OIL STINKS! COMFORT DEMANDS NE-GOTIATIONS NOW! . . . LET'S HAVE A NICE BIG WAR, HARLEY! . . . AMERICA, THE NEW IMPE-RIALIST! . . . U.S. SAYS: KILL NEGROES AT HOME, KILL NEGROES IN AFRICA . . . HOW ABOUT U.S. AGGRESSION, HARLEY?

Off on the edges of the roaring crowd Cullee could see cameras grinding, flashbulbs popping. I hope you're satisfied, he told them grimly. This is the way you want it.

Whether this was a fair comment by a mind that usually tried to be fair, he did not have time to analyze, for it was obvious that he must make some decision at once or their car would be engulfed in the mob with consequences that could literally be fatal. He had a wild, ironic impulse to shout, Go ahead, John, they'll let us through, we're all black! But of course it was gone as it came. It was obvious he and his companions were Americans, the stamp of their civilization was on them whatever their color, and in addition the two small flags on the front fenders were there to advertise it. Already he could see the nearer rioters beginning to turn, he could see their eyes picking out the flags, he could sense the impulse that shot through an ever-larger segment of the crowd.

He yanked open the door, grabbed Sarah's arm and pulled her after him, yelled, "Take the keys and leave the car, John!"—and then the three of them were running back toward 42nd Street, managing to elude the stragglers still rushing toward the riot, managing to find haven, finally, among the morning crowds on 42nd, where he abruptly slowed down. They began walking, winded but as though they belonged there, slowly around the long block until they could come again, unobserved, to the upper edges of the mob.

"I didn't want to abandon government property, John," he said with a shaky laugh, "but I thought, better lose a car than our lives."

"That's right," their driver said fervently. "That is right!"

"Maybe it won't be lost," Sarah said as they turned back toward First Avenue. "Maybe the police got there in time."

But this, they saw as they came in sight of the mob again, was a vain hope. Though the police had noticeably increased in five minutes, the mob still filled the street. It too seemed to have increased, and over at the far side smoke was rising. Through it they could see the wheels of their overturned limousine. It lay on its back, windows smashed, tires ripped. Someone had doused it with gasoline and set it afire, and around its pyre a ring of rioters, holding hands, moved with a lively step and a happy chant. "Down with U.S. mur-der-ers, down with U.S. mur-der-ers, down with U.S. mur-der-ers. Yeaay!" And again, "Down with U.S. mur-der-ers, down with U.S.—" And yet again, as the mindless circle continued its jocular parade.

"I think," Sarah Johnson said in a voice close to tears, "that we did the right thing. How horrible!"

"I know we did," Cullee said grimly. "Officer!" he said to a nearby mounted policeman patrolling the edges of the crowd, "can you get us into U.S. headquarters?" He pulled out his wallet, showed his credentials. The officer smiled, tipped his cap to Sarah, but shook his head.

"I'm afraid not, Congressman. You see what they're doing. I don't think it's even safe around at the back, right now. You'd better stick by me. Or I'll stick by you, rather. As much as I can."

They could see now that the front of the headquarters building was spattered with mud, eggs, and manure. Even as they looked two windows on the second floor were shattered by flying rocks, and an approving shout went up. There was an extra disturbance just in front of the door, a flurry of motion, a sudden great splash of oil across the door and the ground-floor windows immediately adjacent. A great "Yeaaay!" rose exultantly from the crowd. It was repeated with an even wilder, more savage, and triumphant note as the oil was followed by a flare that ignited it instantly, sending a great wave of flame running up the front of the building.

"Excuse me," the mounted policeman said abruptly and swung his horse away, directly into the crowd as his fellows did the same from all around the periphery. There were screams, yells, groans, boos, but the mob at last began to give way. Staring intently into the sea of insanely contorted faces, Cullee saw at last the two he knew must be there. For a brief instant his wife Sue-Dan and LeGage Shelby stared back at him as though from a cavern in hell. Then they were lost again in the crowd, but not before he knew that they had seen him, too, and not before a terrible pain for a moment wrenched his heart. They were lost to him, lost; yet was not he still lost to them? His face must have said as much, for he became conscious again of Sarah Johnson's hand upon his arm.

"What's the matter?" she asked with concern. "Do you feel all right?"

"I feel fine," he said, trying to sound as though he meant it. But the mood in which he had started to address her before the riot, whatever it had been, was gone for now. "I think we'd better try to get on in as soon as we can."

"All right." She shivered and drew her coat more tightly about her. "What an awful age we live in," she said quietly.

He sighed.

"And getting worse."

South 250 miles, in front of the White House, several hundred pickets carrying similar banners pushed and shoved and tried to block traffic along Pennsylvania Avenue. The police fought them back but more kept coming. By 11 A.M. forty-three were seriously injured and one was dead, a white student from Georgetown University who lost his footing and fell beneath the wheels of a patrol car attempting to herd the mob.

A sense of the world unloosed began to grip America and turn decent men everywhere to a somber and desolate mood.

Such was Walter Dobius' mood, and it needed no further turning, as he arrived, walking from the East Side Airlines Terminal, at the UN esplanade just as the mounted police were pushing back the last group of rioters who had attacked U.S. headquarters. One quick look at the building with its coating of filth, its shattered windows, and its great scar of flame and smoke, one quick look at the burned limousine being towed away, the littered street, and the little core of picketers who still obligingly waved their banners before banked television cameras on the UN steps, and the reporter's instinct that never failed hurtled him across the slowly resuming traffic. Out came his pad and pencil as he ran. He was already jotting notes when he arrived at the knot of rioters and reporters who were paying little heed, so fascinated were they by each other's attentions, to the still arguing, angry police shouting to them to move on.

"LeGage!" he called as he recognized the lithe, tense figure that appeared to be dominating things. "Walter Dobius here. What happened?"

"There's our friend!" LeGage cried happily. "There's Mr. Walter Dobius, the man who understands what we're trying to do this morning, the man who's against this crazy deal in Gorotoland! Stand back for our friend there, Mr. Walter Dobius!"

There were cheers from the forty or fifty rioters who remained, respectful looks and greetings from many of the reporters. Helen-Anne's standard advice—don't let yourself be made to look ridiculous—flashed across his mind, but he instantly rejected it. This was no ridiculous cause, this was literally the cause of world peace. Anything his presence could do to serve it he would contribute. Years of conditioned caution against placing himself too obviously in a partisan position found themselves consumed by his absolutely sincere conviction that it was now or never for the world.

"Thank you," he said, stepping forward with dignity. (Behind his head as the eager cameras swung in upon him and LeGage Shelby, a white rioter from the Konference on Efforts to Encourage Patriotism held high a tattered but still-legible placard reading DON'T FALL FOR COMMIE TRICKS! NEGOTIATE NOW!—KEEP. And behind that, looming beautifully for all the pictures, the scarred delegation building made a perfect backdrop across the street.)

"I have just arrived," he said in his most gravely pompous voice to the intent cameras, the hushed and feverishly scribbling reporters, "but it is obvious that there has occurred here this morning a sincere and genuine protest against the irresponsible policies of the present Administration in Africa. I hope it will be noted in Washington. I believe it to be representative of the reactions of most sober and sensible citizens in this period of fearful crisis provoked by President Harley M. Hudson and Secretary of State Orrin Knox.

"America abhors the kind of violent action this Administration has ordered in Gorotoland. America rejects this kind of dangerous gambling with the lives of this nation and all others on the face of the globe. America wants peace, not war."

He flung out his hand with a sudden vigorous gesture and the cameras obediently swung around to climb the glassy monolith of the UN Secretariat looming above them.

"There is where this issue should be decided," he said firmly as they swung obediently back. "There in the UN. Not with guns and planes and squadrons of Marines, in violation of all the rules of civilized behavior, but *in the UN!*

"I applaud the genuine outpourings of protest that are apparent throughout the nation this morning. They are in the great tradition of a free people. May Washington take heed and bring this matter speedily to a peaceful settlement here in the world organization where it belongs."

He stopped and again there were shouts of approval, cheers, and applause. LeGage shook his hand fervently, a clever fox-faced girl whom he remembered from Washington cocktail parties as Congressman Hamilton's wife came forward and did the same while further pictures were taken. He bowed, waved gravely to the crowd, and pushed through the respectfully opening ranks of his fellow journalists. With his steady, trudging gait he moved forward across the broad esplanade toward the doors of the UN. Behind him his older colleagues looked at one another with some skepticism, but his younger colleagues assured each other with a genuine excitement that they had seen one of the authentic greats of their profession, brave enough to lay his reputation on the line for what he believed. It was a real inspiration. They assured one another that they would never forget it.

"Have you seen this quote on the news ticker from Walter Dobius at the UN?" the President asked half an hour later when the Secretary of State entered his oval office in the west wing of the White House. "Walter's taking himself seriously indeed."

"Do you still want to go to his luncheon on Thursday?" the Secretary's wife asked when she talked to him fifteen minutes later after hearing about it on the hourly news roundup.

"Hell, yes, I want to go," Orrin snapped. "It's time somebody pinned his ears back."

"Right now," Beth said thoughtfully, "I'd say he's the one who's doing the pinning."

And so he believed himself, as he stood just within the entrance to the Delegates' Dining Room waiting for Vasily Tashikov, while the multicolored garbs and faces of the peoples of the earth went by. Many recognized his stocky, determined figure and proud, self-confident air; frequently he was flattered with their polite and respectful greetings.

"Walter!" Krishna Khaleel said, bowing low and shaking his hand vigorously. "We are honored by your presence, dear friend. You will be here for the Security Council debate this afternoon?"

"I will indeed. What do you think will happen, K.K.?"

The Indian Ambassador frowned.

"It does not look good for America, I am afraid," he said sadly. "These are difficult times. I think the President and Orrin have"—he sucked in his breath and shook his head with a worried air. "I do not know exactly what they *have* done, goodness gracious!"

"Gone to war, I think," Walter said grimly. Krishna Khaleel nodded quickly.

"I read your column. I thought it was magnificent."

"Will we be ordered out, do you think?"

"I do not see how it can be otherwise," the Indian Ambassador said.

"I hope so. I hope we are forced to leave at once."

"Of course," K.K. noted with a wistful delicacy, "there is just one thing, you know. We can order, but . . . if you do not want to go . . . what then?"

"I cannot conceive of an American Administration so brutal and so unresponsive to world opinion as to do such a thing!" Walter Dobius said, and the Indian Ambassador could see that he was genuinely shocked at the concept.

"Possibly not," he said gently, "but Orrin and Harley, you know . . . would it surprise you?"

"They would destroy themselves politically," Walter said somberly. "They would destroy the United States in the eyes of the world. I cannot conceive of it. I simply cannot conceive of it."

"Well," K.K. said with a worried frown, "I hope for all our sakes you are right, dear Walter. We shall see as events develop. You have a luncheon companion?"

"Vasily Tashikov has invited me to be his guest. It seemed to be a worthwhile invitation to accept. Although I did not know when he called me yesterday that we would have quite so many things to talk about."

"My, yes," the Indian Ambassador said. "I am waiting for the delegate of Brazil."

"How does he feel?"

"Our governments are quite agreed, I think."

"I doubt that we have a friend in the world," Walter said, and was aware as he spoke of a cheerful presence coming up to him out of the throng of arriving delegates.

"I heard that!" Lafe Smith said, giving his arm a jocular squeeze. "I heard it! Shame on you, Walter, you old warmonger. We've got millions. Literally millions."

"I don't think the occasion is one for levity, if you'll forgive me," Walter said coldly, disengaging his arm.

"O.K.," Lafe said, matching his mood instantly with obvious relish. "I think that was the God-damnedest column you've ever written this morning, and I think that was the God-damnedest stupidest performance you ever put on, out there in the street. I think it was close to treason, if you want my frank opinion."

"My goodness," Krishna Khaleel said in an alarmed tone. "My goodness, Lafe, what are you saying!"

"What he always says," Walter said through lips compressed with anger. "The most fatuous nonsense in the United States Senate."

"You're getting too big for your breeches, boy," Lafe told him with the same infuriating air of enjoyment, while a number of delegates, seeing their expressions and hearing the tones of their voices, drifted nearer with attentive faces. "You think you run this whole country, don't you? Maybe you're wrong."

"We'll see who's wrong, after this little episode in Gorotoland," Walter said harshly. "If you'll excuse me, I see my host. Goodbye!" But he found his way blocked by the giant frame of the chief American delegate, who was holding a copy of the *Daily Mirror* in his hand.

"Before you go," Cullee said softly, "just one little word with you, Walter. Do you realize what happened out there this morning before you came along and gave it your grand endorsement? Take a look. You see that burned car? I was riding in that car, with Sarah Johnson and a driver. We got out just in time, Walter, while your grand, democratic, liberty-loving friends were rioting against your country. Would it have made you happy if we'd been killed?"

For a long moment Walter Dobius stared up at him with a look of studied contempt. When he finally spoke it was in his most clipped and heavy tones, biting off the words as though he would spit out each one.

"No, it would not have made me happy if you had been killed. How infantile can you be? As for my grand, democratic, liberty-loving friends, as you call them, I was happy to endorse their protest against the irresponsible, inexcusable act of a war-mad Administration. I would do it again. I *will* do it again, in my column and in everything else I say. Is that clear?"

From his compact height, Cullee looked down with an

equal contempt. Again he spoke softly, while all around the watching nations goggled and stared.

"What you overlook, Walter, dear, is the fact that some thirty-five or forty people have been killed, that American property has been destroyed, that honorable American rights guaranteed by honorable arrangement with a legal government have been violated. . . . It's always the same, with you and your crowd, isn't it? You always succeed in turning everything upside down so that you get the whole world arguing about what the United States has done—instead of about what has been done to the United States. Ignoring, of course, very conveniently, the fact that if nothing had been done to us—we wouldn't be doing anything. I swear to God I don't see how you people can do it with a clear conscience. I swear I don't."

"Well, now, Cullee," Krishna Khaleel said nervously. "It is not only 'Walter and his crowd,' as you put it, who feel the great measure of concern about what the United States is doing. It is all of us. It is because of your greater power and your greater potential to do damage to the world. We are all concerned."

"I can understand you," Cullee said, making his voice less contemptuous with an obvious effort. "But"—and the contempt came back—"I can't understand him and his friends. They're beyond me and they always have been. Now go have lunch with your pal, Walter. Who is it, Tashikov?"

"Yes!" Walter spat out.

"That figures," Cullee said in a tired tone. "That sure as hell figures. Come on, Lafe."

"Dear me," Krishna Khaleel said to no one in particular as three angry Americans strode away toward their respective tables. *"Mercy!"*

5

FOR QUITE A few moments after he and his host had claimed their table and ordered drinks, America's leading philosopher-statesman found it almost impossible to think coherently, so angered and embittered was he by the degrading and inexcusable humiliation to which he had been subjected by his countrymen before the avidly interested eyes of the nations. If anything had been needed to alienate Walter Dobius permanently and implacably from the Hudson administration and its present course of action in Africa, his public tongue-lashing by Congressman Hamilton and Senator Smith would have done it. Everything was now in place, all things were clear, his own course was finally and completely justified. Behind Cullee and Lafe, as vividly as though they had actually stood there, he could see the figures of the incompetent President and the irresponsible Secretary of State, the warmakers who were challenging all the principles of civilized and orderly international behavior to whose strengthening Walter and his friends had devoted themselves in all the difficult years since the end of World War II. Their policies were so violently contrary to those Walter knew in his heart to be right, their attitude toward him personally so mocking and disrespectful, that he was convinced now that he had been absolutely sound in his column, absolutely correct in the statement he had made after the riot, absolutely justified in everything he was doing and intended to do to hinder, defeat, and discredit permanently if he could, the present policies of Washington and the men responsible for them.

Despite this righteous certainty, however, it was not until the drinks arrived—the Soviet Ambassador had ordered Dubonnet on the rocks and Walter in spite of his whirling anger had retained enough caution to do the same, for he was not about to engage in any conversation with Vasily Tashikov half-drunk—that he finally calmed down enough to be able to pay attention to the comments with which his host was setting the stage for their discussion.

He was pleased but not surprised to find that Tashikov was stating opinions exactly paralleling his own concerning the painful episode in which he had found Walter involved when he stepped off the escalator into the dining room.

"It is disgraceful," the Soviet Ambassador said. "Disgraceful, for your countrymen to make of their greatest journalist such a cruel public spectacle! It is typical," he added matter-of-factly, "of those who have gone mad in the pursuit of their imperialist ambitions."

"It was not pleasant," Walter admitted, taking a long

swallow of Dubonnet and stilling the last erratic thumpings of his heart by a sheer effort of will. "But," he added grimly, "I think events will prove who is right."

"They will prove it is you who is right. There is no doubt of it, for I ask you, how could they do otherwise? You *are* right! The United States is engaged in insanity, as you said in your column this morning. Civilized peoples everywhere regard it so. The world, I think, will show the United States what happens to neo-colonialist warmongers!"

"I would hope the Administration could be forced to withdraw," Walter said, ignoring the anti-American rhetoric—they always felt they had to use that, and anyway it was more important to have them opposing the Administration than it was to quibble over words. "I should think that would be sufficient to place the matter back on a reasonable basis on which the UN might then consider the merits of Prince Obifumatta's complaint versus ours."

"Mr. Dobius!" Vasily Tashikov said in a disbelieving tone. "Mr. Dobius! Surely you do not believe the imperialist warmongers in Washington have a case in Gorotoland? Your writings do not indicate this."

"I believe there is some merit," Walter said carefully, for by now he was calm enough to be on guard against what he knew from long experience with Communist diplomats in Washington could easily turn into an attempt to entrap him into saying things he didn't mean, "in the argument that missionaries working peaceably in a country have a right to be unmolested. I also believe—although," he said with a smile indicating that in this he and his host were probably close to agreement, "I feel that one may legitimately be suspicious of American commercial enterprises in underdeveloped lands—that once a company has entered into a legal arrangement with a government, it has some right to just recompense if it is dispossessed or damaged."

"Legal arrangement with a government?" Vasily Tashikov demanded, his squat little body swiveling indignantly in its chair, his sharp-featured face with its gold pince-nez peering angrily across at his guest, while at the next table the delegates of Nicaragua, Honduras, Ghana, and Mali pretended a casual inattention as they did their best to overhear, and farther away the two United States delegates, the British Ambassador, and the French Ambassador stopped eating for a moment to give them a speculative glance. "Now, Mr. Dobius, you are not being consistent with your recent columns. Surely you do not consider an arrangement of the illegitimate colonialist lackey Terry to be legitimate. Mr. *Dobius!*"

"I don't agree with Prince Terry's policies, no," Walter said calmly, now curious to see what he could provoke, "but he is the legitimate government. You cannot deny that."

"Can I not?" the Soviet Ambassador cried. "But I am! I do! It is accomplished, my denial! What then?"

"Please do not excite yourself," Walter said coldly, feeling it time to bring the conversation down to earth. "I agree as you know with your opposition to the basic United States position in Gorotoland. Certainly you are aware I agree 100 percent with your opposition to our latest action there. There is no point in confusing our understanding of each other with semantics."

"Ah!" Tashikov said with a sudden smile. "Semantics! Now you touch upon one of the great difficulties in bridging the gap between the two worlds, Mr. Dobius. Your use of words in the West is so foreign to us. It is so contrary to the way we use them. Democracy and freedom to us are perfectly clear and understandable terms. But we have learned to know that when the United States and the West uses them they mean imperialism, exploitation, dictatorship over helpless peoples, and tyranny. It took us many years to realize this. But we know it now."

"Well, Mr. Ambassador," Walter said dryly, "you know perfectly well that I cannot accept that. It seems to me we are getting far afield. I repeat, I trust the Security Council this afternoon will order American forces withdrawn from Gorotoland. After that, the issue can be discussed on its merits free from the threat of war."

"It is not only the threat, at this moment," the Ambassador said. "As you have written, it is war."

"Then I surely hope it will be condemned as such," Walter said firmly. "The Administration deserves no less."

"Mr. Dobius," Tashikov said with a sudden embracing smile, "you are an inspiration and a strength to those of us who oppose your government's fatal neo-colonialist policies. It is so comforting to know that America's greatest journalist and his friends are on our side in the endless battle to defeat America's imperialist aggressions all over the world."

"America's greatest journalist," Walter said calmly, for it did no good to become angry with them, it only got you lost in competing rhetoric, and anyway, he was America's greatest journalist, "is interested above all things in helping to preserve peace in the world. I believe you will find if you examine my writings that there have been occasions on which I have condemned Soviet aggressions too."

"I can remember nothing as devastating as your column this morning, Mr. Dobius," the Soviet Ambassador said cheerfully. "And may we thank Lenin for that! Shall we order?"

After they had done so, Tashikov requesting a filet mignon and Walter scallops in a wine and curry sauce he remembered fondly from his last visit to the UN, the Soviet Ambassador leaned forward confidentially.

"For your information in writing about events here, Mr. Dobius"—and Walter was pleased that he was doing this, it was the sort of inside information he was seeking and he was gratified that Tashikov was volunteering it, it showed a real confidence in his integrity as a reporter, which Walter prized above all else—"for your information, I understand that your government will offer an amendment to the resolution of condemnation this afternoon. This amendment will attempt to bring condemnation of the People's Free Republic of Gorotoland. We will veto it. Then the resolution condemning your government will come to a vote. Your government, the United Kingdom, and the alleged representative of the illegal Government of Taiwan, as is customary in such cases, will abstain. The Council will then proceed to approve the resolution of condemnation and your government will then stand convicted before the world, as it should be, for its unprovoked imperialistic invasion of an innocent country. That will be the procedure we will follow today."

"That is very interesting, Mr. Ambassador," Walter said solemnly, though he had already heard the same prediction from his sources in the State Department and none of it was news to him. "I appreciate your confidence. The only thing I question is whether it will be quite so easy to defeat the United States amendment criticizing Prince Obi's government."

"I have told you," Tashikov said with a shrug. "The U.S.S.R. will veto it. Then, Mr. Dobius, the world will turn upon the United States, as you invited it to do in your column this morning, and punish it for its insane crime against civilized humanity."

Again Walter decided not to challenge this interpretation. He was anxious to learn other things.

"Suppose the United States refuses to withdraw even though the resolution is passed by the Security Council?"

"Then the United States will also stand convicted by the world's opinion as the destroyer of the United Nations!" Tashikov said promptly.

"Even though the Communist powers have similarly ignored resolutions of the Security Council?" Walter could not help suggesting blandly. The Soviet Ambassador gave him a look equally bland.

"Communist powers do not act in violation of the civilized rules of mankind, as the United States is doing. Therefore Communist powers do not recognize condemnation by anyone. It is not pertinent. It is not worthy of recognition. Communist powers act for freedom and justice, Mr. Dobius. They do not act for war and imperialist conquest. The world is aware of that."

"I am glad to hear you explain the difference."

"I did not think I would have to," Tashikov said with a humorously chiding air, "after your magnificent column this morning, Mr. Dobius. It appeared to me as I read it that you thoroughly understood the difference! So has it appeared to all of us here in this house. I think you will find your position almost universally applauded here. America's greatest journalist—perhaps the world's greatest journalist—having the courage to criticize his own country because he loves peace and justice. It is an inspiring thing, Mr. Dobius. We are all inspired!"

"Thank you," Walter said, even as he told himself again that he must avoid traps. "Providing the Security Council action today saves the peace and lays the groundwork for reasonable UN discussion of the situation in Gorotoland, I shall be content."

"I think you may be assured that there will be ample discussion of the situation in Gorotoland." Tashikov gave his short, barking laugh. "Ample, Mr. Dobius! Ample!"

"I'm glad everything's funny over there," Lafe observed

from across the room where he was starting dessert in the company of Cullee, the French Ambassador, Raoul Barre, and the British Ambassador, Lord Claude Maudulayne. "I wonder who's doing what to whom?"

"I think," Raoul Barre said, "that Vasily is congratulating Walter on saving the world and Walter is congratulating Vasily on the same thing."

"With the assistance of France, as I understand it," Lord Maudulayne suggested. The French Ambassador nodded matter-of-factly.

"Certainly. My government feels it has no choice but to join the U.S.S.R. in this resolution of condemnation. We cannot possibly support the good Harley and his industrious colleague, Orrin, in their little enterprise. The risks are too great."

"And the possibility of assisting the United States too great," Cullee suggested dryly.

"And the possibility of hurting her too attractive," Lafe added.

Raoul Barre smiled and shrugged.

"You take it personally. You Americans always take it personally. It is quite impersonal, I assure you. My government simply does not agree with these tactics of pressure and invasion. Have we not a right to express ourselves?"

"No one challenges your right," Cullee said slowly. "It's just that in recent years it always seems to be expressed against us."

"Someone must argue for sanity," the French Ambassador said. "Someone must try to stand in the middle." Lord Maudulayne chuckled.

"And who better equipped, eh? Certainly not we, God knows, who find ourselves with no choice now but to support the United States."

"Would you not if you had the choice?" Lafe asked. "Just what would you do, Claude?"

"Absolutely what you are doing, I suspect," Lord Maudulayne said. "But with a little more feeling that it was our own idea, possibly."

"I don't think the President could have waited," Cullee said. "In a case like that I think the decisive act is worth any number of battles."

"You will get," Raoul predicted calmly, "any number of battles before this is finished, I think, my friend. May they all go as decisively as the opening act—though I think they may not. . . . I understand the United States intends to introduce an amendment to the French-Soviet resolution which would condemn Prince Obifumatta's government. You do not expect it to pass, of course."

"No," Lafe said with a glance that flicked across Cullee's for a second. "We do not expect it to pass."

"It will be vetoed," Raul said. "We can rely upon Vasily for that."

"But it will serve a purpose," Lord Maudulayne suggested, "as things in the UN do serve a purpose in these days of dissolution—the same purpose. Propaganda—headlines —attention to a problem, even though nothing comes of it —possibly a little delay before things rush on toward wherever they are going, in this odd world of ours. At least it will remind some of our friends in Africa and Asia that there is another side to this."

"There is no other side for most of them," Raoul said flatly. "Why pretend that they are sophisticated enough to be appealed to? Their minds are closed. If they needed further closing, the President's action has closed them. It is an exercise in nothing to try to appeal to them on this issue."

"Except for the historical record," Lord Maudulayne said thoughtfully. "It pays to make a record, even in these times when all records may be summarily destroyed by the blast of a bomb. Someday there may be a history to be read, of these times. If there is, it will be important to know how the United States came to take the action she has taken, and who it was who provoked her. And how my Government happened to associate itself with her, and the things we believed in."

"That is assuming that it will be people like us who are there to read the record," the French Ambassador said dryly. "I consider it rather unlikely."

"It will be unlikely if we don't stand together," Lord Maudulayne agreed. "Where stands France?"

Momentarily the French Ambassador looked genuinely annoyed. Then he spread his hands and shrugged.

"France stands where reason dictates." He smiled ironically. "It is not always comfortable, but it is intellectually satisfying."

"If you survive it," Lord Maudulayne said. "And, of course, in such excellent company"—he gestured in the direction of the Soviet Ambassador, grinning and rocking and making some obviously flattering comment to Walter Dobius—"there is no question that you will."

Raoul Barre shrugged again.

"To survive in these times one method may be as good as another. The frustrating thing about it is that one may not know for a hundred years if one has chosen the right course. And by then it will be much too late." He looked thoughtfully at Cullee Hamilton. "Much, much too late."

"Don't look at me," Cullee said. "I haven't any doubts about our course. If you doubt yours, that's too bad. But I'm not worried. It had to come sometime."

"If one accepts the premise that it 'had' to," Raoul agreed, "then perhaps this is best. Not all of us are that positive. In fact, nine-tenths are not."

"If France would stop fishing in troubled waters and stop trying to pick up adherents in Africa and Asia by playing the anti-American game," Lafe said calmly, "she might be positive about something—if she had a more positive purpose than mere mischief-making. But I suppose that's too much to ask of a power that has substituted spite for policy."

"That I resent," the French Ambassador said sharply. "That I do resent as an unwarranted attack upon my country."

"Sometimes the game gets real," Lafe said laconically. "I'm sorry if it hurts. Are you through, Cullee? I expect we ought to go down to the Delegates' Lounge and politick a little before Security Council begins. Coming, Claude?"

"Right-ho," Lord Maudulayne said.

"I shall go and speak to Walter," Raoul Barre said stiffly.

"Good luck with him," Cullee said, rising and turning away with scant courtesy. "He's on your side. . . ."

"I'm sorry we let ourselves become annoyed, Claude," Lafe said as they left the table and started for the Lounge, "but every once in a while I get fed up with that damned superior attitude which is nothing but a screen for trouble-making. It gets a little wearing now and then."

"Delusions of grandeur," Lord Maudulayne suggested with a smile. "The grandeur goes, but the delusions remain."

Yet this might have been a somewhat too-cavalier way

in which to dismiss the French Ambassador, who was angrily convinced, as he moved toward Walter Dobius through the bowing, greeting nations, that it was impossible to reason with colleagues so bent upon self-destruction as the Americans and the British. He did not mind an occasional slap at his country, certainly he contributed enough of them himself in the opposite direction. But he did resent the accusation that France had no other purpose than troublemaking. He was quite convinced that his government was following the only correct policy in joining the Soviet Union in sponsorship of the resolution demanding U.S. withdrawal from Gorotoland.

Only if American forces were withdrawn could the situation be restored to some semblance of normalcy so that negotiations could be undertaken to create a permanent stability and remove the threat of major war. France's position, he was convinced, was very practical. He could not always remain patient with the Americans, who were so impatient themselves. France wasn't siding with the U.S.S.R. all the way. France had a plan, if her friends would just be patient enough to let her achieve it. France always knew what she was doing. He found it hard at times to be properly tolerant of those who could not perceive it.

But here, at any rate, was one who did. His columns on many occasions had reflected his approval of France's busy anti-American activities—or, at least, if not approval, then a sympathetic understanding so perceptive of French motivations that Paris had justifiably taken it to be approval. Raoul Barre extended his hand cordially as the Soviet Ambassador half rose and gestured to a chair beside him.

"Walter," Raoul said, "it is good to see you. May I—?"

"Please do," Vasily Tashikov said. "I have been explaining to our friend the strategy that will be followed in the Security Council this afternoon."

"Does he approve?"

Walter nodded.

"I do," he said in his most judiciously contemplative voice. "While I could wish that certain details might be handled differently, still the basic purpose of removing the American forces so that stability may be restored to Gorotoland seems to me perfectly justified and indeed imperative if a full-scale war is to be avoided."

"So it seems to us," the French Ambassador said. "It is

good to know that we may expect further commentaries by you which will help your countrymen to understand why the decision of the Administration must be reversed at once."

"I shall certainly continue to write against it until it is reversed," Walter said. "And speak against it, too."

"Yes," Raoul said. "I have been pleased to receive from Patsy Labaiya an invitation to attend your banquet Friday night."

"I, too," said Tashikov. "It should be an interesting occasion."

"I hope to make it so," Walter said with a tight little smile. "There is much to talk about."

"Including, no doubt," the French Ambassador said, "some discussion of possible presidential candidates and how the present crisis will affect the coming campaign."

"It would appear to be a logical subject of comment," Walter said, his smile a little less humorless. "I intend to go into it."

"Why has Governor Jason not commented?" Raoul inquired. "I should think it would provide him with his opportunity."

"I really do not know," Walter confessed. "I'm puzzled, quite frankly. I haven't talked to him yet, as I've been assuming that at any moment the news would come. But so far—"

"Possibly he is going to support the President," the Soviet Ambassador suggested. "Stranger political things have happened, in your country."

"I don't see how he possibly can," Walter said. "It would be counter to everything he believes."

"I repeat," Tashikov said, "stranger things. . . . But perhaps in your speech Friday night you will be able to persuade him."

"I have no doubt whatsoever," Walter said firmly, "that long before Friday night he will have made his position clear. Events are moving too fast for him not to."

"Let us hope so," Tashikov said. "His support would be helpful."

"It also," Raoul Barre suggested, "might be decisive in helping him become President. In which case a more sane and responsible policy might be followed by the White House hereafter."

"If this ends in a week or two," Walter said slowly, "it

probably will not affect the campaign. If it drags, it will. If we are still involved six months from now, or even two months from now, the effect may be decisive."

"Then I would think the Governor would have no choice," Raoul said.

Walter smiled.

"If he hasn't gone on record by Friday night, I hope to make it clear to him in my speech that he has no choice."

"It is amazing, your influence in the United States," Vasily Tashikov said in an admiring tone, his eyes briefly meeting the French Ambassador's. "Absolutely amazing."

"And so deserved," Raoul Barre agreed smoothly. "It is of inestimable help in persuading the American people to support a sound and constructive policy."

"It is a *great* help in the fight for peace and justice everywhere," the Soviet Ambassador said solemnly.

"A major weapon in the cause of sane and rational international behavior," Raoul affirmed. "Indispensable!"

"Except," Walter said with a wry expression, "that sometimes in the White House, where it is most needed, it is totally ignored."

"But you have the last word, Walter," Raoul said soothingly. "You journalists always have the last word."

Walter Dobius looked solemn.

"I have devoted my working life to being worthy of the responsibility."

"And have succeeded brilliantly," Tashikov assured him.

"Thank you," Walter said gravely. "I do my best. . . . By the way," he said abruptly as the waitress brought the bill and they prepared to leave, "what do either of you hear about Felix Labaiya?"

It seemed to him that for a split second the Soviet Ambassador looked knowledgeable about something, but as quickly the expression vanished; and he could sense that Raoul Barre knew nothing. He said as much, in a puzzled tone.

"I do not know, except that he departed abruptly last night for Panama. I was not aware of any crisis down there. It seems odd, on the eve of the Security Council meeting, though I suppose his deputy will represent him."

"Nor do I know of any crisis down there," Walter said, "which is exactly why I wonder if perhaps there isn't one. What do you hear, Mr. Ambassador?"

But Vasily Tashikov was ready for him. He shrugged.

"The comings and goings of the Ambassador of Panama," he said with a bland smile, "are almost as unexpected and unexplainable as those of his wife, the surprising Patsy. I do not know. I am puzzled too."

They were still discussing the mystifying nature of Felix's sudden flight home when they caught up with the Indian Ambassador, and with him walked slowly along to the Delegates' Lounge, a-buzz as always with the greetings, gossip, and rumors that comprise 75 percent of the UN's business on any given day.

The subject of Felix was of interest in Washington, too, where, among all the other business of the onrushing crisis —the notification of the arrival of the first American ships off Tanzania, the landing of the first squadron of fighter-bombers in Leopoldville, the crash of a Marine transport on takeoff from Libya, with fifteen killed—(U.S. GOROTOLAND TRAGEDY, the afternoon newspapers cried with triumphant headlines and news stories that dwelt with loving attention on America's shortcomings. OWN PLANES CROWDED US, SURVIVOR SAYS)—the President still had time to check with the Secretary of State on what was going on in Panama. He received from him a puzzled but intuitive guess. Helen-Anne Carrew, equally intuitive, was at that same moment going right to the source.

"Patsy, love," she was saying as she leaned confidentially over Patsy's shoulder in the closing moments of the special luncheon the Women's National Press Club was giving for the First Lady at the Mayflower, "what's this I hear about your hubby dashing home? My sources tell me Panama may explode at any minute. Is it true?"

"Helen-*Anne*," Patsy began in an annoyed tone and then hastily modified it—"darling—I don't know WHERE you pick up all these silly rumors you peddle all the time. Really, I don't. I told Walter last night and I'll tell you today that Felix has gone to 'Suerte,' the family estate down there. I believe there's some problem with the workmen. His mother and grandmother are too old to tend to it, so he's gone home for a day or two. He'll be right back, for heaven's sake. What *is* everybody so worried about?"

"I didn't know anybody was, except Walter and me," Helen-Anne said, giving a dutifully cordial nod to the First

Lady, four seats beyond Patsy at the head table. She emitted her sardonic snort. "If we are, I can assure you the whole world soon will be. But if you say he'll be back, I suppose he'll be back."

"He WILL be back. Before you can even print it. So why bother?"

"I don't know," Helen-Anne said with a speculative look in her eyes. "I still heard something funny last night at the Indonesian Embassy."

"Indonesia!" Patsy said with a sniff. "What do they know about anything?"

"They're experts on Australia," Helen-Anne said with a wry chuckle. "You ought to hear them rave. Well, O.K., sweetie, if that's all you'll tell Auntie Helen, I guess it's all you'll tell her. Don't let Felix make a liar of you, now! I'd hate to have to drag the whole stinking mess into the open."

"Oh, Helen-Anne!" Patsy said as she turned back to the Ambassadress of Guinea on her left. "You do run on so."

"Maybe," Helen-Anne agreed. "But it usually adds up to something, sooner or later."

But what it would add up to this time, the small, neat, dark-haired, dark-visaged figure standing on the terrace at "Suerte" and gazing far down the valley between the mountains was not quite sure at the moment. Don Felix Labaiya-Sofra, oligarch of Panama, son of a President, his country's Ambassador to Washington and the United Nations, generator of many plans, focus of many discontents, had been home twelve hours, and out of them no clear picture as yet emerged.

To his mother and to ancient Dona Anna his grandmother, huddled away in their far corners of the rambling old *estancia*, he had said merely that he had felt it was time to check on the work of the estate now that spring was almost here. Dona Anna had received this with the inattention of age, his mother with a certain silent skepticism that annoyed him but which he did not feel he need expend the energy to combat. They had retired together to their rooms and, as far as he knew, had not been aware of the steady stream of visitors who had come furtively through the night from Panama City to the brooding acres at the foot of Chiriqui. Or if they had been aware they had not emerged to say so, and so he had felt free to proceed without reference to the nagging feeling at the back of his mind that of course they would not approve, could they know what he was undertaking.

That he should be undertaking it, finally, after so many years of preparation, of planning, of dissembling, and making do with half-best at the hands of the hated creators of his country, was, he believed, a tribute to his own ingenuity and skill in profiting from *Yanqui* mistakes. He had watched, with a semblance of tolerance but an inward contempt, while the blundering homeland of his wife and brother-in-law had staggered from one defeat to another down the slippery slopes of the later twentieth century. Six months ago the tempo had appeared to accelerate, when he had successfully steered through the United Nations and brought close to final victory the motion to censure the United States in the wake of Terence Ajkaje's visit to South Carolina and all its consequences in focusing world disapproval upon America's racial practices. Briefly the Americans had seemed to recover, there had been a lull. Then had come the rebellion in Gorotoland, the American intervention on the old-fashioned, no-longer-valid theory that missionaries should be protected, that a country's nationals should be safe on good behavior, that commercial rights granted by a legal government should be protected— and the Achilles' heel of America's persistent naïveté concerning the cold-blooded realities of a cold-blooded age was once again revealed.

It had seemed the opportune time to advance certain plans that first began at "Suerte" fifty years and more ago, in the time of his grandfather, Don Jorge.

He had sent word that he was coming home, and obediently, some from the professions, some from the university, some from the slums but quite a few, also, from the opulent homes where they suavely entertained the rulers of the Canal Zone, his friends had slipped away and come to him in the night.

Whether this was indeed the time, he did not know for sure, even though many of them told him so. He was close enough to America, both by marriage and from all the years he had spent there, so that he was not one to underestimate the United States, for all its fumblings and its often wide-eyed incompetence in world affairs. Its action in Gorotoland might furnish the ideal opportunity, but it also demonstrated that the Colossus was quite capable of moving, and moving fast, when it thought it had to. Therefore Felix hesitated, though in his final conversation before leaving the UN yesterday he had been assured that all was in readiness; had been reminded of the distance between Panama and Gorotoland; and had been urged to take the step that would, in his colleague's opinion, irrevocably commit the United States to a course it could not possibly pursue without disaster.

Felix was not so sure, nor was he so sure that he should move before his brother-in-law made his position known. Governor Jason was one of the few men Felix feared, both because of the economic pressures his companies could exert upon Panama, and because of something more personal, a brain as shrewd and cold as his, a personality as self-assured and forceful, the suspicion that in both these respects there might be more than equality. Felix was never sure how completely Ted Jason saw through him, nor was he certain what Ted Jason could do to thwart him if he really set his mind to it. And while he thought the Governor would oppose the move in Gorotoland and so, consistently, oppose any other move that might follow, he could not be sure. Ted wanted the White House in the worst way, and when men want that, consistency does not always apply. Ted had never granted Felix much consideration in his own right, and now that he and Patsy were in the midst of an uneasy separation teetering on the edge of divorce, Ted no longer need give him even minimal consideration as a brother-in-law.

Felix, too, belonged to the many who wished on this hectic morning that the Governor of California would declare himself. He might know then more certainly what he would do.

For the moment he expected to continue as he was, talking to friends, conferring with supporters, quietly making arrangements that he might, before long, decide to implement. There was no immediate hurry. Whatever happened would not happen for several days, and the necessity for concealing his activities imposed a certain slowness on him in any event. It was best that the owners of the Canal not be aware of the traffic to "Suerte." He was sure they did not even know he was home, and he intended to keep it so. His friends drifted in and out of Panama City casually, sometimes singly, sometimes in groups of two or three. There could be no open indication of where they were going, no alerting the hostile ones that Felix was home. He was certain he had concealed it from his friends in the North, and he was certain his presence was unknown to his enemies in the Canal Zone, who in any event were nervously involved in listening to radio and television, wondering what they would be called upon to do as a result of the President's action in Gorotoland and the consequences that might flow from it in the Security Council meeting this afternoon. They were too busy right now, he thought with a grim little smile, to worry about him.

So brooded Felix Labaiya, oligarch of Panama of the new style, generator of plans, focus of discontents, on the terrace at "Suerte," while along the valleys between the mountains his friends continued their furtive pilgrimages and in cities of power far away men who had the responsibility of being aware of such things noted that he was home, read secret reports on his visitors, and wondered, as they liked or feared him, how soon they would be called upon to come to his support, or root him out.

6

AROUND THE familiar green baize table of the Security Council where so many hopes have been born and so many hopes have died, in the room where the world's eyes watch the inheritors and assassins of the dream, they were gathering this afternoon at 3 P.M., as they had so many times before, to go through the charade of promise without redemption, potential without fulfillment. One thing only made it different from all the other times they had staged the same weary, foredoomed performance: the United States was involved today, and the United States could be counted upon to abide by the charade. Where others condemned the game and made it pointless by their intransigence, where others balked and refused to play, the United States went through the motions each time as though it really believed in what was going on. The United States could be relied upon to do the Right Thing, even if nobody else, any longer, felt impelled to do so, or even to pretend it. The United States was True Blue.

It gave them all a comfortable feeling of certainty as they came down the aisles and took their seats, gossiping and chattering and greeting one another with the accustomed cordiality of players who have joined together in the same foredoomed enterprise on many another furious but futile occasion. This was one of the rare times when it might not be futile, since the United States, bless it, would behave.

In the press section, where he was surrounded by the respectful attentions of his younger American colleagues, the flattering deference of his foreign colleagues, the obsequious greetings of the many delegates who turned to stare and smile and bow, Walter could see that his own country's representatives were already in their seats. So too were the British and French Ambassadors, the Ambassador of the Soviet Union, and the Secretary-General. The S.-G., he noted, looked even older and more frail than he had the last time Walter visited the UN, during the first Gorotoland crisis—Terry's crisis—six months ago. Obifumatta's crisis must be imposing a greater strain, and one the old man was less equipped to carry. There would be a strain on many before this was over, Walter thought grimly. Pray God it was not a strain from which the world would not recover.

Yet he was quite sure, so certain was he of what his country would do, that this meeting of the Security Council would mark the turning point. With some grumbling, but bowing to what it had known right along to be the correct procedure, the Administration would halt its invasion of Gorotoland and withdraw. The problem would then revert, as he had told Tashikov, to these halls where it could be discussed in a calmer and more sensible mood. Nothing would come of the discussion, of course, nothing would be achieved to prevent a recurrence somewhere else of the type of thing which had brought U.S. intervention, nothing would be done to stop the steady erosions of the world by Communism, the world's fabric would go right on unraveling. But at least there would be no war.

That was all that mattered, in his mind and in the minds of a majority of his world: not honor, not dignity, not decency, not integrity, not real stability, not real peace.

Just—no war.

And wasn't that enough? he demanded of his mind impatiently. Walter had no truck with those who argued that the condition of no-war was not automatically and by definition a condition of peace. He had only scorn for those who said that peace without honor, without justice, without firm and enforced agreements, without the real stability that could come only with integrity and honesty on both sides, was a butterfly that lasted no longer than the morning of the day the UN brought it forth from chrysalis. Walter brushed aside such negative arguments angrily, and so did Walter's world. They did not believe in pushing mankind's luck. It was all very well to insist that peace without safeguards and good faith on both sides was no peace at all. If everybody got blown up while people were insisting on safeguards and good faith, what good would that do them?

Walter had covered test shots at Bikini and White Sands, he had walked the ruins of Hiroshima and Nagasaki, he knew what the consequences could be if his stubborn nation insisted too much that international affairs should proceed on a basis of just principle and honored agreements. Perhaps the Communists were engaged in a campaign to conquer the world if they could, perhaps they really were dedicated to the death of the free world, including above all his own country, perhaps they never did do anything but inflame crisis and encourage chaos. If the alternative was threatening them with the bomb and perhaps using it —then, so what? In the first place, he could not conceive that the sensible peoples of the world would stand for it (even though quite a sizable number of them had disappeared into the Communist maw while they were busy telling each other it simply couldn't happen); and in the second place, even if worst came to worst and the Communists eventually did take the world—wouldn't that be better than having a war?

Walter thought so, and never had he thought so more firmly than he did at this moment, encouraged as he was by the deferential congratulations of colleagues who obviously agreed with him, lifted up by the respectful greetings of nations who clearly felt that his policies were infinitely more sensible than those of his government.

It was easy at such a moment for a man to feel that he

was bigger than his government. He was quite sure now, as he watched the last straggling delegates enter and Chile, this month's President of the Council, prepare to gavel the meeting into being, that events this afternoon would prove that, yes, he was.

"Mr. President," the Soviet Ambassador began quietly in his native tongue, while the translator gave his words a dutifully heavy emphasis through the earphones, "we are seized here today of a situation known to all the world. At an early hour this morning, using as a flimsy pretext an action by troops of the legitimate government of Gorotoland momentarily exceeding their orders ['Oh, that's what it was,' Lafe remarked to the British Ambassador beside him. 'Quite inadvertent,' Lord Maudulayne agreed], the Government of the United States has launched an unprovoked imperialist attack upon the legitimate government of Gorotoland led by His Royal Highness Prince Obifumatta. American planes, naval units, and land forces are now on their way to, or may even in some cases have actually entered, Gorotoland.

"The world is confronted, Mr. President, with a condition of war.

"A condition of war, Mr. President!" he repeated, his voice rising, his delivery beginning to get into the grand old ranting swing of it that had echoed through this room so many times from the lips of Soviet delegates. "Mr. President, I call your attention to this: a condition of war! War upon the freedom-loving, liberty-seeking peoples of an innocent nation, Mr. President! A war of neo-colonialist, imperialist aggression! War upon us all!

"Mr. President," he said, and his tone changed abruptly to one of heavy sarcasm, dutifully mimicked by the translator, "is there another pretext beside the one I have mentioned, for this attack? Why, yes, Mr. President, there is. The President of the United States tells us that he was 'invited' to send assistance, Mr. President. And by whom? By someone named Terry, Mr. President! By a worthless colonialist lackey named Terry, who cannot even command his own capital, Mr. President! By an international jackanapes who is even now lolling about in New York instead of heading his own troops in the field, Mr. President! An invitation from *this* is worth a war?"

A little titter of agreement ran through the room, and abruptly he halted and turned toward the American delegation with an elaborate irony.

"There will be some, Mr. President, who will say that this is a charitable venture, perhaps. Or perhaps scientific. Possibly they will say they meant to go to the moon and found themselves in Gorotoland instead." He nodded at the quick burst of laughter that came from the press section, the delegates, and the members of the staff and general public who had managed to squeeze into the overflowing chamber. "Well, Mr. President, we say to them this, that they will wish they were in the moon instead of Gorotoland once the world has passed its judgment upon them!"

There was a burst of applause and the President of the Council rapped his gavel impatiently for order. Tashikov concluded in a somber and portentous fashion.

"Mr. President, the resolution condemning the neo-colonialist imperialist aggression of the United States and ordering withdrawal of United States troops from Gorotoland is clear and simple. The conscience of the world demands it. The facts demand it. The conscience, I would estimate, of 90 percent of the American people themselves, demand it. [There was loud applause, but this time he ignored it and hurried on.]

"I urge the Council to adopt this resolution, so that the world may know that American imperialistic invasion of the continent of Africa is at an end. Otherwise, Mr. President—" and his voice sank to an ominous note and his little eyes behind their gold pince-nez snapped and sparkled with anger as he looked again at the American delegation —"no one can say what may happen to the world. My Government cannot be responsible. It will have to take appropriate measures, regardless of the consequences. Regardless, Mr. President!"

Again there was applause, interrupted by the President's gavel. Tashikov sat back, looking about him with a satisfied air, as across the circle Raoul Barre leaned forward thoughtfully around the table for a moment before he began to speak.

"Mr. President," he said gravely, "the Government of France has associated itself with the Government of the U.S.S.R. in sponsoring this resolution for one reason and one only: because we believe that only by re-establishing a condition of peace ['Was that what was there before we

came?' Cullee inquired, not too quietly, of Lafe. There
were a few hisses and the President of the Council gave
him an annoyed look and rapped sharply with his gavel.]
will it be possible to negotiate a reasonable settlement of
the difficulties in Gorotoland.

"My Government does not, of course, attribute to the
United States the motivations implicit in the language of
my colleague from the Soviet Union. Nonetheless, Mr.
President, I have to tell you that France is seriously
shocked and saddened by what appears to be a most irrational and irresponsible act. If I may quote America's most
distinguished journalist, Mr. Walter Dobius—" there was
applause, and several of Walter's colleagues pointed him
out to the audience. The applause became filled with an extra respect, an added warmth—"in his brilliant column this
morning, the action of the Administration in Washington is
'the triumph of idiocy over reason.' ['It must be nice,' Lafe
remarked to Claude Maudulayne, 'to hear yourself quoted
attacking your own country.' The British Ambassador
smiled but made no comment.] Mr. Dobius also refers to it
as, 'a purpose no decent man can defend . . . a hopeless
war far away at a time when the nation's domestic needs
are crying for solution.' He also says that the President 'has
committed his country to what amounts to a state of war in
the middle of Africa.' With these strictures, Mr. President,
my Government agrees."

He paused and took a swallow from a glass of water at
his elbow.

"It is imperative, Mr. President," he resumed soberly,
"that peace be restored in Gorotoland. Only if peace is restored can lasting stability follow. My Government, all
during the early hours of this morning, attempted to persuade the President of the United States to rescind his decision and order the withdrawal of American troops. The
President of the United States, Mr. President, refused to
accept the sage wisdom of the President of France. Therefore my Government had no choice but to associate itself
in this public condemnation and to urge the United Nations, representing the massed conscience of the world, to
order the withdrawal which amicable persuasion has been
unable to secure.

"France urges the Council to approve this resolution,
Mr. President. After its passage, which now seems certain"
—vigorous applause—"we hope the issue of Gorotoland

can be debated calmly and intelligently so that a lasting solution for its problems may be found."

He sat back with a polite smile at his American colleagues, both of whom bowed ironically. A little sound of amusement, turning quickly to annoyance, swept the audience. In the press section Walter could not refrain from shaking his head with a frown that was dutifully noted by all.

Lord Maudulayne raised his hand and leaned forward to his microphone.

"Mr. President, speaking as the delegate of one of the governments—one of the few governments, apparently—which will not support this resolution, the United Kingdom cannot agree with the premise put forward by the delegate of France nor the harsh condemnation uttered by the delegate of the Soviet Union. The United Kingdom may possibly regret some aspects of the American action, yet it cannot deny that the basis for that action was perfectly valid as the United States sees it."

There was a ripple of laughter, and his next words came sharply.

"This does not mean, Mr. President, that my Government does not see it the same way. We do. Our methods of dealing with it might have been different in some respects, but we would have dealt with it, Mr. President. Make no mistake of that. We would have dealt with it.

"The Government of the United States, and by association the Government of the United Kingdom, made amply clear to the rebel forces in Gorotoland that indiscriminate and irresponsible attacks upon innocent and defenseless people would be met with the severest reaction. Apparently this was not believed. The world now has the proof.

"My Government regrets, Mr. President, that things have come to this pass. But the solution is simple. The President of the United States has clearly stated that the American mission is pacification and stabilization, not retribution, and that once pacification and stabilization have been achieved, the United States will gladly withdraw. It was on that condition that the President accepted the invitation of the legitimate government headed by His Royal Highness Prince Terry [skeptical laughter, raucous, rude, welled up] to go in.

"Therefore, Mr. President, we need not fear the outcome. It does not mean war, nor will it mean war, if this

Council and the United Nations as a whole will refrain
from exacerbating still further, with this resolution, a situation already explosive and unhappy enough.

"Mr. President, Her Majesty's Government hope this
resolution will be defeated.

"I join my distinguished colleague the delegate of
France, in the hope that once it has been, and once the
American mission has been completed, this organization
may turn to the establishment of a genuine and lasting solution for the problems that beset Gorotoland."

"I certainly don't think that gained any ground," the
Post remarked scornfully to Walter in the press section. He
nodded.

"The British," he said heavily, "will let us carry them
down, yet."

"I suppose we'll speak next," the *Post* said. "What do
you suppose we'll do?"

"A counter-resolution in the form of an amendment
condemning Prince Obi."

"Oh, really?" the *Post* asked, as respectfully surprised as
though he hadn't heard the same thing himself, hours ago.
"Do you think it will pass?"

"Are you kidding?" Walter asked. A scornful smile
touched his mouth. "I don't see why we even bother to
speak."

But the chief American delegate must have considered it
worthwhile, for he leaned forward in his turn and placed
two huge hands quietly around the stem of his microphone.

"Mr. President," Cullee Hamilton said slowly, "I think
the true nature of the United Nations in this present era of
its decay ['Oh, *no!*' some visiting lady from Boston or Kansas City gasped in the audience. The President of the
Council rapped his gavel.] of its decay," Cullee repeated
calmly, "has never been better illustrated than in the comments of the Soviet delegate and the fact that they have
quite obviously been accepted as fact by most of those sitting around this table—and most of those in this audience
—and most, I am quite prepared to believe, in this world.

"What have we had here this morning, Mr. President?
We have had lying [Again there was a gasp, some mur-
murs, a little booing from the audience. He swung around

and surveyed it with a contemptuous look and then turned back.] lying, deliberate, cold-blooded, calculated, crude. And instead of everyone here rising up and crying *No!* like my friend in the audience a moment ago crying out at the truth, everyone accepts it blandly and calmly and puts the stamp of approval on it.

"Everyone, that is, except the United States and the United Kingdom and perhaps a very few others.

"The Soviet delegate says that the murder of American citizens and the attack on American property—or, rather, Mr. President, he doesn't say that at all. He doesn't admit it. He doesn't even name it. He doesn't even say it happened.

"This is the first lie.

"And we all know it's a lie.

"The Soviet delegate, however, has to acknowledge that something happened, so without saying what it was he talks vaguely of some undefined 'action' by 'troops momentarily exceeding their orders.'

"It was not an undefined 'action,' Mr. President, it was a specific action. It was not done by troops exceeding their orders, it was a cold-blooded, deliberate massacre of innocent people and a cold-blooded, deliberate destruction of property on the cold-blooded, deliberate orders of a cold-blooded, deliberate gang of Communist riff-raff masquerading as a quote legitimate unquote government.

"The pretense that it was done by troops 'momentarily exceeding their orders' is the second lie, Mr. President.

"The pretense that those orders were given by a quote legitimate unquote government which consists of Obifumatta and his Communist mercenary-volunteers is the third lie, Mr. President.

"And we all know they're lies."

"That's not very diplomatic language," the *Post* remarked with an ironic smile.

"Shocking!" Walter said gravely. "Absolutely shocking."

"The Soviet delegate," Cullee went on, "says that the United States has gone into Gorotoland on 'a flimsy pretext.' The deliberate murder of half a hundred Americans and the deliberate destruction of American property is not 'a flimsy pretext.'

"This is the fourth lie.

"And we all know it's a lie.

"The Soviet delegate says that the government of His Royal Highness Prince Terry, 137th M'Bulu of Mbuele in direct descent, is not the legitimate government of Gorotoland. It is legitimate by his birth, by its control of two-thirds of the country [skeptical laughter], and by the recognition of these United Nations scarcely six months ago, Mr. President.

"The UN did recognize this government and bring it into being six months ago, you know, Mr. President.

"We really did.

"To say that it is not the legitimate government of Gorotoland is the fifth lie.

"And we all know it's a lie.

"Lastly, Mr. President, we come to the great eternal everlasting lie of them all, and that is that the United States is a colonialist, imperialist power. The United States gave up its last colonial possession in the year 1946, Mr. President, when it granted independence to the Republic of the Philippines. Since that time the United States has not acquired a single piece of new territory, nor has it imposed its type of government on a single nation, nor has it engaged in any attempts to subvert and overthrow other governments. Neither has the United Kingdom, which is associated with us in the attempt to restore stability to Gorotoland.

"The world knows that the United States is not a colonialist, imperialist power, Mr. President.

"It *knows* this.

"But the Soviet delegate says this isn't true, and that we are an imperialist power.

"This is the sixth and final lie, Mr. President.

"And we all know it's a lie.

"But, Mr. President, observe this great United Nations. Here nobody shouts *NO!* at a lie, like my friend in the audience shouting *NO!* at the truth a while back. Here the lie is king, Mr. President. Here the lie is stated every day, in a thousand ways, on a thousand subjects; and from here it goes out, solemnly sanctified by whatever remains of the dignity of this body, across the world.

"There are no rules by which we can challenge lies before they are sanctified in our proceedings, Mr. President. We give them an implicit stamp of approval just by sitting here calmly and listening to them. A great many of us go further and give them approval with our votes.

"The United Nations is tailor-made for lies, Mr. President. The United Nations is the greatest mechanism for liars in the history of mankind. All liars have to do is open their mouths here and their lies become hallowed. Lie and ye shall be listened to—that is our rule, and the Soviet delegate has proved it once again.

"Because all of us at this table—and perhaps I should not speak for all of us in this room, Mr. President, or for others in the world beyond, because some are ignorant, some are naïve, and some are willfully self-blinded—but certainly all of us at this table, know what the facts are.

"There are no innocents in this house, Mr. President.

"We know.

"And yet most of us at this table are going to vote against the facts. And to justify ourselves we are going to pretend that lies are truth and that truth is a lie. And so King Lie will rule again.

"Mr. President," he said, in a quieter, more thoughtful tone, "the United States had contemplated introducing an amendment to this resolution seeking the condemnation and ouster of Obifumatta's Communist mercenaries. My Government has decided not to do so, but to let events develop—[he paused and all around the room there were puzzled glances, startled looks, questionings, and uncertainties, for this was not like the United States, which could always be counted upon to Play The Game]—and see what may occur," he finished softly, and sat back.

"Well, I'll be damned," the *Post* said. "That was a strange performance. And a strange conclusion."

"I think the whole Administration has gone mad," Walter said somberly. "I really do. I think that was an insane speech, utterly unfounded, utterly destructive of the United Nations, completely inexcusable in every way. There couldn't have been a more graceless or more inept way of preparing for the beating we're going to have to take. I just don't see why we did it. I just do not see!"

"Well, buddy," Lafe said, leaning comfortably against Cullee's shoulder and speaking in his ear as he stared around the buzzing audience, "I guess you told 'em. And more power to you. I thought it was a great speech."

"Quite pertinent," Claude Maudulayne agreed. "Not,

perhaps, quite diplomatic, but"—he smiled—"quite pertinent."

"I thought it was necessary to lay a little groundwork,"
Cullee said calmly.

"For an abstention?" Lord Maudulayne inquired quizzically. "Perhaps so."

Cullee gave him a steady sidelong glance.

"Perhaps not."

"Oh?" the British Ambassador said with a startled look.

"Shh," Lafe interrupted quickly. "Listen to Vasily. He's
going to climb the wall."

And so, for a moment, it seemed that the Soviet Ambassador would do. During Cullee's speech he had shuffled his
papers, bounced about in his seat, stared, squinted, puffed
out his cheeks, sucked them in, popped off his pince-nez,
put them back on, leaned forward, leaned back, spun about
to stare at the audience, spun back, grimaced at Raoul,
glared at Cullee, and generally given a superb performance
of a man about to explode, prevented from doing so only
by sheer strength of character. Now his, "Mr. President!"
cracked across the table like a whip.

"The distinguished delegate of the United States," he
said with a furious calm, "has done his best this morning to
destroy the United Nations. That is the purpose of his remarks. They were ostensibly an attack upon me, Mr. President, but the purpose is crystal clear. The United States,
speaking through this"—he hesitated and spat out the word
—"individual—is engaged upon a deliberate and blatant
attempt to destroy this organization.

"Why, Mr. President, I ask you, why? Again, the purpose is clear: because the United States wishes to embark
unhindered upon a course of imperialist conquest throughout the world. Today it strikes in Africa. Tomorrow it may
strike in Asia. Next day, who knows, it may be in Europe.
Or it may be Latin America, where democratic freedom-
loving peoples have long had cause to fear American
designs.

"Yes, Mr. President, that is what we are seeing here today: the start of the formal United States campaign to destroy the United Nations so that the United States may
launch its long-prepared plan for world conquest!

"I warn delegates, Mr. President," he said with an ominous note in his voice, "and I warn the world: beware

America! Condemn her and stop her *now*—or suffer! Do
not let her do this thing in Gorotoland! Do not let her destroy the United Nations! Help humanity, I beg of you!
Help poor defenseless humanity, terrorized by this giant
about to break out of control! Stop her, Mr. President!
Stop her now!"

"Next week," Lafe murmured, "East Lynne." But in the
press section Walter Dobius said to himself, That's right.
He's right! That's it. That's what we are doing. Oh, you
damned, damned fools, how could you!

And through his mind like spears of flame there stabbed
the words and phrases for Thursday's column, and a plan
for the evening, born of a desperate conviction and an urgent fear, began to take shape.

Cullee again leaned forward to the microphone.

"Mr. President," he said quietly, "the Soviet delegate is
hysterical. He speaks like a child or a fool. No power on
earth has given more money, more time, more patience, or
more support to the United Nations. No power on earth
has been more dedicated to helping it succeed. But we can
only do so much, Mr. President. We have hoped that there
would be an equal dedication elsewhere, and there has not.
But to say that to be honest about its weaknesses is to destroy it, Mr. President, is an appalling statement.

"If to be honest about it is to destroy it, then it is destroyed already.

"Surely that is clear enough.

"No, Mr. President. The magnificent vituperation of the
Soviet delegate, which we have all had so many opportunities to hear, does not change the facts. The facts are that
United States citizens have been cruelly and deliberately
massacred, and that American property has been cold-
bloodedly and deliberately destroyed, and that under this
calculated provocation the United States has responded in
the only way that national safety and honor would permit.

"These are the facts that concern this Council this afternoon, not fantasies of the Soviet delegate. My Government
suggests we get on with the business of the day and stop indulging in nonsense."

"But it has hurt you, you know," Lord Maudulayne
murmured as Cullee sat back. "It has hurt very much."

"I didn't think it would be an unhurtful day," Cullee said shortly, but he nodded.

"Mr. President," Raoul Barre said blandly into the seething silence, "I move that the Council vote."

"If there are no objections," the President of the Council said, and there were none. In the press section Walter leaned forward intently. Never, he thought, had his country been more ineptly managed or more fatally misguided than it was now by Harley M. Hudson and Orrin Knox.

"The draft resolution, as the Council knows," the president said into the suddenly tense and silent room, "states the sense of the Council that the United States invasion of Gorotoland, launched at an early hour this morning, is a threat to peace and counter to the best interests of the United Nations and the welfare of mankind. It calls upon the United States to withdraw its forces immediately from Gorotoland and submit the dispute to the United Nations for negotiation. If there are no amendments"—he said in a puzzled voice, but it was obvious that there would be none—"the Secretary-General will call the roll. The voting will begin with Ceylon."

"Ceylon," the Secretary-General said.

"Yes," said Ceylon, to a rush of applause.

"Chad."

"*Oui.*"

"Chile."

"*Abstención*"—and there were hisses and boos.

"China."

"Abstention"—and there were more.

"Cuba."

"*Sí.*"

"Czechoslovakia."

"Yes."

"Dahomey."

"*Oui.*"

"France."

"*Oui.*"

"India."

"Yes," said Krishna Khaleel with a righteous air.

"Panama."

"*Sí,*" said Felix Labaiya's nervous little second-in-command.

"Uganda."

"Yes."

"Union of Soviet Socialist Republics."

"Da!" said Vasily Tashikov with an air of triumph.

"United Kingdom."

"Abstention," said Lord Maudulayne calmly, and some of the tension in the room lessened.

"United States."

"The United States abstains," Cullee said, and there was an approving further relaxation around the table and around the room. The world could always count on the United States, and thank God for that. It would be too awful if it couldn't.

"Venezuela," said the Secretary-General.

"Sí," said Venezuela.

"On this vote," the President of the Council said, "there are 11 Ayes, four abstentions. Therefore the resolution—"

But the chief United States delegate was leaning forward again, and suddenly the tension in the room increased a hundredfold. Oh, *no,* Walter shouted inside his mind. Oh, *no,* we're *not*—

"Mr. President," Cullee said, quietly but with a noticeable tremor, for this was indeed an eventful thing, "the United States abstained only on the order of voting. It does not abstain on the vote.

"The United States, Mr. President, votes No."

"My *God!*" the *Post* cried as the room exploded in a roar of excited sound. "My God, we've done it!"

"We haven't done it," Walter shouted back bitterly. "Those fools in Washington have done it! For the first time," he added more quietly, in a desolate voice as though he might cry. "For the very first time."

But not the last. When the Soviet and French Ambassadors, confronted with the death of their resolution on the first American veto in history, proposed a substitute motion to send the entire dispute to the General Assembly, Senator Smith leaned forward ("Might as well let me share the mud with you," he suggested with a grim little smile) and said quietly, "On this vote, too, Mr. President, the United States votes No."

And once again the room—and very shortly thereafter the world—exploded.

7

Now IT HAD happened, the event so monstrous that nobody could ever conceive that it would: the United States had actually defended itself with the veto. The fabric of society was ripped indeed, the globe was all awry: horrid things were seen in the streets, graves yawned and geese did fly in the Forum. From all the nations a fearful yawp went up.

The whole world went *"Waaah!"*

Loudest of all, of course, was the *"Waaah!"* from the United States itself.

U.S. DEFIES UN, CASTS FIRST VETOES; FLAUNTS WORLD OPINION IN GOROTOLAND, the New York *Times* roared with stern disapproval; NATIONS CONDEMN U.S. "IRRESPONSIBILITY"; NUCLEAR WAR NEAR.

"On this day," the moderator of the hastily organized CBS special, "Doomsday in the UN," said somberly at 9 P.M., "the United States Government took the step which may end forever mankind's hopes of lasting peace." One political scientist, two historians, Herbert Jason, and a former chief American delegate to the UN nodded agreement with a prim and solemn air, and were off on an hour of quivering attack upon the President and the Secretary of State.

From LeGage Shelby of DEFY, Senator Fred Van Ackerman of COMFORT, and Knight Kommander Rufus Kleinfert of KEEP came violent denunciations strikingly parallel in word and emphasis. In New York the organizers of the HANDS OFF GOROTOLAND ad hastily rewrote their copy to carry the heading STOP MURDERING THE UN, MR. PRESIDENT! An anguished cry came from the president and executive board of the American Association for the United Nations, an equally wounded wail from the National Council of Churches. One vast bleat arose from a thousand frantic newspapers, a thousand radio and television programs. At the Cape, Clete O'Donnell's "One Big Union," in company with several others in major defense installations, prepared for a protest strike. Ministers big and little readied their sermons. Across the nation teachers quivered, students shook: at a hundred campuses tomorrow, school would not be kept. Poets, prelates, and professors returned White House invitations right and left, their primly pompous announcements of discourtesy carried to the reaches of the globe with an eager encouragement by Walter and his friends.

On the continents and over the seas, the world kept pace. In Moscow they bellowed, in Peking they shrieked, in London they managed to be both dignified and aghast, in Paris they spat out disdainful words. Here a U. S. Embassy made a perfect target, there a U. S. Information library gave off a lovely light. In India they rioted. In Rome they ran in the streets. In Africa and Asia, U.S. nationals were hounded to their homes and several were killed. In Latin America nine capitals trembled with anti-American demonstrations. "It is a truly fearful thing," said Britain's oldest, most doddering, most pathetic peer, who had never been moved to comment by more than two hundred Soviet vetoes in the past, "when America decides to destroy the one chance humanity has to escape instant death and eternal damnation."

And everywhere, on every continent, in every land—

Everyone who had access to a microphone spoke.

Everyone who had access to newsprint wrote.

The United States, the world and all, went *"Waaah!"* indeed.

At the storm center, all, apparently, was calm despite the diligent and desperate efforts of the press to stir it up. To a clamoring White House press corps shouting angry questions in an office jammed to overflowing, the President's press secretary kept patiently reiterating one sentence: "The President has retired and will have no comment tonight."

"Will he have one tomorrow?" someone shouted.

"I don't know," the press secretary said.

"Or ever, the old jackass?" somebody else murmured loudly, and there was a burst of approving laughter.

"I repeat," the press secretary said, flushed and harassed but standing his ground, "the President has retired and will have no comment tonight. Now why don't you all be reasonable and go on home."

"We don't know our homes are still there," someone responded bitterly, and with many noisy murmurings and mutterings they withdrew, though not, at first, to go home. For quite a long time, most of them remained milling about in the lobby of the west wing of the White House, condemning in cleverly bitter frustration the man they could not reach.

Nor could they reach the other principals, as it developed. Both the State and Defense Departments refused to put through calls to their respective Secretaries, and all their press officers remained as unresponsive as the President's. Not even Lafe Smith and Cullee Hamilton could be found when the New York press sought to close in upon them for comment. Lafe had called "Oak Lawn," the sanitarium up the Hudson where Hal Fry's son lived, and arranged to get a visitor's room for the night, telling them he wanted to see the boy in the morning, knowing he would never be found there. Cullee had slipped away in the wild confusion as the Council session ended, run quickly downstairs, and disappeared in the night crowds of Manhattan. Now he and Sarah Johnson, unknown and unnoticed, were eating a late dinner in the Village; he thought he would probably stay at her place for the night. Tashikov, Raoul Barre, and any one of a hundred other delegates were eagerly commenting whenever the press gave them a chance (Lord Maudulayne was politely tight-lipped, but this was considered characteristic and no one complained), but it was the Americans the press wanted. The Americans were not to be found.

In his quiet room on the seventeenth floor of the Waldorf-Astoria, Walter wrote. He had only an hour and a half before the meeting he was certain would decide the fate of the Administration, the presidential election, Gorotoland, and many other things. The phrases flew, on the wings of a righteous conviction and a terrible indignation.

"Insanity compounds insanity. Stupidity piles upon stupidity. History's greatest irresponsibility sends the United Nations hurtling into the discard and the world hurtling ever faster into war.

"Yesterday, one could say, 'God help the United States.'

"Today, one doubts that He would dare.

"Never has an action less honorable and more destructive of everything mankind holds dear been undertaken by America—and this under the leadership of an Administration that says it values honor.

"It knows the word.

"It does not know the meaning.

"There is no honor here. There is only the awful, stark face of terror and universal destruction, implacable, inexorable, deaf to all reason, locked away from all appeal.

"And to think it is the United States which has done this thing!

"For shame, for shame.

"Now the United Nations, the shield and protector to which civilized mankind has turned for decades as the hope and guarantee of peace, is made an empty shell. Now the stout defender of a stable world society, the brave and kindly Godfather of Nations under whose helping hand half a hundred newborn states have come to being, is no more. Now the bright torch that was lighted in San Francisco flickers out, plunged into darkness by the one power above all that should keep it alight.

"Vetoes, it is true, there have been in the past. But what, essentially, have they been? Procedural matters, minor items, understandable and perhaps even justifiable acts by the Soviet Government, which has rightly concluded on far too many occasions that the West was combining against it. In self-defense it has exercised the right granted in the Charter. But never, it seems safe to say, has it done so in quite the cold-blooded fashion, or with quite the dreadful consequences, as the United States has done in this fateful and fearful hour for mankind.

"For this is no minor or procedural matter here. This is nothing that can be justified or understood by the decent tenets of decent men, who everywhere today stand aghast before this dreadful deed. This is the wanton act of a wanton Administration, deliberately throwing onto history's slag-heap all the patient work of decades that has slowly but steadily strengthened the United Nations until it has become—until Tuesday afternoon—the bright beacon and brave hope of all the world.

"What is humanity to say of the nation which has thus ruthlessly extinguished the world's dream of peace? What is it to say of the little men wielding great power who have used it in so black-hearted a way to defy the hopes and aspirations of Earth?

"Of the nation it may say: misguided, mismanaged, misled.

"But of the men it should say: blind, bigoted, beyond excuse and beyond redemption.

"And to them it should say:

"Go, Harley Hudson.

"Go, Orrin Knox.

"Go, all ye of little faith and little courage who applaud their deed.

"Leave the stage of history, wet with the blood of the hope you have destroyed!

"Begone and let us rest, in the pain and agony into which you have thrown us!

"You have done enough.

"Not all the cabals of hell could manage more."

And that, he told himself grimly, as he ripped the sheet from his typewriter and prepared to call the syndicate and dictate it for release Thursday morning, was no more than God's own truth.

For the first time in his life he was ashamed to be an American.

"Look, lover-boy," Helen-Anne Carrew was saying sharply at the same moment to the White House press secretary, who congratulated himself that she was arguing with him from the Kennedy-Warren and not from the other side of his desk, "you tell him this is little Helen-Anne calling, and you tell him that I'm *not* interested in anything about the vetoes. You tell him I think the vetoes are great, I'm all for them, and I'm going to say so in my column tomorrow. So I'm not calling to bother him about that. But you tell him I've got to talk to him, because it's very important. Now, damn it, stop stalling and put me through."

"Helen-Anne," the press secretary said patiently, "don't you realize he isn't talking to anybody? There are three hundred press people outside here, all as mad as you are. What makes you think you're different?"

"He'll talk to me if you tell him it's urgent. And I haven't got all night to argue with you, dear. Really I haven't."

"I'm a little busy myself," the press secretary said with a

pardonable asperity. "They're calling in here from as far away as New Zealand, you know. You're lucky to get through even to me, sweetie pie. Now why don't you go to bed and be a good girl?"

"Who wants to be a good girl in bed?" Helen-Anne demanded, and gave her ribald hoot. "I grant you I usually am, but it isn't for lack of trying. Now look, lover. Let's stop the chitchat and put me through, O.K.? You tell him it's something about Panama I picked up at the Italian Embassy tonight. I thought he ought to know it, that's all. Damn it, is that too much to ask?"

"Well—" the press secretary said. He sighed. "Christ, why did they ever let women into this profession?"

"Thank your stars they did," Helen-Anne told him. "You men would be an even lazier bunch of slobs than you are already if we weren't around to keep you on your toes. Ask the man to talk to me now, O.K.?"

"Hang on," the press secretary said in a tired tone. "I'll try."

"Good evening, dear," the President said a moment later in an amused tone. "I hear you've been giving Jack a hard time. Are you sure it's all that important? Have you really heard something about Panama?"

"Probably no more than you have," she said, "but I thought you ought to know."

"Tell me," he said; and after she had, "Yes, that's interesting and a somewhat different angle from what we've already received here. Now what did you really call me about?"

"Walter," she said promptly. "I'm worried as hell about this tack he's taking. I think he's going through the male climacteric and it's driven him crazy. I've never known him to be quite this unrestrained before. I have a feeling it's going to get worse."

"Yes," the President said soberly, "I suppose it is. I didn't think, after I read his column this morning and his statement at the UN, that he had any invective left, but I imagine after the vetoes he'll be inspired to new heights. Of course he's not alone. He's leading a righteous army." His tone lightened but not too much. "I may be shot down at the East Gate of the White House tomorrow morning, you know, if I venture out."

"I'll be there to defend you," Helen-Anne promised. "I like the vetoes. I think you've done exactly the right thing.

And don't you fall for the theory that Walter runs the country. He doesn't. Plenty of people disagree."

"I know," the President said with a rueful little laugh. "But they aren't the ones who have the newspapers and the networks and the magazines. Those are the ones who agree with Walter, and I'm afraid they're making so much noise we can't hear anyone else. In fact, I hate to say it about a noble profession, but on the basis of past performance I rather suspect they aren't going to *let* us hear anyone else. What do you think?"

"Oh, they will," Helen-Anne said dryly. "On page 37, with the worst photographs they can find. Except for you and Orrin. You can always get page 1 and all the networks. And that, if I may advise, is what you'd better do, Mr. President. And fast."

"I expect to have a few things to say as the days go by," the President assured her. "I'm only lying low tonight. Incidentally, I trust you're not writing any of this down and that it's all going to be forgotten the minute you hang up, right?"

"Yes, Mr. President. It won't be forgotten but it won't be written. I am going to come out strong for what you've done. I may not be the female counterpart of America's leading philosopher-statesman, but I have a few million circulation, myself."

"Have you talked to the Knoxes?" the President inquired. His tone became humorous again. "I haven't dared call. I'm sure Walter and his friends have all the wires tapped."

"Oh, yes. I got through there, too. It took a little doing, but—"

"Helen-Anne," he said, "you're the miracle woman of the Washington press. The President and the Secretary of State put an absolute lid on calls, and Our Girl comes through. Sensational!"

"I just figured that along about now you'd both be getting curious about the outside world and so you'd be ready to talk to someone. And who better than Helen-Anne?"

"You're pretty shrewd," the President said. She laughed. "Some of my friends use other adjectives. Anyway, the Knoxes are fine. Orrin wants to blast Walter from here to Timbuktu, but Beth and I managed to hold him down. . . . I *am* worried about Walter," she said with a sudden reversion to more somber concern. "If he wants to destroy himself, let him do it, but he shouldn't be writing such wild things about his own country at a time like this."

"I think we've shattered something, in Walter and his friends," the President said thoughtfully. "I think that for thirty years and more they've lived by a certain rigid pattern of beliefs by which they've judged everything, and into which everything has been made to fit whether it really did or not. The basic premise of it was that the United States would never—really—do anything out of the pattern to protect its own interests. It was all right for us to make protests, and occasionally have a little friction somewhere with the other side, maybe even, now and then, engage in a little military action—but the key word was 'little,' and nobody in Walter's world contemplated anything big because they all convinced themselves years ago that anything big would automatically mean the end of the world. And now suddenly under my Administration the United States has burst out of the pattern and violently disarranged all the beliefs they've clung to all these years. It's no wonder they're hysterical. I probably would be, too. Which doesn't, of course, make it easier to take their hysteria, just because I understand it. . . . You're calling around, this evening, reaching people other people can't reach. Why don't you call him? He's at the Waldorf-Astoria."

"Have you tried to reach him, Mr. President?"

"No," he said slowly. "I've thought about it, but I doubt if it would do any good at the moment. Anyway, he's made it virtually impossible for us to communicate, with what he's written. It'll be a while before we talk again, I imagine."

"What do you want me to tell him?"

"You might give him a warning."

"Oh?" And instantly, though she was on his side, he could sense the instinctive reaction of the press to anything that smacked of coercion.

"Relax, Helen-Anne. I'm not going to censor anybody. Walter's very conscious of history, though—or at least, he's always writing about it. You might tell him that just possibly, when this is long over and he and I and you and Orrin and Terry and Obifumatta and even Vasily Tashikov are rotting in our graves, history may say that he made the wrong judgment and wrote the wrong things in an hour when his country needed all the help she could get from her leading people. You might just tell him that history may say he was wrong."

She made a skeptical sound.

"He'll just come back and say that history may say that *you're* wrong."

"I know," the President said. "I'm prepared for that. But I don't think Walter's prepared that it might say he's wrong. I think he ought to be. It might make him a better man."

"I don't know that he'll talk to me. I don't know that I can stand to talk to him, right now. But I'll try."

"Good girl. And thanks for calling me. He worries both of us. I'm not afraid of Walter, and certainly Orrin isn't either, but he's a problem. There's no doubt of that."

"I still think you'd better grab page 1 in one hand and the networks in the other, and stay there."

"I don't intend to be idle," he said comfortably. "You needn't worry."

"I'm not worried, exactly. Just scared as hell."

"Aren't we all," he agreed. "But that doesn't stop life from pushing us forward. It just means we've got to hang on tighter."

"Well," she said. "Good luck on the curves, Mr. President."

He laughed.

"Thank you. I'll need it."

She reached Walter half an hour later when he finished dictating his column. He was cold and adamant and unimpressed by the possible uncertainties of history. As the President had foreseen, he was unable to conceive that it could ever betray him. His words concerning the Chief Executive were unrestrained and filled with a violence she had never known him to use. Their talk was short, sharp, bitter. It ended when she told him he was a damned fool and slammed down the receiver.

Freed of that annoyance, and after giving himself ten minutes to still the chaotic anger that she could always arouse in his mind and heart, he picked up the telephone again and called Sacramento. The Governor, too, was playing hard to get, and it was only after several minutes, with an obvious reluctance, that he came on the wire.

"Yes, Walter," he said crisply. "I'm a little busy—"

"You aren't too busy to talk to me," Walter said calmly, his voice at its heaviest and most pompous. "Why hasn't the country heard from you?"

"Because I haven't desired to speak," Ted Jason said coldly.

"I think you should," Walter said, unimpressed, because this was a man who needed his help to win the White House and they both knew it.

Ted laughed without humor.

"Many people think I should."

"Why haven't you? Surely you aren't afraid?"

"You're being very offensive tonight, Walter. What's the matter?"

"Don't change the subject," Walter said calmly. "The country has a perfect right to know what you think."

"You won't believe it, but I honestly am not sure right now what I think."

"Even with the vetoes?"

"Even with the vetoes. The world hasn't ended with the vetoes, though I gather you think so."

"It's closer than it ever has been in my lifetime," Walter said somberly.

"I grant your sincerity in thinking so," the Governor said, "but I don't know. Maybe I would have vetoed myself, under the circumstances."

"How long do you expect to take to make up your mind?"

There was silence in Sacramento.

"What have you got to offer," Ted Jason asked, biting off each word, "to convince me that I should?"

"I'll tell you what I have to offer," Walter said, and did. There was another silence.

"How do I know they'll go along with you?" the Governor asked.

"They usually do," Walter Dobius said. "Certainly they won't if I tell them we've got a weak-willed candidate who can't make up his mind to take the only stand the conscience of mankind will permit."

"I cannot tell you yet," the Governor said calmly, "when I shall make my statement. Nor can I tell you what it will be."

"You think we have nowhere else to go," Walter said coldly, a statement, not a question.

"I know you have nowhere else to go," Ted Jason said with an equal coldness. "And so do you."

This time there was a silence in New York.

"I must be able to tell them that you will speak out by Friday," Walter said. There was a silence, somewhat shorter, in Sacramento.

"Very well. That, perhaps, is fair enough."

"This is an unequivocal promise?"

"It is an unequivocal promise."

"Then I think that we can proceed with confidence."

"I hope so," Governor Jason said politely. "Good night, Walter."

"Good night," Walter said, thinking, By Friday you won't be able to go in any direction but the one we want you to, friend.

In his office in mid-Manhattan the executive chairman of The (the capital "T" was very important) Greatest Publication That Absolutely Ever Was thought with a tired sigh that while he was as concerned as anyone about Gorotoland and the nation's future, he did rather wish that America's greatest columnist had not chosen tonight to have a conference about it. He also wished that Walter had not appealed to him to allow it to be held in the G.P.'s executive dining room. In a sense this would put the G.P. in a somewhat partisan position, and a partisan position was what the G.P. never wished to admit it was in, except for those two weeks prior to every Presidential election when it had finally condescended to tell a waiting Republic how to vote and was doing its best to secure the Republic's compliance. For the rest, the G.P. preferred to sit serene upon its particular Olympus, frequently pouring hot coals upon the heads of those below of whom it disapproved, but disguising these attacks as fair, objective news stories which permitted it to cling tenaciously to its non-partisan mantle.

Also, if truth were known, the executive chairman rather resented Walter taking it upon himself to call a conference at all. The G.P. prided itself on setting the tone and calling the tune for the nation's press (its top stories and columns syndicated across the land, its front-page makeup carefully studied by several hundred lesser editors anxious to learn what was Really Important so that they might humbly feature it in their own pages), and it was not about to admit that Walter Dobius had more influence than it did. Actually he had, since the G.P. was to be found following his lead on things far more than he repaid the compliment. But it was one of the basic tenets of the G.P. that no one surpassed it in independence and vigor of thought (were not its anti-Terry, pro-Obifumatta dispatches from Gorotoland sufficient proof of this?) and it acknowledged the leadership of no one. Of course it hurried to hail Walter suitably on state occasions—each new prize elicited a long, flattering front-page story; a special five-page insert full of quotes and columns was being prepared for his twenty-fifth anniversary this Friday—but no one in authority liked to admit that he exercised the influence he did upon its editorial deliberations and ultimate product.

There was also a more modest, more personal reason why the executive chairman resented Walter's intrusion at this particular moment. Down below in the enormous city room, at the interminable typewriters, across the endless copy desks, in the ceaseless editorial conferences, the final editions of the G.P. were at this moment being put together by all its devoted workers great and small. From time to time the executive chairman liked to wander through this solemn process (rather akin, in its attention to detail and general reverence of approach, to the weaving of some great tapestry in a medieval cathedral) and show himself to those who labored to advance the work.

He would chat for a while with some editor, sub-editor, or possibly sub-sub-editor; pass a word or two with some busy reporter, perhaps exchange amiable persiflage with the large group of idle ones that always seemed to be playing bridge or poker down the block at the other end of the city room; and generally make the contribution to morale that his kindly, generous personality always seemed able to give. For he was liked, he told himself with a frequent wistfulness, even if he didn't always know exactly what was going on; even if, at times, he felt that the G.P. was taking stands too harshly intolerant, printing stories too obviously slanted, publishing headlines that clearly placed it on just one side of the great issues that gnawed the vitals of the world.

Once in a while he would express himself in a gently concerned fashion about this, but always some bright young man was instantly at his elbow to soothe away his worries with some politely deferential, glibly rational explanation. So The Greatest Publication That Absolutely Ever Was sailed on: far from objective, but—since it told the country and the world that it was, and was from long habit believed—an institution haloed and sainted in the land.

And now here was Walter with a meeting, and the executive chairman couldn't go down to the city room tonight. The first edition was already gone, with its thundering headlines on the vetoes and Gorotoland, and he had been advised that the later editions would carry much more on the rapidly growing crisis. There would be the EUROPEAN OPINION CONDEMNS U.S. stories, based on quotes from thirty-seven anti-American newspapers and five pro-; the LATIN AMERICA FEARFUL and ASIANS AND AFRICANS UNITED IN OPPOSING U.S. AGGRESSION stories, with their comments from every possible critical source who could be contacted in a hasty two hours of telephoning, interviewing, and cabling; the first pictures from Gorotoland—REBEL WOMAN MOURNS DEATH OF THREE CHILDREN IN SKIRMISH; TRAGIC LOSS BRINGS BITTER "WHY?"— WAR IS HELL FOR REBEL SOLDIER CAPTURED, BEATEN BY TERRY FORCES—and other similar items designed to give a factual and well-balanced picture of how the affairs of America stood tonight.

The executive chairman would have liked to see this, to have uttered, perhaps, a wistful question or two—"Aren't there more people friendly to America who might have been interviewed?" Or, "Wouldn't it have been possible to get a little better balance in these quotes?" Or, "Aren't there any non-rebel women who lose children in the fighting, too?" And, "Isn't war hell for non-rebel soldiers, too, when they get captured by the rebels?"

Not that it would have done any good, of course.

Still, it would have made him feel better to ask.

But, of course, no chance now. Here was Walter. And looking like a storm cloud, too.

"Walter," he said with a kindly smile, "do sit down and stop worrying. The others will be here in a few minutes, I expect. Did you have any trouble reaching anyone?"

"A couple were at banquets," Walter said, "and the head of Newsweek was in Philadelphia. But he's flying back."

"Good," the executive chairman of the G.P. said comfortably. "Then it should be an interesting discussion. Before they come, and just between you and me, Walter—because I think this publication has a right to know, don't you, considering who we are?—what, essentially, do you hope to accomplish tonight?"

"A consensus on the Presidency," Walter said promptly. "I think we already have a consensus on Gorotoland, do we not?"

"I don't know about *Time* and *Life*," the executive chairman said thoughtfully, "or possibly the UPI and ABC. But I would say that *Look*—the AP—CBS, NBC—*Newsweek*—the *Post*—ourselves—are pretty well agreed. Perhaps you can convince the others, too. Your column this morning was certainly a powerful argument."

"The one I've just written is, too."

"You seem very convinced that the Administration has committed a nearly fatal act, I gather."

Walter stared at him.

"Aren't you people? Your editorial this morning wasn't so friendly, was it?"

"Nor is tomorrow's," the executive chairman agreed. "We have not gone quite as far as you in the language we've used, but I suppose that essentially we're just as strongly opposed."

"Your headlines and the newsplay you're giving it indicate as much," Walter said. "You really don't have to say much in your editorials. With your position in the country, you can do the bulk of it in the way you present and emphasize the news."

"Your position is effective too, Walter. I think you have already had, and will continue to have, a great influence as events develop."

"I certainly intend to," Walter said calmly. "And so, of course, do all of us who will be here tonight. We all do have. When we all agree," he said with a trace of smugness that was entirely justified, "I don't think there's a man or an issue in America that can stand against us. Do you?"

"No," the executive chairman of The Greatest Publication That Absolutely Ever Was agreed thoughtfully. "I don't suppose there is. Does it ever concern you?"

"Me?" Walter said blankly. "Why should it? I've worked hard to get where I am; I do a conscientious job of discharging my responsibility to the country; I believe I am by now better informed than almost anyone else in the country; and I feel a profound obligation to guide, to warn, to lead, to oppose, as in my judgment seems best. If by 'concern' you mean do I have any fears or hesitations about stating my honest convictions to my countrymen, the answer is No. Do you?"

"If I do," the executive chairman of The Greatest Publication said with the slightest hint of a dry little smile, "I expect I am alone in this building. . . . Well, then: you think Ted Jason is the man, eh?"

"He's inevitable," Walter said flatly. "Who else is there?"

"The President and the Secretary of State."

"But the crisis and the vetoes have removed them. Surely that's obvious."

"It may be obvious to us," the executive chairman said, "but I'm not sure just yet that it is to the country."

"Then it's our responsibility—all of us who will be here tonight, not just me—to make it obvious to the country. We can do it. We've done it before."

"That is true," the executive chairman said gravely. "We have indeed done it before."

"There will be—what?" Walter said thoughtfully. "Ten or fifteen men, at the most, in this room tonight, controlling publications and networks that blanket this country from one end to the other. If we agree tonight on Governor Edward Jason of California, no one else will have a chance. Ted will be on every front page, in every editorial column, on every television and radio program, over and over, day after day, week after week, month after month. His opposition will get almost equal coverage, but it won't be the same. The headlines won't be as friendly or quite as big, the news stories won't be as flattering or encouraging, the photographs will make him look awkward and inept, the panelists he faces on the programs will be hostile and out to get him, the editorials and columns will emphasize his every misstep and forgive most of Ted Jason's." He gave a curious little smile, sad yet defiant. "That's how it's done."

"That's how it's done," the executive chairman agreed. "But I can't say that it always makes me happy that it's done that way."

"Duty is not always intended to make a man happy," Walter Dobius said, "and our duty is to elect Ted Jason and put an end to this war-mad drive to destroy the United Nations and the peace of the world that has its source in the White House and the Department of State. In pursuit of the duty of driving Harley Hudson and Orrin Knox from all control over their country's affairs," he said with an unamused laugh, "I am prepared to be quite unhappy. Except, of course, that I am not unhappy. I am happy to be doing it. I feel it *is* my duty and the duty of every responsible opinion-maker in America. Which is why I thought we should all discuss it here tonight and get started upon it as soon as possible."

"The Governor hasn't said yet where he stands on the crisis, has he?"

"He will by Friday."

"And will he say what we would like him to say?" the executive chairman of The Greatest Publication That Absolutely Ever Was asked gently.

"By the time I make my speech Friday night," Walter promised, "we will all of us, I hope, have made it impossible for him to say anything but what we would like him to say."

And later, close to 1 A.M., when the meeting finally broke up and he returned through the icy streets to the Waldorf, he felt that he had pretty well achieved what he set out to do. Some of his colleagues had been hesitant, two or three openly opposed, but the majority had seen it his way. The world of Walter Dobius, he was confident, would not fail its leader. There remained for him now only to articulate and express the arguments with which many others would justify their course in the tense months ahead.

He found a message in his box to call Terence Ajkaje when he got in, but he tore it up contemptuously and went straight to his room. He opened his typewriter and began to write. It was very late but there were some things he wanted to add to his speech as a result of the meeting just concluded.

Across town, the final edition of The Greatest Publication was being put tenderly to bed. A hasty last-minute editorial, very short, had been inserted at the head of the editorial column, above the earlier leader entitled BRUTAL BETRAYAL OF THE UN.

It was entitled TIME FOR GOVERNOR JASON TO SPEAK.

The process had begun.

8

AGAIN LAFE saw the broad lawns dropping to the Hudson, the handsome, unknowing boy, wrapped in sweater and blanket, sitting under an ancient oak while the bright sun and gentle breezes hurried the snows to their melting. Again he felt the terrible inadequacy that he knew the boy's father had felt with such anguish on so many occasions; and again, like the boy's father, he braced himself and went forward with a hopeful and encouraging smile. It was a new role for the junior Senator from Iowa, but one he was learning to fill with a surer touch and a greater conviction as the weeks and months went by.

"Hi, Jimmy," he said easily. "How are they treating my pal?"

For a moment he thought there would be a response: just for a second he thought he saw the eyelids seem to flicker, the slightest movement of the head as though it might turn toward him in response. But no. It must have been imagination as always, hopeless hope betraying him again. Jimmy Fry continued to stare straight ahead, the customary polite, heartbreaking smile on the classically handsome face, no motion anywhere as far as Lafe could see—although he insisted to himself stubbornly, he was almost certain he had sensed something. Surely there had been something. Surely the Lord would not permit it to go on forever.

With the terrible and crushing thought that it might go on forever, he knew the late Senator from West Virginia had contended to the day of his death from leukemia six months ago. Hal Fry had never, perhaps, entirely given up hope, but it had diminished to almost nothing in the sad years since the boy had fallen ill. He had commended Jimmy to Lafe's safe-keeping when he had finally discovered that his own end was approaching, in the midst of the hectic days when, as chief United States delegate, he was battling Terry, Felix, and their many-hued and many-sided friends in the UN. It had been a bequest that did not carry much hope with it, but Lafe had accepted it with the determination that if anyone could find the path through the labyrinth of Jimmy's mind, he would. He had told Beth Knox when they met at the airport the morning after the Secretary-General's annual ball, that he felt a sense of responsibility he had never felt before, "now that I have a son." In pursuit of that responsibility he had made the trip up the Hudson twice a week since Hal's death. So far, he was forced to admit, without tangible result.

Yet he could not believe that he was entirely mistaken in the ghostly sense of response he was beginning to feel lately, the intimation, elusive, indefinable, but increasingly there, that somewhere, far inside, some reaction to his visits was beginning to stir in Jimmy. He warned himself that he might be like the devotee of the ouija board whose own hopes and nerves drive the board without his conscious volition to deliver its cryptically garbled messages; but he fought this down. Rigidly he excluded all possibilities of imagination, dismissed things that might otherwise be construed as sentient response, reminded himself constantly that he must not overempathize—and still there seemed to be something. Faint, fleeting, fugitive, not to be stated, not to be grasped, but—there.

And if there were? He asked himself with a sudden mood of bitterness, as he came around and sat down so that the level, hazel eyes were looking into his (now there was the vague, meaningless recognition that came when something was placed directly in front of the boy) why he should be so anxious to bring Jimmy back to the world. What kind of a world was it that he wanted to return him to, and what made Lafe think the boy wasn't infinitely better off locked away in his serene and apparently happy silence, protected forever from that world's terrible torment and travail? What right did he have to force him to face what mankind had to face in these savage days?

He could not honestly say, as he began to chat easily and naturally about events at the UN, using simple language but otherwise talking as he would to any other youthful mind, that he was doing the boy any favor. He could not honestly say it was a world he liked himself, filled as it was with hatred, bitterness, and crisis. "I beg of you," Hal Fry had cried to the silent nations of the General Assembly in his last, searing address, "let us love one another. *Let us love one another!* It is all we have left." They had listened, moved for the moment; thought about it for a day or two; paid it dutiful lip-service; and returned to hate. Why was it so important to make Hal's son suffer with the rest of humanity? Except, the Senator from Iowa told himself grimly, that if he didn't suffer he wouldn't be a part of humanity in this twisted century, and if he weren't part of it then he might as well not have lived at all. Living was worth the suffering, and better to pay the price than exist and die a vegetable.

In this, he recognized, he was reflecting something of the thoughts of Mabel Anderson, expressed in the letter he had received night before last when he and Cullee returned to the Waldorf from Selena Castleberry's party.

He had not corresponded with Mabel in the months immediately after Brigham Anderson's suicide at the height of the Senate battle over Bob Leffingwell's nomination to be Secretary of State, but at Christmas he had sent a card to Provo, Utah, where she and little Pidge were living with her parents. The response had been a brief letter, hesitant and cautious as Mabel was in her human contacts (thanks partly, he could see now, to Brig's unhappy problems and all she had gone through with him), but genuinely pleased. On an impulse he had replied at considerably greater length, telling her the latest gossip of Washington and the Senate, bringing her up to date on old friends, deliberately giving her as much as he could, in his straight-forward and good-hearted prose, of all the busy and exciting life of the great white capital sprawled along the Potomac. She had told the Knoxes after Brig's death that she never wanted to see it again, but her immediate and pleased response to Lafe's letter indicated that now, a year after Senator Anderson's death, she was not so sure that self-imposed exile was what she wanted, after all. Their correspondence had intensified. Now they were writing on an average of once a week. Having exhausted gossip and old friends, they were beginning to get into areas more personal and, as they could sense each other beginning to realize, more self-committing.

Over this Lafe had hesitated, but not for long. His hasty marriage and equally hasty divorce, after years of the activity that had won him the wry reputation of being the Senate's greatest Lothario and the UN's *chausseur formida-*

ble, had left him with the sour feeling that it was about time for him to take on more responsibilities than just Jimmy, if he were ever going to. He had felt, suddenly, quite old and tired after his divorce from little Irene, who had kept him company on the night before the Leffingwell nomination had come up to the Senate, and who had subsequently turned out to be no better than—well, than he was. The sort of easy and endless sex he seemed to have been born with a gift for was always a great fascination to those not similarly gifted, but he had reached a point long since where he knew how desperate and empty and futile it was. A scathing self-disgust had finally come upon him. If he climbed into one more meaningless bed, he thought even as he compulsively did so, he would go stark, staring mad. But of course he didn't—at least consciously, though he suspected that what he was doing was itself a form of insanity, the coldest and bleakest and most empty of all, without heart, without warmth, without dignity, without reward save the same old automatic one that came and went and left nothing behind. He had reached a profoundly depressed state of feeling about it, underneath the sunny good will and casual friendliness he still managed to show the world. He really felt he led an empty and pointless existence, in the most fundamental sense. He was beginning to wonder whether there was anything in the world for him that could give it some meaning and make it worthwhile. And this while outwardly and publicly he was one of the most attractive, most popular, and most effective members of the Senate of the United States.

Then, quite unexpectedly, had come the gift of Jimmy—and he did regard it as a gift from Hal, who had judged him better, perhaps, than he judged himself—and very soon after that the more or less inadvertent re-entry of Mabel Anderson into his life. If a crippled boy depended upon him—as he was beginning to, he told himself fiercely, he *was* beginning to—and if a nice girl like Mabel, knowing him and his nature as she did from the old days of his intimacy with Brig in the Senate, still responded as openly and willingly to his proffer of friendship as she had, then perhaps life could still have some reasonable purpose after all. It was a measure of the desperate nature of his need for reassurance, perhaps, that it had taken him no more than a week or two to reach this conclusion and from there to jump to the near-certainty that there was something inevita-

ble about Mabel. As with Jimmy he fought to preserve his
skepticism, told himself angrily that it was far too trite, assured himself that it was a long way from a few letters to a
bed that would be permanent and a union that might bring
love. But he was too knowing to misread the overtones in
Mabel's letters. He was an old campaigner and he knew the
signs.

Very well, then, he told himself fiercely, this time it was
now or never, and this time he would be worthy. He
wouldn't push it too fast, he wouldn't be tricky, he
wouldn't use any standard techniques—because if this really might be love, then there were no techniques except the
techniques that would suit this one case. He would just let
it develop as it came, writing whenever she did but not
being in too much of a hurry to get out to Utah, letting
events bring them together soon or keep them apart for a
while as events saw fit. They had not even talked on the
telephone yet, and there, too, there was no hurry. If it happened, it happened; it would someday, before too long. She
had mentioned something in her letter last night about
being asked to sit on the platform at a rally in Salt Lake
City next week. For the first time since Brig's death she
had not rejected such a political invitation out of hand, but
had accepted because, "I think maybe just by being there
I can help to carry on a little of what he stood for." Widows of Senators sometimes turned up as members of state
delegations to national conventions, and Lafe knew he
would head Iowa's. Somehow or other, he suspected, life
would work it out for them if it were meant to work out.
His only problem would be to refrain from becoming too
anxious. A technique for that, he thought with a rueful
amusement, had not yet been developed by man. But he
would have to do his best.

Meanwhile, there was Jimmy, and as he went on talking,
quietly and pleasantly, to the vacant, handsome boy in the
steadily warming day, he felt again that tantalizing, fugitive
sense of—something. Deep, deep inside, responding just a
little, beyond sight or grasp of ordinary communication: a
spark. He thought it was growing, but again he told himself sternly that he must not be overly anxious or optimistic. Senator Fry had failed in all his years of trying.
Why convince oneself that a stranger could do what a father could not?

But still there was—something.

He talked for fifteen minutes in a calm, unhurried tone and then got up.

"Goodbye, Jimmy," he said, reaching down for the strong hand lying placidly on the blanket, giving it a friendly squeeze. "I have to leave now and go to Washington for a session of the Senate. But I will be back," he promised, his voice sent clear and distinct and apparently certain of acceptance into the shadows that engulfed the mind before him. "My name is Lafe, and I will be back."

There was no outward indication, the clear, kindly eyes stared straight ahead, the gentle, friendly smile remained unchanged. But he was sure, as he watched for a long moment and then turned away. Somewhere inside there was— something. And he was undismayed.

His name was Lafe, and he would be back.

"Bob?" the familiar voice of the Speaker said. "Are you ready to go? I'm calling from downstairs. My car's here."

"Oh, O.K.," Senator Munson said, from his office near the Senate floor. "We could have taken mine, though, and saved Elbridge the trouble."

"Elbridge doesn't mind driving me," the Speaker said with a chuckle. "As between our two chauffeurs, I think he minds rather less than C.B. does. Don't you think so?"

"C.B. is in love again," Bob Munson said. "His mind isn't really on his work these days. I'll be right down."

"Good. I'll be talking to the cops on the door and finding out what's really going to happen in the Senate. They always seem to know."

"Better than I do," the Majority Leader said. "See you in five minutes. . . . Now," he said, when he and the Speaker were comfortably settled in the back seat of the Speaker's limousine and Elbridge was driving the car slowly out from under the archway beneath the Senate steps into the bright sunlight, "how does it look for Harley's resolution on your side?"

"Puzzling," the Speaker confessed. "Don't know as I quite understand what's going on in the House today."

"That will be the first time in forty years. Has anything changed since I talked to you yesterday?"

"Well, yes: the vetoes."

"Do you approve of them?"

"Oh, yes," the Speaker said calmly as Elbridge swung

the limousine left into Independence Avenue to start the
ten-minute run from the Hill to the White House. "*I* approve. Some don't."

"We have the same problem in the Senate," Bob Munson
admitted. "Arly Richardson and Freddie Van Ackerman
seem to be leading the parade."

"I noticed in the papers that Fred and COMFORT seem
to be right in there. Arly's a little surprising."

"Anything to be in the opposition," Senator Munson
said in an annoyed tone, "Arly's been in the Senate for
twenty years and every single day has been devoted to
making himself stand out from the crowd. It's a congenital
necessity that he be a loner. No matter what it is, there's
Arly, alone against the universe. It's a psychological compulsion."

The Speaker smiled.

"So, will they tie it up?"

"They may for a while," the Majority Leader acknowledged.

"Filibuster?"

"Lord, I hope not," Bob Munson said. "I am so tired of
these grandstand plays. But they can delay it enough to
weaken a lot of the impact, even if they just debate it for a
day or two—or three or four. Or more. You don't know
how lucky you are, Bill. In the House you have galley
slaves, not prima donnas."

"Ho!" the Speaker said with a skeptical snort. "Have I
not? Brother, you get so busy in the Senate you don't notice my troubles. My biggest prima donna right now is the
Honorable J. B. 'Jawbone' Swarthman, distinguished chairman of the House Foreign Affairs Committee. Jawbone is
wrestling with his conscience, and when Jawbone does that
you can hear the groans from Richmond to Philadelphia.
He's refused to introduce the resolution in the House, you
know. He refused to come to this luncheon."

"I know."

"How about Tom August? Is he coming down?"

"To tell you the truth," Senator Munson confessed,
thinking of the will-o'-the-wisp mind from Minnesota that
presided as chairman of the Senate Foreign Relations
Committee, "I don't know about Tom, either."

"Good Lord!" the Speaker exclaimed. "What is this, a
revolt of the masses?"

"Revolt of the asses, more likely," Bob Munson said dourly. "I've already spent two hours arguing with Tom, but he still may not do it."

"And I with Jawbone. I think Walter Dobius and his kind have them buffaloed."

"Not only that," the Majority Leader admitted. "Honest doubts have them buffaloed, too. . . . I'm not entirely happy myself, to tell you the truth."

The Speaker nodded.

"Nor I. But you know what we always do, Bob: you know what you and I have done for twenty years and more. We have our doubts and we have our worries, but when all's said and done we resolve them in favor of the man in the White House." He chuckled. "If we didn't, two other distinguished and able gentlemen would be riding down Pennsylvania Avenue to lunch with the President as Speaker and Majority Leader. It surely wouldn't be you and I."

"I know," Senator Munson said with a sigh. "I wonder how much we've lost, you and I, in actual basic integrity, by going along with the White House."

"You haven't always gone along," the Speaker pointed out. "You jumped the traces over Bob Leffingwell when Brigham Anderson died."

"Finally," Senator Munson said, his eyes suddenly shadowed with the pain of all that unhappy tangle that had cost so much and in which he had, at one point, played a role he could never forget and would give anything to erase. "Finally . . ."

"Of course you did," the Speaker said comfortably, not entirely positive what the problem had been on that sad occasion, though pretty sure he could guess, in the light of subsequent events. "Anyway, I don't feel I've sacrificed much integrity, over the years. Look at it this way: the country elects a man President to do certain things. If you help him to do them on the Hill, then you're helping the country get what it wants. Maybe we have lost the right to eternal challenge that your friend Arly is so fond of, but there's a substitute integrity, you might call it, which is just as valid: the integrity of seeing things through, of getting things done, of having your colleagues know they can trust your word and count on you to deliver the things you promise in return for their support of the man you serve. . . . No, I don't feel regrets about it. The country elects him—we help him do what the country wants. Nothing dishonorable about that."

"No," Senator Munson agreed as the car swung left into Constitution Avenue at the Federal Triangle. "Except that this time—did the country elect him to do what he's doing in Gorotoland? It did not, in fact, elect him at all. He succeeded to the job. Which makes him—and we who support him—that much more vulnerable to attack from Walter and the rest."

"That is true," the Speaker acknowledged gravely. "I confess I'd feel better about it if he were an elected President. Seems to me that's why he's got to run again, doesn't it you? Give folks a chance to say whether they approve or not."

"You think so? What will that do to Orrin and Ted?"

"I'm for Orrin," the Speaker said calmly, "over both of them. Told him so and I'm telling you so. I'll tell Harley, too, if he asks. But everything's changed now. Especially if Ted decides he's going to come out in opposition to what's going on."

The Majority Leader gave a dry little grunt.

"If I know Ted, he's going to wait a while. He's not the impulsive type, much as Walter would like to have him be."

"They're going to make it mighty tough for him to keep still. I imagine the President'd kind of like to have him speak up, too, don't you think?"

"I expect he would," Bob Munson said as Elbridge piloted the limousine swiftly through the noon rush on Constitution, past the Justice and Commerce departments, Labor, and the rest. "Maybe that's why he's asked us down," he suggested wryly. "Good news from the political front."

But when they reached the White House they found little good news there of any kind. The President and Orrin were grave-faced and worried. The first contingent of Marines had reached Molobangwe. Contrary to advance predictions from their confident commanders, the task was not proving easy. There had been a pitched battle in the center of the town, around Barclay's Bank. Quite a few rebels had apparently been killed, but so had seventeen Marines. The first air skirmish had occurred, near the remains of the Standard Oil installation in the highlands. Three Soviet MIG's, piloted by Chinese, had been knocked down, but so had two United States fighter planes. It was an old story, in a repetitious age. They could feel it in their bones: it wasn't going to be easy.

"It's dragging already," the President conceded grimly. "How soon can you get that resolution through?"

"We'll have it passed by midnight tonight," the Speaker said.

"The Senate has problems, as you know," Bob Munson said. "If there's a filibuster we'll break it by tomorrow night. Not, I imagine, before. I'm sorry."

"That's all right," the President said. He smiled, more relaxed. "The Senate wouldn't be the Senate if everything went smoothly. As soon as you get near passage, let me know. I'm going to broadcast again."

"Good," the Majority Leader said. "You don't think you might before?"

The President considered with a frown.

"No, I don't think so. That would make it look frantic. I think it's better to let the Congress operate as it will in its own way. That won't put me in a false position of either begging, or trying to get the country to bring pressure to bear."

"Especially," the Secretary of State observed, "since we're not entirely sure at the moment that the country would respond."

"That's right," the President agreed with a return of his normal good humor. "Trust Orrin to spell it out. I think it will be much better for me to go on tomorrow night, if that's when it is. Just give me an hour or so advance warning so we can notify the networks. We'll have them standing by."

"There are still a few weapons left in this house," Orrin noted with satisfaction. Senator Munson nodded.

"The Senate vote won't be any later than tomorrow night. Arly can always be bought off once he's made it clear to the country that he and he alone is standing between it and eternal hellfire. Once that's accomplished, something for Arkansas can always choke off the rhetoric. Freddie Van Ackerman's a different problem. Him," the Majority Leader said with a grim assurance in his voice, "we'll break."

"I hope so," the President said. "I've been trying to build up John Morgan over in the House, as you know, Bill, to run against him in Wyoming this fall. I think John's in pretty good shape."

"He was, Mr. President," the Speaker agreed thoughtfully. "Until the last forty-eight hours."

"Is it really that bad? Surely not."

"Bob and I were saying on the way down," the Speaker replied in the same musing way, "that for once we're not sure. There's a very funny mood on the Hill right now; a very funny mood in the country. I think in their hearts and their guts most Americans are with you. But the press has 'em confused. Walter Dobius and Company are making some headway. They may make more."

"Well," the President said flatly, and for a moment he did not look at all like the kindly, comfortable, rather bumbling Harley Hudson they had known so long: he looked like what he was, a President of the United States. "I am not about to turn tail and run from Walter Dobius and all his imitative little pals. And I shall tell them so. In fact, I shall tell the country so, tomorrow night."

"If you think you should, Mr. President," the Speaker said calmly. The President stared at him for a moment. Then he smiled and relaxed.

"Don't worry, Bill. I won't dwell on it. But I want everybody to get the message." He pushed back his chair and stood up. "I'm sorry it's going to be a little difficult up there, but I know you can do it. Keep me advised."

"We will," Bob Munson promised as they started for the door. He paused. "I suppose the news of our reverses out there will be released soon?"

The President nodded.

"Surely. The Pentagon wants to hold them back, and"— he glanced with a humorous air at his Secretary of State— "so, I think, does Orrin, but—"

"No, I don't," Orrin said. "It can't be done anyway, there are too many correspondents swarming into Gorotoland. Better let it out and take what we have to take and get it over. Things will get better," he added confidently. "None of us doubts that, I hope."

But though they assured him that of course they didn't, it was in a much more worried mood that the Senate Majority Leader and the Speaker of the House returned, shortly after 1:30, to the Hill. Their ride was silent as Elbridge performed again his practiced maneuvers through the midday traffic. It was only when the limousine stopped to deposit Senator Munson under the arch of the Senate steps that the Speaker finally broke his reverie.

"I wish I were surer of things. I'd feel better."

Bob Munson nodded.

"Yes," he agreed, staring thoughtfully at the crowds of tourists who were already, this early in the season, beginning to jostle and push their way through the Capitol corridors, many of them scarcely apprehending that a good portion of their fate and that of the world was actually being decided right here in these old stone halls even as they passed. "Yes, there have been simpler times and clearer issues. But I suppose," he said with a rather grim little smile, "that's what makes it fun. Let me know how things are going over there."

The Speaker nodded.

"It won't be so bad. Cullee's going to lead off, and you know Cullee. He doesn't fool around."

Nor did he when, a few minutes later, he arose at the microphone at the committee table in the center of the majority side of the House and began the four hours of debate on the resolution that the Rules Committee had allowed. Briefly he sketched the background of recent events, described the provocations that had brought the Administration response in Gorotoland, defended the vetoes, emphasized the importance of the pending resolution in presenting a united American front to the world; paid his respects to Jawbone Swarthman's right not to introduce it if he didn't want to, introduced it himself, strongly urged its passage; sat down. A scattering of applause came from the galleries. The temporary presiding officer, chairman of the Committee of the Whole House on the State of the Union which provides the House's mechanism for opening work on a legislative measure, rapped the gavel in an admonishing way. Jawbone surged to his feet from his chair beside Cullee with his usual combination of hesitancy and belligerence.

"Now, Mr. Chairman," he began, "I want the House to understand what is involved in this little bitty old resolution presented by my distinguished—and yes, he is distinguished, I will say to the House, as we all know—my distinguished friend, whom I am proud to call my friend, the distinguished Congressman from California. I want the House to understand, too, Mr. Chairman, the grave, the very grave situation our beloved country is involved in,

Mr. Chairman. It's a mess, Mr. Chairman. Yes, sir, it is surely a mess."

There was a titter of laughter and, again, some applause. The chairman used the gavel, the titter subsided. Representative Swarthman swung round to stare down at the ebony giant at his side. Cullee looked back with an impassive interest.

"Mr. Chairman," Jawbone said, "my dear friend here says I had a right not to introduce the pending resolution of support for the President in his latest actions, even though I am chairman of the great House Foreign Affairs Committee. Now, I do appreciate—I do, Mr. Chairman—this charity and understanding. I wish I could show it, Mr. Chairman, to the course of action my friend is defending here. I do, Mr. Chairman! But, Mr. Chairman"—and he shook his head sadly and waggled his forefinger suddenly in Cullee's face—"I just can't, Mr. Chairman! I just can't!"

"Mr. Chairman," Cullee said, rising so abruptly that Jawbone had to jump back to escape being toppled. "If the gentleman will yield, what alternate course would the gentleman propose? Didn't the United States have to do something when its people were killed and American property was destroyed? What would the gentleman have done?"

"I would have gone to the United Nations, Mr. Chairman—"

"The gentleman knows that would have been a meaningless thing," Cullee said flatly.

"Well, now," Jawbone said. "Well, now, Mr. Chairman, I'm not so sure, Mr. Chairman, I'm not at all, now. Many intelligent and well-informed people, Mr. Chairman, many people we all know and admire and respect, Mr. Chairman, would have gone to the United Nations, now—"

"If you mean Wal—" Cullee began ominously.

"Whom *many* of us respect and admire," Jawbone amended hastily. "Yes, sir, they would, and I would. I would, now. I would have gone to the United Nations and I would have said, 'Lookahere, now, you fellows, you know we've suffered a right inexcusable attack there, now, and it's up to you to help us.' And I think they would, Mr. Chairman! I think they would!"

"Mr. Chairman," Cullee Hamilton said in a tired voice, "the distinguished chairman of the Foreign Affairs Committee has served on the U.S. delegation to the UN in previous years. He knows the situation wasn't good when he was there and he knows it's worse now. Who's he trying to kid, Mr. Chairman? Surely not this House."

"Now, Mr. Chairman," Jawbone said sternly, "I will say to my good friend the Congressman from California, I will say, that I think we are dealing with a condition here, a condition in the country. I don't think the country wants a war, Mr. Chairman, that's what I mean! I think that's what we've got to face here. I just don't think it does, Mr. Chairman. I know my people in South Carolina don't, leastways the way they're writing and wiring and phoning to me. I bet I'm not alone in it, either, Mr. Chairman." He swung around with a wide gesture to embrace the whole of the attentive House. "I bet most of you-all are getting the very same thing this very minute, now. Isn't that a fact, now, Mr. Chairman? Sure it is, now!"

"If the gentleman will yield," Cullee said patiently, "I will agree with him that many of us are receiving messages opposing the President's course. My own state," he observed dryly, "is always among the most vocal on most issues. It certainly is on this. But I wonder if that's enough, Mr. Chairman, to decide an issue as grave as this one. We all know what inspires mail and telegrams and phone calls. Sometimes it is genuine and sometimes it is whipped up. I think we can assess it pretty well."

"Oh!" Jawbone cried. "Now! Mr. Chairman! That's strange talk from one who aspires to a seat in the other body. How does he hope to win a seat in the other body if he defies his own people, Mr. Chairman? How can he hope to do it, Mr. Chairman? People don't get elected to the other body that way, Mr. Chairman!"

"How do they get elected?" Cullee demanded. "By giving in to every passing fancy of the people of South Carolina? I am not the only member of the House who might aspire some day to go to the other body. I don't know when I might attempt it, but I can tell my friend from South Carolina, Mr. Chairman, that I won't do it his way. I won't do it by appeasing every passing hysteria that comes along. I'll do it by standing for what I believe in and saying, take it or leave it. That's my way, Mr. Chairman, and California knows it."

"Well, now, Mr. Chairman," Jawbone said, changing the subject with a brisk air that brought a chuckle from the House, "now we're getting far afield. My point is the country doesn't like this war, Mr. Chairman. It sympathizes with the slain folks, Mr. Chairman, and God knows nobody does more than I do—it deplores the damage to American property—but I think it doesn't want a war. It wants to negotiate and settle things peacefully, Mr. Chairman. America doesn't want a war."

"Does America want honor, Mr. Chairman?" Cullee demanded, and a snicker of scornful laughter rippled through the galleries. He swung upon them angrily.

"I am not surprised, Mr. Chairman," he said with a biting emphasis, "that many Americans and many of our distinguished guests in the diplomatic galleries find the word corny and laugh at it. There hasn't been much of it around in recent decades. But again I ask my friend," and he turned back to Jawbone, twitching and bouncing about beside him, "does America want honor? If so, Mr. Chairman, she may have to risk war to keep it. Make no mistake about that."

"Well, now, Mr. Chairman," Jawbone said, "I don't mean to be impolite to my friend, now, I really don't, but I wonder if we aren't getting the basic issue confused with words, Mr. Chairman? Words like honor are fine, Mr. Chairman, and we all want honor, but it's a little abstract and relative, now, isn't it, Mr. Chairman? War, now, that's concrete. That's something everybody knows about, Mr. Chairman. Folks may have their doubts about honor once in a while, but there's no mistaking war, Mr. Chairman. When you've got it, you know it. I'm afraid we've got it in Gorotoland, Mr. Chairman, and we all know what that means: on and on and on and on! No end to it! No stop! On and on! The country doesn't want it, Mr. Chairman. It just doesn't want it, now!"

"The gentleman," Cullee said patiently, "overlooks entirely, as do some other very vocal citizens on this matter, the question of who began it. Was it the United States, Mr. Chairman, who attacked innocent missionaries and murdered them? Was it the United States who destroyed property acquired under honorable leasehold from a legitimate government? Who began this, anyway?"

"Mr. Chairman," Jawbone said, "I know the gentleman's feelings about this. God knows all Americans resent what was done. But America is a great power, Mr. Chairman. America can show restraint. America can show tolerance. America doesn't need to start a war to prove her points, now, Mr. Chairman, we do not! That's what I am saying to the gentleman. There are other ways. There may still be other ways, in spite of the vetoes the gentleman and the distinguished Senator from Iowa, from the other body, cast in the UN yesterday. It isn't hopeless, Mr. President. There can be negotiations. We can talk, Mr. Chairman. The vetoes haven't made it impossible. There's still a chance, now."

"Mr. Chairman," Cullee said coldly, "I am not going to stand here and take the implication that the United States has ruined something by using the veto. Whatever was ruined—if anything—was ruined already. The vetoes were used at the direction of the President of the United States, I would remind my friend from South Carolina, *and"*—he added in a contemptuous tone to Jawbone, who looked up at him like a disheveled bantam rooster—"with the full advice and concurrence of the American delegation—to protect the best interests of the United States and, I firmly believe, the best interests of world peace." At this there was a skeptical hoot from somewhere in the galleries, and the chairman patiently rapped the gavel.

"The vetoes were used in support of the principle that murder is not something to be hailed and condoned by the United States *or* the United Nations, and the principle also that international conspiracy and lawlessness should be stopped by civilized powers, not encouraged by them. The vetoes made nothing impossible, Mr. Chairman. They were a matter of principle which could not be avoided and they will, if properly judged and analyzed by our opponents abroad, lead on to negotiations that can really mean something."

"Principle?" Jawbone cried indignantly to the silent House, and, *"Principle?"* Arly Richardson shouted with an equal indignation to the attentive Senate on the other side of the Capitol. "Where, I ask you, Mr. President, is the principle in this brutal casting-aside of the United Nations? Where is the principle in this wanton and ruthless invasion of a helpless African state, committing us to war in the midst of a hostile continent eight thousand miles away?

"The distinguished Senator from Iowa talks of principle, Mr. President? I suggest that we would be in a much better position if we had adhered to the Richardson Principle, Mr. President. The Richardson Principle says that the United States should not resort to force under any circumstances until all other means of settling disputes have been exhausted. The Richardson Principle says that only when its national interests are most gravely and directly threatened should the United States adopt an independent, unilateral course. If we apply the Richardson Principle to the situation existing in Gorotoland immediately prior to the President's decision of two nights ago, or even directly prior to the United States vetoes yesterday, it becomes clear that under no circumstances could the Richardson Principle be used to justify what has been done. I say to my President in the White House that he has abandoned the Richardson Principle, Mr. President! He must return to the Richardson Principle, Mr. President! The world demands the Richardson Principle, I say to my President in the White House!"

"If the Senator will yield," Lafe said dryly, "we are all indebted to him for establishing the Richardson Principle, and for all the other principles of behavior both national and international upon which he has lectured this Senate on so many occasions for so many years. But I do think I must say to him in all candor and respect that I do not recall any great discussion of the Richardson Principle at the United Nations. I am not even sure, Mr. President," he went on, as a laugh went across the Senate, "that members of the United Nations even know that the distinguished Senator from Arkansas has established his principle. In any event, I think the principle we must discuss right now is not the Richardson Principle, but the Hudson Principle. [The laughter grew, and over on the minority side Johnny DeWilton of Vermont murmured behind his hand to Jack Baker of Kentucky, *"Now* listen to Arly start to rave."]

"The Hudson Principle at the moment, Mr. President," Lafe said with an amiable grin that he knew would infuriate Arly, standing with an air of rigid disapproval at his chair four desks away, "is in full control of the White House, and I don't see any way of dislodging it. The Hudson Principle seems to be that when we get stepped on, we step back. It seems to be that when we are wantonly, viciously provoked, we retaliate. It seems to be that when we feel the time has come for us to say, 'Enough'—we say, 'Enough.' That is the Hudson Principle, as I understand it."

"The Senator from Iowa, Mr. President," Arly Richardson said bitterly, "is, as always, full of wit and humor. But, Mr. President, I wonder how long the Hudson Principle—

or perhaps we might call it the Hudson-Knox Principle—
will remain in control of the White House if it produces
such tragically misguided results. Does the Senator have
any inside information on that one, with all his wit and humor?"

"If this is to become a discussion of the presidential election, Mr. President," Lafe said ["How can it help but be?"
Powell Hanson of North Dakota asked Tom August of
Minnesota. The chairman of the Foreign Relations Committee, who had finally decided to introduce the resolution
with a very brief, lukewarm speech, gave him a nervous little smile and nodded agreement.], "then I will say to the
Senator and to this Senate, right now, that I for one am not
afraid to face the implications. An issue has been created
here, not by us but by our enemies, which may very well, I
grant you, decide the presidential election. Very well. I
know where I stand: with the President of the United
States and the Secretary of State. I support the Hudson
Principle, Mr. President, and the Hudson ticket, or the
Knox ticket, or the Hudson-Knox ticket, if that's what it
comes to. ["Oh, oh," Bob Munson murmured to Stanley
Danta of Connecticut, the Majority Whip, "there's a slip."
Lafe obviously realized it too, for he attempted to hurry
on.]

"Now, what is it we are confronted with in Gorotoland,
Mr. President? It is my conviction that in Gorotoland we
face a challenge so serious that—"

But Arly Richardson would have none of it.

"Just a minute, Mr. President," he interrupted sharply.
"Let the Senate understand this. Is the Senator telling us
that he has inside information from the White House that
it will be a Hudson-Knox ticket? Has the President told
him that he intends to run again, and that when he does he
will select the Secretary of State as his running mate? I ask
the Senator, is that his information? That puts a whole new
light on the Gorotoland situation, Mr. President. That
makes it seem possible that—"

"Now, just a minute, Mr. President," Lafe said with an
equal sharpness, aware that all across the crowded chamber and in the galleries above the Senate, press and visitors
were leaning forward with a suddenly increased alertness,
"I have no inside information whatsoever on the President's intentions. He has not talked to me about it, nor has
anyone else in a position to know. In fact, I don't think

anyone does know. He told this Senate a year ago, upon his accession, that he would not run. That is all I know. If I said something in error, Mr. President, I apologize to the President and the Secretary of State. I apologize for distracting the Senate from this very important matter of our entry into Gorotoland, our vetoes in the United Nations, and the pending resolution. I think, Mr. President, that we should return to the very important matter before us now, and—"

But now Fred Van Ackerman was on his feet, and there was a stirring and a heightened tension over the chamber as the Senate perceived that it would probably be a while before Lafe had his wish.

The junior Senator from Wyoming, who had never forgiven Lafe, or indeed any of them, for censuring him for his part in the blackmail that had driven Brigham Anderson to his death, was obviously in a savage mood. This was nothing new, as Warren Strickland of Idaho, the Minority Leader, remarked to Bessie Adams of Kansas, but it did not promise a very edifying or pleasant debate.

"Mr. President," Senator Van Ackerman said, "if the Senator will yield to me—"

"I don't have the floor," Lafe said, "but if the Senator from Arkansas will yield to me for the purpose"—Arly Richardson nodded—"I will accept the Senator's question."

"Very well," Fred said, in his voice the acid note that they all knew so well, "the question is, wouldn't it be a fair interpretation to say that the President and the Secretary of State have deliberately created this crisis in Africa so that they can go to the country as a team and seek re-election with the argument that you can't change an Administration in the middle of a crisis? Isn't that a reasonable assumption, I ask the Senator?"

Both the Majority and Minority Leaders were on their feet at once, but Lafe, for the moment, at least, did not need help.

"Mr. President," he said coldly, "the Senator asked me two questions, as I understand them: is his interpretation fair, and is his assumption reasonable. Fair and reasonable are not words this Senate is accustomed to associate with the junior Senator from Wyoming, I will say to him, and my answer to his questions is no, they are neither fair nor reasonable."

"Well, Mr. President," Fred said, beginning to get the

furious scowl that came so easily to his face in his collo-
quies with his colleagues, "that may be a clever debater's
trick but it isn't responsive. I repeat to the Senator, is it not
perfectly natural to assume that the great President and the
great Secretary of State, whose greatness we in this body
have known for so long, have put us at war in Africa to
bolster their own ambitions for re-election? The Senator
can evade all he pleases, but I think that is the impression
that is going to reach the country."

"I know it will if the Senator has anything to do with it,"
Lafe snapped. "The Senator sounds just like the—just like
some of the people the American delegation has to contend
with at the UN. He, too, Mr. President, seems to forget we
are in this situation because a total of forty-nine Americans
were killed and American property was wantonly destroyed. The Senator is as adept as America's enemies at
forgetting what was done to us in his eager haste to tear us
down by yelling about what we have done. Were the circumstances different I would ask the question, how he
squares this with his conscience. But its absence makes the
question academic."

["Here goes Freddie through the ceiling," Royce Briar of
Oregon chuckled to Alexander Chabot of Louisiana. Alec
Chabot smiled and shrugged, in his dapper way.]

"Mr. President," Senator Van Ackerman said, and into
his voice there came the high, spiraling whine his colleagues knew so well when Fred, as Irving Steinman of
New York liked to put it, "takes off from the human race,"
—"we all know how clever the junior Senator from Iowa
is. Oh, Mr. President, we have had so many examples of
his cleverness! But I say to him, Mr. President, and to the
incompetents down the Avenue whose errands he is running, that he can't fool the country or the world, Mr. President! He can't fool the country or the world! There's a re-
election plot here, Mr. President, and the country and the
world know it! It's all right to be clever, Mr. President, but
there'll be a reckoning. Mark my words," he repeated with
an ugly, snarling emphasis, "there'll be a reckoning!"

"Mr. President," Bob Munson said, making his voice as
calm and scathingly paternal as he could, "will the distinguished Senator from Arkansas, who I believe still has the
floor, yield to me to put this thing back in perspective?"

"Oh, Mr. Chairman!" Jawbone Swarthman cried indignantly to the House. "Perspective! My good friend from California, Mr. Chairman, he keeps coming back to perspective, he keeps telling us about murdered Americans, and nobody feels more deeply for the sobbing widows and the sweet little orphans than I do, Mr. Chairman, nobody does, now, but after all, we have to look at perspectives ourselves, Mr. Chairman, we do, I say to my friend from California!

"I'll tell you the perspective here, Mr. Chairman, the perspective is the great big old United States, here, ignoring the wish of the world for peace and zeroing in on little bitty old Gorotoland, Mr. Chairman. Now, most peoples on this earth, and I think that includes the American people as well, they think, now, that it's best the world keep the peace, Mr. Chairman. They wonder—yes," he cried, as Cullee moved restlessly at his side—"yes, they understand, they see these murdered people, and I will say to my friend from California, yes, I'm with him—but they see them and they see how it could all be settled with a nice little old talk in the United Nations, everybody talk, nobody go to war, nobody hurt, Mr. Chairman, just a nice little old United Nations chat about it, and they say, now, why you suppose that old United States is deciding to go to war, Mr. Chairman?

"They aren't dumb, Mr. Chairman. Oh, Lordy, sweet Pete, they aren't *dumb*. They see this President, now, getting ready to run for re-election, and they see his Secretary of State there, just kind of easin' and oilin' and scrunchin' around, Mr. Chairman, getting himself all set to move in on it if that old President—and he's my President, Mr. Chairman, I love him, I do love him, now, and don't let anybody tell you old Jawbone hasn't supported him sixty-five-million-one-hundred-percent, because I *have*, Mr. Chairman—but anyway, they see him kind of oozin' and oilin' too, and they get to figurin' and they think, Now, if *I* was a President or a Secretary of State and I wasn't exactly sure how to go about getting elected this fall, I think I'd fix me up a crisis so's I could run on it! Yes, sir, Mr. Chairman, I do believe that's what most people think when they look at this. They see that old election roundin' the corner, there, and they see that old President and Secretary of State just a-screezin' and a-scrunchin' up toward it when nobody ain't lookin', and they figure: By dad gum, that's it!

That's *it*, Mr. Chairman! That's what they figure," he ended solemnly, "and I do believe they're right, Mr. Chairman.
I do believe, now, that they're right. Yes, sir!"

"Mr. Chairman," Cullee asked in a tired tone, "what on
earth prompts the gentleman to make a vicious charge
like that, so out of character for him as the House knows
his character? He knows perfectly well that's what it is, a
political charge and a vicious one, against his own Administration. Why does he make it? And incidentally," he said,
provoking the House to laughter as he went along, "if the
gentleman has an answer I think he can give it in plain English. We all know he was a Rhodes scholar and we can all
see the Phi Beta Kappa key hanging from his watch
chain, so I think he can spare us the corn pone and give it
to us in ordinary English."

"Corn pone?" Jawbone exclaimed, looking fit to burst as
the wave of laughter grew and crested. *"Corn* pone? Now,
Mr. Chairman, that's a funny way to talk to a friend and
colleague, I will say to my friend from California. Maybe,
Mr. Chairman, they all speak perfect English out there on
those sunny, windswept Western slopes, but as for me, Mr.
Chairman, I come from South Carolina and—why, by did-
dle-dum-dam, Mr. Chairman!" he exclaimed. "The gentleman from California his-*self* comes from South Carolina
originally, now I remember it, so what's he talkin' about? I
swear, now," he said with an amiable grin that brought the
House to laughter again, "I think my friend's the one who's
forgotten English, Mr. Chairman, not old Jawbone. Old
Jawbone's talkin' like folks back home. Old Jawbone's talkin' like folks ought to talk. Shame on you, Congressman!
Shame, now!"

"All right, Mr. Chairman," Cullee said, laughing in spite
of himself. "We all know the gentleman is one of the great
Congressional comics of all time, and maybe this debate
does need a little humor. But, Mr. Chairman," he said, his
smile fading and his face becoming stern, "that doesn't excuse the gentleman from making a vicious and unworthy
charge against his own President. I repeat, why does he do
it?"

"I'll tell you why I make this charge, Mr. President,"
Fred Van Ackerman cried to the Senate in his tense, nasal
whine, off on the edge of his private hell, no laughter or
good humor here to remind men they were still friends in
their disagreement, while the Majority Leader stared at him

THE WORLD OF WALTER WONDERFUL   231

with a stern and expectant face. "I'll tell you why I make
this charge against the two *mis*-leaders who have plunged
the United States into this, that great President and great
Secretary of State the Majority Leader is so anxious to defend. I do it because it's the truth, Mr. President, and we
all know it's the truth. The President made us a promise
he'd retire at the end of his term and let somebody
worthy seek the office, but now he wants it, Mr. President,
and so he's contriving to get it any way he can, even if it
means dragging the United States down with him. And as
for the Secretary of State, Mr. President—as for that great,
distinguished former Senator from Illinois who used to
stand here and tell the Senate how to jump *and is still
doing it, Mr. President*—as for him, does anybody have any
doubts about the ambitions of Orrin Knox? Does anybody
think there's any limit to what *he'll* do in pursuit of them?
That's a laugh!" he said, uttering a harshly cruel one himself. "Orrin Knox, our old puppet-master here in the Senate! Here he is again, pulling his strings on us, forcing us to
go along once more with his ambitions. Haven't we had
enough of it, Mr. President? *Haven't we had enough of it?*"

"Mr. President," Senator Munson said, an expression of
deep disgust on his face, "if the Senator from Wyoming is
through blackguarding his betters—

["My, my, Bobby's mad," Lloyd Cavanaugh of Rhode
Island chuckled to Grady Lincoln of Massachusetts.
"Damned little Wyoming varmint," Grady snapped. "I
hope Bob murders him."]

"—if he is through," Senator Munson said, "with his
kind and decent and generous and honorable remarks, I
should like to take up with the Senator from Arkansas,
who still has the floor, his original point—the only pertinent point, I think—concerning the action of this government in bypassing the United Nations and in exercising its
right of veto in the Security Council to fend off any hasty
and ill-advised United Nations action until our own action
for peace has been completed."

["That kind of smooth talk isn't going to deflect those
two," Gossett Cook of Virginia predicted dryly to Ed Par-
rish of Nevada. "Me, either," Ed replied. "I'm not happy."]

Nor did it appear, as afternoon wore into evening, lights
came on in Washington, and over the Capitol the great
beam that indicates a night session sent its message to the
city, that very many of them were.

In the House Jawbone concluded, Cullee gave a brief rebuttal, many others spoke, the debate centered more and more upon three things: U.S. defiance of the UN, the fear of general war, the constantly repeated theme of the alleged ambitions of the President and Secretary of State. A substitute resolution was offered by fifty-seven members, principally from New York and the Midwest, condemning the American action and calling on the President to withdraw United States forces from Gorotoland at once: it was defeated 231-163. An amendment was offered to declare the sense of the Congress that the United States should keep its forces in place but immediately cease all hostilities and resubmit the issue to the General Assembly: it was defeated 220-215.

Finally the Speaker came into the well of the House and read the riot act about supporting the President, upholding the United States, politics ending at the water's edge and, in conclusion (using the tone of gentle menace that had long ago brought him the name, "Boss Bill") the fact that in the House "memories are not short, and while loyalty is gladly rewarded, disloyalty deserves—and receives—no charity." That did it, and at 7:48 P.M. the resolution endorsing the Administration's position in Gorotoland passed the House.

Even so, it was only by a vote of 214-206. Disgruntled, embittered, uneasy, and upset, the House went home, most of its members not sure whether their country was right or wrong and not sure whether or not they had done the right thing—a mood in which the House often leaves the Capitol after a session, but one this time lent an extra bitterness and uncertainty by the steadily rising condemnations from around the world and from the voters back home to whom many members felt they owed their first and overriding obligation.

In the Senate, debate was still droning on. Arly Richardson had made his final appeal of the day for the Richardson Principle, Fred Van Ackerman had spewed out his last gobbet of hate for the time being, the argument was settling into the duller regions occupied by such as Walter Calloway of Utah, Taylor Ryan of New York, and Hugh B. Root of New Mexico. Surveying the now half-empty chamber as the dinner hour arrived, Bob Munson consulted across the aisle with Warren Strickland and then announced that it was his present intention to hold the Senate in session until midnight if necessary to pass the resolution. Arly and Fred both protested, and Fred threatened to fili-buster. Senator Munson shrugged and repeated that, as of that moment, it was his present intention to go on until midnight if necessary. He exchanged a casual glance with Warren Strickland, Warren returned a barely perceptible nod, and they went off to dinner, leaving Powell Hanson in the chair and Taylor Ryan droning on into the night in op-position to the President, knowing that the Senate might very well still be there talking at 8 A.M. tomorrow.

Outside in the great world the clamor continued to mount. HUDSON-KNOX GOROTOLAND RE-ELEC-TION PLOT CHARGED IN CONGRESS, the most fre-quently used headline had it . . . HOUSE NARROWLY PASSES GOROTO RESOLUTION. TOP LEADERS RE-VOLT. SENATE FACES POSSIBLE FILIBUSTER . . . NATIONS STEP UP ATTACK ON U.S. POLICIES . . . PRAVDA URGES "SOCIALIST UNITY" TO MEET U.S. THREAT . . . PEKING OFFERS NEW GOROTO VOLUNTEERS . . . BRITISH CABINET IN EMER-GENCY SESSION . . . FRENCH SEEK "MIDDLE FORCE" TO HALT EAST-WEST CLASH IN AFRICA . . . POLITICOS WAIT WORD FROM GOVERNOR JASON.

And much smaller, down toward the bottom of page 1 or, in many cases, on page 3 or 4: BODIES OF SLAIN AMERICANS START FOR HOME.

The evening television programs were equally balanced and informative, filled with disapproving dissertations on the motives of the President and Secretary of State, heavy with analysis of the awful things being done by Washington to world peace and an innocent and dreadfully wronged UN. With a lifted eyebrow here, a skeptical smile there, a chuckle, a frown, a knowing tone of voice, a bland omis-sion, a gracefully damaging turn of phrase, all the lesser Walters went at it with a will. Somberly they sketched the world in collapse as the result of the vetoes, smoothly they shifted the blame from America's enemies to America's President, suavely they telescoped the Administration's ar-guments and gave extra time to the opposition's. Then with a portentous sadness they bade the viewers good night, having spent a brisk thirty minutes blackguarding their country, encouraging its enemies, and doing all they could to undermine its citizens' confidence.

Already it was becoming a little difficult for many people to remember just exactly what had started it all. There just seemed to have been something bad, some monstrous attack on the UN, humanity, and the peace of the world, for which Harley Hudson and Orrin Knox were irretrievably, awfully, unforgivably to blame. The voices that were to be heard defending them were rarely given a chance to be heard above a whisper, the editorials in the quite sizable number of newspapers around the country that were beginning to swing back to an understanding of the President's reasoning after the initial shock, were mentioned with a heavy sarcasm if at all:

"During the day the Administration won support from such prominent publications as the Valdosta, Georgia *Bulletin*. Somehow it did not seem sufficient to stem the criticism sweeping in an almost unanimous tide across the nation's major press."

That was certainly true enough.

At the White House the President received a call from Senator Munson, checking in from the dinner party at the Stricklands' to wonder wistfully again if perhaps the President shouldn't go on the air right away. But he was told pleasantly and calmly that the President intended to hold to his original plan and wait until the resolution passed the Senate. Anyway, the President said, baffling the Majority Leader considerably, Lucille had an idea he wanted to explore before he spoke; he'd call up about it tomorrow morning. Puzzled but perforce silenced, Bob Munson hung up.

At "Salubria" in Leesburg, Walter went over his speech once more, between phone calls, and did some further editing and rewriting. In Spring Valley the Knoxes discussed the situation, and in Dumbarton Oaks, Patsy, too, was on the telephone. But in Sacramento, still, the insistent were not satisfied and the impatient were not appeased.

"Sweetie," Patsy said, "you MUST speak out. The world is waiting for you. Won't you PLEASE say something before it's too late?"

"Pat," her brother said, using the nickname and tone she knew from childhood meant: shut up, "will you calm down? I know perfectly well what I'm doing and I'm going to do it my own way. O.K.?"

"All r—ight," she said doubtfully, "but I still don't think you know the feeling that's developed."

"Of course I know the feeling," he said impatiently. "It's

screaming at me from every headline, radio, and television screen. My papers out here are as rabid to get me committed as any back there. Walter is calling me every hour on the hour, urging me to do something and promising dire things if I don't." He chuckled. "University faculties and students from San Diego to the Oregon line are threatening to march on Sacramento. I know the feeling. Where," he added abruptly, "is Bob Leffingwell?"

"In town."

"What's he doing?"

"Waiting to see."

"Very smart of him," the Governor said dryly. "That's what I'm doing."

"You can't do it FOREVER," his sister said.

"Watch me."

"You'll have to say something tomorrow at Walter's luncheon. You'll just have to. It would make it such an *exciting* meal!"

"It's an exciting age," Governor Jason said, "but don't let it get you down. Meet me at the airport at eleven tomorrow, will you? And don't tell the press I'm coming in."

"Of course I will. You don't think they won't know it anyway, do you?"

"O.K.," he said indifferently. "By the way, what's your damned husband up to?"

"I really don't know," she said thoughtfully. "I haven't heard a word from him since he went down there."

"That would be all I'd need to make my position perfect," he said sardonically.

"It would give you something else to be mysterious about," she couldn't resist. He laughed.

"Who needs it?"

In this he was undoubtedly right, for in Spring Valley his silence was a major topic as it was at many another dinner table around town on this evening of national uncertainty, international outcry, and rising political pressures. Helen-Anne had been invited, and now the Secretary, his lady, and their acid-tongued friend were sitting in front of the fire having coffee and liqueur.

"You realize," Orrin said with a smile, "that you're probably damning yourself forever, being in such awful company at a time like this. I'm one of the two men who's destroying America, the UN, the world, and—so I gather from Walter's columns—the whole damned universe. I admire your courage."

"I admire yours," Helen-Anne said. "How do you stand it?"

"It isn't easy," Beth admitted. "Somebody left a home-made bomb near the back door last night."

"No!" Helen-Anne exclaimed, genuinely shocked. "Did you call the police?"

"No," the Secretary said, "though I did get in one of the department security men to take care of it. It turned out to be a dud. Anyway, I don't want to stir up a lot of trouble. The atmosphere is tense enough as it is. Just suppose what it would be like if I had a couple of cops put on the house. We'd never hear the end of it."

"I don't want to hear the end of *you*," Helen-Anne said grimly. "I don't think you should be a damned fool, Orrin. The country needs you."

"Talk to your ex," Orrin said with an equal grimness. "He and his friends are creating this climate. They may have a lot to answer for."

"I've told him so. He knows how I feel. Of course he thinks you and the President created it."

"Whoever created it," Beth said with some impatience, "when you're dead you're dead. Personally, I think we ought to have guards."

"I'm with you," Helen-Anne said. "There's such a thing as being courageous and such a thing as asking for it."

"I'm not going to do it," Orrin said flatly. "Think of the reaction in the country and around the world! It would transform this whole thing into something that's terribly serious."

Helen-Anne snorted.

"Oh, lover, stop being silly. Transform it into something serious, he says. What in hell do you consider it right now? Stop being disingenuous and phony, Orrin."

Beth chuckled.

"Amen! Let him have it, girl."

"Well, it's ridiculous. You get those guards on this house right away, Orrin, and stop acting like a noble damned fool. And don't go into crowds, and watch when you get out of cars, and for heaven's sake be careful. Some people in this fight are playing for keeps, particularly with a potential President."

Orrin grunted.

"Huh! Not very potential right now."

"Potential enough for me. It's no fun being press officer to a corpse."

"Why, Helen-Anne," he said with a mock astonishment, though she could tell he was genuinely pleased. "I didn't know you cared."

"We weren't sure you could do it, you know," Beth said. "When you talked to me the other night, you were uncertain whether—"

"Oh, yes, I can swing it. The dear old *Star* is agreeable, though slightly convinced I'm crazy, but they'll give me leave if I want it and so will the syndicate. All that's necessary is for you to persuade Harley not to run. And that, my friend," she said with a quizzical smile, "I do not think you are going to be able to do. So it's all academic, anyway."

Orrin looked amused.

"You know, I think you're right? I do believe you are. How about being Harley's press secretary?"

"He's already got one and we fight like cats and dogs. No, I'll stay where I am and help through the column unless you're the nominee. At least," she added automatically in political Washington's favorite phrase, for few in the capital burn any bridges they can retain, "that is my present intention. . . . Tell me," she said abruptly. "How are things going over there in Gorotoland, really?"

The Secretary frowned.

"Not good. You saw the evening headlines. It's deceptively simple terrain, plains in one part and hills and highland plateaus in the other—but it isn't as simple as it looks. Short of gunning down the entire population, which Walter thinks we're bloody-minded enough to do, but aren't, it's a matter of slow, steady slogging. Which means delays—and that means boys dying and families being broken and all the other murderous appurtenances of our age—and that means more chance every day for Walter and his friends to say, 'We told you so.' " He sighed. "It's going to be a tough fight and a long one."

"Will we negotiate?"

Orrin shrugged.

"When they're ready. Which they won't be until we get out. Which we won't do until they'll negotiate. So there we are."

"You paint a cheerful picture."

"I've got a cheerful picture," Beth said lightly, producing it from an envelope on the coffee table beside her. "Take a look at Hal and Crystal Danta Knox, five months pregnant."

"She looks darling," Helen-Anne agreed. "So does he. But then, of course, they always were darling kids." She sighed too. "God, how time rushes in this age. It seems like a million years ago that I went to their wedding at the Cathedral. How's Hal getting along?"

"Fine," his father said. "He's in a law firm in Pekin, Illinois. He may run for the legislature next year."

"Repetitions, repetitions," Helen-Anne said with a smile. "Can't you Knoxes ever do anything but guzzle off the public payroll?"

"It seems to be an ingrained habit," Orrin said. "How about some more B and B?"

"No, thanks, love, I really must run. I thought I might go up to the Senate and see what's going on. They're into a filibuster, aren't they?"

"Van Ackerman is," the Secretary said. He smiled. "I think the rest of his support has dropped by the wayside by this time. Bob Munson called about an hour ago to tell me he'd bought off Arly Richardson and terrified Tom August, so that takes care of them. A lot of Senators are very uneasy but they're going along, sometime tomorrow when Fred gets tired out."

"I hope it kills him, after what he did to Seab Cooley," Helen-Anne said coldly, thinking of what the Senate had come to regard as Fred's murder-by-filibuster of South Carolina's gallant old senior Senator.

"He's a lot younger," Orrin said. "It won't kill him, the way it did Seab. And also, he's on the popular side, this time—just as he was then, actually. I think Fred is out, this evening, to make himself the spokesman for all the dissident groups in the country and then swing them behind Ted Jason, if he can. He may succeed, too," he added grimly. "He's not dumb."

And with this judgment, though they hated his guts, most of the colleagues of the junior Senator from Wyoming were in agreement as he talked on toward midnight, while above him the galleries, emptied during dinner, filled up again with an attentive and sometimes applauding audience. He spoke from a bitter, and apparently absolutely righteous, conviction, twisting the knife in the Administration with attack after slashing attack. Inside he was telling himself with a savage satisfaction that this time he had the pious bastards on the run. Not only the Committee on Making Further Offers for a Russian Truce (COMFORT) was behind him, but around 9 P.M. he had been called from the floor to take a call from LeGage Shelby of DEFY in New York. Defenders of Equality for You, Gage said, was wholeheartedly in favor of any attempt to stop the resolution, and its national executive was even then planning to join demonstrations in key cities tomorrow. Nor was that all. Shortly before Fred had taken over the floor from Arly Richardson at eleven-sixteen he had been called out again.

This time the call came from Dallas.

"This is Rufus Kleinfert," the voice said in its oddly accented tones, traces of York County Pennsylvania Dutch still lingering after forty years in Texas oil. "I am Knight Kommander of the Konference on Efforts to Encourage Patriotism." He paused and added carefully, "K—E—E—P—."

"Sure, sure, Rufe," Fred broke in heartily. "Good to hear from you, buddy. What's on your mind? Going to join me in this great fight against war and these power-mad bastards downtown? I need all the help I can get, Rufe, I'll tell you that."

"K—E—E—P," Rufus Kleinfert said carefully, "believes it must speak out. It believes your gallant battle tonight is the battle of all of us who fear the entanglement of our beloved country in foreign wars and alliances. K—E—E—P believes that our entanglement in Gorotoland is a Communist plot to drain our manpower and resources as they have been drained in so many places in recent decades. It believes that the President and Secretary of State, if not knowing Communist agents, are at best Communist dupes. K—E—E—P intends to oppose this course, not just at this moment, but, if need be, at the national convention of the President's party in July, and in the national election later. K—E—E—P—"

"Say, Rufe," Senator Ackerman broke in, "that sounds like great stuff. Why don't we have a little talk next time you're in D.C. or I'm in Dallas? I think maybe with this issue the way it is, with the national outcry in the press and all against this insane stupidity on the part of Half-Brain Harley and Odd-Ball Orrin, that we just might be able to swing the whole deal for a really great American."

"Who's that?" Rufus Kleinfert asked with an abrupt suspicion.

"Governor Jason, who else?" Fred said briskly. "Now, Rufe—"

"K—E—E—P," its Knight Kommander said coldly, "is not convinced that Governor Jason is really With Us in our fight to preserve America's traditional freedoms from foreign betrayal and entanglement. How do we know where he stands? Has he spoken out? Everything he has said on other issues up to now indicates that he is no better than a dangerous, radical, Communistically oriented liberal, of exactly the sort the Konference on Efforts to Encourage Patriotism was established to combat. K—E—E—P has opposed every such dangerously radical individual it could in recent years. K—E—E—P—"

"You've done a great job, boy, a great job," Fred Van Ackerman said cordially. "I don't know where the country would be without you."

"K—E—E—P also has the feeling," Rufus Kleinfert said, unimpressed, "that you yourself, Senator, have espoused many dangerously liberal causes in your Washington career. What reason does K—E—E—P have to believe that *you* are sincere and dedicated in this great battle to—"

"Now, just a minute, Rufus buddy," Senator Van Ackerman said harshly. "Who made this phone call? It wasn't me, was it? You must think I'm on your side or you wouldn't be talking, would you? Now, cut the crap and let's talk sense on this. We've all got to stand together on the side of keeping the peace and getting the hell out of Gorotoland—the side of upholding the UN instead of destroying it!—the side, Mr. President," he shouted, as his colleagues watched him with something of the apprehension with which they would have watched a rabid ocelot, and the galleries leaned forward excitedly to enjoy the drama he was precipitating below, "of saying to the world that America does not go along with this insane drive of Harley M. Hudson and Orrin Knox to re-elect themselves to another term with the treasure of America's coffers and the blood of America's boys!

"That is the side on which I stand, Mr. President, the side of fighting this madness to the last breath that's in me! That is the side on which the vast majority of Americans stand. And, Mr. President," he said, his voice dropping to a menacing calmness, "I think our two distinguished and oh, so able, former colleagues will find it out in November. Yes, Mr. President, I say to them, let them run! They will learn in November what their countrymen think of their insane course! Isn't that a fact?" he demanded abruptly of the Majority Leader, who had returned from the Stricklands, shortly after eleven and had been sitting at his desk, still in tuxedo, impassive and expressionless, ever since. "Isn't that a fact, I ask their defender, the distinguished Majority Leader?"

"Mr. President," Bob Munson said, rising slowly to his feet, "I'm not defending—or denouncing—anybody. I'm just waiting for the Senator to get through so that we can vote on this resolution."

"Oh, we'll vote on it, I will say to the amusing Majority Leader," Fred Van Ackerman cried as a little scythe of laughter cut its way across the Senate, "we'll vote on it, sometime tomorrow, as he wishes. But before we do, Mr. President—before we do—I intend for this Senate—and the country and the world—to understand exactly what is going on in this city of Washington. I intend for the world to understand how an ambitious pair of politicians, who may or may not be knowingly playing into the hands of the Communists, Mr. President—"

"Now, just a minute," the Majority Leader said angrily. "Just a minute—"

"I say may or may not," Senator Van Ackerman cried. "I said may or may not, I didn't say they were, I will say to their friend the distinguished Majority Leader who is so anxious about them instead of about the American boys who are dying out there in that bleak African country, Mr. President. Why, Mr. President"—and he held up, for all to see, the early edition of tomorrow's *Post* with its banner headlines, U.S. CASUALTIES JUMP AS GOROTO WAR STALLS; REDS RUSH VOLUNTEERS; ALLIES DOUBTFUL; H.H. ELECTION PLOT FEAR GROWS— "who do they think they're fooling, down there in their precious White House? *Their* White House? Why, Mr. President, after the election they won't even be able to get in the front gate! After the election we'll have a man who really thinks of his own country in the White House, Mr. President! We'll have a man who puts America's interests first. We'll have an *American* in the White House!"

"I would ask the Senator," Senator Munson said in a

tired voice, "what interests he thinks the President is defending right now. Except that it's pointless to argue with him. But I would suggest he tell us the name of this paragon who is going to lead us all to the promised land. Would he care to divulge it?"

"Oh, no, you don't, Mr. President!" Fred Van Ackerman cried, and above in the diplomatic gallery Patsy Labaiya, who had come in a little while ago with Bob Leffingwell, sat back with pursed lips as her companion gave her an ironic smile. "Let's just concentrate on one presidential candidate at a time. I'm talking about Hapless Harley and his sidekick Artful Orrin, right now. I'm saying, Mr. President—"

"The Senator, as always, is saying too much," Senator Munson snapped, "most of it impertinent and all of it immaterial. Mr. President, I move that the Seante now proceed to vote on this—"

"Mr. President!" Fred Van Ackerman shouted, his voice sailing up into its familiar snarling whine as three or four others, including Verne Cramer of South Dakota, jumped to their feet. "I have the floor, Mr. President. I'm not through yet, Mr. President. I'm not—"

"Then I suggest the Senator get through," Bob Munson grated, "so this Senate can dispose of this matter and go home."

"You can go home, Senator," Fred Van Ackerman said with a fleering, sneering invitation. "I'm staying here for a while."

And for once true to his word, he held the floor for ten more hours, during which Patsy and Bob Leffingwell and Helen-Anne and many another distinguished visitor, intrigued as Washington always is by news of a filibuster in the Senate, came and went.

After a quiet consultation with Warren Strickland at 2 A.M., the Majority Leader decided not to order cots for the cloakrooms or otherwise give any indication that they expected a full-scale filibuster to develop. By 3 A.M. most of the Senate was either snoozing at its desks or napping in its respective offices and committee rooms nearby. None could go home, because Fred persisted in demanding quorum calls at regular intervals: each time a red-eyed group had to gather itself together and straggle in to respond to the roll call. At 7 A.M., as dawn was beginning to touch the Capitol, the monuments, the great government buildings, the sweep of lazy river, and the broad avenues beginning to swirl with life, Senator Van Ackerman showed his first sign of tiredness. A dragging note came into his voice, his body began to sag against his desk, he looked as though his eyes were not focusing quite right. There would be for him, however, no such gallant last stand as had claimed Senator Cooley's life six months ago. He had no intention of sacrificing his health or even a part of it to his purpose this night, for indeed by the time he got ready to stop he had pretty well achieved it. Some thirty-six of his colleagues, including such respected members as Lacey Pollard of Texas and Shelton Monroe of Virginia, had interrupted with questions or statements indicating support for his position, if not his person, which all of them despised. Many of their number had been interviewed, their words incorporated in news bulletins, analyses, commentaries, and news reports for the coming day. His own savage charges led all the rest.

Shortly after 11 A.M., about the time Governor Jason was being met at Dulles International Airport by his sister and Bob Leffingwell, and about the time the Secretary of State left his office, accompanied by Helen-Anne, to pick up Beth in Spring Valley and start the drive to Walter's farm in Leesburg, Senator Van Ackerman uttered his last charge, repeated his last slur, made his last vicious attack, duly recorded and reported, and sat down. Immediately the Majority Leader, feeling more than a little groggy, rose to his feet and moved that the Senate vote on the pending resolution.

"Without objection," said Powell Hanson in the chair, "it is so ordered, and the Clerk will call the roll."

A weary Senate wandered in and twenty minutes later the President had his endorsement, 54–43. Five minutes later Senator Munson was on the phone to the White House. Two minutes after that he was saying in a startled voice, "Why, yes, if you want to—we could—if you think it would be fitting—"

"What more so?" the President asked sharply. "I think it's time to put this back in perspective. Yes, I do think it would be fitting. I certainly do."

"Little Walter's going to hate you-ou," the Majority Leader said with a wan attempt at a mocking, after-an-all-night-filibuster humor.

"I don't give two cents about little Walter," the President

said shortly. "I want to shock the country into its senses. Plus the fact that it is, indeed, completely fitting and deserved. Will you tell the Speaker for me?"

"Yes, I will," Senator Munson said. "Tell me: is this what you meant last night when you said Lucille had an idea?"

"I think it a very admirable and honorable one," her husband said calmly. Senator Munson sighed.

"I do too, but there are some who won't."

"I doubt very much that the country will listen to them on this," the President said with an obvious inflexibility in his tone.

"Very well," Senator Munson said. "We'll get things ready up here, then. What time will you be speaking?"

"Nine."

"Good luck. I think you have the initiative now."

"I intend to keep it if I can," the President said, with a grimness he revealed to very few.

When their conversation ended the Majority Leader sat for a few moments, as he had on so many occasions in the midst of crisis, staring down the Mall, past the Washington Monument, the Lincoln Memorial, and Arlington to the sweetly rolling hills of Virginia beyond. Presidents, as he had often discovered, were sometimes the most surprising people. And as for their wives—He thought of plump little, fluffy little Lucille. Would she be able to stage-manage it as carefully if—But he dismissed that thought with a shudder and a protest. It would not—it could not—happen, even in a situation so inflamed as the present.

Still he was overwhelmed by her astuteness and calculation. A sound of amazement, humor, and concern combined came from his lips. The Majority Leader had seen a lot, in his time in Washington, but this was going to be one of the classics.

9

THIS WAS THE type of occasion he loved, the owner of "Salubria" acknowledged to himself as he looked in on Arbella, preparing the meal and setting the massive refectory table for eight; checked with Roosevelt, getting ready to park cars, take coats, mix drinks, and serve the food; and thought of all the past occasions on which his house had served as focus and fulcrum for the great world. The last time important people had come to lunch, a month ago, it had been the President of France and the Foreign Minister of Greece, an odd conjunction which had nonetheless produced delightful conversation and, two weeks later, a new trade agreement between Paris and Athens. ("We should call it," the President of France had written just yesterday in his shaky but still decisive hand, "the 'Dobius Entente' in honor of a delicious meal and a delightful host." The letter had gone at once to Yale, where the Dobius Archive already filled a thirty-foot shelf.)

Nor, of course, had that been the only significant gathering in the rambling old Revolutionary home. Presidents, Prime Ministers, Foreign Secretaries, dictators—Senators, Congressmen, Cabinet Secretaries, administrators—artists, authors, dancers, composers, and a constant stream of his more powerful colleagues in the press—a long and glittering parade passed constantly through the lovely countryside to Leesburg, partaking of lunch or dinner, lingering long and talking late about the problems of a puzzling country and a difficult world. Out of their conversations many times had come some significant change in government policy, some otherwise inexplicable diplomatic démarche, some subtle but devastating shift in press opinion toward or away from some individual or cause.

Here at "Salubria," Walter was fond of saying to his guests in his most self-satisfied and pompous voice, a good deal of the latter half of the twentieth century had been decided. Allowing for the exaggerations of a host justifiably proud of his cuisine and the caliber of his company, the comment was not too wide of the truth.

Today, he assured himself with an inner chuckle and something as close to excitement as he, with all his fame and honors, ever permitted himself to come, would be an occasion to rank with the most notable. His original impulse to invite Ted and Patsy had acquired an extra irony when it had occurred to him to add the Knoxes. Helen-Anne, he knew, would be jealous of his success in arranging such a party, and could be counted upon to do her usual profanity-filled, cow-in-a-china-shop act, which would

certainly liven the conversation; and the final addition of
Bob Leffingwell, a guest who had every reason to be embittered and antagonistic to Orrin Knox, made the explosive
potentials perfect. This party had so many undercurrents,
he told himself wryly, that he could hardly keep up with
them. But one thing it meant, he was sure, was great fun.

A serious man who did not have too many pleasures or
amusements, Walter did love to stir up human tensions. It
was free, and it was fascinating. He had some difficulty
keeping his anticipation under control.

And there was, of course, another reason for satisfaction. The savage mood in which he had written his columns had not diminished much. Even though events
seemed to be moving his way, even though American casualties were already occurring and the United States was receiving a still-rising tide of condemnation—so that he
could reflect that the world once again knew how right he
was—his bitterness had not decreased. The rapidly growing
troubles of his own country were making him look better
and better, but he was still suffering from the emotions, literally approaching shock, which had overwhelmed him
when he heard that the Administration, defying his advice
and that of his friends, had plunged into direct action.

The invasion of Gorotoland had been a profound blow
to Walter, as it had been to a majority of his world. Within
twenty-four hours the shock had been compounded by the
vetoes. It would be a long time before he, or any of them,
would entirely recover. Betrayal most foul had been committed upon the world of Walter Wonderful by Harley
Hudson and Orrin Knox. It gave him a visceral satisfaction
now to think that in all probability he had set the stage for
a most hurtful and uncomfortable couple of hours for one
of this murderous duo—the one who actually, in his mind,
was the real motivating force behind it all. He had really
been surprised that Orrin would still come to "Salubria,"
considering what Walter had written about him; but since
Beth had not called to cancel, they must be on their way.
A tight little smile touched his lips as he surveyed the
perfectly appointed table. Orrin Knox would eat henbane
and nightshade this day, of that his host was sure.

Not entirely unsuspecting of this mood which awaited
him in Leesburg, the Secretary of State was even then driving the family car carefully along the winding roads, their

snow cover almost gone now as spring rushed on to claim the land. Beth and Helen-Anne were gossiping casually as they rode, pretending an unconcern they did not feel about the episode ahead, but while he appreciated their worry, he did not need it. He did not feel any particular apprehension. He did not, in fact, feel much of anything. Apparently Walter's original intention had been to bring him out and put him through his paces, on the phony pretext that Walter did not already know whom he would back for the presidential nomination and still had an open mind about it. That mind, Orrin told himself tartly, had closed shortly after it came to Washington and it had never been opened since. It was some measure of Walter's really colossal ego that he thought he could fool the world into thinking that he was fair, objective, and statesmanly in his judgment of men and events. It was some measure of the willingness of the world to be fooled that it accepted this self-promoted image lock, stock, and barrel, complete with hosannas and laurel wreaths.

Well, it didn't make much difference to Orrin. He had written Walter off long ago, and his last two columns and his outburst on television after the riot at the UN had ended forever any possibility of friendly communication. Orrin was driving into Virginia today for just one purpose, and that was to tell Walter Dobius exactly how vicious, slanted, unfair, unworthy, and close to traitorous he really considered him. It was a task he looked forward to with pleasure, and he was not at all tense or excited about it. It would be a rendering of judgment long overdue, in his opinion. The great Washington habit of greeting with the most vociferous friendliness the people you despise, imposed by the necessities of fame and politics upon the most divergent personalities, had finally worn thin with Orrin Knox and Walter Dobius. The Secretary was polishing a few phrases that would match Walter's best, as he drove along responding rather absently to the carefully innocuous chitchat of his two worried companions.

Behind his mood lay also the fact that Gorotoland was very rapidly turning into one more slow, desperate contest, greatly increasing his concern and that of the President for the men in the field. It was a concern that no honorable and compassionate man could escape, despite the violent allegations of his critics. ("Thousands and thousands of American boys will be in Gorotoland within a month,"

Arly Richardson had shouted in the Senate, "and I say to the American people that thousands and thousands of them will be coming home in coffins!")

Underlying compassion, of course, were inevitable thoughts of politics, preferment, the nomination, and the problematic judgments of history. Lifelong politicians possess compartmentalized minds, and all compartments have the ability to function simultaneously; so that while he was deeply concerned about the crisis, emotionally moved by the plight of the fighting men, alertly ready to repel the attacks of his critics, he was also, inescapably, assessing in quite another shrewd and pragmatic place the effect it would all have upon his own political chances. This he could do without in any way sacrificing his integrity or his compassion: it was the Washington habit, ingrained by many years of judging events according to their impact upon the political world, however much they might be affecting one on an emotional level.

Through that glass, Gorotoland at the moment seemed to him neither plus nor minus for his own cause. He had participated fully in the decisions that had led to the intervention and the vetoes, his voice had been second only to the President's in urging the course of action agreed upon at the midnight meeting at the White House. He had sought and accepted full responsibility for present policies. Therefore he stood or fell by them. Despite the outcries of Walter's world and the diligent way in which many of its members had set about propagandizing the country, he did not think he was on especially shaky ground at the moment. A good many of Walter's older and less susceptible ("jealous," Walter would have said) colleagues were reserving judgment; a good many of the smaller newspapers and a few of the larger ones were beginning to take a more approving line toward the Administration's decisions; there was some sense, elusive but encouraging, that a basic common sense was beginning to reassert itself in the country.

Common sense, that is, as Orrin saw it: which was, of course, diametrically opposed to common sense as Walter saw it.

He did not feel entirely without friends as they went through Leesburg, turned right, and neared "Salubria." At the moment friendly voices were overwhelmed by the roar from Walter's world, but roars could not be sustained forever. Other sounds would break through; they always had, in his experience. The radicals and extremists on either side in America usually shouted themselves out, and a fundamental balance in the country reasserted itself in the long run. The run might be a little longer than usual this time, but he was counting on it.

He had the ironic and rather satisfying thought that Ted Jason might be sizing it up the same way, in view of his determined silence so far under pressures Orrin knew must be intense.

With this assumption on the Secretary's part his potential opponent might well have agreed as he rode along with his wife, his sister, and Bob Leffingwell in Patsy's Rolls-Royce.

Patsy had greeted him at the airport with a "WELL?" and he had grinned and said, "Well?" right back, so that she had known at once that he was not about to spend the next two hours arguing about it. He had gracefully fielded a series of insistent questions from the more than thirty reporters who had been waiting for him, leaving them disappointed but still friendly. He could see that his attitude did not disturb Bob Leffingwell in the least; in fact, he thought Bob looked relieved. The glance they had exchanged indicated that there was probably much they should talk about before either of them could move forward wholeheartedly into the campaign, but this was obviously not the time to do it. Their group, too, chatted of personalities and innocuous gossip as they rolled along toward Leesburg.

Behind the screen of their casually joking exchange the Governor was thinking, as he seemed to have done without letup since Monday night, about the situation in Gorotoland and the situation in his party. Like Orrin he was assessing it with a shrewd pragmatism. It was a constant companion, even in sleep: he had actually dreamed about it last night, and he was not given to dreams. The convention had been roaring with excitement, he had just received the nomination by 793 votes, and then with an ominous and commanding emphasis as he struggled to fight his way to the platform through newspapermen, delegates, and grasping well-wishers, a giant voice from somewhere in the hall had shouted, *"JOHN J. McCAFFERTY!"*

By the time he had finally dragged himself, with the frantic slowness of dreams, to the rostrum, Arkansas' eighty-seven-year-old junior Senator was already clasping two shaky old hands above his head and preparing to make his acceptance speech.

Ted had awakened with a start, followed by an abrupt, ironic laugh that had also awakened Ceil. He was thankful she couldn't see him, because he realized he was sweating and his heart was beating with a painful rapidity. It was not really so very funny, when all its implications were considered. It had taken him quite a while to get back to sleep.

His days had been similarly occupied with the subject. Walter was not the only one who had taken occasion to pick up the telephone and call Sacramento in the last forty-eight hours. There had apparently been some sort of meeting in New York, of the same general nature that had occurred on many occasions in the past when certain powerful elements in Walter's world were making up their minds whom to support for the Presidency. It was always denied furiously if anyone mentioned it, but a standard part of America's political processes in the latter decades of the twentieth century was the dutiful parade of candidates to the executive dining room of The Greatest Publication That Absolutely Ever Was—the editorial conferences in other influential places at which the hopeful were put through their paces—the general agreement that came about either in a formal meeting or in more informal talks, meetings, dinners, cocktail parties, and intimate discussions among the movers and shakers. The average voter down in the street might think he had a hand in choosing his candidates, but up above, in the executive suites, they knew. A few men reached consensus and with luck they put it over. Sometimes the luck failed and some independent interloper broke through the cordon to run off with the prize. Far more often, he who received anointment at the starting gate came home first at the finish line.

Almost inadvertently—certainly so with regard to Gorotoland—the Governor of California now found himself well on the way to this fortunate and favorable position. He congratulated himself that he had not really had to do very much open striving to get there, either. The family wealth had been a help, his own decisive and effective personality had been another, his overwhelming victory in his run for the governorship had put the cap on it—but mostly it had come about just because he was there. There in Sacramento; there at the helm of the nation's largest state; there in the public eye, with his dignified good looks, his steel-trap mind, and his wry humor. Then had come the President's move in Africa and, abruptly, he was there as the focus for all those elements domestic and foreign who opposed it so violently.

The honor he regarded as dubious and the responsibility a matter so tricky and full of pitfalls that he would gladly have seen it go elsewhere. Ambitious as he was, and determined to be President, he still did not relish the difficulties inherent in being the leader of forces of discontent against his own Chief Executive. He was first and foremost a shrewd and practical politician, and shrewd and practical politicians do not openly challenge the man at the top if they can possibly avoid it. Sometimes subtler methods are adopted in an attempt to achieve the same end, but the political graveyard is strewn with the hopes of ambitious men who let it be known too openly that they disagreed with their leader's policies.

Now he was being thrust forward by a relentless and implacable pressure whose manipulators, he was convinced, did not really give two hoots about him. Walter Dobius and all his like-thinkers didn't really give a damn about Ted Jason personally, or about what he really stood for. They were out to get the two men who had defied their pet beliefs, and in pursuit of them they were simply seeking the best instrument.

Governor Jason prided himself upon some good principles and policies, and a good record of achievement in Sacramento. He felt a strong annoyance with Walter and his world, whose support was given him for what he regarded as essentially a small, contemptible reason of their own to which his merits bore no relation. Their support was an insult, even as it was a most powerful boost in the direction in which he wanted to go.

He was further annoyed by their egregious bullyragging in telephone call, telegram, and personal letter, to say nothing of their increasingly demanding insistence in programs, editorials, and news displays. ("We're going to put you on next week's cover," the editor of the lesser picture-magazine had informed him brightly only an hour ago in a tone of triumph. "We'll caption it, 'Governor Jason: His Presidential Prospects Boom in the Midst of Crisis.' How will that be?" "Great," Ted Jason had said dryly. "Just great.") He might be ambitious, but he was not a wrecker and he did have an abiding love for the country. So, he supposed, in their own twisted ways, did the interests that were seeking to use him now. But for him, who might conceivably be called upon to exercise the responsibilities of the office they wanted for him, it was not so simple. A term as Governor had given him an acute appreciation of the fact that men quite often were used by power rather more than they used it. He resented the relentless attempts of Walter's world to force him into a position where he would no longer be an independent agent but would be swept headlong before the tide of emotion flowing across the world from Gorotoland.

He had been seriously tempted at several points in the past two days to tell Walter that he would not come out today. What had begun as a pre-convention talk between a powerful columnist and a man he wished to see become President had been transformed by events into another gambit in Walter's battle with the Administration. The Governor did not relish it, though he knew exactly what he would do if pressed: he would remain adamant on his promise to speak by Friday, and he would not be pushed an inch further. He had worked out a careful and ticklish strategy for himself after his talk with Ceil, and in it Walter played a significant part, if in a somewhat different fashion than Walter himself contemplated.

Ted thought with a wry appreciation of his principal opponent. Now, as always, he admired Orrin's guts, and at the moment he also admired the simplicity of his position. The Secretary had no problems, his commitment was complete. He had advocated a certain policy for years and now he had been instrumental in bringing it about, and that was all there was to it. No equivocations for Orrin, no necessity to duck and dodge and beat about in an attempt to avoid the pressures of friends who might as well be enemies. Like Orrin, Ted was quite sure that very soon, now, the reaction against the position of Walter and his world would begin to set in. He was not at all convinced that the Administration was in anywhere near the trouble that they were maintaining in their indignant headlines, caustic editorials, hostile programs, and vituperative columns. They were trying hard to convince the country that it was horrified by a policy of strength, but the Governor was at heart a skeptic and a shrewd, intuitive judge of public opinion. He was as certain as Orrin that there would soon be a swing back; possibly not as complete a swing as Orrin thought, but substantial enough so that he who would go surfing on that sea would need a steady eye and a sure foot. Ted Jason was no irrational gambler with his own career, and he was determined, despite the growing pressures upon him, that he would not permit Walter and his world to force him to be one.

He was brought abruptly out of his reverie by Patsy's exclamation as they turned off the winding lane beyond Leesburg, into the oak-lined carriageway that ran up a gentle incline to the pleasant eminence where the white-pillared red brick house had stood since 1765.

"It is!" she cried. "It's Orrin and Beth and Helen-Anne! I knew it! I just KNEW it."

"Shall we turn around and go home?" Bob Leffingwell inquired. Ted laughed, though he could not escape a sudden tension at the sight of his opponent and the thought of the confrontation to come.

"Not on your life," he said easily. "I wouldn't miss this for the world."

"I always knew Walter had a sense of humor," Ceil said gently, "but I see I underestimated it. The kid's a riot."

In the other car, whose occupants were just getting out when they heard Patsy's machine behind them, the reaction was about the same: a combination of surprise, disturbance, and the ironic, saving humor that enables so many in public life to pass through the tests that circumstance imposes upon them.

"Well, well," Orrin said as Roosevelt stepped forward to take his keys and park the car, "that's the thing I love about the hunt country of Virginia: you never know what you're going to find running around loose out here."

"It's typical," Helen-Anne declared. "Absolutely typical. He thinks he's pulling some really profound stunt here. Walter Wonderful, Master of Men, my God!"

"At least," Beth suggested, "it won't be dull."

Nor was it, as they gathered in a rather awkward group at the door while their host delayed his appearance, peeking through the drapes in the downstairs study and watching with a tolerant amusement their attempts to ease the situation. It was the sort of embarrassment that pleased him: he was so much above it all.

Actually it went rather well. Ceil stepped forward at once and held out her hand to Beth.

"Mrs. Knox, I have so long wanted to meet you and compare notes on campaigning. You seem to enjoy it so, while I"—she shrugged perfectly clad shoulders and tossed back her stunning blond hair—"I'm afraid for my part," she admitted with a down-to-earth laugh, "I get tired awfully easily of sweaty palms and fervent breathing."

Beth responded with a quite genuine amusement.

"I, too. But tied to these two"—and she gestured to her husband, standing beside her with a reasonably relaxed smile, and to Ted, waiting patiently beside Ceil with a wary but cordial expression, "what can we do?"

"Ted," Orrin said, stepping forward and shaking hands, "it's good to see you looking so well."

"It is?" Governor Jason asked, but with a laugh that was friendly. "Well, you, too, Orrin." His expression changed. "Seriously, I wish you well with your burdens."

"Thank you," the Secretary said. He turned to Bob Leffingwell and extended his hand.

"Bob, it's been a long time."

"I'm tempted to say too long," Bob Leffingwell said, with a certain irony but a reasonable amount of friendliness, "except that you might not believe me. How goes it?"

"Busy," Orrin said, and though it was not a particularly funny remark they all found the tension considerably relieved after they had laughed at it.

"Well, I do think this is EXCITING," Patsy said as they turned toward the door. "Except where's our host?"

"He's hiding out," Helen-Anne said. "He's about to appear dramatically in the doorway, hoping we will all have fallen on each other with knives and clubs. God, he is so *tiresome!* Walter!" she shouted, to her companions' startled amusement. "Walter, come out this minute and stop acting like a two-bit melodrama!"

"Drastic methods," Ceil murmured to Beth as the stately door swung open to reveal America's leading statesman-philosopher with his customary lord-of-the-manor smile, outwardly oblivious to Helen-Anne's raucous hail. "But apparently effective."

"I wish I were brave enough to speak to Orrin that way," Beth replied with a chuckle. "It would simplify so many things."

"I, too," Ceil said. "I suppose you have to be an ex, and then all things are possible."

"Welcome to 'Salubria,'" Walter Dobius said with a gravely cordial hospitality, every inch the country squire. "My house is honored."

For a time, as they chatted of innocuous matters with a reasonably relaxed air over Roosevelt's cocktails, and then consumed one of Arbella's famous luncheons, the tensions underlying their little group did not break through, though there were moments when the Secretary of State found it difficult to maintain society's pretenses. His feelings at being thrown unexpectedly with Ted Jason and Bob Leffingwell were nothing to what he felt as he forced himself to be civil to Walter. *"Yesterday, one could say, 'God help the United States.' Today, one doubts that He would dare."* An enormous contempt and distaste for the man who could write such a thing, no matter what his emotional involvement, filled Orrin's mind and heart. It was matched, and he realized it, by Walter's equal contempt and distaste for him. But still the meal progressed with relative ease, as so many meals in Washington do progress, under the stern discipline of a political society whose stability often requires of its participants that they curb their deepest feelings, suppress their truest emotions, hide their honest convictions and smile, smile, smile.

Occasionally in such gatherings, however, there does come a moment when reality insists upon breaking through, when truth, too long denied, will rise again in spite of everything to shatter all about it and lay waste the chummiest confabulations of old, dear friends. It arrived for Walter's famous luncheon—as it very rapidly became, for by week's end at least five different authentic versions had appeared in print—when the meal was done and the guests had retired for coffee and brandy to the comfortable book-lined study. There, before the enormous window (Walter's one concession to modernity in his restoration of the house) which gave upon gentle meadows, Dogwood Creek, and the rolling Blue Ridge beyond, it was Bob Leffingwell, surprisingly enough, who broke through the smile barrier.

"Walter," he said casually, when they were all settled and beginning to look at one another with a wary expectancy, "what's this all about? Just a chance to satisfy your ego that you can get people like Ted and Orrin to drop everything and come to lunch, or does it have some other purpose?"

For a moment Walter looked quite taken aback and later Beth was to claim that she had actually seen him blush. But no one ever believed it possible.

"I have asked you all here," he said stiffly, "rather inadvertently, I must confess. I had first intended to invite just Ted and Ceil and Patsy. I have not had a good visit with Ted for some time. Then it occurred to me that it would also be advisable to talk to Orrin as well—"

"Why?" the Secretary asked, his distaste escaping his control and getting into his voice. "To embarrass me? And Ted?"

"I thought I would like to see what you had to say for yourself," Walter said calmly.

For a second Orrin stared at him, as did they all, in blank disbelief.

"What *I* have to say for *myself?*" Orrin said finally, with an ominous softness. "Oh, I see."

"Walter," Helen-Anne said, "I think you're out of your cotton-picking mind. I literally think so."

"I'm not interested in what you think," he said with a deliberate heavy rudeness. "I have a perfect right to ask Orrin about his views."

"That wasn't exactly the way you put it," Bob Leffingwell pointed out, and the Secretary gave him a surprised and grateful glance. "It was more in the form of an inquisition, it seemed to me."

"And why should it not be?" Walter demanded, a sudden anger coming into his voice. "Here he sits"—and he looked at his guest with what in one of less national and international stature might have been termed a glare—"having put this country into a hopeless war on a continent eight thousand miles away, having virtually destroyed the United Nations, having betrayed everything that America has stood for since World War II—and he acts as though it were nothing at all. He and his President just don't care! They're ruining us and they're ruining the world and he *just doesn't care*. He thinks he knows it all. American boys are dying at this very moment we sit here but nobody can tell him anything, he's so self-righteous, he's so certain he's doing the right thing in destroying us all!"

"Well, well," Ceil said finally into the stunned silence. "What a pleasant luncheon party you're giving, Walter, and how glad I am that we came here early all the way from California so that we could attend."

"Somebody has to speak the truth," Walter Dobius said, breathing hard but managing to speak more quietly. "Someone has to make people realize what this Administration is doing. And don't tell me *you* don't see it," he added, turning suddenly upon Ted Jason, who sat beside him on the big leather sofa. The Governor gave him stare for stare, unyielding.

"I understand that emotions are involved and tempers are high," he agreed presently in an unhurried voice, "but I would not want to charge that the Secretary of State is unaware of what he is doing, or unfeeling about it. Or the President either."

"As a matter of fact, Walter," Bob Leffingwell said, and again Orrin gave him a glance of surprise at support from this entirely unexpected quarter, "some of us have been a little startled by your own vehemence. I think more can be accomplished by maintaining perspective and balance than by indiscriminate attacks on the leaders of the country."

For several moments Walter did not reply, and they could almost see him forcing himself to become calm, to adopt the bland and superior air with which he was accustomed to deliver his opinions, to become again Walter Wonderful, the Instant Wise Man.

"Well," he said finally, "I will make no apologies for my honestly expressed views—"

Orrin Knox snorted.

"You should. To me, and to the President, and," he added with a deliberate insulting slowness, "to all who agree with us, whom you and your crowd blackguard and besmirch the length and breadth of this land every hour on the hour."

Again there was silence in the room.

"I hope you lose the nomination, Orrin Knox," his host said at last in a cold and remote voice. "I hope you are driven forever from public life, and your complaisant President with you. Anything I can do to assist in this result," he added with a wintry smile, "I intend to do. Even though," he said with a sarcastic glance at Governor Jason and Bob Leffingwell, "others may deem me too vehement, and may possibly not be really worthy of my support. Just where *do* you stand, Ted? Anywhere?"

"I have already discussed with the President where I

stand," Governor Jason said with an air of almost insolent calm.

"Does he know," Walter inquired dryly, "or is he as confused as the rest of us about your apparent equivocations concerning the greatest crisis the United States and the United Nations have faced in this generation?"

"Walter can't help talking as though he were writing a column," Helen-Anne remarked. "Every sentence a living gem. Give me another brandy, dear heart. I can't take you without it."

"I hear you're going over to Orrin," Walter said scornfully, as he obliged with an automatic courtesy.

"Keep listening," she suggested cheerfully. "You never know what you'll hear next, in this town."

"I hate to see you sacrifice a reasonably successful career," he said with his most patronizing air. But instead of reacting she gave him a pitying look she knew would infuriate.

"I really think you have no conception of what you are doing to your reputation," she said, shaking her head sadly and looking to Beth and Ceil for agreement. "Those columns. *Poor* Walter."

"Those columns," he said, suddenly provoked to a genuine anger, "state a view held by untold millions of decent and fair-minded people in America and throughout the world. This is all flip nonsense that is being talked here. The fundamental fact has been, and remains, that the United States has invaded a small, helpless nation for unworthy motives and suspect purposes, and that in the process of safeguarding its invasion it has twice used the veto to shatter and destroy the peace-keeping functions of the United Nations. Now that is the fact of it, and cheap rationalizations and appeals to the flag are not going to change it. Men who equivocate now," he said with a sudden heavy emphasis, swinging again upon Ted Jason, "are going to find themselves forced by events into the only honorable position, which is one of opposition to this bloodthirsty insanity. Better they move there now as a matter of free choice, than later as a matter of political necessity."

Ted made a movement as if to speak, but again it was Bob Leffingwell who interceded.

"Riding pretty high, aren't you, Walter?" he suggested mildly. "Some of us aren't so positive as you are about where that honorable position is."

"I am going to make a speech tomorrow night," Walter said slowly, leaning forward, square-tipped fingers on knees. "In it, I expect to state what seems to me the only decent and responsible philosophy that liberal men can follow in this crisis. I expect my speech to have some effect upon the nomination and the campaign." He gave Bob Leffingwell a challenging look. "Do you deny that it will?"

"No," Bob Leffingwell said, still mildly. "I expect it to."

"And after it has been made," Walter said flatly, "when the press comes to you and asks you whether or not you endorse it, you will find yourself in a position where you will have to endorse it or be branded a warmonger along with all the other reactionaries. And so," he finished calmly, once more in command of things, "will Ted."

Bob Leffingwell nodded.

"That is why, my friend," he said with a thoughtful slowness, "I do not think I will introduce you tomorrow night."

"But, DARLING—" Patsy started to protest, even as Walter straightened abruptly and spoke as though she did not exist.

"But," he said with an air of disbelief that anyone could do such a thing to him, "you're a previous award-winner. You said you would!"

Bob Leffingwell continued his thoughtful appraisal for a moment.

"I think it will be best if I just stay out of it."

"Bravo for you, Bob!" Helen-Anne exclaimed. A silence fell, during which the Knoxes looked at each other, Patsy shook her head in dismay, Ted looked perfectly bland, Ceil waited with a polite, attentive air, and Helen-Anne shrewdly studied them all. Finally their host spoke, in a voice heavy with emotion and the effort to keep it under control.

"Very well," he said, leaning forward once again, hands on knees, to stare at them. "You do as you please. All of you, do as you please! But I shall speak for Governor Jason tomorrow night and I shall make it impossible for him not to run as the leader of the untold millions all over the world who oppose the insanity of this Administration. I shall continue to oppose that insanity as long as the blood of life is in me. I think Harley Hudson and Orrin Knox are betraying America, betraying humanity, betraying the world. I truly believe this, and I believe that millions upon millions of people agree with me. I see nothing but disaster

ahead if this course continues. I truly believe this," he repeated almost in a whisper. "I truly do. I cannot abandon
the country to such a fate if I can possibly prevent it. I
cannot."

"Well," Ceil said, standing up with a graceful motion,
"on that note, I think we had best get back in to Washington. Ted has some people to see, and I want to do some
shopping, and—we just have many things to accomplish between now and tomorrow night. It has been so delightful,"
she said, turning to Beth and holding out her hand as the
others rose. "Perhaps another time we can visit more fully.
Although," she said with a wistful little shrug, "politics
being what it is—"

"Yes, I know," Beth said, ignoring, as did they all, their
still-seated host. "That's one of the tragedies of Washington, I think—the people who might have been friends if
only their ambitions hadn't sent them crashing into one another."

"We wish you luck," Ceil said, quite sincerely.

"And we you," Beth replied, turning to shake hands with
Governor Jason as they all moved toward the door, Walter
at last rising slowly behind them and following.

"Bob," Orrin said, "come see me sometime, if you feel
like it. Your ideas would be helpful in this situation."

"I may," Bob Leffingwell said, his tone recognizing, as
did Orrin's, that this was their first really amicable exchange in many months. "I just may."

"I hope so," the Secretary said. "Thank you for the
lunch, Walter," he tossed back over his shoulder without
turning around.

"Yes," Helen-Anne said dryly, "we do thank you so
much, lover."

"It HAS been exciting," Patsy agreed.

But they really hardly looked at him, and the men did
not pause to shake his hand.

The last they saw of him as their cars swung around the
parking circle and started down the drive was a short, stolid
—yet, in some way he would not have perceived and would
have bitterly denied—pathetic figure, standing in the
classic doorway of his lovely old home, staring out across
the Virginia countryside with world's-end in his eyes.

"WELL," Patsy said as the cars reached the road and by

tacit agreement theirs moved rapidly out and away from the Knoxes', "I must say THAT was something."

"You want to watch out, Ted," Bob Leffingwell remarked. "You're apt to get yourself boxed in where you can't move, with that crowd."

"They haven't boxed me yet," Governor Jason said grimly, "and they aren't going to."

"Of course if *you* introduce Walter tomorrow night—" Ceil suggested ironically. Then she looked thoughtful. "You know, I really think—"

Her husband nodded.

"I'm way ahead of you, darling." He smiled. "For once. I'm going to."

"My!" Patsy said. "That will be exciting, too."

"I swear to God," Helen-Anne said as they went through Leesburg and headed for home, "I think he's around the bend."

"I don't," Orrin said. "I think he's deadly serious. It's probably just as well Harley's going to speak tonight and blanket him out."

Helen-Anne looked pleased.

"Good. I told him to."

Beth laughed.

"I think it's so nice: you tell Harley what to do and Walter tells Orrin what to do. That way you both have the situation covered."

"I hope Harley lets him have it," Helen-Anne said in an unamused tone. "He deserves it."

But the President was more subtle than that when, at 9 P.M., he went on the air from his oval office in the West Wing. Outside on Pennsylvania Avenue the Ministers' Vigil for Gorotoland, three hundred strong, was marching solemnly up and down, as it had been all day, while across the avenue in Lafayette Square groups of supporters and critics engaged in occasional shoutings, shovings, and angry japings that teetered uneasily on the edge of conflagration. In the grand ballroom of the Sheraton-Park the hastily organized National University Teach-In on Gorotoland, three thousand strong, was still, as it had been since 10 A.M., wildly applauding the thirty speakers who had been invited to attack the Administration, vigorously booing the six who had been permitted to appear on its behalf. In New York and Chicago, St. Louis and Detroit, Los Angeles, San Francisco, Houston, Dallas, Seattle, and Salt Lake City, the banners of COMFORT, DEFY, and KEEP were flying side by side in parades that seemed to have materialized out of nowhere but appeared to be remarkably cohesive and well organized just the same. All over the land the people who had never said a word of protest while the United States was meekly taking its losses around the world in carefully limited patty-cake engagements with the enemy were suddenly outraged, infuriated, and enjoying a delicious togetherness, now that the United States was acting tough.

O the marches, the speeches, the parades and demonstrations!

O the happy full-page ads in the New York *Times*, the glorious Communications to the Editor, the marvelous statements and petitions proclaimed in televised mass rallies, the wonderful release of at last being able to denounce your own country as you had always hoped you could!

The grand and glorious self-righteousness—the marvelous *sincerity* of it all!

It was the high point of many drab lives in Academe and Theologia.

They would never forget it.

Never.

Yet even upon them, in their teach-ins, talk-outs, pray-downs, and spit-ats, there fell a silence at 9 P.M. when the President began to speak. His address had not been announced until three hours before, and it was not only in America, of course, that his critics and supporters waited anxiously to hear. Long after midnight in Europe, early in the dawn of Asia, wherever the reach of Telstar and Early Bird bound the earth, and that was everywhere, men paused in their riots and demonstrations, their speeches and denunciations, to study the measured words and the kindly, untroubled face that represented to so many of them the hated United States and its fearsome attack upon the shaky pillars of a fantasy world in which the United States was supposed always to retreat, never to stand firm. Now that world was in ruins, as it had been inevitable that someday it would be; but still they could not believe it. They watched the face and heard the words and their shock and horror grew, for again there was no retreating and now the President was moving against his opposition with a shrewdness they were suddenly afraid they could not match. It made their reaction even more violent than it was already.

"My countrymen," he said quietly, "I thought I would talk to you tonight, very briefly, about duty and responsibility and the honor that moves great nations and peoples when they are truly great.

"You have been made aware in the last three days—" and he smiled slightly, an ironic but undismayed smile— "of all my shortcomings as your President. You have been made aware of all the awful things that I have done, and my principal adviser, the Secretary of State, has done.

"At least"—and again he smiled the small, ironic smile —"you have been made aware that some people consider them awful.

"Some very prominent and vocal people consider them awful. Some people who would rather condemn their own country, perhaps, in order to preserve an unreal, impractical concept of the world, than defend it against those who have made of international integrity a laughingstock and of collective security an empty phrase.

[On Kalorama Road, watching with friends at a black-tie dinner, Walter Dobius said bitterly, "Oh, it's someone *else* who's destroying collective security, is it?" His host and hostess laughed a trifle nervously, but his fellow guests, including the Ambassadors of Guinea and Pakistan, nodded sagely.]

"What are the techniques," the President asked, "which are used by these people—this small but influential group whose power is out of all proportion to their numbers? You have read them in a hundred crises, you have listened to them on a thousand occasions when your country was attempting to deal firmly with its enemies.

"There is the headline or bulletin so phrased that it instantly gives the American citizen the impression that his own country is in the wrong, no matter what the truth is.

"There are the sympathetic stories about the poor enemy citizens who are being hurt by war, never balanced by equally pertinent and worthy stories about the loyal citizens who are being hurt by war.

"There are the shocked disclosures of how disorganized

and corrupt and irresponsible the loyal government is—and the admiring reports of how shrewd, well-organized and invincible the enemy government is.

"There are the diligent—one might almost say, the eager —reports of American losses and mistakes, somehow never quite matched or balanced by reports of enemy losses and mistakes.

"There are the analyses and commentaries which conveniently refrain from telling you *why* your government has taken certain actions—but always tell you how awful these actions are and how dreadfully critical the rest of the world is of them.

"There is the convenient—and, my friends, since these are highly intelligent people, I can only conclude, the deliberate—forgetting of where the blame truly lies, and the incessant and implacable attempt to pin it always on the United States.

"And there is, finally, the indirect and vicious attack upon those who support a policy of firmness—an attack which concentrates upon their financial practices, or their personal lives, or their private morals, but never honestly comes into the open to tell you that the real argument is with their political philosophy.

"All of these," he said calmly, "are the patterns of the councils of defeat, which you have read and heard from Korea to Vietnam to Santo Domingo to Gorotoland—and who knows where beyond?

"This is the one-sided, unfair, unobjective, biased, twisted, irresponsible, deliberately slanted way in which the world is described to you by a few powerful people who have been given the high privilege of being your eyes and ears upon events.

"This is what has become, in this partisan century, of the once inviolate integrity of a once inviolate profession.

["Wow*ee*," Walter's host said softly, but his guest only turned upon him a scowl so black that he hastily subsided.]

"I reject such councils of defeat," the President said, "as I know the great majority of you do.

"I urge you not to let them confuse you about the situation we actually face—and did face—in Gorotoland.

"We were attacked: we did not attack—until we had to.

"We were injured: we did not injure—until we had to.

"Do not let the councils of defeat tell you the opposite. Do not let them turn the facts upside down.

"You and I know better."

He paused, and when he resumed it was with what seemed an almost abrupt distaste.

"But enough of that. Let us turn, unafraid and united, to the course that honor dictates. There has just been voted, by the Congress of the United States, a resolution of support and approval ["Not too much approval," Walter's hostess ventured, and was rewarded with a tight little smile] of your Government's policies in Gorotoland. Let us go forward in that spirit voted by your Senators and Representatives in the Congress.

"And let us do honor to those who, by their example and their deeds and the sacrifice of their lives, have done, and are doing, honor to us.

"There arrived this day in the city of New York," he said gravely, "the bodies of fifty-eight Americans slain to this date in Gorotoland. Forty-nine are missionaries and business personnel ["Why don't you say Standard Oil?" Walter demanded angrily, and again there was a nervous moment in the room, though the two Ambassadors nodded vigorously.] killed prior to our intervention. It is because of their deaths that we did intervene. Nine are Marines and airmen who have died since.

"These were brave Americans, and it seems to me only proper and fitting that America should do them honor.

"Therefore I shall go tomorrow to New York City and escort these American dead to Washington. ["My God," Walter said in a disbelieving tone, "how can you beat that kind of cruel corn?"]

"I have made arrangements with the appropriate authorities of the House and Senate that here in this city these brave men and women may lie in state on Friday and Saturday in the rotunda of the Capitol ["That's going to hurt your speech, isn't it?" Walter's host suggested, but his guest did not reply]; and that there on Saturday afternoon, in their presence, there shall be conducted a National Service of Tribute and Dedication to them and to the cause of international decency and brotherhood for which they gave their lives.

"This service," the President said, "I also designate a service of Dedication and Support to all those brave men who now carry the American flag in Gorotoland and anywhere around the globe where the honor of the United

States and the security of mankind is threatened by wanton aggression.

"To this service on Saturday I shall ask to accompany me the Supreme Court of the United States; the Congress of the United States; the Governors of the several states ["Oh, oh!" Walter's host couldn't resist. "There goes Ted Jason!"] and all those foreign governments that have diplomatic representatives in this country. ["But—" the Ambassador of Guinea protested in a shocked voice. "But," said the Ambassador of Pakistan grimly.]

"Following this national tribute and dedication," the President said quietly, "the bodies of these American dead will be taken to their respective homes and there interred according to the wishes of their next of kin."

He paused, and when he resumed speaking it was in an even more somber, emphatic tone.

"Respect for our dead—indeed, respect for our living— has not been overly prevalent in the world in recent decades. I intend to see that it is, from now on.

"And I also intend to see, my countrymen, that you are kept advised of the progress of this action your Administration has taken in Gorotoland—that you are constantly reminded of the reasons for it—and that you are not allowed to forget, despite the councils of defeat, why we are there and the reasons why we intend to stay there until this situation is corrected.

"Let me review them once more briefly for you:

"A Communist-backed and Communist-inspired rebellion broke out in Gorotoland.

["That's the first time he's claimed that," Walter's hostess remarked. "He must be hard-pressed," the Ambassador of Guinea replied spitefully.]

"Communist-backed and Communist-inspired rebel troops threatened to overrun the American missionary hospital in the capital of Molobangwe, and actually abducted two American nurses whose fate is still unknown, but they must be presumed dead.

"Communist-backed and Communist-inspired rebel troops also threatened a Standard Oil installation in the highlands which had been granted the right to operate by the legitimate government of Gorotoland headed by Prince Terry.

"Your Government thereupon issued the firmest and most emphatic warning to the rebel leaders.

"Within a week this warning was disregarded. Molobangwe was overrun. The missionary hospital was burned. The Standard Oil installation was destroyed. Forty-nine Americans were wantonly murdered and mutilated.

"These, my friends, are the facts as they happened. They are not"—and, for Harley, the tone became bitingly acrid —"the topsy-turvy, upside-down-cake misrepresentations that are being given you by the councils of defeat. They are what really happened, and if I have to go on the air every hour on the hour to set the record straight in the face of these misrepresentations, I am prepared to do it. . . . I would hope, however, that the common sense, good judgment, and innate fairness of the American people will make this unnecessary.

"We live in difficult times, and I can understand if some Americans let their emotions cloud their judgment and dictate their actions. But I believe the great majority of you agree with me that in the circumstances we face in the world, there can be no other course than the course of honor, unafraid and willing to stand up for what it believes in.

"Any other direction spells suicide, in my estimation, and as long as I am in this office, I shall proceed accordingly. Councils of defeat," he added dryly, "or no councils of defeat.

"I ask you to join me in paying tribute to our brave dead and in reaffirming our determination and dedication to the principles of this Republic and to the survival of the free world. And I ask you to believe that your Government has no other purpose and no other aim than this."

H.H. SETS NATIONAL MOURNING FOR U.S. GOROTO DEAD, the headlines blared; HITS "COUNCILS OF DEFEAT"; BODIES TO LIE IN STATE; CRITICS CHARGE "CALLOUS USE OF DEAD"; PRESIDENT ADAMANT ON INTERVENTION POLICIES AS MILITARY ACTION BOGS DOWN.

"In an extraordinary move," the typical broadcast had it, "President Hudson tonight used the return of American dead from Gorotoland to launch a scathing attack upon the domestic critics of his policies in that distant African land. Shocked observers in Washington could not recall anything to match what one of them called 'a callous political use of the dead.' Typical of the dismayed reaction of many was that of Senator Fred Van Ackerman of Wyoming, who told our Washington reporter, Carole Cooney, 'I can't remember a similar callous political use of the dead. It's a cheap stunt by a mis-leader who claims he's inspired by honor. Does the President actually think he can get away with this?' Other comments, while less personal in nature, were equally condemnatory of the President's latest move in the domestic war he is fighting with critics of his Gorotoland policy. In the harshest public address of his entire Administration, the Chief Executive attacked unnamed 'councils of defeat,' who, he alleged, were misrepresenting . . ."

In Dumbarton Oaks, where Ted and Ceil and Patsy had watched the speech in silence (save for Ted's quizzical exclamation when the President announced his invitation to the governors)—in Spring Valley, where Orrin and Beth listened attentively to the words Orrin had helped to write the night before—at the Shoreham, where Lafe paused in his latest conquest to listen—at the party on Loughborough Road, where Helen-Anne vehemently approved—at Cullee's handsome home off 16th Street where he and Maudie watched—and everywhere else in the politics-conscious city where men were accustomed to appraise events in terms of initiatives seized and advantages won, there was a deeper and shrewder appreciation of the President's speech.

"Seems to me like he got 'em shortcutted," Maudie remarked thoughtfully to Cullee as the flag and the anthem and the Presidential Great Seal faded from the screen. "I think that old President got 'em shortcutted." And this, indeed, was the general impression throughout the lovely capital, across much of the land, and in many a distant city in a world held together by the chains of man's communication if not the bindings of his love.

But though temporarily shortcutted, few of his opponents were under any inhibition that they need abandon what to many of them seemed a genuine and worthy cause. The deliberately malcontent and malicious in their ranks were far outnumbered by the genuinely idealistic and sincere, however much the latter may have been led and misled by the former. One of the most idealistic and sincere of all, in his curious, pompous, egotistical, lonely fashion, was Walter Dobius, leader and led, driven on by a conviction made ever deeper by his outrage at what he could only consider the President's rawly inexcusable use of American corpses to advance his own political cause.

Whole new paragraphs for his speech flooded his mind as Roosevelt drove him back through sleeping Virginia shortly after 11 P.M.

"We shall all be looking forward to your address tomorrow night," the Ambassador of Guinea said when they parted, pressing Walter's hand moistly between his own. "Someone must stop this—this—monstrosity."

"It is very hard," Walter said with a wintry smile, "to combat the man in the White House if he really makes up his mind to fight. But I shall do my best."

"The world expects no less of you, dear friend," the Ambassador said fervently. "You are our only hope."

Walter Dobius shrugged.

"Governor Jason is our only hope. Pray that I may persuade him to do his duty for all mankind."

10

AND SO ONCE again they came, as they always have and always will on such portentous occasions, down from Chevy Chase and Bethesda, over from Alexandria and Arlington, in from the hunt country, up from the fashionable reaches of the Potomac, down from Georgetown to converge upon the Statler in their white ties and formal dresses, their Cadillacs and taxis, their bright, all-knowing archness about the political currents and undercurrents of the world. GLITTERING CROWD EXPECTED TO HONOR DOBIUS, the *Evening Star* reported; PRESIDENT MAY NOT ATTEND . . . WHAT'S WITH H.H.?" the *News* inquired, more jauntily; CAN IT BE HE'S MAD AT WALTER?(!) The possibility lent an extra spice to an event that was already heavy with Gorotoland, the vetoes, the coming election, and all the clashing and dramatic personalities involved.

Of these, the one belonging to the Governor of the State of California was perhaps the least at ease as the evening drew on to the hour of seven-thirty when, with the honor guest and other notables, he must join the pre-banquet reception and then the shambling little parade to the head table that always distinguishes such occasions in Washington. He was very much aware that Walter intended to make his persuasions as inescapable as possible, and to his own introductory remarks he and Ceil had given intensive thought in the hours that had elapsed since the disastrous lunch at "Salubria" and the President's talk. He knew, if the *News* and *Star* did not, that the President would not attend, for the President had called early in the afternoon and told him so. He was not bothering to inform Walter, the President said with an ironic little laugh, because he thought Walter probably suspected; but he did want Ted to know that it was nothing personal as far as he was concerned.

"Of course," he had added, "it does relieve me of appearing to take sides between you and Orrin, which is all to the good, isn't it?"

"I don't know," Governor Jason said. "I had hoped you'd join in the wild enthusiasm and help nominate me by acclamation."

"I doubt if it will be quite that."

"I don't have any doubts what it will be, as I said the other day. It will be Harley M. Hudson, all the way. I thought your talk last night was very effective. You've made it difficult to disagree."

"Though some no doubt may try," the President remarked. "For instance— . . . I wish I could be there to hear you. It's my one regret in not attending."

"I don't think you need worry very much," Governor Jason said. "And I will be at the Capitol Saturday."

The President made a wry little sound.

"I doubt very much that there will be any refusals."

Nor, of course, would there be, the Governor thought with an equal wryness as he got into white tie and tails in the suite he and Ceil had engaged for the evening, helped her with a few last tuckings and zippings, and then stood back to admire the statuesque blond beauty which was always saved from arrogance by her quick wit and genuine friendliness. She was quite an asset, his wife, because she always overwhelmed people on first meeting but had them eating out of her hand two minutes later. Plus, of course, the good looks and the style and, although she professed to despise the word, the glamor.

"I hate to be written about as though I were a movie star," she often remarked, but laughed when he replied that in California, having a Governor's wife who looked like a movie star seemed to arouse some deep atavistic response in the sun-tanned lemmings as they ambled toward the sea.

"I'll bet," he said now, "that you're worth two million votes to me, just as you stand, on the hoof, f.o.b. Sacramento."

"Darling," she said with an ironic smile as she selected a pair of gloves, "you're going to need every one of them this year, and don't think you aren't."

He frowned.

"Yes, I imagine. And I still don't know that I want them."

"I still don't know that you're going to get them," she replied, the smile deepening. "I doubt if your introduction of Walter is going to set the Mall on fire—though it may leave Walter sufficiently baffled to keep him on his toes."

"Leave everyone sufficiently baffled to keep them on their toes," he suggested. "It's a good thing Walter's on my side or he'd be writing columns about what a damned equivocal shilly-shallyer I am." He smiled. "May yet."

"What an extraordinary character that little man is," she said, pausing in her last-minute hair primpings to really think about him. "I honestly believe he thinks the country rises or falls on what he tells it in his columns."

"Why shouldn't he?" Governor Jason asked. "The country tells him it's true."

"His own profession tells him it's true. I don't know whether twenty-five years of studying your own navel in the Reflecting Pool in front of the Lincoln Memorial is really the way to understand the country or not."

"He is one of the great men of our time," Ted said solemnly. "I am about to say so myself. Surely you'll believe me."

"I find him curiously pathetic," she said. "Necessary, I guess, but pathetic. As any ego that large is pathetic, when you come right down to it. How does anyone ever convince himself that he's that important?"

"You have to," her husband said with an amiable smile. "*I* had to. So have we all, in this town. It's the only way to stand the gaff and beat the competition."

"Hmm," she said thoughtfully. "Watch out for Washington. It can give you the world with one hand, but keep your eye on the other. There's usually a price tag in it."

"And for me the price will be?"—he asked quizzically. She shrugged.

"Maybe nothing. Maybe nothing at all. Or maybe"—she gave him a thoughtful stare. "Integrity. Decency. Harley's pet word, honor." She shrugged again. "Who knows?"

"I'll count on you to keep me from paying too high a price," he said softly.

She laughed.

"That's noble enough, all right. But, darling, I discovered many years ago that what little Teddy wants little Teddy goes after, and it doesn't really matter very much what little Ceil thinks about it. Right?"

"You don't do yourself justice," he said, but she only laughed again.

"Oh, it's quite all right. I love you just the same, you understand. If you want to march out of that hall tonight leading a charge on the White House, I'll be right at your side. I'm sure the President will give us soda pop and an ice-cream cone before sending us quietly off to bed."

He grinned.

"You're so good for me. You have no idea."

"Oh, sure I have," she said with a smile. "It's what keeps me going between appointments to have my hair done. . . . Toss me my shoes, will you? In fact, help me put them on. . . . Cullee Hamilton called, incidentally, I forgot to tell you. He said he'd come by and walk us down to the reception."

"Did he?" the Governor said with an expression of exaggerated surprise as he knelt to oblige with the shoes. "What's that about, I wonder?"

"Maybe he's afraid Patsy's really going to run for Senator in California and he wants to beg you to keep her away."

"Patsy isn't going to run for Senator from anywhere," he said with a surprising impatience. "I wish she'd get over the idea that it's fun to get someone like Cullee stirred up. He's too important, at this point."

"Even though he cast a veto and is proud of it?"

He gave an ironic grunt.

"That won't hurt him very much. Some of the teach-in crowd will squeal, but nature has them in a nice box for him. After all, he's black. They may hate him for supporting the Administration in Gorotoland but they've simply got to love him for being a Negro. There's no way they can get around it. God!" he said with a sudden bitter honesty that quite startled her. "How I hate all those damned intolerant little self-righteous, self-centered boors. Somebody ought to wash their mouths out with soap, give them a good licking, and send them to bed. Along with all the pompous little twerps egging them on, that some abortion of justice has put on the faculties."

"My goodness!" she said with a hearty laugh. "Are you ever violent! What have they done to you, except urge you to run, from every stately campus and ivory-covered tower?"

"Oh, I know," he said, relaxing into a grin as they heard a knock on the door. "They're major roots in my grassroots support. Don't worry. I won't tell them what I think."

She nodded.

"I know. That's part of the price tag, isn't it?"

He gave her a long stare, and his eyes did not drop until he was ready for them to.

"Here's Cullee," he said finally, as the knock came again, a little more insistent. "Be nice."

"I always am," she said with a sunny smile. "It's my most wonderful characteristic."

And as they sat and chatted for a few moments before going down to the pre-banquet reception, she was friendly and frank with Cullee, who, an imposing and magnificent ebony giant in his white tie and tails, was very much at ease with them. He asked after Patsy with the ironic designation "Senator Labaiya," and a grin that dismissed her, and the Governor responded with just enough of a grin in reply so that Cullee knew there was no point in worrying about that. There was also a fleeting reference to the incumbent junior Senator from California, Raymond Robert Smith, and again there was something in the tones of both the Governor and the Congressman that seemed to take care of *that*. Ceil realized that in ten minutes' time they were disposing of the political future of California in the fall elections; providing, of course, that the price tag was honored.

She was not entirely sure what it would be until they left the room and started toward the elevator. Then Cullee, who was the man in a position to present it, inquired casually, "I expect you're really going to bawl the President out tonight, hm?"

The Governor smiled.

"Do you think I should?"

"No, *I* don't think you should," the Congressman said, "but a lot of important people who want you to be President think you should. So you will, I guess."

"What would you do if I did?"

Cullee gave him an impassive stare.

"Issue a statement repudiating you at once," he said calmly. "What would you expect?"

"Knowing you," the Governor said, "I'd expect it."

Cullee shrugged.

"Well."

"But," Ted said with a smile as they reached the elevator and Cullee touched the button, "I may not be so easy to categorize as all that."

"Then you certainly won't satisfy Walter and his crew," the Congressman said, adjusting his tie in the mirror beside the door.

"Must I?" Ted asked, seeking Cullee's eyes in the mirror and holding them until the Congressman turned around.

"It's up to you. I thought you wanted to be President."

"Maybe it needn't be quite as drastic a commitment as that," Ted said. Cullee studied him thoughtfully.

"It's got to be. The country's getting so divided that you won't be able to equivocate much longer. If, that is," he added with a little smile, "you are equivocating. Myself, I've been giving you the benefit of the doubt. I've been telling myself that you were genuinely trying to make up your mind."

"I'm genuine," Ted Jason said with a smile. "You've just seen me in one or two ungenuine moments, that's all."

"Such as when old Terry was over here romping through South Carolina last fall," Cullee remarked. "Yes, I know."

"It seemed advisable to support him then," the Governor said. "It may now. I'm not sure."

"I can believe that," Cullee said as the elevator arrived. "There's a lot at stake in Gorotoland."

"Indeed, yes," Ted said as they stepped on and started to descend.

"I hope you will both wind up eventually seeing it the same way," Ceil remarked. Cullee smiled with a certain skepticism.

"We start from rather far apart."

"But Washington brings so many divergent points of view together," she said gently.

His smile broadened.

"Marvelous, isn't it?"

She gave him an amused glance and nodded. "Marvelous. Tell me," she added abruptly, "did you get what you came to get tonight? About the Senatorship, I mean?"

For a second he looked startled. Then he grinned.

"I think so." The grin broadened. "Haven't had to pay anything for it, either, have I?"

The Governor laughed, apparently without rancor.

"Not yet," he said amicably. "Maybe never."

"That would be the best solution," Ceil said, and before Ted could answer, as the elevator came to a stop and through its yet unopened doors they could hear the babble of famous voices halfway through the second drink, she cried, "And here we are!" Linking arms with both of them she drew them forward into the reception. The sound immediately rose in excitement, and somewhere over by the bar someone began applause that surged across the room as photographers hurried forward to take their pictures and record their triumphal entry.

"Is Walter here?" the Governor called out, and someone shouted back, "No, he's going to jump out of a cake at the banquet!" The thought provoked a wave of laughter, and on it they were washed pleasantly along for the next half-hour, shaking innumerable eagerly grasping hands, smiling innumerable automatic smiles, engulfed in the loud "Hi, *there's!*" and "Haarh y'alls?" that always launch a Washington reception. Suitably greeted and made much of, they were then ready for the parade to the head table. Still accompanied by Cullee, who promised that he would break away at the door and "seek my own level" at Table 16, they moved to the little room just off the ballroom where they were to form in procession.

There they found Walter Dobius, who greeted them with a solemn handshake. A slight paleness gave the only indication that he was still remembering the luncheon at "Salubria" and anticipating the speech to come.

"This is an important evening for you," Ceil remarked,

more to be saying something than for any other reason. He bowed gravely.

"It is an important night for the country. I expect many things will be changed after tonight."

"You frighten me," Governor Jason said with a smile. Walter was not amused.

"Don't frighten us," he said coldly. "Too much depends upon you now."

"That frightens *me*," Ceil murmured as Walter turned away to greet Associate Justice Thomas Buckmaster Davis of the Supreme Court and his inevitable sidekick, the executive director of the *Post;* and though she said it lightly, it was apparent to her husband that she meant it. He gave her a contemplative look but did not reply.

Then they were entering the enormous ballroom, led by Patsy, regal in orchids, diamonds, and the great green Star of Boonarapi, followed by Walter, nodding with a grave acknowledgment as the applause welled up from the handsome audience that filled every table and overflowed into the halls beyond. But Walter's applause, though warm, encouraging, and respectful, as befitted his dignity and international stature, was as nothing to the roar of sound that suddenly rose from the room as the Edward Jasons came up the steps onto the dais.

Primordial, animal, visceral, consuming and, to them, frightening in its intensity, it engulfed them. Instinctively the procession halted. After a second's hesitation, as the photographers shoved and jostled frantically to snap their pictures and from the projection booths high in the walls the network cameras and spotlights swung down to focus upon them, the Governor and his wife stepped forward. He raised his arms, his right hand linked with hers, and together they waved. The sound rose yet higher, passing beyond human control, beyond sense, beyond sound to become almost a solid thing, a great chunk of animal hunger that swallowed them up and transformed them in that instant into free individuals no longer but symbols, thenceforth and forever captive to the dreams of other men.

"I think we've got a candidate," the executive director of the *Post* shouted happily to the gray-haired little figure of Justice Davis jumping wildly up and down at his side.

"My dear boy," Tommy Davis cried. "My dear boy, I think we have!"

Launched in so spectacular a fashion, the Jason Foundation Dinner for the conferring of the Good and Faithful Servant Award upon Walter Dobius, columnist and statesman, moved in an ever-tightening tension toward its climax. Not even the entry, ten minutes later, of Prince Obifumatta was sufficient to interrupt its steady progression. (The leader of the gallant fight against American imperialism had decided to delay his departure for the front so that he might appear over the weekend on "Face the Nation," "Meet the Press," a CBS special entitled, "Gorotoland: Foredoomed Adventure?" and an NBC counterpart, "Gorotoland: Why Are We There?" Taken together, these hastily produced programs, rushed to the screen as a major contribution to the calm, dispassionate consideration of the situation, represented three hours of prime time with the American public. No intelligent leader of a modern rebellion ever turns down this kindness of the networks, which sometimes seems to be offered automatically to anyone sufficiently hostile to the aims and purposes of the United States. The only reason Prince Terry was not doing the same was because nobody had asked him. Terry was yesterday's enemy; today he was a friend and as such no longer worth the time. Also, of course, such appearances might win him public support. He was already back somewhere in the bush leading his troops. It was all very sad from his point of view, but great from Obifumatta's.)

Not even Obi could distract for more than a minute or two the dazzling audience that ate a rather absentminded meal as it stared with an avid interest at the handsome Governor and his beautiful lady.

Admittedly, there were a few small areas of skepticism: Helen-Anne Carrew, expressing herself so loudly that she could be heard four tables around and at one point provoked an indignant, "Oh, *hush!*" from the wife of the Norwegian Ambassador—Lafe Smith and Cullee, keeping up a running cross fire at their table against the worshipful comments of Krishna Khaleel and the Ambassador and Ambassadress of Uruguay—Bob and Dolly Munson, maintaining a pointed and effective silence at another table where Senator Raymond Robert Smith of California was holding forth with a nervously insistent enthusiasm about what a great Governor Ted was ("I'll tell him what you think," Senator Munson finally remarked, which was of

course what Ray Smith wanted)—at the next table Bob
Leffingwell and his wife trying to refrain from provocatory
responses to the provocatory comments of Fred Van Ackerman and LeGage Shelby of DEFY—and the principally
diplomatic table where Raoul Barre of France joined Herbert Jason and Selena Castleberry in fulsome praise of
Governor Jason while Celestine Barre smiled in her silent,
enigmatic way and Lord and Lady Maudulayne rather uncomfortably put in an occasional cautious word for the
Secretary of State.

But for the most part it was an audience that had really
awed and overwhelmed itself by the depth of its awesome
and overwhelming welcome for the Governor. Senators
and Congressmen, members of the government, members
of the diplomatic corps and the press, spoke with a
qualified caution and restraint they would not have shown
an hour ago about the chances of the President and
Secretary of State. Quite without anyone planning it—and
even though logic told them it was a friendly audience anyway, which could have been expected to react as it did—an
enormous boost had suddenly been given to the Governor
of California, and to all those forces of dissidence and criticism of America's policies that hoped to make of him
their spokesman and standard-bearer.

Logic had nothing to do with it. Emotion had abruptly
taken over, and with its spur a psychological tide in five
frantic minutes had suddenly been set running at top speed.
Astounding, inexplicable, unexpected—there it was, suddenly and permanently, a fact of political life in this presidential year.

Most gratified of all was the honor guest. Walter, for all
his confident talk in recent days, had really not been at all
certain how his speech would be received, either here or by
the country. Now he had no doubts.

With the end of doubt came a growing impatience to get
at it. When Patsy arose forty-five minutes later and gaveled
the excited room to silence he told himself that he hoped to
God she would have the sense to keep it brief. He had underestimated Patsy. After the generous applause for her
had died down, she kept her introduction very short, reading from text in a voice whose slight tremor alone revealed
her own excitement and tension:

"The Jason Foundation welcomes you tonight to the
biennial ceremony which, for me and my family, repre-

sents perhaps the most worthwhile—certainly the most satisfying—enterprise that we conduct: the honoring of the American citizen who has contributed most to the welfare and the future of our beloved country. Tonight the Good and Faithful Servant Award, always special, is even more special, for it goes to one who for twenty-five years has served America as few men have: with honor, with decency, with integrity, and with an impartial fairness and justice that have made of his name a marvelous beacon to the world.

"To introduce him to you," she said, and permitted a smile to break through, "I present to you one who has always been a beacon to ME, ever since I was a little girl in awe of my big brother who always knew everything—and still does—the Honorable Edward Jason, Governor of the State of California."

And now, little Teddy, he told himself in Ceil's wry phrase as he faced a hall gone mad, you've got to be good. And you will be, he promised himself fiercely: you will be. You're not going to let them stampede you—you can't afford to let them stampede you. These loving monsters will eat you alive if you let them. You cannot, you *cannot*.

"Madame Chairman," he said with a grin when the mass of sound had finally died down ["Five minutes and seventeen seconds, I make it," ABC said to CBS in a booth above, and CBS confirmed it], "Big brothers don't ever admit it, but sometimes they're in awe of little sisters, too." There was warm laughter and spurred by it, another prolonged burst of applause. When it ended his expression changed, became solemn and serious. An attentive hush fell as they strained to listen, and only the vague drunken noise of a too-happy supporter being vehemently shushed by his wife and dinner guests, somewhere toward the back of the room, broke the ravenous silence.

"Ladies and gentlemen," he said gravely, "we meet tonight in a time of unusual tension for our country and the world, to confer upon one who is probably America's leading journalist the Good and Faithful Servant Award. ["Look at Walter," Helen-Anne urged her tablemates. "He doesn't like that 'probably.' " *"Hush,"* said the Norwegian Ambassadress severely again. "Don't hush me, Inge!" Helen-Anne said loudly. "I won't buy any herring next week." The Norwegian Ambassadress looked furious but did not reply.]

"To our award winner, and to his profession," Ted Jason continued, "we look for information, analysis, and guidance to help us better understand and bravely meet the challenges which, so constantly in this century, confront this land of ours.

"For twenty-five years he has indeed been a good and faithful servant to us all. Informed in analysis, astute in criticism, he has rarely permitted partisanship to overcome his sound and objective judgments. No more will he do so now.

["Hm?" said Bob Munson in a startled voice, and at the table adjoining, Bob Leffingwell caught his eye and gravely winked.]

"The same even-handed fairness, the supreme, dispassionate intelligence he has always given us—we need them in present days more than we ever have before. Guidance and stability is what his country wants from him. His country knows he will not fail it.

"There is in this man," the Governor said smoothly, "no intemperance, no irresponsibility. ["Oh, brother! And this is going over nationwide television!" Helen-Anne exclaimed. This time the Norwegian Ambassadress didn't even bother.] Though we may find these characteristics in others, we will not find them in him as the nation works its way through the serious difficulties that now confront it.

["I wondered when he was going to get to those," Krishna Khaleel said brightly, but to his surprise and that of many others, that was the first and last the Governor said on that subject.]

"Decency, integrity, honor—these are the qualities my sister has rightfully attributed to our honored guest tonight. Add to them restraint, dignity, good judgment, the ability to understand points of view with which he disagrees, the ability to accord them graciously their proper place in a free America—these, too, distinguish him. Never has he failed them; never have they been more needed.

"Ladies and gentlemen," he said suavely, "it is my official privilege as it is my personal pleasure to present the Good and Faithful Servant Award to him, and in turn to present him to you: a man who for twenty-five years has written a brilliant column and given his nation brilliant guidance—a man who needs no detailed recounting of his career, for we all know it so well—a man whom we honor, but who even more honors us, by his presence, his writings, and his lifelong symbolizing of the dominant characteristics of present-day American journalism—Walter Dobius."

["Izzat all?" the over-celebrator demanded loudly of his wife and guests. "Whakinaspeechizzat?"]

For a moment it seemed that most of the Governor's audience must be wondering the same thing, for there was a peculiar puzzled little hesitation. Then Bob Leffingwell, a quizzical expression on his face as he caught Senator Munson's eye, began to applaud with a heavy, insistent beat that instantly started them off. At once the puzzlement was forgotten, the doubts were resolved, sound once again rose and overwhelmed the room. A few whose business it was to wonder continued to puzzle thoughtfully over his carefully noncommittal, curiously cautionary remarks, others when they sobered up tomorrow would wake to puzzlement, but for the moment he was once again sweeping nearly all before him as he stood, bowing and smiling and gesturing to Walter to advance to the lectern and receive his award.

Only Ceil, turning to watch with interest as Walter did so and then placed his papers with a slow dignity exactly in the center of the lectern, could see the tight little lines of anger around his eyes. Walter's mad and I am glad, she thought irreverently, and I know what will please him: Harley dead and Orrin's head and little Ted to ease him. Then her husband had gestured her to her feet, and Patsy too, and they were standing with Walter, smiling and waving, while the photographers snapped, the cameras rolled, and the audience cheered, festively at first and then again with the deep animal sound that had greeted and overwhelmed them at the beginning.

"He could be nominated right now!" Justice Davis cried exultantly to the executive director of the *Post*. "I sure wish he could be, it would save a hell of a lot of headaches!" the director of the *Post* cried back.

Finally the Jasons sat down, the final susurrus died away. Walter stood alone at last to face his audience.

Of his thoughts at this moment, some in the audience had their conceptions. Helen-Anne thought she knew, and Senator Munson had his own ideas, and Bob Leffingwell was convinced he could place himself inside that monumentally capable, monumentally egotistic mind, and there were others; but none, of course, could know exactly the combination of defiant conviction and cold determination that filled his heart. His attitude might have offended the Jasons, for the award was nothing, he got awards every day, one more accolade for his genius was no more than he expected and no more than his right. But the opportunity to speak at so crucial a point in his nation's history was everything, an advantage beyond price. Dutifully his colleagues were alert to every word and every nuance. Out to the country in newspapers and magazines, over television and radio his words would fly. Telstar and Early Bird would carry them to as many distant lands and distant minds as ever heard the President's. The world of Walter Wonderful was geared tonight to the task of seeing to it that Walter's opinions covered the globe.

Man and occasion were met.

Gravely he began to speak.

"Governor, distinguished guests, ladies and gentlemen: it is with a profound humility that I accept this great honor tonight. Of all those which can be conferred by Americans upon one another, this, I think, is the most satisfying and most rewarding. No one who receives it could be other than deeply pleased. It is both an accolade and a challenge.

"You will understand," he said, and his tone became heavier and more portentous, the tone that some of his more acid colleagues referred to as "Walter's advising-God voice," "that in the context of the circumstances in which we meet tonight, it is as a challenge that I accept it."

At this there was a stirring and a restlessness in the audience, an eager leaning-forward, an exchange of glances, an anticipatory sucking-in-of-breaths, an excited wave of now-he's-going-to-let-'em-have-its. And so, without further preliminary, he did.

"This nation tonight is in danger as grave—if not graver—than any it has faced in my lifetime. In the short span of seventy-two hours the Administration in Washington has invaded a small, far-off, defenseless nation; cast two vetoes which have for all practical purposes destroyed the United Nations; and defied the astounded and justifiably enraged opinion of the world.

"It is quite an accomplishment," he said with a grim little smile that brought a scattering of rather nervous amusement from the audience, "for so short a time in the life of a country.

"It took us decades to build up world respect.

"It has taken us three days to tear it down.

"We have heard," he said, and a cold contempt came into his voice, "a great deal about honor in these fateful hours. There are various interpretations of this word. My own is based upon the belief that it is honorable to adhere to collective security, honorable to uphold the United Nations, honorable to continue a record of international decency and respect for the opinions of mankind, honorable to refrain from the use of force, particularly in our dealings with smaller countries and particularly where we are not ourselves directly threatened.

"These are what honor means to me. I ask you," he said, and a challenging demand came into his voice as he raised it for emphasis, "if you agree with my interpretation."

There was again a little nervous hesitation, and this time it was not Bob Leffingwell who converted it to applause. But somebody did, and after a second it rose and filled the room with a defiant and excited air.

"And so, I think," he resumed after a suitable pause, "do most honorable and decent Americans.

"Now, Madame Chairman, Governor [and he gave this word a slight but unmistakable emphasis that sent a delicious thrill through many in his audience], distinguished guests, what are we confronted with tonight?

"I say to you we are confronted with nothing less than the end of American influence in the world and the end of world civilization as we know it.

"I say to you we are confronted with the desperate need to find a man who can lead us out of this situation and back to sanity, without which we and the world will perish.

["You tell 'em, pal!" Fred Van Ackerman said loudly to LeGage Shelby, who nodded solemnly, and somewhere someone yelled, "Yeaay!" A wild surge of applause and excitement rolled up from the glittering tables.]

"I say to you," Walter Dobius said, abruptly grave, abruptly solemn, "that without such a man I do not, in all honesty, see hope for us in the months and years ahead."

He paused and reached down for a glass of water, which Patsy placed quickly in his hand. From it he drank and then, with a curious little motion that brought renewed excited stirrings from his audience, lifted it, in what almost seemed to be a toast, in the general direction of Governor Jason before he passed it gravely back to her.

"Of the errors of judgment and misjudgment which have brought us to this pass," he went on slowly, "of the misguided misleaders who have presided in state [there was a startled, knowing laugh, but he ignored it] over this abrupt destruction of America's historic role of peacekeeper in the world, I see no reason to talk tonight. We all know who they are: we all know how sadly they have betrayed their solemn mission to protect and preserve the United States. Their contemporaries abhor them, history will judge them. Let us tonight regard them with sorrow, pity, and horror, but do not let the contemplation of their fearful errors divert us from keeping our eyes squarely upon the future and squarely upon what must be done to save it for us and for mankind.

"Particularly," he said with a calm yet heavy emphasis, "do not let them divert us from our great task of finding the one to lead us safely from this perilous situation.

"What," he asked quietly, and a sudden renewed tension and silence settled upon the room, "should be the qualifications of such a man?

"Firstly, it seems to me, he should be one deeply and sincerely dedicated to human decency, human integrity, and human honor—and when I say honor," he said with a dry little smile, "I mean true honor, not speechifying honor.

["By damn, he's telling 'em!" Senator Van Ackerman said with a grin to 'Gage Shelby.]

"He should be one who believes in America's historic role of moderator and mediator in the world.

"He should be one who honors America's commitments to the United Nations and to collective security.

"He should be one who will always negotiate honorably first, and only as a last resort—the very last resort—turn to force for the solution of any international problem.

"He should be one who truly believes in a liberal and progressive policy for this nation in all her affairs, domestic as well as foreign.

"He should be one who has had the opportunity to serve either as the head of some great private enterprise, such as the management of a corporate empire—or as the head of some great public enterprise, such as the leadership of a major State of the Union—or preferably"—and the next word brought a roar of approval as Ted Jason tried to look interested yet unconcerned and found the feat almost beyond his abilities—"both.

"He should be one whom his countrymen know and love and trust.

"He should be one who makes up his own mind, on his own judgments, without turning to incompetent and ill-starred advisers who tell him, 'Cry war!' when his nation and the world beg for peace.

"Does America," he asked, and again that tense, devouring silence seized the room, "have such a man? I believe it does.

["Tell us, Waller boy!" the extra-drunk one cried out in the silence and there was a burst of laughter, but tense, nervous. Walter picked it up at once.]

"Do I need to tell you?" he asked, and Bob Munson murmured to Dolly, "Well, that's saved him from naming names. I wondered how he was going to handle it." And once again he and Bob Leffingwell bowed gravely to each other and winked.

"Do I need to tell you?" Walter demanded and the audience roared, "No!"

"Do I need to point him out?"

"No!"

"Is there anyone here who has any question who he is?"

"NO!"

"Get behind him, then!" Walter cried as the sound began to build ever more frantically against his words. "Work for him, then!"—the sound grew—"Nominate him!"—there was a roar of endorsement—*"Elect him!"*—and the sound burst at last into its full animal rapacity, frantic, insistent, all-devouring. First one and then another and then, swiftly, all, were on their feet, shouting, applauding, pounding on tables, pounding on each other, laughing, crying, uttering incoherent sounds. If Governor Jason had moved at that moment the event would have passed beyond sanity into some other realm; but that realm, he knew, must be saved for the convention, if ever. He did not dare move now. Very carefully he sat as though frozen and so did Ceil, fixed smiles on their faces, prisoners already though they still hoped against hope they might somehow yet be able to stay free.

Presently, when it had gone on long enough ["Ten minutes, thirteen seconds, I make it," CBS said to NBC. "Fifteen seconds, mine says," NBC amended.] Walter raised his hand for silence. Finally, reluctantly, it was granted.

"My friends," he said gravely, "I shall say no more to-night. The crisis grows, the need is urgent, the way is clear. Let all who love America rally to the cause.

"Destiny—and," he added with a heavy emphasis—"honor—require no less."

And he sat down. And again the room roared. And again the Governor and his lady sat frozen while Helen-Anne's protestations were lost in the tumult, Senator Munson and Bob Leffingwell exchanged their last quizzical glance, Fred Van Ackerman and LeGage Shelby grinned excitedly at one another, and Ambassadors, government officials, Walter's colleagues, and all, found themselves swept along in the wild, consuming tide.

And then presently the audience began to break up, many beginning to shove their way toward the head table to shake hands with the Governor, so that soon there was an enormous push and crush at the front of the room. Responding now, as he knew he must, he and Ceil leaned forward, reached down, shook hand after eager hand thrust up to them from the happy, exuberant, emotionally and alcoholically excited mob below. In the stir and shove of it, few noticed when the Governor straightened up and tilted his head back and to one side to listen to the words of a Secret Service man who had approached from behind the platform and laid a calm, insistent hand upon his arm.

"Yes, what is it?" he asked, still waving and smiling to cover the interruption.

"The President wants you to come to the White House right away," the Secret Service man murmured. "We have a car downstairs."

"Right," Ted said, and with one last wave at the crowd, which uttered a disappointed groan as it realized he was leaving, he whispered the news to Ceil and Patsy. "Oh, dear," Patsy said with a stricken look. "You don't suppose it's"—"I wouldn't be surprised," her brother said tersely. "I'll see you two at the house." Then in a flash he was hurried out and away by the Secret Service man and a colleague who seemed to materialize from the wall.

"What was that?" Walter demanded harshly of Ceil and Patsy, but neither would tell him.

In some puzzlement and confusion but still aglow with the excitement of the anointing of a candidate whom most of them devoutly believed in, the audience dispersed into little eagerly gossiping groups and moved slowly out. In the jostle Helen-Anne happened to come alongside Cullee Hamilton. He paused and offered her his arm.

"What did you think of that?" she demanded as they resumed their slow progress through the crowd. He shrugged. "About what we expected, wasn't it?" "How are you going to stop him?" she asked. He looked down at her with the quick, knowledgeable glance of political Washington. "Only one man can, I think," he said, nodding in the general direction of Pennsylvania Avenue. "And that, only by telling him flatly, No."

But if the Governor of California had any idea that this was what awaited him at a White House outwardly hushed and deserted but inwardly quivering with tension, he was soon disabused. His was not the only limousine to drive straight to the Diplomatic Entrance on the south side of the White House. Orrin was just alighting from one when Ted arrived, two of the Joint Chiefs of Staff and the Secretary of Defense were getting out of another, the Under Secretary of State for Latin American Affairs descended from yet another. Babble greeted him as he entered the beautiful old house that has seen so much of a nation's hopes and agony. He had time only to exchange a few quick greetings with others as baffled as himself, only time to realize suddenly that, whatever it was, the President was seeing to it that he was committed from the start, only time to realize once again with a surprised, ironic little smile that it was wise not to underestimate Harley, when the White House usher appeared at the head of the stairs and said gravely, "Gentlemen, the President will see you now."

And then he and all of them knew what it was that had brought them there, and knew also that, quite possibly, it really did not matter in the long run what such as Walter Dobius said or did not say, since what would happen now really lay in the hearts and minds of a very few men.

Across the room the Governor of California met without flinching the steady eyes of the Secretary of State, knowing, as he could see Orrin did, that in the last analysis probably only three of these really counted; and knowing also that in all probability their future and that of their country had been decided by the events of the last three furious days and this ominous night; and that things were frozen

PART TWO

THE PRESIDENT'S BOOK

1

THE HANDLING by Walter's world of the state funeral of the American dead from Gorotoland, and the simultaneous story out of Panama that Felix Labaiya had finally moved to seize the country and the Canal, was, of its kind, a classic.

In some calmer century there might have been time for the student to observe, during the memorial ceremonies at the Capitol which held the attention of the nation and the world for forty-eight somber hours, how respectfully the dead were treated and yet how suavely, in what hushed and fitting tones, the blame for their brutal demise was somehow removed from those who had killed them and placed upon the President of the United States . . . how tenderly and with what dignified sorrow the cameras dwelt upon the faces of the bereaved, and yet with what loving attention they somehow seemed to keep coming back again and again to the gravely handsome visage of the Governor of California, so that he frequently appeared to be the only mourner present . . . how meticulously and with what careful attention most of the dignitaries were noted, yet how casually and almost absentmindedly the President and the Secretary of State were passed over in fleeting glimpses and casual comments, so that the viewer or reader could almost be excused if he somehow had the hazy impression that they weren't there at all . . . and how profoundly, with what deep sorrow, but with what shrewd and subtle slantings under the shroud, the various "teams," the various "roundups," the various discussion groups composed of Our Correspondent From Here, Our Reporter From There, and Frankly Unctuous, The Anchor Man From The Home Office In New York, were able to link Gorotoland and Panama, and in the hush of benediction use them both to beat the Administration over the head.

Thousands of churches were open, millions upon millions worshiped, the President's desire for a Day of Dedication was amply fulfilled; yet from the members of Walter's world there poured a steady counterstream of cutting-down, weakening the effect, subtly, but effectively destroying the mood.

It was one of their finest hours, and they gave it their best.

So also did they for Panama. The news of Felix Labaiya's coup had not really surprised them much more than it had the government, for there had been fairly clear intimations during the preceding week; but no innocent citizen would ever know it, to hear the reports. Shocked and shattered by America's response, Our Correspondent, Our Reporter, and Frankly Unctuous The Anchor Man announced with a grave dismay the sudden explosion of one more act of inexplicable violence by the United States. The shock and dismay were compounded a hundredfold because, as one of them put it, "in this nightmare world produced by hasty and impulsive action in Africa, the United States Government seems to be heading straight for a repetition six thousand miles away in Latin America."

Endlessly Walter's world repeated the story of the midnight White House meeting, exactly as before; the apparent determination to go it alone once again despite the outraged and embittered outcries from around the world, exactly as before.

"They say repetition is boring," said Frankly Unctuous crisply as he brought to a close the fifth unanimously condemnatory round table he hosted for his network on that fantastically repetitive weekend filled with the ritual of one war and the bulletins of another, "but when repetition could mean the death of a great nation as well as the world's hope of survival, it perhaps behooves us to pay attention."

So they did, and the effort they had expended upon Gorotoland began to seem only rehearsal before they were through. Again there were the violent editorials, the savage commentaries, the headlines that twisted, the news stories that half-told, the photographs that misrepresented, the programs that smeared and subtly undermined—all the customary weapons of Walter's world striving desperately to hold to the last vestige of sanity as they believed it to be. With a mounting hysteria they demanded that the United States submit the Panamanian issue to the United Nations, though the President had announced in his statement early Monday morning that the United States would again use the veto if any attempt were made to interfere with preventive action against what he described as "the clearest and most direct attack yet made upon the safety and security of the Western Hemisphere." With an equal fury they demanded the intervention of the Organization of American States, though that argumentative and uncertain body was again wallowing helplessly in its own mutual suspicions and consternations. The CIA report listing the presence of Soviet and Chinese Communists in Felix's "Government of the Panamanian People's Liberation Movement" was treated with scorn and skepticism in many major publications and programs, almost completely ignored in others. The President's statement that the United States had no choice but to meet an immediate situation with immediate action was dismissed by The Greatest Publication That Absolutely Ever Was as "an empty and obvious cover-up for American aggression, of a type the world has seen before in the Caribbean area."

Repetitions there were, all right: the repetitions of Walter's world, bound and determined that it would force the facts of an ugly century to conform to its own fond beliefs of what the United States should do, if it had to slant those facts, twist them, corrupt them, or suppress them altogether in order to make its case.

Confronted with this continuation, and in many cases escalation, of the furious attacks upon him, the portly man with the kindly face who sits at the big desk in the haunted house does not find it too difficult, on this morning three weeks after the start of hostilities in Panama, to maintain a relatively calm approach to the problems that confront him. He has called a press conference for 4 P.M. this afternoon, his first in almost a month, and in the hours between he is preparing firmly yet unhurriedly to do the things that must be done before he makes the statement he is planning for that time. Some will be pleasant, some painful, some, perhaps, a curious mixture, yet all, he feels, are necessary.

He looks forward to them with interest, for he is, among other things, an amateur but increasingly experienced student of human nature. It always intrigues him to observe how it will react to the pressures of ambition, disappointment, and hope.

Harley M. Hudson at sixty-two has been President of the

United States for a year, and having satisfied himself at Geneva in the first week of his magistracy that he was equal to its demands, he is not about to shiver and shake now, either when he faces major decisions or when he is under attack. It is true that few Presidents have received the condemnation that has been his in the days since he moved in Gorotoland, ordered the vetoes, and then, three days later, found himself forced to move in Panama. But it is also true that few have been more comfortably supported by the conviction that what they have done has been the only thing possible if the country is to survive.

It would have been neater, he sometimes reflects with a rueful smile, if history had given the world time to assimilate Gorotoland before he was called upon to throw Panama in its face: yet history in these times is not neat. Crisis crowds upon crisis, disaster tumbles upon disaster. History never pauses to give men breath before it renders new demands upon them. They find they have survived one challenge with reasonable heroism only to discover that new heroics are required before they have time to get a shave and shower. They no sooner put out one fire here than another bursts out there. A ham sandwich, a gulp of Coke, a quick cigarette, and Marlborough *s'a va t'en guerre* again. It is all rush, rush, rush and the devil eager and anxious to take the hindmost.

It is all, in fact, hectic, dangerous, traumatic and upsetting, and it imposes upon the sheer luck of rapid decision the burden of whether or not the country, and with it some semblance of a free and decent civilization in the world, will survive.

So there was no time in Panama, precious little in Gorotoland.

Things had to be done.

He did them.

Psychologically and emotionally, his countrymen are still reeling, particularly that small but highly influential number comprising what he, in common with many who have felt the sting of its self-righteous savaging, thinks of as "Walter's world." They pay him their disrespects every day in a thousand different fashions, some direct—"The President's Policies Are Foolish," one of Walter's lesser colleagues had entitled a column yesterday; some more crablike—"President May Wish To Protect Associates' Holdings in Panama," Washington's most famous hit-and-run artist had put it the day before—but the essential song is the same. With it, the corollaries: an increasingly bleary-eyed academic community, staggering through its umpteenth teach-in; earnest gentlemen of the cloth almost, though none quite, asking Jehovah to strike him dead; an occasional full-page ad, signed by the more self-conscious members of the cultural community, still appearing with a weary defiance in the New York *Times*. The opposition may be groggy, but it is as grimly determined to thwart his purposes as it ever was. Now, as a month ago, he and his policies remain the issue.

For a soul who really loves peace and quiet, he sometimes tells Lucille with a rather grim humor, destiny has certainly cast him in a strange and hardly believable role. The furniture manufacturer from Grand Rapids, Michigan, who inherited a small family business and parlayed it into fortune, and then into fame when he was chosen by a hard-pressed party to run for Governor, really never wanted anything but to have a nice family in a nice house on a nice street, lead a friendly and productive life, travel a little, do some fishing, read a book or two. Yet here he is, fulcrum of the earth, hero to many, monster to many more, leader of the world's strongest nation and as such repository of the hopes or hatreds of most of mankind.

It has its ironies, and Harley Moore Hudson, though not all his critics or his friends give him credit for it, has the sort of mind that can appreciate them.

If he had to categorize that mind—and once, when he was a half-forgotten, uneasy Vice President, *Life* had asked him to do so for an essay it was preparing on his peculiar office—he would probably say "good-natured," for that is, generally, what he considers it to be. He cannot remember ever having had any particular hatreds, ever having held any particular grudges. He rarely even gets annoyed enough to swear, and then it is usually a mild, "Holy Toledo!" which in the robust Senate always used to delight his more freely-spoken colleagues, and now in the White House is capable of injecting a note of startled amusement into the most somber discussions. Not even Gorotoland and Panama, not even Walter Dobius at his most savage, can provoke much more than some such mild response from the President: the expletive, such as it is, truly reflects his nature. He is not a man of great indignations—or, at least, not of noisy ones—and he is not one who feels, as do some in public life, that he must shout at the top of his lungs to convince the country that he means something. But the convictions are there.

For many years, though the record in Michigan was plain to those who knew him, this fact was overlooked or disbelieved in Washington. In Michigan, where he grew up the son of an earnest Dutch immigrant running a small corner furniture store in Grand Rapids (expanded, before he died, by the addition of two branch stores), Harley was known as a steady, industrious child of an almost uniformly sunny disposition and a quietly determined personality. The oldest of three brothers and two sisters, he was what his Scotch-Irish mother called "my little top," who seemed always to be spinning about the house or the school ground, going after what he wanted and humming with happiness and good will toward the world. Troubles were few and quickly forgotten, triumphs were modest but solidly grounded in the friendliness and encouragement of his teachers and contemporaries. He was not a brilliant student but he was a reliable one, who stood somewhere in the middle of his class scholastically, somewhere near the top in affectionate liking and regard. When his father died, Harley was seventeen and president of his high school student body. He had already decided that he would return after his graduation from the University of Michigan and enter the business. When he completed his studies he did so, assuming command from the junior partner into whose hands it had temporarily passed upon his father's death.

In college his principal achievement, as he often told audiences when he was running for Governor, was to marry Lucille Breckenridge, even then a plump, rosy little soul who had been a class behind him. Theirs had been a mild but enduring courtship that had furnished placid companionship and much serene happiness, and still did. They had married as soon as he graduated, Lucille saying calmly that she didn't need her degree anyway since she knew he would be a success in anything he did and so she would never have to make her own living. He had been both alarmed and flattered, but despite his innate caution about the future she had gone right ahead, and, as usual, had been correct. He has been a success, and she never will have to worry should anything happen to him. Her decision to devote herself to the running of a happy home and the rearing of two delightful daughters has proved to be the best possible for them both.

In a quiet, homebody way, however, she has been fully as much of a political help as Beth Knox to Orrin or Ceil Jason, in her wryly intelligent way, to Ted. Lucille has not been much of a one for campaigning or for making speeches, but she has put in appearances often enough to please the voters, and privately she has given him advice he has usually found to be sound and sensible. She has some instinct for brushing straight through all the rationalizations to get at the heart of things, and with it she also has a shrewd ability to judge human nature, particularly in its more ambitious aspects. It had taken him, for instance, some time to really size up Ted Jason, but it now seems to him that Lucille had pegged him right the first time. "He's an opportunist," she had said after they met the Jasons four years ago at a Governors' Conference in Glacier National Park. "He may be a worrying one, but when the worry's over, he doesn't hesitate. You'll see." It was an analysis that has come back often to the President's mind in this last hectic month. Ted is still hesitating, the worry isn't over yet. Which way will he jump?

In a sense the President has to admire this, because he knows the pressures to make Ted run against him are fully as strong as the pressures to make the President retire—they ought to be, they come from the same sources. He is not giving in to them himself, and every day that Ted withstands them is one more day in the bank for the Administration. The President has not attempted to influence him any further after the weekend of Panama and the memorial service; hasn't seen him in Washington, called on the phone, written.

"It's up to you to decide," he remarked when they shook hands at 3 A.M. after the Panama meeting and Ted smiled, a little wanly, the President thought.

"Decisions, decisions!" he said with a humorous air.

The President nodded.

"They go with this house, and they go with getting here. I wish you luck with yours."

"Thanks," Governor Jason said. "If I'm as calm in mine as you always seem to be in yours, I should be able to stand the gaff."

And in a real sense that is true, the President thinks now

as he prepares to go downstairs, walk the colonnade along the rose garden, and so come to his oval office and the clamoring world that waits to leap upon him from his desk. He always has been pretty calm, now that he looks back upon it. The only rough period came during the seven years when his brilliant predecessor deliberately excluded him from the inner workings of the government so that Harley found himself, more times than he likes to remember now, in the unenviable position of being outside looking in. That had been hard to take, while all the formal pretenses of consultation and cooperation and "making unprecedented use of the Vice President" had been kept up for the benefit of press and public. Harley had known that the President wasn't really cutting him in on anything very important, and he had also known in the President's last year and a half that he might soon be called to fall heir to all of it. It had been a most frustrating time, and only Lucille's support and his own innate stability had permitted him to emerge, somewhat emotionally tattered and torn but otherwise in reasonably good shape, when the news he had been dreading so long arrived at his offce in the Capitol on a night he would never forget.

The first portion of his life, however—"before the blitz hit me and I got into this," he will sometimes tell his appreciative audiences—and, in a sense, the first year of his Presidency, had been comparatively serene. He had returned from college just as he said he would, plunged into the business with interest and enthusiasm, and in a short while led it through a carefully planned expansion to a new level of success. Additional branch stores were opened in Flint, Saginaw, and Detroit, and by the time he was forty the company was doing an annual gross business of ten million dollars. The years appeared to stretch out ahead filled with more stores, bigger grosses, greater fortune—and what?

Although it took him a while to admit it to himself, he was beginning to get bored.

More for that reason than for any deep-seated social motivation, he began to dabble in a mild way in politics. His money was more than welcome and his participation, since it did not involve wounding battles for or against any particular candidate or issue, proved equally so. It was good to have Harley around, the party leaders felt; he could always be relied upon for a handsome check, and he could also be relied upon to provide one shoulder everybody could cry on, one heart and mind that didn't seem to hate anyone. Subtly and quite without any conscious desire or manipulation on his part, he presently became the one man in Michigan whom everybody liked. It was only a short step from that to becoming the one man upon whom everybody could agree. When that happened, destiny took over and the roller-coaster ride began.

Even so, his nomination for Governor came as a complete surprise to him.

"But not *me!*" he had exclaimed blankly when Bob Munson, exercising his prerogative as Michigan's senior Senator to step in and bring squabbling factions together after the sudden death of the party's standard-bearer, came to him with the news. "Why *me?*"

"Because nobody's mad at you," the Majority Leader said. "No other contender can make this claim."

"But I'm not a contender!"

"I know," Senator Munson said cheerfully. "That's why. So you are now."

"You'll let me talk it over with Lucille," he suggested timidly. Bob had smiled.

"Sure, but I'll bet we both know what her answer will be."

And so they had.

"Do it. They think you're just an amiable man they can all agree on. They also think you're an amiable man they can all push around. They don't know you're also a good man, who won't be pushed and who will do some good. Surprise them all. They need it."

So he had called Bob Munson next morning in Washington. His selection had been announced that afternoon. By nightfall pledges of support were flooding in. In the six remaining weeks of the campaign he and Lucille had crisscrossed their huge state by plane, bus, and motor caravan, drawing good crowds and an increasingly warm response wherever they went. There had been a series of television interviews and flattering reports in the papers—he had been fashionable, in those days, and even Walter Dobius had come out from Washington to do a series of columns around the general theme, "A Man of Integrity Seeks A Governorship." On election day he had won by a comfortable margin. He still has among his papers somewhere Walter's letter of congratulations, written in the gravely dignified, fatherly style he likes to effect with newcomers on the national scene:

"I look forward—and I know it will not be long delayed —to the time when you will come to Washington. There I know we can work together in harmony and understanding for the good of our great country."

His year in the governorship had been notable for its smoothness. "Everybody Likes Harley," his campaign posters had proclaimed, and in Lansing, it seemed, they did. The state's problems at that point were not too great, and he handled them with an easygoing efficiency. He was beginning to get heavy-jowled, portly, and gray; his face grew more kindly and likable as he aged. His popularity continued to rise, he could probably have stayed around for quite a while. But then came the famous convention at which Orrin Knox had made his second bid for the Presidency— against, ironically, another Governor of California—and out of its wild turmoil Harley M. Hudson had been flung to the top.

He could still remember that fantastic moment in which he had been trying to reach the podium to cast Michigan's votes for the then Senator from Illinois, only to have Orrin intercept him with a blaze of anger and the charge that he was backing Orrin's opponent. His own reaction had been instantaneous—it had to be, in that roaring sea of emotion —he had cast Michigan's votes for the Governor, Orrin had lost, and not until almost eight years later, in the first hours of his own Presidency at the end of the Senate fight over Bob Leffingwell, had Harley revealed to Orrin what his original intention had been.

To this day he could not entirely understand Orrin's motivations in so affronting him in that crucial moment. But it had made him Vice President—for Bob Munson and the Michigan delegation claimed their price from the winner— and in due time it had made him President. So he was not ungrateful for it. And it had also had much to do with the maturing of Orrin Knox, and that was a gain for the country.

The personality of his Secretary of State, like that of Governor Jason, is a matter of endless fascination to the President. He has watched that shrewd, calculating, volatile, impulsive, dynamic, skeptical, impatient, sometimes arrogant, often domineering, generous, and idealistic mind at work for a good many years now, and there are areas of it that still don't add up, from his standpoint. But there has been a steady growth, a maturing and calming-down from more extravagant extremes, which he has watched with approval and relief. Although Orrin is taking a pounding from Walter's world fully as savage and severe as the President's, there is still an excellent chance that he may yet be President himself. And even if that should not develop he will continue to have, in office or out, a major influence with a great many of his countrymen who, the President suspects, are loyal and unshaken despite the bitter criticisms to which the Secretary is being subjected.

These criticisms, and the events in Gorotoland and Panama which have brought them down upon Orrin and himself, are, the President has long since concluded, just part of the normal burden one has to bear if he wishes to remain true to certain principles in carrying out the office of Chief Executive. It would be nice to be loved, and in his first few months he certainly had been, so he knows how that feels; but sooner or later there comes a time when personal popularity has to be put in the balance against doing what judgment and the facts say is best for the country. There had been some Presidents in the twentieth century who, faced with this choice, had taken the easy way and sought to hold personal popularity to a maximum while doing the minimum necessary to meet the imperatives that challenged them. That has not been his concept of the Presidency.

What that concept is he had been forced to decide, of course, the moment he assumed office, for there had been waiting for him the Soviet demand that the United States meet in Geneva under the threat of the successful Russian manned landing on the moon. His predecessor had already accepted this challenge when he died, and Harley, though he could gracefully have used the excuse of his sudden new responsibilities to evade it, had accepted too. There had followed that flat defiance of the Soviet threats which had won him such universal popularity. When he had walked out of the Geneva Conference and brought the American delegation home, leaving behind a sputtering Russian Premier, his personal stock had shot up to a fantastic peak, and the self-confidence and pride of his countrymen in their country had reached heights it had not known for many years and would not, perhaps, know again for many more.

"The only place I can go now is down," he told Lucille ironically when he saw the nation's most influential opinion poll two weeks after his return from Geneva. (Now, of course, that poll, following as always the line of Walter and his world, is telling a different story. COUNTRY DIS-APPROVES OF GOROTO-PANAMA POLICIES, its latest headline had said only yesterday. "One in five American voters is concerned about the President's policies in Gorotoland and Panama," its report began. Some fifteen hundred in a population pushing 250,000,000 had, indeed, been interviewed.)

He had known at Geneva, however, that he must decide then and there, without any chance for second guesses, what kind of President he intended to be. It was true that the Soviet demands, encouraged by the euphoria of beating the United States to the moon, had been presented in such a harshly exaggerated fashion that it would have been impossible for any President to accept them and stay in office. Yet there would have been some who would have made counter-offers, who would have stayed and "negotiated," to use the favorite word of Walter's world, who would somehow have submitted to some face-saving compromise that would have yielded a few more ells of advantage to the Communists while retaining some small inch of American face to bring home to the country.

He could not. Fortunately he had been surrounded by Orrin Knox and Bob Munson and some other strong-minded friends from the Senate, rather than with the sort of timid and tentative minds that had accompanied too many Presidents to too many conferences. So the delegation had been almost unanimous, and it had been relatively easy to be strong. But he knew he would have been, anyway.

Surprisingly, Harley M. Hudson, the easygoing, amiable, outwardly timid and uncertain soul who had been thrown off his psychological underpinnings by his predecessor's equivocal and wounding treatment of him as Vice President, had emerged—as one of Washington's livelier humorous columnists had put it—as Harley M. Hudson the Fearless Peerless. And for nearly a year—until Gorotoland and Panama came along—he had remained so in the eyes of the great majority of his countrymen. Even Walter and his friends had been forced to concede his courage and integrity. Their only mistake had lain in hoping it was just the one time, and that he would not again subject them to the nervous shock he had when he went counter to their cherished beliefs and actually defied right out loud, in an absolutely irretrievable manner, the demands of imperial Communism.

For him to have done so in the first instance had been gauche, it had been chauvinistic, it had been stupid, it had been one of those things that absolutely wasn't done in the best of circles—and it had worked. But to have him try it again, on two more occasions—to have him go to the heart of the matter, brush aside the pious hypocrisies about "wars of liberation," "genuine democratic freedom-loving revolutions," and the rest, and actually meet the challenge again, head-on—*well*. Who does he think he is, anyway? Does he think he has been given a warrant to be Fearless Peerless forever?

Yes, as a matter of fact, he tells himself now as he opens the door and steps out of the lovely spring day into the pleasant green hush of his office, he does. He has come to terms with the Presidency and with himself, and he has made up his mind that he will not look back and will not hesitate. He will do whatever needs to be done and do it firmly, and as swiftly as he can persuade the ponderous machinery of government to move. He would have liked to have sat down and consulted with the United Nations and Walter and everybody else about Gorotoland, but there it was: he had to act at once or see everything get out of control. He would have liked to have spent weeks of gracious chatting with the O.A.S. about Felix Labaiya's coup in Panama, but there it was: he had to act at once or see everything get out of control. And whose control? His and the United States'. And does anybody object? Well, let 'em bellow.

And so they are. Of course neither situation has gone too well, it is almost inevitable nowadays that in difficult terrain, unless the United States wishes to use its major weapons, decimate the earth, and destroy its peoples, it has to move slowly and be prepared to take temporary reverses. American troops have recaptured Molobangwe in Gorotoland and driven the rebels out of most of the lowlands; Terry's control is now restored almost everywhere except for an area roughly the size of Rhode Island in the rich highlands, where Obifumatta holds out. But Obi is holding out very well, and in the lowlands constant rebel bombings, stabbings, spearings, and ritual massacres are keeping the populace agitated and uneasy. In Panama, although the Americans and a small, extremely reluctant O.A.S. detachment have recaptured most of Panama City and a good part of the Canal, things are at a virtual stalemate at the moment. Felix is doing very well with his appeals to the UN and friendly nations to help his "Panamanian People's Liberation Movement" so that he may stabilize the country and reopen the Canal to commerce. This appeal from a native leader seems to have won more support around the world than a similar appeal from the United States, though no one has dared test the President's calm announcement that he will again employ the veto if necessary to halt UN obstruction of his policies.

So there is a good deal to bellow about, at the moment. And again he thinks grimly: Let 'em!

He smiles at himself as he sits down and presses the assorted buzzers that will summon his staff. Old Fearless Peerless is really eating fire this morning. Slow down, Harley, he tells himself, slow down. It will be a busy day, and this is no mood in which to begin it. He takes a deep breath, finds that it calms him considerably, and looks up with his usual unruffled smile as his secretary comes through the door.

"I have quite a few people I want to talk to today," he says, "so you might as well get started on putting through the calls."

While the first call is being arranged he thinks again, as he has so often in these past weeks, of the discussion that preceded Ted Jason's rather wistful, genuinely envious comment upon his capacity to make decisions calmly. The hour previous had been a good testing ground, a crucible in which the bitter challenge of desperate events had shown most of his colleagues for what they were. Himself, Orrin, the Joint Chiefs of Staff, the Secretary of Defense, most of the Cabinet—the response had been almost automatic. It had not been quite so automatic with the Majority Leader, the Speaker, and the chairmen of the major Congressional committees.

"We're getting the heat from home," Bob Munson had said. The Speaker had nodded agreement.

"Seems like this scare talk from Walter and his pals is getting through to some of 'em. You saw what we did on the Gorotoland resolution. It reflected the way the mail's been running. It was a leeettle close."

"Hasn't there been a turn?" the President asked. The Speaker shrugged.

"Oh, yes, some. But not enough yet to make the Hill feel really happy. We have a lot of skedaddlers up there, you know. Doesn't take much to make some of 'em run for cover."

"Some of them never get out from under it," Senator Munson said tartly. "Panama on top of Gorotoland will really make them quiver." He turned on the chairman of the Senate Foreign Relations Committee with a suddenness that made the senior Senator from Minnesota jump. "Isn't that so, Tom?"

"Oh, I don't know, I'm sure," Tom August said in his customary timid, don't-look-too-hard-at-me-I-don't-know-anything manner. "I—I think there may be some question."

"On Panama?" the President demanded. "Now, Tom, surely that's an obvious enough case of national security being involved."

"But Panama has a right to run her own affairs," Senator August said with a surprising stubbornness. "And she has some good arguments on the Canal. I just don't know whether we should barge in and—" His voice had trailed away, but he had looked, for Tom, surprisingly defiant.

"That's the way it seems like to me, too, Mr. President," Jawbone Swarthman blurted out. "Now this here may be a little old bitty crisis, possibly, it may upset us a little, but I know Felix, now, Mr. President. Why! Felix just wants what's best for his country down there. He isn't mad at *us*, Mr. President. He'll sign up with us the minute you give him his rights down there. What we doin' in his back yard anyhow, that's the way it seems like to me!"

"You see what we mean, Mr. President," Senator Munson remarked. "It's complicating. . . . However, that doesn't answer your question on the consensus here tonight. Yes, I'm for going in, I don't think Felix leaves us any choice, do you, Bill?"

"Nope," the Speaker said. "Let him have it."

"And you, Tom and Jawbone?" the President inquired in a tone that brooked no evasion. Senator August blinked and looked about, rather like a worried rabbit, Representative Swarthman puffed and pouted and looked indignant; but finally they both nodded.

"I guess so," Tom August said. "But it isn't going to be any picnic!"

"Nobody said it was," the President said shortly. "Orrin?" And even though no one in the room expected any surprises from the Secretary of State, there came an extra tension as they realized that of all who were being tested tonight, he and their visitor from California had the most to lose or gain.

"What would you expect me to say?" Orrin Knox inquired impatiently. "Of course we should go in. Of course we should meet the challenge. I just don't see how anyone can hesitate. Again we face a situation, not nice theories about it. Certainly: act." An ironic glint came into his eyes for a moment. "Nobody's going to hang us any higher than we are now."

"Governor?" the President said thoughtfully, and the attention of some forty men swung upon Ted Jason with an intensity he might have found frightening were he not already becoming used to it from voters who examined him as though their eyes would turn him inside out, if need be, to find his true essence.

"I invited you here," the President said, "rather irregularly, probably, because of a fact none of us need blink, which is that you are potentially, and perhaps soon to be actively, a contender for this office." He smiled without much humor. "I thought this would be an admirable chance for you to find out how it's done. And also," he added, quite seriously, "we need all the help we can get, and quite likely you can help."

For a moment Governor Jason returned his gaze impassively. Then he smiled and spoke in a measured and careful voice.

"And also," he said, "I can be committed to the Administration's policy—which is another aspect none of us need blink."

The President looked at him without expression for a moment. Then he gave him a little mock bow and a cheerful laugh.

"How astute people are. How astute! I am afraid I shall never be able to hide my crafty ways. . . . But," he added with a calm insistence, "tell us what to do."

"I'm in a somewhat difficult position, you know," Ted Jason said with an engaging grin, "since it is my brother-in-law, as a matter of fact—a matter of present fact—who happens to be leading this revolution down there. I do not know," he said with a tight little smile, "how long he will remain my brother-in-law. You aren't interested in family secrets, I know"—the smile broadened—"but for some time things have not been too frightfully cordial in that household. So we shall see. Presently, it is the fact.

"It will not, of course, influence me in any way in doing what seems best for the United States. Were he my dearest friend, Felix is still an enemy of my country, and for that, I think he should be brought to book and I think his effort should be overthrown. . . . I do wonder a little, though," he said slowly, "whether the course proposed here is exactly what we want to do at this particular moment. Have we exhausted all the good offices of the UN, for instance? Has the O.A.S. been given time to consider it? Have we made use of neutrals who might be able to help? Obviously, no. The event has only just happened, as I understand it—"

"Two hours ago," the President said.

"—and yet here we are—here *you* are, the Administration—preparing the most forceful and most direct reply, apparently without consultations with anyone. I wonder," he remarked thoughtfully, "if this is really warranted, and what effect it will have upon America's reputation abroad, particularly since it comes on top of similar direct action in Gorotoland."

"Ted," the President said, "you bespeak a certain point of view, and you bespeak it very well. I admire you for having the courage to do it in these circumstances—"

"Oh, I'm not afraid of you," Governor Jason said pleasantly, and again the President gave him a little bow, and smiled.

"I should hope not. But, have you tried to get the good offices of the UN applied to a situation at once, right now, this minute, before it deteriorates to the point where the Communists take over? Have you ever asked the O.A.S. to stop squabbling with itself and move, move fast, on an issue where something must be done at once or disaster will occur? Have you ever approached a professional neutral like India, for instance, and asked for help immediately and without equivocation in negotiating a difficult problem? Holy Toledo, man!" he demanded as their laughter rose to accompany his words, "have you ever tried to get Krishna Khaleel to tell you the time of day in one sentence? It can't be done!"

"I know, I know," Ted Jason agreed. "I don't minimize the difficulties at all. I just wonder if it wouldn't look better if we waited, say, forty-eight hours, tried all these things openly on the record, and then, having failed, moved in. Surely Felix can't do a great deal of harm in that time."

"He can be recognized as the official government of Panama by a great many non-friends of ours," the President said. "We can get ourselves bogged down very neatly in appeals and counter-appeals to the UN. We can find ourselves in the middle of next month still arguing with the O.A.S. We can let ourselves be drawn into a sea of molasses with K.K. and Company. Meanwhile Walter and his friends can start a great hamstringing clamor around the world against our doing anything. And Panama and the Canal can be lost to us and the free world."

"Suez wasn't," Ted remarked.

"Suez was somebody else's jugular," the President said grimly. "This is ours. No, I will not have it. The choice is action—or endless jawing, and defeat. I won't have it."

Governor Jason shrugged and smiled.

"Well, if you won't have it—you won't have it. You're the one man in a position to say."

The President studied him thoughtfully.

"Are you with me?"

The Governor gave him look for look, and though a good many in the room disagreed with his position, it was impossible not to admire his guts.

"I'm not against you, certainly. Neither am I wholeheartedly for you. There must be a middle ground, there always is, in democratic experience—"

"These takeovers are not democratic experiences," the President said quickly. Ted nodded.

"I still think middle ground could be found. But obviously," and he smiled calmly at them all, "you don't think so, so what I think doesn't matter."

"At least here," the President agreed. "Well," he went on, as the Governor remained impassive, "let me see you to the door. There's no reason to embarrass you with the press. Nobody, I think, will tell the press you were here. Gentlemen, I'll be right back."

"Oh, no," Ted said politely, "that's quite all right. I want them to know I was here. After all, it was an honor to be invited."

The President gave him a long look and sat down again.

"Yes," he said softly. "So it was."

And that was what Ted made of it when later, after his somewhat wistful farewell as the meeting broke up, he went forth to be surrounded by the clamoring reporters outside. The meeting had begun in secrecy, but as usual in Washington the secrecy hadn't lasted long. The Chief of Naval Operations had left abruptly at quarter to eleven from a dinner party at which the UPI's Pentagon man had also been present; across town the Assistant Secretary of State for Latin American Affairs and his wife, pleading the excuse of a call from the baby sitter about one of the kids having an upset tummy, departed with equal speed from a similar gathering; the AP's State Department man was there. Within five minutes both journalists, acting on hunch, instinct, and the off-chance, had telephoned their offices and said they were going to drop by the White House, just in case. A number of other newsmen, going home from the Dobius banquet, had been intrigued to see a rash of official limousines, going—somewhere. In no time the word was all over town, and two hundred reporters were clamoring at the door. Ted Jason made the most of it as he stood before the cameras in the driveway, his gray hair ruffled a little by the cool wind that had risen after midnight:

"I have no statement to make, except that I have been here as the President's guest, and that of course if I were to have any criticism of what has been decided here tonight—"

"What has been, Governor?" a frantic voice cried from the back.

"I assume he will tell you himself, very shortly. If I were to have any criticism of it, I should not voice it here. There are times and forums—"

"Do you?" another voice insisted. He smiled.

"Sometimes," he said, "there is a patriotic duty to support. Sometimes there is a patriotic duty to disagree. Conscience must decide the issue."

"Now what in hell did that mean?" a puzzled voice inquired as he waved for the cameras and stepped into the limousine that waited to take him to Patsy's in Dumbarton Oaks.

"I don't know," another voice responded dryly, "but it will look good on a campaign poster. I can see it right now: Conscience Must Decide The Issue."

And now he is about to get the word, the President

thinks as the buzzer sounds and he picks up the phone.

"Ted?" he says with a little smile. "How are things in the Great West?"

"If only," Lafe said to Cullee, standing again on the beautiful lawn dropping away to the Hudson, the sun warm and happy on the trees, the handsome boy smiling his polite and gentle, faraway smile, "I could get *through*. But I can't seem to."

"Maybe it isn't meant that you should," Cullee said thoughtfully, studying the level eyes that looked so directly yet so blankly into his. "Maybe he's meant to stay this way. After all," he said with a sudden bitter note in his voice, "it isn't much of a world if he should come back."

"I've thought of that, too," Lafe said, staring away across the rolling fall of palisades to the river. "But I think Mabel has the right idea."

Cullee smiled.

"Oh? When have you talked to her?"

"I haven't, yet," Lafe said, and at his friend's kind but amused expression, added defensively, "well, it's just seemed best not to. I've just decided to let it develop as it comes, and if it does, well—then it does, and if it doesn't—it doesn't. I mean, I'm not about to push anything that could mean something, at my age."

"And with all your other interests," Cullee suggested. Lafe shook his head with a peculiar little grimace.

"Ah, *them*. You can have 'em."

"Don't need 'em, thanks," Cullee said with a grin. "I think I'm getting fixed to get married again, soon's I can shake Sue-Dan. Which won't be until after the election, probably."

"You and Sarah hit it off pretty well, don't you? Well, that's good. I think it's wonderful."

"At least," Cullee said soberly, "it's peace of mind, I think . . . and you know something? The older I get the more I value that. Didn't used to be very important alongside a couple of hours in bed with nothing else on your mind, but it is now. Sarah's very calm and peaceful and I need that, now. I've had enough of the other." He smiled. "My brains have been beat in long enough."

"Good," Lafe said. He looked at the silent youth sitting between them, eyes somewhere beyond the valley of the river now.

"Mine, too, I think. Mabel and I write quite often, you know. She's been very interested in Jimmy, here. She sees your point of view about why try to bring him back, but she says if he doesn't come back there will never be any point in his having lived at all. I guess I reflect her thinking on that." He looked thoughtful. "I didn't at first."

"How is she? She had it pretty rough, didn't she?"

Lafe looked somber for a moment.

"When Brig—died—she almost went to pieces for a while. But she's come back fine. Getting into politics and everything. She may be a delegate to the convention. That's where I plan to see her, if it works out that way."

Cullee smiled.

"It will. It's fate . . . Jimmy," he called gently. "Can you hear me, Jimmy?"

For a second as they leaned forward intently there seemed the slightest trace of attention, the faintest flicker of response. Then it was gone, if it had ever been.

"Just for a minute," Cullee said softly, "I thought—"

"So do I," Lafe said unhappily. "It's always that way. Something so elusive you can't catch it—and then it's gone."

"Maybe someday it will stay. If you're just determined enough and patient enough."

"I am," Lafe said, "but sometimes it seems it's a hard task the Lord has set me. . . . What are you going to do about running for Senator from California?"

Cullee gave him a thoughtful look and frowned.

"I think I'm going to do it. There's still time to file. Ted isn't going to stand in my way." He smiled. "Or Patsy either. She was just having fun, with that rumor. So, I guess Ray Smith and I will have a little argument out there about the Administration's horrible policies."

"Will he beat you for the nomination?"

Cullee's eyes narrowed.

"He may, but I doubt it. In spite of all the howling, I still think a majority of the country approves of what Harley's doing. I may be completely mistaken but that's my belief. Even with things dragging the way they are."

"Yes, I know," Lafe said with a worried frown. "I wish we could get something decisive in one place or the other. We could carry one inconclusive commitment if the other were settled, but with both unsettled it poses quite a political problem."

"How about your own campaign?"

Lafe shrugged.

"No sweat. Iowa's uneasy but they like me awfully well, and the only competition in sight at the moment is a political science prof at the University who hopes to beat me on a wave of teach-ins. I don't think he can do it. . . . What do your people say about your waiting so long to declare?"

"Everybody's waiting," Cullee said. "It's slowing the whole campaign down, but you can't move without the Old Man."

Lafe snorted.

"If you'd told me a year ago that that timid soul wandering around the Senate under the title 'Vice President' would ever be referred to as 'the Old Man,' I somehow don't think I would have believed it. 'The Old Man' sounds like somebody pretty powerful."

"Harley is."

Lafe nodded.

"Harley is. What time have you got?"

"Ten-fifteen."

"The White House left word at the hotel for me to call him about this time. Want to go find a phone?"

"Sure," Cullee said, surprised. "Is something coming up in the UN we're supposed to know about?"

Lafe shook his head.

"Not that I know of—but who knows? . . . Jimmy," he said, firmly, holding out his hand, knowing there would be no response but making the gesture as part of his customary, determined routine, "take care of yourself. Congressman Hamilton and I have to go now. We'll see you soon. Goodbye."

And he started to turn away. But even as he did so, he froze and the hairs rose on the back of his neck.

"*Cullee!*" he said in an excited whisper. "Did you hear what I—"

"I did!" Cullee responded with an equal excitement. "It was either—"

"It was either 'goo' or 'guh,' " Lafe said in an awed tone, his voice trembling as he stared at the handsome head that was turned away from them, apparently not responding, but from which sound at last had come.

"It was certainly the start of 'goodbye,' " Cullee agreed, "that's for sure. . . . Why, you old sentimentalist!" he said, giving Lafe's arm a squeeze. "You actually have tears in your eyes."

"You, too, you superior bastard," Lafe said with a shaky laugh. "Jimmy!" he said again. "Jimmy? Goodbye! Goodbye, Jimmy! Goodbye!"

But this time there was no answering sound, and after a moment Cullee said softly, "Don't push your luck. It will come. Now it's started—it will come."

"Oh, God," Lafe said fervently, and it was more prayer than expletive, "*I hope so.* Golly! I want to go tell Harley! Let's find that phone!"

And a couple of minutes later he was saying eagerly to fatherly Washington, "Harley—Mr. President—you know Hal Fry's boy Jimmy—that he sort of left to me? Well, Cullee and I have just been up here seeing him, and I think he spoke to us, Harley! I really think he did. He started to say Goodbye. Yes, sir, he really did. . . . Well, thank you, we're very excited, too." Then his voice changed and his expression became more intent as the President began to talk. "Yes. . . . Yes, we're both running this year. Yes . . ."

"What is it?" Cullee demanded in an insistent whisper, but Lafe gestured for silence.

"Yes," he said. "Yes, Mr. President. . . . Oh, I think so, yes. . . . I think both of us will be. . . . I'm sure of it."

After he has called Lucille to tell her about Jimmy, the President sits for a few moments staring thoughtfully out at the rose garden. There had been no particular reason for him to talk to Lafe and Cullee, they were not so material to his plans this day as all that, but it had pleased him to do so simply because they are old friends who will inevitably be affected, and he is fond of them. Now he is glad that he did, because it thrilled him, too, to hear about Jimmy. It had quite broken up Lucille for a minute or two.

"I only wish Hal Fry were here," she said. "But maybe he knows."

"I think so," the President said. "Somewhere. . . . Why don't you call Beth and tell her? She's always been so interested."

"I will, right away. Have you talked to Orrin yet?"

"Oh, no. I have a few others to get out of the way, first."

"All right," she said, "then I won't say anything."

"Just concentrate on Jimmy," he suggested. "That will be enough"—adding to himself as she went off the line,

Knowing Beth and her intuition, I hope so.

While he waits for the next call to go through—it neces-
sitates arranging for two very busy men to be in the same
office at the same time—he thinks with a reminiscent fond-
ness of the parts they are playing, and have played, in his
life in recent years. If it had not been for the Senate Majority Leader, he supposes, he would not be President now:
Bob Munson had forced the warring factions in Michigan to
choose him for Governor, Bob Munson had fought his way
across a frantic convention hall to secure his nomination
for Vice President, Bob Munson had almost literally held
his hand and mopped his brow and calmed him down four
years ago, when Harley, fed up and frustrated with the deliberate disregard of his predecessor, had been on the point
of declaring that he would not run for second term as Vice
President even if the President did want him, which he
doubted. Bob had told Harley he must run again, and, no
doubt—though Harley had never known the inside story
on that one—had told the President that he must again
choose Harley to be his running mate. Bob had a lot of
I.O.U.'s lying around Washington, and he had cashed some
of his most important for Harley Hudson. And although
Bob had reached a point of being quite annoyed and impatient with him just before his predecessor died, the President likes to feel that since that low point, Bob has held
him in good regard. He likes to feel that this is especially
true since Geneva, and more recently, since events in Gorotoland and Panama have brought from Harley a strength
many in Washington did not know he possessed. ("Like all
weak men confronted with the need for decision," Walter
Dobius had written just the other day, "Harley M. Hudson
overreacts—when he reacts at all." Bob's view, the President likes to feel, is somewhat more generous than that.)

By the same token he likes to feel that the Speaker also
holds him in fair esteem. That powerful gentleman, who
runs his branch of the government with a placid air that
comes from an absolute lack of political fear and an absolute toughness—which in turn come from years of seniori-
ty and influence that no one in the House would now
dream of seriously challenging—is not one given to fulsome compliments. Yet in his taciturn, no-nonsense way,
he too gives evidence of considerable faith in Harley M.
Hudson. Certainly his support through this past hectic year
has been stanch and unshakable. If he has had criticism to

offer, and he has not had much, it has been constructive
and helpful; if he has had doubts, they have never appeared. The only qualifications he has ever had have been
the same expressed wryly three weeks ago on the night Panama exploded: the thought that some of his boys in the
House might be wavering under pressure, the practical
contemplation of the possibility that the President might
not have quite as much "silent support" in the country as
he thinks he has. But the Speaker has never indicated in
the slightest that these things worry him, nor has he ever
suggested to the President that he change his course or
moderate his policies to meet the clamor of his critics. He
has been to Harley what he has been to four other Presidents: an unwavering supporter, a good right arm, an invaluable ally, and an indispensable lieutenant. A politician
in the grand style, is the Speaker. The President is grateful
indeed that their tenure of office should have coincided.

But it is to Bob Munson that his thoughts keep returning, for with Bob, because of his decisive interventions
in Harley's life, there is a special relationship. It is especially important that he stand well with Bob, because Bob has
had an opportunity to judge him for what he is for the full
span of his political life. Bob, too, is one of the grand ones,
and even if he had the gravest doubts, he too would go
along and do his best and the President only rarely would
be made aware that he had misgivings. But with Harley he
is under no compulsion, personal, traditional, political, or
sentimental to act this way if he doesn't mean it. If he
doesn't approve, he certainly has the right to say so. Knowing Bob, the President is sure he wouldn't hesitate.

Yet though he is extrasensitive about it, and alert to every possible nuance of tone and statement, the President so
far has found no evidence. They talk to one another about
legislation two and three times a day, sometimes oftener,
and never once has the Majority Leader expressed the
slightest doubt about the course the President is following.
Like the Speaker, his only worries have been for his colleagues in the Senate. Some, like Tom August, are genuinely
wavering under the pressures from Walter's world. Some,
like Arly Richardson, are using their country's torment to
demagogue themselves into all the political advantage they
think they can see in opposing their country's policies.
Whatever the motivations, there are enough doubtfuls to
make Bob uneasy. Yet when the President last week finally

asked pointblank, "Do you think I should change what I am doing? Are they really genuinely worried enough for me to revise my policies?" Bob dismissed it tartly. "I should say not," he responded. "The genuine doubters we'll always have, the professional demagogues like Arly we'll always have. Neither bunch is worth endangering the country for. If you believe you're right, stay with it."

"Do you believe I'm right?" the President asked. The Majority Leader didn't hesitate a moment.

"I do indeed." A certain humor entered his voice. "Don't you?"

"Certainly," the President said, "but I happen to feel that it's important that you do."

"I'm flattered," Bob Munson said, "but don't worry about me. You'd know if I didn't agree."

"I hope so," the President said.

"Count on it," said Bob Munson.

And now he will need Bob's help again, and the Speaker's too, and many another's before it is successfully over. He wonders what the reaction will be, and when the buzzer sounds once more and they come on the line from Bob's office, his voice is humorous but they can sense a little worry in it as he asks, "Are you both sitting down? I think you should be."

These were the visits, the director of the President's Commission on Administrative Reform thought with an ironic little inward sigh, that tried men's souls. Busy, bright, interested, and didactic, his caller's sharp-featured little face peered at him earnestly from across the desk, its expression as eager for agreement as it was avid for gossip. Pushing seventy if he was a day, Mr. Justice Thomas Buckmaster Davis of the Supreme Court was one of the more famous monuments of Washington and knew it. He fixed Bob Leffingwell now with a determined eye and leaned emphatically forward.

"My dear boy," he said, "my dear *boy!* You mean you *still* haven't decided what to do about Ted Jason?"

"What has Ted Jason decided to do about Ted Jason?" Bob Leffingwell inquired. "Does anybody know?"

"There has been," Tommy Davis admitted thoughtfully, "there *has* been some—hesitation, shall we say—since the banquet. Not enough, you understand," he added hastily, "to affect in any way the ultimate success of a marvelous

candidacy, but enough to—perturb, you might say—those
of faint heart and little faith. I am not one of them," he
added stoutly. "I believe in Ted Jason. Conscience Must
Decide The Issue!"

"Mmmmhmm," Bob Leffingwell said. "Conscience
seems to be having a lot of trouble."

"I was talking to Patsy only yesterday," the little Justice
said, "and SHE said"—he fell into an unconscious parody
of her manner—"that she simply KNEW her brother was
going to make his position formally known before much
longer."

"That's good and specific. Personally, I don't think she
knows a thing."

"I think it would help everyone," Justice Davis said, "if
we could get a clear statement of the need for Ted to run
from someone in a really unimpeachable position—*really*
unimpeachable."

"No one more unimpeachable than Ted," Bob
Leffingwell said with a shrug.

"Now, my dear boy," Tommy Davis said, "I do hope
you won't be willfully obtuse and obdurate. I really hope
not."

"Me? I'm not being obtuse and obd—"

"Yes, you are, my dear boy," his visitor said severely.
"Yes, you are. I was saying to Ned over at the *Post* just last
night that if you would only step forward and seize the
opportunity that events have now given you—if you would
only take the step the country is waiting for you to take—
if you would only grasp the nettle—"

"Tommy," Bob Leffingwell demanded, "what on earth
are you talking about? What nettle have you and Ned
planted for me to grasp this time? And who in the country
do you think gives a damn whether I grasp it or not?"

"You minimize your own importance, my dear boy," the
Justice said, still severely. "You occupy a unique position.
You really do. You influence a great many people you
don't realize at all. You mustn't minimize them, or yourself. They are waiting."

"I don't influence anybody any more," Bob Leffingwell
said, "and if this is some elaborate scheme you and the
Post have cooked up for me to bring pressure to bear on
Ted Jason—well," he said with an ironic smile, "you really
must be hard up. I thought Walter Dobius was in charge of
lining up people to pressure Ted Jason."

"Walter has done a superb job," the Justice said. *"Is* doing, a superb job. And of course many others in comparable position are doing all they can, but—"

"But what? What more do you need?"

"Well, there is the danger, you see, that it may all seem like a press and television campaign. That Ted is really just —just the press and network candidate. That it's all just— propaganda, you know? That there really isn't any grassroots demand for him. . . . There's a possibility people may think that."

"Yes," Bob Leffingwell agreed solemnly, "I can see that there is a possibility. However, I don't think there was any doubt at the banquet that he has plenty of support outside the press. You don't get that kind of ovation just on headlines and help from the networks. That was genuine, all right."

"But it's what people *outside* think that counts," Justice Davis said. "You know, in Washington we sometimes get a little—self-centered, you know? There are lots more people in the country than just—*us,* dear boy."

"Oh, are there really?" Bob Leffingwell inquired. "I've been in this town sixteen years and I've never been sure of that since the day I arrived. Are they really out there? Well, well."

"Yes, they are," Tommy Davis said sternly, "and it is time for you to speak to them. They need to be told by someone besides Walter and the metropolitan press and the networks that Governor Jason is the man for them. They need to have it said by someone they look up to—and respect—and admire as an *individual,* not just as a—as a columnist."

"Careful, now, Tommy," Bob Leffingwell said. "You're coming close to treason."

"Well, it should be someone outside Walter's crowd," the little Justice said stubbornly. "Anyway, you'd get reams of publicity on it. You'd be on the front page of every paper in the country and you'd be interviewed on every program there is. It would amount to the same thing, really. It would just *seem* like a fresh point of view, that's all, and that's what we need, right now."

"Tommy," Bob Leffingwell said, and began to move papers about on his desk as though resuming work, for there was no point in prolonging this, "I think it's very flattering that you and Ned still think anybody gives a damn what I say, but I'm afraid I can't help you. Since I got beaten for Secretary of State, I haven't exactly been the white knight on a charger, you know, in the mind of the country." His eyes darkened as he thought of his error of judgment in lying to the Senate Foreign Relations Committee about his long-ago, innocuous Communist associations, an error he would regret for the rest of his days for reasons far more fundamental than just being defeated for Secretary. "Let's face it, I was a damned fool." He gave his visitor an honest look, suddenly so naked and tortured that Tommy Davis averted his eyes. "No one respects me any more. I don't respect myself. What makes you think that anyone at all could be influenced by what I say about Ted?"

"My dear boy," Justice Davis said solemnly, "you entirely underestimate your own character. What you did was—regrettable, perhaps, from one point of view—though I supported you in that decision, and always will—but you have recovered magnificently. Magnificently! People *do* respect you. You haven't complained, you haven't gone around whining about it, you haven't rationalized or justified. You've taken the job the President gave you and done very well with it, and you've come out all right. You really have, believe me. Now surely you know that."

"I know," Bob Leffingwell said honestly, "that I've come back pretty well. I'm not going to overdramatize myself. But the fact remains, Tommy, that when a great many of my countrymen think of me they think"—and his mouth gave a sudden bitter twist—"*liar*."

"They do not!" Justice Davis exclaimed. "They do not, Robert Leffingwell! I don't ever want to hear you say that again, do you hear me? They may think misguided, or—or misled, or—mistaken—but they don't think—*that*. They've gotten over that. Now don't you *ever* say that again!"

Bob Leffingwell sighed and shook his head.

"Well. In any event, Tommy, when you said 'the job the President gave me,' you said it all. I'm not going to speak until he decides what he's going to do. I owe him too much. He saved me, that rather bumbling but very kind gentleman you and Ned and Walter and the rest of you despise so much. I'm his to command, and the last thing I would do is attempt to force his hand or make things difficult for him. Besides which," he added with a certain coldness in his voice, "I am not so sure as you apparently are that I disagree with what he's doing. There's always that to consider, you know."

"My dear boy," Justice Davis said, and there was genuine dismay in his voice. "Surely you don't—surely you can't—surely it isn't—but, *surely!* When things are going as poorly as they are? When we're bogged down everywhere you look? When we have the whole world against us? When it seems as though everything he does is stupid and ill-advised and ruinous to the country? When all he does is what *Orrin* tells him to? My dear boy! Now you do appall me!"

"I'm not so sure I disagree with Orrin, either," Bob Leffingwell said, feeling a real satisfaction at the way the bustling little face across from him appeared to be disintegrating in abhorrence and confusion. "They may have a point, Tommy. We don't know yet whether they do or not."

"Very well," his visitor said coldly, standing up with an abrupt motion that almost tipped him over, so that he had to support himself with one quivering little old hand against the desk. "I must say I am most disappointed in you, Bob. Ned will be too, and so will Walter and—and so will everyone. You occupy a unique position. You have a chance to do a great service to the country and the world by issuing a statement calling on Ted to run. You refuse to do it. You simply refuse, and for the basest of motivations —because you *agree* with this insane policy! I must confess I do not understand you, my dear boy, I simply do not. . . . However," he said, and it was obvious that he was making a great effort to speak with calm and tolerance, "I may be able to forgive you, ultimately, for I am sure it is simply a temporary aberration. I am sure you will be found when the time comes on the side of Right and Justice. Even though," he couldn't help concluding sadly, "we could *so* use you now!"

"Conscience must decide the issue, Tommy," Bob Leffingwell told him. "Thanks for coming by."

"They will be *so* disappointed at the *Post*," Mr. Justice Davis said with a last wistful glance as he turned toward the door.

"Tell them not to cry," Bob Leffingwell said.

But although he said it as a parting shot, and though it gave him genuine satisfaction to show the busy little Justice and all his friends that he was no longer captive, as he once had been, to either their friendship or their enmity, it was

with an unhappy restlessness that he resumed the duties of
the day as the door closed behind the Court's most ubiquitous member. He was not out from under all the burdens
of the bitter battle over his nomination to be Secretary of
State, though he knew he was on his way. But he still had a
way to go.

It was with a genuine surge of gratitude, as though he
were about to talk to someone who, in his kindly, fatherly
way might have all the answers to soothe a still-regretful
heart, that he heard his secretary say over the intercom,
"Pick up the phone, please, for the President."

Where is he now, the clever, arrogant little man who
thinks the world skips to his tune, the President wonders
half an hour later, and what is he doing and what will he
think when he hears my voice, and what it has to relate?

Probably sitting at his typewriter at "Salubria" damning
me up and down again; and whatever he thinks or says will
have a snarl in it, and there will be further damnations and
maledictions forthcoming.

Well, Mr. Walter Dobius, he advises in a silent dialogue
while he reads absentmindedly through the National Aero-
nautics and Space Agency report on the plans to send another manned expedition to the moon now that the first is
safely home after its protracted stay, as far as I am concerned you can continue to do your twisted worst and I
can survive it. I have so far, and I shall continue.

He reflects with some wry amusement, as his secretary reports a little difficulty in finding her quarry, that Walter
since the banquet has reverted to the image he has so carefully created over the years. He has not, in any speech or
column since, poured forth quite the venom and invective
he disgorged immediately following the American intervention in Gorotoland. Although obviously strongly opposed
to Administration policies, he has resumed the mantle of
objective statesmanship and maintained it even when his
world again ran amuck in flame and froth following Panama. Walter's tone since the banquet has been one of cold
disapproval and acrid pity for policies so misguided, but
his views have been stated with a clever regret for misguided men rather than a bitter open blame of them. The naked
feeling that overwhelmed him with Gorotoland and the vetoes has not been permitted to appear again. His faithful
followers, in all their dutiful millions from Harold and

Reggie in London to Dottie and Dick in Minot, North Dakota, are reassured and comforted. Because he is shrewd enough to realize how unrelieved invective sounds over a period of time, Walter has conquered his runaway emotions and become dignified again. And since the attention span of the general public in these days of overproduced news is roughly two days, it has not taken long for his worshipers to accept the quickly refurbished portrait of the statesman-philosopher. Now most of them only remember vaguely that Walter Dobius got a little hot under the collar, back there when things first broke—but he's really back on the ball, now, giving them the real inside scoop on Washington with a background of twenty-five years of unimpeachable integrity that a few days of forgivable human irritation can't diminish.

Washington knows, however, that his animosity and his opposition are basically as grim and unrelenting as ever. For some reason Gorotoland, the vetoes, and Panama are personal issues between the Administration and Walter. Having set the tone and hied on the pack, however, he no longer has to lead it: its members continue to function dutifully without him, aware that he is giving an over-all respectability to their unrelenting campaign, which will continue as long as the Administration dares to follow a course that ignores what Walter and his world are determined the course should be.

And now, of course, with the situations confused and chaotic on two continents, there are meaty matters to bite into.

GOROTOLAND: ANOTHER VIETNAM? queries a CBS special; the answer of course is Yes. PANAMA: CAN INTERVENTION SUCCEED? wonders NBC; the answer of course is No. THE GRIM, UGLY WAR OF BOG-DOWN AND BETRAYAL, *Look* describes Gorotoland, and the inescapable conclusion is that the United States had better get the hell out of it as fast as possible. THE PANAMA CANAL: A BITTER ISSUE SPARKS A PEOPLE'S PROTEST, *Newsweek* reports, and Felix Labaiya emerges a mighty sweet-smelling democratic rose, while the "alleged Communist infiltrators seen by U.S. spokesmen behind every bush" are dismissed with the skeptical sneer which half-a-hundred "genuine people's revolutions" in recent decades of course make fully justified and completely mature.

Daily the headlines gloat on U.S. reverses, hourly the bulletins emphasize the bitter choices and handicaps of an Administration struggling to make some sense of the international chaos deliberately created by the Communists, history's most irresponsible wrecking-crew. A month has passed without absolute, eternal victory everywhere, and already the phrase "an American policy which obviously is not succeeding" is beginning to appear in column after column, commentary after commentary, program after program.

Bog-down and betrayal, the President is logically being forced to conclude, are quite all right as long as the enemy isn't being hurt too much in return. They can go on for years and nobody in Walter's world will say Boo. But let the other side be hurt, let the United States really go into action, and at once the chorus swells: America is awful, the policy isn't succeeding, the peace of the world is being dreadfully damaged by the rude, crude, brutal, bad United States.

The other side *is* being hurt, the President knows, and far more than Walter's world is willing to tell the public that depends upon it for information. Slanted photographs and slanted stories and the ruthless twisting of the news to blackguard his Administration do not change the private reports that come steadily in. Obifumatta's hold on the areas of Gorotoland he occupies is tenuous at best, dependent more and more upon a policy of fearful atrocity that is blandly ignored by Walter's world as it sends its tender dispatches about "Rebel Village Devastated by U.S. Attack," or, "Son of Rebel Chief Loses Leg in War's Holocaust." Felix Labaiya is fighting as desperately against attempts of "the alleged Communist infiltrators seen by U.S. spokesmen behind every bush" to capture his revolution, as he is against attempts by the United States to recapture the Canal, yet somehow this is not the message which gets through to America.

The President knows, however, and so does Walter and so does his world; and it is with some difficulty that the President manages to show them even a minimal courtesy, so deliberately are they suppressing and distorting the facts in their attempt to bludgeon his Administration. It is not something which can any longer be sluffed off with an easygoing, "Well, they're as human as anybody else," or,

"It's only natural to be a little prejudiced," or, "They mean well." These things used to suffice, but the world has moved on. Walter and his particular clique are no longer content to report policy. Now they seek to arrogate to themselves the right to make it, using all the powerful weapons of communication which are theirs. No more is this something which can be dismissed with a forgiving wisecrack. It is a deadly serious business, now, against which every President and every Administration has to be constantly on guard and with which they must constantly contend.

Walter's world is out for high stakes, indeed: to run the country, regardless of who sits in the White House, or who on Capitol Hill.

The reasons for this the President, because he is a fair-minded and basically very tolerant man, has to conclude are not particularly sinister or unpatriotic. Rather they spring from idealism carried to arrogance, patriotism carried to intolerance, egotism carried close to the point of insanity. *Nobody* is more sincere than Walter's world; *nobody* has a greater concern for the country; *nobody* knows better how the universe should be run. And in corollary, *everyone* who questions must be attacked, *everyone* who disagrees must be vilified, *everyone* who opposes must be slandered and condemned no matter how sincere and justified he may be.

Very well, little Walter, he thinks grimly as the buzzer sounds and his secretary reports that she has found America's statesman-philosopher in the Senate Press Gallery: having another fit, on me. He realizes this mood is unworthy of him, and he knows he is making this call purely for spite, but he cannot help himself. To this extent, at least, they have got to him and pulled him down to their level.

"Good morning, Walter," he says crisply. "I have something to tell you that you are to keep confidential until after my press conference this afternoon. You can't use it before anybody else does, but"—his tone becomes dry—"in view of your extreme interest, I wanted you to be one of the first to know."

"Well, dear," Lucille says calmly at the cheerful luncheon table set by a window overlooking the South Grounds, the Monument, and the Ellipse, "how has it gone, so far?"

"Very well, I think," he reports with an equal calmness. "What's this, some sort of fancy omelet?"

"It's a recipe Dolly Munson brought back from Italy last fall. Who have you talked to?"

"Wouldn't you like to know," he says with a chuckle. She responds with a smile.

"Not particularly, if you don't want to tell me. You looked a little grim when you came in, that's all."

"That was talking to Walter. I'm afraid I've really let him annoy me more than I should, over the last few weeks."

"I hope today you annoyed him."

It is his turn to smile.

"Yes, I think so. He wasn't dreadfully surprised, but I think he'd been hoping against hope."

"And Orrin?"

He frowns.

"I haven't talked to Orrin yet, I suppose actually I'm a little afraid to."

"Don't be. You can always trust Orrin to understand."

But can you, he asks himself as he returns along the colonnade to his office shortly after getting up at 2 P.M. from the nap he takes conscientiously every day after lunch. Can you trust Orrin to understand, when what you have to say is exactly what Orrin—

Instantly and unbidden a thousand pictures of his volatile Secretary of State leap to mind. He sees him on the Senate floor, his face flushed, his positive, didactic voice raised in impatient anger with some colleague he obviously regards as stupid, his body swinging vigorously about as he thrusts forward an extended arm and jabbing forefinger to make his point . . . in private conversations with constituents needing his help, shyly gentle and kind . . . in committee hearings, his glasses sliding down on his nose, his keen eyes peering sharply at a recalcitrant witness, his manner growing acrid as he pins down an eel-like evasion or squirming equivocation . . . at that strange conference in Bob Munson's office at the height of the Leffingwell nomination battle when Orrin asked for advice on the fantastic, unbelievable bribe offered by Harley's predecessor . . . at the fateful convention of eight years ago, his contorted face confronting Harley's on the ramp out to the podium—and his crestfallen face, a classic study, a year ago when Harley had finally disclosed what his intention had been that night . . . Orrin's unimpressed responses to the Soviet threats in Geneva, his unwavering support in the crises caused by Terence Ajkaje in South Carolina and the UN six months ago, his unwavering support now . . . at parties, at receptions, in corridor conversations, at lunchtime talks over a quick hamburger in the Senate restaurant, at late-afternoon drinks in the Speaker's office after the legislative day was done . . . in Washington, in San Francisco, in Paris, Tokyo, London, Johannesburg, wherever the winds of diplomacy and politics blow him: idealistic, practical, sentimental, tough, iron-firm on issues, sometimes too soft on people, predictable one minute, unpredictable the next; the great ambition, the great ability to accept ambition's denial—a many-sided man, not entirely understood by his President, who now is about to seek understanding from him.

Yet surely Orrin will grant it, for it is something he can grasp as a logical man; and whatever the sudden gusts of emotion that sometimes conquer his heart and befog his mind, Orrin is always, in the long run, a logical man. Surely that sensitive and perceptive brain, falsely labeled cold by those who hate him, known to be an odd combination of warmth and calculation by those who like him, will respond, as it always has eventually, to the imperatives of the situation.

Surely Orrin the loyal and forgiving servant will be the loyal and forgiving servant again.

Or will he?

It is with real trepidation and a nervous heart that the President lifts the receiver and personally puts through this call.

"Good afternoon," he says when Orrin comes presently on the line. "How many new disasters are you struggling with today? . . . Only the old ones? That's good. . . . Orrin," he drops the banter and becomes completely serious as he extends a courtesy he has not extended to anyone else this day, "would you be free to come over here at three? There's something I want to talk to you about."

He knows, as he hangs up and stares out upon the pleasant springtime lawns, that Orrin knows; and it is with a rather helpless expression and a sad little sigh for all the things in this world that cause men to do what they feel they must, that he turns back to his desk and takes up more of the endless items of public business that will occupy him until the door opens at three and the Secretary of State is ushered in.

2

"OF ALL THE damned places to hold a news conference," the Chicago *Daily News* remarked with some asperity, "this East Room of the White House always strikes me as the worst. I feel like a flea on a plate with someone about to scratch me."

"Harley would love to," the New York *World Journal Tribune* told him from the row behind. "Damn, these chairs are uncomfortable."

"This is the Punishment Room," the Baltimore *Sun* remarked, looking around at their inconveniently close-packed, chattering ranks as they waited for the President to arrive. "He has us in here when he's going to give us a lecture. When we've been good, he lets us be comfortable in the New State Department Auditorium."

"Haven't we been good?" the New York *Times* inquired. "I thought we had."

"I don't think he likes what we've been saying about him lately," the Washington *Post* suggested. "Harley is a man who loves to be loved, you know."

"Oh, is that his trouble?" asked The Greatest Publication That Absolutely Ever Was. "I thought he reveled in opposition."

The AP snorted.

"Harley? That man has to be popular. He's so thin-skinned he wants the babies to kiss *him*."

"I don't think many are nowadays," the Los Angeles *Times* remarked.

"How could they," asked the San Francisco *Chronicle*, "with a policy like he's got? At the rate Harley's wars are going, they'll still be running when the babies are ready for the draft."

"I hear we lost six more Marines in Panama today," the Philadelphia *Inquirer* said.

"And two more bombers collided in Gorotoland," the Newark *News* contributed.

"And that's 'an affirmative policy looking toward conclusion of hostilities'?" the Denver *Post* asked. "God, it's wonderful."

"I think it's time for Dobius to give him another blast," the New York *World Journal Tribune* said. "Does anybody see him?"

"Yes, he's here," the New York *Times* said. "See, over there on the right with Henry Wilson."

"Tittle and Tattle," the Chicago *Tribune* remarked with an acid chuckle. "As a matter of fact," he added more seriously, studying their famous colleague across the room, "Walter doesn't look very happy today, does he? I wonder what's on his mind."

"Walter never looks happy," the *Christian Science Monitor* commented. "He just looks profound."

"What the hell are we here for anyway?" the Baltimore *Sun* inquired impatiently. "What's Fearless Peerless have to say? Does anybody know?"

"Maybe we're going to withdraw from Gorotoland and Panama," The Greatest Publication That Absolutely Ever Was suggested dryly.

"Maybe we're going to withdraw from the earth," the Washington *Evening Star* suggested, even more dryly.

"Whoops, boys and girls, on your feet!" the Chicago *Sun-Times* admonished. "Here comes Democracy's Noblest Symbol."

"Is it 'Hail to the Chief' I hear," the New York *Post* murmured as they obediently stood up and the gossipy babble of three hundred voices died away, "or is it 'Goofus'?"

"Please be seated," the President said pleasantly, smiling out upon them as they surveyed him with varying degrees of amiable and not-so-amiable attention. "It has been several weeks since I met with you, and I thought perhaps you might have a few questions. I also have a small announcement to make, but I expect it will keep until you're finished. Ray?" he said, singling out the UPI from the seven correspondents who were instantly on their feet.

"Mr. President," UPI said, "have you received any indication from the rebels in Gorotoland or the Labaiya Government in Panama that either would be willing to negotiate a settlement?"

"No," the President said, "we haven't. As you know, there have been efforts made by the British Government, using the good offices of the Government of Kenya and the Government of Malawi, to bring about some informal meeting with the rebel leaders in Gorotoland, but so far these overtures have been repulsed."

"Would this government be willing to enter such discussions, Mr. President?" the Baltimore *Sun* inquired.

"Not as long as the rebellion continues, no," the President said. "We didn't go in there to sanctify a rebellion, if you will recall."

"Then you want unconditional surrender from Prince Obifumatta," the New York *Times* said. The President shook his head, a little impatiently.

"We want pacification of the country and re-establishment of the legitimate government of Prince Terry. Surely that's been clear enough, right along."

"Then what grounds are there for negotiation, Mr. President?" the New York *World Journal Tribune* inquired.

"Who wants them, aside from you fellows?" the President retorted with an asperity so unusual that there was a murmur of comment over the room.

"But, Mr. President," the *Christian Science Monitor* said hesitantly, "if we insist on unconditional surrender, in effect, of the rebels in Gorotoland, then isn't that simply going to encourage them to go on fighting? What would they have to gain if they stopped?"

"An end to bloodshed," the President said promptly. "A peaceful situation in their country. Safe passage, which the United States is prepared to guarantee and enforce, for rebel leaders out of the country to asylum in some friendly nation of their choice. Not too cold a one, I hope, after that hot African climate. . . . But you see, what they're after isn't a peaceful conclusion. They don't give two hoots about the condition of their country. What they and their friends are after is a power center in central Africa. That's why they aren't going to negotiate on any terms except our complete withdrawal."

"And that's why we aren't going to negotiate," the Washington *Post* suggested, "on any terms except . . . " his voice drawled ironically away.

"Do you think we should?" the President demanded. "Of the two alternatives, which do you and your paper prefer?"

["Well, well," the Philadelphia *Inquirer* murmured to the Los Angeles *Times*. Fearless Peerless is getting nasty."

"Must be that thin skin again," the L. A. *Times* agreed with a laugh.]

"I'm just asking the questions, Mr. President," the *Post* said after a moment. "My editors didn't send me here to answer them."

"I know what they sent you here for," the President said tartly, telling himself he mustn't give in to this uncharacteristic temper, smug and superior and infuriating though his questioner was deliberately trying to be. "As a matter of fact," he said more calmly, easing the tension which had abruptly risen in his audience at his challenging tone, "the original question asked about negotiations in both Gorotoland and Panama. The situation is on the same footing in both places. We do not recognize the rebels in Gorotoland nor will we negotiate with them until they end their rebellion. We do not recognize the rebel junta in Panama—we certainly don't recognize what you call 'the Labaiya Government,' Ray, we prefer to call it the P.P.L.M. as Felix— Señor Labaiya—does. And we certainly won't negotiate with them until their rebellion ends. So I'm afraid there isn't much to report in that area this afternoon."

"Isn't it true, Mr. President, that the UN and many of our allies are demanding an end to both conflicts?" the Denver *Post* asked.

"No more than they have right along."

"Don't you think an end to them is advisable?" the Denver *Post* persisted.

"On rebel terms?" the President said. "We don't."

"Then we think our judgment is superior to their collective judgment, Mr. President," the New York *Times* suggested.

"We happen to believe so, yes," the President replied. There was a little gasp of surprise at his tone, followed by an ironic murmuring.

"Is it planned to send more troops, planes, and supplies to both places, Mr. President?" the Chicago *Sun-Times* asked.

"When they're needed."

"Not *if* they're needed," the *Sun-Times* said gently.

"I answered it, Bill," the President said, and there was a tension-releasing amusement, not at his sentiments, which many of them abhorred, but at his tartly humorous tone, which they could enjoy even if they did not agree with him.

"Well," he said, "if there are no more questions—"

"Mr. President," Walter Dobius said heavily, and there was an insant quieting and swiveling-about in the room to see what he was up to. "Can you tell us anything about your political plans?"

The President gave him a cheerful smile.

"Thank you, Walter," he said. "I was afraid I was going to have to raise the subject myself. I just happen to have an item here—" and he reached in his pocket as if to pull it out while an excited buzzing erupted and the Washington *Evening Star,* leaning forward to poke the back of the Baltimore *Sun,* said, *"Now* you know why we're here this afternoon."

"Can't seem to find it," the President remarked amiably. "Anyway, I expect to repeat and enlarge upon it on television at 9 P.M. Eastern Standard Time tonight, because I think the country deserves a full accounting of my reasons for reaching this decision.

["He's going to run?" the New York *World Journal Tribune* hissed to the AP, and the AP, scribbling furiously, snapped, "Shut up and don't bother me!"]

"But for now," the President went on in the same friendly tone, "I wanted you to have the gist of it so you can get it out right away—and I hope," he said with an amused candor, "help me arouse sufficient interest to get up a reasonably good audience.

["God, this man kills me when he gets coy," the Chicago *Daily News* muttered to the Houston *Post*. "He does it so perfectly."]

"You will recall," the President said, more seriously, "that when I succeeded to the Presidency a year ago, I told the Senate in a formal speech that I would not be a candidate for this office this year—that I would retire from the Presidency, and from public life.

"That was my firm intention at that time. I told the Senate and the country—and I meant it—that the decision was irrevocable.

"But, as all of us who live and work in Washington

know, words do not always have meanings that stay the same from year to year or month to month or even day to day.

"I think"—he smiled—"that 'irrevocable' is perhaps the most flexible word we have in the entire Washington vocabulary—perhaps outranked only by 'permanent' and 'final.'

["Get on with it, *damn* it," CBS whispered vehemently. "Stop the damned sideshow!"]

"Events since then," the President said, now completely serious, "have made it imperative, at least in my mind, that I run for re-election.

"I shall not attempt any defensive rationalization for my change of mind. I was completely sincere a year ago when I said that I would not run. I am completely sincere, believe me, when I say that I am convinced that now I must run.

"I must run," he said, "because I am the principal initiator of a policy of meeting treachery with force which has aroused very loud and violent criticism from some of you gentlemen and your publications, and from some segments of the national and world community.

"I must run because I believe this policy to be the only one consistent with the honor and security of the United States that can safely be followed in this present era.

"I must run because it is my policy and because it is not fair to ask someone else—even if," he said, and they stirred and murmured for they knew who he meant—"he might have been closely associated with it—to carry the burden of criticism which rightfully falls on me.

"I must run because I should not ask anyone else—particularly if he were not closely associated with it"—and again they knew who he meant—"to carry the criticism and fight the battle.

"It is my policy.

"I want to defend it.

"And I will.

"Furthermore," he said quietly, "I want to defend it because I do not believe that some of you gentlemen are completely correct when you tell the country that it does not agree with me.

"I think the country should have a chance to say whether it agrees with me or not. I expect to explain to the country again tonight why I have taken the road I have in Gorotoland and Panama and the United Nations, and I expect to keep on explaining, right straight through to November 3. And then I expect the country to say, with its votes, whether I am right or wrong.

"For once," he said, and smiled, "this will be a campaign that really discusses some issues. That in itself will be a service to the country, I hope, whether I win or lose."

For a moment he paused and there was a nervous upspringing of wire-service correspondents, tensed to dash for the telephones. But he held up a quick, warning hand, and amid the laughter of their colleagues they also laughed and sat slowly down again.

"However," he said, and something in the word and in his voice made the room very quiet again, "if I am to foreclose a contest for the nomination for President by asking the party and the convention to choose me again—which I think you fellows will agree," he said with a sudden chuckle, "much as you hate the thought, is what will happen now that I do ask for it—if I am to foreclose a contest for President, then it seems only fair that I should throw the convention open to an uncontrolled contest for Vice President.

["My God," the New York *Times* said in an explosive whisper to the *Christian Science Monitor*, "what a fiendishly clever idea! If Orrin gets it, Harley can say the country's for his policies, and if Ted gets it, the whole issue will be so fuzzed up that nobody will know what they're voting for and Harley will get re-elected anyway. This guy's one of the master politicians of all time!"

"I've always thought," the *Monitor* said gently, "that some people underestimated Harley a little too much."]

"Therefore," the President said, "I think this is the way it should be, and I ask the managers of the convention to arrange things so it will be done. Or, to be candid," he said with a grin that brought an answering amusement even in the midst of their furious scribbling and concentration, "I hereby tell the managers of the convention that they should run things the way they always do—only this time the President won't intervene. . . .

"I may anticipate a question by saying that I have communicated these decisions to both the Secretary of State and the Governor of California today, and they are agreed that this is the fair thing to do and they are willing to have the convention proceed on that basis." He smiled and his next words brought laughter. "I will say that their feelings when I told them were mixed. They had to weigh the advantage of being chosen by the President against the gamble of losing an open contest. But, on the other hand, if one were to be chosen the other would certainly lose, and if there's an open contest, who knows who will win when the votes are finally counted?

"Of course," he said amicably, and this time, in a releasing of tension and a readjusting to the situations created by his announcements, there was a genuine roar of laughter, "I don't know that either of them intends to run, and maybe you'll want to ask them about that after this conference breaks up. But if they do, that's the situation.

"And now," he said, joining comfortably in their laughter, "I think that's enough for one day."

"Thank *you*, Mr. President!" the AP cried, and they were off on the pell-mell race for the telephones along the stately corridors of the White House.

3

So SIMPLY the world changes, the Governor of California thought in Sacramento that night, listening to the calm and explicit voice of the President, studying the kindly face as he explained his decision to his countrymen. A man—if he is a certain man in a certain place—makes up his mind and says a few words at a press conference and over the air, and the lives of millions of people and hundreds of nations are changed in five minutes irrevocably and beyond recall. The power of it, he told himself with awe, the power of it!

The power he would like to have; but from the President's first words on the telephone this morning he had known it would not be his—at least, not this year, and perhaps not ever—if he wished to remain in his present influential position in American politics. It was, as the President had made clear, fish or cut bait, cooperate or forget it. The tone had been amicable but the import had been clear.

"Ted," he had said after the opening felicities (a little

too fulsome and casual, the Governor thought, sensing it already), "I am announcing a decision to the press this afternoon, but I thought I would communicate it to you first, as one of the directly interested parties."

He paused, as if inviting comment, and Ted said cheerfully, though a terrible sinking feeling was already gripping his heart, "I appreciate that, Mr. President, and whatever the decision is, you know I will support it wholeheartedly."

The President laughed, in a friendly way.

"Well, that may or may not be—the 'wholeheartedly,' I mean—but I am sure you will support it. . . . You of course have been correct right along."

"I knew I was," Governor Jason said. "I didn't see how you could avoid it, with the prospect of a dogfight between me and Orrin coming up, and with your policies and your Administration under such bitter fire. You've almost got to."

"More than almost," the President said. "I have got to. Not because of you and Orrin"—he had sounded amused again, and Ted had been alerted at once, "you and Orrin may still have your dogfight, if you want to—but because of exactly the point you make about being under fire. I can't ask either of you to carry the burden of that. At least," he interjected again, and again Ted's curiosity grew, "alone. They're my policies and by rights I should have to defend them. And I intend to. So, that's what I'm announcing at my press conference. Confidentially to you, of course, until after it's over. Except for that lovely Ceil of yours. She might be interested."

"I'm just about to join her for lunch. I think I can assure you she will be . . . Well, Mr. President, I wish you luck, and of course I am yours to command in the campaign any way you like."

"No," the President said thoughtfully. "I don't want to bind you that much, Ted."

"But—" the Governor said, his mind immediately filled with a vision of himself being quietly left out of things, in effect dumped from the party's top councils because of his attitude on Gorotoland and Panama. The man he was talking to was still the boss. He suddenly wished he hadn't been so equivocal.

"In fact," the President said, "I want you and Orrin to be engaged in the most vigorous possible way, and yet in the most independent and self-reliant one, too. He represents a very definite position, which of course is the same as mine. You represent, I think, a different position, though you have not yet expressed it very clearly."

"I know," Ted Jason said quickly. "You realize I have been under considerable pressure to be much more adamant than I have." He gave a rueful little laugh. "I have some very ruthless friends. In a sense, Mr. President, silence from me has been the equivalent—for you—of active support from Orrin. At least I haven't let them make me damage you."

"I know, and I appreciate it. However, you do, as I say, represent a somewhat different position. I'm prepared to grant it's a valid one in the minds of many people, and I think it should have representation in the convention . . . if that's what the convention wants."

"What do you mean by that?" Ted asked cautiously.

"I think you should run for Vice President."

"Do you mean," Governor Jason demanded, "that you're going to pick me for running mate?"

"Oh, no," the President said calmly. "I'll admit that would be a neat way to balance the ticket and win over at least some of your supporters. It's been done before. No, I meant what I said: I think you should run for Vice President."

"Nobody 'runs' for Vice President. You didn't."

"I was sort of created," the President said with a chuckle. Then his tone became serious again.

"When I say run, I mean run. That's happened too, once in a while."

"An open convention for Vice President?" Ted asked incredulously.

"Why not? As I said, you represent one position, he another. Popular sentiment will have to give one of you the victory."

"And either way," Ted Jason said slowly, "you win."

The President chuckled again.

"That may be, but at least there will be a fair fight in the convention and all sides will have a chance to state their case. And nobody can say I rigged it, because I give you my word, having made the decision to stay out, I'm going to stay out. And if you get the nomination your friends can breathe easier, because that great statesman, Ted, is running with that warmonger, Harley—who may drop dead at any minute and give Ted a chance to change the whole picture. . . . So you see," the President concluded gently, "why I think it would be very smart of you to run, from both our standpoints. . . . However," he added crisply, "I of course cannot and will not make any attempt to commit you to it . . . unless you want me to." He paused for a moment, but the Governor said nothing, and he went on."I will tell the press conference that it's going to be an open convention. What you do after that is your own affair. Watched with great interest," he concluded humorously, "by me."

"Thank you, Mr. President," Ted said suavely. "I appreciate your confidence, I appreciate your alerting me in advance, I appreciate—everything. It will of course take a little time to decide what to do, as this is rather surprising and startling news with many ramifications. I assure you," he said with a sudden amusement of his own, "that you are not the only person who will be watching me with great interest. I will be too!"

"Just so you don't drop the mirror," the President said pleasantly. "It means seven years' bad luck. . . . Goodbye, Ted. Have fun."

"Thank you, Mr. President," Governor Jason said evenly. "You too."

And now he was watching the rationale and the presentation as it came with a quiet dignity, a firmness of purpose, and an unassailable aura of integrity, to the country. The President was doing a good job, there was no doubt of that. He had, Ted was forced to admit to himself ruefully, done a good job on him.

When he returned to the baroque old Governor's Mansion for lunch, Ceil had seen at once that he was much disturbed, and in her candid, friendly way had asked straight out what it was. He had managed to muster a rather wan smile.

"One of the things I love about you," he said, "is that you know when to be tactful."

She laughed.

"When you look like you just did, I know it's time to be. I can be the most devious old bush-beater-arounder you ever saw with the ladies of the state party. But not with the head of the greatest state in the Union when he looks like that. So what is it?"

She frowned a little as he told her, while she went about the business of getting lunch, a task she always liked to reserve for herself without the aid of the servants, when he was able to come home for it.

"Hmmm," she said thoughtfully when he finished. "He's got you in kind of a neat box, hasn't he?"

"He's kind of a neat politician, when you come right down to it. It's one of those things being President has brought out in him, I guess. Nobody ever knew it before. . . . Yes, he has, to answer your question. How am I going to get out of it?"

"Do you want to?"

"Don't I have to?"

"Yes," she agreed, serving the soup and salad, sitting down across from him with a cogitating air, "I suppose you do. You could always do exactly what he suggested, you know. That might be the simplest out of all. Since," she gave him a cheerful smile, "you're quite sure you'd win such a fight in the convention."

"Hah! Don't *you* start giving me a hard time. I'm not at all sure I could win in the convention."

"Against Orrin?" she said with a surprise he could almost believe was genuine.

"Come on," he said. "Yes, against Orrin. I have no doubt I could win against anyone else—well, do you?—but against Orrin—who knows?"

"I repeat, the simplest way to find out is to try," she said. "Also, perhaps—the most honest."

"There are situations in political life," he said softly, "in which honesty isn't always enough."

"But a pretense of honesty," she said with the encouraging smile he couldn't always fathom. "At least a *pretense* of it." This time he thought he could fathom it.

"When it comes," he said shortly, "it won't be pretense. They'll know how I feel."

"Well, I don't know. You've managed to stand them off for a month under some pretty terrific pressures. You could probably do it longer."

"I could," he agreed calmly, "but would it be worth it to me to do so?"

"It might be worth more to the country if you didn't. The country might like to have you speak right out, now that the President's offering you the opportunity."

"He's offered me more than that. He dangled his own corpse in front of me."

"My," she said with a little laugh. "That sounds ghoulish."

"Well, in effect. The old Secret Weapon of Vice Presidents, you know, that enables most of them to stand it—the thought that No. 1 may drop dead any minute and I could then, as he put it, 'change the whole picture' as quickly as I pleased. This of course, as he very well knows, is why it would be a great advantage for him to have me on the ticket—because that's exactly the thought that would be in the minds of people like Walter Dobius, for instance, and therefore they would work and vote for him in the hope that the Lord or some little psychopath would answer their prayers and make me President."

"It is ghoulish, isn't it?"

"And practical. But I'm not so sure I want it on that basis. I'm not so sure I want to help him that much. I'm not so sure, either, that I want to be his pawn and let him move me around on the board like that."

"But if you don't run for Vice President," she said gently, "you're through, aren't you? He'll have given you the chance and you'll have turned him down. And parties and conventions don't like that kind of thing. They remember the people who were too proud to try. They don't forget."

"And if I do try, and lose, then I'm finished, too." He smiled without humor. "Clever, our Harley. He's quite a boy."

"But if he really keeps hands off, what on earth have you got to fear from an honest try? You won't be through if you lose, if you do it in that spirit, because you will have made a record and fought a good fight, and, I hope, done it with dignity and good heart and won a lot of respect from it. Parties and conventions don't forget that kind of thing, either."

"You want me to," he said. She gave him a long, thoughtful look, and smiled.

"I want you to do whatever you think is best. I'm your most loyal camp-follower, you great big handsome man. Every day after the battle I'll be there to wash your feet and scrub your back and fix you a dry martini. You know that."

He smiled.

"And dispense subtly disapproving advice along with it."

"Why," she said blandly, "I don't disapprove. I learned long ago that there's no room for disapproval in the entourage of a man who's really going places. Capitalize that," she added with her silvery little laugh as she began to clear the table. "A Man Who's Really Going Places."

But there was always room for it where she was concerned, he thought without resentment as the President concluded his talk, the Presidential Seal came on the screen, and the national anthem began its crashing statements. He caught her studying his face with an intent, appraising glance as he reached to turn off the set. Always room for it with her, because it was almost always sound, even when he didn't take it.

At the moment, how could he? Literally within seconds now, he expected the phone to begin the clamor he had successfully avoided after the President's press conference by simply refusing all calls. Now they had a right to reach him, and they would. "Governor, what did you think of the President's speech? Are you going to run, Governor? How soon can we expect a formal announcement, Governor?" And very soon, no doubt, pompous and heavy and filled with the weight of the nation's burdens which its owner had carried so long: "Ted? This is Walter. How much longer are you going to keep the country waiting?"

Well: at this moment, he did not know. Orrin, of course, had left no doubt, but that was Orrin's way. Slam-bam and into the middle of it, that was the Secretary of State. His own path was more delicate. Orrin could state his point of view, but his supporters wouldn't own him: they never had. Ted's supporters wanted to own him, with the great, devouring, all-consuming, all-obliterating love of the animal ovation at the banquet. There would be other such ovations, there already had been, wherever he went. They saw in him the embodiment of all their fears of present policy, their desperate hopes for a return to weakness. All they asked in payment for their love was the complete surrender of his mind, his independence, and his individuality.

At this point. Later, if he was nominated for Vice President—if the ticket won, as it almost certainly would with him on it—if Harley did drop dead—then they would own him no longer. Then he would be their master once again, as he had been in all his public life up to the day of strangely mixed blessings when he had suddenly become confused with an issue in too many highly intelligent and inflammatory minds.

But if he didn't run—or if Harley didn't drop dead—if

he, Ted, went into political limbo for a term or two—

So what should he say, when the phone rang?

"I don't know," he said aloud, and Ceil smiled as though she understood what he meant, which, being Ceil, she no doubt did.

Insistent, inexorable, inescapable, the bell roared at his elbow.

"Ted?" said a heavy, pompous voice across three thousand miles. "This is Walter. How much longer are you going to keep on playing games with us—now?"

Through the closed door of the upstairs study he could hear the rise and fall of their contentious voices as he came slowly to the foot of the stairs from the library where he had gone to put through his call. He hesitated for a moment, then turned to stare out through the big window into the soft velvet night of Virginia. Slowly he went toward it, took a seat in the armchair left permanently facing the view, put his fingertips together, and leaned his chin upon them with a thoughtful frown. Two conversations today, and a third about to begin. He would dictate his careful memories of them later for the Archive. Right now he wondered where they were leading him.

"Good morning, Walter," the President had said crisply when he reached him in the Senate Press Gallery, and at once Walter could tell he was in a hostile mood. "I have something to tell you that you are to keep confidential until after my press conference this afternoon. You can't use it before anyone else does, but"—his tone had become dry—"in view of your extreme interest, I wanted you to be one of the first to know."

"Thank you, Mr. President," Walter had said without, he congratulated himself, a trace of inflection one way or the other in his voice. "I appreciate your thinking of me." Then his feelings had momentarily won the upper hand and he had asked with a dryness of his own, "Is this something the world will be upset about?"

"The world?" the President had said. And then: "Oh, the world. Yes, I expect it will. All sorts of worlds, including yours. It doesn't involve military action, though, if that's your worry."

"It seems a legitimate one," Walter said with an edge to his voice, "under all the circumstances."

"Well," the President said, "I'm not going to debate that

with you, Walter. You just go ahead and write another column about it, if you like. No, this concerns me; and your favorite candidate for President; and other people. . . . I really," he said thoughtfully, "don't know why I'm bothering to call you—unless it's just spite, which isn't a very worthy motivation for a President of the United States to have." He laughed, surprisingly. "I'm afraid, Walter, that you've got me into rather bad habits, lately. I didn't used to feel spiteful toward anyone."

"I'm sorry, Mr. President," Walter said, his eyes straying over his gossiping colleagues sitting about on the sofas and chairs of the Press Gallery, the inevitable gin rummy game that starts when the Senate is not in session going at the table by the fireplace. How astounded they would be if they knew the extraordinary conversation going on fifteen feet from them.

"So am I, Walter," the President said. "It's a sad commentary on the times. And some people in it."

"If you mean me, Mr. President," Walter said, and his tone became pompous and emphatic, "I have only done my duty as I see it."

"I'm not sure I grant you that," the President said, "since you so bitterly refuse to grant it to me. However, I repeat: I didn't call to debate it." He laughed, a brief, unamused sound. "Actually, I just called so you could get a head start on the column you'll write tomorrow condemning me. . . . I'm going to run."

There was a silence on the phone in the gallery. It lasted long enough so that the President finally said, "Walter?"

"I'm here," Walter Dobius said heavily. *"Why?"*

"Because you—and other people—have forced me to. Because you've been so extraordinarily savage and unfair that I feel I must defend myself and my policies and the only way to do it is to go to the country and get a mandate, if I can."

"Do you think it will be large enough to be called that?" Walter asked in a tone close to insolence. This time the silence occurred at the White House.

"No one can say until the votes are counted," the President said finally. "But at least there will be a decision, one way or the other. If it were no greater than a hundred thousand for your side, you know you would claim it as a mandate. I shall certainly do no less."

He paused and Walter wondered what more he had to say, this odd, extraordinary, foolishly blind and destructive man who was ruining the world.

"There's an aspect of it which may give you hope, however," the President went on. "I'm throwing the convention open for Vice President. Perhaps you can find a candidate for that office who will suit you." He uttered a small, ironic sound. "If you can persuade him to run, that is."

"That *is* extraordinary," Walter conceded. "But of course I think you are very wise. Very shrewd, too," he added with a grudging honesty. "I will say, Mr. President, whatever else I may think of you, that you have become quite a remarkable politician in the past year."

"Thank you so much. I treasure these small items of your regard. . . . I wish you luck with your candidate."

"You want him to run, don't you, Mr. President?"

"It's part of my shrewdness. I hope you can persuade him. I don't think I have."

"I hope I can," Walter Dobius said calmly. "I regard his election as absolutely imperative for world peace."

"You know," the President said dryly, "that's exactly how I regard my own. Strange, isn't it?"

It was indeed, Walter thought as the fantastic call ended, and strange he thought it still as the fatherly face faded from the television screen and his guests expressed themselves with suitable scorn and indignation. He had come downstairs to find privacy for the call he had intended to place ever since the President had told him of his intentions. He had deliberately waited until after the speech because he thought delay would carry some element of surprise and perhaps increase the psychological pressure. He had known, however, that the project would not be easy and might well be unsatisfying. But damn it, he told himself as the phone began to ring in Sacramento, there had to be a decision sometime. There had to be.

"Ted?" he said, and he deliberately made his voice as emphatic as he could, "this is Walter. How much longer are you going to keep on playing games with us—now?"

"Is that what I'm doing?" Governor Jason asked blandly. "I didn't know."

"Don't fence. This may not be the first call you have received; certainly it won't be the last. They will all ask the same question and seek the same answer. I trust you have it ready."

"For Vice President?" Ted Jason said dreamily. *"That* office?"

"I said don't fence. You know all the possibilities."

"I also know why the President wants me to run," the Governor told him tartly. "To balance the ticket, to futz up the image, and to blur the issues so that he can be elected."

"But if you're elected with him—"

"What will you do?" Ted asked like a shot. "Find another Lee Oswald?"

There was a silence.

"That," said Walter angrily, "is a vicious, unprincipled, evil remark."

"Oh, come, Walter," said Governor Jason, unimpressed. "You'd be delighted if Harley died. You wouldn't care how it happened."

"I repeat, that is a vicious, unprincipled—"

"Listen to me, friend," Ted Jason broke in coldly. "If there is any one man in the United States responsible for creating the climate in which such a thing could happen, it is Walter Dobius the great philosopher. Now, you examine your own conscience for a change and leave mine out of it. If I decide to run, I'll run, and if I decide not to, I won't. From now on I'm not taking any more pressure from you or anybody."

"Those are brave words," Walter said, and over three thousand miles the Governor could hear his breath come heavily with anger. "You are a very difficult man for those who know you to like."

"But those who don't know me worship me, don't they?" the Governor asked in a nasty voice. Then his tone changed and became quite matter-of-fact and impersonal. "You think now, don't you, that I'm in a spot where I'm really vulnerable—where I've really got to do something and where I can really be pressured. I don't see it that way. I think I'm in a spot where anyone who wants me to run has got to come to me and pay for the favor. Why should I take the gamble of a second-best office for you, just so you can write your precious columns about 'a balancing influence on the ticket,' and kid yourself that there'll be somebody inside who can subvert the President's policies? He'll swallow me up if I take second place. I wouldn't be able to subvert anything—even if I wanted to, and I'm not sure I do."

"You remain the one hope for a return to sanity in this

Administration," Walter said with a dogged insistence, "and if you think the progressive and decent forces of this country are going to give you up or let you evade your responsibility, you can think again. The situation was unclear as long as the President withheld his intentions, but now that he has announced them the way is open. It is imperative that you become Vice President. At the very least, it will inevitably have a moderating influence upon the Administration. And anything can happen once you're in there. Nothing may, of course. He may live eight more years in office. The important thing is to have you there in case he doesn't. To that end," he concluded with an adamantine coldness to match the Governor's own, "my energies and those of many other powerful people in the country are being directed, and the tempo will increase as we approach the convention. If you think you can halt it now, you are a fool, Ted Jason. And you're not a fool."

"No," the Governor agreed pleasantly. "But I warn you not to take me too much for granted. You may be trying to fabricate me into a symbol that doesn't exist."

"I may be trying to fabricate you into a straightforward and unequivocal man," Walter Dobius said with a biting scorn, "and that, I grant you, may be impossible. Whether you announce or not you are, from today, a candidate, and all the energies and activities of a great many top people in very influential places are going to be devoted to placing you on the ticket. So prepare to accept your martyrdom with grace, because it's coming."

"In that case," Ted Jason said, still pleasantly, "I really don't have to say a thing, do I?"

"If that is your concept of honor," Walter said coldly, "I wish you joy of it."

"Goodnight, Walter," the Governor said cheerfully. "Thanks for calling."

"You will be hearing from us," Walter Dobius promised with a ponderous portentousness in his voice. "By the millions."

And yet, what could you do with him, and what did a conversation like that portend for the future? He would be nominated, all right, Walter was sure he and his colleagues could bring that about, but then what? Suppose he did become President someday, how could you ever count on him? He would never listen to advice, he would never take guidance from those most capable of giving it, he would never—he would never *behave*. You could never be sure of him, even if you did succeed in giving him the prize he wanted. He would be a disappointing President, should he become one.

Ted simply had no respect for those who saw clearly how the world should go. He had too many ideas of his own.

But for now, Walter thought grimly, he was a prisoner of the political tide and nothing he could do would stop it. Too many powerful factions and forces were too deeply committed on his behalf.

For example, the rather odd trio that waited in his study now. Their coming out here tonight had not been his doing, but he had agreed to it when they called, partly because he was curious to pick their brains, partly because he knew that they symbolized the coalition from which Ted's basic strengths would come, and partly because they had told him flatteringly that they needed his advise.

"I talked to him," he announced, opening the study door. "As always, he loves to be equivocal. But he'll run."

"Then all we have to do is get organized," said Fred Van Ackerman of the Committee on Making Further Offers for a Russian Truce (COMFORT), "and we've got it made."

With an air of savage satisfaction LeGage Shelby of the Defenders of Equality for You (DEFY) nodded his darkly equine head, and Rufus Kleinfert of the Konference on Efforts to Encourage Patriotism (KEEP) gave the awkward and uneasy grimace which, with him, passed for a smile.

"Wait 'til Orrin comes up against *this* combination," Senator Van Ackerman said with an ugly pleasure. "I'll bet he's wetting his pants already."

"You heard his statement," Walter said. "He's setting about as coldly and efficiently as he knows how to get on that ticket."

But in this glib assumption the Secretary's reputation for political pragmatism was perhaps playing him a little false, for it was in a mood not quite so unemotional as Walter believed that he was contemplating what appeared to be the ruin, for the third and probably final time, of his hopes of ever becoming President. He too of course had seen the obvious the moment Harley disclosed his intention to throw the convention open. Harley himself had succeeded to the Presidency as a result of death, the event had happened before in one way or another, it could happen this time.

Equally could it happen that the President would live to retire at some distant date full of years and dignity, and Orrin could end his own political career as a Vice President having far less direct control of policy and events than he did right now as Secretary of State.

One thing he realized at once, however, and that was the immediate need to support the President and to indicate by his own actions that he endorsed and defended the policies he had done so much to help formulate. The slightest hesitation on his part would be read as a drastic weakening of an Administration already hampered to a considerable degree by the hesitations of the Governor of California. Overriding every other consideration in Orrin's mind at that moment was the necessity to speak out at once in support of the President. Being Orrin, it had taken him five minutes to reach the decision. Half an hour after the President's press conference ended he had acted upon it.

In a sense this had been easier to do because of the kindness with which the President had disclosed his intentions. When he had called to invite the Secretary over, Orrin had known instinctively at once what the subject would be; and some other element, the necessary escape clause that most experienced politicians carry always in some defensive recess of the mind—"Things probably won't work out the way I want them to, so I'd better not get my hopes up too high"—prepared him for the likely decision. Yet Harley could not have been nicer.

"Sit down, Orrin," he said cordially, and the Secretary could sense at once that he was not entirely at ease. A moment later he admitted it, with a self-deprecating smile that aroused Orrin's sympathies at once.

"This isn't too easy a conversation for me," he confessed. "I hope you'll help me with it."

"You know I will, Mr. President," Orrin said gravely. "What does it concern?"

"I expect you know," the President said.

The Secretary stared out at the bursting gardens, the beautiful lawn, the sweet felicity of the weather, committed at last to Washington's lovely spring. He sighed.

"Yes, I expect I do."

"I don't feel too good about it," the President said with a wry little smile. "I don't like to go back on my word, or abandon a position and a conviction that have been entirely sincere—though you may not think so now."

"Oh, yes," Orrin said. He too smiled with some wryness. "Of all the people concerned with your decision, I expect I can probably grant your sincerity almost more than anyone else does . . . even though I probably have more to lose from it than anyone else."

"Don't be too sure," the President said, and Orrin looked puzzled. "I do want you to understand why I do this," he went on before Orrin could speak. "It really is because I am under such vicious attack that I feel I must defend my own policies and not ask anyone else to do it. I wouldn't consider it for a moment, otherwise."

"I realize that plays a major part in it," Orrin agreed. He smiled with a genuine amusement. "At least I think that's how most Presidents rationalize it—they have to defend the record, isn't that it?"

The President laughed in a completely relaxed fashion, and from that moment their talk went forward without strain.

"You may be right. But certainly the immediate practical reason is exactly what I say: I have got to defend myself. The division in the country is sharp enough so that I really—at least as I see it—do not have a choice. I must meet the situation head-on because basically it's my responsibility."

"And you want to."

The President smiled.

"I'd kind of like to see it through. I'm making a great experiment here: whether a policy of complete candor about what needs to be done to save America and with it the free world from another Dark Ages of the mind can work in this century of ours. I'm not sure it can. But," he said with a somber emphasis unexpected in one usually so calm, "I intend to accomplish it if I can."

"I admire you for that," Orrin said. The President's next remark came with a gentleness that took him by surprise and almost destroyed the tight grip he was maintaining on his swirling emotions.

"I regret very much the destruction of your hopes to run for this office."

For a moment, absurdly, Orrin found himself unable to answer. By a great effort of will—another moment, he told himself with a hasty scorn, and he would probably be blubbering like a schoolboy, if he didn't watch it—he forced himself to concentrate his gaze upon the rose garden and think of something else, while the President, too, stared tactfully out the window.

"It is of course a disappointment to me," he said finally, managing to keep his voice steady, but just. "You know how long I have been—interested." He smiled, at considerable cost. "Nobody knows better than you do, Harley— and how much, foolishly, I suppose, I have been depending upon the word you gave the country a year ago. But we talked about this a month ago right here, didn't we? And I went home and told Beth you were going to run." He smiled again, a little better this time. "But it's still a disappointment. You can't keep yourself from disbelieving the things you don't want to believe. I do understand—I do accept your reasons—I do see how you consider them valid." He smiled again, though it still cost him something to do it, but it was getting easier every second. "It's a long way across this desk from this chair to that one, but if I'd ever made it, I think I would do exactly the same thing."

The President gave him a long look, obviously touched himself.

"Thank you," he said at last. "And Orrin: don't sound so elegiac about it. Don't say 'if you'd ever made it.' You still may."

The Secretary shot him a glance that was, the President was relieved to see, good old skeptical Orrin Knox again, in person.

"Huh!" he said with a snort. "How?"

"I'll tell you," the President said. When he finished the Secretary studied him for several moments with a shrewd, appraising gaze.

"Do you want me on the ticket?" he demanded.

"Do you want to be there?"

Orrin laughed.

"I asked first."

The President chuckled.

"That, I am afraid you will have to determine yourself," he said lightly. Then he dropped it and became serious. "Given a choice between Ted Jason, who hems and haws and doesn't really agree with me, and you, my right arm who has participated in all these decisions and helped to make all these policies, who do you think I want on the ticket with me? Of course I want you on the ticket. But suppose you had gone that long distance across this desk from that chair to this—would you think you were in a position to make the outright choice? You're a practical politician, so I've been told—"

"You know I'm not at all," the Secretary interrupted with a rueful grin. "I'm sentimental and impulsive and emotional, and I let my feelings run away with me sometimes when I wish I hadn't. But go on."

The President smiled.

"I'm just saying what I've been told—and you know there are many reasons why I've got to do it this way. Not the least important is that there really is a serious split in the country, and it really should have a chance to work itself out in the convention. That contest for Vice President is going to be a safety valve. There's got to be one, and that's where it's got to come." He paused and shot the Secretary a quick, shrewd look. "Doesn't that make sense?"

Orrin's glance was equally shrewd.

"It also takes you off the hook."

"I know that," the President said impatiently, "I'm admitting that. But you do concede there are other elements, just as valid."

"Oh, yes, of course there are. It's a very astute idea all around, and, I grant you, probably a necessary one. . . . The one thing I've got to do, it seems to me, is announce at once so there won't be the slightest doubt that I, at least, am supporting you." He gave an ironic smile. "How do you know there'll be a contest? Have you talked to California?"

"I have," the President said with an equal irony, "and there may not be. In which case, you'll be even better off, won't you? And so will I. I really will keep hands off, but don't forget: I don't *want* to do it this way. I think it's best. Things might be a lot different if I had my druthers."

"If you'll excuse me," Orrin said, "I think I'd better get back to the Department and call in the press."

"Why don't you just issue a statement after my press conference? I wouldn't lay myself open to questions at this point, if I were you. You don't have to."

"That's true," Orrin said. The President rose and came around the desk, holding out his hand.

"Orrin, my friend: thank you and good luck."

"Thank you, Mr. President," Orrin said, and found he

must turn hastily away, for it was not so easy to say farewell so fast to so many long-held hopes. "I'll be in touch," he tossed over his shoulder in a muffled voice.

Promptly at 5 P.M. his statement was issued through the State Department press office:

"I shall be a candidate for the nomination for Vice President of the United States.

"I make this announcement, happy to know that if I should be nominated, I will be on the ticket with a President whose policies I believe to be the only safe and effective policies for America to follow in these troubled times.

"Those policies I endorse 100 percent.

"That President I support 100 percent.

"Let no one anywhere have any doubts where I stand.

"I ask all who have been my friends in the past to rally to me now. The task is hard, the road difficult, but with the help of all who uphold the courage and honor and above all the survival of the United States of America, we shall win."

And now—having begged off from a dinner at the French Embassy, which he regretted but felt was best under the circumstances—he had eaten a quiet dinner with Beth, watched the President's speech, and was just beginning to realize what had happened. It was only now when Beth snapped off the set to leave a sudden terrifying silence in the room that the event and its full implications came rushing upon him in such a fierce attack that he thought for a moment his being might not be able to stand it. Everything up to that moment had gone so well and so fast that he had really not had time to think about it very deeply. Now nothing stood between him and that abyss from which men's hopes, once toppled, rarely re-emerge.

He tried to hide the reaction, in a mobile and candid face, but he was in the presence of a close student of thirty years' standing.

"Now, just take it easy," she said quietly, coming to sit beside him on the sofa. "It isn't the end of the world."

"My world," he said with a wry shrug.

"What nonsense!" she said comfortably. " 'Your world!' Poor old Orrin Knox, all he is is Secretary of State, a likely Vice President, and maybe President someday." She chuckled and took his hand with an elaborately pitying squeeze. "Poor old fellow, I feel for you!"

"Well," he said with the trace of a smile, "it is, in a way. 'Maybe President someday.' My somedays are running out, Hank. I'm getting past the first fine, fresh bloom of presidential likelihood. This is the third time around the track, and now it's only Vice President if I do get it."

"But—"

"I know all the arguments. If they didn't require the death of a man I have always been fond of and in the past year have come to really admire, I'd be sold on them too. But not wishing Harley any bad luck, and having to think of him as being, obviously, in very good health, I have to contemplate eight years as Vice President, after which I shall be well into my sixties and too old to seek the Presidency. I'll have been around too long, Hank." He grinned ruefully. "Plenty of people think I have been already, but they'll be sure of it, then."

"You just never know," she said. "You literally don't. What's the alternative? Let Ted take it by default and maybe have him become President someday, with all his wishy-washy ideas?"

"He isn't so wishy-washy," Orrin said thoughtfully. "He's just cautious. More so than I am, that's for sure."

"The millions of people who believe in Orrin Knox— and millions do, my boy, don't forget that—believe in him exactly because he isn't cautious every time, he doesn't always hesitate and trim. Once in a while he has the guts to state some principles, dream some dreams, and go for broke."

"Lady," he said with some return of his normal humor, staring into the fire, lit for coziness though they were now safely into spring, "would you like a job writing campaign copy? I have just the spot for a nice young copywriter like you."

"Well, it's true," she said, flushed and indignant, "so don't make fun of it. That will continue right along, you'll carry it into the Vice Presidency with you just as you have at every step of the way since Illinois. Don't knock it. It can't be said of everybody in this town."

"True enough," he said, "true enough. And of course if I do get it, it will strengthen Harley's hand considerably in his policies, there's no doubt of that. . . . Even though, of course, having Ted get it would strengthen him even more in the immediate contest in November."

"Will it be much of a contest? Who do they have in the other party? Surely you don't think Warren Strickland can beat Harley?"

"No," he said, considering for a moment the able, amiable, and not overly aggressive Senate Minority Leader from Idaho, who appeared to be the likeliest choice of the minority party to be its sacrifice candidate this year. "In the first place, his heart isn't in it, in the second place there's no real opposition stand he can take that wouldn't be entirely too extreme for his own temperament to accept, and in the third place the registration's against him. Plus the fact that he likes Harley and has supported him right along in foreign policy. No, they're just going to be going through the motions this time. The real battle's with us, as it usually is. But, Hank," he said soberly, "can I win that convention? Do I really have a chance? Hasn't the outcry of people like Walter Dobius created such a mood in the country that a candidate upholding the Administration's policy will be beaten? Isn't Ted really riding the popular wave?"

She studied him thoughtfully before replying.

"You don't think so for one minute," she said finally. "Neither do I, or lots of people. Helen-Anne called, for instance, right after your statement was released, to say she's ready to work for you for Vice President, if you still want her. She thinks you've got a terrific chance. So do I. And so, old dear, underneath all the heroics about Orrin Knox on his way to pasture, do you. So suppose you buckle down, Wynsocki, and get to work. O.K.?"

He smiled.

"Oh, yes. I will, of course, you know that. But, Hank"—and his expression changed suddenly to a strangely young and vulnerable wistfulness that took her back to Illinois and other dreams and the long road that now appeared, in truth, to be ending short of the goal he had set himself when they were first married, so long ago, "it would have been nice—to be President."

"Oh, my dear," she said softly, taking his hand again in hers and turning her head to the fire so that he would not see the tears in her eyes, "one can't tell on these things. If it's meant to be, it still will be. If it doesn't happen, then we'll just have to conclude that we were the only ones who meant it to be—not someone else. . . ."

But he did not reply, nor, for a while, did she dare glance at him. They sat for a while in silence, there before the fire, while in many places and many hearts others were determining what position, if any, Orrin Knox should occupy from now on in the peculiar but oddly magnificent history of his country.

4

AND SO, HE thinks as he steps out on the Truman balcony for a last moment in the soft spring air and his ritual look at the Washington Monument before bedtime, the deed is completed and Harley M. Hudson, an honorable man who has never yet broken his pledged word, has done so. There have been many opportunities in the past year to realize what is meant by the loneliness of the Presidency and its hard, cruel choices, but he knows that this is the sharpest and most poignant moment of them all. He had meant it with all his heart when he stood before the Senate a year ago and said, "I shall not be a candidate for the Presidency next year." He had meant it up to three weeks, or even two, or maybe even two days, ago. Then he had changed and betrayed the hopes and plans of many men . . . betrayed himself.

But, he honestly believes, saved the United States, which is why Presidents do these things. He tells himself, as he sits down for a moment in one of the chaise longues and lets himself relax a little from the great tensions of this most momentous day, that it is probably the height of egotism—or insanity—or something—to equate his own political fortunes with the preservation of the United States. And yet this, too, is something Presidents have to believe, if only to rationalize what they do through the imperatives of ambition.

There comes a point in this office, he realizes now, at which it is literally impossible for the occupant to distinguish any longer between his own interests and the interests of the United States. The White House in time, even for the most determinedly idealistic, gradually obliterates the line between self and service. Presidents after a while—and sometimes a much shorter while than in his case—reach a point where they simply cannot regard themselves objectively any more. A few have made the decision to retire, and stuck to it, but history does not record many; and none with the complication of problems that bedevil him, in a world that hourly grows more complex and more dangerous to every living thing.

So—pledges are broken. Decisions are reversed. Yesterday's absolute becomes today's maybe and tomorrow's negative. History bends Presidents to its will as it bends other men. So be it.

Yet he cannot help but feel a sad regret for the self that used to exist until, at some time in recent days and hours, he had come finally, perhaps subconsciously, to the conviction that he had to run. He had wanted to keep his word, but events wouldn't let him. People wouldn't let him. The country wouldn't let him.

He had known, when he set out upon the course that led through Gorotoland to the vetoes and then to Panama, what the reaction of certain very noisy segments of the populace would be. You could always count on the shouters, the joiners, the conveniently short-memoried idealists, and the professional phonies to clamor against every strong stand you might take anywhere. But though he had been prepared for the dimensions of their outcry, he had not been prepared for its extraordinary violence. It had created in him a real alarm that its practitioners would succeed in twisting the realities of Communist imperialism permanently out of shape in their countrymen's minds, so that America would be even more confused than she was already in her appreciation of the dangers that beset her. The alarm in turn led directly to his decision to run. It came down to something as simple as the picture he had seen on the front page of The Greatest Publication just last week. It showed two Marines training their rifles upon a hut in Gorotoland. ALL IN THE DAY'S WORK FOR MARINES, the caption read, with a snide air of arch disapproval. "Two U. S. Marines get ready to respond to alleged 'ambush' in rebel-held Goroto town."

"Good God!" he had exploded with a sudden uncharacteristic profanity to Lucille. "Why in the hell haven't they got a right to respond if they're being fired upon? And who the hell said it was an 'alleged' ambush?"

It is ten thousand little things like that, all adding up to one great big slanted misrepresentation of both Gorotoland and Panama, that have finally made him lose his last trace of tolerance for Walter's world. Its members haven't wanted him to run, but now he is going to, and lick them soundly. He hopes they are happy.

They probably are, he thinks with a contempt that is also unusual (the pressures must really be getting to Harley Hudson, he tells himself dryly, he is beginning to react like a nasty old man to his critics' discomfiture), since he is giving them the sop of a contest for Vice President. On one level—their level—he does not have the slightest doubt that this is exactly what it is: a sop. He knows who his own choice is, and he has told him so frankly in their talk this afternoon. He does not believe for a second that the convention will select anyone else. His reasons for throwing the contest open are what they have all surmised and discussed with him during the day, plus one more reason locked in his own mind. He is counting on the implacable enmity of Ted Jason's supporters toward himself to guarantee that they will fall into the trap, make an all-out fight for it—and lose, discredited and defeated and pushing their reluctant candidate willy-nilly into the discard along with them, all in one neat package.

Thus he has been able with a relatively clear conscience to take a step which he knew would greatly disappoint Orrin: because he is sure the disappointment will not last long. He is convinced Orrin will become Vice President, and four years from now will be another day. Certainly by that time Gorotoland and Panama will be long decided, or the world will be gone, one of the two; and he will be sixty-six, if he lives. Then he will retire, and no changes. Orrin will be the logical and only choice to succeed him. Or if he doesn't live, Orrin will succeed him sooner. Either way, it is a good bargain he is offering the Secretary of State.

The whole thing, however, has to be done openly and democratically and in exactly the fashion he has announced. He has told Orrin truthfully that he has no intention of intervening. And he has not been disingenuous about the need for a safety valve, either. Out of it, he is certain, the country will get a needed catharsis for raw nerves and frantic emotions, and he will get the running mate he wants.

So he turns to go in, after his little ritual of looking at the Monument and pondering the choices of Presidents; a little startled but not surprised to find that Lucille is standing just inside the doorway watching him.

"How long have you been there, spying on your President?" he demands amicably.

"A few minutes. Have you got it all worked out?"

"I think so. Are you pleased with what I'm doing?"

"It's exactly what I've wanted," she says with her rosy smile. "Why shouldn't I be?"

"I'm glad you're pleased," he replies with a rather grim humor as they walk along toward bed together. "Have you any concept of the number of places on this earth in which my name is mud tonight?"

But here, as the full weight of night descended upon Washington, the last woozy political argument ended at the Press Club bar, the last loudly arguing dinner party broke up in Georgetown, and all but one restless political heart succumbed at last to the even rhythms of sleep, he was perhaps a little harder on himself than the facts warranted. But there was no doubt that the world was thinking of little else.

I MUST RUN: THE PRESIDENT'S PLEDGE, the *Times* said in London. PRESIDENT CHANGES MIND, DECLARES HE WILL RUN, the *Times* said in New York. H.H. SAYS "I GOTTA," the Washington *Daily News* reported cheerfully in the capital. VICE PRESIDENTIAL RACE WIDE OPEN, the other big news went. PRESIDENT INVITES BATTLE FOR SECOND PLACE; KNOX ANNOUNCES, PRESSURE GROWS ON JASON.

Endlessly the event was discussed, analyzed, turned inside out, taken apart, and put back together around the globe. Hardly a soul escaped it as the hours went by. Five in particular were enthralled.

In recaptured Molobangwe, sputtering through the night with sporadic exchanges of fire between rebels and Marines, His Royal Highness Terence Ajkaje, 137th M'Bulu of Mbuele, joined his top American military advisers at his ramshackle palace in a quiet unofficial toast to the President's success; and then later, after his guests had gone, he slipped away, accompanied only by a single bodyguard, to the sacred baobab tree near the royal compound where, on a thunderous night when he was six, his mother had taken him to croon her successful prayer: "Make my son M'Bulu —make my son M'Bulu—make my son M'Bulu!" There was no storm now, only the great soft sky of Africa, and the M'Bulu's words were not said aloud: but Harley M. Hudson was prayed for most sincerely this night by one who, in one more of life's endless little ironies, had only six months ago been his spiteful and determined enemy.

In the ancient and no longer used (until he and his friends from beyond the Bosporus and the Yangtze had chosen to revive it as his official seat) capital of Mbuele in the highlands, another prayed too, in his own rather colorful way: the self-styled 138th M'Bulu of Mbuele, leader of the People's Free Republic of Gorotoland, lover of liberty, fighter for democracy, small kernel of power caught, though he only dimly preceived it, between the millstone of Moscow and the nether millstone of Peking: His Royal Highness Obifumatta Ajkaje, cousin and bitter enemy of Terry who besought the gods in Molobangwe. Obi besought them too, with the ritual murder of a child, followed by suitable signs and incantations, while his advisers stood about in their dusty uniforms and self-consciously proletarian dungarees and wondered, a little fearfully and not for the first time, whether they might not be venturing into a world where they really did not belong. Harley M. Hudson was mentioned in prayers in Mbuele, too, and obscene little objects that represented him, or parts of him, were dipped in the blood of a dying child and destroyed while he slept peacefully far away in Washington.

And in Panama at "Suerte," which he held and from which he directed his campaign, Felix Labaiya, a shrewd and pragmatic soul, killed no children, prayed no prayers, burned no filthy little objects. Instead he appraised, as cautiously and carefully as his half-Panamanian, half-American upbringing and background enabled him, the consequences of the decisions announced by the man, and in the capital, that he knew so well.

There were times when, to use his own phrase, he would deliberately put aside his native habits of thought and let himself drift into a state which he described to his friends as "thinking American." In that frame of mind, which he was now inducing as he stood, very late, on the terrace at

"Suerte" and listened to the murmurous jungle sounds of his home, he could appreciate Harley Hudson's move as astutely as any would-be Vice President. Felix knew that the President's decision meant a continuation of the drive to destroy him, and like the President he was convinced that Orrin Knox would become Vice President, and so the policy would be continued whatever happened. He must be even shrewder, Felix told himself, even more determined and alert to use all the means of publicity and international pressure that he could bring to bear upon America. The policy must not succeed: not in Panama, and not against Don Felix Labaiya-Sofra, oligarch of Panama of the new style, leader of the People's Liberation Movement who did not, at that moment, know whether he could overcome his ravenous and never-resting allies, let alone the American enemy.

And in Washington and Sacramento, two men still lay awake. Now and again they prayed, though not for Harley Hudson.

PART THREE

TED JASON'S BOOK

1

HE IS SURE that sometime in the night he must have slept, though he has no memory of it: it has been the second such night he has known in two months, the first following the President's announcement, the second now on the eve of the day he must put on his best clothes and his best smile, step into a limousine, and be driven from Sacramento to San Francisco, there to face his party in convention assembled. Apparently his wakeful hours have not disturbed Ceil, for glancing at the other bed he can see that she is curled up in her customary fashion, a pillow over her head and the well-worn scrap of black velvet she calls "my security blanket" jammed over her eyes to kill the light of dawn. He is glad one member of the family has been able to rest untroubled, and is not surprised, though some might be, that it should be his own wife.

All he can remember of his own night is a constant turning, an endless battle of alternatives racing back and forth across the darkened ceiling, a little dance of unclear choices thumping and carousing on his head. It has left him exhausted and not as prepared as he would like to be to face the start of what he knows will be an extremely hectic and wearing week.

For a man as outwardly confident and self-possessed as the Governor of California, this is an unusual and uncomfortable state to be in. It does not go with the picture of the always assured, always calm, always competent executive his supporters like to believe in; the picture that has, in fact, usually existed until this latest, most confusing time in a life that heretofore has known little but the swift success that inherited wealth, plus ambition, plus charm can so easily confer in the catch-as-catch-can world of American politics.

He had been about five, as nearly as he can establish the period now, when he first began to realize that Jasons were different; that not everyone lived in four houses, two in California, one on Long Island, and one in Portofino, each with its permanent staff of maids, houseboys, and gardeners; that many people were not driven but had to drive their own cars; that many women were not as beautifully dressed or constantly publicized as his mother, that many men failed to command the instant respect, the automatic springing-to-assist and leaping-to-please that seemed to be accorded his father; that in many families there was often a noticeable and sometimes insurmountable gap between "I want" and "I've got"; and that as Jasons got, so were they expected to give, of their money, of their power, and of themselves.

This theme of service, happening as it did to coincide with the great energy and ambition that seemed to run in the family, was an easy one to follow. They were a relatively small clan, as the nation's moneyed hierarchies went, but by the time he entered school he knew that the nation and the world knew that the Jasons were around. The family had dwindled from the old Spanish land-grant days to his father and mother, his sister Patsy and himself; his uncle, the thermonuclear scientist Herbert Jason; and his twin aunts, the painter Valuela Jason Randall and the one *Time* called "the First Lady of Philanthropy," that peroxided, persistent party-giver-for-worthy-causes, Selena Jason Castleberry. But his father, managing with an iron hand the steadily growing number of Jason enterprises at home and abroad; his mother, constantly featured in society columns and national periodicals for her perfect clothes and stunning beauty; Herbert, recipient of award after award, culminating in the Nobel Prize six years ago, for his scientific contributions, recipient of headline after headline for his participation in parades, riots, and protests against practically everything the United States had ever stood for; Valuela, the flamboyant and repeated marrier who also happened to be a really excellent painter; and Selena, always in the papers either as Lady Bountiful or as wild-eyed, hair-askew partner with Herbert in his less scientific adventures—none was the silent or unnoticed type. All were good copy, and it was a rare day that there did not appear, somewhere in the United States or abroad, some reference to one or another of the Jasons.

With the mention there also went, inevitably, a mention of the family wealth and some reference to the romantic family history, both of which had begun long ago in Spain with the scrawl of a royal pen. Don Carlos Alvarado Montoya y Montoya had been an impoverished grandee with a wandering foot and a roving eye. The first took him to California and the second led him to the family's most legendary figure, the Indian girl christened Valuela whom he discovered working in the fields managed by Mission Santa Barbara, conquered in a day, subsequently fell in love with, and, with a suitably dashing arrogance, defied his family and his King to wed. Six months later his King forgave him, recognizing in his lively spirit and firm abilities exactly what the stabilizing of California required. Within a year Don Carlos was possessor of a land-grant filled with oak-furred valleys, brown, tumbling hills, and gorgeous coastline that compared very favorably with anything held by Sepulveda, Duarte, Pio Pico, or the rest.

For perhaps twenty years an idyllic life prevailed on the great ranch "Vistazo" in the Santa Barbara range. Don Carlos settled in to cultivate his acres, participate in the government of the province, and rear two sons and four daughters, of whom one son and a daughter died of smallpox in infancy. The distant political upheavals in Spain and Mexico did not affect the family fortunes, which soon were solidly grounded in cattle, horses, sheep, and vines. The surviving children were sturdy and well, growing steadily toward a promising maturity; Valuela, largely self-taught, had become a lady not only of beauty but of dignity, grace, and great strength of character; Don Carlos was well respected, popular, and increasingly active in the affairs of the province, now a part of Mexico. In 1840 he became Governor of California, a fact which would be made much of in the next century when his descendant decided to seek the same title under a different dispensation. With a level head and steady hand he presided for a year and a half over the increasingly uneasy province, disturbed by the jealousies of its old families and the steady pressure of immigrants from the westward-growing United States. Then at fifty, no longer as quick as he used to be, he tried to break one wild stallion too many, was tossed against a rock, and died within the hour. Doña Valuela was left an enormously wealthy widow of forty-two with a son nearing his majority, three beautiful daughters, and holdings that comprised the original grant and some hundred thousand acres in addition that Don Carlos had managed to acquire by shrewd purchase and careful husbandry.

The daughters Doña Valuela had no difficulty in marrying off in rapid order, one to a collateral branch of the Sepulvedas, the other two to Americans. The son, Carlos Alvarado the Younger, was filled with dreams of the old life and an uneasy despair about the apparently inevitable approaching acquisition of the province by the lively and ambitious country of his brothers-in-law. On his twenty-first birthday he announced that he was going to Mexico and make his fortune there. His mother told him angrily that he was betraying the family, but added with a mixture of contempt and satisfaction that she could no doubt be woman of the house, and man, too, if he did not care to be. Then she softened, sold off five thousand acres to an enterprising young American speculator named Mathias Jason, gave Carlos Alvarado the proceeds, and sent him on his way with her blessing. (To this day, well over a century later, "the Montoya cousins" still come up at regular intervals to visit Ted in Sacramento and Patsy in Washington, arriving laden down with trunks and suitcases from Mexico City, where their branch of the family has successfully survived wars, revolutions, and economic upheavals. Young Carlos Alvarado's stake from his mother has grown to encompass ranches in Sonora, mines in Yucatan, resort developments on both coasts, heavy industry in the middle states, and a combine of banks, investment companies, and real estate firms in the capital, together with joint ventures with the Jasons' "JM Enterprises" in Panama, Chile, Argentina, France, West Germany, Italy, Israel, and Japan.)

For Doña Valuela, presiding alone two years later over her great estate, remarriage was at first an idea to dismiss with a shrug. But Mathias Jason, who was ten years her junior and sincerely stricken both with her still stunning beauty and her fantastic properties, set out to change her mind. Six months later he had succeeded, and at forty-four she took the Montoya Grant into the Jason family.

In 1846 John C. Frémont in his dashing way set about to precipitate the American conquest of California by starting the short-lived "Bear Flag War." Three weeks later Captain John Sloat, somewhat more practical of nature, followed suit by raising the United States flag over Monterey and declaring the province to be a part of the Union. Two years after that a defeated Mexico ceded California to the United States. In 1850 Congress declared it a state.

By that time Mathias Jason was already in position to bring his wife's inheritance and his own steadily expanding activities safely through the change. He had decided immediately after his marriage to establish the name "JM Enterprises," the second initial a tribute to the Montoya holdings. The gold rush gave him his first great opportunity. Leaving "Vistazo" in the experienced hands of Doña Valuela, then pregnant with the future Mathias Edward Jason, he went north to San Francisco, opened a general merchandise store at the corner of Grant and Sutter, and proceeded to collect his share of the gold pouring into the city through the hands of the happy 49ers. With one of these, whose shrewdness and uncharacteristic care of his newfound money impressed him, he went shares on gold claims; the "New Reliable" near Marysville came in as one of the biggest strikes of the entire rush. When Mathias returned to "Vistazo," leaving the store in the hands of his partner, he had cash in hand of sufficient amount to cause Doña Valuela to admit with a smile that now the "J" was almost as important as the "M." He assured her the day would come when it would be equal, if not greater.

It came with the birth of Mathias Edward, for with his mother close to forty-nine it was clear that he would in all likelihood be the only child Doña Valuela would contribute to her second marriage. Her daughters she had taken care of with ample dowries when they married, Carlos Alvarado was far away and already successful in his own right, and nothing stood in the way of the future inheritance of the new child or the love that could be lavished upon him by two middle-aged parents.

Then, as abruptly as it had taken Valuela's first husband, death took the second.

Mathias was gone at forty-one of a heart attack, and almost simultaneously with his death the United States announced that it was establishing a special commission to review the tangled land-grant situation. Two things brought the Montoya Grant safely through: the fact that it had been given direct from Spain before the Mexican domination, and the fact that Doña Valuela fought for it through four bitter years with every ounce of character and almost every bit of fortune she possessed.

Her first reaction when the American government informed her that the grant was invalid and all her properties subject to suit and confiscation was one of stunned disbelief. The reaction lasted perhaps an hour, in a locked bedroom from which terrible sounds of anger and despair emerged to frighten the maids and mestizos who huddled outside on the broad patios of "Vistazo." Then the sounds ceased, the door opened, and Doña Valuela, red-eyed but composed, emerged and went to work.

Her first move was to seek an injunction staying the government's hand. It was granted in Santa Barbara, and later extended twice. With the pressure somewhat relieved, she then began the endless round of visits and conferences —the lobbying that would for four years consume her thoughts, her energies, and nearly all her fortune, necessitating the mortgaging of the "New Reliable" and the store in San Francisco before it was over.

But when it was over, she had won, partly through the merit of her case and partly through the sheer force of her personality, which had brought her support from many influential leaders in both Sacramento and Washington. The tall figure of Doña Valuela, striding down the corridors in traditional black dress, comb, lace mantilla, carrying an inevitable fan, was one of the sights of the decade in two capitals. The classic Indian simplicity of her face became traced with somber lines, something bright and happy left her eyes, but an iron that was in its way as beautiful replaced it. One of the family's prized possessions now is the portrait painted of her a month after the news came from Washington that all her claims were confirmed and the Montoya Grant would rest undisturbed thereafter. Somber, stately, and still stunning at fifty-five, she stares forth upon a world that has obviously met one of its conquerors, self-possessed, unyielding, indomitable.

Ted's father had it copied for them all as a Christmas present twenty years ago, and now she looks out upon Ted's uncertainties in Sacramento, Patsy's whirligig of a life in Washington, Herbert as he lopes in and out of his apartment in San Francisco between demonstrations and scientific conferences, the present Valuela turning from canvases to men and back again in Portofino, Selena presiding with squawks of excitement over her motley crews and causes in New York. Whether they admit it or not— and at times they all do—she gives them something to this day: some strengthening, some assurance that underneath it all they are of a good blood and a fighting heritage.

"Even when we're at our most crackpot, by God, we've got style!" today's Valuela once put it to a friend. They owe it to Valuela the First, and they know it.

There followed a California story similar to others in the second half of the nineteenth century. The threat removed, once again the man of the family, Doña Valuela concentrated her energy, shrewdness, and skill upon rebuilding JM as swiftly yet as soundly as she could. She moved into the financial worlds of California and New York as surefootedly as she had moved into Sacramento and Washington. Within five years she had recovered her losses, paid off her mortgages, was launched upon new investments. The store in San Francisco grew rapidly into one of the city's most popular and successful. The "New Reliable" continued in production until 1873 when it finally petered out after yielding to JM Enterprises close to eight million dollars as its share of the total profits. "Vistazo" continued to show a steadily increasing return from cattle, horses, sheep, and vineyards. There were opportunities to invest in banks, lending institutions, and land, to purchase a steamship company, to have a share in the railroad developments that were taking Leland Stanford and his friends to mansions on Nob Hill. By the time young Mathias Edward reached his majority already well trained by his mother, who shrewdly began giving him more and more responsibility from the age of sixteen onward, JM Enterprises was one of the four or five prime financial forces on the Western slope.

From then on the story was one of almost monotonous success, threatened now and again by depressions in the nation but never seriously damaged and always recovering to go on to new investments and new profits. Doña Valuela died at a great age in the Nineties, one of California's authentically legendary figures from the old days. Mathias Edward married flawlessly in San Francisco, produced Herbert and Matthew Edward and the twins, Valuela and Selena, served in the state legislature, went to Washington as Senator for two terms soon after the turn of the century, died in 1930. Matthew Edward in his turn married flawlessly, this time in New York, produced Edward Montoya and Patsy, pushed JM Enterprises into Europe, Asia, and Latin America with the aid and cooperation of the Montoya cousins, died of a heart attack in 1947, leaving Ted and Herbert jointly in control. Herbert relinquished his direct interests in 1965, and a young but capable Ted became sole manager for the family.

Ted pushed JM Enterprises still further across the globe; established the Jason Foundation which eight months ago honored Terence Ajkaje at "Harmony" in South Carolina and two months ago enhaloed Walter Dobius in Washington; sold off much of "Vistazo's" excess land for real estate developments, diversified the remaining compact ranch, raised it to new profits; married flawlessly, in San Francisco, produced no children, to his and Ceil's deep regret; decided to run for Governor of California, won; decided to run for Vice President of the United States, won; became President of the United States in 19—

Or did he? Is that what the history books really said of him, when it was all over? He wonders as he eases out of bed and walks softly into his bathroom to prepare for the day. And if so, where in his life or current course is there to be found warrant for such a golden conclusion?

After the realization that Jasons were different, he remembers now, came the realization that Jasons had power and that, having power, they were to use it, first for the good of mankind, secondly for the business, and only incidentally for their own financial gain. It had, indeed, been forty years and more since anyone really needed to worry about the company's stability or the family's personal fortune, so that by the time he came along it was an established principle that Jasons were, and should be, free to participate in whatever movements for human betterment they deemed worthy of their support. If this occasionally took somewhat erratic forms with Herbert and Selena, if Patsy sometimes seemed to fly off in oddly exaggerated directions, if Valuela now and again appeared to devote her time and fortune to improving the lot of the individual male instead of the species as a whole, these were simply instances of strong character modifying a universal principle. In his own case, for the most part, he had devoted himself to causes and activities that were respected and applauded by a majority of his countrymen. If they generally seemed to lean toward one side of the political spectrum, if they were the sort that automatically seemed to draw the most favorable publicity from such as Walter and his world, certainly no astute and perceptive man could be blamed if a sincere heart and a lively ambition found it easy to make common cause.

These were considerations, however, that were far from his mind in his earliest years when the family was moving about from house to house, when his father was shuttling over the earth in pursuit of JM's interests and his mother was riding the crest of society. During that period he was just another little rich boy, acquiring the proper manners, doing the proper things, attending the proper schools, assuming the proper polish of that careless and artificial world of wealth that has its roots in the grubbiest and most realistic areas of American business. It was a world of servants and governesses, constant travel, changing scenes, and changing people, held together by its own seasonal patterns of movement, a list of resorts and institutions that were proper and acceptable, a consciousness that all who belonged to it were automatically superior to everyone else.

He entered Choate School at the age of six and from the first established himself as a leader. He had a quick and intuitive mind, a commanding air, a physical presence that even at that age brought him an automatic following. His were the blond Jason good looks, aided by some lingering trace of Indian blood that produced deep-set dark eyes and dark eyebrows for startling contrast; a proud and sensitive mouth; and a certain high-boned fineness of feature. It also produced a sometimes mercurial, sometimes secretive and elusive personality that was capable of retreating into itself where others could not follow, to reach decisions that sometimes surprised and even dismayed them.

His years at Choate passed sunnily enough, with superior grades, good friends, and a recognized position of dominance that caused his headmaster to predict great things for him, over and beyond the achievements that would come automatically from his role as ultimate master of JM. By his own choice—his father, Matthew Edward, was astute enough to realize, in his pauses at home between travels in the company's service, that his son had an innate independence of judgment that should be encouraged—he decided to leave Choate and complete his pre-college training at Thatcher School near Ojai in California. The East was fine, he said, but his future naturally lay with California, and he thought it was time to come home. He did not realize how much he meant this until he saw again the dusty little river valleys, the startling seacoast, the pines, the oaks, the bare brown hills, and knew that from now on he would remain among them. He felt then that he had indeed come home, and imagined with a thrill of recognition that he was the first Don Carlos, riding through the hot, dry, beautiful land in command of all the thousands of acres that were his.

From Thatcher, where he maintained his high grades and again asserted almost automatically his easy dominance of his fellows, he went to Stanford, where the story was the same. He was not one of those political fortunates whose early life must be reconstructed out of all recognition for the sake of the legend required by later events. Ted Jason began as a leader and continued as one to the end of his school career. At Stanford he was president of the freshman class, president of his fraternity, president of the junior class, and finally president of the student body. He went out for swimming, tennis, and debating, excelled at all three, took a liberal arts course as an undergraduate, made Phi Beta Kappa, got a graduate degree from the Business School; emerged at twenty-two healthy, handsome, in command of himself and his world and ready to move on to find others to conquer.

The inevitable one was JM Enterprises, but his success there was hereditary and guaranteed, and neither he nor anyone who knew him had the slightest doubt that he could handle it when the time came. He had other ideas. Although he knew that for some years he could be expected to do his duty for the company and certainly wanted to —for he had great pride of inheritance and family and was not about to break the long parade of triumph from Doña Valuela on down—there were more exciting ambitions that now intrigued him. His classmates had four times given him proof that he was a popular and effective candidate. He put aside the thought of politics for the time being to plunge into business, but he knew when he did so that it was only a temporary farewell. He would pass that way again.

His first job with the company, his father told him, was to travel, and so he did for a year, familiarizing himself with JM's offices through the country and the world, getting acquainted with its top people, making himself at home with its plans and programs. He came back to settle into the headquarters office in San Francisco with a lively respect for his inheritance and a head full of ideas for its improvement. His father was amused by his impatience but impressed by his grasp of the business. Within a year young Ted was a vice president whose title meant something. He was determined, decisive, forthright, and force-ful. No one ever called Ted Jason an equivocator in those days.

Two years of faithfully attending the opera, the sym-phony, the art galleries, the theaters, the seasonal round of San Francisco's balls and parties presently reached their in-evitable conclusion one night at the opera when he was a guest in the box of a family almost as old and distinguished as his. A heart that had gone through college mildly inter-ested but seldom really involved suddenly found itself very much involved. A cousin of his hosts was in the City from Redlands for a couple of weeks to do some shopping. She was his partner for the evening, and before it ended he was convinced she should be for life. They were married almost six months to the day. For all that he was never quite sure that she always approved of what he did, he nev-er regretted it.

The adjectives used by the press to describe Ceil Robert-son at the time of their marriage and since were the usual clichés about charm, intelligence, grace, and stunning blond beauty, and of course they were all true; and of course they did not penetrate very far into a mind as shrewd as any he knew and a wry little sense of humor that was constantly challenging his assumptions about himself. "They know you're intelligent," he had remarked, tossing aside a typical interview in one of the nation's major wom-en's magazines, "but somehow they can't quite believe any-one as beautiful as you are really has *brains*." "That's my secret weapon," she had replied with her silvery little laugh and a toss of that golden hair that always bedazzled the onlooker. "I early learned not to reveal too much. Only you know what a crafty witch I am." "Not crafty," he had said thoughtfully. "Just—aware."

And aware she was, in ways that continued to surprise and catch him off balance to this day. She was also rigidly honest in her personal standards and, in the main, the stan-dards by which she judged others. There, too, however, there was a saving grace: she did allow people to be hu-man. Sometimes when she most disapproved she would finally conclude, "Oh, well, I suppose they can't help it. I guess I'm not perfect either"—a sentiment given lip-service by many, but used in her case with a genuine tolerance.

Physically and socially, of course, she could not have been a more perfect wife for Edward Jason, heir-apparent to JM Enterprises, and Edward Jason, candidate-presumptive for public office. She really did look like a movie star. She really did have golden hair, beautiful eyes, a superbly chiseled face, a perfect figure, and the perfect clothes to set it off. She really was a lovely woman. And automatically, from their marriage on, she was the darling of society pages, women's magazines, photographers, and painters. "When in doubt, use Ceil Jason," the society editor of the San Francisco *Chronicle* advised one day when a picture was needed to complete the makeup of a page. The advice was followed there and in a thousand other offices all over the country, all the time.

"People know you a lot better than they do me," Ted had said, with a rueful humor when he decided to run for state office. "You'd better be the candidate."

"I'll furnish the glamor," she said with a certain dryness, because she often got tired of being constantly on exhibition. "You bring the brains."

When he finally did decide to run—after all was moving smoothly at JM and he felt his duty was done there—he realized again how lucky he had been to attend the opera that particular night. Despite her self-deprecating remark to Beth Knox when they met at Walter Dobius' luncheon, there was no better campaigner than Ceil. She *was* glamorous, and when she added to it her perfectly natural friendliness, courtesy, kindliness, and grace, there was virtually no group or audience she couldn't take command of in a matter of minutes. "Perhaps of all his many attractive assets," the Los Angeles *Times* had remarked during his first campaign, "none is greater than the lovely lady who happens to be Mrs. Jason."

In addition, he developed many of his own. As a businessman he was practical, pragmatic, perceptive, and shrewd. Doña Valuela's descendant was as tough-minded and astute as she had been. In the close-knit financial, social, and political world of California he had been born into a major place, and everything he did after he received his inheritance seemed to enhance it. Being head of JM automatically involved him in many areas of the state's business, kept his name and picture constantly before the public. Now and again he deliberately sought prominence, there was an occasional artful courting of publicity, but most of the time it came to him without his having to exert any effort.

Presently there came the time when the idea he had always treasured for his future was first stated definitively by someone else. He could remember the place, the occasion, and the speaker. It was at Bohemian Grove in the summer of his fortieth year, and there, with dull Care cremated and the enchanted canyon echoing in the night to the sound of music everywhere and the laughter of happy voices, he had been walking along River Road after midnight past the camp known as River Road Ramblers when he was hailed and welcomed aboard. Turning toward him from his place by the fire was that complex and brilliant personality who was to precede him in Sacramento and then go on to precede Harley Hudson in the White House. He was then in his fifth year as Governor and beginning to get in position for what he liked to call "the big try." Now he greeted Ted merrily, and turning to the group around him called out, "You were wondering who you ought to have in Sacramento after I leave? There he is right now! His great-granddaddy made it. Why shouldn't he?" And although Ted protested that Don Carlos had not actually been his great-granddaddy but only his great-grandmother's first husband, the Governor had won agreeing laughter from their attentive audience when he said, "Never admit it, Ted! Never you admit it. He was in your family, wasn't he—some way? And he was a Governor of California, and a pretty damned good and romantic one too. Don Carlos—Don Eduardo! With the romance of Old Spain—and JM—and that wife of yours—and your own good looks and ability—hell's fire, boy, how can you lose?" There had been much good-natured joking and agreement before someone began playing the piano and River Road Ramblers became diverted again to song. Two days later every political columnist in the state was reporting that, "The Governor exploded a political bombshell at Bohemian Grove this week when he named Edward M. Jason as his handpicked successor." And for the remainder of the Grove, Ted found himself hailed as "Governor" wherever he went through the lazy days and happy nights among the towering trees.

Six months later, however, the Governor proved that his jesting had been in earnest when he called Ted one day in JM's Los Angeles office and asked him to run for state comptroller. "I'll be leaving in a couple of years," he said, "and we've got to give you a little experience up here before you take over." "I'm not going to take over," Ted said skeptically. The Governor chuckled. "There's nothing you want more, at this point. I know the disease, I suffered from it myself until I got the more malignant type I have now—the one that makes you itch for Washington. Let yourself come to Sacramento, Ted. You won't stop here."

So he had run, with Ceil's quick agreement—"Who am I"—with the elusive little smile she sometimes got in discussing the family—"to stand in the way of destiny?"—and had won without much trouble. Two years later, in the election that took the Governor to the White House, he succeeded him in Sacramento.

"Everything comes easy to the Jasons," skeptics said sourly. "What can you expect, with all that money?"

But hard work had gone into it, too, and much planning on his part, both in the selection of a management team he could rely upon to safeguard and improve JM in his absence, and in the organization of his campaign. It was conceivable that money alone could carry a candidate into office, but that had not been his observation of American politics. The candidate had to be attractive, and he did not minimize his own assets, or Ceil's, in that; and to be sure of the outcome, he also had to have the best organization that could be put together. Here the Jason money was indeed a major factor, because it made all things easy. Top people were hired, top publicity outlets were purchased, California was saturated with the Jason name and record in a way that his more modestly financed opponents could not possibly match. His most effective campaign points were exactly those his shrewd predecessor had outlined at the Grove: the romantic tie-in with Don Carlos (an appearance in Spanish costume at several Southern California parades put his picture everywhere, including the cover of *Life*); his record as a successful businessman, his success as comptroller; Ceil's beauty, his own good looks, his pleasing personality and excellent record. ELECT A *CALIFORNIAN* FOR CALIFORNIA his most effective billboard cried. His handsome graying head against a background of misty mountains, *caballeros* near at hand, and in the distance Indians working the fields of Mission Santa Barbara, made the point in a way his Kansas-born opponent could not answer.

So he became Governor of California, with an ease that embittered many ambitious men who considered themselves more deserving, and so persisted in attributing his success to his money. But he entered upon office determined to prove that he had the ability as well; and for a time, in a honeymoon period that enabled him to move safely through his first session of the legislature without difficulty, there were no successful challenges. Then what his predecessor had called "the itch for Washington" began to assail him, and from then on, in some subtle, curious, and almost indefinable way, he seemed—to himself at least —to lose something.

To himself, and to Ceil. "You're more cautious than you used to be," she remarked thoughtfully in his second year when he was hesitating to challenge the lumbering interests on an amendment to a bill designed to prevent further destruction of the redwoods by the slide-rule-happy maniacs of the state highway department. "No I'm not," he had said indignantly, and to prove it, forced the issue and won.

"You see?" she said after the vote. "It wasn't much of a battle, was it?"

But they both knew that another time she would have to make her challenge even stronger, he would have to make his response even more a deliberate effort of will—if he made it at all.

Some essential of the younger Ted Jason, some automatic and unhesitating response to what was right, that perhaps went back as far as Doña Valuela, was beginning to atrophy. Now he was beginning to pause and calculate, now the pragmatic and forceful approach which, linked with integrity, had been invincible, was beginning to give way to a more devious approach. He was beginning to think of dreams ahead in a way that sometimes hurt realities at hand.

"I don't want to say anything," Ceil had remarked at last, and not unkindly, "but I wonder a little if maybe you aren't beginning to loose a little of your *virtu*—in the old sense."

Again he had denied it with some sharpness, but in his heart he had wondered too. Compromise was so easy to rationalize, and indeed so much of it was perfectly good and perfectly necessary: the line was easy to slip over. A compromise with elements in Southern California that wanted certain concessions on offshore oil drilling—which would probably guarantee his re-election as Governor—which in turn would permit him to go on being a statesman—which in turn would help him, perhaps, to become President—who was to say that it was wrong? Only Ceil, of course, and his own heart; and, perhaps, Doña Valuela, hanging on the wall. But her he could appease, he thought. Passing her picture on the night of his triumphant re-election, he made his habitual little bow to the comb, the mantilla, the dark, brooding eyes, and somber but beautiful face.

"I'm going to hang you on the White House wall yet, old girl," he promised her with a sudden smile. "You wait and see."

But he was not entirely sure that she would have wanted to go there, could she know the paths he must follow to make good the pledge.

Not that there were any major betrayals of principle, of course; not that he engaged in anything notably shady or devious; not that he was, by any standard of politics, a dishonest man. It was just that somehow, step by step, daily, hourly perhaps, imperceptibly beneath the outward show of firmness and determination that remained unchanged, he was becoming more careful, more calculating, more equivocal. In some subtle fashion that he was partly aware of but seemed powerless to stop, he was no longer the direct and straightforward individual he used to be.

Occasionally Ceil would repeat the suggestion that this was really not necessary, that he could achieve what he desired without going the long way 'round to get it. But it always seemed to him that he had perfectly good reasons. It could even be argued that a certain amount of deviousness and equivocation was a necessary concomitant of being a good President: it had characterized some of the greatest, on occasion.

"It takes flexibility to be a leader," he had explained once.

"My point is," she said in one of her rare impatient moments, "that you really don't need to be 'flexible.' You've got everything going for you. Nobody was ever more favored, certainly. Nobody ever had less reason to compromise. Why be indirect?"

"Being a leader means you lead, doesn't it?" he inquired with a defensive sharpness. "People. And that means you can't always be direct. You have to persuade, you can't bludgeon."

"I know that's the rationale," she said, ending one of their few open arguments on the subject. "But it isn't always what I like to think of as Ted Jason."

But it was, obviously, what a great many other people liked to think of as Ted Jason. In fact, as he moved farther into politics and climbed higher toward the top, he became aware, with a curious combination of distaste and gratitude, that people were not really interested in Ted Jason, himself. They were interested only in what it satisfied them to think Ted Jason was.

By now it was second nature to him to do as he had on the Administration's policies, to emerge from a meeting and say something like, "There is a time to support. And there is a time to oppose. Conscience must decide the issue."

He had not said whether he would support or oppose, yet look what had happened. With a glad cry Walter and his world and millions of his countrymen had leaped upon the phrase and interpreted it to suit themselves, written columns, printed editorials, held rallies, presented programs, taken full-page ads in the New York *Times* under that heading to urge him to run, made it, inevitably, his campaign slogan: Conscience Must Decide The Issue! What issue? And whose conscience? And what made them so sure they knew what it would decide?

There was, however, no doubt that they *knew*. The phrase was sweeping the country. Conscience—theirs and Ted Jason's—was automatically enlisted against the Administration.

They didn't have to ask Ted Jason what he meant.

They *knew*.

He feels again, as he proceeds with his dressing and in the bedroom hears Ceil begin to stir, that sense of terror and fear of being devoured that comes to the intelligent when they are given the love of the mob—doubly terrifying and fearful when the mob is intelligent, too, and possessed of the means of coercing the beloved into the image the mob desires . . . doubly treacherous when the mob has within its grasp, or thinks it has, the means of giving, in return, what the beloved desires.

For two months he has been the plaything of the mob as it has prepared the country for his candidacy for Vice President. Not once has he broken his private vow of silence on the subject, but it hasn't mattered: the mob has launched him anyway. *Look* and *Newsweek*, working overtime for a point of view, have put him on their covers, made him the subject of their lead articles; *Time* and *Life*, less ideological but faced by the imperatives of the news, have done the same. His views on finance have appeared in *Fortune,* his views on California as a tourist paradise in *Holiday. Sports Illustrated* has discussed his opinions of tennis, the *Saturday Review* has carried a guest editorial (written, because, he told himself, he simply didn't have the time, by one of the higher-paid young men on his publicity staff) on the perennial dream of nuclear disarmament. *U. S. News & World Report* has interviewed him in depth for eight pages of graceful dodging that somehow, in print, sound firm and positive. The *Library Journal* has discussed his reading habits, the *National Geographic* has run an article on the romance of California's Spanish land-grants, prepared some months ago and shrewdly held in reserve for the proper moment; the Montoya Grant, with many flattering photographs of its present inheritors, is featured throughout. The nation's leading opinion poll seems to be releasing his latest ratings every other hour on the hour: they are always up. He has appeared at least twice on "Face the Nation," "Meet the Press," "Today," "Tonight," "Talk," and "Monitor." (Orrin Knox has been invited to appear once, on two of them.)

His clipping service reported only yesterday that in sixty days there have been a total of 1217 profiles or personality sketches of him in the nation's newspapers; that he has appeared in front-page articles on fifty-three of those days; that his picture has appeared on some front page somewhere on every one of the sixty, and that on many days it has appeared on the front pages of all the metropolitan papers throughout the country. A collection of his speeches, published two weeks ago under the title, *Where I Stand: Governor Jason on the Record,* has been reviewed most favorably to date in 673 newspapers and periodicals; a competing volume, *A Consistent Policy: As Orrin Knox Sees It* has been reviewed by 231, not so favorably.

(In a front-page report in its Sunday Book Review, The Greatest Publication That Absolutely Ever Was commented gravely:

("Governor Jason's book is a major contribution to current American thought, the fine and moving statement of a dedicated public servant. Every American—and particularly all those delegates to the convention that will convene in San Francisco next month—owes it to himself and his country to read this powerful presentation before he votes. It is an absolute must."

(In a brief item on page 23 of the same section the same publication reported:

("Secretary Knox's rehash of old speeches and, it must be confessed, rather tired statements of policy, have, inevitably, a passing interest in view of his declared intention to seek the Vice Presidency. But there is here no fresh opinion, no such vigorous and commanding point of view as we are receiving from many others in the political arena. His book will probably be of interest to his most rabid partisans. Others may wish to seek enlightenment elsewhere."

(Dutifully the same type of treatment was accorded in journal after journal across a free and independent land.)

And as for Ceil—Ceil is everywhere. THE LOVELY CEIL JASON, *McCall's* described her in a fawning interview. . . . The *Ladies' Home Journal* reported HOW MRS. EDWARD JASON RUNS HER HOME. . . . CEIL JASON, *Life* said, putting her on the cover in a really sensational pose against the pines and sea at Big Sur (Beth Knox, who knows a thing or two herself, appeared a week later on the same cover, standing at the stove in the dowdiest, old-shoe dress she could find). . . . *Look,* reluctantly delaying its 521st twelve-page spread on the Kennedy family, countered with an almost equally sensational cover taken at the Wawona Tunnel entrance to Yosemite: CEIL JASON: WILL A WOULD-BE SECOND LADY SOMEDAY BE FIRST?

Woman's Day has featured her recipes, *Vogue* her hair, *Harper's Bazaar* her clothes. *Good Housekeeping* has described HOW CEIL JASON AIDS HER MAN. *Redbook* has called them, simply, CEIL AND TED: AMERICA'S TOP POLITICAL TEAM. And in Hollywood each new week brings a new sensation: CEIL JASON'S MOST DIFFICULT DECISION (how to decorate the Governor's Mansion in Sacramento). . . . WHEN CEIL ALMOST LOST TED (he had been fifteen minutes overdue on a flight from "Vistazo" to New York). . . . THE SECRET FRIEND WHO HELPED CEIL MOST (her mother, who told her how to decorate the Governor's mansion in Sacramento). . . . CEIL JASON'S TRAGEDY (that politics doesn't give her enough time for painting, at which, as a matter of fact, she is actually rather good). . . . CEIL'S

MOST SACRED LOVE (for Doormat, an English sheepdog she owned in childhood). . . .

And she, too, has appeared in so many articles on so many days in so many papers, has been guest on so many programs, had her picture on so many front pages so many times. . . .

By now, Ted realizes, completing his dressing and calling out, "Hi!" as she goes by his bathroom door with a sleepy wave, the two of them no longer exist. They are creations.

And he realizes also, on the opening day of the convention that will decide his future and that of many other things, that he is no longer an individual named Edward Montoya Jason, occupying the office of Governor of California, an independent being with an independent judgment and independent course to follow in the world. He is the prisoner of his creators, bound hand and foot, hogtied and delivered up upon the altar of their ravenous love and their terrible desire to punish Harley M. Hudson and Orrin Knox and remake the world in their own image.

He has equivocated too long.

He is a candidate, announced or not, and Walter and his world have won.

2

SOMEWHERE A BAND was playing—a band is always playing, that Great Eternal Band of American politics that is always on hand every time, everywhere, its happily excited tootlings and thumpings forming the backdrop for arrivals, departures, rallies, parades, speeches, picnics, hand-shakings, barbecues, baby-kissings—and the July sun shone bright and sparkling on lovely San Francisco as the delegates arrived.

Some—the chairman of the National Committee, the vice chairman, principal sergeants-at-arms, head doorkeepers, the chairman of arrangements, the publicity director, officials of the press and communications galleries of the Senate and House, staffs of the Jason Headquarters, the Knox Headquarters, the Hudson Headquarters, members of the Credentials, Housing, and Platform Committees, parliamentarians, secretaries, stenographers, hundreds of eager college kids who swarmed the corridors and now and then managed to be helpful—these had arrived a week or ten days ago, together with many working reporters and a large number of detached and analytical observers from Walter's world. As a result of their preliminary hustlings and bustlings much drama had already emerged—JASON WINS FIRST ROUND IN CREDENTIALS COMMITTEE, for instance; SERGEANT-AT-ARMS RULING UPHELD. . . . KNOX FORCES FIGHTING HARD TO RETAIN PLATFORM PLANK. . . . REPORT MICHIGAN DELEGATION SPLIT. A steadily rising tension gripped the magical city and the nation, fascinated and frequently dumbfounded, which watched its portentous story unfold.

But today was the day of the delegates, and all that had gone before was only preliminary to their shouting, whooping, lighthearted arrival. Old hands stood about the lobbies of the St. Francis, the Palace, the Mark Hopkins, the Fairmont, the Hilton, making disparaging remarks about the naïveté and exuberance of the newcomers, but on this day nothing could detract from their carefree enthusiasm. "They think it's real," the New York *Times* remarked to the Deseret *News* at the Mark, as they watched a noisy troop of delegates from Pennsylvania swarming in to pay their respects at Jason Headquarters on the third floor; but for the delegates it was real. "They think what *they* think is important here," CBS commented in the same mood to The Greatest Publication That Absolutely Ever Was as they stood in the lobby of the St. Francis and watched a similar group, from Ohio, storming up to Knox Headquarters on the mezzanine; but it would be a while yet before the delegates realized the acrid wisdom of the comment.

Right now the convention was young and it was happy, and in some strange, mysterious way that no one has ever entirely defined, it would work, as it usually has, to send into the field two reasonably good men, perhaps no better, perhaps no worse, than most of their countrymen—two men to carry the hopes of millions—two men to reaffirm

what America is all about—two men to become Symbols
instead of eating, sleeping, lusting, sweating, stinking, defecating men—two men to bear witness to a great experiment's long, continuing life.

The convention might not work the way a majority of
the delegates thought it was going to—but it would work.
They might not have quite the influence on its deliberations
that some of them thought they would—but it would work.
Their votes might not be quite as free and independent as
some of them believed right now—out of their tumultuous,
swirling, agglutinous mass on the convention floor there
might not come quite the solemn, profound, and dedicated
judgments that some of them fondly fancied—but it would
work.

Conventions don't get together to fail. They get together
to pick candidates. And somehow, in some way, at some
point in three or four frantic days and nights—but best not
ask too closely exactly how, for sometimes it is a little far
from the textbooks that children read in school—they
work.

This, however, was a knowledge that would come later,
and in some cases with some lasting bitterness, to the happy souls who were arriving literally every minute from air
terminals, train stations, by car, by chartered bus, and
even—in the case of a well-publicized rebel section of the
Illinois delegation which was going to go for Jason instead
of Knox—by hovercraft across the Bay and thence by helicopter to Union Square in front of the St. Francis. This
was their day, and it was possible as one watched, no matter
how old a hand, no matter how sophisticated, how experienced, how skeptical and cynical and know-it-all, to yet
feel a thrill along with them, to believe for just a moment
that it was all real, that everything was as bright and shining and free and glorious as America was in her days of
beginning, and as she sometimes still is in the hearts of
her people.

For here came good old Joe Smitters from Ashtabula,
chairman of the county central committee for nigh these
twenty years, and Mrs. Joe Smitters—Belle—head of the
Ladies' Auxiliary. And right after them came Bill Smatters
from Atlanta, biggest contributor in town to the last campaign, and Mary-Clare, daughter of the late Senator Ri-
vage, smartest old Sentuh theh evuh was. And right after
them, Bob Smutters and Lulie, from Punxsutawney, Pa.,

and John Smotters and Susie from Phoenix, and—h'aar
y'all?—ding, dang, if it wasn't Buddy and Vangie Smetters
from Little Rock, and how have you-all *beein?*

And the Governors and the Senators and the Congressmen, and the state senators and the assemblymen, and the
Cabinet officials and the state officials and the society gals
preparing their big shebangs and the members of the diplomatic corps ready to observe—ready to observe, on an average, fifty martinis, thirty gin and tonics, fifteen bourbon
highballs, two bottles of rosé, four of burgundy, and three
of sauterne—at innumerable cocktail parties, receptions,
private dinners, and public banquets before the week was
over.

And Walter Dobius and Helen-Anne and all their
friends and colleagues of the communications media, the
teams, the groups, the lone wolves, the sages, and the work-
ing-stiffs, prepared to fill endless reams of newsprint and
endless hours of newstime with an awful, abysmal, appalling expanse of absolutely nothing—and on four or five vital occasions, at four or five electrically decisive moments,
with something really important and really exciting.

And Ted and Ceil Jason, arriving at the Mark, to face a
wild surge of reporters, cameramen, and shouting delegates, speaking a few hastily innocuous words into the insistent microphones, being whisked by their campaign staff
into a crowded elevator and rushed to their suite on the
twenty-third floor—there to have the last half-hour of quiet
they would know for five days—before leaving to attend an
11 A.M. reception given by the Massachusetts delegation at
the Palace.

And Orrin and Beth Knox, arriving at the St. Francis to
be greeted by a similar wildly excited crowd, speaking a
few hastily innocuous words into the insistent microphones, being whisked by their campaign aides into a
crowded elevator and rushed to their suite on the eigh-
teenth floor, there to have an excited reunion with a Hal
looking older and more settled and more—"husbandly," as
Beth put it—and a Crystal radiant and glowing with her
pregnancy—before being hurried away to the Fairmont for
a reception given by the ladies of the Ohio delegation.

And Bob Leffingwell, also arriving at the St. Francis,
carefully noncommittal; and Fred Van Ackerman, arriving
at the Mark with a flat prediction of victory for Ted Jason;
and LeGage Shelby and Rufus Kleinfert, arriving together

at the Palace, which caused some startled comment from the press, Rufus silent and uneasy but 'Gage making the same firm prediction. And the same prediction from Patsy Labaiya, arriving in a flurry of lights and cameras at the Fairmont, accompanied by Herbert Jason, Selena Castleberry, and Valuela Randall, Valuela come all the way from Portofino "to help my favorite nephew." And Cullee Hamilton, smiling quietly and slipping in behind them with Sarah Johnson, almost unnoticed in the Jasons' characteristic uproar. And Bob and Dolly Munson, equally unobtrusive, managing to elude the press at the St. Francis by coming in a side door. And the Speaker, following seconds after, at the Hilton. And Justice Thomas Buckmaster Davis and his friend from the *Post*—"Let's slip in this way, dear boy, we don't want too much publicity, you know, it might detract from Ted." "You old fraud, Tommy, you want all the publicity you can get and we all know it. Hey, boys! Here's Justice Davis! Better ask him a few questions!"

And the delegations from Indiana, Michigan, Montana, Hawaii, Alaska, Mississippi, South Carolina, North Carolina, Louisiana, Georgia, tumbling in on one another's heels at the Palace; and Kansas, Pennsylvania, the Dakotas, New York, and a riotous, exuberant California jamming into the Hilton; and the others scattered all over town. And the cable cars beginning to move more and more slowly up and down Powell as the crowds grew in Union Square and in front of the St. Francis; and the taxi drivers beginning to curse, and the buses along Geary beginning to honk impatiently; and at the Cow Palace in Daly City, ten miles south on the Peninsula where the convention would actually be held, the last lights being tested, the last cameras and microphones being checked, the last sound trucks being wheeled into place, the last briefings being held for the cops and the sergeants-at-arms, the last consignments of hot dogs, soda pop, banners, and programs being unloaded for the booths beneath the stands. And the sun bright and sparkling everywhere, and the waters of the Bay competing with the sky to see which could be bluest. And at the Fairmont, almost unnoticed in all the shouting, running, moving, shoving people, a conservatively dressed, quietly pretty young woman with a big "UTAH" button on her coat, getting out of a cab with an excited little blond girl of seven—almost unnoticed but not quite, because a stocky, pleasant-faced man with a big "IOWA" button stepped forward and called, "Mabel! Mabel Anderson!" And the young woman stopped and turned and blushed and the little girl screamed, "Uncle Lafe!" and rushed into his arms.

"Why, there you are," Mabel said, and he bent and kissed her lips as though he had done it a million times, while Pidge jumped and squealed and wriggled in his arms.

"Yes," he said with a gravely gentle smile. "Here I am."

"I find these Knox men," Crystal confided to her mother-in-law at the St. Francis as they changed and made ready to depart for the Ohio Ladies' reception at the Fairmont, "quite something to live with."

Beth smiled.

"No complaints, I hope?"

"Heavens, no," Crystal said. "But it's—intriguing—to watch the wheels go around, you know?"

"Yes," Beth agreed, briskly getting out of the tweed suit she had traveled in, briskly getting into a light blue dress, neat but matronly, "I think I do know. In what particular respect, though?"

"Oh—I don't know. The ambition, I guess. And the drive. And the sudden spells of being so sentimental and human, and so—overcome by it all. When Hal came back to the room after his first speech at the state convention six months ago, he started to tell me what a wonderful greeting they'd given him and tears came into his eyes and he had to stop. He really got all choked up." She smiled, her own eyes suddenly brighter. "So did I, as a matter of fact."

"They care," Beth said seriously. "People don't believe that about the Knoxes, or at least about my Knox, but they do care. Such a hatchet job has been done on them by people like Walter Dobius that the public has an automatic association of 'Knox—old-blooded.' At least some of the public. Thank God there are others."

"Plenty of others," Crystal said, starting to struggle into a stylishly cut maternity dress that was as efficient a matching of purpose and pretense as maternity dresses ever are. "Look at the crowd downstairs in the lobby."

"For heaven's sake, girl, let me help you with that," Beth said impatiently. "Haven't you learned to be waited on, yet? . . . You're a politician's daughter; you know what crowds mean."

"Thanks. . . . It depends on the crowd. I'd say from the tone of the one downstairs that there are plenty of people here who want Orrin Knox on that ticket. I think they're going to get him."

"They've wanted him before," Beth said, her eyes suddenly shadowed by the memories of two lost conventions, the endless speeches, the endless campaigning, the shattered effort, heartbreaking and destructive of all but the toughest. "They didn't get him. What makes you think they will now?"

"A hunch," Crystal said, moving to the window and staring down at the swirling crowds far below. Faintly the sound of a band in Union Square came up through the cool, shining air. "And this time, a principle and a cause that maybe are greater than any he's fought for before. Before, I've felt, it was Orrin Knox-the-efficient-leader who was running, and that was a powerful argument. But not enough. Now it's Orrin Knox the man who symbolizes a specific policy and program, and that's a little different. Man and issue have finally come together, I think."

"What does Stanley think?"

At this reference to her father, senior Senator from Connecticut and Majority Whip of the Senate, Crystal looked surprised.

"He's heading up the campaign, isn't he?"

"I know," Beth said, pinning to her blouse a rose taken from one of the bouquets sent to the room by the ladies of Illinois, the ladies of Michigan, the ladies of Pennsylvania, the ladies of Nebraska. "But what does he really think?"

"The Dantas are like the Knoxes," Crystal said, a little stiffly. "He wouldn't make the commitment if he didn't believe in it."

"Now, now," Beth said calmly. "Don't get upset. I know Stanley. I mean about the chances. Is he as confident about it as we'd like to have him?"

"I think he is," Crystal said slowly. "He's pretty close-mouthed, you know, even with me, but I think he thinks there's a very good chance."

"I hope so," Beth said soberly. "I do hope so. I don't know whether Orrin could stand it again if——"

"Oh, of course he could. Others have taken it and survived. He could too."

"I'm glad you have such faith in the Knoxes," Beth said with a sudden smile. Her daughter-in-law smiled back with perfect candor.

"It grows."

There was a banging on the door of the adjoining room. Crystal laughed.

"There they are, ready to start the grind. Hold on a minute!" she called cheerfully. "We'll be right there. . . . Really, you know," she said as she started for the door, "I feel like a cow on exhibition."

Beth laughed.

"You look rather like one, too, as a matter of fact. But a nice one."

"Thanks so much," Crystal said, giving her an affectionate peck on the cheek as she went by. She opened the door for her husband and the Secretary of State, both of whom looked alert and a lot more rested than they would in twenty-four hours—or forty-eight—or seventy-two—or whenever it all ended. "O.K., boys. The girls are ready!"

They were at the Mark Hopkins, too, or almost. Patsy was trying on orchids, and having discarded a cerise, three whites, and a purple, was now experimenting with a deep yellow flecked with green. Selena, gin and tonic in hand, was standing by the window staring down at the crowds that swarmed atop Nob Hill. Here, too, a band could be heard, faint shouts and celebrations ascended, the whole great hotel seemed to vibrate with excitement. Valuela sat on one of the sofas, surrounded by newspapers: KNOX-JASON CONTEST DOMINATES CONVENTION ON OPENING DAY, the New York *Times* said. JASON AIDS CLAIM VICTORY ON FIRST BALLOT, the San Francisco *Chronicle* announced. JASONS, KNOXES ARRIVE; PRESIDENT DUE WEDNESDAY, the San Francisco *Examiner* reported. KNOX-JASON DEADLOCK COULD OPEN WAY FOR DARK HORSE, the Washington *Post* advised. Herbert, looking rather morose, sat in a rocking chair and read *Time:* his nephew and the Secretary faced one another on the cover against a background of campaign banners, Goroto assegais, and the Panama Canal. In the next room a murmur of voices indicated Ceil and the Governor, busy with their dressing. In the hall outside other voices gave evidence of adoring supporters, the few interlopers who always manage, by dint of much pleading and assistance, to get past the first barrier of guards to stand chattering excitedly before their hero's room.

"Val," Patsy said in a sudden explosive voice, "you're

the artist. Will you PLEASE tell me WHAT color orchid to wear with this dress?"

"Darling," Valuela said with a lazy smile, tossing aside the *Chronicle* and surveying her niece from head to foot, "with that dress you could wear anything. Who gave it to you, Joseph?"

"Patsy's noted for her clothes," Selena said spitefully. "I read about them all the time in the New York papers. 'Señora Labaiya, in a startling combination of green and magenta,' or, 'Señora Labaiya, as usual trying to outdo the rainbow.' Good Lord, girl, you have the money. Why haven't you ever learned how to dress?"

"I do know how to dress," Patsy said, "and you're certainly no example, Sel. Just look at you! A rag, a bone, and a hank of hair—"

"Worth fifty million dollars," Herbert spoke up with a sudden chuckle. "You can get away with quite a lot with that kind of backing."

"And you shouldn't talk," his niece told him sharply. "If that suit has been pressed in the last three weeks, I'll eat my hat. The shabby Jasons! We're a fine lot for a presidential —vice presidential—candidate to have for a family."

"At least *I*," Valuela said, "am presentable"—and she did look stunning at sixty-three, in a sleek black sheath, enormous rhinestone earrings, an upswept hairdo, a slash of brilliant lipstick, and a Spanish comb, also alive with rhinestones. "Anyway, Pat, I think we make up in shock value what we lack in couture. I've already been tagged for sixteen interviews in the next three days. How are the rest of you doing?"

"I'm doing all right, too," Herbert said, his pop-eyes puckish beneath their crown of frizzly white hair. "I've been invited for ten or so, plus a scientific round table under the auspices of the University of California which for some reason, probably attributable to my presence, is, I understand, to be rather extensively covered by the press."

"Lord!" Patsy said. "I pity those poor reporters stuck with an assignment like that just because you're there."

"But who knows," Herbert said blandly. "I might blow up something. Or commit Ted to overthrowing the government by force and violence. Or something equally astounding."

"Now, THAT," Patsy said severely, "is exactly the sort

of levity we can't have. I do hope you and Sel will try to act halfway sensible this week."

"Pet," Selena said, running a hand through her hacked-off hair, turning her perennially startled eyes upon her niece with a blandness equal to her brother's, "that is the last thing you have to worry about. Bert and I have nothing more in mind than picketing Knox headquarters with ban-the-bomb banners. No one will notice that."

"Oh, stop it," Patsy said, suddenly no longer amused. "This is so serious for him, and for all of us—for the whole country. Now, do stop it, PLEASE! He's *got* to win, and we've got to help him in every way we can. Now, please."

"Relax, child," Valuela said calmly. "When did you ever know the Jasons not wanting to win? We're going to help him, all right. I might suggest," she added a trifle acidly, "that perhaps his biggest embarrassment may lie in the fact that his sister is still married to a man who so far seems to be leading a successful military action against the United States."

"That isn't fair," Patsy said. "That really isn't fair, Val. I've filed for divorce. It has to be done in absentia, obviously. That takes time, particularly with the Church involved. I don't see how anyone can claim that I'm not doing all I can to clear it up."

"I wonder what Felix will do to JM's holdings in Panama," Valuela said dreamily, "if he wins?"

"He won't win," Patsy said shortly. Her aunt looked surprised.

"But don't Ted's backers want him to win? Isn't Ted the idol of all those who oppose the Administration's attempt to stop him from winning? I think Ted is in quite a position."

"He isn't as long as he keeps his mouth shut," Herbert said.

"My thought exactly," the Governor agreed with an amiable smile, entering on the remark. "Are we ready, all?"

"We're ready," Ceil said in a noncommittal tone. She straightened her back, squared her shoulders, gave her glorious hair a toss, and grinned. "Once more unto the breach! Dear friends, we may be dead already."

"Oh, CEIL," Patsy said. "You're always so—so—"

"Aren't I, though?" Ceil said cheerfully. "Awful, isn't it?"

"Here they come!" the crowds roared in front of the St. Francis, screamed in front of the Mark. Two families hurried out into the gorgeous blue day amid bursting flashbulbs, snapping cameras, microphones, reporters, shoving, clamoring, frantically eager people straining to see. ON THE ROCKS WITH ORRIN KNOX, a placard held by a grinning college boy summed up one view, at the St. Francis. HASTEN, JASON, GET YOUR BASIN, a placard held by another grinning college boy summed up the other view, at the Mark.

At this point everyone was still happy, and everyone laughed.

Elsewhere, the mood grew grimmer.

"Bob," the Speaker said in a worried voice from his room at the Hilton, "I'm going to Credentials Committee. Things seem to be getting out of hand a little bit."

"Right," the Majority Leader said from his room at the St. Francis. "They are in Platform Committee, too. I'm going there. How about meeting us for lunch at one-thirty in the room here, and we can call Harley?"

"O.K.," the Speaker said. "See you."

"Can I come too?" Dolly asked. Senator Munson smiled.

"I thought you had to stay here and plan for your party tonight. Can you tear yourself away?"

"Everything's ready," Dolly said. "I can steal an hour or two."

"Be my guest," her husband said. "It may be brutal."

"What are you doing here?" Cullee asked in a pleased voice, bumping into familiar figures in the crush in front of the Palace. The Maudulaynes greeted him with beaming smiles and shook hands cordially with Sarah Johnson.

"Just observing," Claude said airily.

"It's so fascinating," Kitty remarked. "This is our second, you know. We went to the last one, too."

"Not under quite such dramatic circumstances, though," Lord Maudulayne said, pointing to the *Chronicle* he was carrying. It had headlines on NEW LOSSES IN GOROTO-LAND . . . AFRO-ASIANS AGAIN DEMAND UN INTERVENTION IN PANAMA . . . PRESIDENT RE-

ITERATES WILL TO STAND FIRM, NEGOTIATE, and a column by Walter Dobius entitled WHAT CAN THE WORLD'S COP DO NOW?, wrapped around four bloody (and of course not at all inflammatory, one-sided, or biased) photographs of GOROTO REBELS GET TORTURE TREATMENT FROM U.S. ALLIES. "What will happen on all of this?"

"I'm just on my way to Platform Committee to see," Cullee said.

"Oh, that's where we're going," Lord Maudulayne said. "Wouldn't miss it for the world."

"It's closed," Cullee said. "There may be a more significant fight in Credentials, in terms of the convention. Why don't you go there?"

"Can you get us in?" Kitty asked, and took Cullee's arm. Sarah smiled.

"Looks like we've got some company," she said with a smile as Lord Maudulayne offered her his arm. "If we can get through the crowd, that is."

"You do things so much more quietly in your country," Cullee told Kitty as he began gently but firmly pushing people out of their way.

"The blood flows," she said cheerfully. "It usually seeps under the door instead of being splattered all over the hall. But it flows."

"I only hope we can get through this without too much being spilled here," Cullee said grimly. "I'm not too confident."

"Hey, there, boy!" Fred Van Ackerman cried, slapping LeGage Shelby on the back in the midst of the shifting, shouting crowd at the Palace. The chairman of DEFY winced and turned on him with a flaring anger.

"I've told you a million times," he said savagely, "don't 'boy' me. What do you want?"

"Look, pal," Senator Van Ackerman said in a suddenly tight voice, while a dozen delegates, college kids, and reporters looked on with interest. "We've got to stand together on this, so don't go flying off the handle every time I say hello to you, will you? Where's that fat fool Kleinfert? Are his people ready to demonstrate?"

"They'll be ready when yours are," 'Gage said shortly, "and so will we. What do you hear?"

"I hear there's a hell of a fight in Credentials Committee

over the Ohio and Alabama delegations. What about you?"

"They tell me Jason's got fifteen of the Illinois delegation and may get some from Michigan and Washington state by tonight."

"Got any over-all figures yet?"

"Somebody said Knox was claiming 672."

Senator Van Ackerman uttered a short cloacal expletive
that made two elderly lady delegates from Massachusetts
jump and exchange indignant looks.

"What Knox claims and what Knox gets will be two
different things, boy. Yes, sir, two different things. Take
care, now. You and Rufe keep in touch with us over at the
Hilton. Drop in 'The COMFORT Room' and have a drink,
when you get a chance. We've got a real live-wire bunch at
work over there. Let us know when you want to demonstrate."

"We'll call you," LeGage said, without much humor.
"Don't call us."

"You're a kidder," Fred said, but he laid his hand on
'Gage's arm with a grip that made him wince again and
look furious. "Don't forget this is damned serious business
here. The world may depend upon it."

"I don't need you to give me lectures!" 'Gage said, his
handsome face contorted with anger. He flung off Fred's
hand, and flung himself away.

"And that's what we have to depend upon to help nominate the greatest leader this country's got," Senator Van
Ackerman announced to their wide-eyed audience. "Jeeee
—zus!"

"It would be my thought," Walter Dobius said with a
contemplative gravity to three eager young reporters who
were hanging on every word at a table in the Garden Court
of the Palace, "that what happens today in the Credentials
and Platform Committees will indicate pretty definitely
which way this convention is going to go. I'd keep an eye
on them, if I were you."

"Yes, sir," they said, as fervently as though they had not
read this prediction fifty times in every place including his
own column in the past twenty-four hours. Coming from
him, it sounded new and profound, somehow.

"Watch, credents., pltfm.," they scribbled.

It was sound advice.

Everybody was.

"The committee will now hear the distinguished delegate from the District of Columbia," the chairman of Credentials (Old Joe Smitters from Ashtabula) said in the public conference room at the Hilton. "I believe the delegate is the chairman of the vice presidential campaign of the distinguished Governor of California, is he not?"

"I am," Bob Leffingwell said, "and it is our position that of the two delegations purporting here to represent the great state of Ohio, the one headed by the distinguished former Governor of that state is the one that should be seated in this convention."

"And that, of course, is the one favorable to your candidate?" Old Joe Smitters suggested with a knowing smile.

"I am not quite so charitable as to support one that didn't," Bob Leffingwell said, and all down the table— Mrs. Mary Buttner Baffleburg, National Committeewoman from Pennsylvania, Homer Amos Stanhope, National Committeeman from Masachusetts, Miss Lizzie Hanson McWharter, National Committeewoman from Kansas, and all the rest—they rocked and chuckled.

"Present your evidence," Old Joe directed, and Bob Leffingwell leaned forward confidently.

"It is our contention, Mr. Chairman," he began in a thoughtful, measured tone, "that certain illegalities existed in the selection of the delegation that purports to represent Ohio in the name of the distinguished Secretary of State."

"Are you charging a 'steal'?" Old Joe Smitters asked, thinking, That will make good headlines, that's what they want, I have a hunch Jason is going to get this and if he does maybe I can get something out of it if I play it right.

"I will have to let the committee decide that," Bob Leffingwell said smoothly.

"But you wouldn't deny the term?" Old Joe asked, thinking, How clever I'm being.

"No, I wouldn't deny it, if you prefer it, Mr. Chairman," Bob Leffingwell said after a moment's hesitation.

"Would you use it?" Old Joe pursued, his crafty little eyes narrowing, all the skill and shrewdness that had made him the biggest feed dealer in Ashtabula coming into his voice.

"If you insist, Mr. Chairman."

"Now, see here—" Mary Buttner Baffleburg of Pennsylvania began indignantly, but it was already too late. UPI and AP were both hurrying from the room. JASON

FORCES CHARGE KNOX STEAL OF OHIO DEL-
EGATES, the next edition's headline would read. It was
Fate.

"Mr. Chairman," Senator Munson said smoothly in the
private conference room at the Fairmont, "it does seem to
me that in considering this proposed plank in the platform
it would be well to remember that a little more than a fight
between potential Vice Presidents is involved here. I suppose we're presenting a defense of the Administration to
the country, are we not?"

"We are that," Chairman Bill Smatters from Atlanta
agreed, thinking, These smart boys from Congress always
think they can come to convention and push us around,
but by God, we've got the whip hand here and we don't
have to take it. "Is the distinguished delegate from Michigan," he added blandly, "implying that this committee
wishes to *denounce* the Administration? We thought we'd
leave that to the opposition, didn't we, friends?"

And all the way from Walter H. Hanna, National Committeeman from Montana, to Esmé Harbellow Stryke, National Committeewoman from California, they rocked and
chuckled.

"Very well, then," Senator Munson said calmly, "let's
act like it. You've been squabbling for a week here in a
way that makes it look as though half of you aren't for the
Administration at all. How about you, Esmé? Are you for
it?"

"Well!" said Esmé Harbellow Stryke indignantly, her
sharp-featured little face and hard-bitten little eyes awash
with annoyance. "Mr. Chairman, I don't know that I have
to sit here and be cross-examined by—by him."

"O.K.," Bob Munson said with a shrug, "so you're not.
Just keep in mind the other party's watching, that's all. I
think it's time you got to business and stopped this nonsense."

"If this were an open committee, I'll say to the Senator,"
Bill Smatters from Atlanta said huffily, "he wouldn't be
talking to us like this."

"It might as well be," Bob Munson said, unimpressed.
"It leaks like a sieve. Now, what is this language here that
purports to be backed by the Jason forces? Tom?" he said,
swinging abruptly around to the senior Senator from Min-

nesota at his left. "You put this thing in, didn't you? What does it mean?"

"It means," Senator August said with his customary air of timorous asperity when pressed, "just what it says."

"And what does it say?" the Majority Leader demanded in a dramatic voice, holding it up for them to see. "It says" —and he peered at it closely—"damn, it looks as though eighteen pigeons have been walking on it. Isn't there a clean draft somewhere?"

"We're trying to work one out, Senator," Bill Smatters said with some annoyance. He didn't know what the Senator's game was, or who he was for, but he was sure there was some tricky business going on somewhere and he wasn't about to be caught. "Can't you decipher that one?"

"I'll read it," Tom August said stiffly. "It is proposed by myself as chairman of the Senate Foreign Relations Committee and by my distinguished friend, Representative J. B. Swarthman of South Carolina as chairman of the House Foreign Affairs Committee, because we wanted to try to arrive at something that would be fair to everybody. It says—"

"Got your pencil, Esmé?" Bob Munson interrupted. "You'll want to tell the AP."

"If you please, Bob," Tom August said in an aggrieved tone. "Do let me proceed."

"I should hope *so!*" said Esmé Stryke.

"It says," Senator August repeated in a dogged voice, "Believing that the interests of world peace can best be served by halting armed aggression wherever it may exist, we applaud the intention of the President of the United States to conciliate and settle world differences in such areas of conflict on a basis of peaceful negotiation.' "

He gave the Majority Leader a defiant look. "What's wrong with that?"

"Well, I'll tell you," Bob Munson said thoughtfully, looking around the room at faces which were about evenly divided between those which appeared to be friendly and those which appeared to be openly skeptical. "In the first place, I've read the rest of the foreign policy plank—that highly secret document whose major features strangely appeared in the Sunday New York *Times*—and while it's a fine defense of the past in ten beautifully written paragraphs, this seems to be the only place at which you touch,

even by remote control, on such"—his voice became dry—
"interesting issues as the trouble in Gorotoland and the
fighting in Panama. Is that right, Tom?"

Senator August gave him a stubborn look.

"It has taken us a week, Bob, to arrive at this much. It
has just seemed best, here in the committee, to avoid a
direct mention of either Gorotoland or Panama."

"Is it that bad?" the Majority Leader demanded with an
air of not being able to believe it, though of course he had
been hearing for the past five days from inside the committee that it was.

"It isn't good, Senator," Jawbone Swarthman spoke up
suddenly from down the table where he was wedged between Elbridge W. Elbridge, National Committeeman from
Rhode Island, and Anna Hooper Bigelow, National Committeewoman from New Hampshire. "No, sir, I tell you it
isn't good! It's all very well for you to fly in here from
Washington and in ten minutes decide what we ought to do
in this committee, but I tell you, Senator, we've been here a
week already and we've got our troubles here on this issue.
We have certainly got our troubles." He looked around the
table and nodded vigorous agreement with himself. "Yes,
sir."

"People who want assistance from the Administration in
seeking other offices such as United States Senator may
have their troubles, too," Senator Munson said coldly, "if
they can't come up with something better than this paragraph."

"Senator," Jawbone said, "I'm not so sure the Administration could help me right now in South Carolina, and
that's the God's honest truth. We're faced with a bad situation here, I'll tell the Senator frankly. You don't know the
temper of this convention. You wait 'til you've been here a
day or two and you'll feel it, Senator. It's not comfortable."

"I've been here an hour or two," Bob Munson said dryly, "and I know what it is. I only regret the Speaker and I
couldn't get the session wound up in Washington in time to
get out here last week. But we didn't, and apparently the
people the President should have been able to count on"—
and he looked thoughtfully at Jawbone and Tom August,
both of whom looked uneasily defiant in return—"haven't
been able to do the job."

"It won't do any good, Bob," Senator August said in a
doggedly stubborn voice, "to keep after us. I'm telling you

frankly, and this whole committee will support me, and you've been reading hints of it in the papers, too, that if we mention either Gorotoland or Panama in this plank it's going to blow the convention sky-high. People are too upset."

"But, my dear old friend," Bob Munson said, and in a sense he really meant it, for Tom, for all his old-maidish ways, was a dear old friend with whom he had worked on foreign policy matters for many years, "Gorotoland and Panama are what this convention and this election are all about. Surely you know that."

The Senator from Minnesota shook his head.

"I don't think these people will take it, Bob. I just don't think they will."

"He's right, Senator," Congressman Swarthman agreed, and across the table Esmé Stryke and Anna Hooper Bigelow nodded vigorously. "It just won't do any good to argue-fy. It really won't."

"Mmmm," Bob Munson said. "Well, this week isn't last week. In a certain sense, you've been operating a vacuum this past week, surrounded by the press which has been telling you incessantly that you don't dare support your own Administration. Now the delegates are here and the convention is really beginning. Maybe I don't know the mood of the convention, Jawbone, but neither do you, really. You've all been sitting in a closed room working on each other, and letting the press work on you, and you've convinced yourselves that the problem is tougher than it is. . . . *Whatever you think,*" he said in a flat, firm voice as a number of committee members stirred restively, "the White House will not settle for less than a specific endorsement of the President's policy. Why, Good Lord!" he added with a disgusted snort. "Whatever made you think you could get away with less?" His tone became tougher. "Now this is the language the President wants. The *President* wants, I will remind you. *Your* President, of this party, with whom this party sinks or swims. With whom *you* sink or swim, as party leaders, in your own states and districts. So pay attention."

"You needn't use that tone to us, Bob," Senator August said mildly. "We're paying attention."

"We're paying attention, Mr. Speaker, I will say to you," Old Joe Smitters from Ashtabula said testily at the Hilton.

"You don't have to lecture us about our duties in this Credentials Committee, or this convention, either. We're doing our best to work things out here in fairness to all parties concerned."

"Hmph," the Speaker said. "Seems to me you've been mighty quick to use the word 'steal' this morning. That's fairness?"

"It's an open convention, Mr. Speaker," Old Joe Smitters told him, not without some insolence—an insolence, the Speaker told himself impatiently, that he wouldn't have dared to show if the President had picked his Vice President flat-out as he ought to have done, instead of causing all this mix-up. "This committee has its opinions, too."

"If this committee had an ounce of self-respect," the Speaker said, "it would disqualify any chairman who used a hate-word as partisan as that."

"Now, Mr. Speaker," Old Joe said, turning a furious red, while in the audience Belle—Mrs. Smitters, head of the Ladies' County Auxiliary—let out a little cry and clapped a handkerchief to her mouth—"you can't speak to the chairman of this committee like that, even if you are the Speaker and everybody's scared of you. Joe Smitters isn't scared of you, Mr. Speaker, and this committee isn't, either. Now, is it?" And he glared around the table. Mrs. Mary Buttner Baffleburg of Pennsylvania held up her hand for recognition.

"I think," she said, turning her round little head upon her round little neck above her round little figure until she was glaring straight back at Old Joe Smitters from Ashtabula, "*I* think, Mr. Chairman, that the Speaker is exactly right. I think the whole mood of this committee chairman and this committee for three days, now, has been hostile to the greatest Secretary of State we have ever had, the next Vice President of the United States—"

"Mrs. Baffleburg," Joe Smitters shouted, while the committee began to break into a babble of talk and protest, Lizzie Hanson McWharter of Kansas waved and shouted frantically for recognition, the press scribbled furiously, the television cameras peered delightedly, and the audience sat forward with an eager anticipation on the edges of its spindly gold-gilt chairs. "Mrs. Baffleburg! Mrs. Baffleb—"

"I want to endorse that, Mr. Chairman!" Lizzie Hanson McWharter cried. "I want to join my dear, distinguished sister from Pennsylvania in that! I've never seen a more one-sided, more intolerant, more vicious attempt to railroad anything than I've seen in this committee. I think the chairman should be impeached, Mr. Chairman! Or removed or something! I do, Mr. Chairman! And that means you, Mr. Chairman!"

"It isn't enough," Mary Buttner Baffleburg took up the cause, as Old Joe Smitters began pounding his gavel with a heavy, battering beat that threatened to split the veneer on the table, "for you to choke off witnesses, including such a great and distinguished witness as our dear Mr. Speaker here who has served our party so long and wonderfully in the House of Representatives of the United States and in these conventions, Mr. Chairman"—she paused and drew a great gulp of breath before she turned completely crimson —"it isn't enough to do that, but you've consistently favored every witness that has appeared here to speak for the other side. We've just spent an hour and a half listening to Mr. Leffingwell tell us how noble this Jason delegation from Ohio and this Jason delegation from Mississippi are. And who's Mr. Leffingwell?" She glared around the table. "A man who lied to the United States Senate, Mr. Chairman, that's who he is!" Her voice rose as Old Joe Smitters crashed the gavel heavier and heavier, and in the audience Bob Leffingwell winced with an expression of sudden, deep pain. "A liar, Mr. Chairman! That's who comes here for Governor Jason, that's who, a liar!"

Abruptly the Speaker stood up—so abruptly that he succeeded in stopping the uproar, which was what he wished to do. The room fell silent and he let it stay that way for several minutes as he stared at its occupants with the coldly impassive look that his youthful colleagues in the House were wont to refer to as "Mr. Bill's deep-freeze."

"Now," he said finally, "we're going to stop making a public spectacle of ourselves and we're going to conduct this business like decent men and women should. Mrs. Baffleburg, you will apologize to Mr. Leffingwell."

"I will not!" she cried, quivering like an indignant bowl of jelly. "It's the truth and I won't apologize for it!"

At this there was a scattering of applause from the audience. The Speaker swung around so sharply that it stopped at once.

"I'll wait," he said.

"You aren't the chairman!" Lizzie Hanson McWharter of Kansas began. "What right have you got to—"

But Mr. Bill's deep-freeze, if anything, became deeper, and her voice faltered.

"Well, you're not," she said.

"It's only twelve forty-five," the Speaker remarked to no one in particular. "We've got plenty of time."

"I won't do it," Mary Buttner Baffleburg said, still breathing hard but speaking more calmly. "He's—what I said, and you can't make me apologize for it. I'm sorry that I stated it like that in a public place. I'm sorry if I hurt anyone's feelings. But I'm not sorry for speaking the truth."

"Mr. Speaker," Bob Leffingwell said, and they would never know what it cost him to rise with dignity, as he did, and speak in a calm and courteous tone, "I don't take Mrs. Baffleburg's remarks personally—["How can you take them any other way, for Christ's sake?" the New York *Times* demanded of the Chicago *Tribune* at the press table] and, like you, I deplore the fact, if it is a fact, that partisanship has entered the committee's deliberations. If I contributed to it, over and beyond the amount that the chairman of a candidate's campaign can normally be expected to show, then *I* apologize—to Mrs. Baffleburg, to Miss McWharter, and to anyone else I may have offended." He started to sit down, then paused midway for a final comment. "Incidentally, it was not I who introduced the word 'steal,' Mr. Speaker."

"Or repudiated it, either," Lizzie Hanson McWharter couldn't resist in an indignant undertone. The Speaker chose to ignore it.

"Very well," he said, subsiding slowly into his chair and turning back to face Old Joe Smitters, who looked as though he didn't quite know how to take hold of things again. "Now, maybe we can all proceed like ladies and gentlemen. . . . I've been doing a little talking around, Mr. Chairman, and it appears to me there is a genuine split in this committee on these two disputed delegations. Am I correct?"

"Yes, you are, Mr. Speaker," Old Joe said, still breathing hard himself and thinking, Damn it, Doc told me not to get too excited this time or I may have a stroke, feeling the pressure behind his eyes, having intimations of mortality right there in the Hilton, thinking, Oh, God, why did I want to attend another one, I've been to eight already, why can't I let go and let the young fellows take over.

"Well, then," the Speaker said blandly, "I think some sort of compromise ought to be worked out, don't you?"

"The compromise the President proposes," Senator Munson said calmly at the Fairmont, and at his use of the word "compromise" there was a snort from somewhere in the Platform Committee, "goes like this—ready, Esmé?—I quote:

" 'Believing that the interests of world peace can best be served by opposing Communist aggression and infiltration, armed or otherwise, wherever they may exist, we applaud the action of the President in opposing such Communist aggression and infiltration in the nations of Gorotoland and Panama. We wholeheartedly support his determination to bring peace and stability to those troubled areas through the medium of peaceful and honest negotiations as soon as the Communist threat has been removed.' "

There was a silence when he concluded, and into it Esmé Harbellow Stryke wrinkled her permanently disapproving nose, and sniffed.

"I doubt very much, Mr. Chairman," she said in a spiteful tone, "that the people of California would support such language."

"The distinguished National Committeelady has the duty of speaking for twenty-five million people, which she handles magnificently," Bob Munson said smoothly. "I only have the duty of speaking for one." He paused for a moment to let them think about who that one was. "This language, Mr. Chairman, is what your candidate for President wants. Surely the committee will not wish to ignore his wishes."

But at this there was an uneasy stirring in the committee. Roger P. Croy, former Governor and now National Committeeman from Oregon, a regular troublemaker in Platform Committee for four conventions hand-running as the Majority Leader could well remember, raised his hand.

"That's another thing, Mr. Chairman," he said dryly. "This assumption that everything's all cut and dried here. Except for Vice President, that is, and I'm not so sure that that isn't, either, in spite of what we hear. [Well, foo you, Roger P. Croy, former Governor and now National Committeeman from Oregon, the Majority Leader told him in the privacy of his own mind.] I don't doubt, of course, Mr.

Chairman, that our great President will be the unanimous nominee of this convention, but wouldn't it be a little more polite, now, to just at least pretend a little humility about it? We may be sheep," he said, and there was an appreciative snicker from a good many areas of the room, "but at least we like to think we're *independent* sheep. We don't like to be told we've got to bleat when some of us, maybe, might like to try a whinny." The snicker grew to laughter and with an elaborate haste he added, "Not that we'd dream of trying it, Mr. Chairman. Certainly not. It's just a thought. And so's the language of this proposed plank in the platform, which the Senator assumes will be so easy to get through just because our candidate for President wants it. It may not be, Mr. Chairman. It may not be. Some of us might want to start a little whinny, Mr. Chairman, just to see how it sounds, and this is the place where some of us might try—aside from voting on the Vice President, of course. Tell me, Senator," he said, suddenly dropping the pseudo-banter and sounding hard-boiled himself, "I assume this language you propose also has the endorsement of the Secretary of State?"

"I don't know whether the President has consulted him or not," the Majority Leader said. There was a skeptical snort somewhere down the table.

"But you wouldn't seriously say that the Secretary would oppose the President's language, would you?" Roger P. Croy pressed, and Bob Munson thought impatiently, Oh, why don't you go back to your law practice in Salem and run for Governor again.

"The Governor knows I wouldn't say that," he said calmly. Roger P. Croy's next remark was inevitable.

"Then we can of course regard this as a Knox as well as a Hudson substitute, can't we, and we can regard the present committee language as Jason language. That puts the whole thing in a different light."

"You can if you're looking for headlines," Senator Munson said sharply. Roger P. Croy of Oregon shrugged.

"That's how the battle's going to be won, Senator," he said. "With headlines."

And by one o'clock, of course, it looked as though Ted Jason was comfortably ahead in the opening skirmishes. CREDENTIALS COMMITTEE IN UPROAR OVER KNOX DELEGATE "STEAL," the typical banner had it.

REPORT PLATFORM COMMITTEE BALKING AT
KNOX FOREIGN POLICY PLANK. ADMINISTRA-
TION SENDS MUNSON, SPEAKER TO QUELL RE-
VOLT.

By the time the two gentlemen met in the Senator's room
for lunch at one-thirty they realized they had their work cut
out to keep the convention from breaking wide open. They
so reported, somewhat glumly, to the President when they
called him at two. His calmness annoyed them rather more
than the situation perhaps warranted at that moment, but
they were in the midst of a steadily tightening tension and
he was not. However, they were unable to budge him from
his plan to wait until Wednesday before flying in, nor
would he yield a word on the foreign policy plank. At the
two vice presidential headquarters the incessant stream of
visitors who come and go at headquarters came and went,
bringing their characteristic burden of information, rumors,
worry, and advice. In two inner rooms that looked much
the same, sounded much the same, and had the same electric smell and feel of mounting though not yet overwhelming crisis, two ambitious men and those closest to
them tried to assess what was going on as objectively as
they could: though objectivity, along with many other vir-
tues of a quieter day, was increasingly difficult to achieve
in the increasingly hectic tempo of the increasingly blur-
ring hours.

"They look bad," the Secretary said, pushing back the
remnants of a hasty late lunch, surveying the early afternoon papers from all over the country with their near-unanimous chorus of triumph for the Governor of California.

"They're slanted," Hal Knox said bitterly. "Just as
slanted as hell."

"That may be," his father said, "but it doesn't have
much bearing here. The point is, how much are they going
to stampede the delegates. Stanley?"

Grave, judicious, gentlemanly, and calm as always, the
senior Senator from Connecticut shook his head.

"Not much so far. We have good men in almost every
delegation, and all the reports I get are that nobody much
is slipping at the moment. I don't think we need to worry
just yet."

"All my life," Hal said, "it seems to me I've been attending conventions at which good men assured my father that

he wasn't slipping. Then they began counting and suddenly it appeared that all the good men were mistaken. I'm afraid I haven't much confidence in good men. I've seen complacency at Knox headquarters before."

Stanley Danta gave his son-in-law a startled look, began to smile, and then thought better of it.

"If you're worried, why don't you get out and around and do some checking yourself? You're a good man. I've been wondering where to use you. You may be able to find out things the staff can't."

"Cultivate the press," Orrin suggested. "They'll be glad to see you. Just be very guarded in what you say, though. They're waiting to put the worst light on everything out of this headquarters."

Hal snorted.

"You don't need to worry. I can see them coming. When are you going to have a press conference?"

"I think I'll stand by my original plan to have one at ten tomorrow morning."

"That's too late," Hal said flatly. "The Jason people are starting a tide. You've got to get a few headlines yourself."

"With what?" his father asked skeptically. "Claims of strength every hour on the hour? I've gone through that phony business in two conventions and I don't think any more of it now than I did the first time."

"It helps, though," Hal said. "At least it gives you headlines."

"For once," Orrin said with a certain weariness, "I'd like to fight a convention on issues instead of headlines. I know it isn't done, but I'd like to do it. Look: Hotspur. When I make a claim tomorrow morning at ten it's going to be a solidly based one with as much of the water squeezed out as Stanley and I can possibly squeeze. I think right now I've got close to six hundred delegates, which isn't too bad at this stage. But I'm not going to claim them until we're as near to certainty as it's possible to be in this game. I notice Ted isn't rushing into a press conference either, today."

"As far as we know," Hal said darkly.

"O.K.," his father said, "if you're worried, go out and find out what's going on." He smiled. "We're always receptive to inside information, Stanley and I. Bring us some."

"Well," Hal said, somewhat mollified and with the start of an answering smile, "I just don't want *you* to become complacent, either. And if Ted suddenly pops a press conference, I want you to hold one, too. I don't care what you have to say. Say something."

"Yes, sir," Orrin said obediently. "If the occasion arises. Meanwhile, thank you for your excellent advice, Mr. Knox. Give my love to the family, and when you're in Washington, do stop in and see me. It's great to know that this great convention is composed of such great delegates from such great states as—where did you say you came from?— and if there is anything I can do to make things any greater, *let—me—know*. Now, skedaddle, and let us think for a while. O.K.?"

"O.K.," Hal said, "but you remember what I said."

"I'll remember," Orrin said. "Stanley," he added when the door closed, "the solemnity of the young."

"That's a good boy," Senator Danta observed comfortably. "I like my son-in-law. Thank you for him."

"Thank you for my daughter-in-law," the Secretary said. He grinned. "Wasn't it nice we chose them for each other?"

"As I recall," Stanley said, "that is one claim we cannot make. It was all decided before I even knew they were really interested."

"Me, too. Ah, well, it seems to be working out for the best—Grandpa."

Stanley smiled.

"Not just yet, but it won't be long. . . . You really do want to wait until tomorrow morning?"

"Oh, I think so; if he will, anyway. I agree with Hal— if he makes a claim, I suppose I've got to counter, just to show I'm alive. But I'd really rather wait until the picture is a little clearer."

"You came through the outer offices," Senator Danta said. "A hundred people are working out there, and as many more are out with the delegations. We do have a really good organization this time, Orrin. If we fail the reason won't be there. It will be things like"—he gestured to the newspapers strewn over his desk—"the Knox Steal."

"Two months from now, if they've licked me," Orrin said dryly, "they'll be writing pitying, patronizing columns and editorials about 'an obviously bewildered Secretary Knox, who just didn't realize what hit him in the Ohio-Mississippi issue.' Hell, I know what's hitting me: they're hitting me."

"And Bob Leffingwell, I suppose," Senator Danta suggested. The Secretary frowned.

"No, I don't think so. I don't think he really wanted to use the term 'steal.' It was Joe Smitters who got him into it. Honestly, I have observed that old fool for twenty years and if he has ever done one uncrafty or generous thing in his entire political life, I'll eat it. Good old grassroots America, that's our friend from Ashtabula: salt of the earth!" He started to chuckle, then his expression changed. "I must say I feel sorry for Bob, though. Apparently Mary Baffleburg really let him have it."

"Speaking of the salt of the earth," Senator Danta observed. "But," he added softly, "he did lie, didn't he?"

The Secretary sighed.

"Yes, he did. But I'm not as adamant about it as I was then. I can understand it better, maybe. We're all human—we're none of us perfect—who knows what we might do—and so on. . . . Well," he said, suddenly brisk, "the Speaker called to tell me he hopes to submit a compromise idea on credentials to me by tonight some time, which"—he frowned—"I think we may have to accept, I'm not sure, yet —and Bob Munson's busy in Platform Committee—so we'll just have to see what develops. Can you have a report on delegates for me by tonight?"

"Oh, yes, I think so. Are you going to Dolly's party at the Palace of Fine Arts?"

"*Everybody's* going to Dolly's party."

"I'll have it for you then."

"Good," Orrin said. He nodded toward the television set, where crowds, faces, commentators, newscasters, reporters, delegates, Governors, Cabinet members, Congressmen, and Senators had been steadily marching past, uttering profound things, giving portentous analyses, all in absolute silence in this room, though elsewhere in the headquarters stenographers were recording every word and campaign aides were studying every hint of sentiment. But now the scene was shifting to the Cow Palace, and it was obvious that things were soon to get under way. "Better turn up the sound, I guess. We wouldn't want to miss the opening prayer."

Stanley Danta smiled.

"I should say not. Some of us need it. Present company excepted, of course."

"I think we should all listen to the opening prayer," Governor Jason said solemnly. "It may improve us all."

"Perhaps," Bob Leffingwell said with a halfhearted smile but a sad expression he could not entirely conceal. Ceil, who had been standing with Patsy staring down at the crowds milling back and forth between the Mark and the Fairmont, turned and put a hand on his shoulder.

"Don't feel so badly," she said softly. "You know Mary Baffleburg. She's one of the characters of these conventions. It's a special type you see in politics: Mary Buttner Baffleburg, Lizzie Hanson McWharter, Ann Hooper Bigelow, and—God help us here in California—Esmé Harbellow Stryke. The old biddies—or in our case, the young ones —who have the time and the money to make politics their hobby and finally reach the National Committee, there to appear at convention after convention, four years older and four times more irascible each time you see them. I wouldn't worry about her too much."

Bob Leffingwell sighed with a grateful but unconvinced smile.

"You're very kind, Ceil—genuinely so, which is one of the things that makes you a great lady—in case you don't know it," he said to her husband, who replied, "But I do, I do!" with an elaborate bow that was quite genuine beneath its mocking air. "But," Bob Leffingwell said, and his smile faded and his voice became somber, "it isn't just Mary Baffleburg, of course. She isn't alone. . . . I don't think I'm good for this campaign, Ted. I think I ought to get out right now. This would give me an excuse. I could issue a statement that I don't want the slightest hint of scandal to detract from the great campaign of a great—you know the routine when somebody has to be sacrificed. I think I should be. I'm too much of a handicap to you. I'm not worth it."

"And your heart isn't in it," Patsy said with a sudden note of genuine anger that brought them up short. "It never has been. I remember talking to you three months ago before anybody had done anything about this campaign, including the President, and you weren't sure then that you wanted to back Ted. You aren't sure now. You want OUT, and this is your excuse. That's what comes," she said, turning upon her brother, "of trying to work with a weakling."

"Patsy," Ted said in a level voice. "I think you had better leave us, now. Go back and talk to Val and the others, or go get a drink, or something. You're not contributing much here."

"It's true," she said, beginning to cry but not yielding an inch. "I'm not retracting one word of it. He's the President's stooge in this campaign and he always has been. He thinks the President's policies are right. He doesn't really know what he wants, but it isn't you. You mark my words, he's going to wind up backing Orrin Knox. You wait and see!"

"That," the Governor said softly, "will be enough. Do you hear me, Pat? Enough."

"Well—" she said, and then cried, "OH!" and hurried from the room in a flurry of defiantly swinging hips and agitated garish colors.

"My goodness," Ceil remarked gently. "Let me add Patsy Labaiya-Sofra to the list of characters at conventions."

"She's tired and upset," Ted said, "and it's been a long strain for her, about Felix, and about trying to get me to run. That's what comes," he echoed with a strange little ironic pain about his mouth, "of working with a weakling. We're in the same boat, Bob. I still don't know what's best, either. But"—and his voice became increasingly stronger —"here I am. And here you are. And although some people have fancied a convention as the best setting in which to admire themselves playing Hamlet, I've about decided against it, myself. So I think we should both snap out of it and get ready to win." He gestured wryly at the glaring, helpful, eager, encouraging, partisan headlines. "We've got plenty of help, haven't we? If they ask me about you at my press conference I shall simply shrug and point and say, 'He's here, isn't he?' . . . Now," he said, suddenly brisk, and for the moment there was no mistaking who was Doña Valuela's descendant, "have you spoken to Stanley Danta so that Orrin and I won't have a conflict with our press conference times?"

"Yes, I have," Bob Leffingwell said, throwing off his depression with an obvious effort. "But it's Orrin's idea that you should conflict. What he means is that if yours comes first then he can attack what you say, and if his comes first you can attack what he says—so the fairest thing probably is to have them at the same hour. Which will annoy the press," he said with a shadow of a smile, "no doubt. But I guess they can stand it."

"So typical of Orrin," Ceil said gently. "Worrying about fairness! Will the man *never* learn."

"It seems eminently fair to me, too, Ceil," her husband

said mildly. "O.K., Bob, send out the word. Ten A.M. it is for both of us, and let them howl. I hope we will have some good specifics to report by that time."

"Oh, yes. We have some very good men with the delegations. I would say you have somewhere in the neighborhood of six hundred right now. We'll pin it down tighter by tonight."

"Somewhere," the Governor said dreamily, "in some column, news story, headline, program, broadcast, hint, rumor, marijuana jag, or pipe dream, I have seen the figure of six hundred for my distinguished opponent, too. Don't tell me we go to the wire even."

"You won't go to the wire until Thursday. You won't be even then."

"I hope not," the Governor said. "Now what?" he added in some annoyance as the sound of voices raised in bitter altercation sifted through the door. "Don't they have orders not to let any—oh, yes," he said, as they recognized the pompous, familiar tones. "I might have known. Come in, Walter!" he called loudly. "Let him in, out there! It's all right."

"Thank you," Walter Dobius said, breathing hard and straightening a coat which had obviously been tugged at by somebody. "I must say," he added, adjusting the red-ribboned PRESS badge which had also been knocked awry in the sort of tussle no philosopher-statesman should ever have to go through, "you have some ignorant and officious people out there. They didn't even know who I am."

"They were chosen for brawn, Walter," Ceil said soothingly. "Obviously not for brains. *Obviously*. Have you been having a pleasant time covering the convention?"

"Conventions aren't pleasant," Walter said with a rudeness so obvious as to bring a sudden smile to her lips. "They are serious matters, involving the fate of a great nation."

"I shall go to the foot of the class," she said gravely. "With my little balloons and my little badges and my little banners."

"What do you want, Walter?" Ted asked shortly. "Do you want to watch the opening session with us? We're about to turn it on."

"Certain people have come to me with offers of help for you," Walter said calmly. "I want to discuss them with— you."

"You are in the presence of my wife and my campaign manager. Discuss them."

"Very well," Walter said, sitting down and leaning forward, legs spread, hands on knees, in his characteristic posture. "You know that at a convention anybody can become a go-between at a moment's notice. I seem to have been selected by a rather odd combination whose spokesmen first came to me two months ago on the day of the President's decision."

"Yes, I know, you told me. COMFORT, DEFY, and KEEP."

"Yes. After that I thought the flurry had died down, as they didn't approach me again. Did they you?"

"I had a letter from LeGage Shelby about two weeks ago promising the support of DEFY," Ted said, "and of course Fred Van Ackerman has been on the horn several times. 'Look, buddy' "—and his voice dropped into a savage imitation of the hypocrite-heartiness of the junior Senator from Wyoming—" 'we've really got to go all-out to elect the greatest Vice President this country's ever had.' " He laughed with genuine delight. "Imagine! Launching a campaign to elect the greatest *Vice* President this country's ever had! How esoteric can you get? As for Rufus Kleinfert," he added, still laughing, "I haven't heard from KEEP."

"Last night," Walter said, "all three of them called on me at my suite at the Hilton. It seems they want to take over the demonstrations for you. They'll do all the organizing, furnish all the supplies, all the financing, all the people—all they ask is that Bob, here, coordinate things with them so that everybody will work together."

"And so their plans will become our plans," Bob Leffingwell said. "Not on your tintype. Isn't that right, Ted?"

"Are they operating alone?" the Governor asked. "I got the impression from LeGage's letter that most of the more active Negro groups are working with him."

Walter nodded.

"They seem to have selected DEFY to spearhead it for them. I think what they do will pretty well decide where the bulk of the Negro vote goes, both now and—if they get the man they want, here—in the future."

"Not on your tintype, Ted," Ceil remarked, to no one in particular. "Isn't that right?"

"And what about COMFORT and KEEP?" the Governor pursued, his eyes intent.

"The Committee on Making Further Offers for a Russian Truce?" Walter said thoughtfully, as though the others were not in the room, which for all the practical purposes of this discussion they were not. "It was never stronger now that the President is getting us mired deeper and deeper in Gorotoland and Panama. Fred Van Ackerman tells me they're planning a series of full-page ads in the New York *Times* and twenty other major papers across the country, together with a program of TV spots, between now and Election Day. He says they'll be largely devoted to supporting you, providing you can establish a position close enough to Harley's to get by, but independent enough so that they can hold the hope that you may throw your weight against him once you're in the Administration—and take a different course if you should become President."

"A nice trick if you can do it," Ceil observed brightly to Bob Leffingwell, who was staring at Walter with a disturbed expression. "And, I should say, an open invitation to somebody to assassinate the President right after Election Day."

"How many members has COMFORT got right now?" the Governor asked.

"Fred tells me at least three hundred thousand, a lot of them in communications, the unions, the schools, and the churches. It's become very respectable since Gorotoland. I'll wager you every time another American boy dies, COMFORT picks up another thousand members."

"Good for the boy," Ceil said. "Good for him!"

"As for KEEP," Walter said thoughtfully, "they're still afraid of your domestic record, which Rufus Kleinfert still considers Communist-tinted if not outright Communist-controlled."

"Then how——?" Ted asked in a puzzled voice.

"It's that boy," Ceil explained to Bob Leffingwell.

"Rufus told me last night," Walter said, "that any candidate who would stop what he called 'this insane plunge into overseas war and endless international involvement at the behest of Communist tricksters' would have their support."

"There you are," Ceil said triumphantly to Bob Leffingwell, who gave a hopeless little shrug.

There was silence in which a band far below, stripped by distance of its melodies, sent up a solid, thumping beat.

"You can tell them," the Governor said slowly at last, "that any assistance they deem me worthy to receive will be welcome."

Walter stared at him blankly for a moment.

"That isn't as specific an answer as they are expecting, I believe."

"I'm afraid it's as specific as they're going to get," Ted said pleasantly. "Where else can they go if they don't support me—anywhere? Why, hell, Walter, my friend, try to look at this for a second objectively. The responsible Negro vote—yes, I want that. The genuine idealists who join COMFORT and oppose the Administration, as distinct from the Communists and the fatheaded far-out fools who join it for their own egomanic purposes—yes, I want them. The genuinely troubled conservatives in KEEP, as distinct from the insane reactionary weirdos like Rufus Kleinfert— yes, I want them. But to let them control my campaign? To sell myself to them in return for their support? I won't do it."

"But you won't repudiate them, either, will you?" Ceil asked softly, and finally her husband looked at her and replied with an almost defiant impatience.

"No, I won't, because this is politics and it's a practical business and I need their help. But I'm going to get it on my terms, because I'm in a position to do it that way. They need me more than I need them. There isn't any alternative to Ted Jason: there are plenty of alternatives to them. They can be split. A lot of them will go for me, anyway. Now, Bob," he said, abruptly all business, "I want you to sit down with that unholy three sometime later this afternoon and coordinate plans with them. And get in the College Kids for Jason, the Volunteers for Jason, the Former Knoxmen for Jason, and the rest of them, and all of you sit down and get it organized. I think we should have virtually around-the-clock demonstrations from now on. Somebody should be whooping it up for Jason in a definite, organized fashion somewhere in this city every minute of every day and every night. The first thing is a big show at the Palace of Fine Arts before, during, and after Dolly Munson's party tonight. Have a few people crash it, if they can, but keep it under control. I don't want any rough stuff, and you can impress that on Fred and his friends. O.K.?"

"I believe," Walter Dobius said, "that they would like to talk to you personally about it."

"I'm not ready to talk to them yet. Starting tomorrow morning I'm going to have to be talking to fifty delegations as well as a lot of other people, and somewhere along the line I'll talk to them. Right now, I'm going to stay aloof and get a little rest. I didn't sleep very well last night and I intend to get a nap before Dolly's party. . . . You're welcome to stay, however," he added politely to a Walter becoming increasingly watchful and still, "to see the opening with us. Bob, turn it on, it must be almost time."

And time it was, as in his office and in his opponent's, all over the city, all over the country, all over the world, suddenly on the screen the convention took form. First came the shots of the outside of the Cow Palace, the banners flying, the flags snapping, the delegates and spectators hurrying and pushing in. There was a small Knox parade, a small Jason parade. There were placards, not terribly inspired, but willing: CONSCIENCE MUST DECIDE THE ISSUE: END WAR WITH JASON . . . HAS GOVERNMENT GOT YOU BILIOUS? TAKE EX-KNOX—TRY JASON! . . . KNOX EQUALS HONOR—THEY GO TOGETHER . . . WE'LL STAY FREE WITH KNOX FOR V.P.! There were souvenir stands and barkers and long, sleek limousines driving up. There was fog beginning to come over the hills from the ocean. There was excitement.

And then inside to the great hall itself, the orchestra playing "Dixie," the faces of Hudson, Knox, and Jason dancing everywhere on poles and placards in time to the music, the banners flying, the streamers stretching across the rafters, the escaped balloons floating around them, the party dignitaries gathering on the long ramp out to the podium, the enormous pictures of the party's heroes on the wall, the spectators in the galleries eager and ready, the delegates taking their seats on the floor, the newsmen and TV cameramen jamming the aisles, moving restlessly up and down, the hissing, rustling sound of a thousand typewriters, the electric tension and excitement, the insistent, incessant, pulsating roar of sound—sound—sound . . .

And then the temporary chairman and keynoter, veteran Governor of Kentucky grown gray in his party's service, raising the gavel and bringing it down with a thundering crash; and the mellow tones of the Bluegrass bellowing, "I hereby declare this great convention of this great party to be in session!" And a roar of applause, quickly silenced as the band played the national anthem, the vast assemblage stood silent, and the first churchman—a Jew, who would be followed in due course at later sessions by a Protestant, a Catholic, and a Mormon, so that all God's chillun would be happy—delivered the invocation.

Then the ritual disposition of minor details of necessary business, the resolutions of thanks to the host city, to the arrangements committee, to the chairman of this and the chairman of that, the resolutions of praise and tribute to the departed great, the chance to reward all the good little party workers, each of whom in his or her turn was allowed to step to the microphone and shout his little portion of the ritual into the great sea of faces before him and receive its good-natured, perfunctory applause.

And the waves of competing applause and boos, still basically good-natured but with an increasing edge to them as the convention moved inexorably forward, when the names of Jason or Knox were tossed slyly out by their partisans at the podium. And the applause—"dutiful, troubled, and uneasy," Walter and his friends gravely interpreted it for the millions who were watching—that rolled up at each mention of "our great President" or "our great leader."

And the only really solid opportunities for partisanship, the arrivals of the families: Patsy, Valuela, Selena, and Herbert taking their seats in a box on one side to great shouts, cheers, spotlightings, and picture-snappings; and Beth, Crystal, and Hal taking theirs in a box on the other side, to great shouts, cheers, spotlightings, and picture-snappings. And surprisingly and electrifyingly, her entrance causing great excitement in the press and among the more knowledgeable delegates, startled wonderment and concern in two headquarters which found her appearance completely unexpected and quite disturbing, (for who knew what it meant at this particular early moment)—Lucille Hudson, all alone, rosy, dimpled, and smiling, waving to the roar of greeting that went up as she was led forward to the podium to take a bow.

Then the last minor resolution offered by the last minor party-worker-to-be-rewarded, and the voice of the Bluegrass once again: "This convention will now stand in recess until 2 P.M. tomorrow!" And everybody pouring out into the late afternoon sharpness to go back over the freeways to the city, to the banging bands, the great hotels, the lobby conferences, the corridor gossip, the drinks, the comparings of notes, the guesses and speculations and rumors; the exciting knowledge that tomorrow the real blood-letting would begin; and then, finally, the going out, showered and lotioned and dressed to the nines, into the cool foggy night, the drive to the Palace of Fine Arts, and Dolly's party.

There were a great many, of course, who were not invited; who went out into the excited streets, in the sharp, exhilarating night, under the scudding fog-black skies, to ride the Powell Street cable car to the Top o' the Mark or the outside elevator at the Crown Room of the Fairmont, and then on to Fishermen's Wharf, there to stand in line for hours waiting to eat; who met one another, laughing and exchanging cordial greetings or cordial hostilities depending upon who wore which campaign button, at Ernie's or the Blue Fox or Jack's or Tadich's or Omar Khayyam's or Johnny Kan's or Mingei-Ya or Ritz Old Poodle Dog, or whatever; who then emerged to wander along the streets or back to their hotels, well-oiled, raucous, good-natured, and happy.

These were what the press liked to refer to as "rank-and-file delegates," already, though they would have been offended to know it, statistics: carefully annotated cards in files at Knox and Jason headquarters, impersonal digits on big charts where numbers were written excitedly, erased forlornly, put back with whooping joy, erased with growing disillusion, put back with—

These were the dark, mysterious, unknowable herd, whose motivations the analysts thought they could understand, whose reactions the experts thought they could predict, whose final decision the managers thought they could rely upon—who yet remained, right down to the very last minute, no matter how analyzed, no matter how interpreted, no matter how predicted, dark, mysterious, and unknowable, possessing the power, at any second of wild emotion or bitter reaction, to overturn all plans, cancel all triumphs, blast all hopes.

Tonight, unaware of many things moving beneath the surface of the waters, they were generally happy and lighthearted; and of course quite a few of them did get to Dolly's party, some by invitation, some (like the rather disorganized group of Jason demonstrators who swirled angrily out of the night, forced their way through the door, and were promptly overwhelmed with drinks and food ordered by their quick-thinking hostess) in less formal fashion. There they were privileged to socialize with many a famous figure.

Mary Buttner Baffleburg of Pennsylvania and her three lovely sisters were there, Lizzie Hanson McWharter of Kansas stunning in a stringy gown of yellow, Anna Hooper Bigelow of New Hampshire smashing in a gaunt-sized purple sheath, Esmé Harbellow Stryke of California eye-stopping in a black silk-and-sequin concoction as pursed and pinched and expensive-looking as she was. The Smitters, the Smatters, the Smutters, and the Smotters were there (the Smetters had relatives in Berkeley and had to cross the Bay for dinner but would be back later, Vangie assured Dolly); Roger P. Croy of Oregon was sidling about, Senator August and Representative Swarthman came in together, the Maudulaynes, Krishna Khaleel, and Raoul and Celestine Barre could be seen circulating busily with others of the diplomatic corps. All in all, it was a striking, distinguished, and significant group, "the cream of the convention" as the San Francisco *Examiner* put it, who gathered more than fifteen hundred strong in the handsome room where two orchestras played softly, and where the constant yelps of greeting, the rising babble of voices, and the steady clink of ice against glass gave proof through the night that the political processes of the world's greatest democracy were functioning smoothly and well—that The Opportunity Was Being Seized, The Challenge Was Being Met, The Future Was Being Faced, and The Great Problems Which Confront Us Were Being Successfully Overcome.

If there were some attending who had a more serious aspect—if the Speaker and the Majority Leader looked, now and then, a little worried—if Tom August and Jawbone Swarthman looked a trifle belligerent—if the two candidates for Vice President and their families watched one another somewhat warily behind the outward show of cordiality they presented to the avid, insistent eyes of all around them—if everyone appeared to be treating Lucille Hudson as though she were a case of dynamite being passed gingerly from hand to hand around the room—these were things of which the happy revelers in the heart of the city, and even a good many at the party, were entirely unaware. Tomorrow in the newspapers and on the air they would learn surprising things about the evening and would ask one another with an envious dismay, "Was *that* going on? We didn't know about *that!*" But it is unlikely that, even had they been sober enough to notice, they would have known about it. This was the inner business of the convention, the sort of thing that always takes place behind the screen of rollicking bands and roistering delegates, behind the backs and only rarely before the eyes of the innocent or at least uninformed pawns in the game who get moved about by its masters—as long as they allow its masters to move them.

So it was that several separate conversations came together to make a whole; that the Speaker and the Majority Leader, just happening to step aside for five minutes privately with the First Lady, discovered that she did indeed bear words of recommendation and even compromise from her husband; that Secretary Knox and Governor Jason, posing together with a dutiful show of good-fellowship upon their almost simultaneous entries, found themselves approached separately later, Orrin by Senator Munson, Ted by the Speaker, with Lucille's suggestions; that Cullee Hamilton, dancing with Sarah Johnson, still later found the Speaker murmuring in his ear, while Lafe Smith, happily getting reacquainted with Mabel Anderson in an evening that was turning out to be quite enchanted for them both, received the same message from Bob Munson; and that Joe Smitters and Bob Smutters and Roger P. Croy and even Mary Buttner Baffleburg, Lizzie Hanson McWharter, Anna Hooper Bigelow, and Esmé Harbellow Stryke were permitted to receive intimations, before the evening was over, that something was in the wind; and that Walter Dobius and his colleagues, moving diligently through the crush buttonholing, questioning, hunch-gathering, came rapidly to the alarming conclusion that bad people might be cooking up something that could conceivably hurt their hero, and rushed accordingly to their typewriters and microphones to sound the tocsin and call upon all Right Thinkers to come to the aid of the righteous before a carefully planned steam-roller went off the tracks.

HINT PRESIDENT OFFERS COMPROMISE ON JASON-KNOX COMMITTEE FEUDS, the first-edition morning-paper headlines said when the jovial throng, considerably better-fed and better-lubricated than it had been five hours before, began to straggle from the Palace of Fine Arts around 1 A.M. . . . JASON FORCES SEE AT-

TEMPT TO UNDERCUT GOVERNOR . . . KNOX
DELEGATE STEAL (no longer in quotation marks)
MAY GET HUDSON SUPPORT . . . KNOX WAR
PLANK (similarly unfavored with quotes) MAY BE
FORCED INTO PLATFORM . . . CONVENTION
TAKES PRO-WAR TURN AS KNOX STRENGTH
GROWS.

"SAN FRANCISCO—What is happening here in this
lovely city [Walter Dobius typed swiftly at 3 A.M. in the
press room at the Hilton, where a wandering *Life* photographer conveniently came upon, and recorded, genius at
work for next week's convention roundup] is so old and
obvious a replay of the shabbiest closet dramas of American politics as to leave one almost as stale and jaded as the
thing itself.

"The old pros are moving in on the young idealists, and
the young idealists may soon find themselves fighting
back-to-wall to rescue their young, idealistic candidate
from one of those murderous deals that sicken democracy
and move it some appreciable distance further on the road
to its ultimate self-destruction.

"Secretly and surreptitiously, with an almost Renais-
sance cleverness that goes surprisingly with his rather monotonous middle-class mentality, the President of the
United States has apparently sent his wife on ahead of him
as a sort of advance guard to prepare the way for his own
direct interference in a convention he stoutly proclaimed he
would not control. The First Lady has not heretofore been
considered to belong to that history-shaping sorority that
includes the first Elizabeth, Catherine the Great, and Madame Pompadour. Yet unlikely as it seems, this is the role
her husband apparently has assigned her. She has performed it, and from it events of dire potential to the hopes
and fortunes of Edward M. Jason have immediately begun
to flow.

"Now it appears that an attempt by supporters of the
Secretary of State to assume control of the delegations of
Ohio and Mississippi may succeed—because of a compro-
mise proposed by Harley M. Hudson.

"Now it appears that a foreign policy plank that betrays
international morality, defies collective security, and gives
endorsement to two of the most inexcusable and foredoomed interventions in American history may be riveted

into the platform of this convention—at the insistence of Orrin Knox and Harley M. Hudson.

"Now it appears possible—only, at this moment, just possible, but nonetheless possible—that Edward M. Jason may be defeated for the vice presidential nomination, and the candidacy of one of the most devious Secretaries of State ever to grace the Cabinet may thereby win an endorsement that could permit him to succeed at some later moment, without hindrance or challenge, to the Presidency.

"It is a somber hour here in this delightful metropolis, perhaps the most gracious and charming, sharing only with Washington the title of most beautiful, of all American cities.

"In Gorotoland and Panama the wars drag on, increasingly wasteful, increasingly deadly, as the President—and Orrin Knox—step up the American commitment to fifty thousand troops in Gorotoland, seventy-five thousand in Panama—and no end in sight.

"In the United Nations, United States prestige sinks ever lower, as the President—and Orrin Knox—reject attempt after attempt by its desperately worried member-states to bring about negotiations that could end the bloodshed.

"Every day the nation is taken further into a darkness from which only the most enlightened and liberal leadership can extract it.

"Now the only possible means of securing that leadership is threatened. The one man who could bring some restoration of sanity into Administration councils—the one man who, should events take at some time some tragic turn that placed upon him unsuspected burdens, could return America to the high point of influence, honor, and prestige that America possessed before little men betrayed her—may be defeated here in San Francisco.

"It is a time for all Americans to search their hearts and decide what they would like this convention to do—what their own futures and those of their children and their children's children, make it imperative that the convention do.

"It is a time to send the word crashing across this great land, over forests and rivers and plains and peaks, until it rolls at last all the way from the Atlantic to the Golden Gate like the thunderclap of ages.

"It is a time to abandon concepts of 'fairness' and 'honor' which have up to now hampered and hindered the Governor of California and his supporters. It is a time to be as ruthless and tough as Orrin Knox and his master in the White House.

"It is a time to act."

3

"DID YOU SEE this God-damned thing of Walter's?" Helen-Anne Carrew demanded six hours later when, a little bleary-eyed—as who wasn't? After all, it was the second day of the convention and from now on each succeeding morning was going to be considerably more bleary-eyed than the last, for everybody—she happened upon Bob Leffingwell, eating breakfast alone in the coffee shop of the Fairmont. "I swear I think he's going crazy again. Of all the open invitations to—kill Harley—or start a revolution—or something. What *is* the matter with the man?"

"I don't know," Bob Leffingwell said, coming out of a brown study with an obvious effort. "Here, sit down and let me buy you breakfast. What do you hear?"

"I hear things are going to get very ugly," she said, taking the chair he offered, staring around the room already filling with delegates and newsmen. He could see her nodding to a few, ignoring others, making quick mental notes of who was eating with whom, calculating, as all Washington correspondents do, the significance of various combinations. "I suppose you know—of course you do—that COMFORT, DEFY, and KEEP have consolidated their headquarters at the Hilton this morning. They're already out in the streets in full force in front of all the hotels and from Union Square on up the hill here, and they aren't being very pleasant—I suppose with your connivance."

"That's not exactly a friendly word," he said with a fairly good attempt at a smile as the waitress came up. "What'll you have?"

"Just orange juice, toast, and coffee, thanks. I have to

keep my girlish figure. . . . Say," she added, pausing to really study him for the first time. *"You're* not feeling very happy today. What's the matter?"

"Oh," he said, and shrugged. "Mary Baffleburg, I suppose. My past—still my present, and apparently destined to be my future as well."

"That was rough," she agreed. "But," she added with an impartial judicious thoughtfulness that robbed it of much of its sting, "you deserved it—and surely you expected it, at some time or other. The only thing to do is ride it out. Your friends know you regret it, and they include a surprising number of people—even Orrin Knox, I think, and obviously the Speaker. So to hell with the rest of them. . . . But that isn't all that's bothering you, is it? Something else. . . . What's the matter, is Ted really losing ground? Is Walter really right? Have we all got to rise up from the Atlantic to the Gate to stop big, bad Orrin? *Must* we shoot Harley?"

He shook his head.

"I think we're holding very well"—he smiled and gestured to the headlines in the papers she carried, he carried, everyone carried—"in spite of the helpful scare-campaign launched for us by Walter and his friends. Ted and Orrin this morning are holding at about the same level they were last night, I think. . . . No," he said, suddenly serious again, "I'm as worried about the mood as you are, Helen-Anne. I think it's going to be very disturbing, before we're through. Mary Baffleburg attacked me, but that was just an expression of something much deeper underlying this convention. That was an advance warning, whether she knows it or not in her fat little pudding-head. There's something very nasty waiting to break out, I think. Contrary to my man's confidence about it, I'm not so sure it can be controlled once it gets loose."

"My man won't start it, sweetie."

"Nor will mine, at least consciously. But there are people who feel bitter enough so that it may not take much."

"What can we do to stop it?"

He frowned.

"I don't know. That's what disturbs me. Maybe"—he said somberly—"maybe the best thing to do is just get as far away from it as possible."

She snorted.

"Hell's fire, that's no solution. I'm amazed at you, Bob

Leffingwell, with all your history as a fighter in this government! You know perfectly well that's no solution at all. You're the last man I ever thought would break and run."

He smiled a twisted little smile.

"Maybe Mary won her point." Then he sighed and straightened up. "No, of course I don't mean that. But I am disturbed, Helen-Anne, genuinely so, as you are. And I don't know what to do about it. Ted thinks he can control COMFORT and DEFY and KEEP, but they represent powerful forces and now they've worked out an alliance that's going to be terribly difficult to keep in hand. And violence begets violence, even though Orrin, too, of course, will do his best to prevent it. It isn't going to be that easy. I can feel it in the air."

"Maybe," she said thoughtfully, nodding an absent greeting to Esmé Harbellow Stryke, who had come in with the Smetters and Roger P. Croy to take a table across the room, "maybe you should reconsider—where you do want to stand. Possibly you don't want to get completely away . . . but just to the other side."

"Orrin?" he said, and for a second she thought she had misjudged him and gone too far. Then he went on, and she knew with a good deal of relief that she had not. "No, I don't think so." He stared at her with a thoughtful frown. "I don't see how I could. . . . I really don't see how I could." He smiled with a sudden genuine humor. "He's as bad as Mary Baffleburg. . . . Of course," he said presently, and she held her breath and concentrated carefully on her coffee, trying not to give the slightest hint of her growing excitement, "he has much to recommend him. He was only doing what was right about my nomination—what I invited. I don't feel as bitter toward him as I did. . . . And of course the President—" Then he broke off and it was all she could do not to blurt out, "The President *what?*" But somehow she managed to keep still (Good girl, Helen-Anne! she told herself. Oh, God-damned good *girl,* we didn't know you *could* keep your God-damned mouth shut). But he only said, "Well—" briskly, and she knew the moment was over.

But it was enough, she crowed to herself, it was enough, and did *she* have a scoop she couldn't use!

"I must not," he went on thoughtfully after a moment, "as the Governor of California puts it, use the convention as a stage on which to admire myself playing Hamlet.

What I've got to do now is figure out how to control our new-found allies, because it's going to be tough. I think we've all got to help on that one."

"I repeat, it isn't my man who will start it."

"Well, tell him to warn against it," he said, "and I'll try to get Ted to do likewise. Maybe that will help. Are you working for him now?"

"Not yet," she said, gathering up her newspapers, her bulging purse, her scribble-filled pad and worn-down pencils. "Not until he wins the nomination, sweetie. Then I will."

"He isn't going to win," he said, waving to the waitress for the check as she stood up and he stood with her to say goodbye.

"Sure he is," she said, and took a chance: "And you're going to help him."

"Oh, no!" he said with a laugh. "Oh, no. Don't go spreading anything like that."

"I won't spread it, but I'll be expecting it."

"Don't wait up nights," he advised. She laughed as she turned away.

"About one more, I think. That ought to just about do it."

But he only laughed back at her and made a shooing motion with his hands. When she glanced back from the door he was paying the check, his face serious and withdrawn again. All right, buster, she thought: you wait and see what you do in the next twenty-four hours. Unless Helen-Anne misses her guess you're going to be making quite a bit of news before this convention is over. And Helen-Anne doesn't usually miss.

"You two look very serious," Cullee said with a smile in the Oak Room at the St. Francis. "Is that any way to act at a reunion breakfast?"

"Our second reunion breakfast," Mabel Anderson said with an answering smile. "We had one yesterday."

"And," Lafe said gravely, "we will have one tomorrow —and tomorrow—and tomorrow—and—Mabel, I don't think you've met Sarah Johnson?"

"No, I haven't," she said, extending her hand. "Are you working on Cullee's campaign?"

"I'm working on Cullee," Sarah said with a laugh as she sat down.

"About got me, too," the Congressman said, giving her a satisfied look as he took the fourth chair. "I think the title at the moment is secretary to the candidate in my campaign for the Senate, but as soon as I win and get rid of my other encumbrances, I'm going to take on Sarah."

"Congratulations," Mabel said. "Are you going to win?"

Cullee shrugged.

"Who knows? I beat Ray Smith for the nomination and that isn't bad, beating an incumbent." He chuckled. "Even if it was by only nineteen thousand votes out of five million cast. . . ." The chuckle faded. "It isn't going to be easy, Mabel, I can tell you that. California's very divided on the war issue right now. I may just lose, if the other side decides to become the peace party. I don't think my opponent will, himself, but he may not be a free agent."

"And you are?"

He smiled.

"You're quite the cross-examiner. Watch out, Lafe, she may give you a hard time."

"It'll be good for me," the Senator from Iowa said complacently. "It's a good question, too. Are you?"

Cullee got a stubborn look.

"I'm acting as though I am. Some of 'em tell me I've got to cut and trim because of that nineteen thousand squeakthrough, but I tell 'em, no, sir, I've got the nomination and I'm the candidate and if anybody doesn't like it, he can lump it."

"That's what I'm telling them in Iowa," Lafe said. "We may be taking quite a gamble, old buddy, but I'd rather do it that way than take a stand I couldn't live with later."

"Aren't they noble?" Sarah said innocently to Mabel.

"They are noble," Mabel agreed innocently with Sarah.

Cullee laughed.

"We operate on a simpler level. We're just little Senators. I guess when you get up to the top you have to make come concessions and acquire a few peculiar bedfellows, isn't that right, Lafe?"

"So I hear. What's the news from your old pal LeGage?"

"Him!" Cullee said, scowling at the thought of the chairman of DEFY, his onetime Howard University roommate and bitterest friend-enemy. "He was after me again last night—came to the room and we had a terrible row. He wants me to join this big movement for Ted he's working up with Van Ackerman and Kleinfert."

"But you're not for Ted," Lafe suggested.

"No, I'm not for Ted! I issued a statement right after I got the nomination"—he laughed suddenly—"that's how noble I am, Sal, I waited until I got it—that I was leaving the door open as to what I'd do here. But it was pretty obvious which way I thought I'd walk when I went through that door."

"And 'Gage couldn't change you?" Mabel asked.

"He couldn't change me if he had the last drink on earth and I was a dying man," Cullee said flatly. "If I were Ted," he said somberly, "I'd damned well watch out for what I was getting into."

"Maybe you should warn him," Lafe said.

"I'm going to see him, sometime today. I'll tell him. I don't expect it'll do any good, but I'll tell him."

"Maybe it had better be before the committees meet," Lafe said, "if you got an assignment last night like I did."

"Oh, did you?" Cullee asked with a pleased smile. "Yes, the Speaker came by and gave me the word. I'm on-stage in Platform Committee in about one hour from now."

"And I in Credentials," Lafe said. He smiled with a frank enjoyment. "I'm looking forward to it. I'm not sure Orrin's going to win but it will be a chance to state a few home truths."

"In Platform Committee, too," Cullee said. "Too bad you girls can't come see me, but I guess you can go listen to Lafe, all right."

"Why don't we?" Mabel said. "I have a young lady who was still sleeping when I got up, so I asked one of the maids to sit for me, but I'll go get her and give her a quick breakfast and then we'll meet you at the Hilton, Sarah, O.K.?"

"My pleasure," Sarah said. "I'll be there."

"Excuse me, then," Mabel said. "I'll see you soon. Thanks, Lafe."

"*My* pleasure," Lafe said.

"How's it going?" Cullee asked as they watched her, a pleasant girl, a little dowdy, perhaps, but obviously as nice as she could be, go through the door, saying hello to a couple of her fellow delegates from Utah as she went.

"No rush . . . no rush at all. We've got a lifetime."

"Ho!" Cullee said with a smile. "Like that, eh?"

"Like that," Lafe said quietly. Then he smiled. "If you'll

tell me what the Speaker told you to do I'll tell you what Bob Munson told me to do."

Cullee laughed.

"Oh, no, you don't! We've got secrets, you and I. Big, dark secrets."

"Which boil down to: *fight like hell*," the Senator from Iowa said. His expression became serious. "I only hope they work."

Congressman Hamilton nodded somberly.

"I only hope Ted's people let them work."

The President, too, hoped they would work, as he sat at his desk in the White House and, like most of his countrymen, tried to do his job with half his mind on the little box blabbing from San Francisco. Something was rising there he did not like. Twice in the last half-hour there had been shots of Powell Street from Union Square to Nob Hill, companion glimpses of the major hotel lobbies: in each the demonstrators stood solidly packed, virtually expressionless, barely moving, hardly speaking, silent, hostile, and, yes—menacing. The easygoing college kids of yesterday, the happy delegates who formed the impromptu parades and whooped it up in the convention's opening hours, seemed to be still there but pushed back, shoved aside, elbowed out, relegated to the outer fringes where the cameras still caught them from time to time, but only briefly, sporadically, almost absentmindedly. Some people might still be having a good time, the ubiquitous lenses seemed to be saying, but they were rapidly becoming a minority. Not since the pictures of the defacing of the U.S. delegation headquarters at the UN three months ago, the President thought, had such grim and unpleasant white and black faces appeared upon the screen—and at least those had been screaming and yelling and there had been some animation, no matter how forced and phony. These were deliberately cold and impassive, deliberately ominous; pompous and childish in their ostentatious posing, yet with the pomposity and childishness of monstrous idiot infants who might at any moment go mad. And their banners were all of war, and of the fear of war, and of the hatreds of vicious minds let loose, as though their masters had pried open some giant manhole cover and out of it they had crawled from the sewers of the race to hold their savage placards denouncing Orrin and calling with a threatening insistence for Edward Jason.

"What in thunderation is going on out there?" he asked aloud, looking out suddenly at the beautiful lawn sloping to the Ellipse, silent and somnolent in Washington's sweltering July. A squirrel bounced across his vision, bound on its secret business from tree to tree, a cardinal called hurriedly and was still. He could not see the distant cars or hear the muted hum of the half-deserted summer city. He might have been one of his predecessors a hundred years and more ago, in some older, sleepier, perhaps as difficult, yet basically much gentler, time.

Not so, apparently, the convention of his party, which was being transformed before his eyes and the eyes of the world into—well, he didn't know into what. A Nuremberg rally, he was tempted to say, except that the bland voice accompanying the pictures (Frankly Unctuous the Anchor Man, using the same plum-pudding tones with which he had commented upon conventions, moon shots, astronauts, racial crises and other phenomena for twenty years) assured him suavely that it was not so.

These new demonstrators, the voice said confidently, "seem to have sprung spontaneously from the three democratic groups that are gradually coalescing behind Governor Jason as the forces of Secretary Knox prepare to make their all-out bid to win this convention." These groups, the voice explained, were "COMFORT, DEFY and KEEP—a combination that under other circumstances might well cause surprise, since their domestic politics range from the most liberal to what some might call the most conservative." But, the voice went on smoothly, "their cooperation here is being brought about by an apparently genuine fear of the foreign policies of the Hudson administration—which might almost be termed [and Frankly Unctuous smiled a trifle coyly] the Hudson-*Knox* administration—and a determination to aid, if they can, the man they believe—rightly or wrongly [and again he smiled], we would not presume to say—to be more genuinely concerned with America's safety and good name than either the President or the Secretary of State." The lifeless faces of the new demonstrators, the voice went on, "if they seem somewhat more serious than some faces you saw on the screen yesterday, may be due to the fact that the convention itself is becoming more serious, as delegates begin to grasp that they are truly charged here with a great responsibility—to choose, in effect, between two policies: one which many believe can lead only to deeper involvement and greater war—and one which can ultimately lead to a restored and revitalized American prestige in a peacefully united world."

In fact, Frankly Unctuous concluded with an approving blandness, the injection of "this new, united, democratic force behind Governor Jason may perhaps guarantee that this convention will truly be what the President has said he wants it to be—a genuine expression of grassroots American democracy at its most vigorous and thrilling. This may, indeed, be America's finest hour."

So it must be, the President thought tartly as the plum-pudding tones died away, the shrewd, patronizing face faded from the screen, and the cameras moved once again along the grim, sullen ranks up Powell Street, because television says it's so. And if television says it's so, then everybody must believe it, right?

On a sudden impulse—though he had talked to them only a couple of hours ago, and to Lucille more recently than that—he picked up the direct telephone to Senator Munson's rooms at the St. Francis. (JASON FORCES CHARGE SECRET COMMAND POST IN MUNSON SUITE DOMINATING CONVENTION, the Washington *Post* had cried this morning, and the view—halloo had been taken up by most of the others by this time.) His voice was disturbed but determined as he asked Bob and the Speaker for their opinions, received them, and began to make his plans accordingly.

Even as he put down the phone and turned back to the set, a bulletin appeared upon the screen. KNOX DEMONSTRATOR SEVERELY BEATEN IN CLASH AT PALACE HOTEL, it said: followed by a phalanx of grim faces meeting a straggling group of college boys, running figures, contorted bodies, raised clubs, viciously pounding placards, and then a bloodied and battered face, perhaps nineteen, hanging from a limp and dangling body being hastily carried away by police.

The plum-pudding tones, slightly shaken but still suave, were back immediately to assure the country:

"It is believed the incident occurred when the youthful Knox demonstrator made some joking comment to the

Jason group standing in the lobby of the Palace. The remark apparently was misinterpreted, but our reporter, who was standing close by, tells us he is convinced there was no real malice in the spontaneous and probably quite unthinking reaction of the Jason backers. They were apparently just carried away for a moment by the feeling here, which is beginning to run"—and Frankly Unctuous gave his comfortable, soothing smile—"a little high, as you can see."

"I certainly can," the President said grimly to George Washington, whose eye he happened to catch as he swung away from the set with an angry concern. "And I'm going to do something about it, too," he promised George, who looked back with his rather prim and disapproving stare from the wall and offered his successor only the memory of courage and integrity that always enfolded him. It might be enough, the President thought stoutly, if he could only manage to apply its lessons here.

In their press conferences at ten, both candidates discussed the same general topics with the shoving, pushing reporters who jammed their respective offices to overflowing. Each claimed at least six hundred sure votes as of that moment. The Secretary was asked again to explain the Administration's position in Gorotoland and Panama and did so in blunt, uncompromising terms. Governor Jason was questioned on the same subject and managed to get through a graceful little discussion of the world's need for peaceful negotiation without once mentioning either conflict. Both were asked about violence in the convention, both pledged themselves to oppose it whenever and wherever it cropped up. KNOX REAFFIRMS PRO-WAR POSITION, the Knox headlines said. JASON CALLS FOR "FAIR-PLAY CONVENTION," HITS "EXTREMISTS," the Jason headlines said. Their questioners hurried back to their vigils at the Platform and Credentials Committees. The convention tumbled on, steadily picking up speed and tension as it went.

"Ladies and gentlemen," Chairman Bill Smatters of Atlanta said calmly at the Fairmont, looking around the closed and tightly guarded room at Esmé Harbellow Stryke, Roger P. Croy, Senator August, Congressman Swarthman, and the rest, "this committee this morning faces the duty of completing work on this platform so that it can go to the convention this afternoon. It seems to me, therefore, that it is about time to conclude discussion of the foreign policy plank, which is really the only remaining issue, and take some votes."

"That's all right with me, Mr. Chairman," Roger P. Croy said in his lazy, homespun drawl, "providing it is understood that we vote first on the committee language, then on the so-called Knox substitute."

"Mr. Chairman," said Cullee Hamilton, towering up suddenly out of the audience, "I would like to speak to that point, if I might."

"Mr. Chairman," Rogert P. Croy said blandly, "I don't believe the Congressman is a member of this committee, is he? I think the distinguished National Committeewoman from California, Mrs. Stryke, is quite competent to speak for her great state here."

"Esmé," Cullee suggested, "defend me."

"For what purpose," she inquired in a hesitant voice, "do you want recognition?"

"I want to speak to this plank in the platform," Cullee said patiently. "Now, surely, you aren't going to join a conspiracy to silence a Congressman from California, your candidate for the United States Senate, are you?"

"Now, Mr. Chairman," Roger P. Croy said with a show of annoyance, "I don't believe this committee should permit the distinguished committeewoman to be bullied by the Congressman, here. I really think we must maintain order."

"Nobody's violating order here, Mr. Chairman," Cullee said, calmly but allowing a hint of anger to enter his voice, "and nobody, except the delegate from Oregon who is trying to silence me, is doing any bullying. Esmé, dear," he added, "I think you'd better decide whether you're siding with me or with this gentleman. I'll want to tell the press about it if you aren't siding with your own candidate for United States Senator."

"Why," she said hastily, her pinched little face looking flustered, her shrewd little dark eyes for once perturbed and defensive, "I can say to my distinguished fellow delegate from California, our great candidate for the United States Senate, that of course I am for him. What else would I be, Mr. Chairman?" she demanded indignantly. "Whatever else would I be? Of course you can speak, Congressman. I ask the committee to please allow our distinguished Congressman Hamilton, the next United States Senator from California, to speak to us on the pending amendment—plant—substitute—whatever it is!"

"I'm sure the committee has no objection, Congressman," Bill Smatters from Atlanta said blandly. "You-all just tell us all about it, now, and we-all will just sit here and listen."

"Thank you, Mr. Chairman," Cullee said, refusing to rise to the bait offered by Bill Smatters' deliberately patronizing tone, "and thank you, Esmé. I can't tell you," he said, keeping it solemn, "how much your support means to me. Mr. Chairman, my friend from Oregon, that great distinguished former Governor, Mr. Croy, calls the language pending before this committee 'the Knox substitute.' That's the label the press would like to have us use here, so they can attack the Secretary of State with it. We know differently, don't we? This is the Hudson substitute—or rather, I should say it isn't a substitute at all. It is what your President wants in this platform. Anything else is the substitute. *This* is the official language."

"Now, just a minute, Mr. Chairman," Roger P. Croy said angrily, while stirrings and grumblings came from around the table. "I'll just ask the distinguished chairmen of the Senate Foreign Relations and the House Foreign Affairs committees of the Congress whether this language the committee has been getting ready to approve—up until yesterday when the Majority Leader of the Senate barged in here with this new disruptive language—I'll ask Senator August and Congressman Swarthman whether they agree that the President's language is the only language and we can't discuss anything else. How about it?"

He swung demandingly upon Tom August, who quivered a little and then replied in the aggrieved voice he adopted when he felt he was being pushed into too much controversy.

"It is my belief," he said, "that the language in the tentative draft before this committee is the language a majority of this committee wants."

"That's right, Mr. Chairman," Jawbone Swarthman spoke up from down the table next to Esmé Stryke. "I will say to my dear old friend from the House, there, whom I hope to see along with me in the United States Senate next January, that this *is* the case here. We tried to tell the distinguished Majority Leader that yesterday but he wouldn't believe us. I guess now he's sent you to do the same thing, but it won't work, Cullee, it just won't. These folks are so riled up—this whole convention is so riled up—that any language stronger than what we've got here is going to cause a terrible rumpus, Cullee, it really is, now."

"The President is aware that there is some division in the committee and in the convention," Cullee said calmly, "but the only thing that matters is that he *is* the President, he's our candidate for re-election, and we've got to stand by him. That's all there is to it. Let me read this language again, and then let's stand by our President. Anything else will blast this convention wide open and make us lose the election. We've got to present a united front. We can't win divided."

"I would suggest to the Credentials Committee," Lafe Smith said quietly at the Hilton, "that unless we can work out some reasonable compromise on seating these delegations, the convention may get into a situation of such bitterness that it could have serious effects on the campaign and the election. After all, we're here to select a winning ticket and back our President for re-election. We can't jeopardize his success because of a petty squabble over what is essentially a vice presidential matter. We can't expect to win if we're divided."

"Mr. Chairman," Mary Buttner Baffleburg said, "it seems to me every convention that's ever held, sooner or later we get soft-soaped with this talk that we've got to bury all our troubles or we might hurt the President. I say there's a matter of principle involved—"

"Hear, hear!" said Lizzie Hanson McWharter, barely able to keep her eyes open after last night's partying but full of combativeness still.

"A matter of principle," Mary Baffleburg repeated firmly. "This is no 'petty matter' as the Senator from Iowa calls it. This is a deliberate attempt to steal delegates—not," she said, her face flushing and her voice rising sharply, "by Orrin Knox, who's the most honest man that ever lived, but by a slick, conniving schemer from Sacramento that the press seems to let get away with blaming everything he does on Orrin Knox! That's who's stealing, Mr. Chairman!" she cried as the committee began to stir, the audience leaned forward with excited anticipation, the press went to work, and the television cameras trained upon her pudgy, indignant face. "That's where the problem is! Tell the Senator to go talk to Governor Jason! He's the smart boy behind all this!"

"Mrs. Baffleburg," Old Joe Smitters from Ashtabula said with as much force as he could muster after staying up until 3 A.M. drinking with some old cronies in the Texas delegation, "I must remind you that these proceedings are being carried to the nation by television and we should conduct ourselves with some dignity here. Now, the Senator, as I understand it, is about to propose a compromise which is agreeable to both sides—"

"That's a lie, Mr. Chairman!" Mary Baffleburg cried. "That's a lie!"

"The distingushed delegate from Pennsylvania," Lafe Smith said with some asperity, "is awfully free with her charges of lying these days, it seems to me. Maybe she has information I don't have, but I have been given to understand by both campaign chairmen, less than half an hour ago, that the proposal I am about to suggest is agreeable to both sides."

"Campaign chairmen!" Mary Baffleburg cried scornfully. "That's the trouble with these conventions, Mr. Chairman! We're always being told what somebody higher up wants! We're always being pushed around! What do the delegates want, that's what I want to know? You feel the same way, Mr. Chairman, you know you do, we all do! What do *we* want, for a change? That's what I'd like to know!"

And with this there did seem to be general agreement, for from all along the table and throughout the room, regardless of favorite candidate, there came sounds of approval and endorsement. Apparently Mary Baffleburg was speaking the popular voice. Lafe realized suddenly that this was not going to be so easy.

"The suggestion has been made," he said carefully, as even Old Joe Smitters stared at him with a hostile gaze, "that rather than have a bitter fight on the convention floor this afternoon, which we all know would have very serious effects upon the party, the committee should agree on a compromise that would be fair to all sides. After rather lengthy consultations—"

"A phone call from the White House!" Mary Baffleburg shot out, and Lizzie Hanson McWharter said solemnly, "You are so right. You—are—so—right."

"—after lengthy consultations," Lafe went on with dignity, "the suggestion has been made that the Mississippi delegation pledged to Secretary Knox be seated."

"No!" somebody shouted, but he went on, as calmly as possible.

"In return for that concession by the Jason forces, it is proposed that the competing delegations from Ohio be equally divided, with half of each delegation being seated and with the other half of each delegation being declared alternates; the present alternates for each competing delegation to be declared special guests of the convention and given special seats in the official galleries."

"No!" somebody shouted again, and this time the voice was joined by many others, exclaiming, protesting, indignantly arguing. Out of them the voice of Old Joe Smitters could be heard rising in what was, for several minutes, a futile demand for order.

"Now," he said, breathing heavily when it was finally honored, "the committee will be in order. Does somebody wish to put that in the form of a motion?"

"I want to speak to it first, Mr. Chairman!" Mary Buttner Baffleburg cried.

"It has to be a motion first, as you know perfectly well, and then you can speak to it," Old Joe Smitters said angrily. "Will somebody make a motion?"

"Yes, Mr. Chairman," Lafe said. "I'm sitting in for our delegate to this committee, State Senator Wood, who is unavoidably absent this morning—"

"Oh, *I'll* bet!" Lizzie Hanson McWharter said with a raucous chuckle.

"—and I do so move."

"Second!" said Homer Amos Stanhope of Massachusetts.

"Mr. Chairman," Mary Baffleburg said, "Pennsylvania does not, and it will not, accept this compromise, whose net result will be to lose Secretary Knox at least fifteen votes, no matter how you slice it. I say to all on this committee who favor justice and decency that we should reject this so-called compromise and stand by our candidate!"

"But this has the approval of your candi—" Lafe Smith began, but his protest was drowned in the general uproar.

"Question!" somebody called frantically. "Question!"

"All those in favor—" Joe Smitters began, but before he could complete the sentence, Mary Buttner Baffleburg, Lizzie McWharter, and at least twenty other committee members were on their feet.

"Mr. Chairman!" Mary Baffleburg shouted, while the press and the audience craned to see and the television cameras had a field day, "Pennsylvania refuses to vote on this so-called compromise! Pennsylvania is leaving this committee! Pennsylvania urges all who believe in fair play and decency and Orrin Knox to join her in this move. Pennsylvania has had enough of this farce! Pennsylvania—"

"Take it to the floor, Mr. Chairman!" Lizzie Hanson McWharter barked sternly as the press counted at least thirty delegates from twelve states moving toward the door. "Take it to the floor!"

"Damn it," Old Joe Smitters cried, trying to wave his arms and pound his gavel on the table at the same time, "oh, God damn it, sit down! If you *ladies* and the rest of you will sit down, I'll entertain a motion to take it to the floor. I can't do it just because a pack of—a pack of—just because the distinguished National Committeewoman from Kansas says I have to. I have to have a motion, damn it!"

"I move, Mr. Chairman," Lafe Smith said, shaking his head with a tired expression, "that the committee report to the convention that it has been unable to reach an agreement on the seating of the delegations from Ohio and Mississippi, and that it asks the convention to dispose of the matter when the committee files its report this afternoon."

"I second!" Mary Baffleburg and Lizzie McWharter shouted together.

"All in favor—" said Old Joe Smitters.

"AYE!" roared the committee.

"That tears it," said the Senator from Iowa, leaving the room in undisguised disgust to find a phone and call Bob Munson.

At the same moment, in Union Square, a fistfight was breaking out between a Knox supporter and a Jason supporter. By the time police converged upon the square the fight had turned into a riot in which several hundred persons were battling wildly in the bright sunny day. Again the grim-faced minions of COMFORT, DEFY, and KEEP showed no emotion, displayed no anger, went about their business with an impassive efficiency that sent a genuine thrill of fear through many delegates on the spot and many watchers around the nation. A total of thirty people were injured this time, two of them so seriously that first reports raised the possibility they might not live. Frankly Unctuous' plum-pudding voice was stern and harsh as he set the tone for his fellows:

"It is clear at this moment that an angry spirit of violence unusual in an American political convention is beginning to play an increasing part here. Whoever started this latest clash between Jason and Knox forces—and it seems a fair presumption that some Knox supporters, angered by this morning's earlier episode in which a backer of the Secretary was roughed up a bit at the Palace Hotel, sought to retaliate and thus touched off this newest bloody business— the time has obviously come to put a stop to it. Governor Jason scarcely two hours ago demanded a 'fair-play' convention. It is time for his opponent and all associated with him to heed this call."

KNOX FORCES START UGLY RIOT IN UNION SQUARE, the next batch of headlines said; IGNORE JASON CALL FOR FAIR PLAY.

On five hundred newscasts across the country five hundred newscasters began their reports: "A bloody riot which observers believe was started by supporters of Secretary of State Orrin Knox today turned San Francisco's Union Square into a shambles."

And at five hundred typewriters five hundred editorialists and columnists began to write, in words that were synthesized, as so often happened, by The Greatest Publication: "Extremism of any kind is deplorable in American politics. When it is extremism in the form of physical violence, apparently condoned by a major contender for public office, it is doubly deplorable. While Secretary of State Orrin Knox may not be personally responsible for the ugly riot that has just besmirched a great convention, nonetheless—"

"To refresh your memories," Cullee said—and he and his audience were just as straight-faced as though the full text hadn't been leaked to the New York *Times* and already appeared in today's edition—"the President's foreign policy plank reads as follows:

" 'Believing that the interests of world peace can best be served by opposing Communist aggression and infiltration, armed or otherwise, wherever they may exist, we applaud the action of the President in opposing such Communist aggression and infiltration in the nations of Gorotoland and Panama. We wholeheartedly support his determination to bring peace and stability to those troubled nations through the medium of peaceful and honest negotiations as soon as the Communist threat has been removed.'

"I assume most of you have had time to consider that language overnight, and therefore I wouldn't think we would need much more discussion before bringing it to a vote, Mr. Chairman—"

"Now, Mr. Chairman," Roger P. Croy said testily, "again the Congressman acts as though he were a committee member, or maybe even the chairman himself, or something. He's trying to tell us what to do. In fact, he's trying to railroad this right through the committee. I think he ought to be told right now that a good many of us aren't going to stand for it, Mr. Chairman. So he can stop it right now and we'll all save time."

"If the distinguished delegate from Oregon wishes to lead a revolt against the President of the United States, Mr. Chairman," Cullee snapped, "let him start—right now—and we can all save time on that, too. How about it, Governor? You going to lead the troops?"

"The Congressman doesn't have to get insolent, Mr. Chairman," Roger P. Croy snapped in his turn. "We have a perfect right in this committee to study this language very thoroughly and even oppose it, if we like. I'm going to. I don't know whether others are going to tuck their tails between their legs because the President sends a messenger boy, but I'm not." And he glared at Cullee, who had tensed at the term "messenger boy" and glared right back.

"Well, now," Bill Smatters from Atlanta said soothingly, "it seems to me like you people are getting a little too hot about it. We're just starting to discuss it and already you-all are practically banging each other's heads on the floor. The Congressman's a nice fellow, we all know that, and he isn't insisting on anything. I'm sure he understands that this is a pretty serious matter here and some of us want to consider it pretty carefully before we vote. Isn't that right, Congressman?"

"That's right, Mr. Chairman," Cullee agreed, more calmly, "insofar as discussion isn't used for delay, or just to oppose. I do think, though, that it's quite clear what the issue is: you're for the President or you're against him. The whole world is watching. I grant it would be great if we could all pretend Gorotoland and Panama don't exist, but how can we? I think there's some danger of making ourselves look ridiculous if we try."

"Mr. Chairman," Esmé Harbellow Stryke said with a disapproving sniff, "I do hope my distinguished fellow Californian isn't saying that this committee is ridiculous when it tries to suggest language that will produce harmony among the very sharply conflicting opinions represented in the convention. The committee language may not satisfy everyone, but it represents many long hours of trying to work out a compromise. I can only repeat what has been said here before, that to mention the two nations in which American aggression has occurred would only—"

"Now, just a minute, Esmé!" Cullee exclaimed. "Just you wait one minute! What was that term you used? 'American aggression,' was it? That's what the Communists call it but I didn't expect to hear the National Committeewoman from California call it that. Is that what you really think it is?"

"I have my opinions," Esmé Stryke said darkly, "and so do a good many people in this state, I say to the Congressman. He's found that out already in one campaign. I hope he isn't going to have to find it out in another."

"You really believe," Cullee said in a wondering tone, "that the United States began all this. You really honestly believe. . . ." He shook his head and said, "Whew!" in a quiet voice. Then his head came up in a challenging fashion and he looked up and down the table. "Isn't there anyone here who believes in the honor and integrity of this Administration?"

"Well, now, Congressman," Bill Smatters said in a comfortably patronizing tone before anyone could reply, "I don't think it's necessary to put anybody on the spot here, I really don't. I think, as you said earlier, that we could just go ahead and vote, now, and see what happens. I think this committee pretty well knows where it stands on these issues and I think most of us are ready to make our positions clear. So why don't we have a vote now?"

"On which proposition, Mr. Chairman?" Roger P. Croy asked quickly.

"Parliamentary procedure would indicate, would it not," Bill Smatters said smoothly, "that the first vote should come on the committee language—unless," he added slowly, "it's amended."

"I so move," Senator August said suddenly. "That it be amended, I mean, by substituting the language just read by the distinguished Congressman from California."

"But—" Roger P. Croy protested with an almost comical dismay.

Tom August looked upset but stubborn.

"The distinguished delegate of Oregon knows how I feel about this," he said in his soft, precise voice, "and he knows how long and hard I have worked in the past week to find reasonable language. But I am not going to have it said, when this leaks to the press as of course it will, that this committee refused to give its own President a fair hearing. Now," he demanded with what was, for him, a startling show of anger, "is the great former Governor of Oregon going to tell me that he wants that? Go ahead and tell me!"

Roger P. Croy, for once, looked nonplused. Both his homespun logic and the enormous egotistical arrogance beneath it were suddenly stripped bare. There was a long silence while Tom August stared at him.

"Of course," he said at last, "we must give every point of view a fair hearing. But we have already given that point of view a fair hearing, for a week, and we haven't been able to come up with anything else. So I don't see the point. But . . . Mr. Chairman, I will put the motion that the language just read by the Congressman from California be substituted for the committee language."

"I second the motion," said Esmé Stryke promptly.

"All right, then," Bill Smatters said swiftly. "Do I hear the question?"

"Question!" someone said as the room grew very still.

"Will the distinguished National Committeewoman from California serve as secretary for this vote? Very well, Mrs. Stryke, call the roll."

"Harry Bill Johnson of Alabama!" Esmé Stryke said, and Harry Bill Johnson of Alabama said, "Aye!"

Ten minutes later, in a voice that shook a little with nervous strain, Esmé Stryke said:

"On the substitute amendment offered by the Congressman from California, and moved by the delegate from Oregon, there were four abstentions. The Ayes are 15, the Nays are 15, and the amendment is defeated."

There was a gasp from the room and, "Mr. Chairman!" Jawbone Swarthman said hurriedly, "I move we vote now on the committee language."

"Is there a second?"

"I second!" said Roger P. Croy in a suddenly excited voice.

"Harry Bill Johnson of Alabama," said Esmé Stryke, and Harry Bill Johnson of Alabama said, "Nay!"

Ten minutes later, in a voice even more agitated, Esmé Stryke said:

"On the committee language, there are again four abstentions. The Ayes are 15, the Nays are 15, and the committee language is defeated."

"But that's ridiculous!" someone shouted as order dissolved in a babble of raised voices and indignant cries, "that—is—*ridiculous!*"

"Mr. Chairman," Tom August said, in a voice that was not very loud, but insistent. "Mr. Chairman. Mr. Chairman. Mr. Chairman."

"If you-all will hush," Bill Smatters cried, banging his gavel on the table, "if you-all will just hush, the great chairman of the Senate Foreign Relations Committee wants to speak. Do hush!"

"Mr. Chairman," Senator August said when the clamor finally subsided into a few indignant murmurings, "it seems quite obvious that we have, indeed, reached an impasse. There are two alternatives, I believe. We must find some further substitute language that will satisfy the conflicting viewpoints here. Or we can admit failure and throw the whole matter to the convention, with consequences of great bitterness and controversy. I suggest that we follow the former course, even if it means delaying presentation of the platform to the convention. It is better to thrash it out here than on the floor, I think."

"Why?" demanded Roger P. Croy, and several voices said, "Yes, why?"

"After spending a week trying to remove the bitterness and soothe inflamed feelings," Tom August said sharply, "the delegate from Oregon apparently suddenly wants to throw it all over and invite the convention to tear itself to pieces. I will ask *him* why."

"Mr. Chairman," Roger P. Croy said carefully, "the distinguished Senator from Minnesota has put his finger on it when he mentions impasse. It is clear from these two votes how narrowly, yet how implacably, opinion is divided on this issue. What right have we, Mr. Chairman, to deny to the convention the right to work its will? What right have we to arrogate to ourselves the role of censor and dictator? The President said he wants a free convention, Mr. Chairman. Very well, *let it be free!* Let the convention decide! I move, Mr. Chairman," he said with a growing excitement as his fellow committee members began to stir and talk, "that the chairman report to the convention the two proposed planks on which we have just voted, together with the record of the votes cast upon them, and invite the convention to work its will."

"Mr. Chairman!" Cullee Hamilton shouted.

"I second that, Mr. Chairman!" shrieked Esmé Stryke. "I second it, second it, second it!"

"QUESTION!" somebody bellowed.

"All those in favor say Aye," cried Bill Smatters from Atlanta.

"AYE!" roared the committee.

"Mr. Chairman," Tom August called futilely into the uproar, "Mr. Chairman, that isn't fair, Mr. Chairman, there should be a roll-call vote, Mr. Chairman—"

"The AYES have it!" Bill Smatters shouted.

"I move the platform committee stand adjourned sine die!" shouted Roger P. Croy.

"I second!" screeched Esmé Harbellow Stryke.

"All those in favor—" cried Bill Smatters.

"But—" shouted Cullee Hamilton.

"AYE!" roared the committee.

"This committee is hereby adjourned," cried Bill Smatters.

Five minutes later they emerged from the room redfaced, still arguing, shouting and furious, to face the waiting reporters, read the headlines of the Union Square riot, and contribute some of their own:

PLATFORM COMMITTEE DEFIES ADMINISTRATION ON FOREIGN POLICY PLANK . . . WAR HAWKS LOSING GROUND AS BITTER FLOOR FIGHT LOOMS.

It was, said Walter Dobius comfortably to his three young friends when they queried him eagerly in the St. Francis lobby a few minutes later, only to be expected. He did not tell them that in his mind, and he knew in some others, a sudden wild idea had taken hold. One headline-writer, at least, he noted, had caught it too.

Not Orrin Knox, his headline said, but PRESIDENT FACES REVOLT IN CONVENTION.

4

"But I was *there*," Hal Knox said bitterly, shortly after noon at the St. Francis. "*I was there. I know* our people didn't start it. I saw it begin. You've got to say something. You can't just sit here and let this—this—" he gestured with a wild anger and helplessness at the glaring headlines —"*assassination* go on. Stanley," he appealed abruptly to his father-in-law, "Stanley, *make* him issue a statement."

"I think you should, Orrin," Senator Danta said gravely. "I quite agree. I think this is rapidly getting beyond any rational point. I think you've got to speak up, in your own defense."

"With what?" the Secretary asked with a skeptical smile. "A denial that will be instantly drenched in sarcasm by the networks and the Dobius crowd? What's the point in that?"

"The point," Beth said crisply, "is a record, which has to be made whether you win or lose. If your people didn't start the riot, say so. You only confirm lies with silence."

"So say I, too," Crystal agreed from the bed where she was resting with a damp washcloth over her eyes. "I think you must."

"Let's see something," the Secretary said, reaching suddenly for a phone, dialing a number. "Let's see something, first. The only way it would do any good would be if—"

"Yes, Orrin?" Governor Jason said pleasantly. "What can I do for you? . . . Oh? . . . Well, yes, I think that's understood, isn't it? At least, I understand it. I know some of our people—or, rather, you'll understand if I put it a little differently, some of the people who are volunteering their support for me—seem to be getting a little out of hand. I deplore it as much as you do. . . . I *am* doing something about it. I have issued the sternest orders to Bob Leffingwell to pass the word along that this sort of thing must stop at once. . . . A joint statement? What good would that accomplish? . . . Oh, you mean if I were to acknowledge that my people started it? Well, now—are we entirely sure? I mean, I understand myself that they did, but—after all, I don't believe anyone has definite proof. The TV and the newspapers seem to think it was your people. . . . Oh, Hal saw it and says so, does he? Surely you're not telling me that Hal is an objective witness. . . . No, no, no, of course I'm not saying your son is a liar. I'm just saying that very naturally he sees things from the Knox point of view. I certainly don't criticize him for that, who would? I'm just saying it tends to discount—well, no, since you insist on an answer. No, I won't join in it. . . . Because I don't know that it *was* my people, Orrin, really. And why should I offend them if it wasn't? . . . Well, I'm sorry you feel that way. Each of us has to judge this convention according to his own lights and do what he thinks best. . . . Yes, I appreciate that. . . . Yes, I know. I wish you luck with it. . . . All right. . . . Good luck. Goodbye."

"That twisting son of a bitch," Hal said softly. "That slimy, shifting, two-faced son of a bitch."

"I think he's right, you know," Ceil said thoughtfully. "I think you should join him and make clear it wasn't done with any approval of yours. You have your own record to think about. I think you should issue the strongest possible denunciation. After all, I heard you say it to Walter right here in this room: they haven't anywhere else to go. And," she added with a look at Bob Leffingwell, "the few people left in America who still deplore violence and believe in fairness will think better of you for it. And that might be worth even more than a nomination to you, some day."

"It would also, I am convinced," Bob Leffingwell said gravely, "represent the last chance to turn this convention away from something very deeply serious toward which it seems to be racing at this moment. I think you are the one man who has it in his power to decide which way this convention will go. It's a sad cliché with sad consequences, but the world *is* watching what we do here in San Francisco, and we do have some duty to help preserve certain things in America if we can—those old-fashioned things," he said with a sudden bitterness that should have been a warning, "that Walter Dobius and his friends have such a good time making fun of all the time, like decency and integrity and kindliness and honor and being halfway fair to other people even if you are opposing them. . . . I agree with Ceil, I agree with Orrin: I think you should. Platform and credentials—those can be fought out on the floor, and while it may be bloody, at least it's a relatively mild and accepted part of the system. But this thing that's developing in the streets—it frightens me, Ted, it's up to you to stop it, and I think you had damned well better."

But the Governor, staring out the window with a frown of concentration on his handsome face, made no reply, being gone into what his wife had once referred to as his "fastnesses." He stayed so for quite a few minutes, while far below a band played "Dixie" over and over and the silent watchers of COMFORT, DEFY, and KEEP frowned portentously upon the passersby. Nor, indeed, was it really necessary for him to say anything, for when Ceil finally walked over and turned on the television, more or less for something to do, Frankly Unctuous in his plummy tones was saying it for him.

"The one man," he was saying sternly, "who has it in his power to decide whether this convention will sink deeper into a violence that is truly un-American, or be restored to those traditional principles of justice and fair play which have always characterized this great nation—Secretary of State Orrin Knox—has just issued a statement which would hardly seem to satisfy the harsh imperatives of this moment. The Secretary denies that his supporters are responsible for the frightening mood of hatred that is developing here. He denies that they were responsible for the tragic riot this morning in Union Square which may yet claim the lives of two Jason supporters, even though many competent observers who were there are convinced beyond a doubt that—"

"You know," Ceil said pleasantly to no one in particular as she snapped off the set, "I am really becoming quite terrified."

"Bill," Senator Munson said in the lobby of the Hilton,

"I think we're going to need more protection out there this afternoon."

"I've asked the city for extra police," the Speaker said, "and the mayor thinks he can let us have a hundred or so more. I don't like it, Bob." He shook his head. "I don't like it."

"Maybe the fight on credentials and platform will let off enough steam to calm it down," the Majority Leader suggested. The Speaker frowned.

"The people behind this don't want it calmed down. Their only chance is to keep it tensed up."

"I begin to wonder," Senator Munson said thoughtfully, "if they aren't out for something more than a vice presidential nomination—or even a presidential, for that matter."

"I don't know," the Speaker said. "But I know one thing," he added grimly. "Ted Jason is a fool if he thinks he's still in charge of it."

"I'm afraid," she said, amid the tinkling glasses, clinking silverware, and softly murmurous music in the Garden Court of the Palace. A shadow of pain touched her eyes. "It's like the sort of thing that—that killed Brig. It's akin to the kind of thing I heard on the phone and got in the mail before he—stopped being with us. . . . Politics is so evil, Lafe. It is so *evil*."

"It can be," he conceded, taking her hand protectively in his where it lay upon the gleaming tablecloth, "and it's so hopeless to say: it needn't be—it isn't always—it can accomplish wonderful things—it can be good and noble, worthy of a man's lifelong devotion and a nation's respect. Because it's so easy to say: yes, but so often it isn't. . . . Which is true." He sighed. "Which is true."

"I think," Mabel said, "that after this convention is over —if," she remarked with a sad, wry smile, "we all live through it—I shall take Pidge and go back to Provo and never, never, never stir out of my nest again."

"Oh, come," he said with a smile, though a genuine alarm touched his heart, "that's no way to talk, when I have other plans for you. After all, you can't be much help to me 'way out there. Or," he said, more soberly, "to Jimmy, either."

"Are you going to bring him down to Washington?" she

asked with some interest and he congratulated himself that he had hit on the proper subject for the moment.

"Yes, I think so, providing"—he grinned—"I'm there myself, after November. I think I will be, but you never know."

"I'm so thrilled that he's finally trying to talk."

"It's a beginning. It may never go beyond that one moment, but at least I have a witness. Cullee was there and heard it, too, so we know it happened. And maybe, someday, if I keep at it. . . . You did that for me, you know it? And for him. I said why bring him out into the world to be hurt, and you kept writing that if he didn't get out—even if he did get hurt—he would just exist and be a vegetable and might as well not have lived at all." He squeezed her hand. "There's an analogy there, if you will let me state it in my gauche Midwestern way: you and Provo. You can go back and hide in your nest, and you might as well be a vegetable, too."

For a moment he feared she might be offended or upset, and the Mabel Anderson he had known a year ago in Washington would have been. But Brig's death, which had done so many things to so many people, had also, apparently, helped his widow to some maturity she had never known before. She smiled a little, without offense.

"Oh, it won't be that bad. After all, it's my hometown, I have many friends, many things to do, clubs, parties, the outdoors, the Church. . . . I won't be isolated."

"Insulated," he suggested. "Safe from being hurt. . . . Snug . . . smug."

She laughed, quite genuinely amused, gave his hand a squeeze in return, and spoke in a much lighter tone.

"Oh, Lafe, you're good for me. I won't be smug. You won't let me."

"Not if you're in Washington."

She smiled.

"Well. We'll see."

"I think every American citizen who loves his country must be aghast at the mood of viciousness which is gaining control of this convention," Herbert Jason said to the NBC reporter who held a microphone to his lips as he emerged from the Fairmont. "My nephew certainly does, I know."

"Darling," Selena said to the society editor of the *Exam-*

iner in her fifth interview of the morning, "Orrin Knox should be shot. He should simply be shot!"

"I am sure," Valuela said to the society editor of the *Chronicle* in her sixth interview of the morning, "that my nephew knows nothing of these dreadful things. They really seem to be coming out of the Knox group, don't they?"

"Orrin Knox should be ashamed of himself," Patsy said to the local lunchtime radio snooper who was sharing his microphone with her at the brunch given by the Michigan ladies in the Crown Room at the top of the Fairmont. "He should be ASHAMED."

"It does seem," Krishna Khaleel said to CBS, who had cornered him at the Clift, "that there should be some civilized way to decide these nominations without all this violence. I am afraid it is giving other countries, such as my own India, a most unfortunate impression."

"Sorry, old boy," Lord Maudulayne said cheerfully to NBC, who grabbed his arm as he and Kitty swung aboard the Powell Street cable car to go to Fishermen's Wharf for lunch, "but I don't mingle in these American family quarrels, you know. . . . Actually," he murmured to Kitty as the car began its clanging, swaying, ineffable lurch upward, "I wouldn't give the fellow the satisfaction of getting me to say it, but I'm damned upset."

"The poor United States!" Raoul Barre said with a placid complacence to The Greatest Publication That Absolutely Ever Was (for use in a roundup on DIPLOMATIC OBSERVERS AT CONVENTION APPALLED BY KNOX BACKERS' VIOLENCE, which would run at the bottom of page 1 tomorrow morning alongside EUROPEAN CAPITALS SHOCKED BY KNOX FORCES' OUTBURST). "Somehow with the best will in the world, her people *always* manage to put her in a bad light. It amounts to a genius."

"Beth, dear," Lucille Hudson said from her penthouse at the Huntington, "do come up here and have lunch with me. The strain must be terrific for you."

"You, too, isn't it?" Beth responded from the St. Francis. "Have they left you alone at all?"

"There's been a steady stream of grubby politicians," the First Lady said with a chuckle, and Beth could see in mind's eye the satisfied little smile on her plump little face. "They seem to think I hold the keys to the castle."

"And don't you?"

"That's why you'd better hurry over, dear. Today may be the day I pass them out. Oh, and bring Crystal, too, if she'd care to come. The poor girl must be exhausted after visiting all those delegations."

"Only ten this morning," Beth said. "A mere nothing. I'd like to bring her but she and her husband have already left, announcing that they were going to find some secret little hideaway for lunch and—as my son, who is getting increasingly short-tempered, put it—'get away from the whole God-damned convention for a while.' "

"These things are wearing on the young," Lucille said comfortably. "Isn't it nice to be old enough to take it. Do you want me to send a car, or have you one?"

"I have one. Who else do you want me to bring?"

"As a matter of fact," the First Lady admitted, "I have asked Ceil Jason. But Ceil has her own car, of course."

"Of course," Beth said. She paused. "Very well," she said finally.

"And, oh," the First Lady added. "Not a word to Orrin, of course."

"No," Beth said. "Of course."

From where they sat, far up toward the rafters in the middle of the last section just under the roof, the great hall spread out before them vast and echoing in the remaining hour before the session was scheduled to begin. Faintly there ascended the voices of the television crews making their final adjustments of equipment, the banter of the janitors making a casual pretense of sweeping up the last vestiges of yesterday's session, the calls of the sergeants-at-arms across the floor to one another. Almost at eye level they could see the lost balloons of yesterday floating out of reach against the girders, trailing their messages of admonition, encouragement, enthusiasm, and hope: CONSCIENCE MUST DECIDE THE ISSUE . . . EVERYONE FLOCKS TO ORRIN KNOX . . . STOP WAR —ELECT JASON . . . KNOX WILL DEFEND

AMERICA'S HONOR . . . JASON . . . KNOX . . .
ORRIN . . . TED . . . HARLEY AND ORRIN WILL
PULL US THROUGH . . . HARLEY AND TED—A
BALANCED TICKET . . .

"I think we've lost already," Hal said gloomily, finishing
his hamburger with a last, vicious bite. "They've got the
press and TV sewed up. And these damned pickets have
some of our delegates really scared. And Dad won't fight.
And I don't see how we can possibly pull out of it."

"It isn't going to be easy," Crystal agreed. "But on the
other hand," she said with a sudden fierceness, staring
down at the little figures busy around the crowded television platforms, "I cannot believe—I will not believe—that
the general public is going to fall for the kind of twisting of
the truth that's going on here."

Hal shrugged.

"They have before—how many times? So many the
mind loses count. They will again, because that's what
they've been carefully conditioned to do. Some very astute
people have been at work on them for a long time, particularly where Orrin Knox is concerned, and all it needs now
is a little more push and they'll have it done. They've got
two things going for them this afternoon. One is the 'steal'
and the other is 'violence.' " His mouth twisted with bitter
contempt. "And where in the headlines, or where on the
air, do you find the truth about either one of those?"

"I don't care," she said. "I just don't care. I don't believe
the public is going to fall for it this time."

"But my dear girl," he said with an exasperation that
made her grin suddenly and snuggle against him for a moment, "you have read the headlines and the news stories.
You have heard the broadcasts. How do you think they're
going to get the truth? And what difference will it make if
the public does, if a pack of weak-spined delegates starts to
panic? That's what counts here. I think we're licked before
we start."

"Now, see here," she said. "I didn't climb 'way up here
at seven months pregnant, my boy, to hear you give me
Gloomy-Gus-on-the-slide-trombone. That doesn't sound
like you at all. You don't even sound like a Knox. Sir!" she
exclaimed dramatically. "Is this The Father of My Unborn
Child?"

He smiled, though with some reluctance.

"It better be . . . I don't care, Crys, I feel licked. I really do. And I'm scared of this—this mob that seems to be taking over on the other side. I don't even think you should be here. I think you ought to stay at the hotel. I think all the women ought to. I don't think it's safe."

"Oh, come," she said. "I'm not going to hide and I don't think anyone else should, either. It's an ugliness, but it's temporary. Even if the Governor wouldn't join in a statement, I know they're working over there to quiet things down, too. I'll bet by the time the session is really under way this afternoon the mood will be back to normal."

"I don't know where you get this blind optimism," he said, "but I think it is blind. You saw how they looked at us when we left the hotel. I'm sorry now I had this screwy idea. We should have eaten right there."

"They didn't look friendly, I'll admit, but I really got the feeling they were just pretending to be stern—like little kids, you know. They were so determinedly grim and self-conscious, and so pompous about it all."

"You know what happens when you make fun of the pomposities of little kids," he said. "They get mad. So will these. They already have, in Union Square. Two people— two human beings, Crys—are near death, because they got mad this morning. What else is going to happen?"

"And is that a reason to turn tail and run?" she demanded, while below the television crews turned on lights experimentally, focused cameras on the rostrum, shouted instructions back and forth. "Is that a reason for giving up what you believe in, just because evil people get mad and try to stop you? I'm ashamed of you, Hal Knox. I think that's a time to fight twice as hard."

"It's a time to protect what you have," he said grimly, "and that, at the moment, consists principally of you and little Thumper, here. . . . No, of course not. I'm not saying we should turn and run, you know me better than that. But I am saying there's no point in having any false optimism about it. We're up against a really vicious battle here, today and tomorrow, and if Walter Dobius and his crowd keep fanning the flames, it's going to explode into something really nasty. Ted Jason could stop it, but the bastard won't, and Dad can't, because it isn't his responsibility and they all laugh at him, anyway. God damn them," he said with a sudden, level anger. "Oh, God damn them in hell, these monsters of the age who inflame every tension in the world and then blandly tell you it's your fault, not theirs, when kindness and decency are destroyed. I hate them, the awful, monstrous hypocrites."

"Well," she said softly, placing a hand on his arm, "at least the Knoxes don't belong among them and that's some satisfaction."

"Shouldn't they have?" he asked bitterly. "Wouldn't Dad have reached the White House long ago if they had? Wouldn't I do better in Illinois, if I stay in politics, to side with the hypocrites? They can do a lot for you if they love you. Look at their headlines, listen to their programs, read their editorials and their columns! Oh, yes, they can do wonders, if you're their boy. All they demand in return is that you become a hypocrite, too. You have to be one of them and mouth their dirty, upside-down, bass-ackwards version of what's going on in the world. *Then* you're all right, and they'll sing you hosannas from New York City to the Golden Gate."

"But you don't want to get out of it," she said quietly. "And you don't really want him to. Because, now, suppose: suppose all the people like the Knoxes and the Dantas and the rest of us did get driven out by the hypocrites. What kind of a world would it be if we all stopped fighting —if we all stopped insisting on what the truth is, even when they shout us down and write us under—if we all gave up because it's just too hard to fight and we're too tired and disheartened and too occupied with other things? That's what they're counting on. But what kind of a world would that leave for"—and she gave herself an impatient pat on the stomach—"him—or her—or"—more lightly— "whoever you are, in there?"

She stopped and stared down thoughtfully at the great hall. It was beginning to come to life a little more, the janitors and television crews had withdrawn, a few ushers were coming in and taking their stations, the sergeants-at-arms and police were beginning to take their posts at the entrances and aisles, a few band members were already in their chairs starting their first tentative trills and squawks and thumps of sound, and on the floor and in the press section an advance guard of early arrivals was beginning to straggle in and get ready to go to work.

"So," she said after a moment, "that's what I think."

He chuckled, suddenly himself again for the moment, stood up and held out his hand.

"You looked about ten just then—so solemn and positive, after your rhetoric. It's good rhetoric, too. I agree with it. Always have and always will, more fool me. Come on, I'll take you down to the box, and then I've got to be on the floor. I'll check in whenever I get a chance, and come around to see you back to the hotel, later."

"If you can," she said, standing up with some awkwardness, "but it isn't necessary. I'll be with Beth, and I believe Dolly Munson is joining us too. We'll be all right." She frowned. "You're the one who's more apt to get hurt. Suppose you be careful."

"I will," he said, with a return to somberness. "It's going to be a night to be careful, all around."

So thought they, too, in the penthouse at the Huntington as the little luncheon broke up.

"I'll do my best," said Ceil.

"I'll do my best," said Beth. "But I don't think either of them is in control of the situation, any more."

"And if you will forgive me, Mrs. Hudson," Ceil said, "I don't think the President is, either. I hope he's going to arrive soon."

"He must," the First Lady agreed quietly, and suddenly they realized that she was under a great strain, too. "He simply must. This is not going to be a pleasant night."

5

WITH THIS the Speaker and Senator Munson were also in agreement when, an hour later, they rode out to the Cow Palace in the Speaker's limousine, watching on the small television set in the back seat the gathering delegates, the placards, the banners, the bands, the competing groups of demonstrators, the great numbers of police who guarded the entrances and mingled with the crowd. The Texas delegation managed to arrive, as always, whooping and hollering, but the levity of the rest was worn very thin: no matter how dutifully they waved their banners and shouted their slogan for the cameramen, the majority of the delegates who had their little moment on the screen looked sobered and edgy. And time and again the cameras kept coming back to the reason for their nervousness, and the sight was enough to make any perceptive citizen shiver: the somber, sullen, blank-faced rank-on-rank, both white and black, who lined the main entryways and held with a portentous solemnity their standards proclaiming COMFORT WANTS A MAN OF PEACE—NOMINATE TED JASON! . . . OUR LEADER FOR PEACE AND BETTER JOBS—DEFY WANTS JASON! . . . KEEP FOR JASON—NO MORE FOREIGN WARS! And, with an uglier, more ominous note, FAIR PLAY, MR. KNOX! NO MORE STEALS—NO MORE BEATINGS! . . . AMERICA WANTS A DECENT MAN, NOT A RIOTER! BACK JASON!

"Seems to me, Bob," the Speaker remarked softly as the car inched along with the traffic, "that we've got our work cut out for us, tonight and tomorrow."

"Yes," the Majority Leader agreed glumly. "I'm going to feel a lot better when you get your hands on that gavel as permanent chairman this afternoon."

"Me too," the Speaker said. He gave a grim little smile. "At least I'll be able to maintain a little order in the convention, if nothing else. About one more ounce of pressure and this crowd will turn into a pack of screaming maniacs. I don't think Harley knows what he's going to find when he gets out here."

"I wish he'd hurry," Senator Munson said. His expression became ironic. "I never thought the day would come when I'd need Harley more than he needs me, but the moment is here. Why, Bill, I tell you, I don't know that we can even hold all of the Michigan delegation, if things really get rough. And I get the same reports all over. The Jason people are well-heeled, well-organized, and absolutely ruthless—and they've got a new element on their side now: fear. Actual, physical fear."

The Speaker grunted.

"I've got an element on my side, too: A hundred extra police. And I'm not going to hesitate to use 'em, either, Bob, if I have to. This convention is going to proceed in an orderly way and we're going to maintain the dignity of the party, at least inside the hall. I can't be responsible for what happens elsewhere, but inside, people are going to behave."

And so they might have—just possibly might have, though no one could ever be sure, had things continued just as they were, what would have happened on that tense and foredoomed evening—had it not been for two people. One was named William Everett Hollister II. He was in Central Emergency Hospital. The other was named Booker T. Saunders. He was in Mount Zion.

Both William Everett Hollister II and Booker T. Saunders were twenty-two. William Everett Hollister II had grown up in Hillsborough, witnessed the breakup of his parents' marriage, been bounced along from boarding school to boarding school, wound up at the University of California, discovered in himself little aptitude for study but great aptitude for protest; organized riots, planned campaigns, uttered fiery slogans, screamed dirty words, toppled chancellors, harried legislatures, protested everything, graduated at twenty-one with nothing to do but hang around the grown-up world and keep on protesting.

Booker T. Saunders had grown up at the unfashionable end of Divisadero Street, been unable to witness the breakup of his parents' marriage because they had never been married and he didn't even know who his father was; mumbled his way through grammar school, dropped out in his freshman year of high school, joined a street gang, launched his own form of protest, drank, took dope, raped, robbed, murdered, found himself at twenty-one with nothing to do but more of it.

William Everett Hollister II joined the San Francisco chapter of COMFORT when the President of the United States decided to launch his shameful and unprovoked invasion of innocent Gorotoland. EX-CAMPUS REBEL JOINS GROUP PROTESTING U.S. AGGRESSION, said the *Chronicle;* and there was a flattering fifteen-hundred-word interview and two fine pictures. Booker T. Saunders didn't join anything, because he didn't know about Gorotoland, or indeed about much, before or since. He just stood around on street corners drunk, which was where he had happened to be that morning when some fellows came along in a truck, gave him a twenty-dollar bill, stuck a placard in his hand that said something about somebody named JASON, and carted him off to Union Square where there seemed to be bands playing and a lot of people and quite a bit of excitement. William Everett Hollister II marched into the square with head held high, going to glory: he knew what he was doing and reveled in it. Booker T. Saunders shambled into the square with his newfound buddies: he had twenty dollars, he was already drunk, and that twenty dollars was going to make him drunker after a while, and he, too, reveled in it.

When William Everett Hollister II thought he saw a smart-ass college kid with a KNOX button in his lapel laughing at him, he didn't stop to think. Something exploded in his brain at the sight of the grinning, capitalistic, imperialistic, rich-bitch monkey (William Everett Hollister I had fifty million dollars, but of course William Everett Hollister II didn't get much of that from the crazy old reactionary), and he swung on him without thinking twice. The college student was startled but instinctively swung back, and, happening to be well balanced at the moment, knocked William Everett Hollister II down. Immediately William Everett Hollister II's friends sprang to his defense, the college student's friends sprang to his, and the riot was on.

Somehow William Everett Hollister II became separated from his friends after about five minutes and found himself surrounded by eight or ten Knox supporters, still not entirely ill-natured, shouting, "Give up, give up!" But he wasn't about to give up to the reactionary warmongering destroyers of humanity and even though he knew that he was guaranteeing violent retaliation, he raised his standard and brought it down like a claymore across the head of his nearest opponent. The reaction was just what he had expected—just what he had invited—just what he wanted. "Get that bastard!" somebody shouted, and in another couple of minutes, somebody did. He was battered, bloody, unconscious, but even so there was a hint of smile about his lips: he was a glorious sacrifice to a great cause, and obviously that had been his last thought before blackness closed in. Ten minutes later he was in an ambulance being rushed away to Central Emergency; critical, at that time, but with a reasonable chance for recovery if no complications set in.

Booker T. Saunders' saga was much less glorious, though in days to come, he would have been surprised to know, his name was destined to echo somewhat more loudly around the globe than that of his fellow hero. Booker T. Saunders had simply stumbled about when the riot began, striking out aimlessly with his standard, really too drunk to know much about what was happening, really too happy to care. But others were watching Booker T. Saunders, and when a desperate police officer, striving without much success to contain the riot's outer fringes, suddenly drove his squad car right up on the Geary Street curb (POLICE BRUTALITY CHARGED IN RIOT, the headlines said later. It was a nice extra dividend.) it was decided that the time had come for Booker T. Saunders to make his sacrifice for a great cause, too. He never did know exactly what happened. There was a terrific shove in the middle of his back—he spun half-around in loose-limbed desperation—caught just a glimpse of another savagely triumphant black face and a waving placard that said something about "DEFY"—felt himself fall to the sidewalk—felt the beginning of a terrible crushing weight on his chest—felt no more. Five minutes later he, too, was in an ambulance, on his way to Mount Zion Hospital; terribly hurt, critical at the moment, but also given a reasonable chance if no complications set in.

But now the time had arrived, as the Speaker's limousine drew up before the entrance to the Cow Palace and he and the Majority Leader were carefully escorted in past the sullen watchers, for the sort of event, relatively small in itself, which usually concerns only a few, yet can sometimes concern great leaders, states, and causes. In Booker T. Saunders' case it could normally have been expected to concern no one, in William Everett Hollister II's case only a bitter old man hidden away in a mansion in Hillsborough and a raucous thrice-divorced harridan at that moment playing roulette at Harold's Club in Reno. But it was destined to concern many more. Unknown to anyone at that moment in or around the Cow Palace, complications had indeed set in. At Central Emergency, William Everett Hollister II, and at Mount Zion, Booker T. Saunders, noble battlers in a noble cause, were dying.

"And so I say to you, my dear friends of this great party," the temporary chairman, that rich rolling trumpet of the rich rolling Bluegrass, was finishing the keynote address with a suavity almost, but not quite, concealing his inner nervousness—"there rests upon us here the happy duty of backing a great leader and a great program—

"A program which has encouraged and increased the greatest economic prosperity this nation has ever known—

"A program which has educated our children, saved our poor, brought new medical benefits to all sections of our society and all age groups—

"A program which has seen ever-increasing gains in the field of civil rights—

"A program which has seen new advances in labor-management relations—

"A program which has improved housing and urban development a hundredfold—

"A program which has—"

"What about foreign policy?" a voice shouted suddenly from some microphone on the floor, and instantly there was a confused chorus of boos, catcalls, hisses, and an applause which, beginning a little hesitantly, took strength and increased rapidly until it inundated the hall. A wild scramble started in the Illinois delegation, apparently a fight to grab the microphone. Other scuffles seemed to be breaking out elsewhere on the floor. In the public galleries JASON placards suddenly appeared everywhere, and out of the maze of sound a solemn, insistent, curiously mechanical chant broke through:

JA-SON MEANS PEACE. JA-SON MEANS PEACE. JA-SON MEANS PEACE. JA-SON MEANS PEACE.

"I'm coming to foreign policy," the temporary chairman snapped into the uproar, but his words were lost; nor was his gavel, pounded with a will on the quivering lectern, of much more effect. For perhaps five minutes the foofaraw continued. In that period the press, standing on its benches to stare out over the crowd, and the television reporters, frantically squeezing up and down the aisles and shouting into their walkie-talkies, were able to count six scuffles, five shoving matches, and one genuine fistfight, scattered through the delegations in no discernable pattern. Someone in Illinois, presumed to be heavily for Knox, had apparently started it; someone in California, presumed to be solid for Jason, had been observed fighting with another Jason delegate in neighboring Connecticut. None of it made sense by ordinary political standards of political analysis. What it did seem to mean was what the managers and the experts and the smart boys had already begun to conclude, that there was no pattern, no consistency, no predictable conformity, but instead a rebellion and uneasiness that cut far across the country and, more importantly for what was going to happen in the next few hours, far across the floor.

"As I was saying when somebody tried to interrupt me," the temporary chairman went on with an uneasily hearty laugh that did not, however, produce the tension-easing response he had obviously hoped—"we have the happy duty of backing a great leader and a great program which has, in the field of foreign policy that my friend down there is so concerned about, placed the United States squarely on the side of justice and peace—"

Again there were wild hoots and hisses, but this time he did not pause but continued to shout into them—

"—and peace; which has provided this world with perhaps its only chance to re-establish a system of international stability free from aggression, free from revolutions, and free from so-called 'wars of national liberation' which are really only wars of Communist conquest."

Abruptly the flurry died, as if by some signal. A silence almost stealthy descended upon the great room. His peroration received no objections. It was so quiet, in fact, that his voice began to sound a little uncertain as he concluded:

"So I call upon you, my friends, to go forth armored in righteousness and truth, to do battle for a great President and the great cause he leads: the cause of freedom, dignity, human decency, and human peace—seeking solutions of justice for this sad world's problems, so that you and I and our children and the children of all mankind unto the last generation may live in dignity and honor.

"It gives me great pleasure," he said, and a certain genuine relief in his voice brought a titter of amusement in the press section, "to turn the gavel over now to our permanent chairman, that great leader of our party who has, through sunshine and shadow, through thick and thin, through triumph and through adversity, carried high the standard of our great party and done it credit in the eyes of all men —our beloved Speaker of the House. Mr. Speaker!"

And for a moment, as the Speaker came forward with his plodding, matter-of-fact gait that looked as stolid, pragmatic, and practical as he was, their great party was briefly reunited in affectionate tribute to one of its giants. But his comments in the Credentials Committee had been pub-

licized enough, his obvious dedication to orderly procedures was well enough known, he was so obviously on the
side of the President in seeking some sensible compromise,
that the moment swiftly passed. For the first time in the
five conventions at which he had served as permanent
chairman he could sense as he stood before them that he
was facing an audience containing not only dutiful and
affectionate friends but genuinely hostile and resourceful
enemies who were no longer impressed and held docile by
his legend. This time legends were not going to be enough.
He looked slowly about at the aisles, the entryways, the
tiers of seats climbing into the blue haze above. He saw
what he wanted to see, and he made very plain to them
what it was: the police. An ugly little murmur, a ripple of
muffled yet insistent hisses and boos began to accompany
his slow surveillance of the hall, and when he finished they
knew they were in for a fight: he was a tough old bird and
he meant them to realize it. Abruptly he slammed down
the gavel, so abruptly and so harshly in the silence that had
gradually fallen upon them that almost all of the eighteen
thousand souls under the balloon-specked roof jumped.

"Now," he said calmly, "this convention will be in
order. . . . It is customary at this time for me to make
you a little speech on the four years past and the four years
ahead.

"That's simple: the past four have been tough and the
next four are going to be tougher.

"The only way to get through them is with a united party and a united nation. Those who would tear either apart"
—he paused and then went on calmly—"are fools."

Immediately there were renewed boos and hisses, a little
stronger and defiant now. There was also an inarticulate,
choking half-yell, as though someone had started to shout
something into a microphone and been yanked down. He
ignored it.

"In the next few hours, you will have plenty of time to
fight out these issues of credentials, of foreign policy, and
of anything else you please. But as long as you are in this
hall and I am chairman of this convention, you will settle
your differences *here* and you will do it like ladies and
gentlemen with a decent respect for one another's opinions."

Again there was an outbreak, and this time the applause
overrode it; but there was a tentative, almost frightened,
quality to the applause that he could sense and did not like.

"I say to you, that is the only way for one of our great political parties to do it. It is the only way for decent men and women to do it. It is the only way for Americans who love their country ["My God, not *that* old chestnut," *Newsweek* groaned to the Washington *Post*, and the *Post* shrugged and smiled back] to do it. I don't like," he added bluntly, "these odd elements who are trying to take over this convention. I don't like the kooks and oddballs I see trying to start demonstrations and frighten decent people. I don't like the element of violence that has come into this great gathering—and I don't like candidates who are too cautious to speak up about it, either."

Again, as he had planned, there was a sound of protest, this time louder and uglier.

"Let me tell you something," he said with a grating anger. "You can call on the scum and the slime of America to come out of its gutters to help you, if you're that idiotic and besotted with the lust for power—but you can't put them neatly back when you're through. They'll take you over if you let them. They'll take over this party if you let them. I say to you, my old friends who have stood with me for so long, stand with me now! We have a problem here, and it isn't going to do anybody any good to pretend we don't. It's a tough problem and we're going to have to be tough about it. I have one hundred extra policemen in this hall tonight, and if anybody wants to start a rumpus in here that isn't strictly within the rules of free and orderly debate, he's going to jail. Right—now. . . . So keep that in mind.

"Now," he said, more calmly, "just so you won't forget a couple of things: we have a President in the White House. He is about to be our candidate for re-election. He's the only President, and his is the only program, we have. If you have disagreements with him, state them. There is an area for reasonable disagreement and reasonable debate—and then, if a majority of the delegates wish it, there is an area for amendment and revision. But we are here for one purpose and one only: to write a winning platform and choose a winning ticket.

"Let's get at it.

"The first order of business," he concluded quietly, "is the report of the Credentials Committee. The Chair recognizes the distinguished delegate from the great state of

Ohio, the Honorable Joe Smitters, chairman of the committee."

There came, while Old Joe Smitters shuffled out the long ramp to the podium, one of those hasty moments of pause and reflection which, snatched out of time in the midst of the furious contentions of men, sometimes provide them with sound judgments on which to move ahead, and sometimes do not. In this instance it served only to make the uncertain more nervous and the determined more grim. The Speaker's effort had been well meant, and it had been delivered in the manner he had found effective many times before, in the House and in convention; but there was a new breed and a new mood present here. Even as Joe Smitters approached the lectern and, adjusting the black-ribboned pince-nez he affected, opened his report to begin reading, there came again from somewhere in the enormous room the level, measured, monotonous, and curiously menacing chant:

JA-SON MEANS PEACE. JA-SON MEANS PEACE. JA-SON MEANS PEACE.

And though in response there came an immediate outcry of WE WANT KNOX! WE WANT KNOX! WE WANT KNOX! somehow its exuberant enthusiasm, its uneven, raucous, and undisciplined nature, contrasted oddly—frighteningly, many thought—with the deliberately uninflected, deliberately dispassionate, heavy, somber, steady chant that met and gradually overcame the cries for Orrin Knox. Someone, as Cullee remarked to Lafe when they paused in mid-aisle near the Oklahoma delegation to compare notes, had studied his textbooks on mob psychology well. A disciplined force was present, and it was becoming more effective with each passing moment.

After that flurry, however, and while Joe Smitters spoke, the hall remained surprisingly silent. To Orrin, watching with Stanley Danta at their headquarters at the Fairmont, and to Ted, doing the same with Bob Leffingwell at the Mark Hopkins, it appeared that the agreement was going to hold in spite of the brief excitements that broke out as Joe Smitters described it. Mary Buttner Baffleburg billowed to the microphone to shout an indignant protest, Lizzie Hanson McWharter and six or seven others followed, but despite Mary's stanch claims even her own

Pennsylvania did not support her. When she made a motion to separate the two cases of Mississippi and Ohio so that the convention might vote individually upon them, she was shouted down so unanimously that the Speaker did not even bother to order a roll call. The question came upon the full text of the compromise, which would give Orrin all of Mississippi's fourteen votes and divide Ohio's sixty equally. Esmé Harbellow Stryke for California demanded a roll call, but it turned out to be pro forma. The lines held all the way.

The vote for the compromise was 1037–256.

Briefly there was a wistful hope in many minds that perhaps the whole convention could go like this, so quickly had the great headlined battle over delegates dissolved, so short and mannerly had been the debate, so easily had the charges of "Knox steal" been allowed to disappear. It had, as Hal Knox put it with some dryness to Mabel Anderson when he stopped by the Utah delegation to say hello, "served its purpose until they decided to concentrate on bigger game." Now it was all right to let it go.

Five minutes later the Speaker recognized Senator August to present the majority report of the Platform Committee, and abruptly the convention narrowed itself down to the only real issue before it, the only purpose for which history, looking back, would ultimately record that it had met: to reach a judgment on foreign policy. Far away in Gorotoland a platoon of American soldiers, cut off in the highlands by Obifumatta's forces, was even then learning— as long as consciousness remained, which mercifully was not long—what it meant to be subjected to ritual death. Nearer at hand in Panama the first two jets to be shot down by Soviet missiles installed along the Western reaches of the Canal had just crashed into the sea with the loss of six American lives. At the Cow Palace the convention hushed to listen as the senior Senator from Minnesota began to review the ten bitter days of controversy that had brought the committee to an impasse—"this deadlock of sincerely held opinions," as he put it, "to which we hope this great convention has the key."

At Central Emergency and at Mount Zion, in almost identical gestures at almost identical moments, doctors glanced at nurses across two bodies and shook their heads.

The convention had a very few minutes of even its present rather tortured calm left to go.

"Therefore it was decided," Tom August concluded, and his audience was silent and tense as it listened, "that the committee would return the matter of this disputed plank on foreign policy to this great convention for decision. After the vote and the adjournment of the committee," he added rather uncertainly, "a minority report was filed by the distinguished National Committeeman from Oregon, former Governor Roger P. Croy, and the distinguished National Committeewoman from California, Mrs. Stryke, embodying the language of the so-called 'committee plank' which I have just read to you and declaring it to be the sense of the committee that it should be adopted by the convention. . . . Apparently"—he looked around vaguely, while below in the Michigan delegation the Majority Leader deplored in violent private terms Tom's inability to ever take a firm, definite stand on anything—"this is an attempt to bring the matter even more emphatically before the convention, though it seems to me that . . ."

His voice trailed away and he looked puzzled as there were sudden indications of a disturbance at the other end of the ramp. The parliamentarian came forward and murmured hastily in his ear, he turned and looked and then turned hastily back to the microphone.

"But it seems," he said, "that the distinguished delegate from Wyoming, Senator Van Ackerman, is here to speak in behalf of the minority report—"

"No, he isn't," Bob Munson shouted, prompted by some intuition he could not have explained as Fred Van Ackerman strode furiously forward. "Stop him! Stop him!"

But of course Tom went mildly on, "so I shall be happy to yield to him for that purpose."

And with that air of obvious relief with which he always concluded his speeches in the Senate, his speeches to the electorate, and other onerous public duties, he stepped back, holding out his hand for the handshake that inevitably accompanies all such comings and goings at the lectern. Fred's normal discourtesy, however, was heightened by an agitation so obvious that he brushed past the Senator from Minnesota as though he did not exist. Something in his haste and his manner electrified the convention. Here and

there across the floor and in the public galleries where delegates and guests had transistor radios or small television sets there were startled outcries and word of mouth began to travel like lightning through the hall even as Fred started to speak.

"Mr. Chairman," he cried, and already his voice held its high, demagogic whine, "Mr. Speaker, I want to report to this great convention two cases of murder. Yes," he cried as there were shocked shouts of protest and a scattering of boos, automatic and nervous, *"murder!* Evil, monstrous, deliberate murder! Two young men are dead, Mr. Chairman—victims of an unprincipled campaign for high office —victims of a devouring, corrupting ambition that would sweep everything ruthlessly before it—murdered as a result of the riot in Union Square this morning—*murdered by the gangs of Orrin Knox!"*

There were furious outbursts from many sections of the floor and galleries, angry shouts of protest from people too angry to be frightened. But even as they tried to shout Fred down—even as Bob Munson, pausing only to give a hasty order to Hal Knox, who happened to be standing at his side, began to fight his way forward—even as the Speaker, looking furious, strode toward the lectern—there broke from the galleries a somber, measured chant, mechanical, robot-like, which spoke three times with a slow, massive deliberation:

WITH-DRAW, MUR-DER-ER. WITH-DRAW, MUR-DER-ER. WITH-DRAW, MUR-DER-ER.

As abruptly as it began it ceased, while in their box Beth and Crystal and Dolly Munson looked absolutely stricken, and in his office at the Fairmont Orrin shifted in his chair as though yielding to a physical blow.

Into the shocked silence Fred shouted:

"Yes, he should withdraw, Mr. Chairman! Orrin Knox should withdraw! Two young heroes have been murdered, Mr. Chairman! Fighting for what they believed in, a free and decent world without wars and without aggression! *Murdered,* Mr. Chairman! Murdered by the gangs of—"

But now the Speaker had reached him and clamped a hand upon his shoulder so heavily that the Senator winced as the Speaker spun him around and shouted, his face scarcely six inches from Fred's, "Get off this platform, you monster! Get out of the sight of decent men, you—"

But the Speaker was sixty-eight and Fred was thirty-

nine, and with a furious contempt the Senator wrenched his shoulder away and struck down the Speaker's hand.

"Leave me alone, old man," he shouted in his enraged psychotic whine; and then, as he saw the Speaker wince, his voice changed abruptly to a level, sneering nastiness. "Yes, you are an old man! An old, used-up man who has been around too long! This convention belongs to the young men, now, not to old men who are friends of the friend of murderers. This convention doesn't want murderers! It wants the only hope for a decent peace in the world —Governor Ted Jason of California. And it's going to get him!"

WITH-DRAW, MUR-DER-ER, the galleries rumbled in a flat, mechanical thunder. WITH-DRAW. MUR-DER-ER. JA-SON MEANS PEACE. JA-SON MEANS PEACE.

For a long moment Fred and the Speaker glared at one another, suspended above the convention on a private cord of hatred. Then the Speaker reached out, with the slow deliberation that called on all the reserves of all the years, and drew the microphone to him.

"Captain Hughes," he said sharply, "remove this man."

"I'm a United States Senator!" Fred shouted as four policemen came forward along the ramp, and the press stood on its worktables, and on the floor in a great wave rising the delegates stood, too, and watched in a strange, indefinable silence. "You can't arrest me, I'm a United States Senator!"

"And more shame to the people of Wyoming who sent you there," the Speaker roared, letting go at last. "More shame to the Senate that allows you to remain! And shame to you, you vicious being! Take him off this platform and throw him out!"

After that, for a while, there was no particular order to things, as Fred, adopting a sudden satisfied smirk in one of his lightning changes of mood, stepped forward to meet the policemen, gave them an elaborate sardonic bow, and marched out ahead of them, untouched, off the ramp, out of sight and presumably out of the building; as Senator Munson, finally achieving the platform, conferred hastily with the Speaker; as fistfights and scufflings broke out in the galleries and across the floor; as the band desperately played "Dixie" and "Yankee Doodle" in a nervous attempt to restore some jollity to the proceedings; as the reporters furiously wrote and the commentators furiously commented; and as the angry sounds of eighteen thousand agitated voices filled the Cow Palace to the point of near-explosion.

"The Chair," the Speaker said at last in a voice that trembled slightly in spite of him, when the noise had begun to drain itself out a little, "will recognize the distinguished National Committeewoman from California, Mrs. Esmé Harbellow Stryke, to speak in support of the minority report on the foreign policy plank."

And for twenty minutes Esmé Stryke did, while the delegates and galleries listened with an almost desperate attention. The demonstrators of COMFORT, DEFY, and KEEP did not perform again during her speech; their opponents were similarly silent. By a sort of tacit agreement, everyone for the moment seemed too emotionally exhausted and too involved in letting tensions relax to do more than give her a few perfunctory moments of applause, a few dutiful boos and hisses. A great many in the hall were thoroughly frightened, not so much by what had occurred as by what it revealed of the capacity of the human animal to go suddenly berserk. *Who knew what they might do together next?* It was a thought that left many deeply shaken. Esmé Stryke was one of them. Her voice was not too steady, her usually positive manner was uncertain, and although she did make one quick reference to "those who have paid a tragic price for their belief in a peaceful world," she raced over it and hurried on before there could be any reaction one way or the other from the convention.

When she concluded by moving adoption of the minority report as an amendment to the committee report, there was again a rather perfunctory burst of applause. Roger P. Croy followed her to the podium to second the motion; said the one brief sentence necessary to do so; announced that he would reserve further comments for rebuttal, if necessary; and retired to a seat with Esmé toward the back of the ramp.

The Speaker came to the podium and with his words the tension began again to build.

"To speak in opposition to the minority report," he said, his voice still showing strain, though his manner seemed as impassive as always, "the Chair has the great honor and privilege to introduce one of the gentlemen of this party—one of the decent and honorable men who serve this nation with the integrity and dignity befitting the great office of United States Senator"—there was an ominous little flurry of boos, but he went calmly on—"the Majority Leader of the United States Senate, the *Honorable* Robert Durham Munson, senior United States Senator from the great state of Michigan."

While Bob Munson smiled and waved the band swung into the Michigan Fight Song, the Michigan delegation seized its standards and began a snake dance up the aisle which was soon joined in good-naturedly by delegates from many other states. For a few minutes it seemed that the convention had been restored to being just like any other, brutal in spots but basically good-tempered and decent both in its instincts and in the outward display of them. It seemed so until the demonstration began to subside, the delegations returned to their seats, and an attentive silence settled over the hall. Then, just as Bob Munson leaned forward to place his hands upon the lectern and begin speaking, there came a flat, sardonic greeting that put it all back in perspective:

WEL-COME, LI-TTLE RO-BERT.

There was a gasp from the convention, a sudden furious move to pound the gavel from the Speaker, a restraining hand on his arm from Senator Munson, who murmured rapidly, "What can you do, they aren't breaking any rule. Better not make it worse." "All right," the Speaker said grimly. "Handle it your own way. God give you luck."

"I thank you," Bob Munson said calmly, "for that kindly, warm, and cordial greeting." He was rewarded with laughter and applause, not so intimidated now. "I do not know exactly who you are, for you do not speak with bands and bunting and happy, open sounds like my friends from Michigan and other states have just done. You speak as though you live in a cave, or under a rock, which is perhaps where you came from."

WATCH—IT, the claque admonished coldly, and on the floor, many delegates swung around and stared, trying to find the source. But the claque's members had been so carefully distributed through the galleries that they could not be singled out. It was clear only, from their disciplined chorus, that there must be a great many of them, instructed and captained by walkie-talkie from some superbly organized central point with all the money in the world and the ruthless brains to use it.

"I suggest," Senator Munson said with an equal coldness, "that whoever is guiding you and directing you,

watch it; for he is attempting to introduce here methods in
the pursuit of his ambition that are repugnant to America
and will be repudiated by the common sense and decency
of America. I say to him, watch it, for he is trying something that will destroy him before he is through. Take that
message back to him from this convention!" he shouted
with a sudden calculated vehemence that brought an answering, growing wave of cheers from the floor. "Tell him
we don't want his Hitler methods here! This is an American convention and we want to keep it that way!"

There was a great roar of applause, and against it the robot-like voices were temporarily overwhelmed, though
there was some deep-growled indication they might still be
trying.

"Now," Bob Munson said before the enthusiasm could
subside, "what is proposed here? That we actually refuse to
support our President by naming the places where he has
honorably and courageously committed American power in
the interest of re-establishing world peace. That we actually
be afraid to say the words 'Gorotoland' and 'Panama.' Are
we, my friends? Are we such cowards in this great convention that we are afraid to say 'Gorotoland' and 'Panama'?
Tell me if we're cowards!"

"NO!" roared the convention, or enough of it so that
even the skeptics of Walter's world had to admit that he
was carrying a good majority with him.

"I should hope not!" he shouted. "I should hope not! All
right, then, if we aren't afraid, let's say so! Let's take the
only action we can take, consistent with supporting our
great President and his policies. Let's write it into the platform of this party in words that will ring from San Francisco to Peking and back again. Let's repudiate this attempt
by a minority of the platform committee to tiptoe past the
realities of the age we live in. Let's vote down their amendment, let's adopt the committee report, and then as a free
and fearless convention, let's vote a foreign policy plank
that will show the world that we stand behind our great
President united and unafraid! Mr. Speaker, I ask the convention to vote down the minority amendment!"

Once again came a roar of applause, the Michigan
delegation raised its standards and waved them wildly, the
band broke into a few bars of the Fight Song, quickly
stilled as the Speaker stepped forward to introduce Roger P.
Croy. The ex-Governor of Oregon came forward from his

seat beside Esmé Stryke with a grave and thoughtful air.

There was a brief demonstration from Oregon, a welcoming hand from floor and galleries, no sound whatever from the claque. Had a vote been taken at that moment, Bob Munson knew, he could have carried the convention with him. But parliamentary procedures would not permit it, Roger P. Croy had reserved the right of rebuttal and now he claimed it. He began in gravely measured tones and it was apparent at once to the Senator from Michigan that he was mounting a very skillful attack. The issue still was any man's.

"Mr. Chairman," Roger P. Croy said slowly, "I want to tell you about two young men. I shall not," he said, raising a graceful hand as a murmur of protest began to come from many places across the floor, "make any attempt to assess blame for their deaths, or attribute invidious motivations to any man or any group where they are concerned. The candidate I favor in this convention completely and finally repudiates any such type of argument."

"We don't hear him say so!" somebody shouted, but Robert P. Croy ignored it.

"Picture, if you will," he said gently, "two fine, upstanding young Americans, one white and one"—there was the slightest perceptible emphasis—"black, come to the heart of their beautiful city of San Francisco to participate in all the fun and excitement that goes with the selection of candidates at a great national convention. Fun and excitement, yet serious things, too—for both these young men were earnest students of affairs, sincerely concerned for their country's welfare, sincerely concerned about such things as foreign policy and war. One of them was, in his student days, something of a rebel against authority in these areas, so deeply concerned and so dedicated to the cause of world peace that he did, on occasion, make public protest. All honor to him," Robert P. Croy said gravely, "for having the great sincerity and courage of his convictions.

"The other, less favored in education and upbringing, was yet moved by the noble aspirations of his race to seek answers for the troubling problems he saw everywhere in the world about him. In his quiet, less publicized way, he too made up his mind what was right and proceeded to seek it out.

"So, Mr. Chairman," said Roger P. Croy, and it was some tribute to his well-known powers as an orator that he now had the convention, 99 percent of which at that moment knew absolutely nothing about William Everett Hollister II or Booker T. Saunders, quite spellbound, "so they decided, separately, not consulting, not together—these two brave young men who were destined to die together in a great cause never even met, as far as we know, never even knew each other, never even smiled the smile of brotherhood or exchanged the glance of a shared conviction—these two brave young men decided that in the person and the candidacy of the great leader of their great state they had found the answer to their doubts and worries . . . they had found, if you please, Mr. Chairman, the way to world peace.

"So we see them come, laughing and confident in the cause of their candidate, to Union Square in the bright sparkling sunshine that only San Francisco knows how to confer with such sweet beneficence upon her children and her guests. Earnest, sincere, dedicated—yes, Mr. Chairman, *noble*. One white and one—black, we see them come, not knowing one another but linked in the great bond of the great cause of world peace—to Union Square in the sun.

"But wait, Mr. Chairman! Wait! There are shadows on that sun. Something ominous underlies the sparkling air. Evil things are moving beneath the palm fronds and the sweetly swooping doves of Union Square. An ugly spirit is abroad, walking in the name of another candidate for high office—*not,* Mr. Chairman," he said sharply as an angry murmur of protest began to rise from many Knox delegates—"*not* that he knows it, *not* that he directs it, *not* that he has ever consciously said or ever would say, 'I want the deaths of two noble young men who favor my opponent.' No, *no,* Mr. Chairman! Never that!

"But, Mr. Chairman"—and his voice dropped sadly—"even that great man is subject to error. Even he can miscalculate and set in motion forces whose outcome can only be evil . . . and destruction . . . and death. Even he, who cannot, as captain, escape responsibility for his ship, can set it upon a course whose end can only be tragedy.

"And so he has, Mr. Chairman, so he has! In error—human, understandable—but, alas, how inevitable! For see them, our two young friends as they enter the Square, innocent—happy—excited—eager—dedicated—*alive*. How many minutes remain to them, Mr. Chairman? *How many seconds?* Alas, too few! The hostile glance, the angry word, the quick, vengeful act—the blows, dealt in the name of Orrin Knox—yes, I *know,* Mr. Chairman," he said harshly as indignant protests rose from the floor—"not with his knowledge, I *know* that. But *in* his name—and alas, how tragically—*for* the cause he represents, which is the cause of foreign entanglement, the cause of destroying international law, the cause of ruthless aggression by this great power against two tiny ones, the cause of endless war!

"That is what has killed our two young friends, in Union Square in the glorious sunshine shadowed by the harsh ambitions of a candidate and his ruthless backers. They have come seeking peace and life. They have found war—and death. . . .

"Mr. Chairman," Roger P. Croy said solemnly, "surely this convention will not, now, repudiate the cause of peace for which they died. Surely it will not now write into the platform of this great party the bloody names of two little countries, and an open endorsement of war. Surely this language is sufficient, and I quote—'Believing that the interests of world peace can best be served by halting armed aggression wherever it may occur, we applaud the declared intention of the President of the United States to conciliate and settle world differences in such areas of conflict on a basis of peaceful negotiation.'

"Can honest men argue with that? Can decent men argue with that? Can our two young friends, wherever they may be, and we pray God their rest is peaceful and quiet with a peace and quiet a ruthless political ambition has denied them on this earth—can they argue with that? I think not, Mr. Chairman. It approves the President, which seems to be the worry of my distinguished friend the Senator from Michigan. It endorses the President's program of peaceful negotiations. It states the danger to the world as reasonable men see it. What more can possibly be asked of us, ladies and gentlemen of the convention? What is the issue here, what is the trouble? Why was it necesssary for two brave young men to die? Surely this language says it all, firmly and effectively and fearlessly as befits this great party and its great President. Surely there is no argument here!

"My friends," he said solemnly, "in the name of honor, in the name of decency, in the name of national interest, in the name of two brave young men, one white and one—

black, who have so bravely made the last, great sacrifice for the cause of peace, I urge you most respectfully to approve the minority report which embodies this language and thus affirm our support of our great President and the cause of peace."

And he turned and walked, soberly and slowly as befitted an ex-Governor of the great state of Oregon, back along the ramp past Bob Munson, who did not bother to look up from his earnest conversation with a Hal Knox whose sad eyes looked as though he had just about had it.

"Are there further seconds or rebuttals?" the Speaker asked. There was a pause for a moment, then a stirring back along the ramp. One of the assistant sergeants-at-arms hurried forward to murmur in his ear. He turned to the convention.

"The distinguished Senator from Michigan wishes to speak in rebuttal after a fifteen-minute recess," he said. "Without objection the convention will stand in recess until"—he glanced at his watch—"9:17 P.M. Good Lord," he added to the sergeant-at-arms, "is it that late already? Time goes."

"The convention, as you have just seen, has entered a recess period for fifteen minutes," Frankly Unctuous the Anchor Man said smoothly in his booth above, while in the distance delegates and audience could be seen stretching, eating, gossiping, going out to the toilets, milling about. "In this time, it perhaps would be helpful if we reviewed briefly what has occurred here this afternoon and in the opening hours of what promises to be a long and possibly hectic evening. We have asked Walter Dobius, America's leading philosopher-statesman, whose column, 'The Way It Is' is read by many millions of you, to assist us. Walter"—with a smile of brotherhood, a glance of shared conviction—"you will amend, revise, correct, dispute, or interject, as you deem necessary."

"I doubt that I shall deem it necessary," Walter said with a calm, judicious air. "It does promise, as you say, to be a hectic evening."

"Yes," Frankly Unctuous said, and his expression became suitably solemn. "What we have seen so far represents, I think, an extraordinary departure from the pattern of most previous American political conventions. We have seen a United States Senator hustled bodily from the platform as he sought to oppose the candidacy of a Secretary of State. We have seen a growing spirit of ugliness and hate. It is an old truism, I suppose, Walter, that violence begets violence, and certainly we have had proof of that here at the Cow Palace today. Because supporters of Secretary Knox—apparently without his personal knowledge, Walter, I am sure we are all agreed on that—"

Walter shrugged.

"He said so in his statement," he observed in a tone that destroyed with indifference.

"Yes, he did," Frankly agreed. "But because his supporters were responsible for a riot this morning which has now claimed the lives of the two young men you have just heard described by former Governor Roger P. Croy of Oregon, the supporters of Governor Edward M. Jason of California have apparently decided to meet fire with fire. They seem extraordinarily well organized, don't they, Walter, and quite determined to counter every misstatement of fact from the other side with some notable rejoinder of their own. Their presence lends a certain spice to the proceedings in the Cow Palace tonight which might otherwise be lacking. And it further demonstrates a new and fascinating alliance in American politics. Perhaps you could describe this alliance for us, Walter."

"I should be happy to," Walter Dobius said. "Its leaders, of course, are the foreign policy organization known as the Committee on Making Further Offers for a Russian Truce, otherwise known as COMFORT; the leading Negro organization, Defenders of Equality for You, known as DEFY; and the Konference on Efforts to Encourage Patriotism, known as KEEP."

"Right there, Walter," Frankly Unctuous said, "how does it come about that three such disparate organizations —COMFORT, with its constant search for new, peaceful accommodations with the Communist world; DEFY, which has heretofore been principally concerned with furthering the Negro drive for better things; and KEEP, with its somewhat adamant opposition to foreign wars and agreements of any kind—should be able to see eye to eye on the candidacy of Governor Jason? Doesn't it seem like a rather strange mismating, so to speak—a case of political bedfellows being even stranger than is sometimes the case at a convention?"

"Perhaps even more than Governor Jason," Walter said, "I think the President and Secretary Knox are the keys to it. This is a great movement of protest we are seeing here, one of the authentic rebellions of thought of our history. It is inevitable, it seems to me, that COMFORT, for instance, should oppose the Administration's utter repudiation and betrayal of all forms of international cooperation, as exemplified by the prolonged and fruitless struggles in Gorotoland and Panama. It is inevitable that DEFY, having achieved so many of the political and educational goals of the Negro, should now be seeking a speedy and complete equality in the economic field—and that its leaders should realize that in alliance with other groups it will be ten times more powerful and successful than it is now. Obviously opposition to the Administration's ill-advised and foredoomed foreign policy forms the easiest and surest basis for such an alliance. And finally, it is not surprising to find KEEP, which has always opposed foreign adventures of any kind as being Communist-inspired plots to drag us down, willing to join, perhaps somewhat uneasily, in an alliance with groups it has always feared and despised.

"The main issue for all of these is opposition to the Hudson-Knox policies, whose defeat they consider more important and more vital than anything else before the country. It is from this feeling, I think, that Governor Jason draws his principal support and will, in my opinion, conquer this convention."

"Certainly he will, I think we can all agree," Frankly Unctuous said smoothly, "if further violence is forthcoming from the Knox camp. Why don't you just stand by here, Walter, while the Majority Leader renews his appeal, and perhaps from time to time we may be able to offer comments or interpretations that may assist our viewers in understanding his remarks and their effect upon this convention—which now stands," he concluded gravely, "at the crucial moment for many things and many people."

"Not the least of them," Walter said with a sudden grimness, "the President of the United States."

"Why, yes," Frankly agreed, obviously a little startled by his guest's abrupt change of subject and mood. "The President, too."

"Mr. Speaker," Bob Munson said slowly, and this time no chant from the galleries greeted him, only an expectant silence everywhere, "I hesitate to do what I am about to do, yet I think it is necessary in order to put the remarks of the distinguished National Committeeman from Oregon in proper perspective.

"He has talked to you about two young men, unfortunate victims of a riot in Union Square this morning. I am going to talk to you about them too. Unlike Governor Croy, I am going to deal in facts, not fictions. Because of the time —no more than half an hour—in which I have had to find these facts, they are not entirely complete. But they will give you the picture.

"The names of these two youths were William Everett Hollister II and Booker T. Saunders. Both were twenty-two.

"William Hollister was the product of a wealthy broken home who, the record shows, was ousted successively from six private schools before he finally was able to matriculate at the public high school in Burlingame, California. There he had a record of indifferent scholarship and repeated clashes with authority. At the age of seventeen he entered the University of California at Berkeley, and promptly became associated with all the radical-extremist elements on the campus. He had a record of thirteen arrests for disturbing the peace, seven for malicious destruction of University property, three for illegal breaking and entry. Although considered to have a mind of some brilliance, he did just enough academic work to remain in school. He was a perennial troublemaker, a constant leader of so-called 'student rebellions,' a constant protester against anything, apparently, as long as it was something the authorities—any authorities—were for.

"He was, in short, an academic tramp with a flair for publicity—of which," Bob Munson said dryly, pausing to take a sip of water before completing his sentence—"certain local newspapers thoughtfully saw to it that he received a great deal."

"The Majority Leader," Frankly Unctuous broke in to say with a deprecating smile to Walter, "seems to disapprove of youthful independence. But I must confess I can't see how it has any bearing upon the fact that the youth is dead. That is all that really matters, wouldn't you say?"

"I am sure it is all that interests the delegates, the country, and the world," Walter agreed.

"Booker T. Saunders," Senator Munson continued, "was born into the poorest economic conditions and never made much attempt to get out of them. He barely managed to get through grammar school where he, too, had a record of constant disciplinary infractions. He dropped out of high school at the end of his freshman year. After that he drifted through a succession of menial jobs, presently joining a street gang and embarking upon a criminal career which in the past four years had made him a familiar figure to police. He was arrested four times for possession of narcotics, three times for attempted rape, six times for breaking and entering, five times for chronic alcoholism, once for suspected murder. On various technicalities, most of these were dismissed though he did serve six months in one rape case.

"These were the two noble, dedicated youths whom the distinguished National Committeeman of Oregon called upon to buttress his case. I submit to you that their deaths, while regrettable as all violent deaths are regrettable, were perhaps no more than their lives and characters had made inescapable. Certainly I do not think any fair-minded persons can regard them as martyrs to anything but the general chaos and waste of our present society with its general loosening of every restraint required for stability.

"Now let me turn for a brief concluding moment in this distasteful but, I think, necessary recital, to the riot in Union Square which brought about their deaths."

He paused and then went on in a steady, hammering tone.

"Despite the immediate assumption and assertion by television commentators—made instantaneously without any checking at all, and dutifully echoed by certain powerful segments of the press as soon as they could rush it into print—there is no slightest evidence from any source whatsoever that this riot was started by backers of the Secretary of State. [There was a wild burst of applause from Knox delegates. He went steadily ahead over it.]

"Not one single, solitary witness of any credibility whatever has come forward to claim, with proof, that it was Knox-inspired, Knox-authorized, or Knox-started. The so-called 'Knox riot' is the pure and simple creation of a handful of commentators and a group of powerful journalists, all of them deeply hostile to the Secretary of State and deeply committed to the candidacy of the Governor of California. It is they who have charged the Secretary of State with fostering violence—in order to cover up the violence from the other side. That is the truth of it, if anywhere in this convention—or anywhere in this country—or anywhere in this world—men still honor the truth!"

Abruptly the hall was once again in an uproar with shouts of approval, applause, and a wave of boos, some directed at him, some directed at the press sections and the television booths Olympian above.

"Well, well," Frankly Unctuous said directly into the camera with a humorous, candid smile and a mock pretense of wiping his forehead. "I guess we're to be the villains of the piece once again, eh, Walter? I guess the poor old television and the poor old press must once again serve as whipping boys for those who have no genuine arguments to support them. The really interesting thing, of course," he added, resuming his judicious gravity, "is that all of this that has happened here in the past few hours seems to place both the Majority Leader and the Speaker squarely on the side of Secretary Knox in this contest, making of this a convention about which one might say, at the least, that it is influenced, if not completely controlled."

"Even more interesting than that," Walter Dobius said with a spiteful distaste he made no attempt to conceal, "is the fact as you noted a few moments ago, that these young men are dead. However much he may attack their characters when they can no longer defend themselves, and no matter how much he attacks you or us in the press, *the boys are dead*. They were *murdered*, and no amount of personal smearing of them or of the press can change that fact."

"And while no one may have come forward to prove that the Knox forces did, in fact, start the riot," Frankly agreed smoothly, "by the same token, no one has come forward—nor, one suspects, can come forward—to prove that they did not. So there it stands. Our own reporter on the spot is of the impression that they did. I would suggest that his judgment is as good as any—including that of the Senate Majority Leader," he said, permitting for a second a genuine contempt to break through his careful suavity, "who at the time was some distance from the scene, in a suite at the Hilton Hotel plotting strategy to assist the Secretary of State. . . . But," he added swiftly, all smooth, profound, plum-pudding analysis again, "let us see what he has to say now."

"I submit to you, my friends of this great convention," Bob Munson said, "that we cannot in all conscience base our votes upon the crucial issue of foreign policy, or the crucial issue of a nominee for Vice President, upon emotional and unfactual appeals such as those made by the National Committeeman from Oregon. No amount of emotionalism can conceal that the issue is a very simple one: we are for our President or we are against him. We approve what he has done and is doing in Gorotoland and Panama, or we do not. We support him, or we fail him— and we all go down together. It is not a time to quibble or be emotional. It is a time to endorse the only course consistent with the honor and integrity of the United States and this great party.

"I urge you to reject the minority amendment, adopt the committee recommendation that the convention write its own foreign policy plank, and then write into the platform the courageous and forthright endorsement of our great President that the hour and the crisis demand."

"Mr. Chairman!" someone shouted from the California delegation as he left the lectern. "Mr. Speaker, California demands a roll-call vote on the minority amendment."

"I don't think there will be much disagreement with that," the Speaker nodded, and for a moment the convention was laughing together in some relief and reasonable friendliness again.

"And now we shall see," Frankly Unctuous said dryly, "whether so-called 'emotionalism' or Senator Munson's notably calm and dispassionate appeal for support of the President carries the day. And also whether the ancient injunction to 'say nothing but good of the dead,' so strikingly followed just now by the Senator, is still respected and honored by his countrymen."

"Al—a—bama!" cried the Secretary (Anna Hooper Bigelow of New Hampshire, her bony frame clad in a mustard-green sheath, wearing a purple toque topped by ostrich feathers pinned with an enormous rhinestone buckle, exercising the office of glory she had held for three successive conventions).

"Madam Secretary," Alabama said in deep bass accents,

"the great State of Alabama, where Southun hospitality flourishes and the win's are sof' an' gennle—"

"All right," the Speaker said as a few good-natured boos began across the floor, "all *right*."

"—casts 14 votes NO on the minority amendment."

"A—laska!" cried Anna Hooper Bigelow.

"Alaska, the forty-ninth State, where summer's suns and winter's snows grace the fastest-growing State in the Union—"

"All *right*," the Speaker said.

"—casts 9 votes YES for the minority amendment."

"A—ri—zona!"

"Arizona casts 8 votes NO on the minority amendment."

"Arkansas!"

"Arkansas, health resort of the nation, casts 20 votes NO on the minority amendment."

"Ca—li—fornia!"—and there was a sudden waiting silence.

"Madam Secretary," the strident voice of Esmé Harbellow Stryke announced, "there seems to be some division in the California delegation. We request a poll of the delegation."

Twenty tense minutes later Anna Hooper Bigelow announced, "California votes 54 YES, 40 NO on the minority amendment!"

There were wild yells from the Knox camp, boos from the Jasonites, excited figurings and analyzings everywhere.

"Colorado!" Anna Hooper Bigelow said.

"Mrs. Knox," said a lady from CBS, leaning over the box railing to peer with an intense brightness into Beth's face, "how have you enjoyed the proceedings so far today?"

"Let me ask you a question," Beth said coldly. "How have you got the gall to ask me such a thing after what has happened here tonight?"

"I'm paid for it, Mrs. Knox," the lady from CBS said, flushing angrily. "Believe me, I don't enjoy talking to you."

"Nor I you," Beth said, turning away.

"Mrs. Knox," the lady from CBS appealed to Crystal in a placating tone, "Mrs. Knox, perhaps you can help me. I don't mean to offend, honestly, but my network does want me to get a little interview, and I—well, I'm embarrassed and I really didn't know what else to say to your mother-in-law to start it off. Have *you* any comment to make?"

"Just a minute," Crystal said, pausing to listen as Delaware cast six votes YES on the minority amendment. "Yes," she said slowly. "I think there has been a deliberate attempt to smear my father-in-law, to attach to him blame for something for which neither he nor his people are responsible; to place these whole proceedings on a basis of violence, demagoguery, and fear. I think this is foreign to our way of doing things in this country. I think Governor Jason will live to regret it."

"Then you think," CBS' lady said, "that these charges against the Secretary of State that we have heard here are exaggerated?"

"I said untrue," Crystal snapped. "I didn't say exaggerated. What are you trying to do, anyway?"

"Just get an interview," CBS' lady said, apparently close to tears.

"I think you've had enough," Crystal said shortly.

Dolly Munson was the only one left, but after a glance at her expression CBS hastily removed her elbow from the railing, got up, and walked away. "Darling," she said with a chuckle as she met the lady columnist of the *Reporter* in the walkway beneath the stands, "I've just given the Knox women a fit, and am *I* going to have fun with them in my broadcast!" Five minutes later she was seated before the cameras, oblivious to the roll call still booming along over her head, saying sweet as cream:

"The women of the Knox family appear to be at the point of anger and tears tonight as the tactics of Secretary of State Orrin Knox are apparently backfiring in this explosively dramatic convention. In a mood of near-hysteria, Mrs. Beth Knox, the Secretary's wife, refused to answer my questions just now about the violence which has claimed the lives of two young supporters of Mr. Knox's opponent, Governor Edward M.—"

"Mrs. Jason," the lady from *Newsweek* said with a chatty air on the other side of the auditorium, "isn't this a thrilling and exciting evening for you!"

"It's very interesting," Ceil said cautiously. "Excuse me, did you hear Florida's vote?"

"Against the minority amendment, I think," *Newsweek*'s lady said. "Do you think your husband is going to win this roll call?"

"I have no idea," Ceil said. "What do you think?"

"Oh, I *hope* so," *Newsweek* said. "Tell me, how is the Governor? Is he confident?"

Ceil smiled.

"All candidates are confident at this stage, aren't they? That's part of it."

"Mrs. Jason, Mrs. Jason," *Newsweek* said coyly. "You're being evasive with me, now!"

"No, I'm not," Ceil said calmly, and after a second her interrogator decided to drop the coyness and try another approach.

"Are you looking forward to being in Washington?" she asked. Ceil gave her a polite smile.

"I always look forward to whatever I'm going to be doing, wherever I am. It's part of leading a full life, don't you think, to anticipate things rather than look back? I find it so."

"Yes," the lady from *Newsweek* agreed, momentarily stumped, while over the loudspeakers Idaho could be heard voting NO on the minority amendment. "Did you ever think," she said doggedly, "when you married the Governor, that some day you might be the wife of the Vice President of the United States—perhaps even the President?"

"I was sure life with Ted would be interesting and rewarding and not dull," Ceil said pleasantly. "I was right in that."

"I see," *Newsweek* said, thinking, God, she's being a tough bitch. Doesn't she know we're on her side, for God's sake?

"Tell me, Mrs. Jason," she said in a deliberately nasty tone, "do you agree that Orrin Knox is a murderer, as your husband's people said, and do you agree that he is responsible for the violence in this convention?"

This time, finally, she got a direct reponse. For just a second Ceil flashed her a look of naked dismay, followed by utter hostility. Then the courteous mask went on again.

"I think you are completely despicable," she said politely. "Why don't you go somewhere else?"

"Well!" *Newsweek* said, changing colors like some waspish little chameleon, "Well, I *will!*"

And she did, and for several minutes, as she walked back to the periodicals section, had quite a struggle with herself. But discipline and training and knowing what was Right decided the issue. "Just saw C. Jason," she began typing her memo to New York. "She, Ted both confident. Looking forward D.C. because quote I always look forward, 'spart of leading full life, anticipate sted look back. Always knew life Ted be interesting wherever going, V.P., P. or what." She had a story, did the lady, in Ceil Jason's obvious horror of the way her husband was permitting his people to act in the convention, but it wasn't going to appear in *Newsweek* even if the editors would have permitted it. She, no more than they, intended to help Orrin Knox with *anything*.

"Illinois!" Anna Hooper Bigelow cried sharply. There was a pause and again the great hall hushed to a tense attention. One candidate's home state was divided, what would the other—yes, there it came:

"Illinois demands a pole of the delegation, Madam Secretary."

"The Secretary will poll," the Speaker said.

"I don't like it, Ted," Bob Leffingwell said quietly at the Mark Hopkins. Its corridors were deserted now, only one guard remained on the door, no bands thumped and shudered from below. Everyone was either at the Cow Palace or sitting enrapt before television. The candidate, his manager, a couple of secretaries in the outer office and a cop to bar the door were all that remained at headquarters tonight.

"I'm sorry for that," Governor Jason said with an equal quietness. "I think it's been quite effective so far. We're leading in the vote right now, aren't we?"

"So far," Bob Leffingwell agreed. "I don't think we're going to win it, but—"

"But it's going to be close. Very close."

"Perhaps so. But I still don't like—what's been going on. I think it's going to turn against you, before long. I think reaction is going to set in. This is an American crowd. They enjoy seeing people pushed, but sooner or later they react against it."

"Just let them stay with me another twenty-four hours," Ted said softly, "and I won't care."

"Won't you?" Bob Leffingwell said thoughtfully, not looking at him, staring at the television set where Anna Hooper Bigelow was repeating, "Mrs. Harvey S. Rodebaugh, NO." . . . "I should think you might."

"Why? I'm not responsible for what's going on there. I

didn't organize the chorus, that was Fred's and LeGage's and Rufus' idea. I didn't ask Roger Croy to take off into the stratosphere on a couple of no-good tramps—but I must say he was damned effective, and I don't think Bob Munson managed to kill it much, either, particularly with the television boys helping us out and knocking down his remarks for us. I think it's all been damned effective."

"I'm not saying it isn't effective," Bob Leffingwell said slowly. "I'm interested to know you're satisfied with it. And that you think you're not responsible. 'The captain of his ship,' to quote Roger Croy. . . . I thought you were."

"I'm a passenger," Ted Jason said. "I've been a passenger for six months and more."

"You didn't sound like a passenger yesterday. You told me to let COMFORT and DEFY and KEEP into this. You were giving all the orders then. It wasn't my idea."

"What has your idea been," Ted inquired pleasantly, "except to issue sounds of warning and worry? I've been a little puzzled, sometimes."

"My idea has been," Bob Leffingwell said coldly, "that you should fight an honorable campaign and win or take your licking as the event turned out."

"I don't like to take lickings," Governor Jason said blandly. "It isn't part of my family pattern. . . . Look!" he said, turning toward Bob Leffingwell and tapping him firmly on the knee. "If the wild-eyed Negroes, the half-assed liberals, and the crazy conservative kooks want to link hands and dance around my Maypole, that's their problem, not mine. I think it's great to have their support, if it helps me win"—he hesitated for an infinitesimal fraction and some little warning thought flashed across Bob Leffingwell's mind, so fleeting as to be almost subconscious —"this nomination."

"You know Orrin's people didn't start that riot," Bob Leffingwell said, "and you know he didn't have a thing to do with it. 'With-draw, mur-der-er.' My God, Ted, what are you getting into? And these blank-faced semi-storm troopers standing around like sick children playing games! We're going to be lucky if we get out of this with no one else hurt. What are you letting it build up to?"

The Governor gave him a calm glance.

"You heard me talk with Orrin this morning. I told him I had told you to issue orders against any form of violence, didn't I? And I had, hadn't I? What more—"

"You know what more," Bob Leffingwell said flatly. "You seem to think you score a point when the scum of San Francisco calls Orrin murderer. Who scores when the Majority Leader of the United States calls you Hitler?"

"I don't lose in the minds of those who believe in me," the Governor said softly, "because they don't believe it."

"But decent people do," Bob Leffingwell said, and quick as a shot, Ted said, "Oh?"

His companion flushed but stood his ground, while somewhere in front of them, quite forgotten now, Anna Hooper Bigelow reported patiently, "Horace B. Stevenson votes AYE."

"Yes," Bob Leffingwell said, "they do. And they are going to leave you because of it."

"Oh, are they?" Governor Jason asked, still softly.

"Yes," Bob Leffingwell said, unflinching.

"How soon?"

"Not long, if this continues."

"I shall have to take this into account in making my plans," the Governor said.

"You should," Bob Leffingwell agreed.

There was a silence, while Anna Hooper Bigelow polled Justin B. Thompson, who voted NO, and Alicia Tiburoni, who voted AYE.

"So Patsy was right," Ted said finally in a thoughtful voice. Bob Leffingwell shrugged.

"Patsy is often right, for the wrong reasons. I think we'd better listen to Illinois, now."

"On a pole of the delegation," Anna Hooper Bigelow announced, "Illinois casts 53 votes NO on the minority amendment, 20 votes AYE."

"Orrin isn't in very good shape," the Governor said with satisfaction. "Even if," he added gently, "the decent people *are* flocking to him."

"You don't care as long as you win, do you?"

Ted smiled pleasantly.

"Oh, I'm determined to, now . . . whatever I run for." His expression suddenly became dead-serious. "Because, look you, my friend: no man tries for these offices at the top unless he has some conviction that he personally knows what is best for the country—unless he personally feels that he has a mission to try to put it into effect. There has to be—there is in all of us—some inner conviction that *we know best* and that we have simply got to try to do it. This may be mistaken, I grant you. Obviously history eliminates many who share the conviction equally. But underneath everything else, there's that—the feeling of '*I* want—*my* program—for *my* country.' "

"But what would your program be?" Bob Leffingwell asked. "At the moment you're nothing but a focus for discontents—a sort of political back fence on which all the unhappy little boys in the neighborhood are scribbling their dirty words against the President and Orrin Knox. . . . What do *you* stand for, in your mind? What positive program are you offering?"

"Just myself," the Governor said calmly. "Which, in contrast to the opposition, is not too bad a selling point for many people, obviously. As for the other—I'll develop a program, once I'm in. It won't be difficult. I'll have plenty of help."

"Of the same kind you have now in seeking this nomination," Bob Leffingwell said flatly.

The Governor shrugged.

"Listen," he said, nodding to the set. "What's Indiana going to do for her great neighbor from Illinois?"

"Stay with him, I think," Bob Leffingwell said, deciding to drop it, for it was all over, anyway, "though there will be some interesting breaks further down the list."

"I don't like this, Stanley," Orrin said at their equally deserted headquarters at the Fairmont as Anna Hooper Bigelow called, "Innn—dee—anna! . . . It's too close. They told me five defections in Illinois and it's fifteen more than they said. He's going to get a big vote on this."

"He isn't going to win, though," Senator Danta predicted calmly. "I've just checked with our people on the floor. It's still holding."

"Hmph," the Secretary said. He rubbed his eyes and shook his head as if to clear it. "How strange it is, Stanley: I've been accused of the most monstrous things, two young men who may have been worthless but were still human are dead, the ugliest sort of menacing element has been introduced into the convention, I've been most unjustly and viciously blamed—and here we sit counting votes, just as though the world were still entirely sane. That's what conventions can do for you: they establish their own logic, which is like no other logic known to man, and you ride with it because to do anything else would be to go stark, staring mad. . . . I don't really know what else I can do, do you, to counteract this violence charge? I've issued my statement—Bob and the Speaker, bless their hearts, have done what they could—our people are under strict orders to refrain from any provocation whatsoever—"

"And so everybody is being successfully paralyzed into inaction and successfully browbeaten into allowing what could be a Jason walkaway, if carried a bit further," Senator Danta said soberly. "The man I really feel sorry for is Ted, because I don't think, for all his cleverness and intelligence and skill and force, that he really realizes, yet, what he's letting himself in for."

"I could feel sorry for him, too," Orrin Knox said tartly, "and maybe I will—some other time. Right now, I find his methods vicious, underhanded, unprincipled, and dangerous, and if his bullyboys swallow him up I think he deserves it. . . . What's Indiana doing?"

"Indiana," Anna Hooper Bigelow said obligingly from the screen, "casts 31 votes YES for the minority amendment, 12 votes NO."

"Stanley—"

"I'll go and check again," Senator Danta said, "but they assure me there's enough to stop him."

"But he's got to be stopped big," Orrin said. "And he isn't being stopped big. Look at that!" he exclaimed as the cameras cut abruptly from the vote to the outside of the Cow Palace. The ranks of sullen-faced demonstrators had substantially increased since the cameras' last visit. Now there were several hundred, standing in groups around the entrances and near the parking lots. A new element seemed to have been added: now they had been provided with black leather jackets and helmets, on each of which the words JASON MEANS PEACE had been painted in white. They permitted no slightest flicker of intelligence to break through as the cameras traveled across their deliberately somber faces. They intended to appear, and they succeeded, lifeless, cold, and menacing.

"What *is* that man encouraging?" Orrin said in a wondering voice. "We'll be lucky to get out of this without somebody else getting hurt."

"As long as it isn't one of yours or mine," Stanley Danta said softly.

The Secretary looked grim.

"It better not be." His voice changed and an expression close to horror came into his eyes. "I swear to God, Stanley, I do not know what I would do."

"Kansas requests a pole of the delegation," the Speaker was saying as the cameras cut back inside. "The Secretary will poll."

Flying through the night across the enormous country that was his to lead, the President was thinking of his own concerns and of the things the sensitive always think of when flying across America: how vast it is, how fast it goes, what was it like to cross it by oxcart, how did the pioneers ever do it, how brave, how brave—and what do we have left in us now to match their courage as we slide through the reaches of the sky at six hundred—eight hundred—one thousand—two thousand—who-knows-what-thousand—miles an hour? He thought, inevitably, too, of his predecessors, what they did, how they felt, how they managed this great, unwieldy nation as it grew and grew and grew, in size and power if not always in charity and grace.

He was tired tonight, and he knew he would be tireder before the week was done; yet he had known for some hours that he must advance the time of his arrival in San Francisco. The reports he had received from Lucille, Bob Munson, the Speaker, Cullee, and Lafe and half a hundred others at the convention had been filled with a steadily growing concern giving way, in recent hours, to open alarm. The appearance of the strange demonstrators, their robot-like aspect and articulation—the cleverest psychological touch of the whole business, he conceded grimly, was that blank-faced look and the menacing, mechanical outbursts in the galleries—had given to the convention an atmosphere unlike any in the memory of most of its participants. Then had come the growing violence, the riot in Union Square, the deaths of two young no-goods—worthless as human beings, like so many of the world's symbols in the twentieth century, but absolutely invaluable as propaganda—and now a bitterness building to some further outbreak whose nature could not be foreseen.

It was all, he supposed, typical of what seemed to be the century's major theme as it sank rapidly and perhaps irrevocably into a welter of chaos, uncertainty, and violence almost everywhere: a pointless, insensate rebellion against everything, for no reason, no purpose, no logic, no nothing. Out of the great creeds of liberation, uplift, and reform had come finally—nihilism, heartless . . . mindless . . . pointless . . . useless. Millions had died already in the names it put on for a day and lost as easily, many millions would die—just so somebody could have the sick emotional thrill of being against.

It didn't matter against what.

Just against.

But now, as had happened here and there, clever and astute managers had arisen to try to channel nihilism behind their own ambitions; and he was sure they were going to find, as so many had before them, that nihilism destroyed both its participants and its would-be profiteers. When it had all ended—when the whole world-wide orgy of slaughter and insensate rebellion had come to its final horrid end—what would be left to preside over the echoing graveyard of humanity's hopes? No individual, surely, no cause in whose name it had all begun. Just more slaughter . . . and more rebellion . . . and more awful, pathetic emptiness of mind and heart and spirit.

This he had to stop in America, if he could, for his was the responsibility to do it. Never once had he grandly sided with rebellion, placed himself in ringing tones on the side of the nihilists, said blandly that it was all a healthy sign of natural exuberance or long-deferred justice for society to be torn apart. He didn't believe in letting the devils out of the box. He believed in sitting on the lid, for history had shown on too many bloody occasions lately what happened when you let it open. You couldn't tuck the Thing that came out neatly back inside, once it had broken loose to ravage the world.

Harley M. Hudson, in short, was a damned old stick-in-the-mud, not at all enlightened, and someday, perhaps, if his country lived that long, he would be given grateful credit for it.

At this moment, the problem was complicated by the parallel developments in what he and Bob and the Speaker and other old hands were already beginning to think of as "the regular convention." The Jason forces—or, rather, the forces that had chosen to make the Governor of California their instrument—were simply using foreign policy to inflame their adherents in the country. But people like Roger P. Croy and Esmé Stryke were by no stretch of the imagination to be placed in that category. Roger P. Croy was a notorious troublemaker and Esmé Harbellow Stryke was a smart, shrewish little political climber who had clawed her way to the National Committee over other smart, shrewish political ladies, but neither was frivolous concerning politics itself nor the issues that engaged the country. Particularly were they not frivolous about Gorotoland and Panama or the prolonged and unsatisfactory struggles that were going on in those two countries.

He knew that their concern bespoke a perfectly genuine concern on the part of a great many people in their states, and in all the states. Down under the demonstration level, there were many millions of sincerely worried Americans who did not parade, demonstrate, seek headlines, or otherwise use crisis for the care and feeding of their own egos and ambitions. These were deeply troubled about Gorotoland and Panama. The problems in the Platform Committee had been quite genuine, and on an entirely different plane from riots in Union Square and JA-SON MEANS PEACE.

Nonetheless, the two strands in the convention, the one of genuine concern, the other of calculated self-serving protest, were beginning to come together in his mind, as in so many minds, into a single force which he must oppose with everything he could command. Inevitably he and others of good will were being forced into a more and more intolerant position by the deliberate intolerance of the other side. It was true that the intolerance of the other side, commanding as it did great mediums of public communication and many powerful means of carrying its case to the watching country and the world, was of course quite skillful—as always—in putting the blame for its own crimes upon its opponents. But that could not deter him now, nor could it deter, much longer, decent men. The time was coming for them to go ahead regardless and do what they felt they had to do to save the country.

Therefore he was coming early to San Francisco, and as Air Force One swung slowly over the glittering city and the great Bay awash with lights in the clear cold night, his mind was made up on what he must do. Tonight he would lay the groundwork, tomorrow he would act. It did not occur to him at that moment, as the plane began gliding gently toward the airport and clearly below he could see the floodlit Cow Palace surrounded by searchlights sweeping the skies, that tomorrow might already have arrived, a little more quickly than he thought.

"The Secretary reports," the Speaker said into the tense silence—after all the States had voted, after the Commonwealth of Puerto Rico had fulfilled its quadrennial duty of giving everyone a good laugh, after Guam and the Virgin Islands and the Canal Zone—"which will soon be 100 percent American again from Panama City to Colón!" had cast their ballots—"the Secretary reports that on the minority amendment the vote is 643 AYE—["My *God*," Lafe exclaimed to Cullee, against the rising roar of excitement from the floor and galleries]—and," the Speaker concluded in a voice he could not quite keep from sounding excited, "650 NO. The minority amendment is defeated."

SEVEN VOTES, the claque said suddenly, in a monotone that cut heavily across the shouting uproar that filled the hall. SEVEN VOTES, SEVEN VOTES, SEVEN VOTES . . . WHAT NOW, LI-TTLE MAN?

"How exciting it all is!" Krishna Khaleel said to Lord Maudulayne with an ecstatic hiss, and over beyond Kitty Maudulayne, Raoul Barre leaned forward to gesture at the wildly excited delegates on the floor below.

"I wonder," he said with a speculative expression in his eyes, "which li-ttle man they mean."

"Mr. Chairman!" Cullee cried from the California microphone, and here and there, including his own delegation, there were shouts of "Sit down! Sit down!" But he went on unimpressed, "I move that the majority report of the platform committee, which in effect empowers the convention to write the foreign policy plank here on the floor, be adopted."

"Mr. Speaker!" Mary Buttner Baffleburg shouted from the Pennsylvania microphone, "Mr. Speaker, Pennsylvania asks a roll call—"

But there was an enormous "NO!" of impatience and disgust, and the Governor of Pennsylvania grabbed the microphone from her hand and bellowed, "Pennsylvania withdraws that request and urges a voice vote, Mr. Speaker!"

"All those in favor—" the Speaker said quickly.

"AYE!" roared the convention.

"All those opposed the ayes have it," the Speaker said in

one breath. "The Chair recognizes the distinguished delegate from South Carolina, chairman of the House Foreign Affairs Committee, the Honorable J. B. Swarthman. . . . Anna!" he said, hastily turning to her where she sat behind him at a little wooden table with the parliamentarian, "take the gavel for a few minutes, will you, please?"

"But—" she protested with a frightened look. He thrust it into her hand impatiently.

"I'll be close by if you need me. Go on, take it!"

And with an expression at once annoyed and worried, he left the podium hurriedly and began to work his way toward Bob Munson, kneeling in the aisle murmuring in the ear of the chairman of the Illinois delegation.

"Now, Mr.—Madam—Chairman," Jawbone Swarthman began, as the clock on the wall reached 12:07 A.M. and the endurance-contest atmosphere that begins to come over conventions about that time in the morning began to come over this, "what is the issue here?"

"It is, as nearly as we can see it," Frankly Unctuous the Anchor Man said, smiling candidly into the camera in his booth above, "whether the Administration can now succeed in persuading this convention to supinely rubber-stamp the President's foreign policy. Wouldn't you say that's what it's suddenly come to, Walter, after this astounding 650–643 vote that has just barely saved the Administration from defeat?"

"It has come also, I think," Walter said gravely, "to a serious question, not only of whether Orrin Knox can be nominated for Vice President, but even more fundamentally, whether *anyone* associated with the Administration can be nominated."

"This would seem to give the Governor of California a most dramatic boost in his drive to capture that nomination from the Secretary of State, then," Frankly said, "and also would seem to give him some kind of mandate to work within the Administration to moderate the President's policies. Is that how you see it, Walter?"

Walter Dobius gave a smug little smile.

"That is one way to see it, yes."

"If there are other ways," Frankly Unctuous said with a sudden gleam of comprehension and the start of a glorious smile, "then it should be a most dramatic convention, indeed!"

"Madam Chairman," Jawbone was saying as the camera cut abruptly away from Frankly and his smile, back to the rostrum, "now, Madam Chairman, what does the Platform Committee propose here? Why, it just proposes that we affirm our belief in stopping aggression and we applaud our President's actions in attempting to do so. That's what we've just almost voted on, Madam Chairman, it only lost by seven votes, and—"

SEVEN VOTES, the claque said solemnly.

"Yes, I said it, seven votes," Jawbone cried hastily. "You-all up there don't have to parrot everything, I'll say to you, I can do my own speechifyin'. Seven votes is right, Madam Chairman, and that shows one thing. It shows—"

JA-SON MEANS PEACE, the claque observed.

"It *shows*," Jawbone repeated angrily, "that there's a big sentiment in this convention and in this country *against* what's going on in Gorotoland and Panama, Madam Chairman, that's what it shows. We oppose aggression, yes: we hail our great President in his attempts to fight it and negotiate peaceable settlements, yes; but we are *against* the way he's gone about it and the *places* he's chosen to do it. We see what he's tryin' to do, Madam Chairman—why, I sat in those White House conferences myself, I know what he was thinking, but when my famous friend from the Senate, the chairman of the great Senate Foreign Relations Committee, Senator Tom August of Minnesota— when he and I, Madam Chairman, speaking in our respective capacities as chairmen, as well as delegates to this great convention, send up a signal and say, Go slow, Watch out, Rest easy there, boy, why, you-all know there must be some sense behind it, now! Don't you, now?"

There was an upsurge of sound, but so evenly divided between applause and protest that no one could be quite sure which predominated.

"Yes, sir!" Jawbone cried. "That's what we say, Madam Chairman, and that's what this vote of this great convention just now has said! We applaud our great President, we *love* him—"

SEVEN VOTES, the claque reminded, and there was a scattering of boos, applause, and some laughter from the delegates.

"—but we just think we've got to go a little bit easy here, that's all. Folks around the country are mighty upset about this drag-on in Gorotoland, my fellow delegates, you know they are, and they don't like what's going on in Panama, either. The President says he wants negotiations, and *we* want negotiations, but nobody's negotiating yet. They're still shooting, Madam Chairman, yes, ma'am, they're still shooting, and our boys are dying and our money's going down the drain, and my fellow delegates, it just isn't the right time and the right place! We want to stop 'em, yes, but six thousand miles away in Gorotoland? In Panama, where our rights are shaky at best and where these people ought to be our friends and *want* us there instead of us having to always be forcing ourselves on them? And it's dragging, my fellow delegates. It's dragging. We aren't getting anywhere. We just aren't getting anywhere!

"So, Madam Chairman, I move, now that this matter is again before the convention in this little old parliamentary rigamarole, I move the committee language be adopted and again I quote: 'Believing that the interests of world peace can best be served by halting armed aggression wherever it may exist, we applaud the declared intention of the President of the United States to conciliate and settle world differences in such areas of conflict on a basis of peaceful negotiation.'

"I submit that says it all, my fellow delegates and Madam Chairman. I say to you, let's pass it now and stop holding everything up, here!"

"With which sentiment," Frankly Unctuous said with a wry smile to Walter Dobius as the camera returned to them, "I think we must all agree. It is well past midnight, now, and all of us are growing a little weary. But what's this—?" And over his shoulder little figures could be seen moving on the rostrum, down below—"I believe it's Congressman Hamilton of California, one of the few California political figures, and one of the few Negroes, who is apparently not enthusiastically behind Governor Jason. He is evidently going to restate the Administration arguments for stronger language in the platform. While he repeats them, Walter, perhaps you and I might take over the cameras for a few minutes and review just what has gone on here so far. It began, you will remember—" and the convention faded away, and it was guaranteed by two intelligent, earnest, sage, and thoughtful faces agreeing with each other diligently for the next fifteen minutes, that on one network, at least, the sentiments of one of the few Negro leaders not backing Governor Jason would be very smoothly, logically, and skillfully withheld from the country.

Inside the Cow Palace, of course, no such convenient method of obliterating the opposition existed, and so Cullee came to the lectern sure of the attention of the only people who mattered at that moment, 1293 nervous, skittish, tense, upset, unpredictable, and—at this point—quite probably unmanageable delegates. Their little round faces looked up at him from the floor like a basketful of pink pennies; the balloons drifted among the rafters, the banners hung limply, the standards and placards sagged in weary hands. But the explosive potentials were there, even if it was past midnight. The late hour, the increasing exhaustion after more than ten hours of session, made an explosion even more likely. He glanced across at the box where Sarah Johnson was sitting, nodded though he could not see her through the drifting blue haze and the lights slamming straight into his eyes, and spoke briefly and to the point.

"Madam Chairman," he said—the Speaker had left the floor entirely, now, following a phone call whose import— "He's here"—he had just had time to confide tersely to Cullee as they passed on the ramp. Where, Cullee had no idea; possibly right here in a back room somewhere, waiting to state his case, if need be. But he did not think it was time for that yet, and he assumed the Speaker agreed and would tell Harley so, if Harley needed to be told. For the moment, the job was his:

"Madam Chairman, my good old friend from the House has, as usual, confused the issue. This so-called committee language is an insult to the President of the United States. We are here to support the President of the United States, not to insult him.

" 'Believing that the interests of world peace can best be served by halting armed aggression wherever it may exist—' Well, where does it exist, and who began it? And what kind is it? I'll tell you. It's Communist, and it exists in Gorotoland and Panama because the Communists began it there.

"This language is an open, deliberate, and direct insult to the President of the United States, since its clear implication is that there is no distinction to be drawn between kinds of armed action—that they are all 'aggressive,' in the most invidious sense of the word, whatever their motivation and uses, and that the United States is equally guilty in these two situations with the mortal enemies of mankind, the Communist imperialists.

"Let me read on: '. . . we applaud the declared intention of the President of the United States to conciliate and settle world differences in such areas of conflict on a basis of peaceful negotiation.' The 'declared intention,' if you please; the *declared* intention. Is the committee implying here—do *you* want to imply—that your President is telling a lie? *Is* it his intention or is it not? I suggest you stop and think about this for a minute.

"And let me comment briefly on the remarks of my good friend from South Carolina. Gorotoland and Panama aren't the right time and the right places, he says. Is any sane person in this world so naïve as to think that the Communists are going to force an issue with us at times and places that are *convenient* for us? Is anyone so foolish as to think they're going to tailor their subversion of peace to what is best for *us*? Unless we strike first, we are never going to fight at the best time and the best place for us; and I assume that neither my friend from South Carolina or his friends are going to be so awful as to suggest or even contemplate that we strike first. Heaven," he said dryly, "forbid.

"So what makes him think it's ever going to be easy, or quick, or comfortable? It never is. It's always going to be, just as it has been for decades now, awkward and difficult and unsatisfactory and frustrating. But I would suggest to him—and to his friends—and to you—that if we all just hang on a while, it will work out all right.

"Not neatly.

"Not smoothly.

"Not painlessly.

"But all right. . . .

"My fellow delegates," and the hall was very silent, he had them listening with a genuine respect, "the hour is late and we have had enough contention on this issue. You have a man with guts at the head of your party and at the head of your country. For God's sake, stand by him and show a few guts yourselves. It's time.

"Madam Chairman, I move to amend the motion of the delegate from South Carolina by striking all after the words 'Believing that the interests of world peace can best be served by' and substituting after the word 'by' the words 'opposing Communist aggression and infiltration, armed or otherwise, wherever they may exist, we applaud the actions of the President in opposing such Communist aggression and infiltration in Gorotoland and Panama. We wholeheartedly applaud his determination to bring peace and stability to those troubled areas through the medium of peaceful and honest negotiation as soon as the Communist threat has been removed.'

"I ask for a roll-call on my amendment."

"Madam Chairman," Jawbone Swarthman said, returning hastily to the rostrum, and grabbing the microphone, "I think I speak for my friends on my side of this issue when I say we join in that request."

"In the absence of the Speaker, and in my absence," Anna Hooper Bigelow said hastily, and couldn't understand why there was a sudden delighted roar of laughter, "I ask the parliamentarian to call the roll of the States."

"He states it very effectively," Beth said.

"He has the ability," Dolly Munson agreed. "It needed to be put in perspective."

"Yes," Beth said thoughtfully. She smiled with a certain wry grimness. "For the moment, at least, they seem to have forgotten Murderer Knox. I think Bob helped a lot on that."

"Somebody had to," Crystal said with a sudden deep yawn. "It was way out of hand."

Beth studied her for a moment.

"How are you feeling? Shouldn't I take you back to the hotel to bed?"

"I'm going to fold pretty soon," Crystal agreed with a sleepy smile. "But you don't have to take me back. I know you want to stay for the voting. The car's waiting, it won't be any problem. I'll go along pretty soon."

"I think we'd at least better see you to it," Dolly remarked. "I'd feel better."

"And I," Beth agreed.

"Oh, poof!" Crystal said, as a wandering UPI photographer stuck his camera over the edge of the box and took a couple of quick shots of her, just to have something to turn in to the office when he went off duty at 2 A.M. "Don't overdramatize. . . . Isn't that my battered and bewildered husband down there near Ohio? It is! He's waving! He's smiling! He's still alive! Well, bless his heart. I thought he'd be the one in collapse by this time."

"I think he's coming over," Beth said in a pleased voice, and in another couple of moments he did, looking drawn and exhausted, but obviously determined to keep going.

"Hi, Dolly," he said with a tired smile, standing just below them in the press section. "Hi, Mom. How are you?" he asked his wife seriously. She covered his hand on the railing with hers and gave it a reassuring squeeze.

"Thumper and I are tired," she admitted, "but still kicking. What do you hear?"

"Well!" he said. His voice dropped to a confidential murmur, he stood on tiptoes to raise himself toward them, and they leaned down to hear. "I just ran into Cullee a minute ago, and the God-*damndest* rumor is going around the California delegation."

"Alaska requests a poll of the delegation, Madam Chairman."

"The parliamentarian will poll the delegation."

"Is that your intention?" Bob Leffingwell demanded at the Mark.

Ted Jason smiled.

"Let's see how the vote goes," he said, as five telephones began to ring almost simultaneously. "Then we'll argue. Help me with these, will you?"

"I think you must," the Speaker said flatly at a secluded mansion in Burlingame, just down the Peninsula from the Cow Palace. "It may be the only thing that will—"

"Not yet," the President said calmly.

"But you don't know the feeling—"

"I know it as well as though I'd been here," the President told him. "My only psychological and emotional advantage is that I haven't been here—and now I am. But when to make it known, and what to do with it after that, I have to decide."

"But—" the Speaker said angrily.

"Let's listen to the vote," the President suggested. "I'll know better after that."

"This one's going to be too close, too, Stanley."

"Let's listen to the vote and see," Senator Danta suggested, though he was too honest to say it with much conviction.

"Right at this moment," the Secretary said soberly, "I'd say this was anybody's convention."

"At this moment, Walter," Frankly Unctuous said thoughtfully, as behind him on the screen the convention could be seen squirming and stirring like some great basket of eels, "I'd say this was anybody's convention, wouldn't you? The surprises of this night may not yet be over."

"There may," Walter Dobius agreed with a little smile of such savage contempt for a second that it quite puzzled and disturbed millions of viewers, "be more to come."

"On this vote," Anna Hooper Bigelow said an hour later in a voice that trembled with tension and tiredness, "the Yeas for the motion of the delegate from California, Congressman Hamilton, to write in stronger language, are 645—"

"NO!" went up a great roar.

"—and the Nays are 648."

"NO!"

"*Yes!*" she cried in a shaky voice, "and the motion is defeated!"

"What we are seeing here, Walter," Frankly said with great excitement as the hall exploded, "is one of the most startling revolutions in the history of—"

"He has deserved it," Walter Dobius interrupted like an avenging angel, for he thought he had won at last his long battle with the evil men who had betrayed the world, "and now it has come to him."

"Madam Chairman!" Jawbone Swarthman shouted into the bedlam, "I demand a roll-call vote on my milder Platform Committee language, Madam Chairman!"

"Alabama," Alabama shouted even before the Parliamentarian had time to call its name, "Alabama intends, and it hopes other delegations will *all* follow suit, Madam Chairman, to request a poll of the delegation!"

"The Parliamentarian will poll," Anna Bigelow yelled, and sagged against the lectern mopping her forehead furiously with a vermilion handkerchief. "Lordy, lordy!" she said to nobody in particular. "What a night!"

"You're looking awfully pale suddenly," Beth said in a worried tone. "I think we'd better go. Come on."

"No, *no*," Crystal said with a genuine impatience in her voice. "You stay here, you don't want to leave this for one minute, and I'm not going to have you."

"But, really—" Beth protested.

"Don't be foolish, Crys," Dolly Munson agreed quickly. "We'll both go."

"You will *not*," Crystal said, standing up abruptly, staggering a little, steadying herself with one hand on the railing. "I'm not going to spoil the rest of it for you. Hal's back down there somewhere. I'll get one of the sergeants-at-arms to find him for me, and I'll even ask them *both* to go out to the car with me. So there." She leaned down quickly and kissed each of them on the cheek. "Now, you young things have a good time and I'll see you in the morning—what am I saying?—in the afternoon. Not too early. About 5 P.M., in fact."

"Well—" Beth said doubtfully.

"Bye-bye," Crystal said, gave them a little wave and began making her way slowly along the aisle to the stairs going down to ground level.

TOUGH LUCK, ORRIN KNOX, the claque said, reviving suddenly as Alabama reported 9 Ayes, 5 Nos on the milder language. TOO BAD FOR YOU.

"You can't do it," Bob Leffingwell said harshly.

"If it's too much for you," Governor Jason said pleasantly, thinking with contempt, He wouldn't leave me, he's too weak, "I'm sure we can make other arrangements."

"How much longer—" the Speaker demanded, and the President thought it was the only time in his life that he had ever seen Bill really perturbed. But again he only shook his head.

"I think it's all over, Stanley," the Secretary said.

Senator Danta gave him a long, slow look.

"Orrin Knox," he said finally, "doesn't run away. Now, or ever."

"I'm Mrs. Hal Knox," she said pleasantly at the entrance to the floor, "the Secretary's daughter-in-law. Could you find my husband for me? I think he's over near the California delegation. Ask Congressman Hamilton."

"Walter," Frankly Unctuous said, with the excitement and pleasure difficult to contain behind his bland smile and plum-pudding tones, "I think this is an historic night, to-night. I think we are seeing a real revolution in American politics and in the country, here. If this vote carries it is difficult to see how the President—"

"Kansas requests a poll, Madam Chairman."
"The Parliamentarian will poll."

"Oh, all right," she said with a smile. "I guess he's off somewhere getting votes. And I guess you're stuck here, guarding the door, right? . . . Oh, no, you can't leave. I'll make it all right. How do I get to Entrance J and the official parking lot?"

"I don't know what he's going to do," Patsy said impatiently to *Newsweek*'s lady who was back on the prowl again, "but *I* hope he runs for President."

"Pardon me?" she said politely in the dark night, on the swirling, dripping, trash-strewn ground with the fog racing and tumbling all around, "am I heading in the right direction for the official parking lot?"
"It's over th—" somebody began, and then somebody else said with a quick excitement, "Wait a minute! Isn't she Knox's daughter?"
"I'm no relation," she said suddenly terribly frightened. But someone else said in a tight, suppressed voice, "She's his daughter-in-law. Let's show the old man a thing or two!"
Then she began to scream. She was still screaming some ten minutes later, though she did not know it, writhing as she was upon the ground, when the police finally came. The blank, sullen faces had faded back once more into the blank, sullen ranks that stood, impassive and unmoving, around the Cow Palace in the cold, wet night.

6

THUS IT WAS that Crystal Danta Knox and Edward Montoya Jason entered the world's headlines together, though before either could do so it was necessary first for Anna Hooper Bigelow, herald of history in greens and purples and an ostrich-feather toque gone rakishly askew over one eye, to announce to a convention about to go mad:

"The vote on the milder platform language proposed by the delegate from South Carolina is 644 Yeas—"

"NO!"

"—and 649 NAYS—"

"OH, *NO!*"

"*Yes!*" screamed Anna Hooper Bigelow. "The proposal is defeated!"

After that everything dissolved in a great confusion, while she looked about in wild uncertainty until Bob Munson, rushing forward along the ramp, grabbed the gavel from her hand and shouted desperately, "Does the delegate from California have a motion?" and from somewhere in the din Cullee Hamilton bellowed, "I move this convention stand in recess until 2 P.M. this afternoon!"

"FavorsayAyeopposedNayAyeshaveitconventionstandsrecess!" Bob Munson shouted in a single breath, slammed down the gavel, and turned to Anna Bigelow with an exhausted smile to press her hands and give her a kiss of thanks on the cheek.

It was then 2:56 A.M.

At two fifty-eight, while they were slowly making their way out, a youthful seargeant-at-arms, his face white and his voice trembling, stopped Mrs. Orrin Knox and Mrs. Robert Munson to blurt something to them. At about the same moment, as Mrs. Knox swayed and almost fainted and Mrs. Munson caught her in her arms with a sharp cry, another young sergeant-at-arms fought his way through the departing delegates to Hal Knox, whom he found talking

excitedly to the junior Senator from Iowa and Mrs. Mabel
Anderson beside the Utah standard. Those nearby stopped
and watched curiously as he too blurted out some words
they could not quite hear. Immediately after they heard
Mabel Anderson also utter a sudden sharp cry, heard Senator Smith say in a terrible voice, "Oh, God, *no*," and saw
Hal Knox, uttering an indescribable sound, begin to fight
his way savagely out through the mob, ignoring the indignant cries and angry protests of those he elbowed aside in
his frantic passage.

At approximately the same moment, two telephone calls
came in, one to an office in the Fairmont, the other to an
office in the Mark Hopkins.

At the Fairmont, two dignified men who only a moment
before had looked vigorous, if tired, exchanged a ghastly
glance and suddenly looked very old.

At the Mark Hopkins, two handsome gray-haired men,
somewhat younger, also exchanged a glance. It was followed by a long silence, and then Bob Leffingwell said,
"Goodbye," in a quiet voice and started for the door.
"Goodbye," Governor Jason said with an equal quietness.
Then he raised his head with a calm defiance. "On your
way, will you do me one last favor, please. Will you call
the press room at the Hilton and tell them I shall hold a
press conference there in half an hour." "I will," Bob
Leffingwell said and went without looking back.

At three-ten, their front pages remade, the local papers
were on the streets with extras. CONVENTION DEAD-
LOCKS ON FOREIGN POLICY, RECESSES WITHOUT
DECISION, the *Chronicle* said; CRYSTAL KNOX
BEATEN BY UNKNOWN ATTACKERS OUTSIDE
COW PALACE. JASON CALLS CONFERENCE, AIDES
HINT NEW MOVE.

CONVENTION STALLED ON FOREIGN POLICY
AS KNOX DAUGHTER-IN-LAW SUFFERS BEATING
AT COW PALACE, the *Examiner* said; WITNESSES
CLAIM JASON BACKERS GUILTY. GOVERNOR
MAY STATE NEW PLANS.

And at three thirty-five, looking solemn and serious,
Frankly Unctuous was back on the little screen to tell his
countrymen what they should think about it. They could
see that he was alone this time, his distinguished companion was not with him any more, and he hastened to say,
with just the proper ghost of a wistfully weary smile, that

"Walter Dobius, ladies and gentlemen, has left us to return to work at the press room at the Hilton Hotel, from which we shall very shortly be bringing you the surprise press conference called by Governor Edward M. Jason.

"Mr. Dobius asked me—" and Frankly's richly rounded tones became somber and suitably grave, his expression respectful and properly sad—"to express for him as well as myself our profound shock and horror at the unfortunate episode involving Mrs. Harold Knox, the pregnant young daughter-in-law of the Secretary of State.

"Mrs. Knox, as you know, was savagely beaten by a group of unknown assailants outside the Cow Palace during the final dramatic vote of this highly dramatic evening. All that we know so far from Central Emergency Hospital where she was taken—the same hospital, ironically, in which, earlier in the evening, death claimed one of the two young victims of the riot started by her father-in-law's backers in Union Square yesterday morning—is that she is in serious condition, though still, apparently, alive.

"Mr. Dobius joins me, and I am sure all Americans, in wishing her a swift and successful recovery from this tragic episode—an episode which only proves once again—" and now his expression became gently, regretfully, and oh, so judiciously and fairly, stern—"that violence has no place in American democracy, and that those who condone violence, whether openly or simply by tacit, even innocent, acceptance, may sometimes, themselves, offer violence. . . ."

And at 3:33 A.M. at the Hilton, in a room so full of reporters, cameramen, and electronic equipment that it seemed impossible to squash one more human being or squeeze one more machine into it, the Governor of California began to speak to his country in the glare of the pitiless lights.

"First," he said gravely, "I wish to join all decent Americans in deploring the savage and inexcusable attack upon Mrs. Harold Knox.

"I am told," he said, as cameras rolled and pencils raced frantically over paper, "that competent witnesses believe this attack was made by individuals carrying my banners and supporting my cause. If this is true, I condemn them, and I condemn all like them.

"Obviously I knew nothing of this. Obviously it was either an emotional, or a drunken, or a doped-up action by individuals little better than human beasts. Obviously they must be hunted down and punished like the mad dogs they are. Obviously also, all elements involved in this convention must unite at once to oppose, once and for all, the element of violence which has seemed to creep, almost without our knowing it, into these deliberations.

"Anything I can do, of course," he said, looking straight into the cameras with an honest, candid gaze, "I will do. One thing in particular I have done already: the Mayors of San Francisco and Daly City have requested me to assign units of the National Guard to the Cow Palace and to the central area of San Francisco. Fifteen minutes ago I signed the appropriate orders. Within the hour, one thousand troops will be on their way here to take up their stations and maintain order. They will be on duty for the remainder of this convention.

"I regret," he added quietly, "more deeply than I can say, that violence was ever permitted to begin. The question of who began it is of course academic now. We can, only unite in sorrow that it came. Violence begets violence, and we have had tragic proof of it three times in the day just past. Whoever began it," he repeated, and his gaze became, if anything, more honest, more candid—"*who*ever began it, the end result has been ghastly. I am sure all Americans join with me in condemning all those who have permitted such a thing to develop at a free and democratic national political convention.

"To them I say, as all Americans say: change your tactics, forget your violence, and let us work in peace!"

There was a sudden burst of applause in the room, but quickly stilled, for the inhabitants of Walter's world are not partisan and they do not wish their countrymen to think they are, even though honest human emotion will sometimes escape (but only momentarily) their rigid and objective control.

"Now we come," Ted said, and his voice acquired at once a certain tenseness and tightly suppressed excitement that instantly altered his audience, "to another matter raised by the events of the evening just past.

"It is obvious now, I think, after three votes in open convention, that this Administration does not have sufficient support, in this convention or in this country which this convention reflects, to carry its foreign policy views successfully to the electorate.

"It is obvious, on the basis of those three votes, that I"—

and he used the pronoun with a new force, and repeated it —"that *I* do have sufficient strength in this convention, and in the country which this convention reflects, to provide a middle way for all those Americans who sincerely believe that threats to world peace must be stopped, and that only through preserving world peace can America be preserved.

"If these votes had resulted in overwhelming, or even moderately severe, rejection of my position and that of my many loyal followers in this convention—and, I believe in this country [and there was a little, affirmative stirring in the room that came across clearly on television]—then I should not, of course, take this public position or do what I am about to do.

"But you will perceive, my countrymen, that this is not the case. Three times the Administration and I met head-on. In the first vote, on adoption of the mild language of the Platform Committee, their margin of victory was only seven votes; 643 delegates to this convention of 1293 souls voted for me. On the second ballot, the proposal of Congressman Hamilton to write into the platform a strong, uncritical endorsement of the Administration failed by a margin of three votes; 648 delegates to this convention voted for me. On the third ballot, to reinstate the mild Platform Committee language in the platform, the Administration beat it by only five votes; 644 delegates to this convention voted for me.

"In other words, this convention is so closely divided on the issue of how to approach and handle foreign policy in these difficult times that it is, for all practical purposes, half the Administration's, and half mine. And certainly it is, as of this hour and after these three fair tests, deadlocked.

"In such a case, does the better chance of success at the polls lie with those who favor a rigid and unyielding policy, or does it lie with those who have retained sufficient flexibility to be able to maneuver and adapt to what conditions bring?

"And by the same token, does success in the world lie with the rigid and unyielding, or does it lie with those who are flexible and able to maneuver and work out necessary compromises with those people with whom we have to try to live on this globe?

"I submit, my countrymen," and once again he stared directly into the cameras, handsome, distinguished, grave, and powerful, "that it lies with those who can move—not with those who are standing still, bound hand and foot to past misconceptions and past mistakes. It lies with the future, not with the past. It lies with new blood, new vigor, new solutions, new approaches. It does not lie with the dead hand of yesterday.

"Conscience must decide the issue, my countrymen. I may be excused, I think, if I say on the basis of the votes this evening, that it will, I believe, decide it—my way. . . ."

He paused, took a drink of water, a deep breath, returned his gaze steadfastly to the cameras.

"I shall be a candidate this afternoon for the nomination for President of the United States. I invite the support of all who believe, as I do, in America's honor and in America's duty to herself and to the great cause of world peace.

"Ladies and gentlemen, thank you very much."

And he arose in the midst of press chaos to wave confidently—smile—nod—wave again—and depart.

"Lafe," the President said a few moments later over the line to Central Emergency, "I want you to be my messenger, if you will. First of all, how is she?"

"Coming along," Lafe said, sounding as though he himself were in shock. "The baby was born dead, of course—"

"I didn't know," the President said quietly.

"Oh, yes. It hasn't been announced yet. But she's a healthy girl, and young, and the doctors seem to think she'll make it all right. It was a boy. There was quite a bit of kicking and stomping, but not enough to do any lasting damage, apparently. Except, of course to the baby. It was born dead."

"Yes, you said that. Well: I'll express my condolences later in the day when the opportunity comes. Right now, there's something else. Is everybody there?"

"Pretty much."

"All right. How's Orrin doing?"

"Terrible. He wants to issue a statement—"

"I know what he wants to do," the President interrupted, "and I want you to tell him, and if Bob and the Speaker are there I want you to tell *them* to tell him—and tell Beth, too, especially tell Beth—that he is to do *absolutely nothing* until he talks to me. I don't want him issuing any statements or seeing anybody. Is that clear? Use force if you have to, to keep him away from the press."

"They're here, of course," Lafe said, sounding a little more like himself, "but at bay. I think we can persuade him. He's so dazed right now he's almost helpless. His idea about a statement is just blind nervous reaction, I think."

"Good," the President said. "Keep him quiet. Now: I want him to meet me in the penthouse at the Huntington at 10 A.M. today. Got it?"

"They'll probably put him under sedation," Lafe said. "That's only six hours away."

"Well . . . make it noon, then. But without fail I want him there then. All right?"

"Yes, Mr. President," Lafe said. "And—Harley," he added, deliberately but awkwardly, for they were a long way now from the old times of everyday intimacy in the Senate—"don't worry about this afternoon. It's going to be all right."

"Thank you, old friend," the President said, and the Senator from Iowa could tell from his tone that he meant his concluding words: "I'm not."

"Here we are," Ted Jason said, thinking to himself that no one at all, so great had been the excitement at the press conference, had thought to ask after her; thinking that of course she must be here; thinking—

"One of you on the door will be enough, I believe," he added pleasantly. "The rest of you get some sleep and I'll see you in a few hours."

"Thank you, Governor," the four state troopers said; tossed coins quickly to see who would get the duty; left the loser on guard; and departed.

He opened the door and went in to a lightless, lifeless room; snapped on the light; saw staring back at him the high cheekbones, the silver comb and mantilla, the beautiful deep-set eyes and strong old face he had known all his life; saw on the mantel beside it a hastily scrawled note:

"I saw your broadcast. I've gone to Vistazo for a few days to try to sort things out a little. I want you to sit and look at this old lady and think about her for a while."

But he knew, as he stood alone in the silent room and gazed into the calm, dispassionate eyes, that it was too late for Doña Valuela now—much too late.

And besides, he thought, with the first wrenching beginnings of defensiveness against the only two people in the world he really felt accountable to, she was tough herself. She would have understood.

He might have spent a much happier night and rested much easier than he did, had he been able to believe it.

There remained only one episode to make that historic night complete, and although it became a thing of song and story in the Washington press corps and along the shady lanes of Georgetown for many a year, none of the twenty or so reporters who witnessed it ever put it into print.

It was too rich to put into print, in a way: it was too choice to let out of the club, too good to share with the public. And also, it would have embarrassed Walter, and it was rather imperative, now that his candidate had decided to go for broke and he was needed so badly to help, that none of his true believers and dutiful colleagues do that.

He was sitting at his typewriter in the press workroom at the Hilton when it began, and rarely had the words come more smoothly or with such a strong, emphatic flow:

"At last America has a leader, washed to the top on a wave of repugnance against both the Hudson-Knox foreign policy and the violence which its supporters have brought to this otherwise decent convention.

"For one unhappy family, violence has brought its own bitter answer of violence in return. But for the nation, in one of those ironies that history adores, it has brought, one hopes, a great beneficence.

"What has happened here in these last fourteen dramatic hours marks one of the great watersheds of our political story: the repudiation of a sitting President by his party in convention assembled, and the very likely emergence of a new man to head both the party and the nation.

"Only the most profound public uneasiness and concern could have produced such a result. Only a people sincerely convinced that America must turn away from aggression and war to a policy of peace and stability—only a people—"

It was at that point that he realized that someone was reading over his shoulder, something which always annoyed him even though he recognized that it was basically a form of flattering tribute. But before he could look up and give the intruder a discouraging glance, "Only a people," she said loudly, "who have been fed lies and hatred and misinformation and ten thousand other kinds of crap by that great statesman and philosopher Walter Wonderful Dobius, that vicious demagogue of the press and all his vicious friends, that's what people!"

"You're drunk, Helen-Anne," he said coldly, and then he did glance up at her and saw her looking like the wrath of God or a 4 A.M. convention reporter, her face smudged, her hair sloppy, her dress wilted. But there were tears in her eyes, and a cold glint too, and he knew she wasn't drunk, except possibly with rage.

"Worthless," she said bitterly. "Worthless, worthless, worthless! Sitting at your typewriter telling the boobs what to think, the great vast herd you regard with such contempt in your heart, such monstrous intellectual contempt! But they see through you, Walter. They see through you, never think they don't. They let you play your little pompous game with them because it amuses them to watch you perform like a monkey on a stick, but they see through you! Oh, they do!"

"You don't make sense," he said, a righteous disgust in his voice but trying to keep it down in the hope it would lower hers which had already brought everything else in the room to a standstill. "If they see through me, they obviously don't swallow the lies I give them. You can't have it both ways. Why don't you go to bed?"

"Listen!" she said. "Listen to me, Walter! You have almost killed Crystal Knox. You have actually killed two other people. You and your friends have created a climate in this country in which it will be a miracle if the President himself isn't assassinated before this is over. You and your friends have destroyed every pretense of objectivity, fairness, decency, nonpartisanship, honor, that the press was ever supposed to have. The lot of you have spewed out a steady stream of deliberate misinformation, deliberate misrepresentation, twisted, slanted, dishonest reporting, photography and analysis from the day the crisis began in Gorotoland right on through Panama to this very hour."

She yanked the copy out of his typewriter and he grabbed for it with a sudden instinctive lunge. But she stepped back out of his reach so that in his haste he almost lost his dignity and fell out of his chair before he remembered who he was sufficiently to curb his blind anger and sit slowly down again.

" 'For one unhappy family, violence has brought its own

bitter answer of violence in return.' My God, you *monster*, how many times do you and your crowd have to be told that Orrin Knox didn't start any of this? You *know* he didn't start it, yet from the minute it began you've blamed it on him as deliberately and cold-bloodedly as you know how, and that's plenty! You've lied and lied and lied, the lot of you, and the horrible thing, you horrible individual, is that *you have known you lied*. You've done it tongue-in-cheek as though it were a lark for you, or a nice, happy game. Well," she shouted, beginning to cry in earnest, so that her voice came choked and harsh, "it isn't a nice, happy game! It's a killing game and it's killing America, and God damn you, you'd better stop it!"

There was only one way to handle this, he knew from past experience, and he did it, sitting very quietly and sedately, telling himself how calm and dignified and controlled he was, not giving in to it, not giving in, not—until presently her sobs subsided in the absolutely silent room where old friends from Washington and respectful, awe-struck admirers from the country press watched in astounded silence. Then he reached out his hand and said quietly, "May I have my copy back, please?"

"Take it!" she said, ripped it across and flung it at his feet. For a moment he was literally blinded with rage, a great red cloud that seemed to envelop his head and his whole being. But once again the knowledge that he was Walter Dobius whom all the world admired and to whom nobody said or did such things, if they were sane, came to his rescue. Obviously she was not. He had known it for years, and now he had the proof.

Slowly, deliberately, he reached down and picked up the two halves of his copy, arranged them on the table beside his machine so that he could read them. Then slowly and with equal deliberation—though his hands visibly trembled and he could not really see the paper, so violent were his emotions—he put a piece of carbon between two new sheets, inserted them in the typewriter, and began doggedly to copy it over. But she was not through yet. Suddenly her purse was flung across the platen so that the keys would not strike, and again she was standing close to him.

"Listen to me, Walter," she said, more quietly now, in a shaky but controlled voice that was, in its way, more frightful to him than the other. "No one else has ever said this to you and no one else ever will, because you've gotten beyond it. But somebody," she said, and her voice sounded quite slow and awkward, so that he glanced up sharply, but she looked all right, or anyway no worse than before except for a few new tear-streaks, "somebody should, before it's too late.

"You *are* a monster, Walter," she said carefully. "You are an ego grown so great, so convinced of its own infallibility, so fawned upon and made much of by the world, that you have just about lost touch with reality. You have become all mind, and it's a mind that thinks a thousand times a day how wonderful Walter Dobius is. It isn't a mind that really thinks—*really* thinks, way down under—how it can make life more kindly for people, or help them be more decent to each other, or make the world happier. That takes heart and you've got a mind without heart, Walter. You've got a mind, now, that thinks it knows better than anybody else what ought to be done. You've got a mind that rejects anything that doesn't agree with it because *it knows best* and it can't even acknowledge anybody's right to differ, any more. Anybody who differs now has to be destroyed, if you can do it. Walter Dobius *and what he says* means more to you than anything on this earth. . . . I feel sorry for you, Walter," she concluded more quietly, and in some wildly curious way he sensed that possibly she did, or at least thought, in her strange, twisted mind, that she did, "because I think you are a sad case. I think you are a genuinely pathetic being. . . . Just about," she said with a sudden bleak despair, "the saddest and most pathetic I know."

But this he could not take, he had been patient and tolerant too long under this extraordinary outburst, some last tight rein of control was abruptly broken by her monstrously—*monstrously*—patronizing conclusion.

"How—" he cried, half-rising, sitting back, starting to rise again, turning his head blindly, almost gasping with rage, "how could you—how could you say such things to me! How do you have the *nerve* to say such things! . . . What am I doing, what has my crime been? Well, I'll tell you!" he cried with a consuming bitterness while all around the room was absolutely still, his colleagues, looking, could any of them have had the time and detachment to note it, really quite funny in their drop-jawed amazement, "All right, I'll tell you! It has been to oppose as strongly as I know how a policy that I believe—I *believe*, whether you think I do or not!—is leading this nation and the world to disaster. Is it wrong to believe in world order? Is it wrong to believe in the United Nations? Is it wrong to think that a President of the United States and a Secretary of State should not launch armed aggression against smaller states? Is it wrong to say they should abide by international law? Is it wrong to say that—"

"Oh, don't give me that crap!" she cried again, and he shouted, "Oh, stop using that cheap, two-bit word!" so furiously that she blinked and stepped back a little. "I ask you, is it wrong for me to use my column and my position to fight for the policies I believe in, and against those I honestly think—*I honestly think*—are destroying the last chance of ever arriving at a workable arrangement with the Communists?

"You tell me it's just a game, to fight for what I believe in!" His face contorted and his mouth twisted with a terrible, affronted bitterness. "Well, God damn you."

For several minutes she said nothing. When she finally spoke it was in a curiously soft, regretful voice.

"God hasn't given you a mission to run the world, Walter. He hasn't, Walter, love, he really hasn't. . . . Poor Walter!" she said abruptly, and turned away, murmuring to herself from some deep pity that shattered, terrified, and enraged him, "Poor, poor Walter."

"Don't you 'poor Walter' me!" he shouted at her back as she went out the door. "Don't you 'poor'—I'm Walter Dobius! I'm not poor Walter! I'm Walter Dobius!"

And breathing very heavily, his vision so blurred with anger that he could hardly see the paper, his hands trembling so violently that he could hardly control them, he sat down slowly and began pecking, hesitantly at first and then with a surer rhythm, at the keys, while all around the room there was an audible release of breath and one by one his colleagues, not daring to look at him or even at one another, turned back to work.

"Hi," he said softly to the white, bandaged figure in the bed, his eyes red and haggard, his voice choked with weeping. "How are you feeling?"

There was a little stirring, a muffled sound that he could just sense was, "All right," and on the coverlet the hand closest to his moved ever so slightly. So he took it and sat for several minutes trying to get his voice under control again.

"Crys," he said finally, "it's no good. Dad's going to withdraw, and I'm going to give up any idea I ever had of going into politics." Again there was a little stirring, he knew it was protest, and he hurried on. "Yes I am, it just isn't worth it. There's plenty of money in law, it's a good career, and there's no reason why I should subject my wife and"—he hesitated, his eyes filled with tears, but he forced himself to go on—"my family, to this sort of thing. You were almost killed and he—he was, and I'm just not going to do it. I'm just not."

The little motion came again, the faint but unmistakable impression of argument and denial, and his voice sharpened with an impatience grown from horror and fright at what might have been, and what was.

"And you don't have to be noble about it, either! You don't have to tell me it's worth it to keep on fighting, because it isn't! They're too much for us, Crys, the evil are on top, now, and the world isn't going to recover, in our time or maybe for hundreds of years. They're in control of everything, they've got it all their way, and they aren't going to relent now, because why should they? Oh, yes, the bastards may deplore it in their TV shows and their columns and their editorials, but you just watch: there'll be a knife thrown in along with the hypocritical sob-stuff. They'll use it to slam us again, in some twisted way they always know how to manage. They're glad this happened to one of Orrin Knox's family, they're glad you got hurt and we lost our son and Dad has been knocked for a loop. They want him out, and they want us out, they want everyone out who doesn't agree with them. And, Crys," his eyes filled again with tears and he could hardly go on, "they've succeeded with me. I give up."

But once again—and of course he had expected it—there was the slightest movement, the elusive but emphatic sense of protest and stubborn denial. And presently, though he tried to fight against it, he found himself caught helplessly somewhere between tears and laughter and apparently attempting both.

"I know," he managed to get out at last, "I know what you mean: you're in no condition to fight now, but you will later. Crys, Crys! What would I do without you?"

Again there was a little stirring, but this time it seemed to be a settling and relaxing. The faintest ghost of what could have been an amused sound came from the head entirely swathed in bandages; and the movement and the sound ceased. For just one terrified moment he started to rise, his hand tightened on the hand in his. Then he realized that a deeper, steadier rhythm had come into the breathing, he searched quickly for her pulse, found it, and relaxed.

So he sat as the first faint light of dawn rode the fog into San Francisco, while under his fingers he felt her life beating on, steady, sure, young, and on the way back.

In the press room at the Hilton, Walter Dobius continued to write, the powerful phrases coming ever more quickly, the fingers flying ever more rapidly, as years of training joined with a great conviction and a talent in many ways close to genius to calm his nerves, still the swirling angers in his heart, restore him once again to what he was—what he was and would be for the rest of his life, and no one could take it away from him, *no one*—America's leading philosopher-statesman, in whose presence the great and the little of the world bowed down.

And in her room at the St. Francis, Helen-Anne Carrew, columnist, career woman, brilliant figure of the Washington scene, safe, successful, confident, secure, stared into the mirror at Helen-Anne Carrew, columnist, career woman, brilliant figure of the Washington scene, safe, successful, confident, secure; and found, quite suddenly, that she was crying, hatefully, horribly, dreadfully, and with such agony that she did not know that she would ever be able to stop.

PART FOUR

CAPABLE
OF HONOR

1

FROM SOMEWHERE, in some distant place, he begins to be aware that a voice is speaking gently, that a hand is moving on his arm, that it is time for him to return to the world he left six hours before with a tiny skin-prick, a second's swift swirling, and oblivion. He sighs heavily and shakes his head to clear it.

"Yes?" he says dully without opening his eyes.

"It's time for you to get up and eat a little breakfast, Mr. Secretary," the nurse says calmly. He opens an eye.

"Thank God you're not one of the cheerful ones," he says, and for a moment she permits herself a smile.

"That's better. Your clothes are in the closet. I'll be back with breakfast in fifteen minutes."

"How's Mrs. Knox?" he asks, sitting up. "My Mrs. Knox?"

"She'll be along soon. Your son's Mrs. Knox is doing all right, too. She isn't skipping rope, but she's coming along."

"That's good," he says inanely, and she remarks, "Yes, I should think so. Now get up and get dressed. I understand you have a very important engagement at the Huntington at noon."

"The President?"

She shakes her head.

"I honestly have no idea. I was just told it was very important and to get you up. So please continue when I go out, all right?"

"Nurse," he says, "what do you think of all this? Would you be happier if Governor Jason were President of the United States?"

She stares out the window for a moment, watching the galloping fog with a native's thoughtful and approving eye.

"What does my opinion matter?" she asks finally. "Things are going to happen whether ordinary people like it or not, aren't they?"

"I'm too tired," he says with a touch of returning tartness, "to give you my Civics 1-B lecture this morning. Of course they're going to happen, you silly girl, and ordinary people—of whom I'm sure you're not one, that's part of the cliché too"—she smiles and looks quite unimpressed —"can do a lot to influence how they happen, if they will just realize it and take hold. I repeat, would you be happier if Ted—"

"No," she says crisply, "since you ask. I would not. Now, will you get moving? It's getting late."

"I think I'm going to withdraw," he says, abruptly crystallizing all his horrified, tumultuous reactions of the dreadful hour before he was put under sedation.

"I think you're a fool," she says bluntly, "since you've invited my opinions. And quite inconsistent, too. But that's your problem. I shall be back with the tray in fifteen minutes."

"Thanks so much," he says, knowing that as soon as she leaves the dark terrible unhappiness that Seconal killed will return.

Sure enough, it does.

How arrogant he has been, he thinks, and how deserving of punishment from the Lord! As he had remarked wonderingly to Stanley—how many years ago, in what other world?—two deaths had occurred, and still he had not been humbled. However worthless the dead and however slight his own responsibility, at least they had been human beings; and it still had taken an attack upon his own daughter-in-law, the loss of his own grandson, before he had been moved to abandon his selfish worry after votes and realize the monstrous position into which ambition and events had forced him.

And how could he honestly say that his own responsibility was slight? It was slight in the vicious sense that Walter and Ted and all their friends and allies were trying to maintain, it was slight in that he had not ordered, condoned, or excused any of the violence that had crept into the convention . . . but was there not a general guilt in which he inevitably shared, a joint responsibility for the swift deterioration of decency that was his through sheer lack of attention, sheer self-absorption, if nothing else?

Two are dead—three are dead if one remembers the child—and he remembers it now with a sudden despair so great that he actually staggers and has to sit down again abruptly on the bed. His own grandson, *his own grandson,* Hal's first child—maybe, though his mind can barely admit it, so agonizing is the thought—Hal's last child. This is what he, Orrin Knox, has done, simply by not being strong enough, not selfless enough, simply by not speaking out with sufficient firmness and insistence.

Simply by not speaking out . . . simply by not getting out.

"Orrin Knox doesn't run away," Stanley Danta had said, and it was a tribute to all the years that lay between the Secretary and the idealistic boy who had married Elizabeth Henry, gone on to become state senator in Illinois, Governor of Illinois, United States Senator from Illinois, Secretary of State, one of the great powers of Washington and of his time. He never had run away—but that had been when he faced antagonists he could understand and fight with all the vigor of a candid and impatient heart. Now he was contending against something alien, the monster of violence that stalked the unhappy twentieth century: an evil grown great, come to visible life, rampant and voracious in a land that perhaps had been lucky too long in escaping it, and now must be made to pay the price by the jealous Furies.

How could he fight that? He could condemn it, as he had—he could order his people to refrain from it, as he had—but it came nonetheless. Good intentions and decent behavior were not enough, when confronted by this Thing; certainly not enough when the citizenry were not unanimous in their rejection of it. The Thing only needed a few friends to open the gate and let it in; unless everyone stood firm it entered. And where it entered, the world tore open and society collapsed.

It has entered in Union Square, it has entered in blankly hostile faces at the Cow Palace—it has entered, at the start, in savage columns and hysteric editorials and slanted headlines and one-sided photographs—it has entered in suavely supercilious and blandly ruthless rearrangements of the facts in commentaries and roundups and special programs and news reports. The marvelous things that can be done with an adverb, the masterful ruinations of character and purpose that can be accomplished with an adjective, the delicious ability of one lying picture to destroy the effectiveness of a thousand truthful words! And how well the little knowing smile, the ironic expression in the eyes, the polite reservations in the voice, the cordial, chuckling deprecation, can reinforce and keep them company!

It is amazing how many weapons the age provides for the misusers of truth.

It is not surprising that so many should succumb, with so few pangs of conscience, to the temptation to employ them.

No qualms of conscience because, when all is said and done, many of them utterly and sincerely believe in the righteousness of their own point of view. Thus the constant implacable attack upon opposing thought becomes, not the result of a struggle of conscience but the result of the suave use of practiced techniques in the service of a genuine conviction.

Orrin has been in Washington too long to discount the sincerity of his enemies in Walter's world. A few are hypocrites and self-servers, but by far the majority absolutely and sincerely believe that he is a detriment to the country and must be exorcised from public life without the slightest mercy or regret. He knows that they acknowledge his character, respect his integrity, calculate him to be a most determined and formidable opponent—who deserves, therefore, their biggest and most ruthless guns.

Now again, as they had in the bitter battle over the nomination of Bob Leffingwell to be Secretary of State, and later in the controversies arising from the visit of Terence Ajkaje to the United States and the UN, they are in effect dismissing the President and concentrating their fire on the man they consider most responsible for events and the most dangerous to the future success of their own beliefs. They do not fully know—of course they have not had the insider's privilege of knowing—the iron that has come into the soul of Harley Hudson; they still cling to the lingering belief that someone else is putting it there, and that only one man could logically be responsible. The raucous attacks upon the Administration's foreign policy, the pre-convention campaign, the general tone of the opposition speeches within the convention, have come down essentially to an attack upon that one man. He is the target, now, as he has been before. This time his enemies have succeeded. He can survive their attacks upon him personally, he has taken their measure a hundred times and found himself strong enough to stand it. But he cannot stand the results, now, for his family.

Probably no one from Walter Dobius to Frankly Unctuous and back again has seriously desired real hurt and damage to Orrin Knox and his family; still he knows the horrible yet fascinating feeling that has gone through their ranks nonetheless. "That'll show the bastard," they have thought, though he doubts that any has been so crude —or so honest with himself—as to say it aloud: but a sort of tortured, quivering satisfaction, a visceral elation they have doubtless been ashamed of but have not been able to withstand, has shivered deliciously through them all.

None would of himself or herself have raised a hand against the Knoxes. But they have been responsible, as surely as though they have done, for they have deliberately and knowingly created the atmosphere of hatred and hysteria in which the deed could happen.

That is the trouble with these terribly righteous people who play so cavalierly with the explosives of the age, he thinks: quite frequently the explosives go off. And they are really not too sorry about it, they really rather enjoy it, in some sick, near-vomiting fashion that nonetheless enthralls them, so deeply has violence penetrated the fabric of their age.

But it is time, now, to end such philosophizing and acknowledge that they have won. Ambition and idealism and the conviction that he was right carried him triumphant through the testing posed by Harley's predecessor when he offered Orrin the Presidency if he would drop his opposition to Bob Leffingwell; carried him six months later through the difficult decisions and violent attacks connected with Terrible Terry's visit; carried him through many and many a crisis in his long public life. But they cannot carry him through his grandson dead and Crystal alive only by the miracle of her youth and good health. His opponents have reached him at last, and the battle is over.

It is over because of what they have done, but even more —and he realizes it with an agonized self-reproach he knows they could not conceive him feeling and for which they would not give him credit—it is over because of his own sense of guilt for what has happened.

They can settle the argument with their own consciences, if any.

He knows only one way to settle it with his, and that is by offering expiation in the form most meaningful to public men—the voluntary abandonment of dear ambition.

He cannot forsee now, as he slowly rises and begins to apply himself seriously to the business of getting dressed, how Harley will make out in this new contest with Ted Jason. However it is, he realizes with a disheartened exhaustion, he will be unable to help. He would like to, but his heart is out of it—out of him. He just wants to take his family and go away somewhere, out of sight and out of mind—even though he knows, with a sudden contemptuous self-anger, that of course he can't do that, he's Secretary of State. Life is rushing on, policy is rushing on, there's a job to be done and he can't get out of that. But he can get out of this—this madness, here in San Francisco, and that he will.

He knows what Harley wants to say to him, at the Huntington at noon, and he knows equally well what he is going to say to Harley.

"And don't you try to argue me out of it!" he calls out in a strange, harsh voice that his wife and son hardly recognize as they tap on the door and come in. "We have a right to be let alone," he adds, and in a curious, defiant, crazy fashion he is half-crying as he speaks, "and by God, we're going to be!"

2

"THERE YOU ARE," Ted said, glancing up with his pleasant smile, strained and tired now after his restless night and all the strategies that had kept it company. "Thank you for coming to see me."

"How could I refuse," Cullee asked with an answering smile that held many curious things including irony, tension, and something the Governor sensed was probably contempt. "A candidate for President—the Governor of my state—my leader—"

"Never that, I suspect," Ted said with a sudden serious sigh, aware of how quiet the room was, although in the corridors and through the streets below there swarmed the jostling, wondering, rumor-ridden members of the reawakening convention. "Never that. . . . And yet I'd like to hope so. That's why I invited you here."

Cullee raised a giant hand and shook his head.

"Maybe. That isn't why I am here. I'm here to see how a man looks when he's been responsible for what you've been responsible for in the last forty-eight hours. I want to find out how you rationalize it."

"How does one rationalize anything in politics?" Governor Jason asked with an abrupt sharpness. "In terms of power and in terms of what can be accomplished by what has been done."

"And what has been accomplished?" Congressman Hamilton inquired. "Crystal Knox has lost her baby and Orrin's probably been driven out of it. But what else has been accomplished?"

"I have moved within a handful of votes of being the nominee for President of the United States," Governor Jason said quietly. "That's what's been accomplished."

"It's great if you can live with it," Cullee remarked politely. He glanced at the painting that now stood propped atop the television set. "I see Doña Valuela's here. What have you been doing, praying to her or asking her forgiveness?"

"LeGage Shelby thinks I can persuade you to put me in nomination," the Governor said quietly. "I told him he was crazy."

"He is," Cullee said with the dark annoyance that the name of his ex-roommate could always arouse in him. "He always has been. Why doesn't he nominate you himself? That would look good, the head of DEFY up there on the platform telling the white folks he hates what to do. DEFY's the black Ku Klux Klan, isn't it? You need their support, don't you? Have your boy LeGage do it."

"I would rather have Cullee Hamilton, next United States Senator from California, do it," Ted said calmly. "I would much rather—if you would like me," he said with a sudden acid, "to put it in the terms you people seem to love to lacerate yourselves with—I would much rather have a respectable Negro do it than a tramp. Clever tramp though he is."

"Oh, yes, he's clever," Cullee agreed. "So clever that I'll

bet you're not going to know exactly what to do with him, if by any chance you make it. What does he want to be, Secretary of State? He's about that modest."

"He hasn't said and I haven't asked."

"The time may be coming when there's going to be an awful lot of saying and an awful lot of asking. I hope you're going to be ready for it, if you have the chance."

"I may not have it," the Governor conceded quietly, "though I think I will. Tell me: what would it take to get you to nominate me?"

Cullee smiled, a not very pleasant smile.

"You don't have the price. What it would take for me to nominate you would be for you not to run, and that's a little contradictory, isn't it?"

"You feel very confident about California, don't you?" Ted remarked thoughtfully. An expression almost of distaste crossed his visitor's handsome face.

"Hell, I don't feel confident of anything. All I know is that I've told them what I believe and they've given me the primary—just barely. I'm going to keep on telling them what I believe and they may give me the election in November. But I don't know."

"And you don't need any help?"

The Congressman snorted.

"Of course I need help, who doesn't? But not from you, Ted. Or anyway, not as much as you need mine."

"Will I have it if I win the nomination?"

Cullee shrugged.

"I don't know. I'd have to think it over pretty carefully, wouldn't I?"

"But you don't know now."

"Nope," Congressman Hamilton said, getting slowly to his feet. "I don't know now. Where's Ceil?"

"She's gone down to the ranch."

Cullee nodded.

"That figures. Under the circumstances."

"Who are you going to nominate?" the Governor asked. Cullee grinned down from his great height.

"Whoever makes me the best offer."

"I hope you really know what you're doing, Cullee," Ted Jason said softly. "Because the consequences of a mistake could be quite serious for your future."

"That makes two of us," Cullee observed. "See you at the Cow Palace."

"Indubitably," the Governor said.

After his visitor left he sat for several minutes staring straight ahead, his face devoid of expression. He knew who the next claimant to be his nominator would be, and he did not see exactly how he was going to avoid him, now that the choice he had maneuvered 'Gage Shelby into suggesting had reacted exactly as he had expected. A sudden look of sadness, surprisingly frustrated, surprisingly deep, touched his face for a second. Then he turned back to the television set murmuring softly to itself, the newspapers strewn across the beds. His expression hardened and became secure again. His friends were with him and the battle did not loom so frightening after all. He could not, in fact, have wished for endorsements more effective or encouraging than he had:

JASON BANDWAGON ROLLING TOWARD VICTORY, the *Chronicle* said. CONVENTION BREAKING TO JASON IN ALL DELEGATIONS, WORLD HAILS GOVERNOR AS PEACE-MAKER, The Greatest Publication reported. JASON, VICTORY IN SIGHT, PONDERS ANTI-WAR ADMINISTRATION, the *Post* eagerly echoed. . . . T. J. CONFIDENT OF VICTORY AS CONVENTION ROARS TO PEAK. . . . GOVERNOR RACING TO VICTORY IN "CONVENTION OF CENTURY". . . . CONFIDENT JASON MAY TURN TO FELLOW GOVERNOR FOR V.P., cried all the rest.

And there was Walter Dobius' column that began, just as he had written it last night, "At last America has a leader, washed to the top on a wave of repugnance against both the Hudson-Knox foreign policy and the violence which its supporters have brought to this otherwise decent convention. . . ."

And all the columns that dutifully followed his lead, and the earnestly agreeing editorials that chorused solemnly, "America's innate political morality has a great chance to re-establish itself today when the San Francisco convention votes, as we believe it will, to give its presidential nomination to that fighting champion of human decency and world peace, Governor Edward M. Jason of California. . . ."

And the words of Frankly Unctuous the Anchor Man and all his colleagues of decibel, kilowatt, and little glowing screen, suavely, smoothly, insistently pouring forth to their fellow citizens every fifteen minutes or less from commentary, round table, analysis, and news report: "An apparently almost irresistible tidal wave for Governor Ted Jason of California is sweeping this convention today. The signs of Jason victory are everywhere apparent as the forces of President Harley M. Hudson and Secretary of State Orrin Knox, in obvious disarray, strive desperately to turn back a demand from delegates and country alike that apparently is not to be denied. . . ."

And everywhere through the hotels, in the rooms, along the corridors, over the constantly jangling telephones, in the coffee shops and dining rooms and the hectic lobbies awash with shouting, excited people, everywhere on the streets outside where the crowds swirled and the bands played, the Jason agents traveled, saying, "You see what the *Chronicle* says? You see this headline out of New York? You hear Frankly Unctuous on television just now? Don't be a fool, Manny! Get on the bandwagon before it's too late! We'll know who's for us and who's against us, you know! You think the Governor will forget it if you help him hold that delegation against him? You got another think coming, Manny!"

And so the bandwagon grew even as he sat there, and the psychology worked, or seemed to work, and everywhere in the beautiful city emerging finally from the fog to bask in another diamond day the forces of Harley Hudson and Orrin Knox were indeed, or seemed to be, in disarray.

At the Huntington, however, the Speaker and Senator Munson would never have known it to watch the portly, fatherly, apparently entirely unperturbed figure that leaned comfortably back in an armchair and read the papers clamoring his defeat with an occasional "Tut, tut!" or a mild, "My, my!" or even, now and then, a calm, "Is that a fact, now?"

Finally he tossed them aside and gestured toward Frankly Unctuous, who was just explaining for the twentieth time this morning why a Jason victory was inevitable.

"Will you turn that fluff artist off?" he requested mildly. "I've heard his requiem for my hopes enough times to get the drift, I think. A little silence would now be very helpful."

"Right," the Speaker said, rising and crossing to snap off the machine. "He hasn't convinced you, then."

"Bill," the President said, "on the day I pay serious attention to that biased so-and-so I will cash in my chips."

"Not everybody," Senator Munson suggested, "has your ability to perceive his true nature with such startling clarity. I suspect that a great many people believe he's telling them the truth. A great many people like delegates, for instance."

The President shrugged.

"I think this convention has reached the point where it's utterly impossible to count noses. I don't think anybody can accurately say at this moment how it's going to go. Do you, Bill?"

"N—o," the Speaker said, "except as the propaganda is carrying some weight with some delegates, like Bob says. Could be Ted's people don't have to persuade very many."

"How many are we persuading?" the President inquired. "I assume you haven't stopped your efforts."

"Hardly," Bob Munson said. "Everybody's busy. But I must admit all this—" he gestured at the triumphant headlines, the columns and editorials somebody had marked with a black grease-pencil, the silent television screen momentarily robbed of its many pompous, authoritative presences—"is having its effect. We need—" he paused.

"We need an effect ourselves," the President said. "All right, I've got one. In due course it will appear. In the meantime, keep calm and don't panic. I'm not."

"No," the Majority Leader said dryly. "I can see that. What is this—effect?"

"Oh, you'll be there," the President said, somewhat archly. Then he grinned. "Aren't these pixyish people annoying, though, in the midst of serious business? Part of the effect is Orrin. Who will be here," he added pointedly, "in another ten minutes."

"You don't want us to stay around and help," the Speaker suggested. The President became serious but shook his head.

"No. I don't need any help or any witnesses. What I have to say to Orrin I have to say to him alone. How's Crystal doing?"

"Hal says she's coming along very well," Senator Munson said.

"You've seen Hal."

"Yes, he showed up at the room a few minutes ago. Dolly ordered breakfast sent up and made him eat some, after which he said he'd like to keep busy, so I sent him off to the California delegation with Lafe."

"Good for him," the President said. "Good assignment, too."

"I thought his presence around Ted's own delegation might be salutary in making a few people think about the implications of what happened last night," Senator Munson said grimly. "I want him out on the floor when the session starts, too. I don't want the convention to forget it, even if"—again he made his comprehensive, contemptuous gesture toward Walter's world—"everybody else has apparently agreed to bury it as far out of sight as possible."

"We've got a new rule today," the Speaker said dryly. "Law and order's the ticket now. National Guardsmen all over the place and nary a storm trooper in sight. It's touching."

"And the only place where it all continues," the President said softly, "although he may perhaps think it's not so, is in the mind and heart of the man who let it begin, and in the unforgiving and unrelenting minds and hearts of those who did his errands. Because now they have him in thrall in a way he won't entirely realize until he looks back and sees how far he's gone from the point of integrity where he first accepted their help." He sighed. "Poor Ted."

"Poor Ted," Bob Munson said shortly, "may very well take the Presidency of the United States away from you, you know. I don't think I'd waste so many tears on poor Ted."

"No, he won't," the President said calmly. "And if he does, it's still poor Ted, because he's gone now. He's made his bargain with the devil and the devil won't quit. Which poor Ted, like all men too smart to be humble, doesn't believe. Which is why, poor Ted. . . . Be sure and have Anna Bigelow preside again this afternoon, will you, Bill?"

The Speaker looked surprised.

"Why? The poor girl was a nervous wreck this morning after it was all over."

The President chuckled.

"Because I want to see her face when I make my little effect."

"Shame on you," Senator Munson said with a smile. "I

don't think you're taking this seriously at all, Mr. President."

"Oh, yes, I am," the President said, suddenly sober. "Now, get out, both of you, please. Go out and get votes. I'll see you at the hall shortly after three."

"Good luck with our friend," Bob Munson said.

"Good luck with everything," said the Speaker.

The President nodded.

"I've had pretty good luck with things up to now in this office. I aim to keep it that way if I can."

He could see that his visitors, though they put a good face on as they left, were deeply worried and thinking: poor Harley, he doesn't know what he's doing. But poor Harley did, he told himself as he put in a call to the St. Francis and requested the support of the troubled party at the other end.

"I think it would be most helpful," he said.

"But, Mr. President—" and there was a heavy sigh, lonely and forlorn, which he had never expected to hear from that source. One smart man was humbled, he could tell that.

"You're about to take one step," he suggested. "Aren't you? I have you badly figured if you aren't, I'll say that."

"Yes," his listener said slowly. "I am—I have."

"Then you had best take the other."

"Are you ordering me?"

"Good heavens, no. How could I order you? I'm just suggesting that you remember our talk the day I decided to run—"

"Yes. You indicated you might call in an I.O.U."

"Well," the President said, rather testily, "only if you genuinely agree."

There was a pause and another sigh.

"I think," Bob Leffingwell said finally, "I genuinely agree."

"Good," the President said. "Then we can count on your endorsement—"

"More than that," Bob Leffingwell interrupted abruptly in the tone of one who has reached a fundamental decision and is determined suddenly to get on with it and not look back. "What I would like to do, if you'll let me—"

And that, the President told himself as he hung up five minutes later, was proof enough of his luck. He had a talisman, now, and the way was opening up. He put down the phone and stared out at the Golden Gate Bridge and the tawny reaches of Marin across the Bay. Faintly from the swarming apex of Nob Hill far below the sound of a band playing "Dixie" floated up.

3

HOW MANY TIMES in his life had he talked to Harley? the Secretary of State asked himself with a tired wonderment as his two Secret Service escorts swiftly and efficiently whisked him down a side alley, through a back entrance of the Huntington, and into a closely guarded service elevator for the quick, secret ride to the penthouse.

It must be thousands, and some of them came back to him in bits and pieces now: the tense, uneasy talk in Chicago at the convention eight years ago . . . the wild, frantic exchange on the podium above the roaring crowd a few hours later that had cost Orrin the Presidency that time . . . many and many a talk with a nervous, worried, and apparently hopelessly weak Vice President in the years after . . . their first talk at the White House after Harley took over, the ironic exchange when Orrin had entered with a frowning concentration—"I was just thinking"—"About the President, I suppose," Harley had suggested—"No, about you"—"I am the President," in a kindly but ironic tone . . . the talks in Geneva with a suddenly firm, suddenly matured Harley at the strange meeting when the Soviet leaders had made their grandiose, defeated ultimatum for control of the world . . . their talks about Terry and the UN, and more lately about Gorotoland and Panama—a thousand talks, a million talks, if you like, the talks of busy men dealing with great affairs who had worked together for the better part of a decade.

But none, he knew, quite so fateful or so final as this.

He was feeling a little better, now, but nothing had changed his determination to do the only thing consistent

with what he believed to be his responsibility and his duty;
consistent also with his love for his son and daughter-in-
law, his regard for the safety of his family, the duty he felt
he owed to all those millions in America who still had
great faith in Orrin Knox despite what his enemies said
about him. Someone had to be witness for principle, in this
convention gone sick with the sickness of the age. Someone
had to make a gesture sufficiently dramatic to reaffirm the
decencies and perhaps shock the insane back to sanity.
Someone had to have the integrity to accept blame and
give up ambition.

The bitter thought *Why must it be me?* was only a last,
dying protest, a last wrenching farewell to lost hopes. He
had thought he had bade them farewell on the night Harley's predecessor offered him the Presidency and he refused. They had been revived when Harley appointed him
Secretary of State and opened the way for his candidacy
for Vice President. The door was still ajar, then, for future
possibilities. It had been ajar until 3 A.M. this morning.
Then it had slammed shut in the fog outside the Cow Palace and he knew it could not be reopened.

He had tried too hard and done too much—and now,
finally, suffered too much—for presidential ambition. He
would fill out his term as Secretary of State for as long as
Harley wanted him and then go out of office and devote
himself to those pursuits ex-public men always talk of
vaguely and sometimes do: write his memoirs, lecture and
teach on government, visit the universities that were inde-
pendent-minded enough to have him, try to convince the
young that their self-conscious cynicism about America is
really rather poor reward for the idealism that has prompted
their elders to save their country for them on so many
hard and thankless occasions.

The elevator stopped with a thump, they were out of it
and along the hall almost before he knew it. There was a
sudden leaping up of reporters seated near the door, a startled, "Mr. Secretary—?" Then he was inside, the door
slammed shut, the angry voices of press and Secret Service
contending sank away, and he and the President were
alone.

"Orrin," the President said, gesturing to chairs drawn up
before the view, "sit down. You won't mind if I stand for a
minute. I've just been sitting down talking to Bob Munson
and the Speaker. I want to stretch a little."

"What did they have to say?" Orrin asked, but with only an automatic politeness, for it no longer mattered.

"They're depressed," the President said, staring thoughtfully at the impossible beauty spread before them as though cupped in the palm of some giant, fantastically overgenerous hand. He gave a rather wan smile. "They think I'm not." He sighed. A surprising and, to the Secretary of State, quite alarming melancholy came upon his face. "I am," he said simply, and he sat down abruptly, still not looking at his visitor. "Very."

"I'm sorry," Orrin said with a genuine stirring of concern, the first he had felt for anyone other than his family and himself since 3 A.M. "I wish I could help."

"I don't expect anyone can help," the President said in a moody tone that sounded increasingly, disturbingly, unlike Harley. "Not even Lucille. She tried to cheer me up this morning with one of her little pep talks, but I'm afraid it's too late for pep talks." He glanced at Orrin finally, with an attempt at wry humor that didn't quite make it and thus disturbed the Secretary more. "Old Happy Harley has just about had it, Orrin. I think we're licked."

"Oh, I wouldn't say that," Orrin said, automatically and yet with a stirring of genuine protest against this apparent abandonment of even the will to fight. "Surely there are plenty of delegates who still—"

"How many?" the President inquired, still moodily. "Half? Somewhat more than half? Somewhat less than half? We ought to know better than that, Orrin."

"Well," the Secretary said shortly, and the President was pleased to see that there was a return to impatience in his manner, a revival of combativeness in his tone. "I expect you won't know until the last vote is counted, that's obvious, but that isn't any reason to stop fighting . . . that I can see," he ended somewhat lamely, suddenly aware that he was not being entirely consistent with his own determination to stop fighting. But the nuance was apparently lost on the President, who had swung back to stare out again at the glistening day and was seemingly unaware of any confusions in his colleague's mind.

"Why fight?" he asked finally. "Why fight any more? It seems to me that I have fought and fought and fought and *fought"*—he hit his knee with a sudden protesting fist— "to try to lead this country in ways consistent with safety and honor, and what good has it done me? What is it coming to? Nothing!"

"Oh, now," the Secretary objected, lifted out of his worries about his own position in spite of himself: no one could let that remark pass without objection, no one could let Harley deprecate himself when he had done so much, anyone with an ounce of fairness would have to protest that. "Now, that just isn't true! You know it isn't true, so stop saying it. You've done a great deal. The situation is such that you've got to keep on doing it. You can't stop now."

"And take a licking in the convention this afternoon?" the President asked bitterly. "Be the first President in this century to be repudiated by his own party? Let myself be turned out to pasture? I ought to withdraw," he said darkly, "and nominate Ted Jason for them, if that's what they want, and be damned to them! It's what they deserve."

"You can't do that," Orrin said, genuinely alarmed, forgetting protocol in his concern. "You just can't do it, Harley, *you must not*. Why," he said, and his eyes widened with the enormity of the prospect, "that would be terrible! It would mean the collapse of everything we have tried to do in the world." His jaw set suddenly with the line the President had been hoping to see. "It wouldn't be the convention's repudiation, it would be a self-repudiation. I won't let you do it. *I won't let you do it*. The least you can do is stand on your principles and make a fight for it. Then you'll have an honorable record, no matter what happens."

"Why should I take their smearing and their attacks any more?" the President inquired, still with an air of deep bitterness. "All the violence, and all the rest of it—blaming us for it when we weren't responsible, for heaven's sake! I can't—why should I have to take that sort of thing? So if they've won, they've won, that's all. I've fought them enough. I can't take any more."

"But now, see here," Orrin said, and his voice was its old positive self, the President could see he had forgotten himself entirely and was approaching the problem of changing Harley's mind with all the powerful concentration he had brought to so many problems over the years. "Think what it would be like if you gave up. Why, they would say all the charges were true. They would say you had failed and knew it. It would shadow your name forever. And furthermore," he concluded earnestly, "and this is why you really can't do it—it just wouldn't be you. It would be so completely out of character. You can't just abandon your character and step out of it, you know. You can't just stop being you and be somebody else."

I'm doing pretty well, the President told himself with some amusement, but his expression of gloom remained unchanging, his look of being completely unimpressed remained stubborn and unyielding.

"Mr. President," Orrin said solemnly, "I won't let you do it. Nor will Bob or the Speaker or any of us. I think the only way to win is to stick with it and go straight ahead. It's the only way consistent with your record, your character, your life. Maybe I don't have the right to ask, but"—his jaw set again in a stubborn line—"there's nobody else here to do it, and by God I *am* Secretary of State, so I'm going to: I want you to promise me that you'll stay with it —that you won't withdraw—you won't quit."

For several minutes the President said nothing, his eyes fixed on some distant point in Marin where all the inner imperatives and hidden things of a lifetime were apparently gathered. Orrin hardly dared look at him, hardly dared breathe, so certain was he that the issue hung in the balance and that the slightest word or motion could destroy his purpose.

"If I were to stay in," the President said at last in a tone that was still glum but carried, excitingly, the first glimmer of a returning will to fight, "I'd need help. I couldn't do it alone."

"If you make the decision," Orrin said firmly, "you'll have the help. You don't need to worry about that."

"But how could you help?" the President objected with a slow moodiness. "You say you're going to get out yourself—"

"I didn't say that," the Secretary said flatly, and it was true he hadn't said it to Harley, and now, so intent was he upon persuading the President, he forgot he had said it to anybody or even entertained the thought at all. "Don't worry. I'll help in every way I can."

"You will?" the President inquired, but still in a tone that indicated he didn't quite believe it. "But how can you, if you withdraw? . . . Aren't the arguments you've used on me equally valid for you?" he asked moodily. "You're not going to tell me, after that, that you have any more right to withdraw than I have? And furthermore, I need you to hold your delegates—for *me*, you know, as well as for you. Half of them are going to give up and bolt to Ted the minute you get out. Where would that leave me?" He looked abruptly less moody and more aggressive. "Come on, now, Orrin! If I stay in, you stay in. It's got to be a cooperative effort, here. I'm not going to carry it alone. Surely you can't expect that of me!"

It was now the Secretary's turn to fall silent and look moody. But it did not last long, for he realized that he was fairly caught, and, being Orrin, he had the grace and humor to admit it, though there was a last protest he felt he must make, in fairness to himself.

"You just don't know how I've been feeling these past few hours," he said lamely. "You can't just ask me to jeopardize my whole family. What would Crystal and—"

"They'll be with you whatever you decide. Anyway, I'm sure they don't want you to withdraw, any more than I do or any of your friends do. Isn't that right?"

"They did seem a little vehement about it, half an hour ago," the Secretary confessed with a rueful smile.

The President nodded. "You've given me all the arguments: think them over."

Again there was a pause, and this time it was the President's turn to maintain a careful silence. When the Secretary spoke it was with the reluctant beginnings of a smile.

"I just thought of something."

"What?"

"You said Lucille had given you a pep talk and it didn't do any good. *That* wasn't consistent with your character, either. I should have known then that—"

"This office," the President said, permitting himself a sudden grin, "has made an actor of me, among other things." He held out his hand and said crisply, "All right, then, Orrin?"

The Secretary hesitated for a moment. Then he gave the President a firm handshake.

"All right. I've made arrangements with Cullee to nominate me—"

"Call him off."

"But—"

"Just trust me and don't argue," the President said. He stood up and the Secretary perforce did the same. "Very good, then. Now I'd suggest you get back and write yourself an acceptance speech. I'll be in touch later in the day."

"You think I still have a chance?" Orrin asked, with a curiously wistful hesitation that touched the President.

"I'd say it was pretty good. And if it shouldn't be—what was that lecture I got on being true to one's life and record? You were right. Better us two sad old cases go down fighting than give up to that"—he paused and something of his real outrage at what was being attempted against him finally came through in the tone of utter contempt with which he concluded—"that *gang*."

And so one's absolute resolves became not so absolute under the imperatives of politics, the Secretary thought as his two Secret Service protectors elbowed him through the angrily protesting newsmen again, into the service elevator, out of the Huntington, and back down Powell Street to the St. Francis. He had fallen neatly into Harley's trap, he realized with a rueful smile—but, then, he was honest enough to admit, if he hadn't really wanted, subconsciously, to fall into it, he wouldn't have. He must have known all along that his agonized rejection of his hopes and plans had been only surface, though it had seemed so deep and sincere an hour ago that he had thought nothing could change it. But the President's appeal for help, the President's own doubts and dismays—exaggerated for the purpose of winning him over, the Secretary decided, but still a fairly accurate disclosure of how he must be feeling at this moment of attempted betrayal by his party—these had been too much for one trained to a lifetime of public duty. The President had said he couldn't win without him, and in a sense this was true. It had to be a cooperative effort among all who were loyal to the policies he and Harley deemed best for the country and the world. They were all in it together.

He was not under any illusions about his own future, however, when he reached the St. Francis and gave Beth the news she seemed not at all surprised to hear. When Ted failed in his assault on Harley, as Orrin firmly believed he would, he would inevitably return to his drive to capture the Vice Presidential nomination. There would then be tremendous pressures on Harley to accept Ted on the ticket.

Once again, Orrin would be right where he had been from the outset—on his own. And he did not have many hopes, as he prepared to leave for Central Emergency to see his daughter-in-law and then go on to his headquarters at the Fairmont, that Harley would be able to help him much. Harley would have expended too many energies, cashed too many I.O.U.'s, perhaps have given away too much to the Jason forces by that time, to assist his Secretary of State.

So the outcome would be the same, probably, in any case.

The only difference would be that he would have gone down with honor; and how many troops, he wondered dryly as he walked through the lobby to his car and received a heartwarming surge of applause from many delegates, does honor have?

4

Now IT WAS time to gather again in solemn convention assembled, and out from the gleaming city in the bright blue afternoon the cars and taxis and buses and limousines were beginning to pour down U.S. 101 to the Cow Palace off-ramp and from there back through the pastel residential areas against the hills to the mammoth auditorium sitting stolid in its little vale, filled with the echoes of past climactic moments in the nation's history, stirring now with the portent of new climactic movements on the verge of vociferous delivery. Much would be decided here in the next few hours: the always exciting and awesome moment in which a presidential candidate is chosen, the lesser but still dramatic selection of his running mate given an extra tension today as the forces of the contenders prepared to stretch themselves to the outmost limits of barter, negotiation, promise, and appeal, the farthest reaches of physical stamina and emotional endurance.

The sullen faces and sinister ranks were gone, the menacing chorus from the galleries had been disbanded, National Guardsmen reinforced police in the maintenance of order as the crowds flocked in, but actually fearsome faces, scornful voices, and the smell of violence were no longer needed. The news from Gorotoland and Panama was filled this day with new delays and frustrations, there had been a sudden new outbreak of riots around the world, three American embassies had been attacked, two more U. S. Information offices had been burned, in seventeen Afro-Asian nations and on twenty-three American university and college campuses members of the newly created "Booker T. Saunders Clubs" were at this very moment paying bitterly anti-Administration homage to the fallen hero of Union Square. The Soviet Union had just launched another violent attack on the Secretary-General for not moving vigorously enough to stop American aggression, Cuba had followed with a resolution demanding American withdrawal from all bases around the world, Zambia, Tanzania, and Malawi had introduced a resolution condemning U.S. racial practices. All in all, it looked like a great day for the forces of world law and order gathered around the candidacy of the Governor of California. The forces of the President of the United States were a little ragged and groggy this day, and their complete and final rout seemed only a few hours away as the parking lots began to fill up and visitors and delegates jostled in to take their places beneath the festive bunting and the high free-floating balloons.

So it seemed, at any rate, to many of those who were asked to comment as they entered the hall. Patsy Labaiya and her aunt Valuela Randall, waylaid by CBS on their way to their box, were calmly confident. "Everything seems to point to my brother's victory," Patsy said. "My nephew," Valuela agreed graciously, "really does appear to be the people's choice." Selena Jason Castleberry and her brother Herbert were not with them, as they were out in the staging area in back getting ready to join in the Jason demonstrations, and it was noted, too, that Mrs. Edward Jason was absent. "She will be closely observing too, you can be sure of that," Patsy said coolly, and the world was left with the impression that Ceil would soon be there.

Similarly confident were the Junior Senator from Wyoming, Hon. Fred Van Ackerman, representing the Committee on Making Further Offers for a Russian Truce (COMFORT); Mr. LeGage Shelby, chairman of the Defenders of Equality for You (DEFY); and Mr. Rufus Kleinfert, Knight Kommander of the Konference on Efforts to Encourage Patriotism (KEEP). "Hairbreadth Harley and Oddball Orrin are going to have to put on some burst of speed if they want to overtake the Governor," Fred Van Ackerman said. Rufus Kleinfert, with his pinched little smile that somehow looked always disapproving and never happy, predicted that, "Governor Jason will triumph here today, and then this insane policy of foreign entanglement and endless foreign war will, thank God, be ended." Mr. Shelby was not very cooperative. His clever dark face wore a scowl, and instead of elaborating he simply snapped, "Hell, yes!" when his NBC interviewer suggested, "It really looks as though Governor Jason has it sewed up, doesn't it?"

Also confident, though usually a little more cooperative, were such leaders of the Jason drive as National Committeeman Roger P. Croy of Oregon and Mrs. Esmé Harbellow Stryke, National Committeewoman from California. Governor Croy predicted a Jason win on the first ballot, Mrs. Stryke, a little more cautious, picked the second. Governor Croy was asked if he expected to receive the vice presidential nomination if Governor Jason won; his response was an uproarious laugh and a vigorous, "No, no!" which immediately convinced his listeners that he had second place in his hip pocket. Mrs. Stryke was referred to by her interviewer as "very likely to be our next Secretary of Health, Education, and Welfare," and burst into a girlish giggle which contrasted oddly with her sharply clever, hagridden little face.

For the Hudson forces—or the Hudson-Knox forces, as Frankly Unctuous and Walter's world continued to call them—those who appeared on the screen against the background bustle of the gathering delegates were stoutly optimistic despite the rather skeptical tone in which they were questioned.

"Does it *really* seem to you, Senator," CBS asked after Stanley Danta had just said that it did, "that the President can win the nomination now?"

"Isn't it true," NBC inquired of a Speaker obviously anxious to get away to the platform, "that the Hudson-Knox forces face an almost insurmountable handicap this afternoon?"

"You don't really see any chance of reversing the Jason tide, do you?" they asked Cullee Hamilton.

"Now if the President *should* be defeated, Senator," they said to Lafe Smith, "by what margin would you estimate it will be?"

"It is obvious from the comments we have already heard this afternoon," Frankly Unctuous was able to report cheerfully a few moments later, "that, while the Jason forces are riding a high and confident tide this afternoon, the Hudson-Knox supporters seem to be definitely on the defensive. Wouldn't you agree with that curbstone impression, Walter?"

"I would," Walter Dobius said gravely. "The whole aspect of the Jason campaign is one of a well-organized mechanism, based on idealism and unity in a great cause— that of world peace—preparing to function with perfect smoothness to bring its man the nomination. The whole appearance of the Hudson-Knox camp, on the other hand, is that of a collapsing, disintegrating campaign of loosely-held-together forces, each of which is beginning to find that its selfish self-interest cannot be sufficiently rewarded by the leadership it has chosen to support."

"Would you say that historically this has been the pattern of coalitions formed for political advantage, Walter, as distinct from those that have gathered around some great and stirring idea or ideal?"

"It has indeed," Walter agreed. "Events here seem to be following that classic pattern."

"Can you tell us, Walter, if there is anything to the persistent rumors of the past few hours that Secretary of State Knox may withdraw his candidacy for Vice President in the wake of the outbreaks of nasty violence which marred yesterday's proceedings?"

Walter shook his head.

"That was going around earlier, but it seems to be false now. Or so," he said with a satisfied, pardonable little smile, "I was informed by the President himself just a few minutes ago. Apparently the Secretary intends to remain in the race, presumably supporting the President and then seeking to win the vice presidential nomination."

"Which might be a little difficult," Frankly said with a smile, "should Governor Jason wrest the nomination from the President this afternoon. Allowing Secretary Knox to be on the ticket would be, I should think, the last thing he would permit if he wins."

"Or if he loses," Walter Dobius said, and Frankly Unctuous, after a second's startled look, nodded and laughed and said, "Yes, I see what you mean."

But on the floor among the delegates there was no such aura of confidence, no calm certainties, historical parallels, or encouraging indications to the convention as to the best course to follow. There Lafe and Hal and Cullee and Bob Munson and Stanley Danta and even the Jason aides were finding a great uncertainty and a vast confusion. Even more than usual, many delegates seemed to be feeling that inevitable third-day disillusionment that comes over a convention when what the press refers to as "rank-and-file delegates" begin to get the inner conviction that it doesn't matter a damn what they do, because "the boys up top" have got it all worked out between them. Senator Munson's instructions to his co-workers had taken note of this with more vehemence than diplomacy:

"Go out and tell those silly bastards that this thing is wide open and they've got to stand on their own two feet, damn it, and vote what they really believe."

This attitude of stern realism, itself perhaps a good example of what the "up top" mentality is like, nonetheless accurately reflected the situation on the floor as the band swung into "The Star-Spangled Banner" and the convention rustled to its feet to listen to the ponderously stirring old up-and-down tune and watch the single flag at the podium fluttering in its artificial breeze, experiencing all those swirling, inchoate, inextricably entangled emotions of love, reverence, annoyance, and impatience that the contemplation of one's country can induce at this familiar moment.

There were, in fact, very few indications as to which way the balloting would go. The harried chairman of Illinois told Hal Knox that he couldn't really determine how many would defect to Ted Jason—"Everybody's being so damned close-mouthed." Esmé Stryke, though insisting on her right to be publicly confident, nonetheless had to acknowledge to Cullee that he would be far from the only one in the California delegation to favor Orrin. As for Joe Smitters, Bill Smatters, Bob Smutters, John Smotters, Buddy Smetters and all their friends and cohorts on what might be called the "second level," (below "up top" but above "rank-and-file") they were in a daze from staying up all night, drinking too much, talking too much, arguing and estimating and telephoning and wheeling and dealing, even though they knew in their hearts that all their hectic activity didn't mean much, because of course when the word came down from "up top" they would obediently do their best to throw their delegations onto whichever band-wagon appeared to be heading for the wire.

Basically, everybody was in a daze because nobody could quite believe that the convention had actually reached a position in which it might very well repudiate a sitting President. How had they arrived there? Did they really want to be there? Was there any way to get out of it if they did not? Or must they plunge ahead, as the Jason forces—who seemed to be everywhere—and Walter's world—which assaulted their eyes and ears in a steady hum from every transistor radio and miniature television set on the floor—told them over and over that they must do?

"It's all too much," Mary Buttner Baffleburg, panting and red-faced and fanning herself with a tally sheet despite the air conditioning, confided to Lizzie Hanson McWharter in the aisle near the Kansas delegation. "Too *much*."

"And the Speaker wants poor Anna to preside again," Lizzie said.

"Oh, my God!" said Mary Baffleburg, her shrewd little eyes almost disappearing in their many rings of flesh as she closed them in desperate thought. "What does *that* mean?"

"A busy time for Anna," Lizzie said, not without satisfaction. "But I couldn't say what it means for anybody else."

"I suppose the Speaker knows what he's doing," Mary Baffleburg remarked, opening her eyes to peer about at the corn-fed faces of Kansas, the dark eyes and gay leis of Hawaii.

"If so he's the only one," Lizzie Hanson McWharter said tartly.

And as a matter of fact, as these two ladies, one so tall and bony, the other so short and fat, perhaps rather ridiculous in appearance but filled with hard-boiled knowledge of a dozen campaigns, seemed to suspect, the Speaker was quite as uncertain as anyone else when he stepped to the rostrum after the playing of the national anthem and brought the gavel down with a series of impatient raps.

"Hurry up there, now!" he muttered. "It's half-past three already, hurry it up, come on, hurry it up!"

The admonition, delivered too close to the microphone, boomed out clearly to the nearer delegates. There was a burst of laughter and some indication of annoyance, but prompted by the habit of obeying him for five conventions —though his control was somewhat shattered now by the disrespect shown him yesterday—first the nearer rows, then the farther, gradually settled down. In about five minutes the great hall was reasonably silent except for the delicate splatter of clicking, bell-ringing sound from the racing typewriters in the press section, the low-voiced murmur of television reporters addressing their walkie-talkies in the aisles, the echoes from all the transistors of floor and galleries, the steady susurrus of thousands of excited, whispered conversations, and the endless rush of rumors chasing each other around the floor until it seemed that they must finally, like the Tiger and little Black Sambo, end up in a great pool of butter in the middle of the room.

"Ladies and gentlemen," the Speaker said, "we come now to the unfinished business of approving the foreign policy plank of the platform—"

But he was interrupted by Lafe Smith, who seized the Iowa microphone and shouted, "Mr. Chairman! Mr. Chairman!" in an urgent voice. Immediately the hall filled with uneasy noise.

"The convention will be in order!" the Speaker roared with a sudden show of anger that did quiet them down for a moment. "For what purpose does the distinguished Senator, a delegate from Iowa, seek recognition?"

"To move," Lafe said crisply, "that we defer a vote on the foreign policy plank until after we vote on the nominee for President."

At once the convention broke into a gabble of approving and protesting shouts, about equally matched.

"Mr. Chairman," Esmé Stryke cried from the California delegation, "California seconds that motion!"

"Mr. Chairman," the chairman of the Illinois delegation bellowed into his microphone, "Illinois also seconds that motion!"

"But how extraordinary!" exclaimed Frankly Unctuous, and for once his face showed genuine emotion, in this case a guarded dismay. "Such a step has never been taken in a national convention to my knowledge, Walter. Has it, to yours?"

"It has not," Walter said. "But," he added, managing in spite of his surprise to preserve his omniscience with a little smile, "our knowledge does not, after all, encompass all the national conventions that have ever been held. I cannot remember a precedent for it offhand, but there may be one.

Certainly there is nothing to prevent a convention from working its will in any way it pleases, if it has the votes."

"Will it have, do you think?" Frankly asked, still obviously concerned. "I had thought the Jason forces were counting on one more test of strength on this issue to show their candidate's commanding position before going into the presidential balloting."

"They may have been earlier," Walter said, thinking with distaste that he must tell Frankly not to be so gauche in the display of his feelings, "but obviously the strategy has changed. Mrs. Stryke surely would not be speaking for the California delegation if it had not."

"But if Governor Jason has the votes—" Frankly suggested.

"We must assume he and his advisers know what they are doing," Walter said sternly, thinking, For God's sake, man, shut up. Apparently they *aren't* sure, apparently they don't want to risk losing any votes by a premature test. Shut *up*. "I think," he added, turning firmly away from the camera and looking down pointedly at the floor, "that we had best see what develops next."

"Indeed we must," Frankly said, recovering his professional poise though still looking somewhat puzzled. "Today promises to be lively, too."

For a little while, however, as the Speaker sternly gaveled down the noises of protest that continued to rise from the Jason rank-and-file who obviously hadn't been informed by their second level of the change of plans (because the second level hadn't been informed, either), things remained relatively calm. The Speaker put the question in a level, commanding tone that said, Woe betide any who challenges. None did.

Baffled but perforce compliant, the Jason forces went along; Lafe's motion passed on a roaring voice vote and the Speaker said gravely, "We come now to the high and important matter of the nomination of a candidate for President. I do hope the delegates will be in order and pay attention. This is serious business now. Please let us handle it seriously."

And so he would, the man who sat unnoticed far back along the podium said grimly to himself; so he would. But it was a tired grimness, rather than a defiant one, for now all the assumptions of a lifetime were being called into question, and as surely as though he could see himself picked up by a giant hand from the road he was traveling, to be set down upon another, he knew his life's course was about to change forever.

Now all the friends and sycophants who had fawned upon him so lovingly over the years; the stanch supporters in Walter's world who had stood with him throughout his career in a solid phalanx of adoration and approval that had formed a shield against public criticism even in his darkest moments; the thousands in the academic world, the professors who had so often cited him with warm approval as an example of the perfect public servant, the students who had secretly or openly made him their ideal; all that heterogeneous mass of uneasy and sometimes startling bedfellows who huddled together under the term "liberal," some truly so and some among the most rigid and reactionary, in their complete intolerance, that he had ever known; all those overseas in many lands who admired him as a symbol of what they considered best in the American system—now they all would turn upon him, he knew, with the frantic, hysterical savagery of the tyrannical betrayed.

In their despotic kingdom there was no place for the genuinely humble doubt, the sincerely troubled uncertainty, the honestly changing mind. Everything, with them, was absolute, dogmatic, unchanging, and eternal. Any who were honest enough to question their gods were automatically and ruthlessly damned. And when one of their gods himself betrayed their desperately guarded shibboleths—well, he knew well enough what the result would be. Within ten minutes after he began to speak—on the air, in print, everywhere—the tone would instantly change. He could hear them right now, he knew what they would say, Walter Dobius and Frankly Unctuous and all the rest.

He had roughly fifteen minutes left of being their hero, and he knew it as surely as he knew his own name. Thereafter and forever he would be one of their most bitterly despised examples of apostate, one of their prime hates and principal targets.

But—so be it. He had done a great deal of thinking in the past twenty-four hours, and at some point, he could not say exactly what late hour or early moment, he had come to terms with himself and with what he must do. He knew that in what he was committed to now he was being more of a witness for the truth and more a man of principle and honor than he had ever been in all the years when he was so unanimously hailed as such by those whose concept of principle and honor came down in the last analysis to: "You close your mind and agree with us and we will call you Hero: dare to have an independent skepticism of your own and we will scream you Villain."

He took a deep breath to try to still the uneasy trembling in his chest and stomach, riffled once more hastily through the pages of his brief speech to see that they were in order; heard somewhere in some far-off place the voice of the Speaker saying, "The Secretary will call the roll of the states for the nomination of candidates for President"; heard Anna Hooper Bigelow's strident voice cry, "A—la—bama!"; heard Alabama's hog-jowl and molasses accent say, "Mistuh Chehmun, 'Ahlahbahmah yiel's to *New* Yo-uk"; heard the excited burst of sound begin from the floor and galleries, heard it rise to a frenzy of astonishment and anticipation as he rose and walked forward along the long ramp to the podium; found himself at last at the lectern as a sudden deep hush fell upon the hall; and heard himself, in a last split second of wonderment, begin the destruction of a lifetime's easy riding on the adulation of the automatic thinkers who would now, automatically, turn and rend him.

"Walter," Frankly Unctuous was saying in a booth above in a voice his training could not keep steady, so great was his pleased excitement, "this would seem to indicate that it really is all in the bag for Governor Jason, wouldn't you say? With New York taking the lead and his own man making the nomination, it would seem that it is now all over but the—"

But Walter Dobius, with the inner instinct and intuition that had served him well in covering many a story over the years, snapped, "Be quiet and let us listen!" in so harsh and disturbed a tone that Frankly gave him a startled look and, astounded, obeyed.

For several moments after the Speaker introduced him, Robert A. Leffingwell looked out expressionless upon the shifting, squirming, restless mass before him. Its newly refurbished flags and standards waved proudly, its balloons and festoons danced with a gay and confident air, its bunting and confetti were bright; but it was, he knew, an army uncertain upon a battleground unclear. It was in a mood to be stampeded and he knew now without any hesitation that he genuinely desired it to be stampeded in the direction he wished to send it. He also thought he knew how to do it. He took one more deep breath and abruptly his trembling ceased. A calm, cold certainty took possession of him. He took his prepared text from the top of the lectern, placed it carefully on the shelf beneath, leaned forward, and began to speak extemporaneously in a level, emphatic voice.

"Mr. Chairman," he said, and his amplified voice rang out heavily in the listening silence, "on behalf of forty-three members of the New York delegation, and on my own behalf, I am here to place in nomination for *re*-election to the office of President of the United States—"

"My *God!*" cried Frankly Unctuous.
"Keep *quiet!*" snapped Walter Dobius. "Keep *quiet!*"

"—the name of the Honorable Harley M. Hudson of the State of Michigan."
And the world exploded.

"One of the most intriguing things about this, of course," Frankly said to Walter fifteen minutes later as they watched the demonstration that banged and blared and roared around the hall and showed no signs of abating despite the Speaker's halfhearted attempts to gavel it to order, "is the strange apostasy of Robert A. Leffingwell, who only yesterday was campaign manager for Governor Jason and was known throughout the world as one of the great leaders of American liberal thought. It seems incredible that he should now be found supporting the candidate who represents policies that the world has long believed to be absolutely counter to Mr. Leffingwell's own. But apparently," and his voice became grave, his face saddened, "even Robert A. Leffingwell has his price—and someone, apparently, has paid it. Of course"—and his tone turned harsher, his face was stern—"it is perhaps not surprising, considering the way in which he lied to the Senate Foreign Relations Committee about his youthful Communist associations, a year ago when he was under consideration for the office of Secretary of State.

"Possibly that was the tip-off, would you say, Walter, to some fateful flaw of character which now is being shown to the public again? Some inner weakness which raises serious question as to just how valid and honorable his liberalism has really been all these years?"

"I would not know," Walter said coldly, "what compulsions drive an individual of Robert Leffingwell's type. All I know is that for one who has supped long at liberalism's table to turn now upon liberalism's candidate is to furnish the country with an example of ingratitude and lack of integrity that are surprising, to say the least.

"As to the price, I suppose it was very simple: the President picked him out of the discard after the Senate refused to confirm him as Secretary of State, and gave him a soft, high-paying government job. Now the President has cashed his I.O.U. and demanded Mr. Leffingwell's support. It is that simple."

"And Mr. Leffingwell obviously has been too weak to refuse so crass a proposition," Frankly suggested.

"Like perhaps has called to like," said Walter in the voice of Judgment.

"Although one must admit," Frankly said, and there was now some inkling of genuine uncertainty in his calm, plum-pudding tones, "that the support Mr. Leffingwell carries with him from the New York delegation is quite impressive. Forty-three members of that giant group going for President Hudson, it must be admitted, is a disturbing factor for Governor Jason to consider."

Walter gave him a blank look as if to say, You must be mad.

"I still see no real indication that he need be seriously concerned."

But this was not the way the convention saw it, nor the way it appeared in the minds of the watching millions in the nation and around the world. For the first time in three days there was a subtle but definite pause in the onrushing Jason bandwagon, and along with it some sudden doubt as to just how accurately the famous analyzers of column, headline, airwave, and little screen had really understood what was going on in San Francisco. Charitably, as always, many good-hearted souls assumed that the error had been one of perception, not one of a suddenly faltering attempt to create and manage events; but others, more sophisticated, could not restrain a savage satisfaction at this first crack in the hitherto implacable and unchallengeable front of Walter and his world. With it went a redoubled urgency in their efforts for Harley Hudson, an answering anxiety in the drive for Edward Jason.

In his own person, and in one fateful sentence, Bob Leffingwell had changed not only his own life but the convention. He obviously did not intend to lose his advantage as the demonstration finally ended with a few last shouts and banner-wavings and blurts from the band. He resumed in a level, hammering voice:

"What I have to say in support of this nomination I can, and will, say in a few sentences. All the arguments for and against this candidacy have been amply aired in the past two days.

"Harley M. Hudson is President and Commander-in-Chief of the United States at a time of active warfare and grave peril for the nation and the freedom of the world.

"He has conducted his office honorably, fearlessly, and well from the day he was called, with tragic suddenness, to assume it.

"At Geneva he defied the Communist ultimatum and saved the world from conquest and destruction.

"In Gorotoland and Panama he took the only action consistent with safety and honor.

"His personal decency and integrity cannot be denied by anyone. His official courage and steady wisdom are known to the world. He has not been belligerent: he has simply been firm. He has, I believe, saved civilization so far, and will continue to save it when he is returned to office, as I believe he will be in November.

"To repudiate him now would be to repudiate the entire foreign policy and course of the United States of America. It would put this convention on record before the world as saying that it does not support a strong foreign policy, but a weak one; that it does not support an honest man, but a devious one.

"Yes!" he said, and his voice rose sharply to meet the angry Jason outcry from the floor and galleries that greeted that remark. "A devious one, who has condoned violence, played fast and loose with principle, and whose advocacy of a so-called 'flexible' foreign policy is, in my estimation, the advocacy of a delayed but inevitable defeat, for this country, for her allies, and for everything that good and decent men hold dear.

"I grant you," he said, when the indignant shouts died down, "that he may not consciously know this. But I think it would be the result of his policies nonetheless.

"Some men find honor less difficult to abandon than others. From my observation of him, I believe that he is such a one.

"So I give you an honorable man—a consistent man—a straightforward man—a fearless man—a decent man.

"I give you Harley M. Hudson, President of the United States!"

And again the world exploded, and in the great hall a fearsome tension began to grow as the convention realized that the battle was indeed undecided, and that he who had been so glibly discounted might well be moving out in front.

During the next six hours delegates, including Senator Munson and Congressman Hamilton, gave brief seconding speeches for the President. During the next hour, also, in broadcast, news bulletin, and commentary, Walter's world with delicately regretful adjective and suavely damning phrase assailed the character and record of Robert A. Leffingwell.

He did not care. A new peace had come to him. In some curious, deeply satisfying way he felt that he had regained permanently an honor lost on the fateful morning a year ago when he had decided to deny to the Senate Foreign Relations Committee that he had ever known a man named Herbert Gelman.

The certainty of honor was quite sufficient to armor him, as in the last analysis it armors all the decent, against the attacks of Walter's world.

"The convention will be in order," the Speaker directed shortly after 5 P.M. "The Secretary will continue to call the roll of the states for the nomination of a candidate for President."

"A—laska!" cried Anna Hooper Bigelow.

"Alaska passes."

"Aaaaa—rizona!"

"Arizona passes."

"Arkansas!"

"Arkansas passes."

"California!"—and there was a sudden surge of tension as Esmé Harbellow Stryke's shrill voice announced, "Mr. Chairman, California yields to Wyoming for the purpose of nominating a great son of California who will be the next President of the United States!"

"But *why*—" Frankly Unctuous demanded of Walter Dobius in the booth. *"Why* someone like—"

"I do not know," Walter said with a pompous heaviness that sounded, suddenly, quite tired. "I assume the Governor has his reasons."

"Orrin," Stanley Danta said with great satisfaction at the Fairmont as they watched Fred Van Ackerman come belligerently along the podium, "I think Ted is falling apart."

And at the Mark Hopkins, his secretaries watched the Governor of California watch the Senator from Wyoming stalk forward. None was subtle enough to analyze his strange expression of irony, skepticism, sadness, and resignation, though his wife might have been able to had she been there instead of three hundred miles south, watching alone in the enormous sun-room at "Vistazo," her own eyes widening with unhappiness and protest as she came to a conclusion much like that of Stanley Danta—came to it and knew there was absolutely nothing she could have done about it, even had she remained in San Francisco.

Among the many vignettes of that convention that would live on in the memories of those privileged to see it was the look exchanged by the Speaker and the junior Senator from Wyoming when they met once again at the rostrum. It made up in intensity what it lacked in duration, and the depth of its mutual contempt was, as the New York *Times* murmured to the Chicago *Tribune* in the press section below, a classic of its kind.

"The Chair presents," the Speaker grated, turning away and staring straight out, "a delegate from Wyoming, to make a nomination," and for just a second it was obvious that Fred wanted to make some bitter and violent rejoinder to this terse and disparaging introduction.

Then in one of those lightning changes of mood that his colleagues in the Senate knew so well, he shook his head with a sudden crudely pitying grin and stepped forward to the lectern to acknowledge the dutiful but somewhat uncertain applause of the Jason delegates. No one had expected him to be where he was doing what he was, and it was clear that he enjoyed it. In Fred's mind it obviously ranked as a victory, and so it probably was: a victory over the Speaker, who had no choice but to give him the platform again, and a deeper victory, too—a victory over Ted Jason, that high and mighty bastard who thought he could use Fred and COMFORT and then tell them to run along. He had found out, in a bitter, shouting argument earlier this afternoon (at least Fred had shouted, the Governor had been infuriatingly calm even when surrendering) that he could not. Fred had made the proud son of a bitch with his Spanish ancestors toe the line. The triumph of it was in his face as he raised his hands above his head and clasped them together in a victory gesture that brought some laughter and applause from the convention, though it did not know exactly why it applauded, or what.

He stepped forward quickly to the microphones and began to speak.

"Members of this great convention," he said, ignoring the Speaker, "did you see this morning's headlines?

"Gorotoland is going badly for us.

"Panama is going badly for us.

"The world fears and despises us.

"American boys are dying right this minute.

"And no peace is in sight.

"*This*," he said, and suddenly his voice sailed up into the angry, whining shout the Senate knew—"*this* is what your man of honor—your man of consistency—your straightforward man—your decent man—your fearless man—has done! This is the low state to which Harley M. Hudson and his sidekick the Secretary of State have brought America to!

"And *that*," he said, and his voice dropped to a contemptuous snarl, "*that* is what you want for President of the United States? *That* is the sort of record you want your nominee to have? *That* is the policy, and those are the leaders, we are asked to endorse?

"Mr. Chairman," he said, and this time he did turn around and grin his savagely contemptuous grin straight at the Speaker, "*don't make me laugh.*

"You heard a few minutes ago," he said, turning back, "a renegade that the Governor of California had trusted to manage his campaign because he thought *he* was an honorable and decent man. Well, the Governor found out! He found out what he was, just as a while back we in the United States Senate found out what Robert A. Leffingwell was!"

"Do you remember, Orrin," Stanley Danta asked dreamily at the Fairmont, "all those frantic speeches Freddy made for Bob during the nomination fight?"

"I remember," said the Secretary of State.

"Yes, Mr. Chairman," Fred Van Ackerman cried, and in the New York delegation a chorus of boos began to rise to greet his words, and soon it was taken up elsewhere, so that he found himself shouting ever louder to drown it out, "this man is a Judas goat, pretending to be one thing as long as it suited him and then turning on the great Governor at the last minute and trying to lead you to destruction with Harley Hudson and Orrin Knox!

"Go ahead and boo me, then!" he cried in the sudden wild, psychotic yell that was characteristic of him when hard-pressed. "Yes, get your stooges to boo me when I tell the truth! But it won't change the truth about this Administration and what it has done to America! It won't change the truth about what it has done to the UN! It won't change the truth about what it has done to Gorotoland and Panama!

"Go on and boo!" he shouted. "Maybe you can wake up the American boys who have died for the Hudson-Knox foreign policy!"

"*Jesus!*" Governor Jason exploded in a terrible voice, so savage and uncharacteristic that it actually frightened his secretaries. "Can't somebody do something about that—" But he remembered abruptly that no one could, for he himself had put him there. As suddenly as he had spoken, he was silent.

"Yes," Senator Van Ackerman cried into the shocked silence, "you'd better think about it, I say to all of you in this great convention! This is where we decide, right here and now today, what kind of candidate and what kind of party, and what kind of President we're going to have from now on. So listen to me well.

"We *have* an honorable candidate—honorable in all his life.

"We *have* a consistent candidate—consistent in his support for world peace.

"We *have* a straightforward man—straightforward in his dealings with his state, his nation, and all men.

"We *have* a decent man—decent in his approach to the problems of humanity.

"We *have* a fearless man—fearless in his fight for genuine peace.

"It's time for us to turn away from old tired men and policies of disaster," he concluded, sounding calmer and almost like any other relatively sane convention orator.

"It is time to turn to a youthful, dynamic leader of vision and integrity who can lead the world to peace.

"It is time to turn to the next President of the United States, the Honorable Edward M. Jason, Governor of California!"

And the world exploded again, though this time many who were watching thought they could detect a curious defensiveness in the shouting, dancing, whooping demonstrators, a certain edgy belligerence, a curiously insistent, almost forced enthusiasm that contrasted rather oddly with the claims of Jason victory and the genuine warmth of the Hudson demonstration. But it went on for better than half an hour, and after it ended Roger P. Croy, Esmé Stryke, the Governor of Ohio, the Governor of Hawaii, and two Negro delegates from Mississippi and South Carolina made seconding speeches.

5

THERE NOW HAVE arrived those tense final moments before the vote for President, that time of final tightening-up and gathering-together of all the strands of promise, appeal, threat, commitment, arrangement, alliance, certainty, hunch, impulse, equivocation, Yes, No, Maybe, Could-Be and Perhaps that always precedes that particular Call of the States which above all others gives meaning to the American method. It is too late for anything further: it has all been done. Stand or fall, win or lose, the event no longer lies in the hands of those who have attempted to control it, be they candidates waiting tensely at headquarters, managers frantically shouting last-minute directions over walkie-talkies, campaign aides scurrying desperately about the floor, even Walter's world making its last suavely urgent pitch for its chosen candidate in the booths and along the worktables from which it informs and admonishes a not always obedient world.

Now the event is no longer in the hands of Roger P. Croy or Esmé Stryke, Bob Munson or Cullee Hamilton, Joe Smitters, Bob Smutters, John Smotters, Walter Dobius or Frankly Unctuous. Now it is in the hands of all those hundreds who have come to San Francisco in their noisy anonymity, each called Delegate, each being One Vote or Half-Vote, otherwise nameless and faceless; the hundreds who have not huddled in the confidential rooms where things are decided; the hundreds who have not been buttonholed and interviewed to make pompous or hopeful or self-serving predictions; the hundreds who have just been here, and have spent their time outside convention hours shopping at Gump's or I. Magnin's, eating at Canlis or Pauline's, riding the cable cars, having drinks at the Top o' the Mark and the Fairmont, exclaiming ecstatically at the glamorous City by the gorgeous Bay.

This is their moment and nobody better make fun of them now, by God: this is when they get their revenge for being patronized and pushed around like helpless chips on a table. They have proved already, in yesterday's votes, that they are not to be taken for granted. Now they know, with some grim amusement at the uncertainty they realize must be prevalent everywhere "up top," that they will prove it again.

"The convention will be in order," the Speaker says, pounding his gavel vigorously. (He has taken mercy on Anna Hooper Bigelow and decided to preside after all, calling the roll will be enough of a strain for her today—and also, nobody knows what may happen in the voting and he wants to be in charge should it be necessary to gavel down a disturbance or strong-arm something through.)

"The Secretary will call the roll of the States for the selection of a nominee for President."

For a moment or two longer the world hangs suspended while Anna Bigelow, patriotically clad in a red tweed suit topped by a blue toque with a white feather, fusses a bit at the lectern and looks about with an ill-concealed nervousness. A silence, profound, breath-held, attentive, quivering —the sort of silence that can be triggered in an instant into screaming sound—settles on the enormous room. The voting charts furnished at every seat by the soft-drink companies and the major periodicals are ready, the pens and pencils are poised.

"A—la—bama!" cries Anna Hooper Bigelow, and a great expulsion of breath hisses out from everywhere.

"Mr. Chairman," Alabama says gravely, "Alabama casts five votes for Harley M. Hudson, five votes for Edward M. Jason."

There is a rush of sound. Hudson supporters and Jason supporters attempt to outdo one another. The Speaker gavels it down. The edge-of-hysteria silence settles again.

"A—laska!" cries Anna Bigelow.

"Alaska casts six votes for Harley M. Hudson."

A shout goes up.

"A—rizona!"

"Arizona casts seven votes for Harley M. Hudson," says Arizona matter-of-factly.

"Arkansas!"

"Arkansas casts nine votes for Harley M. Hudson, six for Edward M. Jason."

Again there is a surge of sound, again the Speaker gavels. Frankly Unctuous has just time to murmur to Walter, "It is obvious that the Speaker is attempting to give an air of nonpartisanship to his presiding, even though it is an open secret that he favors the President," when Anna cries, "California!"

Abruptly the great hall is as still as tension will allow.

"Mr. Chairman!" Esmé Stryke shouts, and even as she speaks a wave of sound begins to break across the room to greet her words, "California requests a poll of the delegation."

The Speaker bangs his gavel hard and demands silence.

"The Secretary will poll," he says calmly, and the better part of an hour goes by while the Secretary does. During it people in the galleries rise and stretch, delegates mill about the floor, Walter and Frankly speculate with great perspicacity and knowledge on what is happening. Despite their rather emphatic confidence, however, it is apparent as the marks go on the tally sheets that there is still, the furious all-day efforts of Jason managers notwithstanding, a grave and fundamental split in the Governor's delegation.

"California," Anna Bigelow reports finally, "casts 57 votes for Edward M. Jason, 47 votes for Harley M. Hudson."

And again the hall erupts.

Five minutes later the Speaker has succeeded in silencing it again. Anna goes on. An exhausted lull falls temporarily on the convention as she manages to get through Colorado, Connecticut, Delaware, District of Columbia, Florida, Georgia, Hawaii, and Idaho. None demands a poll, all report promptly, few outcries greet their declarations, and when they have finished the President had gained 61 votes, the Governor 55.

"Illinois!" cries Anna Bigelow. Everyone tenses again.

"Illinois, Mr. Speaker," the chairman booms, "finds it must request a poll of the delegation."

Loud shouts, cries, roars. The Speaker gavels. Anna tries to talk. The Speaker gavels. Everybody shouts and stirs for two minutes. Tension eases—a very little. Anna polls.

"Illinois," she reports half an hour later, "casts 51 votes for Harley M. Hudson, 27 votes for Edward M. Jason."

In Walter's world quick comparisons are made between the Jason inroads on Illinois and the Hudson inroads on California. A certain tension begins to appear in Walter's world. The convention shouts and stamps, exchanges rumors and makes biting and sardonic jokes, for the convention is not really so dumb. It can make comparisons too.

"Indiana!" cries Anna Hooper Bigelow, and is permitted to move on with reasonable dispatch through Iowa, Kansas, Kentucky, Lousiana, Maine, Maryland, and Massachusetts.

The sum total of this is 70 more votes for the President, 64 more for Governor Jason.

The vote now stands at 260 for Harley M. Hudson, 213 for Governor Jason.

"Michigan!" says Anna and Michigan replies with a heavy emphasis that rises to a shout at the end, "Michigan casts 53 *unanimous* votes for its greatest son, Harley M.

Hudson, present and *next* President of the United States!"

A great roar goes up, figures are totaled, gleeful or worried comments are exchanged, analysis is offered, wonderment or satisfaction expressed. Five minutes pass in exultation or concern. So near and yet so far dances the golden prize.

"Minnesota!" says Anna Bigelow.

Minnesota casts 17 votes for Edward Jason, 10 for Harley Hudson. Exultation and concern change sides, remain so as Mississippi, Missouri, Montana, Nebraska, Nevada, New Hampshire, New Jersey, and New Mexico report a total of 69 votes for Governor Jason, 71 for Harley M. Hudson.

"New York!" cries Anna Bigelow, and is rewarded with an abrupt, straining silence.

"New York," says the chairman calmly, "requests a poll of the delegation."

But when it comes the quick-rising hopes of the Jasonites are as quickly dashed. Robert A. Leffingwell—who is booed by many but applauded by more when he firmly casts his vote for Harley M. Hudson—has not told them false. Forty-four members of the New York delegation break to the President; the Governor holds 50.

The vote stands Harley M. Hudson 414, Edward M. Jason 409 as Anna Hooper Bigelow heaves an audible sigh into the microphones that produces a burst of not-really-amused, tension-tight laughter from the convention.

"North Carolina!" she calls, and goes doggedly on through North Dakota, Ohio (which splits 33 for President Hudson, 30 for Governor Jason), Oklahoma, Oregon (where Roger P. Croy manages to hold the entire delegation, to the accompaniment of great whoops and cries, for the Governor), and Pennsylvania (where Mary Buttner Baffleburg and 42 of her colleagues stand firm for President Hudson but Governor Jason still manages to pick up 32).

And the vote stands Harley M. Hudson 526, Edward M. Jason 522.

"It certainly looks as though this is going to be a contest right down to the wire, doesn't it, Walter?" Frankly suggests with a brightness born of worry and unease.

"It certainly does," Walter agrees dryly, his instinct at work, his mind already leaping beyond the outcome, calculating the realities then, the possibilities, the likelihoods, the thing he knows should be, and perhaps can be, done.

"Rhode Island!" cries Anna Bigelow. "South Carolina! . . . South Dakota! . . . Tennessee! . . . Texas! . . . Utah! . . . Vermont! . . . Virginia!"

And now the sound hardly dies down at all, it keeps coming in recurrent waves each louder than the last, as everyone moves in for the kill. No one knows exactly who the victim will be, for from those eight states Harley M. Hudson harvests 80 votes, Edward M. Jason 79.

The President had 606 votes, the Governor 601, and on Washington, West Virginia, Wisconsin, Wyoming, and the U.S. possessions the golden prize depends.

At the Mark Hopkins the Governor's face is impassive as he watches the screen. At the Fairmont the Secretary of State and his wife lean forward tensely. At the Huntington the First Lady is close to tears, but from some deep well of confidence—or just plain bullheadedness, she thinks with a frustrated despair as she observes his comfortable calm— the President has drawn the necessary strength to remain steady, unshaken, and undismayed. Now and then the fingers of his right hand tap out a little rhythm on the arm of his chair, but other than that, his aspect, while sensibly concerned, is not alarmed as Anna Bigelow cries, "Washington!"

"Washington casts 12 votes for Harley M. Hudson, 12 votes for Edward M. Jason," the chairman says and a great "Whoosh!" of sound goes up.

"West Virginia!"

"West Virginia casts 11 votes for Harley M. Hudson, six for Edward M. Jason"—and another whoosh.

"Wisconsin!" cries Anna Hooper Bigelow, her voice thin with the excitement that now is so intense that it seems minds and hearts and bodies must crack wide open with the terrible strain of it.

"Wisconsin casts 15 votes for the next President of the United States, Governor Jason," shouts Wisconsin and the great roar begins, "and nine votes for Harley M. Hudson!"

"Walter," Frankly Unctuous says in an oddly thin and trembling voice far from his warm plum-pudding tones, "you realize this gives the President 638 votes, the Governor 634, and if Senator Van Ackerman can hold Wyoming—"

"You are so right," Walter Dobius says sharply, his expression adding, And so obvious. "Please let us listen!"

"Wyoming!" screams Anna Bigelow and the universe simply cannot stand the tension now.

"Wyoming demands a poll of the delegation."

"Oh, NO!" cries the convention.

"Oh, YES, damn it!" shouts the chairman. "How about it, Madam Secretary?"

"The Secretary will poll," the Speaker agrees, and Anna does.

Nine voices, one by one, record their votes, and by the time the tenth is reached it is all over and the Cow Palace is in so great a sea of sound that he can hardly be heard.

But his voice sails up in a high, almost insane whine anyway, and when Anna Hooper Bigelow can finally screech, "Senator Van Ackerman!" he yells, "I cast my vote for Edward M. Jason! Oh, God damn it, I cast my vote for Edward M. Jason!"

But his nine fellow delegates, perhaps reflecting more clearly what they think of him than what they think of the candidates, have not. And now Harley M. Hudson has 647 votes, Governor Jason has 635; and even if all 11 votes from the Canal Zone, the Commonwealth of Puerto Rico, Guam, and the Virgin Islands go to the Governor, he still will miss by one.

Actually, somewhat later in the impossible torrent of noise, Anna does manage to scream their names and the President receives them all.

"The vote stands"—the Speaker manages to make himself heard ten minutes later—"the vote stands at 658 votes for Harley M. Hudson of Michigan, 635 votes for Edward M. Jason of California, and Harley M. Hudson is hereby declared the nominee of this convention for the President of the United States!"

"Mr. Chairman!" Esmé Stryke hollers from below.

"For what purpose does the delegate from California seek recognition?" the Speaker asks, assuming that Esmé will make the customary gracious motion to declare the nomination unanimous.

But she does not, and as the Hudson delegates realize

that she is not going to, a really angry booing begins that the Speaker has a hard time gaveling down.

"Am I to understand that the delegate desires to recess the convention until tomorrow?" he restates her motion in a disbelieving voice.

"That is correct," she shouts, and again the booing surges up, harsh and menacing now at this display of poor sportsmanship and at what many fear is some last desperate trick by the Jason forces.

"The Chair is in some doubt whether the delegate is in order with that motion at this time," the Speaker begins slowly, stalling for time, and now the booing begins from the other side. As he hesitates a red phone on the lower shelf of the lectern begins to ring. He bends down, out of sight of most of the delegates, and picks it up.

"Let them have it," the President directs crisply. "I know what they want"—and here his tone takes on a finally released anger that makes the Speaker realize what he has been through, and the mood in which he intends to handle his enemies from now on—"and I am ready for them. They want tomorrow, give them—tomorrow."

"The Chair will entertain"—the Speaker shouts, but the Jason delegates are so busy booing that it takes a minute or two for them to realize what he is saying—"the Chair will entertain the motion of the delegate from California. All those in favor—"

"AYE!" roar the Jason delegates.

"All those opposed—"

"NO!" roar the Hudson delegates.

"The Ayes have it and the convention stands in recess until 12:01 A.M.," the Speaker shouts, gives the gavel a mighty bang, turns on his heel, and stalks off the platform as the Hudson delegates utter a sudden delighted shout and from the Jasonites comes an angry roar of outrage and confusion.

6

"YOU ASKED to see me," the President said with no cordiality whatsoever. "What did you want?"

"May I sit down," the Governor inquired mildly, "or am I a schoolchild in front of teacher?"

"How do you think you deserve to be categorized?" the President asked. "Go ahead," he directed, turning away to stare out the window. "Chairs are free. But," he said with a sudden sharpness, "nothing else is. What do you want of me, Governor?"

"The vice presidential nomination," Ted said in a tone to match his own. "What else would I want, as things stand?"

"What makes you think you deserve it?" the President asked, turning around to give him a sharp and, for Harley, quite hostile look.

"Six hundred thirty-five votes," the Governor said crisply.

"Of which, at this moment, you retain perhaps 400."
Ted smiled.

"May be. Or may not be. We still have to vote on the foreign policy plank. That will give some indication."

"That's bluff," the President said shortly. "They'll vote with me on the foreign policy plank, and you know it."

"I do not know it," the Governor said. "Nor do you. Furthermore, how can—" he paused deliberately and then went on, "any other candidate—expect to win the vice presidential nomination against me? After all, the convention can't ignore my vote. If they have any fairness at all, enough of them are going to recognize my claim to put me over. And I expect," he concluded calmly, "that you are aware of this."

"Fairness!" the President said, staring at him with a look in which disbelief and contempt contended. "What a fine one to talk of fairness! I would ask you how you do it, except that I begin to realize that this is a mind that can justify almost anything it wants to do. . . . Well!" he said, as Ted, with a great effort, remained impassive, "I succeeded a man like that, and I can tell you *I'm* not going to be succeeded by one like that."

"I assume," Governor Jason said softly, "that you will be succeeded by whomever the convention tells you that you will be succeeded by. And in this case," he said, still softly, "I don't think it's quite such a simple matter as it's sometimes been for the presidential nominee to tell the convention what to tell him, in that regard."

"So you came to make a deal," the President said, seeming, suddenly, tired and dispirited. "You help me carry the foreign policy plank and I accept you as Vice President."

The Governor looked thoughtful.

"No, that isn't it specifically. I assume my delegates will go along more willingly on a foreign policy endorsement if they know you're going to put me on the ticket. But I'm not saying flatly, Mr. President, that you can't have your endorsement without me. Some of my delegates, of course"—he gave a wry little smile—"are fair, too, you know, and they may very well be feeling, now, that you have a right to have any kind of plank you want in the platform. I don't deny, myself, that you do. It would get a bigger vote, I think—perhaps even a unanimous vote, which would look better to the country and the world—if they know I'm to be Vice President."

"How can they rationalize your joining me, after what you and your people have said about my policies?"

"Let's see how they'll rationalize it," the Governor said. "May I?" And he got up and walked to the television set and turned it on. Frankly Unctuous appeared smoothly in midsentence:

"—nor Jason's truly astounding vote in the balloting tonight. Every argument of justice and national unity, therefore, would seem to indicate, would it not, Walter, that the President really has only one choice in the selection of his running mate?"

"Certainly the best way to heal the party's wounds after this bruising battle for the presidential nomination would be to choose the Governor," Walter agreed. "It must be remembered that to many millions of Americans, and to countless millions abroad, Governor Jason is America's symbol of peace. Nothing would be more just and right—

nor, indeed, more practical from a political standpoint—than for the President to accept him gracefully and gladly on the ticket. It would greatly strengthen the President's hand in the election; it would greatly strengthen his hand in international affairs after the election; and, finally, it would bring again to America the unity of attitude and purpose which the violent and tragic events of recent days have so sadly destroyed."

"And perhaps insofar as the President and his Secretary of State may have been responsible for that unhappy turn of affairs," Frankly suggested suavely, and in the room the President made some inarticulate sound of deep disgust, "it would be a form of needed expiation—of reassurance to the nation and the world that such *truly* un-American activities"—and he smiled a little smile at his own clever use of words—"will not again besmirch and bedraggle our national political life. . . . Yes, it would seem that political logic, simple justice, and the cause of world peace all point inexorably to the selection of Governor Jason as the candidate for Vice President of the United States."

"And there is, of course," Walter said thoughtfully, "another reason for such a decision on the President's part."

"Yes?"

"Should Governor Jason be denied this reward which his vote in the convention, as well as the needs of peace and national unity, all seem to make imperative, there would then, I think, be some serious question as to how loyally his supporters might favor the ticket on which some other name was found alongside the President's."

"You mean," Frankly Unctuous said thoughtfully, "that there would be a major, and perhaps decisive, defection—a deliberate staying-away from the polls—or perhaps even a nationwide swing to the other party?"

"There might be even more than that," Walter said gravely. "There could even be some organized attempt to put another ticket in the field, with the Governor at its head."

"I see," Frankly said with equal gravity. "That would indeed raise implications and possibilities that the President might be well advised to consider. So for all these reasons, ladies and gentlemen"—and he turned to smile with a candid honesty straight into the lens—"it would appear that we can expect still further dramatic developments this night; and we can probably assume that they will, in all likelihood, conclude with the selection of Governor Jason as the vice presidential nominee."

"May I?" the President asked dryly, and snapped off the set. The shrewd, determined faces disappeared into a tiny dot of writhing light, then blackness. "Did you put them up to this?"

Ted Jason shook his head with a wry little smile.

"Walter and his crowd you don't have to 'put up' to things. They react on schedule. They have a whole set of alternative battle plans and they no sooner find themselves blocked in one area than they start fighting in another. They've got a great organization going there, and the wonderful thing about it is they never have to consult one another or exchange instructions. Once trained, they're trained for life."

" 'If you stand tall in Georgetown,' " the President quoted softly, " 'you're all *right*.' "

"You know, it's a funny thing," Ted said in an ironic, musing voice. "Every convention I can remember in my adult life, in either party, they've managed to sell to the public as a desperate, last-ditch battle by a tiny little band of vastly outnumbered liberals, fighting tooth and nail against an enormous, overwhelming conspiracy of conservatives—whereas actually, nine times out of ten, the situation has been exactly the reverse. The liberals have had nearly all the press, all the television, all the radio, all the academic, scientific, publishing, theatrical, communications worlds—every possible means of publicity and favorable presentation to the American people. Time after time, the end result has been inevitable from the moment it began. Yet time after time Walter and his crowd have managed to portray it to the public as a great dramatic contest against almost insuperable odds—by their liberal friends, to whom they have given everything—against their conservative enemies, to whom they have given, relatively speaking, hardly even the time of day. . . ." He smiled with a sardonic amazement. "Life has its little ironies, doesn't it?"

The President nodded gravely.

"And rather frightening ones, too, when you think through all their implications. . . . The thing that amazes me about you, Ted, is that a man as intelligent and perceptive as you are, who can see that and understand it, should so willingly have put himself in bondage to them. You've heard how they've turned on Bob Leffingwell in the last hour or two. If I don't give you that nomination and they decide that you're going to head a third party—then by Christopher, my friend, *you'd better head it.* Or else."

"Wouldn't the simpler thing, then, for all of us," Governor Jason suggested gently, "be to give me the nomination? It really would strengthen you, I think, and certainly"— and again he smiled wryly—"it would, if your belief is correct save me a great many personal headaches. . . . To say nothing," he added quietly, "of doing away with the possibility of a three-way election that you would almost certainly lose."

"But I have a funny concept," the President said, and something in his tone indicated to the Governor that this was going to be his final word on the matter. "It isn't very popular nowadays and many people in my country make fun of it. But I still consider it valid, nonetheless. Some people call it a joke, but I call it honor. And in pursuit of that, my friend," and his voice became soft and introspective and quite, quite firm, "I intend to do what I deem best for my country and my people in the disposition of the powers and favors at my command—in the way I conduct the affairs of the United States of America—and in the provisions I make for their future care should anything happen to me. . . . I refer you," he said with a sudden smile, "to my address to the convention, which will occur" —he glanced at his watch—"at approximately 1 A.M. Can I give you a ride to the Cow Palace?" His smile faded and he gave the Governor a long, intent look. "Who knows? The speculation this will arouse could be quite correct."

"Or quite incorrect."

The President shrugged.

"Doesn't it tickle your sense of the ironic, either way?"

The Governor in his turn studied him for several moments. Then finally he grinned, for despite all of Harley's theatrics there must be, there could be under the existing circumstances, only one outcome of their little duel on which so much depended.

"It does. Let's go."

"Our arrival," the President remarked as he opened the door and invited the Governor to precede him into the shouting crowd of reporters and photographers in the hall outside, "will be the biggest public progress since Cleopatra floated down the Nile with Mark Anthony."

"Which one of us," Ted tossed back over his shoulder, "has the asp?"

But the President only laughed, and after a second the Governor did the same, and so in good humor and apparent cordiality they walked briskly out behind the flying wedge of Secret Service men, descended to the waiting limousine with its presidential flags and its phalanx of motorcycles, and swung away in a roar of motors and screaming sirens to the Cow Palace and destiny.

7

AND SO ONCE again, for the last time, the delegates heard a prayer (now it was a Mormon's turn, from snug, smug, delightful Salt Lake City) again they enjoyed their mixture of fond, exasperated thoughts as the band played "The Star-Spangled Banner"—again the Speaker gaveled them to order—again silence settled and tension rose.

"We come now," the Speaker said at 12:13 A.M., "under terms of the previous motion of the Senator from Iowa, to a vote on the foreign policy plank. If there is no debate, the Chair will—"

But even as he spoke, even as cries of protest began to come from various delegations across the floor, even as Roger P. Croy and Esmé Stryke and Fred Van Ackerman all began to shout for recognition at their respective microphones, a sudden excited murmur began to rush through the great room. It started in the press section, spread with the fantastic speed of such things onto the podium, across the floor, and up into the galleries. In something less than five minutes the same words had been repeated approximately thirty-six thousand times by eighteen thousand people: "He's here!" There was no need to identify the "he," for at this particular stage of a convention there is only one great all-important HE in the universe. But what made it even more unbearably exciting was the word that rushed over the hall immediately after, received in astonishment, anguish, jubilation, or dismay depending upon the political sympathies of the listener: "The Governor's with him!"

That, indeed, put the globe to whirling and, at least for the moment, stopped the convention dead in its tracks before it even got started. Fred Van Ackerman, caught in mid-yell, paused and said, "Oh, yeah?" in a disbelieving voice to the fellow Wyoming delegate who clawed frantically at his sleeve. Esmé Stryke's voice rose suddenly into a screech as she started to shout, "Mr. Chairman, my delegation feels there should be a full debate on this *whaaaaat?*" Roger P. Croy fortunately had his mouth closed when the news reached him, and being a man of great experience and presence of mind, immediately opened it again to start calling, "Mr. Chairman! Mr. Chairman! Mr. Chairman!" with an urgent, insistent rhythm.

It was several minutes before the Speaker could get the convention quieted. When he did Governor Croy was still calling, with a patient, persistent doggedness, "Mr. Chairman! Mr. Chairman! Mr. Chairman!"

"For what purpose does the distinguished delegate from Oregon seek recognition?" the Speaker inquired, thinking with a heated annoyance, I wish I knew what purpose Harley has in mind, but I don't, so we'll all just have to play it by ear until he tells us.

"Mr. Chairman," Roger P. Croy said with a dignified and portentous calmness, "I move, on behalf of a great candidate for *Vice* President"—and there was a roar of excited approval from the Jason delegates at this articulation of what they all knew now must be the actual situation—"that this convention adopt as its foreign policy plank the following language, and I quote:

" 'Believing that the interests of world peace can best be served by opposing Communist aggression and infiltration, armed or otherwise, wherever they may exist, we applaud the action of the President in opposing—' "

There was a great shout as the convention recognized the Administration language, a great tribute to a great candidate for Vice President whose spokesman was now, with the true sportsmanship that characterized his candidate, doing the right, the courteous, the honorable, the decent, the *noble* thing. Roger P. Croy went on, imperturbable:

" '—such Communist aggression and infiltration in the nations of Gorotoland and Panama. We wholeheartedly support his determination to bring peace and stability to those troubled nations through the medium of peaceful and honest negotiations as soon as the Communist threat has been removed.' "

Again there was a great shout of excitement and approval, and into it the Speaker, who at least was in no doubt about what to do with an opportunity like this, cried, "Is there a second?"

"Second!" Cullee Hamilton and Lafe Smith, Esmé Stryke, and Fred Van Ackerman, Joe Smitters, Bob Smutters, John Smotters, Mary Baffleburg, Lizzie McWharter, and half a hundred others all shouted at once from their respective microphones.

"All those in favor!" roared the Speaker.

"AYE!" roared the convention.

"All those opposed!" roared the Speaker, and waited a long, deliberate moment.

Silence, quivering, ecstatic, exultant.

"The Ayes have it and the language of the foreign policy plank is hereby adopted!" the Speaker cried, giving his gavel a violent bang! that shook the podium. Instantly another great shout went up, and across the floor Cullee and Lafe exchanged a glance, grabbed their state standards, shouted to their fellow delegates, and began to snake dance along the aisles. At once others fell into line, in a moment the entire convention was in the aisles, and a wild demonstration was under way, led by laughing Jason delegates holding high JASON FOR PRESIDENT placards on which the word "Vice" had been hastily scrawled in above the word PRESIDENT.

"And so," said Frankly Unctuous with a warm benignity in the booth above, "this great convention, perhaps one of the most historic in American history, roars to its climax in this joyous demonstration of unity that should, very shortly now, produce what everyone here happily expects and eagerly awaits, the nomination of Governor Edward M. Jason of California to the great office of Vice President of the United States. Thus do we see, Walter, that the American system still works, in its mysterious, wonderful way, and somehow, out of the violent contentions of sincere and dedicated men, there emerges what can truly be called the people's choice. . . . This is a thrilling moment, indeed, and you will forgive me a personal note, ladies and gentlemen"—and he smiled, frankly, into the camera—"if I say that it is particularly thrilling for those of us who have been here through all these long and sometimes heated days. It is a real satisfaction to us to witness this great, democratic conclusion to a battle so earnestly yet so honestly fought by all concerned. Don't you agree, Walter?"

"Yes, I do," Walter said. Yet there was in his tone a certain indefinable reserve that might have indicated, to one less enthralled than Frankly by the happy harmony of the moment, that something important was working in his shrewd, experienced brain. What it was actually saying to him was: It's too pat—it's too perfect—*watch out*. But all he had the heart to say aloud to his relaxed and delighted brother-in-arms, and to the many millions who were, he knew, hanging dutifully upon their wise and illuminating words, was, "Perhaps we should see, now, what the President has to say."

"If the convention will permit us," Frankly said with a happy laugh. "Just look at them, Walter! Just look at them!"

And indeed they were a sight for sore-pressed pundits to see, as they danced and frolicked and whooped and hollered around the Cow Palace in a scream of sound that showed no signs of abating. Whenever it did the Speaker gave a little nod to Cullee or Lafe or Bob Munson or whoever happened to be passing below the podium at the moment, and it started up again. "I want them exhausted," the calm voice had directed over the red phone a couple of minutes ago from the closely guarded room behind the platform where the candidate waited with Governor Jason. And the Speaker, who, like Walter Dobius, was beginning to get the picture—though in his case with the start of a great inner amusement rather than with Walter's frantically growing worry and bitter alarm—obliged.

Eventually, however, even the greatest moments end, and so, eventually, did this. They were close to the limits of endurance by now, they had been in session since 3 P.M. the previous afternoon, had gone through the excitement of the nominations, the demonstrations, the presidential vote, the constant tensions and pressures that a recess filled with a jabbering inability to relax—for who knew what was coming next?—had done little to relieve. Ten hours of it, topped by this last demonstration continuing for almost half an hour, and they were beginning to feel more than a little groggy.

The red phone rang and the calm voice said, "Any time you're ready."

"The convention will be in order!" the Speaker shouted, pounding his gavel with a steady thock! thock! thock! of wood-on-wood. "The convention will be in order! Will the delegates please take their seats! Will the delegates please take their seats! . . . I will say to the delegates," he roared with a sudden show of anger, "that they are holding up a most important address by someone they'd like to hear, so will they *please* settle down!"

That did it. Another five minutes of gradual quieting and settling, and they were ready.

"It is my great pleasure and high privilege," the Speaker said solemnly into the restless silence, "to present to you our candidate, the President of the United States."

The band swung triumphantly into "Hail to the Chief," and again there was demonstration, hysterical, delirious, overjoyed, for following closely behind him as he came to the lectern was the Governor of California, smiling and waving, and this was sign enough that God was in his heaven and all right with the world. It could be seen that the President solicitously urged the Governor forward to take a seat to his right, toward the front of the podium, in full view of them all—"I want them to be sure and see you," he shouted into Ted's ear over the cascade of sound pouring upon them, and Ted, obviously pleased, nodded and stepped obediently forward—and it could also be seen that from time to time the President looked toward him with a fatherly, satisfied smile, each glance producing a new roar of gratified, ecstatic applause. In the diplomatic section Raoul Barre did take occasion to lean forward and call to Lord Maudulayne, "But where is Orrin? This doesn't seem to ring quite true, does it?"—and Lord Maudulayne first shrugged, then paused with a thoughtful frown, then looked quizzical and nodded. But this was only the most minor of episodes in the joyous occasion in which all those who saw in Edward M. Jason the harbinger and salvation of their hopes reveled in their moment of triumph at last.

Fifteen minutes later the Speaker began to pound insistently for order and five minutes after that he had it. Without further introduction or formality the President began to speak in a clear and solemn voice.

"My fellow countrymen, delegates to this great convention: I accept with pride and determination your decision that I be your candidate for President of the United States."

They greeted this with the customary roar, touched by his forgiveness, unified and at one now that the battle was over and they could go forward together again; pleased and delighted by his good-sportsmanship, the necessity for which a near-majority of them had forced upon him most ruthlessly; relieved and happy, in some curiously childlike and irresponsible way, that Daddy wasn't mad at them after all, in spite of what they'd done.

"At another time," he said, "and at another place—probably on Labor Day in Lansing where I first entered politics—I shall make a formal speech of acceptance. But I wanted to talk to you this morning at once, for there are matters of urgency which concern us.

"I shall conduct this campaign as vigorously and forcefully as I know how.

"I shall continue—and," he added with a quiet firmness that began to give them pause even as they yelled approval —"I shall strengthen the policies which I have followed and which I believe best for the security of the United States and the peace of the world.

"We have now, I think, a platform which adequately and honestly expresses those policies, and adequately and honestly expresses the honorable duty and unflinching determination of this nation and its people.

"I pledge it my full support, and I expect those who help me in this battle for a strong and fearless America to give it their full support."

Again there were shouts of approval, and it could be seen that Governor Jason, half-smiling yet grave and judicious, was nodding and applauding vigorously with the rest.

"The crisis we face—the long-continuing crisis we have faced ever since the resumption of aggressive Communist imperialism after the end of World War II—does not permit a place for the half-hearted, the half-doers, the half-committed. It does not permit a place for those who do not wholeheartedly, with every fiber of their hearts and beings, support and advance the policy of unyielding, unbelligerent, and *unafraid* firmness which is, I believe, the only salvation for this country and the free world.

"There is no place for the half-committed in the ranks," he said, and suddenly his voice rang with a sternness that brought a sudden hush and the first stirrings of a general doubt across the floor, "and there is no place for them at the head of the ranks.

"This army throughout must be an army of the convinced and the committed. Otherwise it will fail."

He paused, and it was quite obvious that a good many in his audience were uneasy now. Could Daddy be mad after all? It was against all the rules, no matter what had been done to him. How dare he be mad? It just wasn't right.

But perhaps he wasn't, really. Now he was going on, for a moment humor was back in his voice, he sounded more relaxed and fatherly, the way they liked to think of him—good old Harley!

"Certainly no one can say that you have reached your decisions here under compulsion from anyone."—and there was an appreciative laugh from all around the hall. "No one can say that there has not been a free, indeed a very vigorous, exchange of ideas and arguments. No one can honestly claim that we have not washed all our linen in public this time!"—and now the laughter was warm and unrestrained, for it was apparent that he was not resentful, he was a marvelous sport, they loved him so and it was going to be all right.

"But—" and the way he said it brought a sudden cessation of laughter—"but—the time for that has passed. The decision has been reached. We face now, as our friends up there in the booths have been telling us in the last couple of hours"—and he gave them a friendly little wave—or was it friendly? Nobody knew and the laughter which greeted it was uncertain, uneasy, and perhaps a little guilty—"the task of binding up the party's wounds and going forward in unity.

"I submit that this will be impossible if those who cannot be relied upon to act with honor are given too great a hand in what we do.

"It will be impossible if those of faint heart and clouded purpose are allowed to enter the places of leadership."

It could be seen by those who avidly looked, and all did, that Governor Jason's face was impassive, though his color seemed a little paler and the line of his jaw might be said to be a little tense. But no one could really conceive that he had any reason to worry. The imperatives of the situation gave the President no room to maneuver, and his remarks now must be taken for what they obviously were, a human little reaction, natural enough, a fatherly warning that he would expect the loyalty which they were all, of course, eager to give him.

"You have nominated me as your candidate for President. Not, I will admit"—he smiled wryly and there was a sharp little bleat of laughter, suddenly very nervous—"in quite the way, or under quite the circumstances, that I had anticipated.

"Had you done it as I anticipated, I intended to follow the policy I announced earlier and make no attempt to influence you in the selection of a vice presidential candidate—even though every presidential candidate, it seems to me, assumes his role with the immediate obligation to assist in the selection of the man he believes best equipped to succeed him should the necessity arise.

"But," he said gravely, and now nobody at all was laughing, from Governor Jason on down they were giving him an absolute desperate attention, "you did not act as I had expected, and so I think I am relieved of the obligation to act as I originally announced.

"I think what has happened here in this convention indicates that I indeed have an obligation to give you the benefit of my thinking on the selection of my running mate and potential successor.

"I know," he said softly, and it could be seen that Governor Jason's face became whiter and whiter as he spoke, "what he must not be.

"He must not be a man who sacrifices honor and integrity and the decent standards of decent men in the cause of his own avid ambition for public preferment.

"He must not be a man who associates with the worst elements in America to gain his ends.

"He must not be a man who, condoning violence, attempts with the most devious skill and the most ruthless cynicism to shift the blame for it to someone who is innocent."

It could be seen, in the deathly silence that now held the great room, that Governor Jason was very still and his face was very pale.

"He must not be a man who calls for 'negotiations' because it is a popular word, but does not have the honesty to tell you that genuine negotiations demand strength on our part and a willingness to stand firm—not weakness and a readiness to surrender in advance every position we hold.

"He must not be a man who offers you the outer shell of integrity but has sold himself to unprincipled backers"— and now he finally permitted his eyes to rest finally upon the Governor, who stared tensely back—"inside.

"He must not, in short," the President said softly, and now he was staring straight at the Governor as though he had never, really, seen him until this moment—"be a man for whom conscience does not—perhaps never has, but certainly, in the heat of his ambition for office and desire for national power, *does not now*—decide the issue."

At this there was a great gasp from the delegates, yet so astounded were they, so overwhelmed, so delighted, infuriated, happy, aghast, depending upon their personal sympathies, that it was impossible for anything coherent to emerge. Only a strange animal mumbling and grumbling, whose elements were unclear and whose import was uncertain, rose from the floor and descended from the galleries.

In the midst of it Governor Jason sat absolutely still, absolutely white, immobilized by humiliation and dismay; not yet angry, because what was happening to him was so overwhelming that it really could not penetrate, as yet; not daring, and actually physically unable, to move, so stunned was he and so uncertain as to what might be coming next.

"I do know a man of honor," the President resumed, still softly, and there was a sudden burst of applause, nervous yet defiant, from somewhere on the floor, cut off as abruptly as it came.

"He has served his country and his party without stain or blemish for twenty years.

"He has occupied high position in his state, in the Senate, in the Cabinet.

"He has fought hard and valiantly and with great courage all his life for what he believes in.

"He has made enemies, but they have been enemies honestly made, in battles honestly fought.

"He has not been devious.

"He has not been cynical.

"He has not been cruel.

"He has not been weak.

"He is as convinced as I am that only with unflinching firmness and the willingness to accept, and act immediately upon, our international obligations, can this nation, and the free world that depends upon her, survive.

"He is direct, forthright, courageous—and honorable.

"Like him or dislike him, take him or leave him, there he stands—a man, in all senses.

"A man," the President concluded quietly, "I believe the country needs—I believe the world needs.

"I know I need him.

"I nominate for the office of Vice President of the United States," he said, so quietly and calmly that they hardly realized he was doing it until it was over, "a great and *honorable* American, Orrin Knox of the State of Illinois."

His expression became stern in the fantastic hush. It was a moment in which the world could end, so terrible was the tension.

"I tell you frankly now, I will accept no other."

And with a grave little bow of his head he turned without looking at Ted Jason, shook hands quickly with the Speaker who could not resist giving his arm a quick, delighted squeeze, and walked solemnly from the podium, a portly, comfortable, old-shoe figure who did not look at all fatherly or forgiving any more.

Of what happened in those next few minutes no one who was there, or anyone who watched it on television, ever retained any coherent memory, so great was the release of emotion that burst from the convention, so furious and contradictory the emotions and reactions that filled the hall and spun outward from it around the earth. From Frankly Unctuous and Walter Dobius, at last too upset to make any attempt to dissemble their horrified disbelief, to Hal Knox, absentmindedly gripping the Illinois standard and staring transfixed at the platform while tears ran down his face, all were undone and everything was tossed awry. The enormity of it was what overwhelmed the Jasonites; the wonderful audacity of it was what stunned the Knox supporters. The President had defied all the clichés of conventions, had refused to go along with the sickly good-fellowship with which men who hate each other on Wednesday embrace on Thursday for the sake of party unity and the necessities of November; had done, bluntly and honestly, exactly what he believed in doing. It was a deed beyond immediate comprehension, though in days to come many and many a solemn word would be written analyzing its reasons, implications, and effect.

But right now, for perhaps ten minutes, no one was capable of doing much of anything. It was as though the whole convention were paralyzed. Delegates milled aimlessly about, the galleries gabbled, Walter's world babbled, nobody took hold. The Speaker, appearing as dazed and uncertain as the rest, stood chatting to Anna Bigelow in a rambling conversation whose content neither of them would ever be able to recall later, no matter how hard they tried. It seemed that no one would act because no one knew how to act.

The event was temporarily too much.

The human animal, however, is not one to go for long without adapting; and in one benumbed but brilliant mind the glow of a great and growing anger produced presently the action required to get the convention back on course and start the world moving again. One decisive act was needed, and this was it.

The Governor of California stood up.

Instantly the hall fell still.

Slowly, with a terrible controlled tightness, he came to the microphone. The Speaker abruptly left Anna in midsentence to move forward beside him.

"Mr. Chairman!" Ted Jason said in a strained, harsh voice that boomed out with a shocking loudness over the amplifiers. ". . . Mr. Chairman."

"For what purpose does the distinguished delegate from California seek recognition?" the Speaker inquired automatically, his own voice strained and uncertain, staring intently, as though he had never seen it before, at the drawn face at his side.

For a second it seemed that the Governor might not be able to go on, so dreadfully was he struggling to control himself.

"To withdraw a candidacy," he said finally, and a great groan went up from his supporters across the floor and in the galleries.

"Yes!" he said, his voice growing stronger. "To withdraw a candidacy and to withdraw myself from this convention which is now a mockery of all that honorable men hold dear."

There was a roar of applause, met by some booing and, from the Wyoming delegation, a wild, frantic voice that yelled, "Give it to him, Ted! Oh, damn it, *let him have it!*"

"Much has been made of honor in the last few minutes," he said, and now his voice was becoming fuller and stronger as the anger began to take hold and the impact of what had been done to him at last began to sink in.

"It is amazing how the word can be interpreted to suit the purposes of those who use it.

"Honor, the President says—and he allows you to assume that he will favor me so that he can get you to vote a platform endorsing his ill-advised and dangerous policies."

There was a gasp but he ignored it.

"Honor, he says—and he brings me here to make a Roman spectacle of me before the world, with a cruelty that sits oddly with the picture of a kindly President in love with honor.

"Honor, he says—and he steps cold-bloodedly into the deliberations of a democratic convention and ruthlessly attempts to impose his will upon you.

"Honor, he says—and he nominates a vice presidential candidate whose policies of violence in the world and violence in this convention—"

Now there was a wave of booing that grew as he spoke, but he shouted on into it—

"—have contributed to disaster here and disaster abroad.

"Honor, he preaches," he said more calmly, "and nothing but dishonor flows from what he does."

Again there was a gasp and an abrupt, uneasy silence.

"He uses, too," Ted said slowly, "and he chooses to make a mockery of it, the word conscience.

"He says I do not have one.

"He says I have never had one.

"He says power means more to me than conscience.

"He sneers at my campaign slogan and implies that it is nothing but a gimmick to get votes.

"Very well," he said, and his voice again became uneven with emotion, "he can say what he likes. And I leave you to make what peace you can with your own consciences about what has happened here. But I know what I must do to rest easy with mine.

"I care not what others do, and I make no attempt to direct or influence them, but I know what I am going to do."

He paused and when he resumed it was in a still-unsteady but stronger voice.

"When I leave the platform now I shall be leaving this convention and I shall not return."

There was a great groan of protest and anger from his supporters, met suddenly with an equally angry and determined applause from the other side.

"Words cannot express my gratitude to those of you who have believed in me," he said slowly and with great emotion. "I wish you well in your future endeavors. May God give you strength to do what is best for our beloved country. I shall always do what I can to advance her interests—in decency . . . in conscience . . . and in honor."

And without looking right or left he turned and walked swiftly, brushing aside the tentative hands that reached out to him in pity or approval, off the platform, out of the Cow Palace, out of the convention.

Moments come, and sometimes moments do not wait. and those who would control them must act swiftly or not at all.

"Mr. Chairman!" Cullee Hamilton shouted while all around delegates sat stunned, none yet moving, none rising to follow the Governor as they might in another second do, "I second the nomination of Orrin Knox to be Vice President and I ask you to put the question!"

"Question!" Lafe shouted from the Iowa delegation, and "Question!" Bob Munson shouted from Michigan.

"QUESTION!" a giant yell went up.

"The Secretary will call the roll of the states for the selection of a candidate for Vice President," the Speaker cried, and Anna Bigelow barked, "Alabama!" so fast she could hardly be understood.

"Alabama," a tense voice said, and a wild rush of sound went up as floor and galleries sensed instantly what was going to happen, "casts six votes for Orrin Knox and *four votes abstain.*"

"On this ballot," the Speaker reported an hour later in a voice heavy with emotion and strain as the clock once again approached the hour of three o'clock in the morning, "there are 763 votes for Orrin Knox of Illinois, 530 abstentions. Orrin Knox is hereby declared to be the choice of this convention for the office of Vice President of the United States!"

He paused for a moment, obviously awaiting a motion

to make it unanimous, but of course no motion came; only a harsh laughter, here and there, and a restless stirring across the floor.

"Mr. Chairman!" Senator Van Ackerman called out into the uneasy pause.

"For what purpose does the delegate seek recognition?' the Speaker inquired.

"Just to say one little thing, Mr. Speaker," Fred said in a savage, mocking voice. "To say that I'm going." His voice rose in a shout. "ARE ANY OF THE REST OF YOU GOING TO HAVE THE GUTS TO GO WITH ME?"

And he, too, without looking to one side or the other, turned and stalked from the floor; and this time others rose, in many delegations, ignoring the Speaker's repeated gavelings for order, and made their way to the exits, while on the floor and in the galleries and in the press the entire convention stood to watch them go: almost 500, Frankly Unctuous reported with a pleased excitement five minutes later, enough to hold a rump convention, enough to start a third party—"although the Governor of California," Walter Dobius cautioned in a voice finally restored to its normal judicious gravity, once more in command of events and busy upon them, "will undoubtedly have to consider many things before authorizing so drastic and fateful a step."

The convention will be in order," the Speaker said finally. "We still have further business to transact, we still have to conclude things in an orderly fashion. . . ."

He paused deliberately and waited until the room was quiet and they sat, exhausted beyond exhaustion, having endured beyond endurance, silent and attentive at last.

"The Chair wishes to present now," he said, and his voice dragged and showed suddenly every one of its sixty-two years, "your candidate for Vice President, the Honorable Orrin Knox of the great State of Illinois."

8

So it had come at last, his moment of triumph—and what a triumph! The commanded choice of a convention in dissolution—the dictated darling of harassed and embittered delegates—probably the genuine choice of well over half of them, but far from the happily near-unanimous selection he had once imagined in his fonder hopes.

The practical politician's creed—Don't look back now, you've got it—was not quite enough as he walked slowly to the rostrum, Beth and Hal close behind, in the midst of a rising roar of welcome.

It was not until they reached the lectern and a sudden note of genuine warmth surged into the greeting that he began to relax a little; and it was only after the demonstration had lasted for twenty minutes, the delegates finding somewhere some last unexpended ounce of energy to help them dance and rollick along the aisles, the galleries applauding and shouting, that he was ready to say the things he felt must be said on this occasion of such importance to him, the party, the country, and perhaps the world.

But first he had to acknowledge something to his family and he did so as a thousand lights beat down and a thousand cameras clicked.

"I'm beginning to think they mean it," he shouted to Beth after they had stepped forward and waved for the fiftieth time.

She smiled.

"I've always told you, Senator, that things work out."

"So have I," Hal said sternly, leaning forward to speak past his mother.

The Secretary laughed.

"All right," he said as he turned back to wave again, "so have you both. Can I help it if I'm a natural-born disbeliever?"

The sound renewed itself, grew, subsided. He leaned back a little, rested his left arm on the lectern, gripped its front edge with his left hand.

"Mr. Chairman," he began gravely as the hall became abruptly still, "I could wish—we all could wish—that events in San Francisco had been conducted in a different atmosphere and their conclusion reached in a different mood.

"I regret that the speaker preceding me chose to take the position he did and conclude it with the action he did. I hope that sober reflection will in due time persuade him to come again to stand beside us."

There was a roar of approval, and in the booth above Frankly Unctuous remarked blandly, "While one of course understands the perhaps rather desperate mood in which Secretary Knox indulges these last-minute afterthoughts for Governor Jason's feelings, one wonders whether his appeals for help will have much effect."

"I am afraid," Walter agreed with a certain spiteful righteousness, "that the split is too fundamental to be healed at this late moment. And in any event, this is rather contrary to the President's own bitterly expressed feelings, is it not?"

"Orrin the Peacemaker?" Frankly inquired dryly.

"Politics make strange apostles," Walter observed, "but this time I am afraid it is much, much too late."

"Little I can say," the Secretary went on, "can change the difficult and frequently embittered things that have occurred at this convention. Yet perhaps there are one or two things to be said that can, to some extent, moderate and soften their memories.

"When men contend, as men have here contended, for great ideas and great prizes, they sometimes have a tendency to move beyond the bounds of decent argument and decent treatment of one another. We expect this in other lands, but although we know it has happened many times here, we still, each time, I think, retain the hope that it will not happen in ours.

"At least I do not think," he said, and his tone was grave and thoughtful and they were listening to him intently, "that many of us consciously start out upon a contest of ideas or ambitions with the deliberate intent to be unfair. At least I think we retain some memory of tradition, some respect for principle, that persuades us that we must, if we can, be decent and just. The hope is there, and I think by far the greater number of us consciously and deliberately try to do the best we can to see that it does not die.

"Yet there are some"—his expression darkened and his voice became sad—"there have been some in this convention—who believe that this is not the way to conduct arguments in America.

"There are some who believe that every means of attack must be used, that every weapon of destruction must be employed, that if you cannot defeat a man on the fair ground of argument, then you must defeat him by assaults upon his character, and by imputing to him beliefs and impulses and actions against which the decencies of mankind cry out.

"Thus it has been said of me that I have deliberately condoned violence in this convention. I did not, but that is no matter: it has been said, and said deliberately, and no doubt some have been convinced by it, and will remain convinced. For this is the kind of lie that feeds on denial and no man, thus impugned, can ever entirely cleanse himself in the eyes of those who would rather believe evil about someone they disagree with than give him the benefit of the actual facts about him.

"It has been said that the President and I have deliberately plunged America into war, that we have deliberately done things in foreign policy that are hurtful to the United States and to the cause of world peace.

"You would get the idea, to listen to some people tell it, that we actually enjoy sending American boys to die; that we actually revel in spending the national treasure upon wars abroad; that we actually sit around in the White House and the State Department clasping our hands with relish at the thought of how much misery and unhappiness we can create.

"What sort of monstrous madness," he demanded, and his voice filled with a sudden flash of real indignation, "is this? *What kind of insanity are some Americans trying to say about other Americans? What kind of nonsense are they trying to persuade themselves to believe?*"

His voice became stern.

"I will tell you that not many of them believe it. Just a few, deluded by those who would use their gullibility for their own dark purposes, into believing what a moment's mature reflection should convince them could not possibly be true.

"Deluded by deluders deliberate and cold-blooded, who know exactly what they are doing. And what they are doing holds no good for America.

"My countrymen," he said, "the hour is very late and we have been here very long; yet I think we might perhaps take one more moment to consider the principles by which we like to think we live in this country—the principles by which, if this country is to come safely through the situation that confronts her in the world, we have *got* to live.

"I grant you that all of us would like to forget about the world's troubles and concentrate on what we have: our fantastic wealth, our fantastic standard of living, our fantastic level of general well-being.

"I doubt if there is an American in the land who does not, in his inmost heart, wish that we could wash our hands of the world and let it go hang while we enjoy ourselves over here.

"We are basically, still, a very isolationist people—and why shouldn't we be? No people ever had greater reason to be, or more to gain, if they could just forget the world and let it go to hell. We are strong enough so that we could do it, probably, if we really set our minds to it.

"But history does not permit this luxury to those who have power and also have some amount of conscience to go with it. History does not permit us to withdraw and go our own way.

"History has vacuums and it says, You fill them.

"History has needs and it says, You answer.

"History has problems and it says, Get cracking, they can't be solved without you.

"And so we face the world and we do not have the luxury of running away from it.

"And by the same token, we do not have the luxury of pretending that its problems can be settled by turning and looking the other way. Or by deluding ourselves into thinking that we have a right to intervene when the world's would-be murderer is named Hitler but have no right to intervene when he changes his name to Tashikov or Mao Tse-tung.

"We aren't permitted the luxury of being either/or as the moment suits us. We have to be in the world or out of it, all the way. And history made the decision for us long ago, and we are in.

"Now I say to you, my countrymen, that conscience and honor have been discussed at some length here in San Francisco. But conscience and honor are only the way you do things, they are not the things themselves. The things themselves are what history has placed upon us. Conscience and honor are only the style in which we meet them. Conscience and honor dictate only how we handle them. They do not permit us to escape from them, or to pretend that they are not there.

"Conscience does not decide the issue: the issue has long been decided. It is only how we meet it that matters. It is only from our courage and integrity, our fortitude and grace, that honor springs and conscience is upheld.

"I do not believe," he said gravely, "that we can do other than we are doing in the world: be steady, be patient, be firm, be willing to talk—but also be ready and willing to act if we must—and then *do it,* when the challenge comes.

"I cannot, in good faith—or good conscience—persuade you to any other policy. I cannot in decency—or in honor—advocate any other course.

"I call you to a campaign," he said quietly, "which will determine whether America is to be a sometime-fighter for the right when it suits her, as some would like her to be—or a consistent and steady advocate of mankind's hopes and decencies whenever and wherever they are challenged, whatever the difficult cost and bitter price of defending them.

"This is what the President and I offer you, I think, this choice, made clear-cut now as it has rarely been by our recent decisions in Gorotoland, the UN, and Panama.

"We hope you will be with us. We hope a majority of the American people will be with us. But regardless, I suspect"—and a wry and almost wistful little smile touched his face for a moment—"neither of us, in all probability, could do any differently, or be any other, than he is."

And he bowed gravely and waved and turned away, shepherding his family before him; and after a moment, a little puzzled at this rather abrupt and subdued conclusion, this final, personal peroration which raised few flags but touched instead on inner things that they would have to think about a while, the delegates and galleries broke into a generous but somewhat baffled applause.

The Speaker stepped forward, pounded the gavel sharply once, and declared, "This convention now stands adjourned *sine die.*"

And thus on Orrin's introspective note it ended, and in all the bright city, great nation, great world, men approved or disapproved as it suited them and made of it what they would according to their lights.

To the dean and leader of Walter's world the issues still were clear-cut as he began his column in the press room at the Hilton shortly before 5 A.M. There was no Helen-Anne to bother him tonight—she was off with the Knoxes somewhere, plotting strategy, as he had heard, with a bitter, ironic smile, from *Newsweek* as he entered the hotel. Nor was there anyone else to interfere as he sat in a corner of the room, stolid and alone, carefully ignored by his colleagues, pecking out the words on the battered portable that had accompanied him on so many journeys to so many famous people in his endless search for Right. He was through with being part of a two-man show, he had bade Frankly Unctuous farewell with considerable relief, he really quite regretted that he had accepted the television assignment.

It was good to be just himself again, Walter Wonderful, for whose wisdom the nations waited and the world bowed down:

"SAN FRANCISCO—Thus in disgruntlement and dismay ends this convention of errors: on a pure note of power politics, struck by a candidate for Vice President whose use of power politics has brought America to the edge of disaster.

"America must act, he has told us: America has a duty to do what she thinks best: America is so perfect and so arrogant that she cannot refrain from intervening, but must force other nations to her will.

"If Americans object to this, they are deluded. If they don't accept it, they are fools.

"One wonders how this policy will suit the rest of the world, which now confronts the possibility that Orrin Knox will be Vice President, perhaps President himself, some day.

"One wonders how it will suit the American people, whose sons are being called, whose treasure is being used, to follow this policy wherever it may lead, even to national destruction and history's eternal condemnation.

"For the President, this marks the low point of a career which, while not notably distinguished, had not been notably harmful until these recent months. Now he has chosen to cap it with one of the most brutal public attacks upon a fellow American that the nation has ever witnessed. His excoriation of Governor Jason before the eyes of watching mankind must always remain as one of the most extraordinary and inexcusable episodes in American history.

"For this merciless public humiliation of a man whose only crime is the desire to bring about world peace, Mr. Hudson deserves, as he will receive, the condemnation and contempt of decent men.

"For Governor Jason, the almost-candidate and undoubtedly the real choice of the convention had the delegates been free to express their true feelings, several courses are open.

"He can, as Secretary Knox suggested in his rambling acceptance speech, forget his principles, his conscience, and his honor, and come to stand beside the President and Mr. Knox in support of a policy his whole life condemns. Others, such as Robert A. Leffingwell, have followed such a cynical course already, and more, perhaps, may do so.

"Or he can stand aside, an independent, critical voice in the midst of the campaign, pointing out errors, urging reforms: a course that can reduce a man to the status of common scold in a very short time, or, if it leave him respected, leave him isolated and impotent as well.

"Or the Governor can remain true to his principles and his convictions, stand firm on the policy of true negotiation and opposition to war which so many concerned and dedicated Americans believe in along with him, and let himself become what they see in him: the guardian of their hopes, the protector of their future, the leader of their cause.

"Rarely, perhaps, has any American statesman faced so difficult a choice.

"Rarely, also, perhaps, has any had so great an opportunity.

"Now the nation's eyes—the world's eyes—rest upon Edward Montoya Jason. The measure of what he is will be found in the next few days and weeks.

"There, too, quite possibly, will be found the measure of what America is, and what, in so fearful and tragic a time, she may yet become has she but the courage to choose a leader worthy of her heritage and her purposes.

"Honor has been made much of, here in San Francisco. It remains to be seen, now, what it means to the Governor of California upon whose shoulders rest the hopes of so many of his heartsick and fearful fellow citizens of this sad, unhappy planet."

But even as he wrote, three thousand miles away in Manhattan the first crack was appearing in Walter's wonderful world. Someone else was writing, too, old and tired, still shaken and quivering after a violent pre-dawn argument with his rebellious juniors, but triumphant at last.

(There had been a sizable group who had favored an editorial on the sudden worldwide upspringing of the Booker T. Saunders Clubs. It would have been entitled HEALTHY SIGN, and it was to have begun: "Another of those spontaneous democratic movements so characteristic of a world in ferment has found in a simple American boy its symbol of articulated comment on the tragic issues of our times. . . .")

It had been quite a while since he had written an editorial, and his fingers were rusty on the keys, but tomorrow morning The Greatest Publication That Absolutely Ever Was would carry a statement that would make the nations pause, and echo quite as far around the globe as Walter's:

"While it is too early to determine who would be the best choices for election in November, it seems to us that it is time, now, for their party to close ranks behind the candidates chosen by the convention in San Francisco.

"Whether one agrees with the policies of the President and Secretary Knox or not, one must concede the candor and courage with which they have expressed, and are expressing, them.

"For anyone to interject a third element into the campaign would, we believe, serve only to confuse and divide America at a time when her choices must be firm and clear-cut.

"There is some element of sour grapes and bad sportsmanship in a third-party candidacy that Americans just don't like. We, along with many of his fellow citizens, would feel regret if one whose qualities, character, and abilities we have always admired should fall into such an error.

"It would not, we believe, do him honor or his country service."

It was short and hasty and not quite as punchy as he could have turned out ten years ago, but The G.P.'s executive chairman told himself as he pulled it out of the machine and prepared to take it down personally to the city room that it would be heard from. Oh, yes, he thought with a satisfaction he had not felt for a long, long time: it would be heard from.

Alone in his room at the Mark Hopkins, knowing nothing of these comments on his future that so accurately reflected the divergent pressures that were threatening to tear him apart, the Governor of California stared at his great-grandmother. He said nothing, she said nothing. It was six o'clock in the morning. In the past hour the phone had rung twice.

Once it was Rufus Kleinfert, saying in his heavy, oddly accented voice, "Mr. Shelby and Senator Van Ackerman and I, we would like to talk to you, Governor—" whereupon the Governor had hung up.

Half an hour later it had been Fred Van Ackerman, saying, "Now, look, God damn it, Ted, we've got to get moving on this third-party idea—" and he had not hung up. He had waited, not saying a word, while Fred went on:

"You can't just sit on your fat ass, it's time to move fast and get everybody lined up before they all leave San Francisco. We're calling a pre-convention organizing meeting for 6 P.M. in the Hilton ballroom for the walk-out delegates and the press. Now, damn it, *you be there.*"

Still he had remained silent, until Fred had cried with a savage impatience, "God damn it, Ted, do you hear me? Answer me! I said we need you there, do you hear me? Will you be there?"

And he had responded at last with two words, very low and as though dredged up from some infinite well of pain, "All right."

"All right!" Fred had crowed triumphantly. "You're God-damned right, all right!"

Now he was just sitting, all alone, staring at Doña Valuela. He had been doing this for quite a long time before a strange strangled sound occurred in the room and he realized in an oddly disbelieving way, Why, I'm crying. Think of that, I haven't done that in twenty years, I'll bet. I'm crying.

9

AND NOW the suddenly melancholic, nostalgic mood of leave-taking was everywhere, and everywhere could be heard the tender cries of old friends bidding one another fond adieu:

"Y'all come see us now, hear? . . . You jus' swing that old state into line and we'll be seein' you four years from now, y'hear? . . . We're counting on you to hold New Jersey for us, boy! . . . Let me know what we can do for you in Washington on that Rural Electrification matter, if it'll be any help in November. . . . Give my love to all those wonderful people of yours at headquarters, now. You tell them we'll be working with them every moment. . . . Well, it was just *lovely* seeing you folks, too, and hasn't it been a great convention? We'll certainly remember this one, won't we?"

Away were going Mary Buttner Baffleburg, Lizzie Hanson McWharter, Esmé Harbellow Stryke, away Anna Hooper Bigelow, her good work done. Away the Senators, away the Congressmen, away the Cabinet members, away Joe Smitters, Bill Smatters, Bob Smutters, John Smotters, Buddy Smetters, away their Belle, Mary-Clare, Lulie, Susie, and Vangie too. Away National Committeemen and -women, away state chairmen, local chairmen, rank-and-file, second-level and up-top. Away, away, all away. At the Cow Palace the last debris was being cleared to make room for the Small Boat Show due in on Monday. In Union Square the gentle doves of Roger P. Croy were once more defecating undisturbed upon the citizenry. In Gump's and Omar's sank the fire. Once again her calm and leisurely pace was about to reclaim the lovely city.

Had there really been such passion and such agony?

Could it possibly have existed?

At the Mark Hopkins, standing in the midst of mountains of luggage awaiting haulage, jostled this way and that by the crowds pushing out through the still-jammed lobby, the junior Senator from Iowa was saying goodbye to the widow of the late junior Senator from Utah with a tension increased by the fact that neither had slept for more than twenty hours. Certainly they had not slept with each other, Lafe Smith thought with a rather grim humor, maybe that accounted for the way in which their sudden understanding of three days ago seemed to have as suddenly disappeared in this hectic, hasty hour of departure in which the head ached, the eyes stung, and every bone in the body seemed to have its own individual exhaustion.

"Well," he said, with a nervousness that surprised him even as he realized he was powerless to stop it, "I hope you have a good trip home."

"Oh, I think we will," Mabel Anderson said politely, while Pidge tugged and bobbed and jumped beside them, staring eagerly about, trying to see everything, saying goodbye to everyone.

"I expect I'll be coming out your way in the campaign before long," he said, hating his platitudinous words.

"I hope you will," she said. "Let us know."

"I'll let *you* know," he said, and with a sudden rush of urgency, "Mabel, what's the matter? What's gone wrong? I haven't done anything, have I?"

"Oh, no," she said hastily. "Heavens, no." Her eyes darkened with an abrupt sadness that quite devastated him. "It's just that—"

"What?" he asked, trying to keep his voice low, his expression no more than politely concerned as the departing delegates shoved and pushed and elbowed past with a noisy, relaxing exuberance.

"It isn't your fault," she said, "nothing's your fault. It's just that—"

"What?" he said gently.

"It's the same thing I told you yesterday—or day before—or whenever it was." She brushed a hand across her eyes with a tired smile. "One loses track so quickly, in a convention. When the ugliness started and they—they hurt Crystal, it was just like being back in the same old nightmare. It was like what they did to Brig." She turned her head away and he realized she was actually shivering. "Lafe," she said, turning back and staring at him from haunted eyes, "politics *is* so *awful*."

"No, it isn't," he protested lamely, knowing how inadequate the words were in the face of what she, and many another, must consider the unanswerable evidence. "It isn't any more awful than people let it be."

"But good people can't seem to do anything about it," she said in the same sad tone. "It's always the bad ones who seem to run things."

"You can't let the past stand in your way forever," he said, realizing that now Pidge had been attracted by their tone and was staring up at them with round, solemn eyes. "Some things have to be forgotten. You have to have faith that what comes next will be better. You have to give your-self a chance. Remember what you told me about Jimmy," he reminded her desperately. "You may get hurt out in the world, but that's part of living. That's what you told me, you can't just hide."

"I don't see how you can stand it," she said in a musing tone, appearing to be far away, as indeed she was, back a year ago in all the horror of her husband's suicide. "I just don't see how you do it."

"At least let me see you when I'm in Utah," he said. "We have so much to talk about—Jimmy—and ourselves —and Pidge—and all. Can't I do that? Please, Mabel!" he said, so loudly that now a couple of delegates did stop for a second in their headlong farewell rush to give them startled looks.

"I'm sorry," she said, coming back suddenly, placing a hand on his arm, giving him a beseeching look and a shy, sad smile. "I didn't mean to be rude. Do come to see me. We will talk. Maybe you can persuade me to feel differently, once we're out of this—this *evil* here." She placed her hands suddenly against his face, drew it down to her, and kissed him. "Dear Lafe," she said gently. "Don't stop trying. I hope you can persuade me."

"I won't," he promised, as earnestly as though his life depended upon it, as perhaps it did. "I won't. I want you to help me with Jimmy and with the campaign and with—so many things. I want you to help me with myself," he said simply, "so don't go away."

"I'll try not to," she said. She looked down at her lug-gage and counted the pieces once again. "We've really got to go. Write me or call. Come to Salt Lake soon."

"I will," he said, while the crowd pushed and shoved and chattered all about. "You can be sure I will."

"Uncle Lafe," Pidge said earnestly, tugging at his hand. "We like you."

"Thanks, Pidge," he said in a shaky voice, not daring to glance at either of them, turning away and moving from them even as he spoke. "I hope somebody does."

"Hi, buddy," Cullee said quietly at his elbow a moment later when he had arrived, somehow, at the other side of the lobby. "No soap, hm?"

"Oh, you saw," he said lamely. Cullee sighed.

"In this game, somebody sees everything. I hope it isn't all over."

"Oh, no," he said with a weary bitterness. "It isn't over, it isn't on. It's just—there. And I'm tired," he said with a determined change of subject, managing a reasonably humorous tone, "and you're tired and everybody's tired, and what the hell's going to happen next?"

"We're going to elect a President."

"The same one we think we are?"

"I think so. There's going to be the start of a rump convention at the Hilton tonight, but I don't think it's going to matter. They say Ted's going to go for it, but I can't conceive of him being such a fool."

"He may believe in what he stands for, you know," Lafe said, forcing himself to concentrate on the political situation and not be too hurt by the two figures he could just catch a glimpse of across the lobby, going out the door. "An awful lot of people believe he does. In which case, he could mean a lot of trouble for Harley and Orrin. He might very well succeed in splitting the vote enough to throw the election into the House."

Cullee shook his head, studying the hastening leave-takers with thoughtful eyes, waving at several who called his name as they hurried by.

"The worst he could do would be to throw it to Warren Strickland on the other ticket."

"I was talking to Beth a little while ago," Lafe said—"I called to ask about Crystal, who's coming along O.K., and also to ask how the old war-horse himself is feeling, now he's on the ticket—and she indicated that they've heard from Warren. A personal note to Harley, apparently. She doesn't know just what, but evidently some pledge on foreign policy designed to create a solid front against Ted if he does run. Something for Harley to keep in reserve."

"I just can't conceive of Ted being so foolish," Cullee repeated. "But ambition is a fearful thing—" he said, as he prepared to run for the Senate and probably take the licking of his life.

"You'll make it," Lafe said more lightly. "How's *your* love life?"

Cullee smiled.

"Simple. And happy. And going to stay that way, I think. . . . When you going back to D.C.?"

"I understand Harley would be happy to have both of us fly back with him," Lafe said, "but I don't think I can make it. I've got to make a speech tomorrow night in Houston."

"Me, either. I've got to stay here and get my campaign moving. Is Orrin going with him?"

"Different planes, I believe, which is wise enough."

Cullee nodded soberly.

"Yes, I think so. Accidents do happen."

"More than accidents, sometimes," Lafe said grimly, "considering how bitter some of Ted's supporters are."

"Have you read Walter Dobius today?" Cullee asked dryly. "He's keeping it hot."

"The bastard never learns," Lafe remarked. His expression changed to one of ironic humor as he saw a familiar face. "There's the man who can tell us all about it. K.K.!" he called, raising his voice across the jabbering lobby to the spot where the Indian Ambassador stood deep in obviously portentous conversation with his colleagues from France and Britain. They all turned and waved and the Americans went over.

"Well, dear friends," Lafe said, "and what do you think of the great Republic now?"

"Fascinating," Krishna Khaleel said with a hiss. "Absolutely fascinating."

"We know that," Lafe said, "but what's going to happen?"

"Rather difficult to estimate at this point, isn't it, old boy?" Lord Maudulayne suggested. "Looks somewhat like a Hudson-Knox victory, doesn't it?"

"A little somewhat," Cullee remarked. "Not a great big somewhat."

"If Governor Jason runs," Raoul Barre said politely, "it will create quite a dilemma, will it not?"

"It could create a contested election, yes," Cullee said. "Which I don't suppose would disappoint our good friends overseas. Nothing quite so delicious as seeing the United States all tied up in knots, is there?"

"Oh, now," Krishna Khaleel protested. "Oh, now, Cullee, you mustn't say bitter things like that. We all want the United States to succeed, so much depends upon her succeeding. We all want her to have a peaceable election and a new President—that is," he added hastily in a flustered voice, "I mean a new President in the sense of one newly elected to take office next January. I do not mean in the sense—"

"We know what you mean, K.K.," Lafe said dryly. "It's clear enough. So you really think Ted Jason would lead the United States in the way you want her led, do you? You might be surprised."

"I think perhaps he has created for himself—or allowed to be created for him," Raoul Barre said thoughtfully, "I am not, at this point, sure exactly which—a psychological and political prison within which it would not be possible for us to be surprised. His hands would be effectively tied, his choices very limited, I should think."

"Presidents' hands are never tied if they really want to break out," Lafe said, "that's one of the intriguing things about the office. Don't be too sure of what he would do. The office might change him—if he got it," he concluded firmly, "which I do not believe he will."

"Still, you are not sure," the French Ambassador said grimly.

"No," Cullee conceded somberly. "We are not sure."

Nor were they, really, in the penthouse at the Huntington, whose temporary tenants, like all the other temporaries of the convention, were surrounded by luggage, ready to leave. The First Lady and Dolly Munson had already departed half an hour ago to go to "Main Chance" for a week of rest, recuperation, and reconstruction; they would join their husbands in Washington for the campaign's opening strategy meeting. Bob Munson and Stanley Danta had come in and chatted for a while, assessed the prospects for the campaign with a shrewd and undaunted realism, and gone out to catch the *California Zephyr* back East, describing a train ride as the best decompression chamber they knew for the fearful tensions of a hard-fought convention. Bob Leffingwell had called to pay his respects and say that he and his wife were going to fly out to the Hana-Maui for a short vacation and then would be reporting in to Washington "for whatever you would like me to do." The Speaker had come by for a moment to wish them luck, made no pretense about considering the task ahead easy, pledged his help in every way possible, and then left for a week with his sister and brother-in-law at their cabin at Lake Tahoe. The last visitor, the Governor of Nebraska, came and went, the phone at last fell silent, there was a little delay before time for departure to the airport. The candidate for President and the candidate for Vice President at last had a few moments to talk.

"Any regrets?" the President asked quietly, looking for the last time over the beautiful Bay. An unhappy grimace crossed the face of the Secretary of State.

"Crystal, of course. And the bitterness of the whole thing. . . . I have a curious feeling we will be a long time recovering from this convention. I think it's done something to us, and perhaps to America. It could," he said slowly, "be something permanent, if we are not lucky."

"These things come and go," the President said. "For a people who like to think of themselves as calm and easygoing, we are apt to be surprisingly violent, at times. But we have been before, and it has passed. Sensibility reasserts itself. I think it will now."

"I wish I were as sure as you are," the Secretary said. "I never told you about the bomb somebody planted at my house a couple of months ago, I didn't want to worry you. And of course you know what both of us get in the mail. The threats will be even more violent and fantastic now."

"As Calvin Coolidge once remarked," the President said, " 'Any well-dressed man who wants to give his own life can kill the President.' " His expression became both sad and ironic for a moment. "Nowadays, they don't even have to be well-dressed. And someday, of course," he added quietly, "somebody may succeed, with me, or with you, or with anyone else who seems to some unhappy mind to be a worthwhile target. But . . . one can't stop for that."

"Oh, no," Orrin said, "of course not. I had my moment" —he smiled—"of thinking one could, but you talked me out of it. What I regret about it is not the danger to you or to me—or to Ted, say, if somebody on our side gets unbalanced enough to go after him—but the fact that all Americans can get in such a state of mind about each other at all. That we could have the really terrifying things that have occurred at this convention. That out of this seemingly decent land could come such monstrous subversions of decency. That rational people—leave aside the kooks and the oddballs, that *rational* people—who begin with reasoned argument can end with the sort of ghastly sincerity that could produce death for their opponents . . . You expect it in other countries, but somehow it always surprises you here, even though the record certainly has its examples. . . . It's still hard to believe."

The President gave him a somber look.

"We have a job ahead, to calm this situation down—to fight a campaign and win it—to maintain what we believe best in foreign policy—and still not let the country be torn apart any further. Can we do it?"

"We've got to," the Secretary said simply. "And the first step, I think, is not to yield one inch on what we honestly believe to be best for the country and the world: not an inch. If we believe in patient firmness, then patient firmness is what we've got to preserve, regardless of what Ted may say or anyone else may do. It's the only way to survive, I think."

"Patient and *unafraid* firmness," the President said softly. "Don't forget the *unafraid*. It can't be timorous or static. That would be fatal, too."

The Secretary nodded as they stood up.

"Exactly. . . . So: I shall see you in Washington, then. What time will you get in?"

The President glanced at his watch.

"Around eight, I think—five o'clock out here. When are you coming on?"

"I had thought I'd go right now, but I think maybe Beth and I will stay around a day or two with Hal and Crystal, just to make sure everything's coming along all right. I'm going to move them down to Carmel this afternoon. I'll go to the airport with you and see you off, of course. Then I'll come along a little later—unless you need me sooner?"

The President shook his head.

"Oh, no. Get a rest. And give the children my love. It's very rough for them to have to take all this."

"They're standing it well," Orrin said.

"You're right to be proud of them," the President said. He held out his hand.

"Well, old friend: let's see how it goes."

"Whatever I can do," Orrin said very quietly, "I will do."

"I do not think," the President said with a smile that broke the emotion a little, "that our labors will go entirely unrewarded—as long as we have no illusions about what we face."

"None whatsoever," the Secretary said with an answering smile. "I've never felt so un-illusioned in my life."

Then there was a knock on the door, the moment ended. Surrounded by Secret Service men, preceded by a group of frantically shouting newspapermen and photographers running and jostling ahead of them down the corridor, the two principal members of the convention left the hotel and prepared to depart the golden city where they had won the golden prize—or at least the chance to try for it. Not they, nor anyone, had truly won it yet.

10

SOMETIMES HE READ. Sometimes he dozed. But mostly, as Air Force One moved swiftly back across the land through a cloudless summer day, the President thought. Not particularly profound or major thoughts, he was too tired and too emotionally exhausted for that, but just the rather wandering, musing thoughts of a gentle man still surprised by his own capacity for deviousness, his own surrender to anger and retaliation, his own grim pursuit of the power he had once thought himself too mild and generous ever to need or want.

He had meant it when he said he would not run; crisis and those who produced the screaming headlines and the hurtful news stories and the suave, damaging broadcasts had changed all that. (PRESIDENT FORCES BITTER CONVENTION TO TAKE KNOX, they said now; JASON MAY LAUNCH THIRD PARTY IN CAUSE OF PEACE.)

He had meant it when he said he would not dictate the choice of Vice President; Ted himself, and the cynical souls behind him, had changed all that.

He had meant it, years ago, when he thought that all he wanted out of life was a loving family, a good home, a peaceful life.

The strange ways of power and politics in a strange and complex country had changed all that.

So here he was, plan-changer, word-breaker, grasper after power as avid as his fellows: Harley M. Hudson, President and candidate, learner with the rest that certain roads of power, once started upon, sometimes cannot be turned away from.

Nor should they be, he thought as the giant craft passed into Maryland and he wondered idly who would be there to meet him when he landed, providing a man believed that he could see a road that led at last, through whatever dark forest, toward some ultimate benefit for the United States. If a man saw somewhere ahead some shining upland where the puzzled, unhappy, beloved Republic might rest at last, if history had given him the chance to lead her to it, then he had a right to seek for power, a right to get it if he could, a right to hold and use it as the Lord gave him strength to do.

Most things were justified by this . . . for Presidents in pursuit of their fearful duty, he was finally beginning to believe, all things.

Much had been made of honor at the convention, as his opponent had said in his agonized speech. And so there had, and each of them had been forced to come to terms with it in his own way, as best he could. For himself, the President felt he had done what the imperatives of history required him to do. So, no doubt, had all the rest, from Ted to Walter and back again. He was satisfied in his own conscience: let them make what bargains they could with theirs. There came a point where a man could not worry about the peace of mind of others. His own was problem enough.

He closed his eyes, his plain, pleasant face slipping into repose. He wished Lucille were with him. He wished Orrin were, too. For the last time on his journey home, he slept.

"There it is!" cried the New York *Times* at Andrews Air Force Base in nearby Maryland, just outside the District of Columbia. "It's a bird—it's a man—"

"It's Fearless Peerless," the Chicago *Daily News* said dryly, "so cut the disrespectful, irreverent, God-damned chatter."

"Shall we kneel down and touch our heads to the ground?" the *Post* inquired.

"Better lie down in a line and let him use us for a rug to

walk to the White House helicopter, hadn't we?" the Washington *Evening Star* suggested. "That might be more fitting, under the circumstances."

They all laughed, somewhat ruefully but dauntless still; not noticing in the flurry and excitement and sudden bustling all about that in the jostling, police-held crowd pressed up against the fence just behind them, one other, gifted by a sometimes puzzling Almighty with the gift to change the world, laughed too.

In Gorotoland at that moment, at Mbuele in the highlands, Prince Obifummata Ajkaje and his stern-faced Communist advisers were even then rejecting, for the twenty-seventh time, the cautious peace-feelers put out by Britain through the circuitous route of Ceylon, Nigeria, and Guyana; while in dusty Molobangwe on the plains, his cousin Prince Terry was reviewing the latest detachment of U.S. troops, whose arrival, as yet unannounced, would lift the formal American commitment to one hundred thousand men.

In Panama, Felix Labaiya, standing alone as he liked to do on the terrace of "Suerte," staring down the long valley that led from Chiriquí to the sea, was calculating what his brother-in-law's humiliation might drive him to do, and on the basis of what he thought he understood of that brilliant, ambitious mind, was deciding with a renewed determination to order his forces to fight on.

At the UN, the Soviet Union, Yugoslavia, Cuba, and nine Afro-Asian nations were preparing yet another resolution demanding United States withdrawal from around the globe, agreeing that they would reintroduce it regularly each month from now on so that the United States, if she so desired, might keep on affronting the world with her hated and inexcusable vetoes.

In San Francisco, the disgruntled, the hopeful, the idealistic, the subversive, the believers in Ted Jason and the Right Position, and his friends of Walter's world, were beginning to drift into the ballroom of the Hilton, where cameras, lights, and microphones were already, an hour ahead of time, in place for the opening of the organizing session that would prepare the rump convention.

And at Andrews Air Force base, the Mayor and City

Council of Washington, the members of the Cabinet, the members of Congress, the members of the diplomatic corps, the public, the reporters, and one other, waited.

Gracefully the giant craft glided toward the runway, ten miles from the great white city on the Potomac where the hopes and dreams, the triumphs and failures, the pasts and futures of so many men and causes were centered, while all around the lovely rolling green countryside drowsed in the peaceful heat of a soft, exhausted twilight, late in the month of July.

December 1964–December 1965

Frank Yerby's magnificent historical

novels have enthralled millions around the world. . . .

Don't miss —

The Vixens

New Orleans—hotblooded men and passionate women struggling for power, position and wealth in the days of Reconstruction. 75c

The Foxes of Harrow

about a daring rogue who loved and gambled his way to power in Old New Orleans. 75c

The Golden Hawk

about Kit Gerado, the ruthless master of the Caribbean sea, driven by his desire for the girl Rouge, and for vengeance. 75c

The Serpent and The Staff

about a dedicated surgeon, Dr. Duncan Childers, who clawed his way up from a New Orleans gutter . . . all the way to the top. 75c

Odor of Sanctity

The world of ninth-century Spain—and the story of Alaric, the Spanish nobleman whose capacity for love matched the violence of his destiny. 95c

A SINGULAR MAN

J. P. DONLEAVY

A Seymour Lawrence Book/Delacorte Press $6.95
A Dell Book   95c

George Smith, the mysterious millionaire, lives in a world rampant with mischief, of chiselers and cheats. Having sidestepped slowly away down the little alleys of success he lives a luxurious, lonely life between a dictatorial Negress housekeeper and two secretaries, one of which, Sally Tomson, the gay wild and willing beauty, he falls in love with.

"George Smith is such a man as Manhattan's subway millions have dreamed of being."   —*Time Magazine*

"A masterpiece of writing about love."
                    —*National Observer*

First published in the United States in 1963 and England 1964. Re-issued in the United States by Seymour Lawrence/Delacorte Press in Spring 1967.

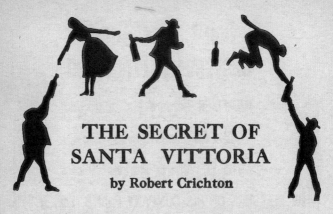

THE SECRET OF SANTA VITTORIA

by Robert Crichton

THE NATION'S #1 BESTSELLER

From time immemorial the Italian hill town of Santa Vittoria had existed as a world unto itself, hostile to strangers, wholly involved in growing and making the fat black wine that was its glory and its lifeblood. As the Allied armies approached, the Germans sent an occupying force to claim the town's great treasure—one million bottles of wine. At this moment a leader emerged—the clownish wine merchant Bombolini. Behind him the town united, forgetting ancient feuds, lovers' rivalries, the division between aristocrat and peasant, pooling its energies and resources to outwit the invader.

"This brilliant novel should be celebrated with a fanfare of trumpets, with festivals in the streets." —*The New York Times*

"Crichton tells his story with grace, pace, warmth, and a wonderful free-reeling wit that skips among the vineyards like an inebriated billygoat." —*Time Magazine*

95¢

Don't Miss These
Bestsellers From Dell

THE FIXER Bernard Malamud 95c

TAI-PAN James Clavell 95c

THE LIE Alberto Moravia 95c

THE PLEASURE OF HIS COMPANY Paul B. Fay, Jr. 75c

LA CHAMADE Francois Sagan 75c

A DANDY IN ASPIC Derek Marlowe 75c

THE LAST PICTURE SHOW Larry McMurtry 75c

IN THE COMPANY OF EAGLES Ernest Gann 75c

THE PAPER DRAGON Evan Hunter 95c

THE EMBEZZLER Louis Auchincloss 75c

ODOR OF SANCTITY Frank Yerby 95c

CANNIBALS AND CHRISTIANS Norman Mailer 95c
